WHEN DAY IS DONE

Elizabeth Murphy

HEADLINE

First published in 1998
by HEADLINE BOOK PUBLISHING

First published in paperback in 1999
by HEADLINE BOOK PUBLISHING

10 9 8 7 6 5

ISBN 0 7472 5620 9

Typeset by Palimpsest Book Production Limited,
Polmont, Stirlingshire

Printed and bound in Great Britain by
Clays Ltd, St Ives plc

HEADLINE BOOK PUBLISHING
A division of Hodder Headline PLC
338 Euston Road
LONDON NW1 3BH

To
Sophia Chapman,
who endured a hard life with courage,
cheerfulness and without self-pity.
May she rest in peace.

When day is done and shadows fall
I think of you.

Chapter One

A gusty wind blew across Anfield Cemetery in Liverpool on a cold October day in 1904, causing the women gathered around an open grave to clutch at their large black hats. The mourners were few: only the dead woman's two widowed, childless sisters, her two young daughters and a few neighbours.

Several of the neighbours sobbed noisily and the two girls, twelve-year-old Kate and ten-year-old Rose, wept as their mother's small coffin was lowered into the grave, but Sophie Drew's two sisters showed no grief. Plump Beattie Anderson, wrapped in a sealskin coat, dabbed at her eyes with a black-edged handkerchief but there were no tears to wipe away, and her sister, Mildred Williams, tall and gaunt, only gazed stonily into the grave.

Rose wept because her elder sister did, but she felt no real grief for her mother. She was enjoying the drama of their situation, and wearing the new black dress and cape and large black hat provided by her Aunt Beattie. Only Kate truly grieved, but their neighbour Mrs Holland had told her that was because she had done so much for her mother. 'She never let you leave her side, girl, so you're bound to miss her,' Mrs Holland had said.

Kate was still weeping when the brief service was over and her aunts led the way from the grave. Rose slipped her hand through Kate's arm. 'Don't cry, Katie,' she said. 'Mama's in heaven now with Dada, the minister said.'

Mrs Holland came to Kate's other side and put her arm about the girl's shoulders. 'Your mama's better off, love,' she said. 'And it will be better for you too.'

'You'll be able to go to school every day,' Rose said, but Kate was not comforted.

'I don't care about school,' she said. 'I'm not clever like you, Rosie. I just want Mama back. I *liked* looking after her.'

Their two aunts had arrived at the funeral carriage and they turned and beckoned to the girls. Kate and Rose followed them into the carriage, feeling shy and nervous. Kate had only seen the aunts once before her mother's death, when they had visited after her father had been killed fighting the Boers in South Africa. Kate recalled that Mama had been hysterical with grief and Aunt Mildred had slapped her face and told her to pull herself together. There had been a violent quarrel and Aunt Mildred had stormed out, followed by Aunt Beattie.

Kate remembered how upset they had all been, but Mrs Holland had come in to comfort them. She had kissed her and Rosie and told them that people said things they didn't mean at such a time, then she had taken a black bottle from under her shawl and poured something into a cup for Mama. 'One hundred per cent proof. It'll do you the world of good,' she had said. It *had* been good for Mama, Kate thought. She had been much calmer although she still wept for Dada. That was four years ago, and Mama had never been well since, but the aunts hadn't called again, not until after Mama died.

The carriage had arrived back at the house in Rowan Road, where a neighbour had food prepared and a kettle boiling for tea. There was little conversation and the few neighbours soon left, intimidated by Mildred's grim silence and Beattie's evident wealth.

Only Mrs Holland lingered to fling her arms around the two girls, weeping and calling them her poor dears. They clung to her and she looked defiantly at Mildred. 'I know I've no rights,' she said, 'but I know what their mama would've wanted and I'd do my best for them.'

Mildred snorted. 'As you did for my sister—' she began, but Beattie coughed warningly and said to Mrs Holland:

'The girls should be with us. We're family, you see.'

'Family!' exclaimed Mrs Holland. 'You never came next or near poor Sophie except to upset her when Johnny was killed by them murdering Boers. She never got over it.

Called out of bed beside her by a bugle blown in the street and she never saw him again. It was enough to break any woman's heart. That's what she died of, poor Sophie. A broken heart.'

'Nonsense,' Mildred said angrily. 'She should have shaped herself and looked after her children like other widows do. Not sat feeling sorry for herself and drinking herself to death with your help.'

Beattie rose to her feet, exclaiming, 'Mildred!' and Mrs Holland said loudly, 'God forgive you. Your own flesh and blood. You're not fit to look after a dog, never mind a child.'

Beattie opened the door wide. 'This has gone far enough,' she said. 'Good day to you, Mrs Holland.'

Mrs Holland kissed Rose and Kate. 'Don't forget – I'm always here if you need me, girls. And never forget your mama and your dada, the best and kindest man—' She mopped her eyes and went to the door, but there she paused for a parting shot.

'Don't think I don't know why you came here like a pair of vultures before poor Sophie was cold, and why you want the girls: one for a toy and the other for a skivvy. God's ways are slow but sure. He knew what He was doing when He didn't give you no children of your own.'

Mildred banged the door shut behind her. 'What a virago,' she began, but Kate was staring at her.

'Mama didn't die of drink,' she burst out. 'She only took it for her cough. It was her heart – the doctor said it was.' She broke into a storm of weeping, sinking on to a stool by the fireplace and covering her face with her hands.

The two women looked at each other and Beattie leaned forward and patted her arm. 'Don't take on, Kate,' she said soothingly. 'Aunt Mildred didn't mean anything. We're all upset about your poor mama, and you're just too soft-hearted like your father was.' Rose came to stand beside Kate and put her arm around her sister's neck, Mildred sniffed, looking uncomfortable.

Beattie looked from Kate's tear-blotched face and mousy hair to Rose, who stood twisting one of her fair curls round her finger. Her dimples showed as she smiled at her aunt, and Beattie beamed approvingly at the pretty child.

'Kate favours Johnny's side in looks too,' she said. 'Rose takes after our side of the family.' She held out her arms. 'Come to Auntie, dearest,' she said, and Rose moved away from Kate and went to lean against Beattie's knee.

Beattie hugged her and looked at Mildred, who nodded. Then Beattie said, 'Now, girls, we've talked it over and we've decided that Rose will come to live with me. Kate, you'll go to Aunt Mildred.'

'And you'll have to behave yourself. No tantrums,' said Mildred. 'My guests are very particular.'

Kate looked bewildered. 'But – but I thought – I thought we'd stay here,' she stammered. 'I looked after Mama and I can look after Rosie.'

'Talk sense, girl,' Mildred snapped. 'Ten and twelve years old to look after yourselves! And what would you live on, may I ask? No, you're lucky you've both got good homes to go to.'

She had been rapidly clearing up and stacking dishes and now she looked with exasperation at Beattie, sitting placidly in the rocking chair. 'Well, come on, Beattie,' she said. 'I haven't got time to waste. Let's get these washed and straighten up and I can get off.'

Beattie smoothed her black silk dress over her ample stomach but remained seated. 'Don't bother, Mildred,' she said calmly. 'Essy will see to them tomorrow.'

'I've never left dirty pots overnight in my life and I'm not going to start now,' Mildred said tartly 'Essy will have enough to do tomorrow anyway.' She looked at Kate, still sitting in stunned silence on the stool, and said abruptly, 'Come on, Kate. You can give me a hand.'

She carried the tray of dishes into the scullery, followed by Kate, who silently dried the dishes as swiftly as her aunt washed them. Mildred glanced at her averted face and said abruptly, 'Don't go upsetting yourself about what I said. I speak my mind and some people don't like it, but that's my way.'

Kate said nothing. She was still stunned by the news

that she and Rose were to be parted, and was wondering desperately what she could do about it.

Mildred began to stack the clean dishes in a cupboard, and before her courage failed, Kate faltered, 'Aunt Mildred, couldn't Rose come with me – or me go with Rosie? She's so little and we've always been together.'

Mildred frowned. 'No, it's all settled,' she said. 'Beattie only wants – she can only manage one and Rose will like living there. She'll want for nothing, and you'll soon settle with me.'

'But what about the house? Our things?' Kate asked.

'Don't worry. That's all sorted,' Mildred said briskly. 'We'll take a few of your clothes with us and Essy can pack up the rest. Now, no more questions. You've too much to say for a child. We'll get off now.'

Beattie still sat in the rocking chair with her arm round Rose. Mildred looked annoyed but said nothing, and went upstairs to bring down two straw bags, which she handed to Rose and Kate. 'Some of your things,' she said briefly then turned to Beattie. 'Well, are you ready? My guests will want their meal, funeral or no funeral.'

Both women still wore their large black hats. Now Beattie rose heavily to her feet and wrapped herself in her sealskin coat, while Mildred and the girls donned their own outdoor clothes. 'Poor Sophie, who would have thought it would end like this?' Beattie sighed, but Mildred only hustled the girls out and locked the door. She gave the key to Beattie.

'Essy will want this,' she said.

Beattie had sent a small boy for a cab, and as they waited, the girls clung together, weeping bitterly. Mildred clicked her tongue in exasperation, and Beattie said, 'Now, now, girls. You'll see each other on Sunday when Aunt Mildred brings Kate to tea with us.'

Tears filled Rose's blue eyes and hung on her long lashes, but Kate dried her face and kissed Rose tenderly. 'Don't fret, love,' she murmured. 'We'll see each other on Sunday and then every day at school, and I'll be thinking of you all the time.'

'I want you to come with me,' Rose wailed, but the cab

had arrived. Beattie drew her away and she stepped into it, followed by her aunt, and was borne away.

Mildred set off briskly along Molyneaux Road and through into West Derby Road, with Kate almost running to keep up with her. As she walked, Mildred muttered to herself: 'Today of all days, and wasting time bringing them back to the house, but that's Beattie! Just because they collected for a wreath.'

Kate suddenly realised that she had no idea of where her aunt lived. Mildred had turned into Everton Road, still keeping up the same rapid pace. Kate was too breathless as she rushed along beside her aunt to ask where they were going, even if she had dared. She felt as though she was in the middle of a nightmare, yet she knew she would not wake from it.

She had assumed without consciously thinking about it that life would go on as before, only without Mama lying on the bed in the corner of the living room, usually with her face turned to the wall. Kate had looked after Mama, and cooked and cleaned with help from Mrs Holland, and Rose had done the shopping and anything else she was asked to do. Other neighbours had helped too. Since Mama had died, Kate had managed to control her grief by thinking that when these dreadful days were over and her aunts had gone, she and Rose and Mrs Holland, who had all loved Mama, could grieve together for her. Now the shock of being parted so suddenly from Rose drove even thoughts of her mother from her mind, and she hurried along beside her aunt in a daze.

Suddenly Mildred stopped before a tall three-storeyed house with a basement and a flight of steps up to the front door. Kate stared up at it in amazement, but still without speaking, Mildred led the way down the basement steps and into a large gloomy kitchen.

Fog had drifted up from the Mersey, and although it was only mid-afternoon it was almost dark, but the kitchen looked more cheerful when Mildred lit the gas mantle and stirred up the fire. She glanced at the clock as she swiftly took off her coat and hat and tied a large apron around her waist.

'Dear heaven, look at the time,' she exclaimed. 'They'll all be in and not a potato peeled. And no help either! That dratted girl walked out on me last night, and the charwoman sent a lad to say her leg was bad – and they knew it was the funeral today.'

She was taking a large stone dish from the oven as she spoke, and Kate said timidly, 'I can peel potatoes, Aunt.'

Mildred looked up. 'Well, you could make a start,' she said. 'I've got six guests, so there's a lot needed. Come through to your room and change your dress before you begin.'

She took Kate through to a room behind the kitchen. Though small, it was spotlessly clean, and the single bed beneath the window was covered with a white counterpane. A bowl and ewer stood on a yellow table, and a curtain covered an alcove. Mildred pulled it back. 'Hang your new dress there and put your hat on the shelf. Change your boots too,' she ordered. 'As quick as you can.' She took a dress and a pair of boots from the straw bag and laid them on the bed, then hurried away.

Kate changed quickly, glad to take off the new boots, which had rubbed a blister on her heel, and to slip into her familiar dress. Then she returned to the kitchen, where Mildred was rapidly chopping cabbage. A large bowl of potatoes stood on the table with a huge pan beside it. Mildred handed Kate a sharp knife. 'Mind you don't cut yourself, but be as quick as you can,' she said.

Kate said nothing, but concentrated on her task, and soon the pan was full.

'Good. You were quick,' said Mildred.

She had been bustling about the kitchen at top speed, opening and closing cupboards, and Kate asked if she could do anything else.

'Come and help to lay the table,' Mildred said. 'Bring that big jug of water.' She picked up a tray of cutlery and started up the basement steps.

Kate followed her through the hall and into a large dining room. She was amazed at the size of it, and at the magnificent furniture. An immense sideboard stood against one wall, and the long table was surrounded by eight dining chairs and two carvers covered in horsehair.

With an exclamation Mildred drew a box of matches from

her pocket and lit the fire which was already laid. 'I forgot the dratted fires,' she said. 'Here, Kate, go and light the fire in the parlour, the door opposite this.'

The parlour looked even more imposing to Kate. It was twice the size of the living room in her home and contained two sofas and several armchairs covered in green plush. There were green plush curtains at the window and green plush draping the high mantelpiece. Many small bamboo tables were scattered about, with plants or framed photographs standing on them. Kate threaded her way through them carefully to light the fire which was laid ready, and then hurried back to help her aunt.

She was sent back to the basement kitchen several times, for glasses and another jug of water and more cutlery. By this time the fire was burning well, and Mildred looked into the parlour where the fire was also bright. She looked satisfied but said nothing.

They went back to the kitchen, and Mildred made a pot of tea and spread dripping on a slice of bread for Kate. 'Eat it quickly,' she said. 'They'll be in before we can turn round.'

A little later there were sounds of light footsteps above their heads. 'The teachers,' Mildred said briefly, then there was silence until a bell jangled on a board on the wall. Mildred made an impatient exclamation. 'Mrs Bradley's coal,' she said. A full coal scuttle stood near the basement stairs, and she took two lumps of coal from it and put them on the kitchen fire.

'Can you manage this?' she asked, lifting the scuttle, and when Kate took it from her she added, 'Mrs Bradley. First floor front.'

Kate managed to carry the coal scuttle up the basement stairs to the hall, but before continuing on up the next flight of stairs, she rested it on the bottom step and bent her head. Could this really be happening? Mama dead and Rosie far away in another house. And herself living here with the horrible aunt who told lies about Mama. She wished that she had died too.

The front door suddenly opened behind her and a tall

young man appeared in the hall. He was wearing a velvet-collared overcoat and a curly-brimmed bowler hat, and was whistling cheerfully, but at the sight of Kate he stopped. 'Halloa,' he said with a smile, then his face changed and he came and took the coal scuttle from her. 'A bit heavy for you,' he said. 'Where's it going?'

'Mrs Bradley. First floor front,' Kate whispered.

As they started up the stairs, he put his hand under her elbow. 'What do I call you?' he asked.

Nervously she mumbled, 'Kate.'

They had reached the door and he put down the scuttle and bent his head to smile at her. 'Cheer up, Kate,' he said. 'It's always darkest before the dawn.'

In spite of her misery, Kate smiled back at him, and the picture of his cheerful face with its bright blue eyes, fresh complexion and silky brown moustache stayed with her and comforted her when he had turned away.

Kate knocked shyly on the door and was bidden to enter. The room was large and comfortably furnished, and the white-haired old lady sitting in a chair beside the fire smiled at her and said kindly, 'Thank you, my dear. That must have been very heavy for you.'

'A man carried it up the stairs,' Kate said timidly. She had put the full coal scuttle by the hearth and picked up the empty one, and was wondering whether she was expected to make up the fire. While she hesitated, Mrs Bradley had been studying her, and now she said, 'I will attend to the fire, my dear. You seem very young for this work. Surely you are required by law now to attend school?'

'I go to school,' Kate said. 'I'll go back on Monday.' And I'll see Rose, she thought, and smiled at Mrs Bradley. The old lady picked up a tin of humbugs from the table beside her and held it out to Kate, who took one, murmuring, 'Thank you,' before returning to the kitchen with the empty coal scuttle.

'You managed it then?' Mildred greeted her. Honesty compelled Kate to tell her aunt that a man had helped her. Mildred sniffed, then said sharply, 'What are you eating?'

'Mrs Bradley gave me a humbug,' Kate said, and Mildred told her not to get too friendly with the boarders. 'They'll

9

only take advantage,' she said. 'Get you doing all sorts of extras for them.'

Kate looked at her aunt with dislike but said nothing. Footsteps and voices could be heard in the hall and Mildred, who was making gravy, said, 'Here they are. I never thought I'd be ready in time.' A few minutes later, when the voices had died away, Mildred went up and banged the gong in the hall. Once the boarders were assembled in the dining room, Kate was kept busy bringing up tureens of vegetables and jugs of gravy to hand to her aunt at the door of the dining room. She was not allowed to enter the room until the boarders had dispersed, then she helped to clear the table.

After they had carried down the last of the dishes, she and her aunt washed up what seemed to Kate a mountain of crockery and cutlery, then sat down to eat their own meals which had been kept warm in the oven.

Although Kate was hungry she was almost too tired to eat and chewed with her eyes closed. She was only dimly conscious of being led to her bedroom by her aunt and helped to undress, and sometimes in later years she wondered whether she had only dreamt that Mildred had leaned over her and kissed her, then said softly, 'You're a good girl, Katie. I couldn't have managed without you.'

It seemed she had only been asleep for a few minutes when she was wakened by the sound of a cart clattering over the cobbles outside the window.

She missed first the warmth of her sister's body beside her, then memory came flooding back. She was in Aunt Mildred's house. Rose was far away, living with Aunt Beattie, and Mama was dead.

Now Kate could allow herself to think of her mother and to weep for her in private. Poor Mama. Kate remembered that awful night when Dada had gone away. She had been awakened by the sound of a bugle being blown in the street and the noise of shouted commands to the soldiers drawn up there.

Suddenly she had heard screaming and had run downstairs to the hall, where Mama in her nightgown was clinging to Dada and screaming, 'Johnny, Johnny, don't go. Don't leave me.' Dada was saying, 'I must, Sophie. You know I've got to go. I'm a Reservist.'

When Rosie had run downstairs too, Dada had managed to pull away and kiss the girls, and Mama had sunk down on the lowest stair, sobbing. Dada had kissed her and said, 'Look after Mama, girls. I'll be back soon.' But he had not come back, and soon he had been killed far away in South Africa.

I tried to look after Mama, Kate thought now, but perhaps I didn't do enough – or perhaps it was just that Mama's heart really was broken as Mrs Holland said. She wept again, then suddenly thought of the kind young man's words, 'It's always darkest before the dawn', and her natural optimism broke through.

Mama would be happy now, at peace in Heaven with Jesus, and reunited with Dada as Mrs Holland had told her. Rose would be safe with Aunt Beattie, because Aunt Beattie would love her and look after her. Rose was so lovable.

I'll be all right too, thought Kate. I'll see Rose every day, and Mrs Bradley was kind and so was the man who helped me with the coal scuttle. She thought of his cheerful face and fell asleep feeling comforted as a nearby clock struck four.

She woke to the sound of her aunt's voice raised in anger, and tumbled out of bed then dressed quickly. When she went into the kitchen she was surprised to find that it was only seven o'clock. Her aunt was shaking her finger in the face of a cowed-looking woman who wore a man's cloth cap on her wispy hair and a pair of battered boots on her feet.

'You let me down like that again and you needn't come back,' Mildred was saying. 'This is your last chance.' She suddenly noticed Kate and added, 'It's a good thing my niece was here to help or I'd never have got through. Now get on with the fires.' The woman limped away through the back door.

The kitchen fire was already burning brightly and Mildred went to a large pan of porridge which was on the hob beside it. 'Pass me two plates, Kate,' she ordered. 'We'll have ours before we start on them upstairs.' Kate was troubled by the charwoman's longing glance at the plates of porridge as she carried a bucket of coal up the basement stairs, but her aunt looked so cross that she was afraid to comment. Mildred made a pot of tea and told Kate to spread a slice of bread with dripping for herself, but she made no offer of tea to the other woman although she had passed through the kitchen several times.

'If you've finished you can help me to lay the table in the dining room,' Mildred said abruptly. 'It didn't get done last night.'

Kate followed her aunt meekly to the dining room where the hearth had been swept and the fire lit by the charwoman. They laid the table, then Kate cut and buttered bread and helped to carry porridge and boiled eggs to the dining room, although again she was not allowed to enter the room while the boarders were there.

When Kate had carried down the dishes and was helping her aunt to wash them, Mildred said abruptly, 'I didn't bring you here to work, whatever that impudent woman said, but you might as well help until you go back to school.'

'I like housework,' Kate said. 'I did nearly all ours—' Her voice faltered, and Mildred said briskly, 'Yes, well, hard work is the best cure for grief. I've got a girl coming today, so you can help Mrs Molesworth until she comes.'

The charwoman appeared on the basement stairs and Mildred said sharply, 'Have you finished the slops?'

'Yes, ma'am,' the woman said meekly.

Mildred was putting on her coat and hat, and now she said to Kate, 'Right. You can dust the parlour while Mrs M. does the steps, then she'll show you how to help with the bedrooms. I've got to go out but I won't be long.' She took a basket from a shelf and went up the stairs to the street.

Kate quickly dusted the parlour with a feather duster, and when she peeped through the Nottingham lace curtain she could see Mrs Molesworth scrubbing the flight of steps to the front door. She went to the door. 'Should I do the brass, Mrs Molesworth?' she asked, and her offer was accepted gratefully.

Kate finished polishing the knocker and door handle at the same time as Mrs Molesworth finished scrubbing. The woman groaned in agony as she straightened up, and Kate ran lightly down the steps and carried the bucket down the area steps to the kitchen. 'God bless you, girl,' Mrs Molesworth said, and Kate asked what she had done to her leg.

'It's a varicose ulcer,' replied the woman. 'I can stand pain but it was that bad yesterday I passed out when I put me foot to the floor. Me poor feller was nearly demented, seeing me lying there and not able to do nothing for me. He thought I'd snuffed it.'

'Couldn't he have helped you up?' asked Kate.

'No, girl. He's lying flat on his back these five years. A bale fell on him and broke 'is back when he was working in a ship's hold,' said Mrs Molesworth. 'He managed to throw some water on me face and I come round, like.'

Kate looked horrified. 'But why did you come today?' she asked. 'Your leg's still bad, isn't it?' She pushed a chair forward for Mrs Molesworth to sit down, and the woman lowered herself gingerly on to it.

'Lord bless you, girl, I darsen't stay off again. I need the money anyhow,' she said. 'I tried to get here yesterday because I knew Emily had scarpered and the missus was going to a funeral, but me boot got full of blood and I had to turn back.'

She had been watching the feet of people passing the window, and now she said nervously, 'Get the cleaning box outa the cupboard, girl, for fear she comes back. That way we can let on we're on our way.'

A minute later she stood up. 'It's no use, girl. I can't settle. She could be back any minute. We'd better get upstairs.' They went up to the bedrooms with Kate carrying the cleaning box and the sweeping brush and dustpan.

They worked together in silence for a while, apart from grunts of pain from Mrs Molesworth, then Kate said timidly, 'It was my mama's funeral that Aunt Mildred went to yesterday.'

'Of course. Me wits are wandering,' the charwoman exclaimed. 'I've placed you now. You're Sophie and Johnny's girl. She's a close one, the missus. She never tells no one nothing.'

'Did you know Mama and Dada?' Kate asked eagerly.

'Oh aye, and I can see where you get your good heart. Your da was the kindest lad that walked the earth. He'd do anyone a good turn. I heard your poor ma had died, so I should've realised that was the funeral the missus was going to.'

They moved on to the next bedroom, where Kate worked quickly under Mrs Molesworth's direction while the charwoman leaned on the footrail of the bed. 'You've got a knack for housework, girl,' she said. 'But don't be *too* handy or she'll take advantage. Bit of a slavedriver she is. Wasn't there two of you?'

'Yes, but Rose has gone to live with Aunt Beattie,' Kate said.

'You'll miss her then, girl,' the charwoman said sympathetically, and Kate's eyes filled with tears.

'Yes. I thought we could stay in our own house,' she said. 'I hope she's not fretting. She's only just ten.'

'Don't you worry. She's fallen on her feet there,' Mrs Molesworth said. 'No shortage of money, and your Aunt Beattie was always easygoing. Mind you, she's had an easy life. Not like the missus here. She was left badly off when her husband died, but she's worked hard to keep herself, taking in lodgers – or paying guests, as she calls them.'

Kate looked up in surprise. 'I didn't know Aunt Mildred had been married,' she said.

'Only for a year,' Mrs Molesworth said. 'She never mentions him.' She looked over her shoulder and dropped her voice. 'He died of a heart seizure in another woman's bed,' she whispered.

'The woman was kind to put him in her own bed, wasn't she?' said Kate innocently. 'Did he take ill in her house?'

'Er – er yes, but don't say nothing to your aunt,' Mrs Molesworth said hurriedly. 'She doesn't like to talk about it. Don't take no notice to me, girl. Me tongue'll get me hung, my feller says. It runs away with me.'

She had barely finished speaking when they heard the kitchen door opening. Mrs Molesworth seized a damp cloth and bent to wipe the skirting board. The next moment Mildred appeared in the doorway. 'Haven't you finished yet?' she demanded.

'Nearly, ma'am,' Mrs Molesworth said, resuming her cowed air.

Mildred sniffed. 'Get on with it then,' she said. 'And you, Kate, you come with me.' As they returned to the kitchen, Mildred said sharply, 'Don't encourage that woman to talk, Kate. She'd rather gossip than work.'

'She was working very hard, Auntie,' Kate said nervously, feeling instinctively that it would be better not to mention Mrs Molesworth's bad leg.

'She'd better,' Mildred said grimly. The basket was on the kitchen table and Mildred told Kate to unpack it and put the food away. 'I've got to go out again,' she added, and went up to her own room at the back of the hall.

Before Kate had finished putting away the shopping, Mildred reappeared in the good black clothes she had worn for the funeral. 'The lads from the butcher and the grocer will be bringing my orders. Check what they bring against the lists before you let them go. Oh, and a girl is coming about the place, so tell her to wait if I'm not back. I won't be long.' She turned back before going up the basement stairs. 'And see that Mrs Molesworth gets on with her work. I'll check what's been done when I come back.'

A minute later Mrs Molesworth appeared on the basement stairs. 'I seen her outa the winda going off in her best clothes,' she said. 'Did she say where she was going?'

'No, only that she wouldn't be long,' Kate said.

'It'll be something to do with your mam's affairs,' the charwoman said. 'Any chance of a cuppa? She usually gives me one when I've done the rooms.' Kate set about making a pot of tea and the charwoman sat down, stretching her leg carefully before her.

'Is your leg very sore?' asked Kate.

'Agony, girl, agony. Still, what can't be cured must be endured, as the preacher said.' She looked about her hopefully. 'Anything left from breakfast – a bit of bread or something?' she asked. 'I'm that empty me belly thinks me throat's cut.'

Kate found two thick crusts of bread in the crock and spread dripping thickly on them. Mrs Molesworth wolfed one down as though she was starving, but the other she wrapped and stowed away among her ragged clothes.

'My feller'll enjoy that,' she said. 'I hope you don't get in no trouble for it, girl.'

'No, Auntie won't mind,' Kate said.

'I'm not so sure, girl. Mind you, she's not mean with food. She keeps a good table and good fires, that's why her rooms are always full, but nobody'd do her outa a ha'penny. She takes after her old feller in that way, though he was that mean he'd skin a flea for its hide.'

'But he'd be Mama's father too,' Kate exclaimed. 'Did you know him well?'

'Me ma cleaned for their ma and I used to go with her to help her, so I knew all of them. Proper lady your grandma was. Different from *him*. Beattie and specially your ma took after her.' She looked uneasy. 'I'd better get on, girl. She'll want to know what I've done.'

Kate said quickly, 'Have another cup of tea. I'll help with the work.' She poured the tea before the woman could protest, and said eagerly, 'Do you know the people here? A man carried the coal bucket upstairs for me. Do you know his name?'

'There's three men, girl but it'd probably be Henry Barnes. Jack Rothwell wouldn't put himself out, and old Hayman wouldn't lower himself. What was he like?'

'He had blue eyes and a nice face,' Kate said. 'He looked very healthy and sort of alive. Very cheerful.'

'Aye, that'd be Henry Barnes,' said Mrs Molesworth. 'He'd be the one to do a good turn. He's a nice feller. Never complains like old Hayman.' They were interrupted by a knock on the door and Kate got up to open it.

A thin girl with an aggressive air stood there. 'I've been spoke for for this place,' she said. 'Me name's Martha Johnson.'

Kate smiled at her. 'Come in,' she said. 'My aunt said you were to come in and wait. She won't be long. Sit by the fire and I'll make a fresh pot of tea.'

The girl, who looked miserably cold, sat by the glowing fire while Kate made tea for her. In spite of her fears about

Mildred's return, Mrs Molesworth lingered to ask questions, but she was forestalled.

'You the other help? Yer not very big, are yer?' Martha said, inspecting Kate.

'No. I've come to live with my aunt,' Kate explained. 'I'll be going to school on Monday but I'll help when I come home.'

There was another knock on the door and the butcher's boy and grocer's boy arrived in quick succession. Kate checked the lists as she had been told, then Mrs Molesworth showed her where the food was stored. 'I'd better get on, girl,' the charwoman said nervously. 'She'll be in on top of us before I can turn round.'

'What can I do?' asked Kate, and Mrs Molesworth told her to scrub the kitchen table. 'Don't leave *her* on her own,' she said in an undertone. 'I'll go and polish the floors upstairs.'

'Why don't you do the table so you don't have to kneel?' Kate said. 'And I'll do the polishing.'

'God bless you, girl. You've a heart of gold,' said Mrs Molesworth. 'Better not let on to the missus though.'

'I won't,' Kate assured her.

After polishing the floors, Kate finished the bedrooms, but when she came back to the kitchen Mildred had not yet returned. Martha still sat close to the glowing fire, but she had lost her pinched, frozen look, and Mrs Molesworth was scrubbing out a cupboard at the other end of the large kitchen. Kate went to her.

'I've scrubbed out the scullery but I kept the door open,' the cleaner whispered. 'I tried to find out a bit about her but she was as tight as a drum. Must have something to hide, but the missus will soon find it out, never fear. Is she the only one coming for a job?'

'She was the only one mentioned,' Kate said. 'Why?'

Mrs Molesworth was smiling and nodding. 'Thought so,' she said knowingly. 'She always had two of them, you know, but Ethel got another place last week and Emily walked out on Thursday because the missus wasn't doing nothing to get no one else. We can see why now, can't we?'

'I don't know what you mean,' Kate said, looking puzzled.

The charwoman shut one eye and placed her finger against her nose. 'Think, girl,' she said. 'When did she find out she could bring you here? That's why she's only got the one. She's got you lined up for the other one.'

Kate was astounded, but to give herself time to think she said, 'I think I'll make another pot of tea,' and walked away.

She remembered Mrs Holland saying 'one for a toy and the other for a skivvy'. Could it be true that Aunt Mildred was going to use her for the other maid? But what about school? She would have to go to school until she was thirteen at least.

I don't like school, and I wouldn't mind leaving, she thought, but if I did I wouldn't be able to see Rosie every day. She comforted herself by remembering that she had only been allowed to stay off school to look after Mama, and because Mama had charmed the School Board man when he called. I'm not going to worry about it, she decided. I'm sure I'll *have* to go to school and be able to see Rosie.

She took a loaf from the crock and cut three thick slices of bread and spread them with jam. For herself she would not have dared, although she was hungry, but the knowledge that Mrs Molesworth and probably Martha were starving gave her courage. The bread and tea were consumed within minutes, which was fortunate, as a little later Mildred returned, her mouth set like a rat trap and her eyes glittering with temper.

Mrs Molesworth had retreated hastily and Mildred said to Martha, 'So you're here, are you?'

Martha seemed too nervous to answer, standing humbly before Mildred, so Kate said helpfully, 'She's been waiting a long time, Aunt.'

'Mind your own business and go and find something to do,' snapped Mildred. Kate did as she was told, wondering what had upset her aunt and resenting her dismissal.

She found Mrs Molesworth lurking in the hall. 'Gorra right cob on, hasn't she?' the woman whispered. 'Beattie must've got the better of her.' Then she added hastily,

'Don't take no notice of me, girl. I'm always talking outa turn.'

They could hear Mildred saying loudly, 'All right, I'll give you a trial and see how you shape. Can you stay now?'

'Yes, ma'am,' Martha said eagerly, and for the rest of the day she rushed from one job to another.

There was less for Kate to do now, but as she passed through the hall from the dining room she had the pleasure of meeting Henry Barnes. He smiled at her and said cheerfully, 'Hallo, Kate. You look brighter today.'

She beamed at him. 'I am,' she said shyly, and he replied, 'Good. Good. Keep it up.' She had to restrain her smiles while she was helping Mildred in the kitchen, as her aunt still looked so grim, but in her mind she went over and over the few words she'd exchanged with him. Mrs Molesworth had gone, so there was no opportunity to ask her more about him, or about her mother's family.

She was less tired when she went to bed than on the previous night, and she lay awake for a while thinking happily about the kindness of Henry Barnes, and that she would see Rose the next day, then after that every day at school. She fell asleep at last with a smile on her face, little knowing the shock that awaited her the next day.

Chapter Two

A few miles away across the city, at Greenfields, Beattie's home, Rose had lain awake for a long time on the night of the funeral after Essy had put her to bed in the large double bed in the guest room. 'Madam's having a room done up for you,' the maid told her, 'but it's not ready yet.' Rose's lip trembled and Essy said briskly, 'Now don't cry. You're a very lucky girl, coming to live here with your auntie. You'll have the best of everything.'

When she had tucked the bedclothes around Rose and gone away, Rose could let her tears flow unchecked. If only Kate was with her. Why couldn't she have come here? There was plenty of room in this big house and in this bed. Her tears fell faster as she thought of her sister with her grim Aunt Mildred. And Kate was so soft, so easily hurt. Born to be put upon, Rose had heard one neighbour say to another. She had always felt older than her sister although she was two years younger. Better able to stand up for herself.

Yet she realised now how much she had relied on Kate. Like last night, when they had been taken to say goodbye to their mother as she lay in her coffin, and suddenly Rose had realised that Mama really was dead. She had cried because sometimes she had been unkind to Mama, but Kate, who was crying too, had held her and comforted her. Aunt Beattie, who was with them, had said, 'Don't be sad, girls. Mama is with Jesus now.'

Rose was glad she had cried, but really, she had thought, it would be better now without Mama and with just her and Kate. They could do as they liked without having to keep Mama company because she couldn't bear to be left alone.

Neither of them had imagined that they could be taken from their home and separated forever.

The pillow was wet with Rose's tears but the feather bed was soft and the room warm, and soon Rose fell asleep.

She slept dreamlessly until she was awakened by Essy drawing back the curtains. 'Oh, you're awake,' the maid said. 'I looked in last night but you were fast asleep. Been crying for your poor mother, too. Don't fret, love, she's in Heaven with Jesus now.'

'That's what Aunt Beattie said,' Rose replied, looking about her at the massive mahogany wardrobe and dressing table and the marble-topped washstand where Essy was pouring hot water into a flowered bowl. 'I was really crying for Kate,' she added truthfully.

'Aye, well, don't worry about Kate. She'll be kept too busy to fret, if I know your Aunt Mildred,' said Essy. 'I've put your clothes out, so get washed and dressed as quick as you can. I've got a lot to do today.'

'You're going to our house, aren't you?' Rose said eagerly. 'Can I come with you?'

'Oh, no, love. You'll have to keep madam company. That's what *you're* here for,' said Essy, and she bustled away telling Rose to go to the dining room as soon as possible as her aunt would be waiting for her.

Beattie was seated at the head of a long table, and as soon as Rose had greeted her and sat down, a slim, dark-haired parlourmaid brought in a tureen of porridge, which Beattie served.

'I didn't know you had another maid, Auntie,' Rose whispered as the girl left.

'Yes, Jane,' said Beattie. 'And there's Annie, and Mrs Phillips the cook, and Maud in the kitchen. Essy's my mainstay, though.'

As soon as the porridge was eaten, Jane brought in eggs and bacon, then a pot of China tea. Rose pulled a face at the unfamiliar taste of the tea, but Beattie told her that only China tea was served in her house. 'Your Uncle Arthur was a tea importer and he insisted on the best,' she said, so Rose drank the tea without further protest.

After breakfast Beattie moved to a comfortable chair beside the morning-room fire, and Rose sat on a footstool beside her. Beattie told her to bring her the parcel which lay on the sofa, then put it back into the child's arms. 'There, Rose, open it. It's a dolly I've bought for you, and Essy made the clothes.' Rose opened the parcel and stared at the doll, not attempting to lift it from the box, and her aunt said rather peevishly, 'Well, don't you like it?'

'Oh yes, Auntie, it's beautiful. Thank you very much,' Rose said hastily, lifting the doll from the box. It had a pretty china face, with blue eyes and long fair curls, and was dressed in a blue coat and bonnet with shoes and socks on its feet.

Just then Essy bustled in wearing her hat and coat, and said officiously, 'There, isn't madam kind to give you such a beautiful doll? What do you say?'

'Thank you, Auntie,' Rose said again, obediently, and Essy began to remove the doll's coat to show an embroidered dress, but Beattie coughed and glanced at the clock and the maid said hastily, 'I'll get off then, madam. Is there anything I can do for you before I go?'

Beattie looked down at the dog basket which lay beside her chair. 'You can straighten Wang's blanket. I don't think he's comfortable,' she said.

Essy dropped to her knees and lifted a tiny pug dog from the basket. He snapped at her as she placed him gently on the carpet. He snapped at her again as she smoothed his fleecy blue blanket, and again as she lifted him back into the basket, and Rose was amazed that neither her aunt nor Essy scolded the dog. He'd better not snap at me, she thought.

When Essy had gone, she undressed and dressed the doll several times, handling it gingerly. She felt that it was not really a proper doll, one to be played with like her rag doll, Belinda. Mama had made Belinda, and Rose felt tearful when she thought of her. She hoped that Essy would bring the doll and her books from the house. She would know they were Rose's books because two of them were school prizes with her name in them.

Beattie had picked up some fancywork but it lay idle in her hand and she seemed to be dozing. Rose stood up and

Beattie instantly opened her eyes. 'Can I play in the garden, please, Auntie?' Rose asked, but Beattie shook her head.

'No, dear, it's too cold,' she said.

'But I could run around to keep warm,' Rose protested.

Beattie appeared shocked. 'Run around,' she echoed. 'Oh, no, dear, it would be most unsuitable. Your poor mama only just laid in her grave.'

Rose felt ashamed that she had appeared to forget her mother's death, and her eyes filled with tears, but fortunately just then the clock chimed eleven and Jane appeared with sherry and fruit cake, and a glass of wine and water for Rose.

'For my health,' Beattie explained as she sipped the sherry and slowly ate two slices of the fruit cake.

Rose disliked the taste of the wine and water but decided that it was better to pretend to like it. She felt that she had already offended by disliking the China tea and suggesting running around the garden. If only Kate was here to tell her what to do, she thought.

Beattie smiled indolently at her niece. 'Talk to me, dear,' she said, but Rose, usually such a chatterbox, could think of nothing to say. She looked around desperately, hastily swallowing some fruit cake, and noticed a large framed daguerreotype on the wall of a severe-looking man with a bushy beard. 'Was that Uncle Arthur?' she asked.

'Oh, no, Rose, that was my father, your grandfather, Thomas Edwin Parry,' said Beattie. 'A fine, upright man he was, respected by everyone.'

'When did he die?' asked Rose.

'A long time ago, dear. Soon after I was married. And my dear mother died a year later of a broken heart.'

'Like Mama,' said Rose, but the conversation seemed to require too much effort from Beattie and she only said, 'Ring for Jane, dear.' She had drunk two glasses of sherry, and after the tray was removed, although she picked up her embroidery frame, her eyes soon closed.

Rose looked about her, wondering what she could do. She was already bored by dressing and undressing the doll, so she went to kneel by the dog's basket, but Wang slept as soundly as his mistress. Rose stood up and wandered around the room. She looked at the photographs and trinkets on the occasional table, and at the huge aspidistra on a stand, and she wondered what Kate was doing now.

If only her sister was here! Dare she ask her aunt if Kate could come to live with them? She knew the answer. Rose was a bright, intelligent girl, and young as she was, she had already realised the reality of her situation and knew that the request would be refused.

Beattie slept on, and Rose slipped out of the room and went to the lavatory, then spent some time in the bathroom, washing her hands and examining the large bath with its mahogany surround and china taps. She went along the landing and peeped into the room which she thought would be hers, as it was newly decorated with rose-sprigged wallpaper, but she heard someone in her aunt's bedroom and ran downstairs quickly.

Beattie opened her eyes when she came back into the room, and Rose said hastily, 'I've just been to the lavatory, Auntie.' Her aunt examined the embroidery frame and inserted a few stitches without replying, but when Rose said, 'Mama taught us to knit and I was knitting a scarf. Will Essy bring my knitting from home?' Beattie looked irritated.

'This is your home now, dear, and you're my little girl. Why don't you play with your dolly?' she said. With a sigh, Rose picked up the doll again and nursed it.

Luncheon was served to them at one o'clock, and afterwards they sat in the drawing room. Beattie nursed Wang instead of the embroidery frame, but otherwise the afternoon was the same as the morning and Rose felt that it would never end. She had never sat still for so long before except in school, and there she had interesting lessons and things to do. Inevitably her thoughts turned to happy days at home and to Kate, and tears filled her eyes and dropped on to her hands, unnoticed by her aunt until Rose gave a loud sob. Beattie held out her arms. 'Come to Auntie, dearest,' she said.

Rose went to her and put her arms around her aunt's neck

for comfort, and Beattie wiped her eyes with her handkerchief. 'Don't cry, child,' she said. 'Your mama is with Jesus now and free from pain.'

'But I want Katie,' Rose wailed, and Beattie tut-tutted.

'You'll see your sister tomorrow when she comes to tea with Aunt Mildred,' she said. 'And I've got a treat for you on Monday.' Rose swallowed and blinked away her tears, and Beattie went on, 'I'm going to take you to town and buy you a lot of new clothes. Of course you'll be in mourning for a year, but you can still have nice black dresses. You'll like that, won't you?'

'Oh yes, Auntie. Thank you,' Rose said. She laid her cheek against Beattie's, and Beattie looked pleased. 'There now, dear,' she said. 'Ring for Jane.'

When Jane appeared she looked with concern at the signs of Rose's tears, and when Beattie told her to take Wang for his walk, the maid asked if Rose could come too. 'Wang could get used to Miss Rose and Miss Rose could get used to him, madam,' she said.

To Rose's relief, Beattie agreed.

'See that Miss Rose wraps up warmly, Jane,' she ordered. 'And bring Wang's coat to me.'

After a tartan coat had been tied on the dog and Rose had changed into her new boots and cape and hat, Jane led her through the kitchen. 'We'll go this way so that you can meet Mrs Phillips and Maud,' she said.

The kitchenmaid was not much taller than Rose, and had the worst squint that Rose had ever seen. She said nothing, only smiled showing broken teeth, but stout Mrs Phillips patted Rose's cheek. 'I'm sorry about your mam, love,' she said. 'But you'll be all right here.'

'The food is lovely, Mrs Phillips,' Rose said.

The cook looked gratified. Wang was sniffing round her and she pushed him away with her foot. 'Take that heathenish creature out of my kitchen, Jane,' she said. 'I don't know how you can bear to touch it.'

Jane laughed, and they went into the garden, where Mr Phillips was tying up some Michaelmas daisies. 'This is Miss Rose, Mr Phillips,' said the maid.

The man smiled. 'I'll be driving you to church tomorrow in the carriage,' he said. 'You'll like that, won't you?'

'I didn't know Auntie had a carriage,' Rose exclaimed, her eyes wide, and Mr Phillips said hastily, 'Don't mention I said anything. Madam might want it to be a surprise for you.' Rose assured him that she would say nothing, and she and Jane walked on round the extensive gardens until they came to a large orchard. Here Jane took off Wang's lead, but he only waddled slowly in front of them and sniffed at one of the trees.

'I'd love to run and jump about,' Rose exclaimed, feeling ready to explode with pent-up energy.

'Go on then,' Jane said, but Rose told her that her aunt had said it was unsuitable as her mama had just died.

'That's only if people can see you,' Jane said. 'No one can see you here,' so Rose went leaping away among the trees. When she came back looking flushed and happy, Jane had replaced Wang's lead. 'Why don't you run a little way with Wang?' she said. 'Not far or fast. Just enough to give him some exercise and for you to cool down.' Rose set off with the little dog, but the unaccustomed exercise made him pant so much that she soon came back to Jane.

'Doesn't he do this every day?' she asked. 'He's far too fat, isn't he?'

'I think so,' Jane said. 'I'd make him take exercise but usually Essy walks him, only she's busy today.'

Rose instantly remembered where Essy was, and looked sad. 'She's gone to our house. I wish I could have stayed there with Katie,' she said.

Jane slipped an arm round her. 'Never mind, love,' she said. 'You'll soon settle down here, and madam will be very kind to you. It's no use looking back. I've found that out.'

Rose put her arm round Jane's neck and kissed her. 'I like you, Jane,' she said. 'Will you be my friend?'

Jane smiled and hugged her. 'I will, Miss Rose,' she said. 'But we mustn't say anything to madam or Essy. You must always be very careful what you say to them in case you upset them, but you can say anything you like to me.'

They went back to the house and Jane took off Wang's coat

and wiped his feet before restoring him to his mistress. Rose took off her outdoor clothes and changed her boots before returning to the drawing room. She felt much happier, partly because she now had a friend, and partly because she had rid herself of her frustrated energy. Beattie, however, seemed cross, glancing frequently at the clock and drumming her fingers on the arm of her chair. Finally she told Rose to ring for Jane.

When Jane appeared, Beattie asked irritably, 'Are there no messages from Miss Mills?'

'Not yet, madam,' Jane said soothingly, but Beattie still looked cross. 'Very well. You may bring in tea now,' she said.

'Very good, madam.'

Back in the kitchen, Jane told the cook that madam was asking for Essy and seemed annoyed. 'She wants tea right away. Seems to be real ratty. Called Essy Miss Mills.'

'But she can't expect a house cleared in five minutes,' Mrs Phillips exclaimed. 'It's a big job, closing a house. Essy won't be in any mood for being scolded when she gets back.'

'Madam will probably feel better when she's had tea,' Jane said. 'Everything's ready, isn't it?'

'Lucky it is, half an hour early,' the cook grumbled, but Jane only smiled and took in the tea.

Rose was amazed to see the variety of dainty sandwiches and small cakes, and tucked in heartily. Her aunt ate as much as she did, and her good temper seemed restored.

Jane reported the change of mood to Mrs Phillips when she took out the remains of the tea, adding that Rose had thanked her and said the food was lovely. 'She's a dear little girl, isn't she?' she said. Maud had been sent on an errand, and the two women poured tea for themselves and settled down to have a good gossip.

'She's very free with her praise, and that'll suit madam. She'd better keep on with it if she knows what side her bread's buttered,' said Mrs Phillips.

'Oh, Mrs Phillips, I'm sure she means it. She's not trying to butter people up. I don't suppose she's ever had food like this before,' Jane protested.

'I'm sure you're right, Jane. She *is* a nice little girl – now,' replied the cook. 'But she'll change, you'll see. She'll be spoiled and given everything she wants, but at the same time she'll have to watch her p's and q's. Make sure she doesn't do anything madam doesn't like. It's the other little one I'm sorry for. She'll have to earn her keep with that Mildred Williams.'

'Your niece worked for her – for Mrs Williams, didn't she?' asked Jane.

'Yes, our Cissie's girl, and she said she never worked so hard in her life as when she worked there. They never stopped from first thing in the morning to last thing at night, yet the missus was never satisfied. The food was good but the pay was a disgrace. Our Cissie soon had her out of there and into another place, I can tell you.'

'I think little Rose will earn her keep here in another way,' declared Jane. 'She's asked me to be her friend, and I will.'

'Watch your step, girl,' advised the cook. 'Make sure madam or Essy don't hear that. You'll never get a place like this again if you lose this one.'

'I know,' agreed Jane. 'I just feel sorry for the child. She seems to be fretting more for her sister than for her mam, mind you.'

'No wonder. The mother was a useless creature. Sweet-natured, like, but spoiled by the family because she was the youngest, then by her husband,' said the cook. 'Always had everything her own way. She took to the bottle, I heard, when her husband was killed in the Boer War, instead of thinking of her children.'

'You worked for the family, didn't you?' Jane said. 'So you know all about them.'

'Yes, I was only a kitchenmaid then, in the big house in St Anne Street, but we all knew what went on. The father, old Mr Parry, was as hard as nails, and mean! He ruled the three girls *and* their mother.'

'And yet madam has got that big picture of him up in the drawing room,' Jane exclaimed.

'Yes, well, people believe what they want to believe about their relations, especially after they're dead,' the cook said cynically. 'The mother was a nice lady, but no spirit. I think he made her feel guilty because she didn't have no son.'

'Was madam pretty as a girl?' asked Jane.

'Oh yes, she was, and a lot of young men wanted to court her, but old Parry seen to it that she married Arthur Anderson. A lot older than her, but plenty of money.'

'Seems to have worked out all right for her,' said Jane. 'I wouldn't mind marrying an old man if he died after a few years and left me as well off as she is. Mind you, I'd probably marry one who lived to be a hundred!'

'Oh, Jane, you're a case,' the cook exclaimed. 'Mind you, the old feller was so busy watching Beattie that young Sophie was able to see a soldier on the sly.'

'Sophie was Rose's mother?' said Jane.

'Yes,' said Mrs Phillips. 'Old Parry died just after madam was married, and about the same time the soldier finished in the army and him and Sophie got married very quiet, like. The old fellow would never have allowed it, but their mother was too ill to care. She died a year after old Parry.'

'What was the soldier like – Rose's father?' asked Jane.

'A nice lad, and it was a real love match. Johnny Drew, his name was, and he was a silversmith by trade. They were happy but they were a soft pair. Little Rose has got her looks.'

'She must've been a beauty then,' declared Jane. 'Rose is lovely.'

'And with more of her wits about her than her parents, I'd say,' said the cook. 'When Mrs Parry died the money was divided between the three girls. Sophie kept hers and his gratuity went into a shop, but they were robbed blind. He believed every hard-luck story and she was as bad. Then he was a Reservist, you see, and he got called back into the army for the Boer War.'

'And killed,' said Jane with a sigh. 'What happened with Mrs Williams?'

Mrs Phillips snorted. 'Mildred?' she said. 'She'd never been courted – she was more like a man than a woman – but when she got her father's money this ne'er-do-well came hanging round and she grabbed him and married him.'

There was a noise outside and the two women jumped to their feet in alarm. At the same moment the drawing-room bell jangled above their heads.

Jane hastily smoothed her hair and settled her cap, but before she hurried off she said quickly to the cook, 'Oo, I *did* enjoy our talk. We never get a chance while Essy's about.'

'Yes, she's got ears like a bat, and everything she hears goes straight back to madam,' said Mrs Phillips. 'Hurry now, Jane.'

When Jane arrived in the drawing room, she found that Essy had returned and was sitting near to Beattie. 'A fresh pot of tea, Jane, and bring a cup for Miss Mills,' Beattie ordered.

Essy looked gratified. As soon as Jane left, she began to whisper to Beattie and show her some lists.

Rose was sitting on the other side of the room, pretending to play with her doll, but her sharp ears caught most of the conversation. She heard Essy whispering that she had brought the sewing table that had belonged to Beattie's mother, and the other things on the list. 'Mrs Williams didn't seem pleased about the trinket set, but she had a donkey cart with her and she took several items of furniture and all the bedding and crockery. I hope that was all right, madam. I made a list of everything that went on the cart.'

'I said she could take the crockery and bedlinen. It wasn't up to my standard,' Beattie said.

'Of course not, madam,' agreed Essy. 'And neither were the other things she took. I threw a lot of rubbish out, but I made sure only quality stuff came here.'

'You did well, Essy,' Beattie said approvingly.

Essy preened herself and said something which Rose was unable to hear, but she did hear her say, 'There were two books with labels in the front saying they were school prizes for Miss Rose. I brought those, madam. I hope I did right. They were spotlessly clean.'

Beattie murmured something about a clean break, but Essy replied, 'I thought you could decide, madam, if I brought them. I thought they'd be proof she was a good pupil.'

Nothing more was said about the books, but when Essy

was putting Rose to bed, she plucked up courage to ask about Belinda.

'That dirty rag doll!' Essy exclaimed. 'I threw it out with the other rubbish.'

'Mama made her for me,' Rose stammered, but Essy said briskly, 'Yes, but you've got your beautiful new doll from madam now. You're a very lucky little girl.' Rose was to hear this phrase very frequently during the next few months and years.

The following day, Sunday, she accompanied her aunt to church, being driven in the carriage by Mr Phillips. True to her promise, she simulated joyful surprise when her aunt led her out to the carriage, and Beattie looked graciously pleased. Mr Phillips appeared relieved, and Rose reflected that although the servants seemed to like her aunt, they were also afraid of her – or perhaps of losing their jobs. They all seemed wary of Essy too.

In the afternoon Kate arrived with Mildred. For a moment the girls looked at each other shyly, then Kate flung her arms around her sister and Rose hugged her in return. Both girls wore the identical black dresses provided by Beattie, but already there was a marked difference in their appearance. While Kate's mousy hair was scraped back into a thin plait tied with a narrow black ribbon, and she wore the boots provided by Mildred for both girls, Rose's glossy fair locks had been carefully brushed into ringlets, and she wore a black velvet bow in her hair and new low shoes on her feet. A richly embroidered black pinafore covered her dress.

As the day was mild the two girls were sent into the garden while their elders talked. Kate eagerly questioned Rose. Was she happy? Did she like living here?

'They call me Miss Rose, the servants, I mean,' said Rose, 'and I went to church in the carriage this morning with Auntie. Mr Phillips drove us. Mrs Phillips is the cook and the food's lovely. We're always eating and we have porridge *and* bacon and eggs for breakfast.'

'But are you happy, Rosie?' Kate persisted.

Rose put her arms around her sister. 'I miss you, Katie,'

she said. 'I wish you could come and live here. I don't like being on my own.'

'I miss you too, Rosie,' Kate said, and they wept together. Kate was the first to recover, and she wiped away Rose's tears with her handkerchief. 'But Aunt Beattie couldn't manage two of us here and Aunt Mildred needs me to help with the guests.'

'I thought we would be able to stay at home, just you and me,' said Rose. 'I'd have liked that, Katie.'

'So would I, but Aunt Mildred says it wouldn't be allowed. We'd have been sent to the workhouse and we wouldn't have liked that, would we?'

Rose shuddered. 'No. Essy keeps saying I'm a very lucky little girl. Auntie gave me a big doll and Essy dressed it. I've called it Kate.'

Before she could say any more, Jane came to tell them that they were to come in. Kate was surprised when Rose took Jane's hand. She herself was very much in awe of the tall, superior parlourmaid, but Jane smiled at her, and Rose said, 'Jane is my friend – aren't you, Jane? – but we haven't told Auntie or Essy.'

Jane said gently to Kate, 'I'm sorry about your mama, and you being parted from Miss Rose, but these things happen. No use looking back. You just have to try to fit in wherever you are, although I know your life will be harder than Miss Rose's.'

Kate only nodded in reply, but she was happy that Rose was with this kind, wise girl.

The sisters went upstairs to take off their outdoor clothes, and Rose proudly showed Kate the guest room where she now slept and the bedroom which was being prepared for her. No work was being done as it was Sunday, but the room was almost ready. Kate was impressed by the rose-sprigged curtains, counterpane and wallpaper. 'It's a feather bed, Rose,' she cried as they pressed the mattress, and Rose said nonchalantly, 'So is the guest bed where I sleep now.'

The floor was fitted with a pink carpet, and a white sheepskin rug lay beside the bed. 'Aunt Beattie must be very rich!' Kate exclaimed.

Rose took her next to see the bathroom, where they washed their hands and Kate admired the large fluffy towels and scented soap.

When they returned downstairs, Rose forestalled any rebuke by saying brightly, 'I've just been showing Kate my room, Auntie, and she thinks it's lovely, don't you, Kate?'

Kate nodded. She felt overawed by the luxury of the house, and was amazed yet pleased that Rose appeared to have adapted so easily to it. Mildred, however, looked grim. 'Kate has a nice room of her own in my house,' she snapped, and Kate eagerly agreed.

Jane brought in tea, and Essy poured, fussing about Beattie, ensuring that a small table was placed in the exact position to be most convenient for her. Rose helped to carry around the plates of sandwiches and the cake stands while Beattie lay back indolently. Mrs Phillips had surpassed herself in the variety of sandwiches and cakes she had provided, and Kate was thoroughly enjoying them until Mildred hissed at her, 'Don't eat as though you've never seen food before,' after which she felt that she must refuse them.

After tea Rose brought out her doll and the two girls played with it, undressing and dressing it. 'I'd rather have Belinda,' Rose whispered to Kate when Essy had left the room. 'But Essy threw her out.' Tears filled her eyes, but Kate whispered, 'Don't cry. You'll soon love Kate just as much.'

It was as Mildred and Kate were preparing to leave that the blow fell. 'I'll see you in the playground tomorrow, Rose,' Kate said happily, but Beattie said languidly, 'I'm taking Rose to town tomorrow for new clothes. We'll enjoy that, won't we, dear?'

'But – but what about school?' Kate stammered.

Beattie waved her hand. 'That's all arranged,' she said. 'Rose won't be going back there. I've entered her for the Select School.'

Rose was as surprised as Kate, and they gaped at each other in dismay.

'But when will I see her?' Kate cried, and Rose gripped her hand.

'You can come to tea again with Aunt Mildred,' Beattie

34

said placidly, seeming unaware of the dismay she was causing the two girls. 'You'll like the Select School, dear,' she said to Rose. 'Very ladylike girls attend there and you'll soon find lots of nice friends.'

It was too much for Mildred. She strode towards the door. 'Come along,' she ordered, and as though in a dream, Kate said goodbye to Beattie and allowed herself to be hustled out by Mildred. They were on the garden path when Rose came flying out of the front door and flung her arms round Kate. 'I didn't know, Kate,' she sobbed. 'Nobody told me.'

'Why should they?' Mildred demanded. 'You're a *child*. Your place is to do as you're told.' At the same moment Essy rushed down the steps and scolded Rose for running out without a coat. 'Come in at once, Miss Rose. You could catch a cold and give it to madam,' she fussed.

The sisters had only time for a hasty kiss before Essy pulled Rose indoors and Mildred marched Kate down the long drive, firmly gripping her arm. '*Miss Rose* indeed! A cold for *madam*!' she muttered angrily. 'And the Select School!'

Kate said nothing. She felt bewildered, as though too much was happening too quickly for her to comprehend. She felt no pain as yet at being parted even further from her sister, but she knew that the pain was there, ready to leap upon her when this numbness passed away.

Chapter Three

Kate was still in a dazed state when they reached home, and Mildred, looking at her white face, told her to sit in a chair by the blazing kitchen fire. She ordered Martha to make tea and said with unexpected kindness to Kate, 'Your sister'll take to that life like a duck to water, and you can just settle yourself here. It's a fresh start for both of you.' Then she began to question Martha sharply about the tasks she had been given to do in their absence. Martha admitted that she had not made up the dining-room fire or prepared the table for the meal, and was scolded roundly by Mildred.

Kate was oblivious to them, sitting in a stupor of misery, trying to absorb the latest blow. It was all too much, she felt. The distress of her mother's death, then of being abruptly parted from Rose when they needed each other most, had been made bearable for Kate because she thought she would see Rose regularly and they could console each other. Now her fortitude was unequal to this latest blow.

Mildred's brief sympathy was soon over. 'Don't change your clothes,' she ordered Kate. 'Put an apron over your good dress and do two platefuls of bread and butter. The blue plates.' She turned to Martha. 'And you – bring up a bucket of coal to the dining room.'

As Mildred went upstairs, Martha whispered to Kate, 'What's up? What's happened, like?'

'I won't see Rose at school,' Kate said. 'Aunt Beattie's sending her to the Select School.' She swallowed, fighting back tears, and Martha exclaimed tactlessly, 'Them snobs. She won't want to know you once she gets with them lot.'

Later, Mildred gave Kate a dish of apple sauce to take

upstairs, and as she left the dining room, Henry Barnes came through the front door.

'Hallo,' he said cheerfully. 'We meet again. Are you settling in?' His kindness was too much for Kate, and she burst into tears. Henry drew her out of the front door to the broad top step, and there in the shelter of a pillar he put his arm around Kate and dried her eyes with his handkerchief.

'There, love, there,' he comforted her. 'What is it? Has the old hag been unkind to you?' Kate shook her head, unable to speak, then managed to whisper, 'I won't see our Rose at school. She's going to the Select School.'

'And you were counting on seeing her at school?' Henry said with instant understanding. 'Look, I know you've been through a lot lately – Mrs Molesworth's been telling Mrs Bradley all about you – and I suppose it seems like the last straw, but never mind. You'll be able to visit each other, won't you?'

'Only every few weeks on a Sunday, with the aunts there,' Kate said, and her lip began to tremble.

Henry said hastily, 'Chin up, Kate. You've been a brave girl and I'm sure this may not be too bad. Perhaps you can arrange to meet your sister in the park or somewhere like that sometimes.' He added jokingly, 'Neither of you are in gaol.'

He succeeded in making Kate smile, as he intended, and they went back into the house. Kate felt comforted and able to speak and behave normally when she returned to the kitchen, and Mildred looked approving.

'It's only a cold meal, and Martha can serve it,' she said. 'You can sit at the table upstairs tonight, Kate. Take that apron off and tidy yourself.'

Kate was apprehensive about eating with the guests, partly from shyness and partly because she was still upset, but she found that she was sitting opposite Henry, who winked at her, and near Mrs Bradley, so she soon felt better. As soon as they were all seated, Mildred announced, 'This is my niece, Kate, who has come to live with me,' and there was a general murmur of welcome. Mrs Bradley leaned forward and said kindly, 'You look very nice, my dear,' and Kate smiled and thanked her shyly.

The meal was cold roast pork from the midday joint and boiled ham, with beetroot and celery, followed by stewed fruit and custard and a large fruit cake. Mildred gave Kate a second slice of cake.

'You need feeding up,' she told her. 'This is better than those fancy fal-lals at your Aunt Beattie's house, isn't it?'

Kate agreed meekly. Rose had told her of the frequent large meals served at Beattie's house but she remembered a saying of Mrs Holland's – 'A still tongue keeps a wise head' – and said nothing of them.

From time to time Kate peeped at the people around the table and identified them from Mrs Molesworth's descriptions. A portly grey-haired man with a full beard must be the shipping office manager, Mr Hayman, and the young swarthy man must be Jack Rothwell, a bank clerk. The two young ladies, straight-backed and ladylike, eating daintily, must be the two teachers, Miss Tate and Miss Norton, but nobody addressed them by name.

At the end of the meal Mrs Bradley leaned forward again. 'Would you like to come to my room, my dear?' she said to Kate. 'I have a picture book which you might enjoy.' Mildred frowned and Mrs Bradley said smoothly, 'It is quite suitable for Sunday reading, Mrs Williams. It was written by a missionary.'

'But what about the dishes?' Kate asked innocently.

Mildred's face grew red with anger. 'What about them?' she snapped. 'You didn't come here to work. I have maids for that.'

Kate looked abashed, but unseen by Mildred, Henry winked at her again, then pulled a face. Kate was smiling as she followed Mrs Bradley to her room on the first floor, where a bright fire burned in the ornate grate. Mrs Bradley sank into a cushioned rocking chair beside the fire, and gestured to Kate to sit opposite her and to pick up the book which lay on a small table.

'Read it to me, my dear,' she said. 'We will look at the pictures later.'

Kate blushed deeply and hung her head. 'I can't read very well,' she mumbled.

'Bring the book to me,' commanded Mrs Bradley. She opened it and pointed to the first word, and Kate tried to read, but it was obvious that she knew only the simplest words. Mrs Bradley closed the book. 'I thought it might be poor eyesight, but obviously you have not been taught to read,' she said.

'I missed school so often to look after Mama,' Kate murmured.

'I thought there must be a reason. You are not a stupid girl,' said Mrs Bradley. She sat thinking while Kate stood meekly beside her, then, with sudden decision, the old lady said, 'Go to Miss Tate's room, Kate. It's the third door from the left round the turn in the stairs. Knock and ask Miss Tate if it is convenient for her to come to see me. Return with her if it is.'

Agnes Tate was the taller and more elegant of the two teachers, with dark hair piled on top of her head. She seemed surprised by the request, and asked if Mrs Bradley was ill, but she willingly accompanied Kate to the room.

'I have a problem,' Mrs Bradley told the teacher. 'I have discovered that Kate is unable to read.' Kate blushed again deeply, but Agnes Tate only asked her in a matter-of-fact way if she could write.

'Only my name,' Kate said miserably, and Mrs Bradley informed Miss Tate that she had missed school to nurse her mother. 'It seems a pity when she is clearly an intelligent girl,' she went on. 'I wondered if you could help, Miss Tate?'

'I would be happy to,' said Agnes Tate. 'But Mrs Williams?'

'Leave Mrs Williams to me,' Mrs Bradley said firmly. 'I just wanted your assurance. We can discuss details later.'

'And what about Kate?' Agnes said, smiling at her. 'Would you like to be able to read and write, Kate?'

'Oh, yes,' Kate said eagerly. 'My sister's very clever, she won prizes at school, and Mama used to write poetry years ago.'

The two women exchanged a glance and Mrs Bradley announced, 'Then you must certainly learn. Now, you must see if your aunt needs you.'

40

When Kate returned to the kitchen, she found Martha alone, as Mildred had gone to church.

'She left me another pile of jobs to do,' grumbled Martha. 'She doesn't half want the worth of her money, doesn't she?'

Kate said nothing. She felt no affection for her aunt and still resented her comment about her mother's death, but she was unwilling to discuss her with Martha. Instead she offered to help with the jobs, and started on a pile of mending thinking of Mrs Bradley and Miss Tate's plans for her.

Mrs Bradley's interest in Kate made a difference in Kate's life, although she was unaware of it at first. Mildred worked hard herself and expected Kate to work as hard. She often reminded Kate of her obligation to her, but a smooth intervention from Mrs Bradley sometimes resulted in less work and more free time for Kate. Mildred valued Mrs Bradley as her longest and wealthiest resident, who gave little trouble, and she was unwilling to offend her.

Even to herself Mildred could not admit that she had taken Kate to be useful to her, someone who would be reliable because she was unable to leave, and hard-working because she was often reminded that she should be grateful to her aunt. Mildred told herself, and believed, that she had given her niece a home out of her sense of duty. Her religion was as bleak and uncompromising as everything else in her life, but at least she did not impose it on Kate.

She had hung a poker-work message in Kate's room – 'Thou God Seest Me' – and insisted that Kate accompanied her to the early-morning Sunday service at the Mission, but apart from that, Kate's work in the house took precedence over any church activities. Mildred felt that by making Kate work hard she was doing her duty by preparing her niece for life. She herself attended the Mission on Sunday, Wednesday and Friday evenings, her only relaxation.

On Monday, the day after that fateful Sunday, Kate helped with the housework before school. When she came out of the school gates at the end of the day Mrs Holland was waiting for her. She pulled a bag of sweets from beneath her shawl. 'Here, love, share these with Rosie,' she said. 'Where is she?'

'Oh, Mrs Holland, she's not coming here any more,' Kate said, bursting into tears. 'She's going to a Select School for Young Ladies.'

'Dear God, she hasn't wasted much time, your snobby old aunt, has she?' Mrs Holland exclaimed.

'I'll only see Rose when I go there to tea,' Kate wept, but Mrs Holland hugged her. 'Never mind, girl. It was bound to come and you might as well get it all over at once. How are you getting on with the other one?'

'I've got a nice room,' said Kate. 'And there's a nice man there, Mrs Holland. His name's Henry Barnes and he said it's always darkest before the dawn and he told me not to cry because I might be able to arrange to meet Rose in the park or somewhere. He said we're not in gaol. He's awful nice.'

'He sounds it,' said Mrs Holland. 'How old is he?'

Kate looked surprised at the question. 'I don't know. Quite old,' she said. 'Over twenty.'

'Ancient then,' said Mrs Holland, concealing a smile. 'What about the others?'

'I only know Mrs Molesworth, the charwoman, and Martha and Mrs Bradley and Miss Tate. They are going to teach me to read better. Henry Barnes carried a bucket of coal upstairs for me.'

'She's got you working then?' Mrs Holland exclaimed.

'Yes, but it's better that way,' Kate said earnestly. 'Aunt says hard work is the best cure for grief.'

'That's handy for her,' Mrs Holland said dryly. 'Make sure the hard work doesn't keep on, though, when you're over the grief.'

Kate assured her that she was quite happy, but Mrs Holland was unconvinced.

'I haven't got no rights, but I could show her up, and I *would*,' she said. 'So don't think you're on your own because you're not. Not while I've got breath in me body. And you know where I live if you need me.'

Kate was comforted by the meeting, but she felt that it was wiser to say nothing about it to her aunt, and she concealed the sweets in her room.

The days passed quickly for Kate. Mrs Bradley had arranged

for her to have two hours' tuition twice a week with Miss Tate so that she found her schoolwork easier, and she was kept busy before and after school with housework. All in all she had little time to think of the past. She still missed Rose, but she was not unhappy, because she found her life so interesting. She spent a lot of time with Mrs Molesworth, who was a mine of information about Kate's family and about the guests. Kate questioned her eagerly about Mr Barnes.

'He's a nice young feller,' Mrs Molesworth said. 'He's some kind of a boss at Bryant's already – y'know, the big shop in Church Street. His mother and his sister live near Delamere Forest 'cos his sister's sickly, like. She's been in a sanatorium for about a year but she's home again now. He goes to see them one Sunday a month. Gorra brother too, but he works abroad – India or somewhere.'

Kate gazed at her, round-eyed. 'Did he tell you all that, Mrs Molesworth?' she asked and the charwoman laughed.

'God bless you, girl,' she said. 'They don't tell the likes of us. No, I keep my eyes and ears open, that's all. There's not much I don't know about this lot. Mr Hayman, now. He's a widower and he never lets on about any family, but I know for a fact he's got two daughters who never come next or near him.'

'That's sad, isn't it?' Kate said. 'Have you got any children, Mrs Molesworth?'

'I've had nine, girl, but I only reared two. Our Billy, who's on the China run, the best lad that ever stepped, and a girl, Florrie, married and in America. Three were stillborn and I lost our Sally with the quinsy when she was two. Then I lost two lads in the one week with the measles. Eighteen months and five months, our Peter and our George.'

'Oh, Mrs Molesworth, that's awful,' Kate exclaimed. 'It must have been terrible for you.'

The charwoman sat back on her heels and rested her hand on the rim of the bucket. 'Aye,' she said sadly, 'but the one that broke our hearts was our little Harry. We knew when he was born he wouldn't live but he lingered on for four months, suffering all the time. We got the doctor but he only said there wasn't nothing we could do. It was some kind of a twist in Harry's inside and he wouldn't last, he said.'

'What a terrible thing to say,' Kate said indignantly, but Mrs Molesworth replied gently, 'No, girl, he was right. Y'see, he couldn't keep his feed down or nothing, and oh God, the pitiful cries out of him.' She wiped her eyes on her sleeve and Kate wept with her. 'Nearly broke me and Charlie's hearts. He'd lay there looking up at us as if to say why? Great big eyes he had in his little tiny face. My feller got laudanum and gave Harry drops of it and it seemed to help. "It's not right, girl, I know," Charlie used to say, "but if it gives him some ease, it can't make no difference."'

'Did he stop crying?' asked Kate.

'Yes, made him drowsy, like, and it must've eased his pain. We'd have given him anything to stop him suffering, and we knew he wasn't gonna live anyhow.' She wept again. 'I remember the day he died as if it was yesterday. He seemed to settle comfortable, like, in me arms, and I sat there with him the livelong day. Charlie came in from work and I said, "I haven't done no tea. He just seems comfortable and I haven't given him laudanum or nothing."'

'"To hell with the tea," Charlie said, and he knelt down by me. "Me poor little lad," he said, and big man that he was he broke his heart crying. "He's so peaceful," I said. "Do you think he's turned the corner?" But he said, "No, girl, he's turned the corner but it's the last one and the best thing for him."' She wiped her eyes again. 'I'd prayed for him to go out of his suffering but when it come to it I couldn't face it. I sat there with Harry so comfortable in me arms and Charlie beside me, and you know what, Kate? The first time Harry ever smiled, and he smiled at us and died.'

She sat back on her heels, her hands idle for once and her eyes empty as she looked back over the years.

Kate was sobbing now, and Mrs Molesworth said contritely, 'I shouldn't be upsetting you, girl, and you with your own sorrow. It's all long ago now, but y'know, it seems like yesterday.' She rubbed soap on her scrubbing brush and began work again, but Kate felt unable to stop crying, and she could see that Mrs Molesworth's tears were still falling even as she scrubbed.

Hearing about the sorrow that Mrs Molesworth had endured made Kate feel even more fond of her friend and put her own troubles in perspective. The loss of her mother and the parting from Rose seemed almost trivial in the light of everything Mrs Molesworth and her husband had suffered, yet she still longed to see Rose.

Mildred had decided that it was her duty to visit Beattie regularly, so Kate was able to see her sister every four or six weeks. On her second visit to Beattie's house the girls were again sent into the garden to play while their elders talked, and Kate produced Rose's share of the sweets given to her by Mrs Holland.

Rose refused them. 'You eat them, Katie,' she said. 'I have much nicer sweets from Auntie.'

Kate put the bag back into her pocket without comment, but questioned Rose eagerly about her life. Rose admitted that she enjoyed the luxury of Aunt Beattie's home, although she had several small complaints.

'I can't do as I like, Kate,' she said. 'Often I want to read but I have to do fancywork in case Auntie wants to talk.'

'Do you like the school?' asked Kate.

'Yes, but if I didn't go to school I'd never be allowed outside the house. Essy thinks winter air is bad for the lungs.'

'So you don't think you could meet me in the park or somewhere?' Kate said in dismay. 'This nice man in our house said we might be able to.'

'No, they watch me like hawks,' Rose said gloomily. 'Essy used to take me to school but sometimes Auntie needed her while she was out, so now Annie takes me and she's even worse. She won't let go of my hand for a minute.'

She looked so woebegone that Kate said bracingly, 'Never mind. We'll think of something. I'm glad you like the school.'

Rose shrugged. 'We don't have proper lessons,' she said. 'I know more geography and English and arithmetic than the big girls.'

'Well, you were always the cleverest in the class, weren't

you?' Kate said fondly. 'What do you learn at the Select School?'

'Deportment and dancing and music. I like them,' said Rose. 'And French. Mademoiselle who teaches French is *really* French but I don't like her. Oh, and sewing, and a little bit of English and arithmetic. I'm the only one who knows her twelve times tables. The big girls say I'm a clever little pet,' she added smugly.

Her hair hung in fat glossy ringlets and Kate touched it gently. 'Your hair looks lovely, Rose. Who does it for you?' she asked.

'Annie, the maid who takes me to school. She looks after the bedrooms but she chiefly looks after me now.'

'What about Jane?' asked Kate.

'She's the parlourmaid,' Rose said airily. 'Essy used to do things for me but sometimes she was busy with me when madam needed her and that wouldn't do, so Annie looks after me now.' As though on cue, Annie, a thin, middle-aged woman, appeared to take them indoors, and Kate was amazed by the imperious manner in which Rose treated her. She felt that she would have been unequal to this lifestyle, but Rose seemed to have settled in happily, in spite of her small grumbles.

Jane brought in the tea and Kate smiled at her, but there was no opportunity to speak.

After tea, Kate and Rose went to the bathroom. When they returned, Mildred was already wearing her hat and coat and Beattie had rung for Essy to show them out.

'I won't get up,' Beattie said languidly. 'My back is aching.' Mildred marched to the door, and as Kate bent over Beattie to kiss her goodbye, Beattie slipped a sovereign into her hand. 'Just for you, dear,' she whispered. 'Say nothing to Mildred.'

Kate was delighted with the gift and felt no guilt about concealing it from Mildred. As soon as she was able to change it to smaller coins, she gave Mrs Molesworth two shillings to buy a treat for her husband.

'God bless you, girl. You've a heart of gold,' the charwoman said when she could speak. 'It'll make that much difference to my poor feller.'

46

She told Kate the next morning that she had bought her husband a pig's trotter, which he had fancied for a while but had been unable to afford. 'He relished every bit of it,' she declared. 'Then I got some shin beef and a penn'orth of potherbs and some barley and made such a panful of broth! I can taste it still. My feller said if he got food like that every day he'd be up and skipping.'

'And would he?' Kate asked eagerly.

'No, girl, he'll never walk again,' Mrs Molesworth said sadly. 'He was just saying, like, how much he enjoyed it.' She smiled again. 'And I've got plenty of money left too. I know how to make one penny do as much as two, so he's gorra lot to look forward too, like.'

Kate was delighted that her gift was so successful. As time passed, her naturally cheerful disposition had reasserted itself, and she was beginning to enjoy life again. She never forgot her parents or ceased to love Rose, but she believed that her parents were happy together in Heaven, and she was glad that Rose was settling into her new life but was still as loving when they met.

She was pleased to feel needed and useful, and felt she was lucky to have such good friends as Mrs Molesworth and Martha and to be helped by Miss Tate and Mrs Bradley. Most of all she was happy to be near her hero, Henry Barnes. She saw him every day, and if he spoke to her she was elated for the rest of the day.

Kate's position in the house was ambiguous. Mildred insisted that she was there as her orphan niece, but Kate was doing more and more of the work of the house before and after school and at weekends. Mildred said no more about engaging a second maid.

Martha was complaining about this one Saturday morning when Mildred had departed on one of her mysterious errands. As soon as she was safely away, Kate made a pot of tea and produced a bag of broken biscuits she had bought for Mrs Molesworth, Martha and herself.

'She's never let on about another girl and she won't while she's got you run off your feet, Kate,' said Martha.

'I don't mind,' Kate said. 'I like housework.'

'You're getting put on, girl, there's no two ways about it,' said Mrs Molesworth. 'She says you haven't come here to work, but she knows we couldn't manage without all you do.'

'I'm gettin' put on an' all,' Martha grumbled. 'A place this size with six boarders and only one maid. It's not right.'

'If it comes to that, I'm only supposed to do the rough, but I've got to turn me hand to anything,' said the charwoman 'But give the missus her due, she does enough for two herself. We can't say nothing anyhow. We're lucky to have a job at all, the way things are.' She stood up. 'I'd better get on now or I *won't* have no job.' She went upstairs with her cleaning box, and Martha followed to make up the fires and polish the dining room and parlour.

Kate washed up and scrubbed the kitchen table, thinking about what had been said. She felt no resentment towards her aunt but she decided she must work harder to help Martha and Mrs Molesworth.

Kate now spent an hour three evenings a week with Agnes Tate, being taught English and arithmetic. She was greatly in awe of Miss Tate, who was a tall, graceful young woman with an hourglass figure and a cloud of dark hair which she wore piled on top of her head and becomingly puffed out at the sides. During the week she wore long navy-blue or black skirts and plain white blouses with small bows at the neck, but on Sundays she wore a long, heavily braided cream skirt and a cream poplin blouse with a cameo brooch at the neck.

She was a very reserved person, and Kate was very nervous when she first knocked at the door for a lesson, but Miss Tate put her at ease immediately. 'I don't know how far you've progressed, Kate,' she said. 'So I've decided to start right at the beginning. The groundwork is so important.'

She was a good and patient teacher, and although Kate found the arithmetic hard, she enjoyed the English lessons and Agnes encouraged in her a taste for books which was to be a delight to Kate all her life. She was finding her schoolwork easier, and was due to take the leaving examination at Christmas 1905, when she was thirteen years old.

Mrs Holland often met Kate at the gates after school. Her

old neighbour was now working in a bag warehouse, hard, heavy work. Her wages went to help her only daughter, Dolly, who had two small children and was married to a man who drank most of what he earned. Kate was worried to see how thin and gaunt Mrs Holland had become and how she kept her hand pressed against her side as she talked, but she was as cheerful and as concerned about Kate and Rose as ever, and brushed aside any concern about her own health.

Shortly before Kate left school, she was shocked to be met by Mrs Holland's daughter, carrying one child and with another clinging to her skirts. She was sobbing hysterically and told Kate that her mam had dropped dead at work. 'She was bad last night but she still went in,' the girl wept. 'She just lifted a sack and fell down dead. She only done it for me.'

Kate tried to comfort her, in spite of her own grief for her faithful friend, but Dolly was inconsolable. Finally Kate picked up the toddler, and carrying the child and supporting Dolly, went back to Mrs Holland's house. There the neighbours had gathered and Kate could leave Dolly to their ministrations. They remembered Kate and consoled her by recalling happier times and telling Kate how much Mrs Holland had loved her.

'She was goin' to meet you today, that's why I went,' Dolly sobbed, and Kate wept with her.

It was late when she arrived home. Mildred was angry at her lateness, and even more angry when she learned the reason for it. 'Drunkards don't make old bones,' she said cruelly. 'And don't worry about the girl. She'll find comfort in a bottle the same as her mother, I suppose.'

Kate was about to make a furious reply, but Martha pulled a face at her behind Mildred's back and put her finger to her lips. Kate swallowed and only said meekly, 'I'll go and change, Aunt.'

'Old cat,' Martha said later, when they were alone. 'She knew you was fond of Mrs Holland, but it wasn't no use saying anything, Kate. She'd only take it out on you some sly way.'

'I know,' Kate said. 'I'm glad you warned me, Martha.'

Kate felt that Mrs Holland's death marked the end of the

last link with her old life, but she was happily settled now in her new one. She was so willing and helpful that she was a general favourite with the guests. Henry Barnes often slipped her small gifts of fruit or sweets, and always joked with her, and everyone else was so pleasant that she could ignore Mildred's constant scoldings. She respected her aunt, but felt that she could never love her.

Chapter Four

The first anniversary of her mother's death had occurred in October, and Kate had longed to visit Rose, but Mildred told her that it was not convenient. She promised to take Kate before Christmas, and true to her word a visit was arranged for December.

Kate had outgrown her dress and boots, and Mildred had bought her a serviceable dark dress and strong boots. She was amazed to find Rose wearing white muslin with a pink sash, and Beattie in a purple dress in rich material heavily embroidered round the cuffs and neck.

'We had a happy day shopping in town, didn't we, dearest?' Beattie said fondly to Rose, then, turning to Mildred, she said, 'I've gone to half-mourning myself for poor Sophie, but I think a year's mourning is enough for a child. I've been able to buy Rose all the pretty clothes I've been longing to get her.'

She smiled at Rose, and Rose came to lean against her chair and kiss her cheek. Mildred made a disgusted exclamation, but Kate was happy to see her beloved sister so obviously cherished.

Before they left, Beattie said in her languid voice, 'So you'll be leaving school at Christmas, Kate? I suppose you will have an allowance when you're helping Auntie full time, but this is just a little extra, dear.' She produced a mesh purse containing five sovereigns. 'I know Aunt Mildred provides everything you need, but this is for extras. A blouse you might fancy, or some pretty ribbons.'

She lay back, apparently exhausted by the long speech, and Kate thanked her profusely, glancing nervously at Mildred. The journey home passed in stony silence and Mildred's temper was still short when they got in. As usual on Sunday evenings, they had their meal with the guests, but Mildred's mood remained black.

It was not a propitious moment for Henry Barnes to speak about Kate's future, but he failed to see the storm signals. He was fond of Kate and felt that she had had a hard life, and he admired her courage and her cheerful willingness to help. As the assistant manager in a large store, he had managed, at some trouble to himself, to secure a junior position there for Kate.

As soon as there was a lull in the conversation, he leaned forward and said eagerly, 'I've spoken for Kate in Bryant's, Mrs Williams, and the manager has promised her a position in the haberdashery department. She'll be in the back room at first, but she's such a bright little girl – I'm sure she'll soon be promoted to the shop floor.'

Kate's smile lit up her plain face, and there were murmurs of pleasure round the table, but Mildred said icily, 'Thank you, Mr Barnes. I'll make my own arrangements for my niece if you please.' Her eyes were like flints and two red spots burned in her cheeks, but Henry persisted.

'Kate won't get a better opportunity. Bryant's are good employers and it would be a job for life if she needed it. Better than a lifetime in service, I would say.'

'Possibly you would, Mr Barnes,' Mildred said caustically, 'but I know what's best for my niece and I intend to train her to take over here when I'm gone.'

Everyone was silent for a moment, then Agnes Tate said hotly, 'I know you mean to do your best for Kate, Mrs Williams, but anything can happen in life. I agree with Mr Barnes that Kate is a very intelligent girl and could go far. A position at Bryant's would be a starting point for her and she would be independent.'

Mildred stared at her coldly but made no reply, and the rest of the meal was eaten almost in silence.

As soon as supper was finished, Mildred rose, and saying, 'Come, Kate,' swept out with only a curt nod to her guests. As soon as they had gone, Agnes said indignantly, 'I think it's a shame. She's made such progress with me. I know she's too good for a life of domestic drudgery.'

Jack Rothwell joked, 'You'll be in the black books now, Barnes. You may be shown the door,' and Joshua Hayman said soberly, 'It's no laughing matter, Barnes. You'd find it hard to get another crib as good as this. Some of my friends envy me when I tell them of the food and comfort we have here, I can tell you.'

Mrs Bradley rose to her feet, but before she left she said reprovingly, 'I think you all misjudge Mrs Williams. She is a Christian woman trying to do her best for her niece in the station to which God has called her. I know you meant well, Mr Barnes, but Kate has led a sheltered life and will be safer here at home.' Henry sprang to open the door for her, and she went out slowly and with dignity.

Kate was unaware of the trouble her future was causing. She had sat through the meal in a happy glow because Henry had bothered to speak for her and because he had called her a bright little girl, but the offer of the position meant little to her.

She would be afraid to go among strangers, she thought, and she was quite happy working in the familiar house with her friends Mrs Molesworth and Martha, and seeing Henry every day. And I've got all that money, she thought exultantly, and Aunt Mildred knows about it so I can spend it openly.

Mildred was in a much less happy frame of mind. She was annoyed and amazed by the interest being taken in Kate. She had expected the girl to slip unnoticed into working full time in the house without the distraction of school, but now first Beattie and then these people were putting their oars in. Why can't people mind their own business? she thought angrily. She felt that now they would be watching everything that happened to Kate.

Mildred went to church as usual and thought things over, and when she returned she rang for Kate to come to the rooms she occupied in a strategic position at the back of the hall.

'Sit down,' she said brusquely. 'I didn't intend to talk to you yet about my plans. I've done my duty by you and I'd expect you to help me out of gratitude, but I don't want nosy parkers saying I'm taking advantage of you.'

'But I *am* grateful, honestly,' Kate protested.

'I should hope you are,' said Mildred. 'Now, I'm teaching you what has to be done here so that you will be able to help in running the place as my niece. I don't like talk of money passing between relations, but I'm going to make you an allowance of ten shillings a month. An allowance, mind you, not a wage. I'll still buy your clothes, but you can buy your own stockings and suchlike. Tomorrow I'll take you to the Co-op Bank and you can put that money from Beattie in and try to add to it from your allowance.'

Kate could see her dreams of what she would do with Beattie's money fading away, but before she could protest Mildred went on, 'Seeing everyone wants to know my business, we'd better have things on a proper footing. Martha has one afternoon off every week, so you'd better have two, but remember you're not here as a maid. You're here as *my niece* and I'm training you. Keep a distance between yourself and Martha and Mrs M., and remember who you are.'

'Yes, Aunt,' Kate murmured.

'Right. Well, nobody can say I haven't done my duty by you,' Mildred said with a satisfied air. 'Get off to bed now.'

The following morning Mildred called Martha and Mrs Molesworth into the kitchen. 'My niece will be working full time here as I'm training her up to help in running the guest house, but she won't be a maid. I expect you to treat her with respect, and from now on you will call her Miss Drew. Now, get back to work.'

As soon as Mildred left to visit the shops, Martha and Mrs Molesworth questioned Kate. 'What brought this on?' asked the charwoman. 'Did something happen yesterday?'

'Mr Barnes said he'd spoken for me in Bryant's,' Kate said, her eyes shining. 'He said it to Aunt Mildred at the table and she said she was training me to take over when she'd gone. Wasn't he good to do that?'

'I see,' said Mrs Molesworth. 'That would've put a spanner in her works. I'll bet that was the first she'd thought about training you, but she's cunning, the missus, and she thinks quick. Did she say any more about it to you?'

'Yes, she called me into her room and she said she'd train me and I could have ten shillings a month and two afternoons off. Aunt Beattie gave me five pounds but Aunt Mildred said I had to put it in the bank, and I could save out of my ten shillings. She said it was an allowance not wages and Aunt Beattie said that too. She said when I was helping Auntie full time I'd have an allowance.'

'I see it all now,' Mrs Molesworth said. 'What happened, girl, is your other aunt was asking questions, then Henry Barnes come up with a job for you, so she thought of this training lark. We won't hear no more about that. Don't worry.'

'I don't want things to be different, but I'll like having an allowance,' Kate said.

'Six pounds a year!' said Mrs Molesworth. 'Well, she can't work you no harder than she does now, anyroad.'

'And we've got to call you Miss Drew,' said Martha, but Mrs Molesworth laughed. 'I give that two days,' she said.

Most of Mildred's guests agreed with Mrs Bradley's opinion on what she would describe as the lower classes, and felt, as she did, that 'The rich man in his castle, the poor man at his gate, God made them high or lowly and order'd their estate.' Agnes Tate, though, held different views.

Although a reserved and conventional young woman, her mind had been broadened by working among poor children and finding that each of them was an individual with differing qualities and abilities, not just 'the poor' in a mass which she had been taught to despise. She was also passionately interested in the emancipation of women, and this made her more receptive to new ideas. Teaching Kate regularly had made her appreciate the girl, and she welcomed the opportunities open to her pupil.

As the guests followed Mrs Bradley to the parlour, Agnes found Henry Barnes beside her. 'Thank you for supporting me, Miss Tate,' he said. 'I'm sure several people agreed with me but they hadn't the courage to speak out as you did.'

'I said very little,' Agnes said with a smile. 'I've grown very fond of the child, and sorry for her too.'

'Yes, I admire her pluck,' Henry said enthusiastically. 'She's had a hard time, losing her mother and then being parted from her sister, yet she always has a cheerful smile.'

Agnes looked surprised at the extent of his knowledge, but she only said, 'Mrs Bradley arranged for me to coach her and I've found her a willing and able pupil.'

'But she will still have to be in service. Her aunt seems quite determined,' said Henry. 'I was so pleased to have obtained the position for her, but it wasn't even considered.'

'But if she is to own the guesthouse eventually, at least she will have a slightly easier life, and more free time,' Agnes consoled him. 'I hope I've widened her horizons by teaching her to read fluently. I believe her sister was taken in by a wealthy relative when their mother died, so Kate was unlucky.'

'Fortunately she doesn't seem to think so,' Henry said, 'which is the important thing.'

Agnes smiled. 'That's very perceptive of you, Mr Barnes,' she said. They were interrupted by Jack Rothwell, but that evening marked the beginning of a relationship between Henry and Agnes which grew deeper and closer as time passed.

It was true that Kate was quite happy. She was pleased to be at home all day and even more pleased that she was now on a proper footing in the house, with money of her own and regular time off.

At Christmas she was surprised to receive gifts from all the guests. Mrs Bradley gave her an uplifting book, *Flora's Dying Wish*, and Agnes Tate a copy of *Her Benny* by Silas Hocking. The other teacher, Dorothy Norton, knitted a scarf and mitts for her, Joshua Hayman and Jack Rothwell each gave her five shillings, and Henry presented her with a lace collar and a box of fondant creams, which delighted her.

'You done better than me,' Martha grumbled. 'I gorra few shillings off them but they never went to no trouble for me.'

'You never go to no trouble for them,' said Mrs Molesworth, who had overheard her. 'Kate often runs out for a paper for them and does bits of washing and ironing when the missus is outa the way.'

'Aye, especially for Mr Barnes,' Martha jeered. 'I think you're soft on him, Kate.'

Kate blushed. It was true that Henry had been her hero since her first day here, when he had carried the coal scuttle for her, but she had thought no one knew how she felt.

'Don't talk daft, girl,' Mrs Molesworth said robustly. 'Kate's still a little girl. You'd better not let the missus hear talk like that outa you.'

'It was only a joke,' Martha said sulkily, but Kate resolved to be more careful about showing her feelings in the future.

At the end of January Mildred handed Kate ten shillings with warnings that it must not be wasted. 'It will teach you to handle money and to save,' she said. 'A regular amount saved will soon mount up, added to the five pounds from your Aunt Beattie.' Kate agreed meekly, but she had already decided that most of her money would be spent in the second-hand bookshops, and some on sweets.

She had skimmed quickly through the moral tale given to her by Mrs Bradley, but *Her Benny* she read at every opportunity, either by candlelight in her room or beside the kitchen fire while her aunt was at the Mission. She wept bitterly at the sufferings of little Nelly and Benny, and Martha watched her with disgust.

'Fancy crying like that over a *book*!' she jeered. 'Why do you read it if it makes you whinge?'

'Oh, Martha, it's lovely,' sighed Kate. 'But so sad. Nelly and Benny lived in Liverpool too, near to Scotland Road.'

'Yer must be mad,' Martha tutted. 'I'm glad I can't read.'

Kate put her ten shillings away in her room. She had gradually given most of the balance of the original sovereign to Mrs Molesworth, and bought a few treats for Martha, without disclosing to her how she was able to afford them. On her first half-day off she took a shilling from her Christmas gifts and went first to a second-hand bookshop in Brunswick Road, feeling a heady sense of freedom.

She was tempted by several books but decided to look through the bookstalls in St John's Lane before buying. Walking into the city, she stopped to buy a pennyworth of stickjaw toffee for herself, and humbugs and toffee for Mrs Molesworth and Martha.

She came to a block of tenement flats known locally as

'the dwellings'. A group of shawled women, girls and young boys was gathered outside them, and a photographer with a tripod and his head under a black cloth was taking a photograph. Although poorly dressed, the girls all wore boots and white pinafores, and the boys had boots and some sort of headgear.

Kate's attention, though, was on a small barefoot boy who stood among the watching crowd, knuckling his eyes and crying bitterly. She bent over him. 'What's up, lad?' she asked gently.

'Them lot won't let me be took on the photy,' he sobbed. 'An' I live in them dwellings and some a that lot don't even live there.'

'But why?' asked Kate.

''Cos I 'aven't got no boots, and Wally and Basher ony borreed theirs and them girls ony borreed pinnies.' And he cried even more bitterly.

In the sweetshop Kate had been given a silver sixpence and three pennies in change, and impulsively she took a penny and the stickjaw toffee from her pocket. 'Here you are, lad,' she said. 'They haven't got a penny and a bag of toffee anyway, and now you have.'

The boy's sobs stopped as though by magic and he clutched the sweets and the money. 'Ta, missus,' he cried, and went leaping with delight down the road.

Kate smiled as she walked away but she looked with more attention at the people around her. It was a time of great distress and hardship among the poor of Liverpool, and the sight of starving, ragged children and gaunt adults had become so familiar to Kate that she had been almost oblivious to it.

A harassed-looking woman passed her with a sickly child held in her shawl and two thin, white-faced children clinging to her skirts, and a skeleton-thin ragged man slumped against the wall, staring at the ground in bitterness and defeat. But it was the sight of so many undernourished and ragged children that troubled Kate most.

All Mildred's guests held well-paid, secure positions, or, in Mrs Bradley's case, had private means, so they could afford to pay Mildred's high charges and she could provide good fires and excellent food. Now Kate looked at people and felt ashamed that she had a comfortable home, warm clothes and good food, and they had so little.

Should she have given the rest of her money to the woman with the children? I wouldn't have liked to do it, Kate decided. She might have been offended or thought I was hard-faced. Anyway, I've done my bit today with that little lad. She smiled again as she thought of his delight and went happily to the bookstalls.

There she bought a well-bound copy of *Bleak House* by Charles Dickens for twopence, and a copy of *Dorrie* by H. Tirebuck for a penny. In a sweetshop she replaced her stickjaw toffee and enjoyed it as she wandered around the shops, where she bought herself a pair of black stockings.

When she got home, she took her books to Miss Tate's room and told her about the poor children she had seen. Miss Tate told her not to worry. Many people were working to help the poor and hungry. 'I am myself a member of a committee which raises funds to provide dinners for poor children, and many others in this city give time and money to similar causes,' she said, and Kate was comforted.

Miss Tate approved her choice of books and told her that Mr Dickens used to give penny readings of his books in Liverpool and Mr Tirebuck was a local man, from Toxteth.

'I wish I knew all these things like you,' Kate said wistfully.

Miss Tate smiled. 'I didn't know these facts when I was your age, Kate. I've had time to learn, as you will. Don't undervalue yourself. You're an intelligent girl and now that you can read well, all knowledge is open to you. It's all there between the covers of books.'

Kate thought often of Miss Tate's words and resolved that all her money would be spent on second-hand books and all her free time in reading. Her guilty feelings had been assuaged by Agnes Tate, and then by Mrs Molesworth.

Kate had told her friend about the little boy and the other hungry people when she gave her the toffee she had bought her. She also told her about Miss Tate's good works.

'I never knew nothing about that,' said Mrs Molesworth.

'But don't you be worrying. There's plenty more posh people who should be worrying, but they don't. You work hard for your bit of money, girl.'

'I know, but a penny or even a ha'penny would mean so much to those kids, and I could spare it,' said Kate.

'Yes, and if you changed your money into pennies and ha'pennies and give it all away it'd only be a drop in the ocean. And when you'd done it once they'd all be waiting for you every time you showed your face. You wouldn't have no peace,' said Mrs Molesworth.

Kate could see the sense in her remarks and decided that she would use any spare money for treats for people she knew – people like Mr Molesworth. Although she had never met him, she felt that she knew him from Mrs Molesworth's frequent references to her 'feller'.

As summer approached, the Molesworth family had even more cause for rejoicing than Kate's frequent small treats. Their son Billy, who had been on a two-year voyage to China, was returning home. 'The only lad I managed to rear,' Mrs Molesworth had once told Kate. 'And I couldn't have reared a better one. The salt of the earth, our Billy.'

Kate asked Mildred to give Mrs Molesworth the day off to meet Billy's ship, offering to do the charwoman's work to free her.

'If it's like the last time he was home, it's tomorrow she'll need the day off,' Mildred said caustically. 'They'll never be sober until his pay-off's spent. It's the way those sort of people live.' But she agreed to the day off.

Mrs Molesworth did seem tired and red-eyed the following day, but Kate believed it was caused by emotion rather than drink. 'Oh, girl, I couldn't stop looking at our Billy,' she sighed. 'He looked that healthy and full o' life. And the presents he brought home.' She produced a delicate fan and a pair of soft kid gloves. 'He brung these for you, girl, because you've been that good to us.'

'But how did he know?' exclaimed Kate, then felt ashamed when Mrs Molesworth said, 'I writ it in me letters to him.'

'Oh, Mrs Molesworth, I'm sorry,' she said. 'I didn't know you could write.'

'I didn't get much schooling,' the charwoman said, showing no offence. 'But my feller learned me. He was a checker,
y'know. Got a good head on him. The difference our Billy's
made to him in one day you wouldn't believe, girl.'

Kate was delighted with the gifts from Billy and sent him a
thank-you note, but she said nothing to Mildred about them.
She was due to visit Beattie and Rose on Sunday, and she
took the fan and the gloves in her pocket to show Rose, from
whom she had no secrets. Rose thought they were beautiful,
but she laughed when Kate said she had concealed them
from Mildred.

'"Oh what a tangled web we weave when first we practise to
deceive",' she quoted. 'I suppose you're afraid she'll wonder
how you could afford to treat Mrs M. She doesn't know about
the original sovereign, does she?' A shadow came over Rose's
face. 'You're luckier than I am. Auntie would never give me
money. She'll buy me anything I want but money might make
me independent, you see.'

'Oh, Rose, I didn't realise,' Kate exclaimed. 'Will you have
some of mine? I get ten shillings a month and I don't need it,
honestly.'

'Don't be silly, Kate,' Rose said cuttingly. 'I'm not complaining, just stating a fact. There's nothing I want that I
can't have.' Except independence, thought Kate, but she felt
snubbed and stayed silent. As though to prove her point, Rose
took her sister up to her bedroom and showed her wardrobes
filled with expensive clothes.

'Aunt and I went to Bold Street and we sat on little gilt
chairs while girls paraded up and down before us wearing
gorgeous clothes so that we could decide what we liked. Aunt
bought me four dresses and an evening cape,' she boasted.

Kate admired the clothes but secretly decided that she preferred her own life, where she could to some extent do as she
pleased. She felt that she had offended Rose and was uncertain how to make amends, but Rose solved the problem.

'Kate, your hands!' she exclaimed, taking her sister's rough,
chapped hands in her own soft ones. 'You must be working
terribly hard. It's not fair. Aunt Mildred should be ashamed
of herself.'

Kate laughed. 'I put lanoline on them when I remember,' she said, 'but they're soon as bad as ever. I don't notice them.'

'But Aunt Mildred should,' Rose said indignantly. 'She's as hard as nails. Would you ever believe she and Aunt Beattie were sisters? Aunt Beattie's like a pink and white marshmallow, and she's like a – a—'

'A stick of liquorice,' Kate suggested, and they linked arms and went downstairs giggling together.

Once they entered the drawing room, as Beattie liked to call it, Rose was transformed from a bitter schoolgirl into a dutiful, affectionate niece, anticipating all her aunt's wishes and gracefully handing round the cakes and sandwiches brought in by Jane. Kate watched her with admiration. She felt that her sister was not being deceitful but was doing her best to keep her aunt happy, and very evidently succeeding.

Kate wanted to wear the gloves from Billy, so she had no scruples about telling Mildred that Mrs Molesworth's son had brought them home and the charwoman had given them to her.

'You shouldn't take gifts from that woman,' Mildred said. 'Next thing she'll be wanting favours. They don't give anything for nothing, that class of woman.' Kate looked at her with dislike. How awful to think the worst of people all the time, she thought, and felt that her white lie was justified.

She said nothing about it to Mrs Molesworth, but it would have taken a great deal to upset her friend at this time. Billy was spending money freely on his parents, and almost the first thing he did was to hire a spinal basket carriage in which his father could lie and be wheeled about the city by his son.

'My feller's made up,' Mrs Molesworth told Kate. 'Billy's took him all over the place. Even down to the docks and to the Pier Head to see the ships in the river. I haven't seen Charlie laugh so much for years when they was telling me about going down the floating roadway. The tide was in and the roadway was that tilted Charlie thought Billy'd have to run headlong down it and they'd both finish up in the river. This chair's doin' him the world of good. I should o' thought of it.'

'But you couldn't have managed it,' said Kate, 'could you?'

'True for you, girl, I couldn't,' agreed Mrs Molesworth. 'With us living over the shops Billy can wheel him along the landing, and he gets fellers to help with the carridge down the steps at each end, but that's a laugh for Charlie and all. He's talked to fellers he hasn't spoke to for years. He said it's like coming back to life.'

Billy's pay-off was soon spent and he signed on again, but his time ashore had brightened his parents' lives and given them much to talk and think about when he was gone.

'He's only signed on for nine months this time,' Mrs Molesworth told Kate, 'and he's leaving me more on me allotment. He wants me to give up work but I dursen't. Wharrif he got married? He hasn't half made a difference, though, buying in plenty of food before he went and the way he's cheered Charlie up. Give him a new lease of life, the doctor said.'

Billy returned in nine months' time, and after that only signed on for short trips, but no matter how small the pay-off, he took his father out in the spinal carriage every time he came ashore. Mrs Molesworth still wore her battered boots and flat cap and sacking apron for work, but Billy insisted on buying better clothes for her to wear on Sundays.

She accompanied her husband and son to a park on several Sundays, but then returned home to rest while Billy wheeled his father round the leafy lanes of Aigburth. 'Me leg give out on me,' she told Kate the first time. 'I cudda done with getting in the carridge with Charlie.' She laughed heartily but after that made only short journeys with them.

'I said to our Billy I should o' thought of the carridge for Charlie, and he said I done more. I kept Charlie clean and comfortable and well fed all these years and he hasn't got no bed sores or nothing. He said he never thought of the carridge himself till he seen a man in Hong Kong in one.'

Kate rejoiced at the change in Mrs Molesworth's fortunes but was pleased that she intended to stay on at Aunt Mildred's. She was fond of the charwoman and felt that she was the only person she could speak freely to or ask for advice. Also she seemed a link with Kate's mother, and often told her tales of the family from the days when she had helped her mother to clean the mansion in St Anne Street.

Martha was becoming ever more dissatisfied and grumbling incessantly, and no one was surprised when she gave in her notice. 'There was something fishy about that one from the start,' Mrs Molesworth told Kate. 'She never had no box for a start, so she must've been outa a place for a while. And she never told us nothing about herself, like.'

Kate smiled to herself. It wasn't for want of trying on Mrs Molesworth's part, she thought, that they knew nothing about Martha. 'Tighter than an oyster' was the charwoman's verdict after one session.

Now Mrs Molesworth said that she could have predicted to the day when Martha would go. 'Just give herself time to get some good food inside her, some good clothes and long enough to ask for a reference,' she said. 'I had her weighed up all right.'

Mildred said nothing while Martha was working her notice, but evidently she had been to the orphanage where their laundry was done and arranged for an orphan to come to work for her. She told Kate about it the night before the girl arrived. 'Her name's Josephine Daulby and she's thirteen. You can help me to train her. It's time you took more responsibility,' she said.

Kate said nothing. Mildred made these pronouncements from time to time, but Kate knew they meant little. She still worked as hard and was scolded as frequently by her aunt, and she was told nothing about the finances of the guesthouse. As Mrs Molesworth had predicted, she was soon plain Kate to everyone again, without protest from Mildred. She still received her ten shillings' allowance every month, although the second afternoon off was not practicable and was never mentioned again.

Kate was nearly sixteen, tall and thin, and although shy with strangers, she was happy and confident with those she knew well. She would never be a beauty like her sister, but she had large hazel eyes and clear skin, and her plain face was transformed by her ready smile. She looked very different to the frightened and unhappy little orphan who had arrived at the house on the day of her mother's funeral.

Chapter Five

Josephine Daulby arrived the following day when the clean laundry was delivered, and stood by meekly while Mildred and Kate checked the linen with the van man. She was a small girl with large brown eyes and dark curly hair. Her arms and legs were like sticks and her cheeks hollowed, but her eyes were sparkling with excitement and she returned Kate's smile with a beaming one of her own.

As soon as the van man had gone, Mildred said, 'Now, this is my niece, Kate, who'll tell you what to do. I expect you to work hard and do everything she tells you to do.'

'Yes, ma'am,' the girl said meekly, but her eyes were still sparkling.

'I'm going out now, Kate, but you know what to do,' said Mildred. 'Put the laundry away for a start, and see that Mrs Molesworth doesn't waste time.'

'Yes, Aunt,' Kate said, remembering her own first day and smiling encouragingly at the girl. As soon as Mildred had gone, she said briskly, 'The first thing we'll do is have a cup of tea. Are you always called Josephine?'

'No, we just had numbers in the Home. There was so many of us, y'see.'

'Well, can I call you Josie? Josephine's a bit of a mouthful,' said Kate.

'Oo, yes please,' the girl said eagerly.

Mrs Molesworth appeared on the basement stairs, and Kate smiled at her. 'Mrs Molesworth can smell tea being made from a hundred yards away, Josie,' she joked.

'Aye, but there's always a cup for me if Kate makes it, and she'll be the same with you, girl. You've fell on your feet coming here.'

As the three of them sat drinking tea and eating biscuits provided by Kate, Mrs Molesworth questioned Josie closely. The girl said frankly that she was a foundling and had been given the surname Daulby because she had been found in a doorway in Daulby Street.

'Josephine's me own name, though,' she said proudly. 'Me mam must've been a lady because she could write. She writ me name on a label and the date I was born, May the third. Every year a doll come for me on that date until I was nine, and then they stopped, like. I think she must of died.'

'You was gettin' a bit big for dolls anyhow,' the charwoman said.

'I never knew about them until I was seven,' said Josie. 'Some woman what got sacked told me and she told me about the label on me clothes an' all. They used to bring the dolls and some other toys out when these toffs come to inspect us, like, so I managed to get one of them and hide it. I brung it with me.' She stopped, looking frightened. 'Will I get into trouble?' she muttered. 'I won't get sent back, will I?'

'Of course not,' Kate said swiftly. 'It's a little secret between the three of us.' She rose to her feet. 'Is this your bundle, Josie? If you've finished I'll take you up to your room.'

Josie was unable to believe at first that she would be the sole occupant of the attic. 'There's another bed from when there were two maids,' Kate said, 'but this is your own room and you can arrange it how you like. You'll have a candle but you must be very careful with it because of fire.' She showed Josie the curtained alcove for clothes and the washstand with basin and ewer, and a small cupboard with two shelves. 'You can keep your doll in there – or in bed with you if you like,' she said with a smile.

Josie settled in happily. She was a cheerful girl used to hard work, and very happy with the plentiful food and her comfortable bed in the privacy of the attic. Mildred provided her with two print dresses and aprons, a sacking apron and a pair of second-hand boots. 'I've made the dresses so they can be let out as you grow, but boots are different. No sense in getting new ones you'll soon outgrow.'

The explanation was for Kate's benefit more than Josie's,

because she felt that her niece was watching her critically, but Josie was delighted. 'I'm made up havin' me own clothes,' she confided to Kate. 'In the Home you never had nothing of your own. You just got a clean dress and any underclothes from the pile and sometimes there wasn't nothing left hardly. Isn't the missus kind?'

Kate smiled but said nothing. Privately she thought that Mildred was taking advantage of Josie. She made her work twice as hard as Martha had done, in spite of Kate's efforts to protect the girl.

Inexperienced and eager to please, and with no one in her background to speak up for her, Josie was vulnerable and Mildred exploited her. Before Josie came Mildred had cleaned her own rooms and spent most afternoons in the kitchen preparing food. Now Josie cleaned Mildred's rooms – usually while Mildred was out at night, often after the evening meal at which she had waited at table – then helped Kate with the mountain of washing-up.

Mildred now spent the afternoons either out at events at the Mission, or in her room, emerging to drive Josie upstairs to replenish bedroom fires or to do other chores she had found for her. Mildred had always worked hard herself in the kitchen, but now her sole contribution was cooking the meals.

'You'll have to learn to skive a bit, girl,' Mrs Molesworth told Josie. 'Pity you wasn't here when Martha was. She'd soon have learned you. A master at it she was.'

'I don't care how hard I work, I'm just made up to be here, and Kate helps me when the missus is out,' Josie said, but she looked exhausted, her face white and dark shadows beneath her eyes.

'Aye, if it wasn't for Kate you'd have cracked up long ago, girl, but you're just getting wore out,' said the charwoman.

Kate said nothing, but she made up her mind to speak to Mildred about it and went to her aunt's rooms the same night, before her courage failed. 'I've come to say I think Josie is working too hard, Aunt Mildred. She hasn't complained but that's what I think.'

'If she's not complaining, what's it got to do with you?' Mildred demanded.

Kate said bravely, 'You said I should have some say in running the place, and I think it's wrong. I'm looking to the future too. Josie's a good worker but she's wearing herself out and we won't get anyone as good to replace her.'

'Nonsense,' Mildred exclaimed. 'Hard work never hurt anyone.'

'Hard work, but not the way Josie's being driven. She works twice as hard as Martha did. She's been here nine months but she hasn't grown at all, and I think that's why,' said Kate.

'My word, you've found your tongue and no mistake,' exclaimed Mildred. 'So you're looking to the future? Don't count your chickens before they're hatched, miss.'

'That's not what I meant,' Kate said, blushing indignantly. 'I'm just talking about the next few years. And there's another thing. I only found out today that Josie's doing all this for just her keep. She should have some pay, no matter how little.'

'Oh, so this is your way of saying you should have had pay the first year you were here?' Mildred said. 'I gave you a good home, miss, the same as I've given that orphanage girl, but there's no gratitude in young people nowadays.'

Kate looked at her in amazement. 'But – but that's got nothing to do with it,' she said. 'You said yourself there shouldn't be talk of money between relations, and my allowance was your idea. I didn't ask for it.'

'Hoity-toity,' Mildred exclaimed. 'But you didn't refuse it either, I notice.' She forbore to say that her hand had been forced in the matter of Kate's pay.

'What about Josie?' Kate said quietly, and Mildred replied sharply, 'Very well, I'll pay her a shilling a week, but I'll expect hard work for it.' Kate looked at her, and Mildred said impatiently, 'Sort it out between you about the work. I'm not satisfied with the way the food is prepared, so I've decided I'll be in the kitchen with you again while it's done.'

'Very well. Thank you, Aunt,' Kate said, and escaped wondering how she had dared to speak so to Mildred. Nevertheless she had achieved her object in getting less work and some pay for Josie. She was not deceived by Mildred's face-saving comment about the food preparation, and knew that she had won a small reprieve from extra work for Josie.

The episode marked a subtle change in her relationship with her aunt, and gradually Mildred left more and more of the decisions about the cleaning of the guesthouse to her niece.

Josie was delighted to receive her shilling a week pay, and before long Kate had also negotiated a half-day off for her. 'What does she want a half-day off for? She's got nowhere to go,' Mildred grumbled, but Kate insisted and gained her point. She also persuaded Mildred to raise Mrs Molesworth's wages because she was so dependable and in spite of her small size such a prodigious worker.

'And she doesn't just do the rough,' Kate argued. 'She'll turn her hand to anything, and she's very good and careful at washing china and ornaments. I couldn't manage without her.'

'Oh yes you could,' Mildred retorted. 'If I sacked her today I'd have another woman in her place tomorrow just as good.'

'You'd have to engage two to do the work she does,' Kate said, greatly daring, but though she grumbled, Mildred agreed to the rise, and humoured her in small ways to suggest that she was a partner. She decided that Kate should accompany her sometimes to choose fresh meat and vegetables, so that the shopkeepers would know her and she could shop for fresh food when Mildred was not free, but she still told Kate nothing about the financial side of the business.

Kate liked Josie, whose cheerful company was a welcome change from the constantly grumbling Martha. Josie, for her part, idolised Kate. She tried to copy the way Kate walked and spoke, and asked her to correct her when she spoke badly. She quickly realised how Kate felt about Henry Barnes, but she never jeered as Martha had done, instead weaving romantic dreams about the pair of them.

Kate now thought she knew the truth, that Henry and Agnes Tate were in love, although they were still very formal and correct with each other in the house. Miss Tate had talked to her about women's rights, and had taken her to a meeting addressed by Eleanor Rathbone. Henry had joined them there, and Kate realised for the first time that he and Agnes were meeting away from the guesthouse.

'We know that we can rely on your discretion, Kate,' Henry said, smiling at her, and she managed to smile back and promise, showing no sign that she was abandoning a dream. Later Agnes told her that they had no hope of marriage for several years so would prefer to keep their feelings for each other private.

'I am still repaying my parents' life savings which they used to support me through college,' she said. 'And Henry has a widowed mother and a delicate sister dependent on him, so we'll just have to be patient and save as much as we can.'

Kate felt hurt that Henry had said nothing of these plans to her, unaware that they existed mainly in Agnes's mind; and often she wept in the privacy of her room. Until now she had drifted along happily, weaving vague dreams of Henry telling her he loved her, but now she had to face reality. He had been kind to her, had comforted her and brought her small gifts, but only as an adult to a child, because he was a kind young man. He likes me – I know he does – she thought, but that was all and she must be content with it. She was at the age to feel most intensely, but she hid her agony during the day, and no one was aware of it. She even managed to smile at Josie's fantasies about her and Henry.

Kate's thoughts had been so full of Henry that she had had little interest in other members of the opposite sex, but Rose, although two years younger, had been interested in young men for some time. One of her many grumbles when they met was that she had no opportunity to meet any.

'The only boys I see are the gardener's boy and the boot boy,' she grumbled. 'If we see any young men on the way to school, Annie drags me past them as though they have the plague.'

Kate laughed. 'Oh Rose, you're a bit young to be worrying yet,' she said. 'Aunt Beattie must plan for you to go to dances or parties, or she wouldn't buy you all those lovely frocks.'

'Oh, I wear those for handing round cakes to the old trouts at her bridge parties,' Rose said carelessly. 'Parties for me are the last thing she'd think about. We were adopted to be *useful*, Kate.'

Kate was sorry to hear Rose being so cynical. Although she accepted that her sister was much cleverer than she was, she felt that in this case Rose was wrong. She was sure that Beattie truly loved her and planned a happy future for her, but she decided not to argue.

Rose was now talking about the dancing teacher at school and declaring that all the girls were madly in love with him. 'He's so graceful, and he wears lavender oil on his hair and sprinkles his handkerchief with lavender water,' she said.

'He doesn't sound much of a man to me,' Kate said bluntly, thinking of Henry Barnes.

'He's Byronesque,' Rose said indignantly. 'Grace Duncan, one of the older girls, crept out to meet him one night in the summerhouse in their garden. She lives in a big house near Breck Park.' She sighed dramatically. 'Grace said he is *all man*!'

'I hope you never do anything silly like that, Rose,' Kate said anxiously, but Rose said flippantly, 'Some hope. They all watch me like hawks in case I do anything to upset dear Beattie.' Kate was relieved to hear it, and not surprised when some months later Grace Duncan was hastily removed from school and sent abroad, and the dancing teacher was dismissed.

The visits to Rose and Beattie were less frequent now that Mildred was becoming more and more involved in the Mission, but in the summer when Rose was fifteen she had momentous news for Kate. The Select School had been sold and taken over by a progressive headmistress, and the lessons in deportment and fancywork replaced by more academic subjects, at which Rose shone.

'The trouble is, I've lost so much time footling about with those silly lessons in deportment and dancing,' she said. 'But Miss Tasker says I'm an intelligent girl and she's taking a special interest in me. She's giving me homework, but the only trouble is getting time to myself to do it.'

'But surely Aunt Beattie will be pleased that you're doing so well, and you don't have any work to do, do you?'

'Not your sort of work, Kate, but I'm kept fully occupied dancing attendance on Aunt Beattie,' Rose said tartly.

'Oh Rose, try not to be so bitter,' Kate exclaimed. 'Think of the good things in your life. Your room and clothes and things.'

'I know, Kate, but they're not important,' Rose said. 'The only way I can do my homework is in bed when I'm supposed to be asleep, and even then Essy creeps round spying on me, so I suppose Aunt Beattie knows but turns a blind eye.'

'Be careful though, love,' Kate said anxiously. 'If Aunt Beattie doesn't like the school being changed, she may move you somewhere else.'

'Not her,' Rose said carelessly. 'She's too lazy to make the effort, and anyway one of her *very* superior friends has a daughter there.' Once again, Kate was distressed that Rose was so cynical, but she dared not say any more in case she made things worse.

On the next visit some weeks later, Rose told her that she was top of the class in English and her essay had been read out at assembly. She was also top in mathematics and was the most fluent French speaker. Miss Tasker, the headmistress, had said that Rose had a first-class brain. 'Not that I have much opposition there,' she said ruefully. Kate, she said, was the only one she could talk to about it. 'Aunt Beattie's so stupid she doesn't know what I'm talking about when I speak about my essays, and Essy's a fool. She said I would overheat my brain.'

'Could you talk to Jane?' Kate suggested, but Rose only sneered.

'*Jane?* Jane's only concerned about her own affairs. She's keeping company with some hobbledehoy and she goes about her work in a dream. If it wasn't that Aunt Beattie was so soft-hearted, Essy would have got rid of her long ago.'

'I hope you're only repeating Essy,' Kate said with spirit. 'I wouldn't like to think you felt like that, Rose.'

Rose laughed and hugged her. 'Still my big sister, aren't you? Yes, I was quoting Essy, and I don't know why because I hate her. She's jealous of me, you know, and she'd do anything to stop me being happy.'

Kate was troubled by Rose's attitude but she only said mildly, 'Be careful, love. Try to keep such thoughts to yourself.'

'Oh, I'm *careful*,' Rose said bitterly. 'That's one thing I've learned here; to play a part.' She looked at Kate's worried face and suddenly flung her arms around her. 'All my moans,' she said remorsefully, 'and you never grumble. It can't be easy living with the stick of liquorice. Does she ever smile?'

'Not often,' Kate said, delighted to see the old Rose that she loved. 'And I do plenty of moaning, but not to you.'

'You don't get much chance, do you?' Rose said ruefully. 'You can't get a word in while I'm complaining all the time.' She kissed Kate, and they wandered round the garden arm in arm.

'I'm sorry,' Rose went on. 'I know I'm lucky to have all this comfort when I think of your life, but honestly, Kate, I'd give anything for some freedom.'

Kate squeezed her arm and Rose laughed. 'Here I go again, moaning,' she said. 'Come down to the orchard and I'll show you how I let off steam.' When they were out of sight of the house, Rose did four high kicks in quick succession, singing 'Ta Ra Ra Boom De Ay', then did handstands with her feet against the trunk of an apple tree. She laughed at Kate's astounded face.

'I come here with Wang. I walk him very sedately while we can be seen from the house, then we come here and I make him run. Then I do my handstands and high kicks. You should see him lying there panting with his tongue hanging out and his eyes nearly popping. I think it's the sight of my bloomers.'

Kate laughed. 'I think I must've looked like him just now, but it wasn't the sight of your bloomers, honestly.'

Now they could hear Annie calling anxiously: 'Miss Rose, Miss Rose,' and Rose grimaced. 'Here we go,' she said, and they started back to the house.

The aunts had evidently been discussing the Select School, and Beattie said immediately, 'Rose is a favourite with the new headmistress, aren't you, dear?'

'I quite like the lessons,' Rose said in a colourless voice.

'And Miss Tasker is very strict. I like to know what I can or can't do. The school seemed to have got very lax with Miss Simmonds.'

Mildred and Beattie exchanged a meaningful glance and Mildred said sharply, 'So I've heard. But you won't be there much longer. You're about fifteen now, aren't you?'

'The girls stay until they're eighteen at the Select School,' Beattie said. 'It's like a finishing school too, you see.'

'But not now, surely, with this new woman?' said Mildred.

'Essy said that,' Beattie said languidly. 'But we'll wait and see.' Rose stood by meekly, secretly rejoicing in the by-play between the two women. She knew that Essy had been pressing for her to leave school and that Beattie's obstinacy would be reinforced by Mildred's interference. Essy's new ally had effectively lost her case for her.

'Miss Tasker called all the girls aged fifteen to eighteen together,' Rose said into the silence. 'She said that we were at the age when we needed most supervision and she would see that we got it.'

The two aunts again looked at each other, and Mildred said triumphantly, 'So I was right in what I heard.' Beattie said only, 'Ring for more tea, Rose dear.'

So Mildred had heard about Grace Duncan, Kate reflected as she and her aunt walked home. Perhaps she could stop worrying about Rose now. At least her sister realised that she was lucky in many ways, and now with Miss Tasker and the interest of the lessons she should feel less frustrated.

Kate was surprised that Mildred had not discovered her feelings for Henry. I suppose the truth is she doesn't realise I'm old enough to feel like this, she thought. Although Josie and Mrs Molesworth knew how she felt, Kate had been unable to tell them about Henry and Agnes, and she'd had no success in trying to discourage Josie from talking about Henry.

Josie was convinced that Henry loved Kate. One morning when they were in the kitchen and had been talking about Rose, she said, 'There y'are. You've got posh relations too, so there isn't nothing to stop youse two getting married, you and Mr Barnes.'

'No, no,' Kate protested. 'Don't say things like that, Josie. It's just not true.'

'Gerraway,' Josie said. 'The way he looked at you and winked this morning and said "Goodbye, Kate. Be good." I went all funny. I'm sure he loves you, Kate.'

Kate said briefly, 'No. It's just that he's a kind man and he thinks I'm still a child.'. She picked up a tray of cutlery and went swiftly up the basement stairs, and Mrs Molesworth emerged from the scullery where she had been scrubbing.

'Do you think I've put me foot in it?' Josie asked anxiously. 'Kate seemed vexed, like.'

'No, but you don't want to be talking like that, girl. Kate just lives in a dream world as far as Mr Barnes is concerned. She never has no ideas about marrying him.'

'But she *could* marry him,' said Josie. 'I'm sure he loves her.'

They heard Kate approaching and hastily began to talk about something else. Kate made no reference to the earlier conversation and was relieved that Josie said no more about Henry. She felt that it was hard enough knowing about Agnes and Henry and, bound to secrecy as she was, being unable to stop Josie romancing, but fortunately the girl seemed to have lost interest in the subject.

Josie was still small for her age, but plentiful food and good living conditions had cleared her skin and given her a fashionably rounded figure, and her sparkling brown eyes and dark curly hair made her very attractive,

All the van men and delivery boys were captivated by her, and a plumber who was called in gave serious pursuit. He constantly handed in notes and posies of flowers and hung about hoping to see her on her day off. Josie treated all of them lightly.

'I'm not getting tricked like me poor mam must've been,' she told Kate. 'And I've got to watch me good name, see, 'cos I haven't got no family behind me.'

'But you could be friendly with them, Josie,' said Kate, whose soft heart was touched by the sufferings of her admirers.

77

'I'll be friendly as long as they take no for an answer,' Josie laughed. 'Look don't touch is me motto.'

Kate smiled. 'But don't think you haven't any family behind you, Josie,' she said. 'We're your family now. Aunt Mildred would make short work of anyone who treated you badly.'

'I wish you was my sister, Kate,' Josie said wistfully. 'Although I know you've got your Rose.'

'In a way you're more like my sister than Rose is,' Kate said with a sigh. 'I see a lot more of you than I do of her.' Then she added cheerfully, 'I'm looking forward to seeing her soon for Christmas. I'll have to get on with the handkerchiefs for my Aunt Beattie.'

'Well, at least I haven't got no needlework to do,' Josie laughed. 'Good job, the way I sew.'

Although Beattie seemed so indolent, she noticed everything that Kate wore on her visits, noting that her clothes were always dark and plain although of good, hard-wearing material, and that she always wore strong boots, even though it was Sunday. She said nothing, but her Christmas present to Kate was a fur hat and muff and a pair of shoes. Mildred's face reddened and her eyes glittered with temper when she saw them, but she only said, 'I don't hold with all this present-buying and Christmas trees. A lot of foreign nonsense!'

'Queen Victoria and Prince Albert started it,' Rose said, and Mildred snapped, 'That's what I said. German nonsense. And don't be pert, miss.'

Beattie sat up. 'My Rose is not pert,' she said, her usually soft voice sharp, and Kate said hastily, 'Oh, Aunt Beattie, this muff is lovely. So warm, and the hat too.'

Rose adjusted the hat and fluffed Kate's hair out round it, and the dangerous moment passed. 'Rose tried the hat so that I could decide,' Beattie said. 'It looked so nice I bought one for her too.'

Mildred snorted but said nothing, and Beattie admired the six handkerchiefs which Kate had hemmed and embroidered for her, then rang for tea to be brought in.

The girls had exchanged books. Rose had bought copies

of *Hard Times* and *The Pickwick Papers* for Kate, who knew her sister loved poetry and had given Rose a copy of *The Golden Treasury* bound in leather. Mildred accepted gloves from Beattie and sweets from Rose with a bad grace.

Mildred cut the visit short and on the way home was still obviously angry. 'Beattie should mind her own business. Shoes indeed. Have you been complaining to Rose?' she asked suspiciously.

'Of course not,' Kate said. 'I was as surprised as you, but I think Aunt Beattie is very generous.'

'She's got too much money,' Mildred said. 'Doesn't know what to do with it. Buying a hat for that girl too. Cheapens the gift to you. It's all nonsense anyway.'

'*I* don't think it cheapens the gift,' Kate said. 'I'm delighted with it, and the books from Rose too.'

'Don't answer back, miss,' Mildred reproved. 'You're as pert as your sister,' and the rest of the journey passed in silence.

Kate still attended morning service at the Mission with her aunt, and on Christmas morning she proudly wore her hat and muff and the new shoes. As they left the chapel, two of the members stopped to speak to them. Kate heartily disliked both of them.

Mr Hopkins was a small, pompous man with a few hairs plastered over his bald head and soft, moist hands. His wife was a wispy woman with a whining voice which she used, under a pretence of Christian concern, to say something unpleasant to everyone. Now she looked at Kate's luxurious hat and muff and said to Mildred, 'Is it wise, dear Mrs Williams, to allow Kate to dress like that? I understand she took the place of your maid who left. Shouldn't she dress according to the station in life to which God has called her?'

Kate blushed, but Mildred's head came forward and her eyes glittered as she stared into Mrs Hopkins's face. 'You should be ashamed to say that you listen to ill-informed gossip,' she hissed. 'Katherine is helping me to run the guesthouse and her station in life is as *my niece*. My mother, Katherine's grandmother was a Miss Green, related to the family of the Marquis of Salisbury, who owns the Manor of Everton. Our family is considerably better than any in this congregation, including your own. Come, Kate.'

She stalked away, followed by Kate, who was full of admiration for her aunt. Mildred walked so fast in her anger that Kate had difficulty in keeping up with her, but she managed to gasp, 'Is that true, Aunt Mildred?'

'Of course it's true,' Mildred snapped, slowing down a little. 'I don't tell lies.'

'I didn't know,' Kate murmured. 'Mama never told us,' and Mildred retorted, 'I'm not surprised. She would never have been allowed to marry your father while our father was alive.'

Kate felt that her father was being insulted, but she was anxious to hear more, so she said nothing, and Mildred went on, 'My mother's maiden name was Green and she was distantly related to the Marquis of Salisbury, and to Mr Bamber Gascoyne, MP, and his brother General Gascoyne. Some day I'll show you the family tree which my father had done. Certainly we're far above that creature who dared to speak like that. I've given them something to think about anyway,' she added with satisfaction.

Kate breathed a long, wondering sigh and Mildred glanced at her and said astringently, 'Don't let it go to your head. I wasn't born to keep a boarding house, but when life deals you a blow, you fight back. Whatever you have to do, you do it better than anyone else, and with dignity. That's how you show your breeding.'

'Yes, Aunt,' Kate said meekly. She still found it impossible to love Mildred, but she felt even more respect for her. She was old enough now to understand what Mrs Molesworth had meant about Aunt Mildred's husband dying in another woman's bed, and to realise what a blow that had been to a proud woman like Mildred. Now she felt that her aunt had explained her philosophy of life to her, and she admired her strength of character.

Kate longed for Christmas Day to be over. Mr Barnes and Miss Tate had gone to their respective homes for Christmas, so there was no hope of a kind word from Henry, and Mrs

Molesworth had the day off, so Kate was unable to ask her about Mildred's revelations. Joshua Hayman had gone to his sister's house, and Dorothy Norton, Jack Rothwell and Mrs Bradley had all been invited out for Christmas dinner.

Mildred and Kate ate their meal in the dining room, waited on by Josie, who then had her own in the kitchen. Kate longed to talk to someone about what Mildred had told her, but she felt that it would be unkind to discuss it with Josie, who knew so little about her own family. She looked forward to talking to Mrs Molesworth the next day. The charwoman might even be able to add some details, though Kate felt that she must be unaware of the aristocratic connection.

Later, in bed, Kate allowed her mind to dwell on Henry. How could she let him know about what she had learned today? And would it make any difference to him if she did? Did she *want* it to make any difference? If he didn't care for me before, would I want being well-born to change things so much? She suddenly buried her head beneath the bedclothes.

I'm a fool, she thought. Henry has never even thought about me like that. He's just been kind to me because he's a kind young man. He's in love with Miss Tate, and she is with him and that's how it should be. Yet a spark of hope still burned in her. If it was to be so many years before they could marry, perhaps he and Agnes might tire of each other and he might turn to Kate. I'll always love him anyway, she told herself, whatever happens.

Henry had given her a flask of lavender water for Christmas, and she had put it on a shelf where she could see it from her bed. Now she got up and took it down. 'I believe it's good for headaches,' Henry had said, smiling, as he gave it to her. Now, as Kate dabbed the lavender water on her forehead and on her wrists, she wondered sadly if it was good for heartache too.

Chapter Six

During the next visit to Greenfields, as soon as they were alone, Kate told Rose about the incident at the Mission and the comments by Aunt Mildred.

'Has Aunt Beattie ever mentioned being related to the Marquis of Salisbury? she asked.

'Dozens of times,' Rose said carelessly. 'I don't take any notice. She's always rambling on and it's about forty times removed anyway. Miss Tasker says class doesn't matter. It's only an accident of birth and it's what people are rather than who they were born that counts.'

'She seems to have unusual ideas,' Kate said doubtfully.

'She has,' Rose exclaimed, her eyes sparkling. 'She's wonderful. She's a New Woman but Aunt Beattie doesn't know, of course. Some of us go to her study at lunchtime and she tells us about women who are doing something with their lives. People like Elizabeth Garrett Anderson, who's a doctor, and of course Mrs Pankhurst and her daughters Christabel and Sylvia. I'm going to be like them.'

She sounded so excited that Kate felt she should warn her, but she knew it would be useless so she only said, 'I wish I knew more about our family. Mrs Molesworth has told me a few things but she doesn't really know much about them. She only helped her mother, who did the rough work.'

Rose laughed. 'I know more than they think about the family. I've been dying to tell you. You know the cook here used to be a kitchenmaid for our grandmother? Well, she got a bit tiddly at Christmas and told me all about them.'

'Drunk, do you mean?' Kate asked.

Rose laughed at her shocked expression. 'Yes. Why not? Her betters do it all the time.'

'I was just surprised,' Kate said. 'What did she say?'

'I told her that Aunt Beattie had said her father was well respected and wealthy and he made his fortune out of sugar. She laughed and said, "And the rest." Apparently our grandfather gambled on the Stock Exchange and did some shady deals as well. When he died he left his money for his wife's use, and after her death to his three daughters, but by the time his debts were paid they only got a small amount each.'

'I think Aunt Mildred bought the guesthouse with hers,' said Kate.

'And Mama drank hers,' Rose said flippantly. Kate gazed at her, unable to believe what she had heard, and Rose laughed. 'Oh Kate, your face! Mrs Phillips said Dada came out of the army just before he married Mama. With his gratuity he went into business with another man, a scoundrel who tricked him and went off with all the money. That's why we had to move from that house they had in Princes Park, but Dada never touched Mama's money.'

'I remember that house!' Kate exclaimed. 'There were servants, I think, but I liked our other house better.'

'Mrs Phillips said Dada worked like a dog so Mama didn't have to do anything, and paid a neighbour to do the rough work there. She said Mama just sat and whinged, and he was probably glad when he got called up as a Reservist.'

'What cheek!' Kate exclaimed, and Rose laughed again. 'I told you she was drunk,' she said. 'And she said after he was killed Mama should've looked after us but she just drank herself to death with the money she wouldn't use to help Dada. Oh, she really loved Mama, I could tell.'

'I'm glad you can laugh about it, Rose,' Kate said indignantly. 'I think she had a cheek to talk like that, drunk or not. Poor Mama was sick.'

'Oh Kate, I don't know how you can make excuses for her. She was selfish to the bone and she treated you so badly. Keeping you off school to wait on her hand and foot, and when you left school it would've been even worse. She wouldn't have cared what happened to you after she died when you wouldn't have been able to earn your own living.'

'I don't see it like that, Rose,' Kate said. 'I was glad to help her.'

'I say Mrs Phillips was right,' Rose said stubbornly. 'People think Mildred has used you, adopting you to be a skivvy for her, but Mama used you just as much. She'd have used me too if I'd let her, but I wouldn't.'

She flung her arms around Kate and hugged her. 'It's not fair, Kate,' she said passionately. 'You got the dirty end of the stick with Mama. You had no childhood, and then to have to go to Aunt Mildred and be worked to death and bullied there with no nice clothes or anything.'

'It's not like that, Rose, really,' Kate protested. 'I'm quite happy there. I know I have to work hard but I've got good friends in Mrs Molesworth and Josie, and the guests are nice.' She hesitated, then said, 'Henry Barnes is lovely. He's been very good to me since the first day.' She waited for her sister to ask for more details about Henry, but Rose only said, 'I wish *I* was, happy I mean. I'm like a prisoner here, just a handrag for Aunt Beattie. I have to be available all the time in case she wants my company or wants me to do something for her. It's not enough that she's got Essy running round after her.'

'But she's very kind to you, Rose, and I'm sure she loves you. And you're happy now at the Select School, aren't you?' Kate looked so anxious that Rose relented.

'Yes, I'm happy at school,' she said, 'and when I get annoyed here now I think about what Mrs Phillips told me about them and laugh to myself. Especially when I look at that picture of our grandfather with his sanctimonious expression.'

'I don't know whether I'm coming or going,' Kate said with a grin. 'Aunt Mildred tells me about our posh relations and before I get used to the idea you tell me about the cook telling you the bad things about the family.'

Rose linked her arm in Kate's. 'Yes, but the bad things are more interesting, aren't they?' she laughed. 'Come up to my room and see my new dresses.'

In the bedroom Rose showed Kate several new dresses, then from the back of the wardrobe she took a faded pink rose wrapped in tissue paper. 'The undergardener gave it to me,' she giggled. 'He said it made him think of me when it was fresh.'

'Oh Rose, isn't that romantic,' Kate breathed, but Rose laughed. 'No, it was daft. He pinched it from the glasshouse and he'd lose his job if anyone knew. I told him so.'

'But you kept it,' Kate teased.

Before they went downstairs again Kate told Rose that she was wrong in thinking that Mildred bullied her. 'She used to be always shouting at me,' she said, 'but not since she told me that I could help her to run the guesthouse. Now it's more like me bullying her. Getting her to agree to all sorts of changes.'

'I'm glad to hear it,' Rose said. 'And I admire your pluck. I don't think I could manage her.'

Back in the drawing room, Kate watched Rose closely, deciding that she was like a chameleon blending into her background. Beattie obviously doted on her, patting her hand or her cheek whenever she was near, and Rose responded with butterfly kisses which delighted Beattie. I couldn't do that just after criticising her, Kate thought, but she told herself that it was necessary for Rose to play a part at home. At school she could be herself and be happy.

Especially with admirers bringing her roses, Kate reflected with a smile. She wished she could talk to Rose about Henry, but although she had mentioned him several times over the years, Rose had never shown any interest or encouraged confidences. Probably when I talk about him she thinks of him as just one of the guests, Kate thought. Now that neither Mrs Molesworth nor Josie seemed to want to talk about Henry, Kate longed to mention his name, but there was no one in whom she could confide.

Perhaps for the same reason, Agnes Tate often spoke of Henry to Kate. She told her a few weeks later that Mr Barnes's sister was ill again but had been cheered because their brother had returned from abroad and was now in the Liverpool office of his firm.

It had become general knowledge among the guests that there was an understanding between Agnes and Henry, although no announcement had been made and no one spoke of it.

Several changes among the guests occurred at this time. Mr Hayman's asthma, from which he had always suffered, had become worse and the doctor advised him to live further inland. He decided to retire, and went to live with his widowed sister in Shropshire. Dorothy Norton left at about the same time. She had obtained the headship of a country church school and announced it triumphantly at the Sunday-evening meal.

'She'd have shown better manners if she'd told me first,' Mildred said to Kate, and Mrs Molesworth said she knew why Miss Norton had found a new position. 'She's been as green as grass since she found out about Miss Tate and Mr Barnes. They never got on like, her and Miss Tate.'

Kate had never liked Miss Norton, a moody young woman given to sulks and always thinking that others were better treated than herself, and she felt uneasy when alone with Mr Hayman. 'Mr Macfeely' the charwoman had dubbed him, and certainly he seemed to like to pat and stroke Kate and Josie. So Kate saw both guests go without regret. Two young bank clerks moved into their rooms, both quiet and pleasant young men.

The spring weather seemed to make Kate restless and unhappy and intensify her feeling for Henry, no matter how much she told herself that he was in love with Agnes and she with him. The general unrest in the country and the city seemed to match her mood, and Mrs Molesworth warned her not to go into town on her day off. Religious riots had started and the charwoman warned that they would get worse.

'You'd only have to be walking past to get battered by one side or the other, girl,' she said. 'Keep away from it all. Strike up into the country.'

Kate took her advice and was glad that she did. It was a beautiful day and she took a tramcar part of the way. She was soon walking in the country lanes which lay near Old Swan. Birds sang from every tree and new growth was everywhere in the hawthorn hedges and the banks at the sides of the lanes.

Numerous plants were in bud and there were even clumps

of primroses in flower. Kate picked one, and as she wrapped it in her handkerchief she thought of the rose presented to her sister by the young gardener and the violets brought to Josie by one of her many admirers. How would it feel, she wondered wistfully, to be given a flower or to wander through this beauty with someone you loved?

'"I have immortal longings in me",' she quoted to herself, and thought how hard it was that she should feel like this when she had no hope of ever satisfying her yearnings. She strolled on, absorbing the beauty around her and letting fancies fill her mind, dreams of rescuing Henry from mortal danger, or better still, being rescued by him and clasped in his manly arms while he breathed, 'Oh Kate, how I've dreamed of this moment.'

She spent several happy hours wandering and dreaming before having to return to reality. She felt guilty when she thought of Agnes Tate, but she told herself that no one knew of her dreams so they did nobody any harm. They had comforted her and made her feel happier, and Josie told her the fresh air had obviously done her good. 'You look worlds better, Kate,' she said.

It was as well that Kate had had this happy day, because only a week or so later, Agnes Tate told her that she and Henry were going to become engaged on her birthday, which fell in three days' time. 'Things are a little easier at home for Henry,' Agnes said, her eyes shining. 'His brother Robert now shares the responsibility for his mother and sister.'

Kate offered good wishes, and a little later, as she went downstairs and Henry came into the hall, she was able to hold out her hand to him and say brightly, 'I've just heard your news, Mr Barnes. Congratulations.'

His face lit up. 'Good, good,' he said. 'Thank you, Kate. We wanted you to be the first to know because it was really you who brought us together. That argument with your aunt about your future, you know. That's when Agnes spoke up for me and we got to know each other.'

'I'm glad,' Kate said. 'I hope you'll be very happy.'

'I'm sure we will,' he said. 'She's a delightful girl, isn't she?'

Kate smiled at his enthusiasm, but she said sincerely, 'She is. I think you're very well matched and I'm sure that you'll be happy.'

Henry was still holding her hand, and now he looked intently into her face and said, 'But what about you, Kate? Are you happy?'

'Yes, I am, Mr Barnes,' she said bravely, although the bittersweet pain of his concern combined with the engagement made her feel that she was being torn apart.

'You work so hard, Kate, too hard I think,' he said, and she said breathlessly, 'I like it. Congratulations again,' and escaped.

Not for the first time Kate wished that she could reach her room without going through the kitchen, but fortunately only Josie was there as she hurried through. She needed time to face the fact of the engagement, but she also wanted to think about Henry holding her hand and asking so anxiously if she was happy. He really cares about me, she told herself, but like a dash of cold water the thought followed, Yes, but he *loves* Miss Tate. She lay down on her bed, covering her face, and at first failed to hear the timid knock at the door. When it was repeated she stood up and composed herself before opening the door. Josie stood there.

'Are you orlright, Kate?' she asked. 'I've been that worried. You looked that queer when you rushed through the kitchen and I couldn't hear no noise from you.' Her careful speech had deserted her, and seeing her concern Kate managed to force a smile.

'I'm all right, Josie,' she said. 'I had a dizzy spell on the stairs and it gave me a fright, that's all.'

Josie gave a sigh of relief. 'Thank goodness. You give me a fright, the white face on you. Lay down again. I'll tell the missus.'

'No, no, don't,' Kate said quickly. 'I'm all right now. Don't say anything to anybody, Josie,' and Josie promised.

Kate sluiced her face with cold water and tidied her hair, and somehow she got though the preparations for the meal without betraying to Mildred that anything was wrong. After the meal Mildred departed for the Mission, while Kate and

Josie washed up the dishes, tidied the kitchen and prepared the dining room for the following morning.

By the time the chores were done, Mildred had returned and it was time to prepare the evening cocoa. Josie had glanced at Kate anxiously several times but had been unusually quiet and subdued.

At last Kate was free to retreat into her bedroom and be alone to think. She realised how tenacious that little spark of hope had been that Henry might one day turn to her. Now she must face the fact that it could never be and try to be satisfied that he liked her and cared about her happiness. If he only knew how much that depended on him! she thought ruefully.

With courage Kate decided that her dreams now belonged in the past and she must firmly put them away and brace herself for the formal announcement of the engagement. She knew it would need all her fortitude to keep a smiling face.

The next day Mrs Molesworth said quietly to her, 'Is there an engagement coming up, girl?'

Kate was amazed. 'How did you know?' she asked. 'Miss Tate told me last night but I thought no one else knew.'

'I was only guessing, girl,' Mrs Molesworth said quickly. 'I asked you 'cos I knew you'd know if anyone did. Someone saw them looking in Brown's window at the engagement rings. I haven't said nothing to Josie.'

'Then don't, please, Mrs M.,' Kate said. 'They want to make the announcement after they've been home at the weekend.'

'Josie's been talking about you and him but it wouldn't have worked, girl. He'd be all right, but wharrabout other people?'

Kate remembered the Mission but said nothing.

The engagement was announced when all the guests were gathered in the parlour on Sunday night, and champagne was produced for a toast.

The young couple were deliberately vague about their plans, but Agnes Tate had told Kate that they planned a two-year engagement. A strange friendship had grown between Agnes and Kate. The lessons had been discontinued long ago, but Agnes had taken Kate to join the Carnegie Library, and on the pretext of guiding Kate's choice of books sometimes invited her to her room.

Adroit questioning by Agnes and willing revelations by Kate about her family had established in Agnes's view the class to which Kate and Mildred really belonged. Misfortune had fallen on Mildred and through her on Kate, Agnes believed, so she had no hesitation in befriending the quiet young girl who spoke good English and loved books, and in confiding in her.

Agnes needed a friend to confide in. She longed to talk about Henry and their plans for the future, but Dorothy Norton had been so incompatible and Mrs Bradley seemed too old. Kate was the perfect listener, never tired of conversation about Henry.

'I've finished replacing my parents' savings which they spent on my education, and Henry's brother coming home has made such a difference. We are really going to save hard during the next two years, because of course I'll have to leave my post when we marry,' she told Kate. 'We're not talking about our plans here because they may have to be changed, but I know you'll be discreet, Kate.'

'Of course,' Kate said.

It was bittersweet to her to hear these confidences. Although she had told herself firmly that she had stopped dreaming dreams about Henry, she was still interested in his well-being and happiness. The conversation was not all about Henry, however. Agnes was too well bred for that, so they talked about books they were reading or which had been reviewed, and Agnes asked if Kate had seen Rose.

'Not for over three months,' Kate said. 'We don't write to each other because Rose says the aunts would want to see the letters, but I'm longing to see her.'

'That's a longer time than usual between visits, isn't it?' Agnes asked.

'Yes, but there's been so much on at the Mission,' said Kate. 'Aunt Mildred has been very involved there on Sundays with visiting missionaries. We're going next Sunday, though, and I'm really looking forward to seeing Rose again.'

Unknown to Kate, a crisis was in progress at Greenfields. Rose, who was now seventeen, had continued to do well at all academic subjects, and with little competition she was consistently top in every class. Combined with praise from Miss Tasker, this had convinced her that she was outstandingly clever, and she had decided that she wanted to be a doctor.

Miss Tasker encouraged the plan and told Rose that she must discuss it with her aunt. 'There are scholarships, but they are very few and difficult to obtain,' she said. 'I'm sure your aunt will be happy to pay the fees.'

Rose confidently broached the subject to Beattie after outlining how unusually clever a girl had to be to be given this chance, but Beattie promptly threw a fit of hysterics. Rose was banished and Essy summoned to minister to her mistress, and afterwards any mention of the subject brought on a fit of weeping by Beattie and declarations that Rose was a wicked, ungrateful girl who was ruining her aunt's health.

Rose knew that the battle was lost. Although she wept and tried to make Beattie change her mind, where her own wishes were concerned, Beattie was inflexible. Even when Miss Tasker called to try to persuade her, it made no difference.

'Rose has such a good brain, Mrs Anderson,' the head-mistress said. 'Even if you dislike the idea of her becoming a doctor, her talents should be used for another profession. She could make you very proud of her.'

'I'll be very proud of her if she is a dutiful niece, Miss Tasker,' Beattie said stiffly. 'Rose knows how much I've done for her. I wouldn't have let her remain at your school if I'd known she would be taught to be ungrateful.' She lay back in her chair, gasping for breath and ringing a handbell for Essy to bring her smelling salts, and the interview was quickly terminated.

When Mildred and Kate arrived on Sunday, Rose immediately bore Kate off into the garden, while in the drawing room Beattie poured out her troubles to her sister. She got little sympathy from Mildred, who told her that she had spoiled the girl from the beginning and made a rod for her own back. Rose, however, found a more sympathetic listener in Kate, at least to begin with.

They sat together on a garden seat with Kate's arms around her sister while Rose raged and wept at the injustice of her life. 'She doesn't give a damn about me or what I want. It's all about what suits *her*. I'm not allowed to be a person with my own hopes and plans. I'm just a toy for her to dress and play with. That woman was right – I can't remember her name – when she said they only wanted me for a doll and you for a skivvy.'

'Mrs Holland,' Kate murmured, and held her sister close. 'Never mind, love,' she soothed. 'It's a shame when you are so clever, but don't give up hope. Aunt Beattie may change her mind.'

'Not her,' Rose said bitterly. 'She's stupid and obstinate and selfish to the bone.'

'But she loves you, Rose,' Kate protested. 'She'd give you anything you wanted.'

'Except freedom!' Rose said dramatically. 'I've said it before. She gave you money, Kate – probably to spite Aunt Mildred – but she's never given me any. Oh, she'll buy me anything I want but money might mean independence, and that's not in the plan.'

'Which plan?' Kate asked, looking puzzled.

'Her plan for me. No doubt Mildred has one all worked out for you as well,' said Rose.

'I don't think so—' Kate began, but Rose swept on.

'I haven't been able to sleep and I've been thinking of the last time you came, when we talked about Mama. Why did they suddenly arrive when she died? They never came when she was ill, but they knew she had two daughters. Beattie wanted a daughter as a doll to dress and play with, and Mildred wanted a skivvy, and there we were, ready-made. They didn't take us for our sakes, Kate. They took us for their own and we owe them nothing – *nothing.*'

For a moment Kate was too taken aback to speak, then she said quietly, 'But Rose, I don't think we'd have been allowed to stay on our own, and Aunt Mildred said the alternative was the workhouse or an orphanage. Josie's told me about the orphanage. We wouldn't have liked it, Rose.'

'I don't care. By now I'd be free,' Rose said. 'Better than being in a cage here.'

'You wouldn't say that if you heard Josie talk,' said Kate. 'You're probably right about when Mama died, but Aunt Beattie's been good to you. This is the first time she's refused you anything. Can't you make the best of it and do something else?'

'You're on her side, too,' Rose said, pulling away from Kate and weeping even more bitterly.

'No, I'm not. I'm worried about you,' Kate protested. 'You're making things worse for yourself working yourself up about old troubles.'

'But I want to do something with my life, Kate, not spend it picking up stitches, changing her library books and generally dancing attendance on her. I could be a good doctor, I know I could.'

Kate thought for a moment. 'Could you help at the Dispensary?' she suggested. 'Aunt would allow that, surely, and it would be useful training for you. Might make Aunt Beattie change her mind too.'

'The Dispensary!' Rose exclaimed, turning to stare at Kate. 'Children with boils and scabies and men with dirty wounds. No thank you, Kate.'

'I thought if you really wanted to be a doctor it would be the next best thing,' Kate said indignantly. 'What do you think you'd see if you were a doctor?'

Rose had the grace to blush. 'Well, perhaps not a doctor. I just want to be *somebody*, Kate. I'll have to leave school soon and I don't know how I'll bear being at home all the time. The days are so long and empty and I won't be able to use my brain at all.'

Kate was silent. She felt desperately sorry for her sister, but whatever she said seemed to make things worse. Rose stood up and walked about the grass and Kate watched her. Why couldn't she be happy? She had so much and she had been blessed with every gift, including beauty. Her gently rounded figure was shown to perfection by the well-fitting dress of rich material elaborately tucked and embroidered, and the colour of it exactly matched her blue eyes. A ribbon of the same shade held back her glossy fair curls.

Kate thought of her own appearance as glimpsed in the large mirror in the hall. She had put her hair up on her eighteenth birthday but it was still straight and mousy, and wisps of it escaped from her bun and hung round her face. She was thin and gawky with an undeveloped figure, and the steel-rimmed spectacles she now wore hid her eyes, her only good feature. Her plain and serviceable clothes did nothing to improve her.

Why? she thought angrily. Why had Rose been given every gift – beauty and charm and cleverness – and she had been given nothing? Poor plain Jane, Mama had called her, and said the good fairy was absent at her birth.

Rose was still pacing about the grass dabbing at her eyes with a lace-edged handkerchief. Weeping had not reddened her large blue eyes or spoiled her perfect complexion, and there was a gloss about her which Kate felt could only have come from years of care, of the best of food and luxurious living. Only the discontented droop of her full red lips marred her beauty, and suddenly Kate lost patience.

'I think you've got a lot to be thankful for, Rose,' she said crisply. 'You can't have everything, and after all, here you can at least be miserable in comfort.'

'You don't understand,' Rose cried, bursting into tears again.

Kate, instantly remorseful, flung her arms around her. 'I do, love,' she said. 'But you're so beautiful, you're bound to meet someone to marry, then all the years of training would be wasted.' Rose said nothing, and Kate, suddenly weary, said, 'I know it's hard to give up your dreams, but you're not the only one who's had to do that. Henry Barnes is engaged to Miss Tate.'

Her eyes filled with tears and she hoped for some words of comfort from Rose, but her sister only said indifferently, 'Oh, is he? We'd better go in now,' and led the way into the house.

Kate followed her, thinking that Beattie was not the only

95

selfish person under that roof. She felt that she would be glad to leave Greenfields and return to the cheerful company of Josie and Mrs Molesworth. At least they never felt sorry for themselves, although their lives were so hard. As Mrs Molesworth said, 'We can't do nothing about it so we may as well make the best of it,' and Kate thought she was very wise.

Mildred and Kate had scarcely left the house when Mildred said crossly, 'I knew there'd be trouble with that girl. Beattie's spoiled her and made a rod for her own back, and so I told her. A few weeks in her room on bread and water would be the best cure for her.' Kate said nothing.

Rose made wild plans to run away and earn her own living, but she was intelligent enough to realise that they were unrealistic. She was too used to living in luxury to face hardship, and it would be impossible to find a respectable job without qualifications or a recommendation.

She went weeping to Miss Tasker, but there was no help there.

'You are dependent on your aunt, my dear, and I can't encourage you to defy her,' said the headmistress. 'You will just have to accept your lot. After all, many people would consider you fortunate.'

'I thought you would understand,' Rose cried. 'I want to *do* something, *be* somebody.'

'I do understand how you feel,' said Miss Tasker, 'but I also see the difficulties, my dear. The time may come when you have more freedom, but for the present you must try to be content. Find other interests and meet fresh people.'

'Aunt Beattie wouldn't agree,' muttered Rose.

'But if you became interested in good works I'm sure she would,' said Miss Tasker. 'Perhaps helping in the Victoria Settlement?' Rose, however, angrily repudiated the idea. She was interested in a career for herself, not good works for others.

As Beattie's indolence increased, she had grown stouter and more breathless, and her doctor had warned her that her heart might be affected. Beattie decided that the trouble with Rose might cause a heart attack, and the doctor was summoned.

He was anxious to avoid offending his wealthy patient, and when his suggestion of more exercise was badly received, he urged instead that Beattie should travel. 'A cruise perhaps, Mrs Anderson, or you could take the waters at Baden Baden,' he said.

A friend of Beattie's had taken the waters the previous year and pronounced them vile, so Beattie decided on a cruise. It would serve a double purpose too, Beattie thought, in distracting Rose from her strange ideas.

Rose, who had been considering her options and realised how much she had to lose by defiance, was just as enthusiastic about the idea, and as affectionate as Beattie had hoped. A three-week cruise was speedily booked for the two of them.

Chapter Seven

Although Mildred had shown little patience with her sister's complaints, one of Beattie's comments had given her food for thought.

Beattie had wept about the ingratitude shown by Rose, then said, 'You got the best of the bargain, Mildred. Kate's a good girl, but be careful she doesn't treat you the way Rose has treated me.'

'What do you mean?' Mildred snapped. 'She's got no hope of being a doctor.'

'No, but she'd be able to get a good job as a housekeeper,' Beattie retorted. 'With better pay and less work. And don't forget she's nearly twenty now. Be careful she doesn't just go off and leave you.'

'Nonsense,' Mildred said roughly, but she was shaken with doubt. Kate had stood up to her to ask for more time off for Josie and more money for Josie and Mrs Molesworth. Perhaps she was also making plans for herself. You couldn't trust these quiet ones, Mildred thought. She watched Kate carefully during the next few days and thought she could see a change in her.

Kate's misery at the ending of her dreams about Henry made her seem quieter and more introspective, and Mildred swiftly decided that something must be done. She needed Kate. Not only did her niece work hard from early morning until late at night, but Mildred now felt free to go out, knowing that she could leave conscientious Kate in charge of the house.

It was many years now since she had told Kate that she was training her to help in running the house and hinted that she intended to leave the business to her niece in her will. Perhaps it was time she reminded her. A few days later she called Kate into her room.

'It's time you took more responsibility, Kate. You're a woman now and I'm not getting any younger. I've been hard with you but it was for your own good because I was training you to take over from me. When I die, this place will be yours – if you are still with me. I've no relations apart from your Aunt Beattie, and she needs nothing from me.'

'Er, thank you, Aunt,' Kate stammered. 'I hope it won't be for a – a long time.'

'In the midst of life we are in death,' Mildred said grimly. 'I want this guesthouse to be kept to the same standard. I've told you that it was necessary for me to earn my own living, and this is how I chose to do it, but I was determined that it would be a superior guesthouse and I select my guests carefully. I provide a comfortable home and choose people who will appreciate it and respect me. I never stint on food or coal, as you know, and my guests pay more for this comfort, yet I never have a room empty for long.'

'Yes, Aunt,' Kate murmured, looking bemused.

'Now, I've decided that sometimes you will do the shopping. I'll tell you what to buy and inspect it when you return, but you will choose the meat and vegetables. Also you will do more in the kitchen. I think you have a knack with cooking.'

Kate was recovering from her bewilderment and said quickly, 'But who'll do the cleaning I usually do in the morning? Josie and Mrs Molesworth couldn't manage it without me. And getting the food ready for upstairs later.'

'I'm coming to that,' Mildred said impatiently but noting Kate's readiness to speak out. 'I'm taking on that deaf and dumb girl from Heyworth Street to help out in the afternoons. Her mother says she can wait on table or prepare food if it's written down what she's got to do, so I'm giving her a trial.'

'When does she start?' asked Kate.

'Tomorrow. We'll see how it goes, but if she's no use *you* can sack her. I'll tell Josie and Mrs Molesworth that in future they'll take their orders from you, and don't be soft with them. Keep them at a distance too. You're far too friendly with them.'

She took a large tin box from a shelf and unlocked it. 'I'm going to show you these books, Kate, but not a word about them to anyone else. Can I trust you?'

'Of course!' Kate said indignantly.

Mildred spread out the books. 'You can see from these figures that the guests pay more than they would in an ordinary boarding house.' She turned several pages. 'Now, these are the household accounts. You can see I have a comfortable margin, but only because I work so hard and spend so little on myself. I don't stint on food or coal but I won't have waste and you must be the same. Servants are always wasteful if they're not watched carefully.'

The figures meant nothing to Kate but she nodded as though she understood, and Mildred said complacently, 'I have a friend who has advised me how to invest my savings, so I will have plenty to leave you – if you stay with me.'

So that's where she goes in her good clothes, Kate thought, but she only said meekly, 'Yes, Aunt.'

'I hope you will be able to share the burden with me now and repay me for giving you a home and looking after you all these years, Kate,' said Mildred. 'It will be to your own advantage. You'll have your rightful standing here as my niece and it's up to you to show some dignity. Keep the servants in their place.'

'Yes, Aunt,' Kate murmured, wondering how dignified she could be while cleaning under beds and washing hearths, and smiling to herself at the thought.

'And another thing,' Mildred added. 'I've decided you can buy your own clothes from now on.' She took five sovereigns from the tin. 'I'll increase your allowance to a pound a month and I'll give you five pounds twice a year for clothes. And there'll be no more talk of afternoons off.

101

As my niece you will come and go as you please. I know you won't take advantage.'

'I won't. Thank you, Aunt,' Kate gasped.

'I think I've been very fair with you, Kate, and I know I can trust you to be fair with me. No silly notions like your sister,' Mildred said with a wintry smile. She stood up to indicate that the interview was over.

Kate said again, 'Thank you, Aunt,' and hurried away, feeling as though she was dreaming.

Later she told Josie what had transpired and Josie declared that it was about time. 'You should've asked for more money and more time off long ago,' she said.

'I couldn't, Josie,' Kate said. 'After all, she gave me a home and bought all my clothes.'

'She never bought you nothing nice, and Mrs M. said you was working from the day you come here,' said Josie.

'I'll be able to buy nice things now anyhow, and I've stopped growing so they'll last,' Kate said. Josie agreed, but Kate thought she sounded wistful and decided that she would buy a nice frock for the girl which she could wear on her day off

Kate had been organising the cleaning for some time, but she found it quite different now that she had a free hand. The plan that she could come and go as she pleased never happened. The deaf and dumb girl came to help as arranged, but Mildred made her so nervous that she never returned, and Mildred was leaving more and more of the food preparation and cooking to Kate. If Mrs Molesworth and Josie had not insisted, Kate would have felt unable to even take a half-day off.

'What'll you do if my aunt doesn't come to help, Josie?' Kate worried, but Josie said airily, 'If she doesn't, them upstairs won't get fed, but that's the missus's worry, not yours. If you give up your half-day she'll let you and not crack on, but if you're out she'll have to help.'

Mrs Molesworth approved of Kate's new status and her extra pay, but she was cynical about Mildred's motives. 'She's got the wind up, girl, because your Rosie's kicking her heels up,' she said. 'She thinks you might leave her. Find yourself a good job as a housekeeper or a cook.'

'But she knows I'd never do that, Mrs Molesworth. I mean, she's my aunt and she gave me a home when Mama died. Anyway, I wouldn't want to go among new people and leave you and Josie,' said Kate.

'Yes, girl, but she judges you by herself. She'd do what was best for herself and she thinks you would an' all. The missus is piling more and more on you, girl, and you'll have to stand up to her,' Mrs Molesworth said. 'You done it for us, now do it for yourself. This is what she always wanted – to be like Lady Muck with someone else doing the work and the worrying.'

'I don't like to say I can't manage,' Kate said, but Mrs Molesworth said robustly, 'That's what she's counting on, girl. You just face her out. Tell her if she's not going to do nothing she'll have to get someone else in place of the deaf and dumb girl.'

It was only now that Mildred had withdrawn most of her help that Kate realised how much her aunt had done in the kitchen. Lacking Mildred's years of experience, Kate found that all the preparations took longer, and it was hard for her to have meat and vegetables all ready to serve at the same time with a pudding to follow. Josie was too fully occupied cleaning to give the help Kate had given her aunt.

'Tackle her about it, girl,' advised Mrs Molesworth. 'But don't barge at her. "Softly softly catchee monkee," my feller always says. Just say you can't manage now she's not able to do so much and try her with the idea of a girl from the orphanage who wouldn't cost much.'

'If we could only get someone like Josie,' Kate said. 'But I wouldn't take advantage of her, Mrs Molesworth.'

'I know you wouldn't, girl, but remind the missus about the mess you was in on Josie's night off. The way they had to wait for their puddens. Say they was moaning.'

Kate went to Mildred and found her surprisingly amenable to the idea of taking another orphan. 'Just as well to get someone trained up,' she said. 'That girl's too flighty. She'll marry young and leave us in the lurch.'

'Josie?' exclaimed Kate, but on reflection she thought that her aunt might be right. Josie still insisted that she trusted no man, but she had grown so pretty that every male who came to the house, and many others, were attracted to her, and she was always willing to flirt with them.

'That's as far as it goes,' she told Kate. 'I'm not going to get tricked by no man the way my poor mother was.'

'Not every man is like that, Josie,' Kate protested, but Josie said firmly, 'I know, but I'm not taking any chances. I haven't met any feller I really like anyhow. Not to be like Mrs Molesworth and her Charlie are.'

'The trouble with you, girl,' Mrs Molesworth told her, 'is you don't give a feller a chance. You know if you fall out with them there's always another one waiting for you.'

Kate had given Josie five shillings for new clothes, and Josie, who said she could do anything with a needle bar sew, had bought one of the ready-made dresses which were now in the shops. It cost two shillings and eleven pence three farthings, and she also bought a new corset for eleven pence halfpenny and a bust bodice for threepence. The material of the dress was of brown cambric sprinkled with orange pansies, and with the remaining coppers Josie bought a velvet pansy for the neckline and brown velvet ribbons for her hair.

'You look lovely, Josie,' Kate told her on the first occasion that she wore the new outfit.

Josie hugged her impulsively. 'It was my lucky day when I met you, Kate,' she said. 'Oh, I wish you could meet a nice chap and be happy.'

'Don't worry about me,' Kate said with a smile, but Josie went on, 'You should be more friendly, like, with fellers, Kate. They think you don't like them and they're afraid to ask you out.'

'I can't, and anyway I haven't got your looks, Josie. But I *am* happy, honestly,' Kate said, laughing. 'Go on or you'll be late,' but she couldn't help thinking wistfully that she wished she had not only Josie's looks but her temperament.

Josie was as lively and adventurous as Kate was quiet and timid, and was the source of endless entertainment to Kate. When the religious riots were at their height in Liverpool in 1909 Kate would go out to the countryside surrounding the city on her days off, but Josie spent her half-days in the thick of the action.

'I don't stick up for either of them so I'll just cheer whichever one's nearest,' she declared to Kate and Mrs Molesworth before setting off joyfully, accompanied by a weedy young grocer's assistant.

'Aye, and you'll get clobbered by both,' predicted Mrs Molesworth, but Josie returned unharmed, her brown eyes sparkling, full of tales of dangerous encounters.

A couple of years after that, when Liverpool was reduced to a standstill by the transport strike and troops were brought in, Kate sympathised with the seamen, chiefly because Billy Molesworth was on strike, but she never attended any rallies or marches in support.

Josie, however, was in the centre of it all at every opportunity, and even a blow from a policeman's truncheon failed to deter her. She was delighted when her half-day off on 7 December coincided with the *Mauretania* breaking her moorings in the Sloyne and drifting down the Mersey on a strong flood tide with sirens blaring. She was among the crowd that followed to see the ship go aground on Devil's Bank near Dingle, in the south of Liverpool, and waited to see her towed off by tugs but break away to go aground again on Pluckington Bank. She knew that she would have to face Mildred's wrath at her lateness but felt that it was worth it.

As it happened, Mildred was lying down with a bilious headache, so Kate was able to conceal Josie's absence, but she had spent anxious hours wondering what had happened to her friend. Josie, who would have endured any amount of scolding from Mildred, was upset that she had worried Kate, and promised never to stay out late again.

The ending of Kate's dreams about Henry, which had filled her mind for so long, left a gap which made her feel restless and unhappy, but her new responsibilities did something to fill the void. The invitations to visit Agnes Tate's room to discuss books and other matters had virtually ceased. Kate was now too busy, and the little time she had for reading was spent on twopenny romances which filled a need in her life. The long books by Thackeray and Dickens were now too demanding for her, so there was little to discuss, and Agnes had a new friend, a teacher who had arrived at her school and who shared her views on women's suffrage and social reform.

Like most people in her situation Kate knew little of what was happening in the country. She never read a newspaper or mixed with people who did, except the guests, and she was never present when they discussed national affairs. Agnes was the only person who had ever talked to her about a wider world.

It grieved Kate to see so many hungry and barefoot children, particularly in the winter, but she consoled herself with the thought that many good people in Liverpool were trying to help the poor. Mr Lee Jones and the League of Welldoers provided dinners for starving children at Limekiln Lane and took handcarts full of hot tea and soup to poor people and to the homeless men who slept under the overhead railway. Quakers and other church organisations provided food and clothing for the poor and all gave treats at Christmas. Even the men of the Mission distributed food parcels at Christmas to people they considered the 'deserving poor'.

It never occurred to Kate that anything could be done to cure the root cause of the widespread poverty, and she knew nothing of the attempts by Lloyd George and the Liberals to introduce reforms such as the Old Age Pension Act of 1908 and the National Insurance Act of 1911. Nor was she aware of the trouble when the 1909 People's Budget was rejected by the House of Lords.

Fully occupied by her own affairs, she knew nothing of what was happening in the world and only learnt that

King Edward VII had died when it was announced at the Mission and shop windows were draped in black. The same shop windows were draped in red, white and blue for the Coronation of King George V, and Kate heard gossip in the shops about the 'Sailor King' and Queen Mary, but it all seemed very remote from her own busy life.

She had little time, either, to brood about Henry's engagement. She still saw him nearly every day and he was as cheerful and friendly as ever, but he never brought fruit or sweets now for her. She surmised that this was partly because he and Agnes were saving hard for their wedding, and partly because he had realised that she was no longer a child.

Kate felt herself that she had changed. She was no longer so gullible, and had foiled attempts by the butcher and the grocer to take advantage of her inexperience in shopping. She still respected Mildred, but she realised now how devious and manipulative her aunt was, and was not afraid of her.

'The missus has gorra shock coming when you start, girl,' Mrs Molesworth chuckled. 'You're not the girl you was.'

'How do you mean?' Kate asked, startled. 'Do you think I've got very hard?'

'No, you're still the kind-hearted girl you always was, but you can weigh people up a bit better and you can stand up to the missus,' said Mrs Molesworth. 'It's a good thing, girl. You was far too soft for your own good.'

'I'd never change my mind about you and Josie, Mrs Molesworth,' Kate said earnestly. 'But I do feel a bit different about Aunt Mildred and some other people. I think I know now what's true and what's false.'

'I'm made up to hear that, girl,' Mrs Molesworth said, smiling at Kate.

Kate felt too that her attitude to Rose was changing. The moment when she had thought of her sister as selfish was the first time she had ever felt critical towards her. She had always seen Rose only as her beloved little sister, to

107

be watched over and guided and have her small worries and complaints soothed away. Now Kate found herself comparing Josie's life and her cheerful acceptance of it with the constant complaints made by Rose, and feeling impatient with her sister.

Kate lacked the experience or the imagination to realise the depth of Rose's frustration and her very real suffering. The years of excelling at academic subjects, of listening to Miss Tasker talking about exceptional women, had opened up new horizons for Rose. She had suggested becoming a doctor because of her admiration for Elizabeth Garrett Anderson, without really thinking of what was involved.

What Rose really craved was knowledge and more education to fit her to become someone of note in the world. She believed that she had the intellect and longed to have it stretched. Now she felt that the doors which had seemed to be opening for her were being slammed in her face without any reference to her wishes or her abilities, and she was helpless to do anything about it.

She was intelligent and clear-sighted enough to see that her years of living in luxury had not fitted her for anything but staying with Beattie, but although she appeared to have accepted her fate with a good grace, the resentment and bitterness she felt stayed with her throughout her life.

Kate was unaware of this and was pleased to hear about the cruise. She thought it was just what Rose needed to reconcile her to leaving school, and hoped she appreciated her good fortune.

Mildred had done nothing about extra help, although Kate had asked her several times about engaging an orphan. 'She always has some excuse about being prevented from going to the orphanage or having a sick headache or something,' she told Mrs Molesworth and Josie. 'I'm determined to do something. I'll tell her I'll go myself.'

'Don't go in them clothes,' Mrs Molesworth advised. 'The likes of that matron judge you by what you've got on your back, and you'll feel better able for her if you've got good clothes on you.'

Josie agreed. 'You said you were going to get new clothes when you got the money. I soon spent what you give me.'

'I haven't had time,' Kate said.

'*Make* time, girl. It's important,' Mrs Molesworth said, and Kate took her advice. She bought a whole new outfit for herself, a suit with a long jacket and skirt in blue, a white blouse and a large blue hat trimmed with white. She added white gloves to hide her work-worn hands.

'You look a proper lady,' Josie told her when she wore the outfit to go to the Mission, and Mrs Molesworth said, 'Aye, class will out, girl.'

Kate had also discarded her steel-rimmed spectacles, now too small and permanently askew, and bought well-fitting gold-rimmed glasses after having her eyes tested. Josie had acquired a pair of curling tongs, and after piling Kate's soft brown hair in a bun on top of her head, she had frizzed the strands which escaped into a fringe.

Kate was especially glad that she had improved her appearance when Agnes met her in the hall and invited her to attend a meeting with her new friend, Winifred Doyle. 'It's about raising funds for a Christmas hotpot for poor children,' she said. 'We have to make plans in good time and I'm sure you're interested.' Kate assured her that she was, and on the night she dressed very carefully and Josie did her hair.

She was amazed to find that Henry intended to accompany them. However, there were several other young men at the meeting and Kate was introduced to several of them, but in her estimation they were poor specimens compared to Henry. He was cheerful and attentive, finding good seats for the ladies of his party and obtaining tea for them.

I feel cherished, Kate thought wistfully. She was pleased that she was able to spend time in his company without betraying her feelings, although she felt that Winifred Doyle was watching her closely. It might only be because Henry was friendly with her, she thought, but later she decided that Miss Doyle was a snob who treated her politely but patronisingly and disliked having her in her company.

She felt that other ladies were patronising too, and shy and timid though she was, there was a vein of independence in Kate which resented it. She held her head high, telling herself that as far as class went, she was as good or better than anyone there. *I* know it, she thought defiantly, even if they don't.

She took off her glove and held out her work-roughened hand to the next young lady to whom she was introduced. Let them see I work for my living, she thought stubbornly. Despite her defiance, she decided that she would refuse any further invitations, though she would make the items for the bazaar she had promised.

Later, as she lay in bed, Kate remembered a conversation she had had with Mrs Molesworth, and realised that, as ever, the charwoman was right. 'You're neither fish, fowl nor good red herring the way the missus has got you here. She should o' reared you as her niece from the start, but she wanted it both ways. She wanted a niece but she wanted a skivvy an' all, and now you don't know where you belong, with us or with the nobs.'

'But I do, Mrs Molesworth,' Kate had protested. 'You and Josie are all the friends I want.'

'But you should be looking higher than us for friends, girl, and wharrabout when you come to get married? You'll want a man what can talk like you about them books and things, not a butcher's lad or the like. Your aunt done you a bad turn being too mean to take on another girl for the work and rear you proper as her niece,' Mrs Molesworth added.

Kate laughed. 'No sign of fellows flocking to marry me, so you needn't worry about that. I'm quite happy as I am,' she declared, and Mrs Molesworth said swiftly, 'Only because you've gorra gift for happiness, girl. It's in your nature, thank God.'

During the next few days, Kate often thought of Mrs Molesworth's words. Until now she had been happy enough taking vicarious pleasure in Josie's many conquests

110

or losing herself in the romances she read, but now she considered the young men she had met at the meeting. Although she despised them, she knew that any one of them would have considered her too inferior for marriage to be considered.

The young men who worked in the grocer's or butcher's shops from whom Josie chose her escorts knew Kate chiefly as Mildred's niece, and would never have thought of asking her out, and even the maids in other houses who were friendly with Josie were wary of becoming too friendly with Kate.

Mrs Molesworth's right, thought Kate, but why should I care even if I never get married? I wouldn't want anybody but Henry anyway.

Kate missed the visits to Greenfields and longed to see her sister, but Beattie and Rose were still away. The cruise had been a success and Beattie had made new friends who intended to spend the winter in the South of France. Beattie decided that there was no reason why she should not do the same, and that it would improve her health.

'It's well for her,' Mildred grumbled when the letter came. 'Able to please herself like that,' but Kate thought that Mildred also did just as she pleased. She had still done nothing about extra help, and Kate suddenly lost her temper.

'Something has got to be done about this house,' she said angrily. 'We can't go on. I can never have any time off and twice Josie has given up her half-day. I'm not having it. Mrs Molesworth has done two hours extra each day, paid for by me although she doesn't know that, and you haven't even noticed. You just don't care about the place any more.'

Mildred had sat in astounded silence as the flood of words washed over her, but now she said sharply, 'Oh yes, I do care, miss, and don't think I haven't noticed how you've fallen below my standards. This is my guesthouse, the fruit of my hard work, and don't you forget it. I can change my will, you know, and I don't have to keep you here. I won't have ingratitude.'

Kate stood up, trembling with anger. 'Very well, Aunt,' she said. 'I'll go, but I don't owe you anything. I've been told that more than once but now I see it's true. I've worked hard since I came here but you've taken it all for granted.'

As she turned away, Mildred said sharply, 'Where are you going?'

'I'm leaving. You'd no right to say that about your will – as though I care about that. And about the standards. I've tried my best but I can't make bricks without straw. All that talk about me being in charge, but I've got no say in things really. Only all the worry.' Kate pulled blindly at the door handle, her eyes full of hurt tears.

Mildred was alarmed. 'Wait a minute, wait a minute,' she said. 'No need to get upset. You know I speak my mind. I realise you've worked hard for me.' It was impossible for Mildred to apologise but she managed to say, 'Come and sit down, Kate. No need for tantrums about this.'

Kate sat down and wiped her eyes, and Mildred went on: 'I do intend to get more help but I've just been too busy with my work with the Mission and the sewing circle. I haven't had time to go to the orphanage.'

'I'll go, Aunt, and I'll take Josie with me because she's kept in touch with the place,' Kate said. 'She can help me to pick a good girl.' She had surprised herself as much as Mildred, but when her aunt meekly agreed she followed up her advantage. 'We need some trained help immediately,' she said. 'I've heard of a woman who was a function waitress before she married. She'd come for three afternoons for six shillings a week. Should I arrange it?'

Mildred looked taken aback. 'You seem to have it all worked out,' she said. 'I'll agree to this, but I don't want any more arrangements made behind my back like this extra time for Mrs Molesworth.'

'It was necessary,' Kate said. 'I know you pride yourself on never stinting on food or coal, Aunt, but we can't manage without help in the house.'

Mildred stared at her, then smiled grimly. 'Maybe you take after me after all,' she said. 'We've both spoken our minds today, but I'm sorry to hear you're not grateful for a good home. I did my duty when your mother died, and so did Beattie. It would have been the orphanage or the workhouse for you both otherwise.'

'I know. I have been grateful all these years really,' Kate admitted. 'I was just annoyed.'

Mildred stood up. 'Very well. We've cleared the air now. No more talk of leaving,' she said. 'You can have a free hand with the orphan and with this waitress woman, but I've got to see them and approve of them before they start.'

Kate wrote to the matron of the orphanage offering to take one of the orphans to train for domestic service and saying that Josie would recommend the guesthouse.

'That'll stick in her craw,' Josie chuckled. 'She hated the sight of me and she only sent me here because she thought I'd have a hard life with the missus. Got her eye wiped, didn't she?'

'I'm glad you see it like that, Josie,' Kate said. 'At least you won't have to work so hard from now on.' She had gone without delay to see the waitress, Dodie, who agreed to work three afternoons. She came to the house to meet Josie and see the kitchen and dining room, and Kate took her to be approved by Mildred.

'She seems clean and respectable,' Mildred said later. 'But why do you want her for three afternoons?'

'For Josie's day off and for when I'm out, and for the orphan's half-day when she comes,' Kate said. Mildred seemed about to say something but looked at Kate and changed her mind.

Josie had kept in touch with the orphanage, and although her friends had now left she still took bags of sweets to the children. She recommended a girl to Kate: 'Her name's Charlotte Higson,' she said. 'She went there when her mam died when she was eight, so she's been well brought up and she's a hard worker.' Kate trusted Josie's judgement and arranged to collect the girl from the orphanage.

She was given a frosty reception by the matron, who told her that she usually selected the girls for domestic service herself. 'I have more suitable girls than Higson,' she said. 'I don't know why you have asked for her.'

'Nevertheless, I *have* asked for her,' Kate said coolly. 'I hope she's ready. I'm in rather a hurry,' and the matron grudgingly rang for the girl to be brought to her office.

Charlotte Higson was a small, skinny girl with brown hair and large frightened blue eyes. She was shy and nervous with Kate at first, but Josie was waiting in the kitchen with tea and cake to welcome them, and Lottie – as they decided to call her – was soon at ease. Mrs Molesworth informed her that she was a lucky girl. 'You've fell on your feet here, girl, with Kate in charge,' she told her.

Later Kate took Lottie up to see Mildred, but after telling the girl she expected her to work hard, Mildred dismissed them, as she was going out. 'My aunt owns this place so she had to approve you,' Kate told Lottie. 'But she doesn't have much to do with the work, so you won't see her very often,' and Lottie gave a sigh of relief.

While Josie took Lottie to see the room she would share with her, Kate told Mrs Molesworth about the matron. 'You were right about the clothes,' she said. 'I wore my best outfit and I think it made her treat me with more respect. It certainly gave me more confidence to deal with her.'

'Aye, you're probably right, but I think you're better able to stand up for yourself now anyway. You've got the missus under your thumb all right. All the help now.'

'Not before time,' Kate replied.

Life was easier for everyone now. Lottie proved to be hard-working and willing. She was especially devoted to Josie, who treated her like a younger sister and did everything possible to help her in her new life. Dodie was an asset too, with a fund of stories from her days as a function waitress which kept all of them amused.

Mrs Molesworth reverted to her normal hours and Kate was able to arrange the work so that the charwoman did scarcely any kneeling. 'I didn't mind doing the extra, like, to help out,' she told Kate, 'but I didn't like leaving my feller for so long. Mind you, he met up with old mates when Billy took him out in the carridge so he wasn't never really on his own, but he's not as well as he was.'

With all these new responsibilities and new people, Kate found it easier to close her mind to thoughts of Henry during the day, and at night she read romantic stories of olden days until she fell asleep. She was happy that everything was going smoothly in the guesthouse, and able to look forward to the imminent return of Rose.

Chapter Eight

Rose enjoyed the cruise in spite of her resentment at being made to leave school. She and Beattie had been on a shopping spree before they left and the cruise was a perfect opportunity to wear all the beautiful clothes provided by her aunt.

Young and beautiful and fashionably dressed, Rose was admired by everyone on board, and Beattie basked in the glow of her niece's success. Young men flocked round, the most persistent being a young man named Benjamin Reynolds. He was travelling with his mother, a rich widow like Beattie, and the two ladies soon became friends.

They were alike in appearance, both plump with blurred features and a pink and white softness, but under their marshmallow exteriors lurked a steely determination to have their own way. They watched Ben and Rose outwardly approving, but both were determined that the affair would begin and end as a shipboard romance.

As they sat together in deckchairs, well wrapped up, Mrs Reynolds said innocently to Beattie, 'Your niece is a beautiful girl. Are her parents living?'

'No, she's an orphan.' Beattie sighed sentimentally. 'I adopted her when my poor sister died after her husband had given his life for Queen and Country in the Boer War. Rose is entirely dependent on me.'

'As Ben is on me,' said Mrs Reynolds swiftly. 'He is devoted to me and he means the world to me.'

'I can see that,' Beattie said. 'A most admirable young man. You must be very proud of him.'

'I am,' said Mrs Reynolds. 'I have two other sons, both married, but Ben was born after a gap of fourteen years.

That's why we named him Benjamin. I was only very young when my older boys were born, of course.'

'Of course,' echoed Beattie.

'My sons married far too young. As I've told Ben, I think forty is soon enough for a man to wed,' said Mrs Reynolds.

'I do agree,' murmured Beattie. 'Of course, girls marry younger, but my Rose is *very* young. Only left school a few months ago. I enjoy her company and it's nice to know she'll be with me for a long time yet. She's a dutiful niece and very fond of me, and of course she knows how much she owes me, although I was very happy to take her when my poor sister died so tragically.'

Both ladies sighed, but both were satisfied, feeling that questions had been answered without having to be asked outright, and that they understood each other. They would each see that steps were taken to deal with the situation if Ben and Rose proved difficult.

Ben would have been dismayed to hear his mother and Beattie. He was a slight, fair young man, quiet and diffident, but he had fallen in love with Rose and everything on board ship made romance easy. They sat at the same table for meals and partnered each other for deck tennis and other activities, or lay in deckchairs covertly holding hands.

At night they walked around the deck arm in arm under a sky filled with stars, or stood clasped in each other's arms as the moon rose, making a silvery path across the water. '"This is the stuff that dreams are made of",' quoted Ben, and was delighted to find that Rose also loved poetry and could quote at length from the sonnets of Shakespeare.

Ben wrote poetry too, and the following night he gave a poem to Rose praising her eyes, 'Brighter than the stars above', and saying that her beauty was 'more potent than the goddesses of ancient myth'.

As poetry it was poor quality but Rose was pleased and flattered. She was not in love with Ben, but she liked him and toyed with the idea of marrying him. Could this be the means of escape that Miss Tasker had hinted at? She was sure that married to Ben she could do just as she pleased, and he would be entirely malleable.

She encouraged him by returning his kisses and pressing close to him, and Ben suddenly became possessive and masterful, objecting when Rose fluttered her eyelashes at ship's officers or talked to other male passengers. Rose became alarmed. Would she be jumping out of the frying pan into the fire if she married Ben? she wondered. She wanted a husband who would be dominated by her and Ben was now showing another side to his character, different from the meek son and pliable lover he had been previously.

With a technique which she would often use in the years to come, Rose withdrew gracefully without appearing to do so, and without giving offence to Ben or his mother.

Ben was bewildered, but remained her friend, although they spent most of their free time during the day with a group of young people playing deck games. In the evening they joined the dancers, but Rose danced with others and gradually less and less with Ben. Instead of the *tête-à-têtes* on deck, they attended ship's concerts with Beattie and Mrs Reynolds.

Rose confided to Beattie that she felt that Ben was becoming too serious and thinking of marriage. 'I don't think he realises how young I am, Auntie,' she said artlessly, and Beattie patted her hand approvingly.

'You're a sensible girl, Rose,' she said. 'You needn't be thinking of that sort of thing for many years yet. You'll have a good life with me, dear. You're all I've got.' She sighed sentimentally, but Rose had not missed her shrewd glance or her gratified smile.

Later, Rose walked along a deserted corner of the deck, thinking of the conversation. It might be a good life for some people, she thought, but not for me. It's empty, empty and futile, and I hate it. I should be studying to make my mark in the world, not frittering my time like this.

She beat her hands on the ship's rail in frustration and anger, and an officer who was passing came to her side. 'Is everything all right, Miss Drew?' he asked, and Rose burst into tears and turned into his arms. Surprised and delighted, the young man held her close, saying belligerently, 'Who's upset you? Tell me. I'll deal with them.'

Rose withdrew and dabbed her eyes with a tiny handkerchief. 'No one. It's just life,' she said dramatically. 'I want to study – to be someone. I wanted to stay on at school and my headmistress thought I could become a doctor, but my aunt said it was unladylike. She made me leave.'

'What a shame,' the young man said indignantly. 'You must have a good brain.'

'I have,' said Rose. 'But what's the use? I *wish* I was a man!'

'Don't wish that,' the young officer exclaimed. 'What a waste that would be when you're so beautiful. Think of the pleasure you give just by looking as you do.'

Rose was too angry and resentful even to notice the compliment, and she went on, 'I can't stand wasting my time like this, playing stupid games and dancing attendance on my aunt. I feel I can't go on, but I'm trapped. I should have been more cunning, made myself unpleasant years ago so she'd have been glad to be rid of me before I got too used to the life.'

Much of what she said was incomprehensible to the young man, and he attempted to draw her closer to comfort her, but Rose slipped neatly out of his grasp.

With a sudden change of mood she laughed. 'I've really got the miseries, haven't I?' she said. 'Thank you for listening to my nonsense. I feel better now.' She stood on tiptoe and kissed his cheek swiftly, then with a wave and a smile she sped quickly away, leaving the bemused young man staring after her adoringly.

Some passengers left the ship at Trinidad, and others joined for the rest of the cruise, including two sisters, Miss Isabel Andrews and her widowed sister Mrs Cecilia Weston. Two passengers had left from Beattie's table and the sisters replaced them and immediately became friendly with Beattie and Mrs Reynolds.

Mrs Weston was the same type as themselves although not quite as lethargic, but Miss Andrews was very different. She was a tall, commanding woman, a born organiser, and before

120

long she had taken control of Beattie and Mrs Reynolds as well as her sister, and had them walking round the deck every morning before breakfast. After their first protests, they found that they enjoyed the walk and felt better for it, and like all recent converts, they preached the advantages of fresh air and exercise to anyone who would listen.

Miss Andrews also took control in other ways, and pillows, rugs and drinks appeared like magic as soon as she ordered them. She firmly took the ball of wool that Rose was winding for Beattie from her hands. 'Go and play deck quoits,' she ordered. 'You're too young and pretty to be sitting here winding wool. I'm neither, so I'll do it.' Beattie was afraid to protest.

The sisters intended to winter in the South of France, and before the ship returned to Liverpool it was established that Beattie and Rose would accompany them. They said goodbye to Mrs Reynolds and Ben with many promises to write to each other and to meet again, but Beattie was sure that Mrs Reynolds would take care to keep her son well away from Rose.

Ben had been downcast and miserable for the latter half of the cruise, and Beattie congratulated herself on Rose's good sense. It might have been difficult to nip the affair in the bud if Rose had been as keen to continue it as Ben was, but Beattie was sure that although Rose promised to answer Ben's letters, the correspondence would soon cease.

She was equally certain that letters between herself and Mrs Reynolds would be few. Ben's mother, although she was unwilling for her son to marry young, was affronted when she realised belatedly that it was Rose who had evidently broken off the affair, no matter how gently.

Rose had learned her lesson, and although there were several eligible young men in Cannes who were attracted to her, she was careful not to become too involved with any of them. She felt that she was not yet ready for a lifetime commitment and could afford to take time to survey the field. Who knows? she thought. Aunt Beattie may even change her mind about letting me study when she sees the alternative is my leaving her to marry.

They returned home in March, both happy to be back, for different reasons. Beattie settled back into having the household revolve round her and being pampered by Essy, and Rose looked forward to seeing Miss Tasker and Kate again.

Rose had determined that before they settled back into the old pattern, she would lay out new structures for her days. She established early on that she would have some time to herself, and also more freedom to socialise with other young people. Beattie had been told by Miss Andrews that she would be wise to allow Rose more freedom, otherwise she might 'kick over the traces', as Miss Andrews put it, so she agreed. Pressing home her advantage, Rose even secured a small allowance for herself in addition to all the money Beattie spent on clothes for her.

'She's changed,' Beattie said mournfully to Essy. 'She's not the loving little girl she used to be.'

'You spoil her, madam,' Essy declared instantly. 'You're too kind and she takes advantage of you.'

Beattie was immediately on her dignity. 'You forget yourself, Essy,' she said. 'Rose is my niece and *I* decide how she's treated. She's bound to change. She's growing up and meeting other people, but she still puts me first.'

Essy sniffed and said no more, but she looked at Rose with even more dislike and did anything she could to make life awkward for her. Rose ignored her, knowing that Essy was jealous but not allowing the fact to worry her. She still hoped for a change of heart from Beattie and used her free time to study in her bedroom, but she had moments of doubt, when she felt that it was a vain hope. She went to see Miss Tasker, but the headmistress had other clever girls whom she was now inspiring, and showed little interest in Rose.

Rose envied Kate, who had written to her telling her how much happier she was now, with the extra help in the house and her new responsibilities. Lottie had proved a great success, always cheerful and willing, and amazed with everything about her new life. She was delighted with the food, her new clothes, her bed in the attic bedroom she

122

shared with Josie, and most of all with the affection shown to her by Josie and Kate.

Josie, too, was in a state of bliss. Shortly after Christmas she had taken a pair of Mildred's shoes to a new cobbler's to be soled and heeled, and after an hour's absence came home to announce that she had fallen in love with one of the cobblers.

'Davy Thomson his name is, and he's lovely. He's got copper-red curls and a lovely smile, and he walked me home. He's coming for me tomorrow on my day off,' she said.

'But I thought you were meeting Stan from the butcher's,' Kate exclaimed.

'I was,' Josie said carelessly. 'But I'll send him a note to put him off. Oh Kate, I'm dying for you to see Davy.'

'He must be well in at the cobbler's,' said Mrs Molesworth. 'To get an hour off this morning and tomorrow off as well.'

'He works for his uncle, and he doesn't mind if Davy takes time off as long as the work gets done. He'll work late tonight,' said Josie. 'He lives with his mam in Baker Street off West Derby Road, and his dad's dead. I've never felt like this about anyone before in me life. I know he's the one for me.'

'So it was love at first sight,' Kate joked, but Josie said seriously, 'Yes, it was, Kate, for both of us.' Kate was astonished at how much Josie had managed to learn about the young man in such a short time, and at how sure she was of her feelings, but when Davy came for Josie the following day she could see why Josie was attracted to him.

He was a tall, thin young man with a pleasant smile and a mop of red-gold curls as Josie had said, and he was gentle and protective with her. 'I'll take good care of her,' he assured Kate and Mrs Molesworth, who had lingered to see the young man.

When they had gone, with Josie hanging on Davy's arm, smiling adoringly at him, Kate turned to Mrs Molesworth. 'I'm sure this is the real thing for Josie,' she exclaimed. 'I've never seen her like this before. It's always the lads who are mad about her and she doesn't care about them. Isn't he nice, Mrs Molesworth?'

'Yes, he's a nice lad,' Mrs Molesworth said cautiously. 'But she'll have to be careful. He looks delicate, like, to me.'

'He's a bit stooped, but that's probably from bending over a cobbler's last,' said Kate, but the charwoman shook her head. 'No, I'm thinking more of them red spots on each cheek,' she said. 'That's not natural, not with that white skin and red hair. Still, I could be wrong, so don't say nothing, girl.' Kate assured her that she would not say anything to spoil Josie's pleasure and pride in Davy.

It was unusual for Mrs Molesworth to linger at the guesthouse, as she now spent as much time as possible with her husband. She confided her worries about Charlie to Kate. 'I can't put me finger on it, but he doesn't seem as well somehow,' she said. 'He says he's fine, but there's something,' and when Billy came home he agreed with his mother.

The doctor was called, but as Mrs Molesworth said to Kate, 'We wasn't no wiser when he went than when he come. He only said Charlie'd done well to have lasted this long after the accident, but he couldn't tell us nothing about the way he is now.'

'Was he able to go out with Billy?' Kate asked, and Mrs Molesworth nodded. 'Billy got the carridge again and we went to the park, but Charlie was asleep most of the time. Billy says—' She hesitated, then muttered, 'But it's a daft idea. What do you want me to do first, queen?'

Kate recognised that the subject was closed and said no more about it, but she grieved to see her old friend so worried. Her affection and respect for Mrs Molesworth had grown with the years, and she knew how much she had always relied on the charwoman's shrewd good sense and advice. Mrs Molesworth had provided affection and guidance for Kate in the early days, when she was a lonely and frightened young orphan, and Kate longed to help her now, but there was little she could do.

She set aside a portion of any tasty food that might

124

tempt Charlie to eat, and arranged more time off for Mrs Molesworth without loss of pay, but otherwise she could only offer silent sympathy.

Beattie wrote to Mildred, announcing their return and inviting her and Kate to tea the following Sunday, and Rose wrote to tell Kate how she longed to see her. 'I don't see why I should go,' grumbled Mildred. 'I've done my duty all these years but she went away for months without a thought for me.'

Kate knew that Mildred would go, but she said nothing. The blow she had long expected had fallen, and Agnes and Henry had set the date for their wedding. '*She's* set it,' Mrs Molesworth said to Josie. 'It's her that's making the running. He's one of them fellows who lets himself be bossed because he's too nice to say no and hurt her feelings. Mind you, it's just as well. It'll be better for Kate to have him outa the house.'

Kate would not have agreed, and wondered how she would bear not seeing Henry every day. The wedding was set for August, and Agnes would leave her teaching post at the end of the school year in July. She told Kate that Henry's sister had been ill again and wanted the wedding to be as soon as possible. She hoped to be well enough to be a bridesmaid.

Kate would normally have been excited about the visit to Greenfields, but now she thought it would only take her mind off her misery for a short time. At Josie's urging she wore her blue suit and hat with the white blouse and gloves, and Mildred looked smart in a black silk dress and carricule coat with a new large black hat. She needed new clothes for her changed lifestyle, and looked forward with grim satisfaction to surprising Beattie and Rose.

There was a new minister at the Mission, with less austere views than his predecessor, and he had introduced social activities in which Mildred, a great admirer of the minister, joined. She often went out to tea with members of the sewing circle, who made hideous garments for 'the heathen', and had taken her turn entertaining the members one afternoon. Dodie, in a smart cap and apron, had served tea, and the ladies had been impressed. Mildred also still made her mysterious visits to town dressed in her best; Kate thought these were connected with her hint about a friend who advised her on investments.

'You look lovely, Kate. Very stylish,' Rose exclaimed when they arrived, and Beattie echoed, 'Yes. Very stylish, my dear, and so do you, Mildred.' Mildred said nothing, and Kate and Rose quickly escaped into the garden, where Rose poured out all the details of the cruise, their lengthy holiday and her many conquests.

Kate was fascinated, but before she could tell Rose any of her own news, they were called for tea. Rose slipped her arm through Kate's. 'I haven't stopped talking – haven't let you get a word in,' she said remorsefully. 'But next time, Kate, I won't say a word, I promise. I'll just listen.'

Kate laughed. 'I enjoyed hearing all your adventures,' she said. 'Much more interesting than mine.'

'Tell me quickly, though,' Rose said as they entered the house. 'What you said in your letters about being in charge. Is it working well?'

'Yes perfectly,' Kate said, 'with extra help, and we all get on well. Aunt Mildred hardly ever interferes.'

'And Mildred's got what she always wanted,' Rose said cynically. 'Playing the lady owner but keeping control of the pursestrings while you do the work and she never has to soil her hands.'

'Oh Rose,' Kate protested, but she looked lovingly at her sister as they went into the drawing room. Rose had not changed from the affectionate little sister she had always been, she thought. Their last meeting had only gone wrong because Rose was so upset about leaving school.

Beattie looked disgruntled, and as soon as they went in she said to Kate, 'You must be a great help to your Aunt Mildred, Kate. Working so hard and taking so much responsibility that she's able to have such a good social life.'

Kate was surprised. Mildred never gave her any praise for her work, but only grumbled sometimes at the bills, so she said with a touch of sharpness, 'I'm glad Aunt Mildred sees it like that. I was not aware of it.'

'I'm not one to gush,' Mildred said. 'But you'd soon have heard about it if I wasn't satisfied.' Kate said no more. I can do without praise, she thought. What you never have you never miss.

Beattie said no more either, but she still looked vexed. She had been as eager as Rose to talk about the cruise and her new friends, but Mildred had not been as attentive a listener as Kate with Rose. She had talked about the new minister and of the many activities she was involved in at the Mission, boasting about how important she was there, and Beattie had been unable to compete with her more forceful sister.

She soon became more cheerful as Essy and Rose fussed about her, and Rose firmly took charge of the conversation, ensuring that Beattie was able to talk about the wonders of the cruise and how highly she was regarded by her new friends.

It was raining when Kate and Mildred were ready to leave, and Mildred asked Essy to call a cab. As they drove home she said grimly to Rose, 'If your Aunt Beattie can treat herself to a cruise, I think we are entitled to treat ourselves to a cab.'

She's jealous of Aunt Beattie, Kate realised with amazement. She had been so used to thinking of Mildred as a model of rectitude, living by her own bleak creed, that it was a shock to find that she had ordinary emotions and failings. She's changed, thought Kate. Her aunt had always been generous with food and fuel as a means to an end, but so tight-fisted with other household bills and wages that Mrs Molesworth declared she would 'skin a flea for its hide'. She had been as mean with herself too, but now she spent money on clothes and entertaining. I don't know what's changed her, but if it means riding in a cab instead of walking home in the rain, I'm all for it, Kate decided.

Kate's mood changed when they reached home and the thought of Henry's wedding filled her mind. She had long ago abandoned hope that her fairy tale might come true and Henry would decide that he loved her, but just to see him

127

and speak to him daily enriched her life. Soon she would not even have that.

Davy Thomson had spent the afternoon with Josie, and it was hard for Kate to join in Josie's joy and excitement about her new love. Her mood was more tuned to that of Mrs Molesworth, who was still very worried about her husband and quite unlike her usual cheerful self.

The White Star liner the *Titanic* had gone down with tremendous loss of life after a collision with an iceberg on 14 April, and Mildred's reaction to the news was to say grimly, 'It was flying in the face of God to say that ship was unsinkable. God is not mocked.' Kate was shocked by her words, and even more so when Mrs Molesworth agreed with her, but Josie said that it was only because Mrs Molesworth was so low in spirits.

Billy had been on the New York run and returned home to find his father no better. The following day, Mrs Molesworth and Kate were working together in the dining room when the charwoman said abruptly, 'Our Billy wants to arrange for his sister to come and see his dad, but I don't want her.'

She had never mentioned her daughter since her first brief reference to her when she had talked to Kate of her family, so Kate had never asked about her.

When Kate hesitated about how to reply, Mrs Molesworth went on, 'You think I'm hard, girl, but it's what she done. She was working on the ships, cabin crew, and when she come home and her dad was laying there with his back broke, she took fright. Got married and scarpered off to America for fear she'd have to nurse him, and I've never forgive her. He thought the world of her and he'd been a good dad, and then to treat him like that. I never mention her name, but Billy reckons his dad is fretting to see her.'

'Do you think he is, Mrs Molesworth?' Kate said cautiously. Mrs Molesworth was polishing the sideboard, and when she looked up, Kate saw that her eyes were full of tears.

'I don't know, girl,' she said in a low voice. 'It's breaking me heart to see the way he is – no life in him. I'd pull the moon outa the sky if it'd do him any good, but he's never spoke about her all these years.'

'Perhaps he didn't want to upset you?' Kate suggested, and Mrs Molesworth shrugged.

'That's what Billy says. He's tracked her down where she's living in New York, and he says she's desperate to come and see us. I'll let her if it'll do Charlie any good, but I won't speak to her.'

'If she's sorry, I'm sure you'll forgive her when you see her,' Kate said, but Mrs Molesworth was implacable.

'Not after what she done to Charlie. Him laying there in agony, worrying about the future, and all she could think of was herself. No, queen, I can't do it.'

Kate said no more. She felt sure, though, that Mrs Molesworth would feel differently when her daughter arrived.

During the following weeks, Mrs Molesworth spoke several times about her daughter. 'The feller our Florrie married, Con Ryan, he was born in America but he come to Liverpool as a baby. He was cabin crew too, but I only seen him the once.'

'Did you go to the wedding?' asked Kate.

'No, girl. We wasn't asked. My feller was too bad anyhow, and we didn't know nothing about it till it was done. She said she done it that way to save me worry. She wasn't expecting or nothing.'

Another day she told Kate that Florrie had written to her from America soon after she had arrived there, but that she had thrown the letter on the fire. 'I was near outa me mind with worry at the time,' she said. 'My feller said, "She's only a child." A child! She was nineteen. When I think what I'd gone through by the time I was nineteen! He never said no more about her, though.'

Kate suspected that Mrs Molesworth was feeling guilty about her daughter and nervous about meeting her, and she asked what Florrie had been like as a child.

'She was real good,' said Mrs Molesworth, 'and tidy! She'd go out to play and all the other kids'd get filthy, but she'd come home like a new pin. I don't know how she done it. Her dad thought the sun shone outa her. I used to put her hair in rags of a Saturday and twist it into rinklets of a Sunday, and he'd walk out with her as proud as Punch. All round the docks, so the fellers doing Sunday shifts could see her.'

Kate felt that at last Mrs Molesworth was softening towards her daughter. She said so to Josie, adding that she was glad. 'It didn't seem like her to be so bitter,' she said. 'I'd never have believed that she could be like that.'

'She probably wouldn't be if it was herself who was hurt,' Josie said shrewdly. 'It was Charlie being hurt that made her so resentful.'

'You're very wise, Josie,' Kate said admiringly and Josie laughed. 'I think I'll need to be,' she said. At Davy's insistence, his mother had invited Josie to tea, but she had not tried to hide her hostility. 'It's not you,' Davy assured her later. 'She'd be the same whoever I wanted to marry. You won't let it put you off me, will you, Josie?' he added anxiously.

'No. It'll make me more determined to marry you,' Josie said, laughing. 'You'd better tell her that.'

Later, Josie told Kate about the conversation, and Kate looked at her with dismay. '*Married!*' she gasped. 'I didn't know you were talking about getting married.'

'Not for ages,' Josie assured her. 'But I told you we were serious, Kate. We will get married, but we'll have to save up for ages first. Davy'll still have to give his mam some of his wages even after we're married, 'cos she depends on him, like. We'll have to have a bit behind us, so it'll take us a while. I'm getting as much as I can in my bottom drawer and Davy'll work late for extra money, so we'll do it all right.'

'I'm sure you will,' Kate said. 'I know it's selfish, Josie, but I'm glad it won't be for a while.'

'A year or eighteen months at least,' Josie said. 'You might be married yourself before then, Kate.'

Kate shrugged. 'And the moon's made of green cheese,' she said. 'I can't see myself ever getting married, Josie.'

'There might be more chance of that after September,' Josie said bluntly. 'Once Mr Barnes is married, you might stop dreaming about him and look at other fellers.'

Kate blushed deeply. 'Oh Josie,' she gasped. 'I don't dream about him. Not since he got engaged,' but Josie looked sceptical.

'I know you don't intend to, Kate, but seeing him every day and that, you haven't got no chance of forgetting him. It'll be better when he's gone. You might take an interest in other fellers then.'

'But will they take an interest in me?' Kate said, forcing a smile. 'They haven't done so far.'

'Only because they think you're spoke for. You're so standoffish,' Josie said sturdily. 'You've got to give lads a bit of encouragement, like, and you'd soon start courting.'

She looked so earnest and concerned that Kate hugged her and pretended to agree, but she felt that she would never marry. Even in the unlikely event that a man asked her, could she be content with second best? No, she thought. No matter what happened, Henry was the only man she would ever love.

Chapter Nine

The summer months passed quickly for Kate, too quickly she sometimes thought, as the wedding day approached. Agnes told her that the arrangements were going smoothly. She went every Saturday to her home in Prescot, a market town a few miles from Liverpool, to help her mother with the wedding plans, and told Kate that wedding presents were arriving every week.

Presents were also arriving at Henry's mother's home near Delamere Forest, and some at the guesthouse. 'At this rate we won't have to buy anything but furniture,' Henry joked as Kate handed him yet another parcel.

Kate was determined to buy them a good wedding present. She was torn between an ornate teapot and stand with matching hot-water jug, and a cut-glass whisky decanter and six whisky tumblers. She decided on the decanter and glasses. Agnes would probably use the teapot for tea parties with her friends, but she thought that Henry would use the decanter and glasses and, she hoped, be reminded of the giver.

She took the gift to Agnes and Henry when they were together, and both enthused over it. 'It's beautiful, Kate, and very generous of you,' said Agnes. 'Such good taste too,' Henry said cheerfully. 'The best present we've had, Kate. I'll think of you when I'm relaxing with a whisky after a hard day.' But Agnes said reprovingly, 'On social occasions only, Henry.'

She needn't have picked Henry up so sharply, Kate thought indignantly. I hope she's not going to change him – and she needn't have sounded so surprised that I had good taste either. But she was delighted with Henry's reception of her gift and his promise to think of her.

The wedding was to be a quiet family affair at the Parish Church in Prescot. The only anxiety seemed to be that Henry's sister Lucy might not be well enough to act as bridesmaid. She had been diagnosed as consumptive several years earlier, and although her health had improved, lately there had been signs that she was losing her brave fight against the dreaded disease. She had set her heart on being a bridesmaid and assured everyone that she was perfectly well, and Henry felt that sheer determination would carry her through the ceremony.

Mr Molesworth, too, had rallied. Billy had arranged for his sister to work her passage home from New York to see her parents in Liverpool. He had planned the visit as a surprise for his father, but Mrs Molesworth insisted that Charlie be warned. 'He can't stand no shocks, the way he is,' she said.

The news seemed to stimulate Mr Molesworth and give him something to which he could look forward. Kate told Mrs Molesworth to take a few days off when Florrie was due, and the others shared her work between them. Lottie willingly scrubbed the steps and cleaned the brass, feeling that she was taking part in a story like those in her ha'penny magazines.

The following day Mrs Molesworth arrived at her usual time. 'I meant you to have a few days at home,' Kate protested, but the charwoman said she was not putting on good nature. 'I was glad I was off yesterday though, queen,' she said. 'My feller was getting that worked up he wouldn't have been a bit o' good by the time she came if I hadn't been there to calm him down, like. She come in as bold as brass, dressed up to the nines, but when she seen her dad she just put her arms round him and cried like the rain. Charlie cried too, huggin' and kissing her. I was sorry I kep' her away for so long when I seen them.'

'But you had good reason to be vexed with her at the time,' Kate said.

'I know, girl, but I didn't know he fretted that much over

her. I still wasn't going to speak to her but he said something to her and she got up off her knees, like, and come over to me. She told me after that she had a speech ready but she just put her arms round me and said, "Oh Mammy, I'm sorry." I couldn't bear no grudge after that, could I, girl?'

'It must have made Mr Molesworth happy that you were friends again,' Kate said.

'Aye, it did. We were fine till I said I was coming here today, and she said all hoity-toity, "What about Dad? Do you leave him to look after himself?" I turned round and told her, "The neighbours have helped us all these years. I don't like putting on them, but there was no one else, was there?" She didn't know where to look.'

'I suppose she spoke without thinking,' said Kate.

'Charlie told her too. He said, "Your mam's worked her fingers to the bone to put food on the table and then come home and seen to me and done the cooking and the cleaning. She's been wore out many a time but she's kept me alive. Been a Trojan," and she started crying again. "I wasn't criticising Mam," she said. "I know all she's done, and I'm sorry." Good job our Billy never heard her or he'd o' given her something to cry about, I can tell you.'

'I thought Billy was on the same ship,' Kate said.

'He was, but he had to stay on board overnight. Home today,' said Mrs Molesworth. 'He won't half see a change in his dad. I done spare ribs and cabbage for them, and Charlie didn't half muck in to his. Hasn't ate like that for ages.'

'That's wonderful!' Kate exclaimed, and Mrs Molesworth agreed but, it seemed, with reservations. Later she said to Kate, 'It's funny. All me and Billy done for Charlie, yet we couldn't do nothing to rouse him up, like. He was slipping away from us, then she arrives and he comes to life again, like.' She tried to smile as she spoke, but Kate could see that her old friend was hurt.

'Only because it was a novelty to see Florrie,' she consoled her. 'Gave him something new to think about. He says himself that you're the one who's kept him alive, and it's for your sake he's struggled on. He must have been tempted to give up many a time but he cared too much about you.'

She was rewarded by a grateful smile from Mrs Molesworth. 'You're a good, kind girl, Kate, and a clever one. You deserve a good husband,' she said.

Kate smiled and changed the subject by talking about Josie and Davy. Davy's mother was still as hostile, and Josie had said to Kate, 'If she was different, me and Davy could get married sooner and live with her, but the way she is it'd mean bloodshed. Either I'd take a chopper to her or she'd poison me. She's only the size of six penn'orth of copper, but bitter in every inch.'

Josie was determined not to allow the woman to spoil her happiness and sang as she worked, until Mildred said irritably, 'Tell that girl to stop singing, Kate. Who does she think she is, the Swedish Nightingale?' Josie only smiled and hummed to herself instead.

When the school year finished in July, Agnes Tate left the guesthouse and went to spend her remaining time as a single girl at her parents' home in Prescot, a few miles outside Liverpool. Henry was still at the guesthouse, and he and Agnes had arranged to rent a large house in Rufford Road in Fairfield, about two miles out from the city centre and not very far from Mildred's.

His brother, who was to be his best man, stayed in Agnes's old room the night before the wedding, and his mother and sister stayed with the Tates in Prescot. Before his brother arrived, Henry met Kate on an upstairs landing. She had been polishing, and felt hot and dishevelled, with a voluminous apron over her dress and strands of hair escaping from her bun and hanging down her flushed cheeks, but Henry seemed to notice nothing amiss.

'I'm glad to see you, Kate,' he said eagerly. 'I wanted to thank you for all you've done for me over the years. It's been a long time, hasn't it?'

'It has, Mr Barnes,' Kate agreed shyly.

'I would have liked you to come to our wedding, but it has to be very quiet, just family, because of my sister's health.'

'I know,' Kate said. 'I hope she will keep well enough for tomorrow.'

'She's determined to,' said Henry. 'You brought Agnes and me together, you know, because we were both concerned about your future.' He seemed to notice her appearance for the first time and said indignantly, 'You work far too hard, Kate. It's not right. All hard work and no pleasure. You deserve better.'

'I'm all right really, Mr Barnes,' Kate said. 'I like the work, and Josie and Lottie and Mrs Molesworth are good friends. I see my sister regularly too.'

'But you should have a better life than this. Don't accept things so meekly, Kate,' Henry urged her. 'We couldn't make your aunt let you go to Bryant's when you were a child, but you're old enough to be your own mistress now. You're a refined, intelligent girl and you could have a better life. Take any opportunity you get to break away. Do what *you* want to do.'

'But I am happy here, honestly,' Kate said. As happy as I can be without you, she thought. 'Thank you for your advice, though.' She smiled at him.

Henry laughed. 'You've got a lovely smile too, Kate,' he said. 'That was the first thing I noticed about you when I saw you with that heavy coal bucket on your first day here. Do you remember?'

'Oh, I do,' Kate said fervently, then, feeling that she had been too emphatic, she added quickly, 'It was a sad day for me, and I appreciated your kindness.'

'Repaid a thousandfold,' Henry assured her. 'By all you've done to make life easy for me over the years.' He kissed her cheek and held out his hand, and Kate took it and said shyly, 'All good wishes for the wedding.'

'Thank you, Kate,' he said. 'And I wish you a happy life, whatever form it takes. I won't forget you.'

They were standing still, holding hands and smiling at each other, when Josie appeared on the landing, and he said cheerfully, 'I'd better get on with my packing or my brother will tell me off.' He disappeared into his room, and Kate smiled vaguely at Josie and went downstairs to her own room.

She touched her cheek where Henry had kissed her, and

then sat thinking of all he had said. I'll never forget a word of it and the way he smiled at me. I'll treasure it all my life, she thought. She sat in a happy dream until the striking of a nearby clock reminded her of the time, and she washed and changed and tidied her hair ready to meet Henry's brother.

The wedding morning was bright and sunny. Henry had said his farewells to the other guests at breakfast, and afterwards to Mrs Molesworth and Josie and Lottie.

While Mildred and Kate stood in the hall with Henry's brother, waiting for the wedding car, Henry slipped out to the porch and returned with two bouquets. The larger one, of mixed flowers, he presented to Mildred, and a smaller one of pink roses to Kate.

'Many thanks,' he said. 'I've been very happy here and very comfortable.' Before they could respond, the car arrived. Henry shook hands with Mildred, then squeezed Kate's hand, saying, 'All good wishes for the future, Kate. Remember what I said,' then he looked into her eyes and added in a low voice, 'I'll miss you, Kate.' He kissed her cheek, and in a moment he was gone.

Mildred said with a sigh, 'He's annoyed me at times but I'm sorry to see them go, I must admit.' Kate said nothing. She had seen a card tucked in her bouquet and she was anxious to carry it away to read in private.

Mildred went to her rooms, and Kate put the card in her pocket before carrying her roses downstairs to be exclaimed over by Mrs Molesworth and Josie. 'I know he's getting married this morning,' Josie said, 'but I still think he was half in love with you, Kate. If Miss Tate hadn't of come along—'

'Or if the missus had let you take that job in Bryant's,' said Mrs Molesworth.

'That's how he got friendly with Miss Tate,' said Kate. 'She took his part when he had words with Aunt Mildred about it.'

'Fancy! I never knew that,' exclaimed Mrs Molesworth.

'See? You don't know everything,' teased Josie. She was making tea and called Lottie to join them.

'It'll seem strange without them all the same,' said Mrs Molesworth, stirring her tea. 'They've both been here a good few years.'

'Were they here when you came, Kate?' asked Josie.

'Yes. Mrs Molesworth was here long before me,' said Kate. She rested her chin on her hand and said dreamily, 'The day I arrived I was so miserable and unhappy. It was the day of Mama's funeral, and me and Rosie had just been separated. We thought we'd stay in the house together, but Aunt Beattie took Rose to live with her and I had to come here with Aunt Mildred.'

'God love you, and I wasn't even here,' said Mrs Molesworth.

'No, you were off with your bad leg and the two maids had just left, so Aunt Mildred had to do everything and I helped her. She told me to take a scuttle of coal to Mrs Bradley's room. It was heavy and I rested it on the bottom stair in the hall. I was so miserable being parted from Rosie and everything, and it was a horrible grey day, but he came in like a breath of fresh air. He looked so healthy and cheerful. His eyes were so bright and his teeth so white and his hair in little curls all over his head. I felt better just looking at him.'

Nobody spoke, and Kate went on in the same dreamy voice. 'He said, "Halloa. A bit heavy for you. Where's it going?" When I said first floor front, he picked up the bucket and walked upstairs with me. He asked my name, and when we got to the door he put the coal down and he said, "Cheer up, Kate. Remember, it's always darkest before the dawn." Then he smiled at me and went downstairs. I never felt as bad again after that.'

'I never knew all that,' Josie said in wonder. Lottie had listened starry-eyed, forgetting to drink her tea. 'It's like a fairy story,' she whispered, and Josie laughed. 'Drink your tea, Lottie,' she said. 'And we'll get on with the rooms.'

'This is a sad day for you, queen,' Mrs Molesworth said when they had gone. 'You'll miss him outa the house,' but Kate only nodded and smiled, still lost in her dream. She fingered the note in her pocket, deciding that she would not open it until twelve o'clock, the time of the wedding.

She was glad the wedding was not at a local church, she thought, where she might be tempted to go and watch it. The fact that it was miles away in Prescot made it seem more unreal, too. At twelve o'clock precisely, in the privacy of her room she opened the small envelope. 'To Kate. With fond gratitude and all good wishes for a very happy life, Henry,' she read.

She sat holding the note, tears rolling down her face, feeling that her heart would break. It's no use pretending, she thought. I love him. I'll always love him, even though he's marrying someone else at this very minute. I can't put him out of my mind and pretend it's all finished and I'll forget him. I never will.

She went over to where the roses stood in a vase on the dressing table, and tucked the card among them, then buried her face in the flowers, her tears flowing. I can't bear it. I'll never see him again and I can't bear it, she thought, her body racked with quiet sobs as she pictured Henry and Agnes at the altar in the Prescot church, being pronounced man and wife.

She had heard voices in the kitchen but had been too engrossed in her sad thoughts to pay any attention. Shortly there was a quiet tap on her door. 'The missus has been looking for you, queen,' Mrs Molesworth whispered. 'I told her you'd slipped out for a minute, but she wants to see you when you come in, she said.'

'Thanks, Mrs Molesworth, I'll be out in a minute,' Kate said in a muffled voice. She splashed cold water on her face and pressed powder leaves round her eyes to try to hide the evidence of her tears, then tidied her hair and went into the kitchen.

'Drink this cup of tea, girl,' Mrs Molesworth said. 'It won't hurt her to wait another five minutes.' Kate finished the tea then, feeling more composed, went to her aunt's room.

'I see those empty bedrooms haven't even been started,' Mildred said abruptly. 'I want them thoroughly turned out, mind. I've got two guests coming for them and they'll be here for dinner tonight.'

'All right. I'll cater for them,' Kate said, moving to the door, but Mildred said triumphantly, 'You see? My rooms are never empty for long.' Kate nodded, trying to make her escape before her aunt noticed the signs of tears, but Mildred appeared to notice nothing and went on, 'One's a widower, a master in a private school, *very* superior, and the other is a lady teacher recommended by Miss Tate. Mr Fallon is to go in Mr Barnes's room and Miss Lennon in Miss Tate's.'

'Very well, Aunt. I'll see to it,' Kate said, thankfully making her escape.

Kate knew that Josie and Lottie would be more observant or more interested in her than her aunt, but they all tactfully avoided looking at her as she told them about the new guests and gave instructions. She was glad to be kept so busy for the rest of the day that there was little time to think of the wedding.

Kate had been nervous about the superior Mr Fallon, but he proved to be a quiet man in his late forties with a pleasant manner and no airs. Miss Lennon was small and slight, dressed in deep mourning. She confided to Mrs Bradley that her mother had died three months previously and she had lost her home.

'You were wise to come here,' Mrs Bradley said. 'You'll be very comfortable and soon feel happier.'

'I won't be happy anywhere without Mother,' Miss Lennon said mournfully. 'We were all in all to each other.'

'Never mind. It's early days yet, my dear,' Mrs Bradley encouraged her, but Miss Lennon made no reply. She was a pretty girl, and Jack Rothwell and the two young bank clerks eyed her hopefully, but she seemed too sunk in gloom to notice them.

Kate had dreaded bedtime, fearing a sleepless night, but before Josie and Lottie went up to bed Josie gave Kate two pills. 'Mrs Molesworth said I had to give you these, Kate. She said she thought you was starting with a cold and these'll help you to sleep it off.'

Kate hesitated, but Josie urged, 'Go on, Kate, take them. She'll batter me tomorrow if you don't.' Kate laughed, and Josie said goodnight and vanished.

Kate took the pills and fell into a deep and dreamless sleep, yet she woke at the usual time, feeling clear-headed but remote from all that had happened.

'Thanks for those pills,' she said to Mrs Molesworth. 'What were they? I've never had such a good sleep or felt like this before.'

'The doctor from the Dispensary give them to Charlie. They make him sleep and he says he feels as if he never worries about nothing when he wakes up. The only thing is, the doctor said only to take them when he really needed them because they were – I can't remember the word, but he'd get too used to them, like. Couldn't do without them.'

'They were just what I needed last night, but I won't need them again, Mrs Molesworth,' Kate said, and the charwoman nodded as though satisfied.

'Aye, that's the way, girl. Forward not back, as my feller says. What's the new people like?'

The unreal feeling induced by the pills gradually wore away, but the sharpness of Kate's grief had been blunted when she needed it and she was able to keep her feelings under control. When the roses faded, she took the card from among them and wrapped it in tissue paper, then put it in the carved box that held her small treasures.

It seemed a symbolic act. During one sleepless night she had decided not to struggle against thoughts of Henry and try to forget him, but to treasure her memories of him. Nobody would know, and they were a comfort to her, growing dearer as time passed.

The new guests fitted easily into the household, although Miss Lennon was still wrapped in grief in spite of Mrs Bradley's encouragement. 'Sorrow affects people in different ways,' Mrs Bradley told Kate. 'We must all be very kind to her until she recovers.'

Over morning tea, Kate told the others of Mrs Bradley's words, but Josie said bluntly, '*I* think she's wallowing in it.

142

Wouldn't do her no harm to smile now and again. I like Mr Fallon, though. He's a proper gentleman.'

Kate liked Mr Fallon too, although she was inclined to resent him at first because he had taken Henry's place. He was a quiet, studious man, almost as recently bereaved as Miss Lennon but never mentioning his loss. He had seen Kate glancing at the newspaper he had left on the hall table, and immediately offered it to her, saying that he had finished with it. 'Although there's not much good news in it, I'm afraid,' he said with a smile.

'Thank you. There seems to be a lot of trouble in Ireland,' Kate said. 'Do you think there'll be civil war there, Mr Fallon?'

He shrugged. 'This man Carson seems dangerous,' he replied. 'He's defying the Crown – raised his own private army of Protestants – and there's all this gun-running in Ulster.'

'But people wouldn't fight each other just over religion, would they?' Kate said.

He smiled wryly. 'It wouldn't be the first time. This is about Home Rule, though. Carson says he would rather be governed by Germany than accept Home Rule for Ireland, but he's playing with fire.' He smiled. 'Let's hope they all see sense.'

After that he often left his newspaper for Kate and spoke to her of items of news, and she was flattered that he thought she had such wide interests. She told Josie and Mrs Molesworth about events in Ireland, but Mrs Molesworth declared that her feller said that it was only the scum on both sides, Catholic and Protestant, who fought each other.

'That feller's got a cheek to threaten our King and Queen,' Josie said indignantly. She had attended a pageant in July on the occasion of the visit of King George V and Queen Mary to Liverpool to open the new Gladstone Dock at Seaforth, and had been intensely patriotic ever since then. The pageant, at Everton football ground, had involved 60,000 children, 15,000 of whom performed Swedish drill dressed in red, white and blue to give the appearance of a huge Union Jack. Josie often talked about it, and always finished by saying, 'I felt proud to be English. I love my King and Queen.'

Now Mrs Molesworth said, 'Aye, the King and Queen are good people. He's a family man, not like his father. King Eddy was a disgrace, running after women. I felt sorry for poor Queen Alexandra, pretending she didn't notice nothing.'

'She was very deaf, wasn't she?' Kate said, and Mrs Molesworth said, 'Yes, but my feller said she'd have had to be blind as well not to know what was going on. I suppose them sort of people have got to put a good face on it.'

'She couldn't very well go and tear the other woman's hair out like Katie Deagan's mother did,' Josie giggled.

Mildred seemed inordinately pleased that she had relet the rooms so quickly. For a time she had been in an ill humour, querying every item on the household bills and grumbling that too much was being paid in wages. At the same time she had been subject to frequent sick headaches, spending much time in her room, and Kate wondered whether this was the reason for her bad temper or whether her aunt had some secret worry.

She never discussed the financial affairs of the guesthouse with Kate, but suddenly the cloud lifted and Mildred resumed her visits to town and her socialising with the people from the Mission. The headaches disappeared and were never mentioned.

'I wish my bad leg'd come and go as easy as them headaches,' Mrs Molesworth said. 'But I don't think it'll ever be any different.'

'Is it very painful now?' Kate asked sympathetically. She was still arranging the work to spare Mrs Molesworth's bad leg, with the willing co-operation of Josie and Lottie, but there were days when it seemed difficult for the charwoman to walk.

'Aye, a bit, but I can't grumble, not when I think of me poor lad laying there all these years with never a moan outa him.'

'He enjoys going out with Billy, though, doesn't he?' said Kate. 'And Florrie's visit made a change for him.' Florrie had returned to New York now, but with promises to keep in touch and to come again, and Mrs Molesworth had told Kate that her husband still talked about the visit. 'It's given him a lot to think about,' she said. 'Done him good.'

So the shock was all the greater when, two weeks before Christmas, Mr Molesworth died in his sleep. A young boy brought the news to the guesthouse, and Kate went immediately to see Mrs Molesworth. As she passed along the landing above the row of shops, she saw that all the neighbours had drawn their curtains as a mark of respect, and several neighbours were sitting with Mrs Molesworth when she arrived.

Mrs Molesworth was dry-eyed and dignified. 'His heart just give out, the doctor said. He said Charlie didn't suffer. I told him Charlie done his suffering all these years and never a word of complaint outa him. He was real nice, the doctor. He said Charlie'd had a cross to bear but he was blessed with a good wife and a loving son.'

Mr Molesworth's body had been laid out on the bed where he had spent so many years, and Mrs Molesworth and Kate stood beside him. 'Doesn't he look young? The way he looked before the accident,' the charwoman said fondly. 'I always used to be that proud walking out with him.'

'He looks noble,' Kate said. 'I'm glad Billy had that idea about the spinal carriage. He enjoyed going out and seeing people, didn't he?'

'Yes, and going round the docks, seeing the ships and his mates again,' said Mrs Molesworth. 'I'm glad he seen our Florrie too. Maybe that's what he was hanging on for,' but Kate said swiftly, 'Oh no. Don't think that. His heart could have given out at any time. He fought to live because he couldn't bear to leave you. You kept him alive, but this had to happen sometime.'

Kate looked about her at the row of books, the feeding cup of water and bag of mint imperials close to his hand, and on the mantelpiece at the foot of the bed a gaudy fan, carved elephants and canoes and a tiny bamboo rocking chair brought home from abroad by Billy. Mrs Molesworth had told her that she changed the items on the mantelpiece every day so that Charlie would have something different to look at. What devotion, thought Kate, when she must have been exhausted by her work in the guesthouse, and then the nursing, cooking and cleaning at home, all done with the handicap of a painful varicose ulcer. She looked at her old friend with even greater respect.

The neighbour who had admitted Kate had whispered that Billy was on a three-week coaster run and was due to dock on Friday. As it was now Tuesday, he would be home for the funeral. A wire had been sent to Florrie. Kate asked if she could do anything, but Mrs Molesworth said her neighbours had everything in hand. 'We're used to death round here,' she said with a sigh.

'The undertaker's coming,' the neighbour said. 'We've made room for the coffin in the bedroom so Mrs M. can have a fire in here.' Kate realised that they were both sympathetic and practical, and left feeling that Mrs Molesworth was in good hands.

Josie and Lottie were grieved for Mrs Molesworth, as Kate had expected, but she was surprised when Mildred called her into her room.

'Is she all right? Mrs Molesworth, I mean,' Mildred asked. 'She's done so much for him, she's bound to feel it.'

'She's upset but very quiet and dignified,' said Kate. 'I suppose she's been expecting this for a long time. Her son's due home on Friday.'

'Good,' said Mildred, then she added abruptly, 'Has she got money for the funeral?'

'I think so,' Kate said. 'I never thought about that. Anyway, Billy'll be home.'

'Try and find out as soon as you can and let me know, Kate,' said Mildred. 'She may be worrying about it.' Kate promised, and left the room thinking that people could always surprise her. I suppose no one's all of a piece, she thought.

The following day she went again to see Mrs Molesworth. There were still neighbours sitting in the kitchen with her, and she took Kate into the bedroom, where the coffin stood on trestles, with candles burning at the head and foot.

Kate whispered to Mrs Molesworth how peaceful Charlie looked.

'Aye, he's outa all his pain now, me poor lad,' the widow said with a sigh.

Kate took the opportunity to tell her of Mildred's words. 'You're not offended, are you, Mrs Molesworth?' she said.

'No, girl, and I'm not surprised neither. Me and the missus have been sparring partners a long time, but I always knew she was a good woman for all her funny ways, like. Tell her thanks, queen, but I kept up me policies and Billy's put money away for me and all. We'll be able to give my feller a good send-off.'

Kate begged to be allowed to supply the food for the funeral breakfast, and Mildred instructed her to order a wreath from herself and Kate. Josie and Lottie also sent flowers, and to Kate's surprise Jack Rothwell organised a collection among the guests and sent a wreath from them. Mrs Molesworth was pleased and her neighbours were impressed by the wreaths, and even more by the fact that Mildred, accompanied by Kate and Josie, attended the funeral. They left Lottie in charge of the house.

Mrs Molesworth, in deep mourning, walked behind the coffin, leaning on Billy's arm. They were followed by a few distant relations and friends. The charwoman was composed and dignified, and probably because of her example, there were no loud outbursts of grief at the graveside. 'All the more genuine for being quiet,' Mildred remarked to Kate.

Billy decided not to sign on for another trip but to take his chance at dock work for a few months, to ease the blow for his mother. Mrs Molesworth returned to work after the funeral. 'Youse have all been very good doing me work for me, but I don't like putting on good nature. I'm better off working anyhow, and our Billy's there at night for me,' she said.

Kate and Josie and Lottie were loving and supportive with Mrs Molesworth, but she never paraded her grief in the way that Miss Lennon did. 'I've no patience with her,' Kate said to Mrs Molesworth. 'She seems to *enjoy* her grief. Always saying that she and her mother were all in all to

147

each other. It's embarrassing for everyone. Very different to you!'

'Yes, but I done me best for Charlie, so I'm not blaming meself for nothing, only leaving him to go to work and I had to do that to keep us. Maybe she's thinking she never done what she should of for her mother, or they'd fell out before she died,' Mrs Molesworth said shrewdly. 'That's when it's hardest for anyone to get over a death, 'cos they're always wishing they could make it right, like, and it's too late.'

How well she understands human nature, Kate thought, and whenever she recalled these words she was able to feel more sympathy for Miss Lennon, and to value afresh the wise guidance she had always received from Mrs Molesworth.

Chapter Ten

The regular visits to see Beattie and Rose were resumed, and on the second visit after her return from France Rose said gaily to Kate, 'Now, Kate, I'm going to keep my promise and *listen* instead of talking all the time. Tell me all your news.' Kate, however, found that her impulse to confide in Rose about Henry had gone. So she talked about the death of Mr Molesworth, Josie's skirmishes with Davy's mother, and the new guests.

'But what about *you*, Kate?' said Rose. 'I mean, you're nearly twenty-one. No sign of a possible husband for you?'

Kate shrugged. 'No, but I don't care, Rose. I like reading about romance but I haven't got time for the real thing.'

'Don't be silly. You'd soon find time if you met Mr Right, but how will you ever do that?' Rose said indignantly. 'You work far too hard for one thing, and Aunt Mildred should introduce you to people. See that you spend time in suitable company.'

'I don't want anyone from among her friends from the Mission,' Kate laughed. 'And they're the only people she mixes with. No thanks. I'd rather just read love stories with handsome heroes in them.' And think about Henry, she thought, but said nothing of that to Rose.

'You could get a bicycle. Join a group,' Rose said. 'Everyone is bicycling now. It's all the rage with my friends.'

'I see groups when I walk in the country,' Kate said. 'Most of the ladies clip their skirts to the guard on the machine, but I saw one lady wearing *bloomers.*'

'Was she old?' asked Rose.

'Yes, about forty, and such a strange shape.' Kate laughed,

and the conversation moved away from the subject of potential suitors.

Rose had now completely given up studying and become friendly with a set of frivolous young women, most of them the daughters of Beattie's friends. They boasted of leading freer, fuller lives than their mothers' generation, and said that things would change even more when they had the vote, but they made little use of their much-talked-about freedom.

They were empty-headed, foolish girls, their conversation always about men or clothes, and at first Rose despised them, but they welcomed her warmly into their set and freely admired her beauty and her wit. Charmed and flattered, Rose quickly jettisoned her plans for the future and slipped easily into their thoughtless, hedonistic way of life.

Kate felt that Rose had changed, without understanding how or why, but she still loved her sister with an unquestioning love.

Kate had herself made a new friend at this time. The house was running smoothly and as a result she had more free time and often visited the public library. There she became friendly with Nell, one of the young assistants, and they often discussed the books which Kate borrowed.

From that they progressed to sometimes having tea together in a small café, or, as the evenings grew lighter, walking along the Pier Head. Nell was a quiet, studious girl, and she and Kate never tired of discussing books, finding that they agreed on favourite authors and the ideas they expressed.

They talked about their lives and their hopes too, but Kate never spoke about Henry. She still kept her memories of him locked away in her heart, and found immense comfort in them.

A friend of Josie's had successfully applied to Agnes for the position of general maid in the newly-weds' house in Rufford Road. Josie often saw the girl, Hetty, on her day off and brought back the information Hetty gave her about Agnes and Henry. 'Hetty's made up with the job,' Josie said. 'She said she was just a drudge with Mrs Jennings and never got no decent food or anything. But now she gets the same food as Mr and Mrs Barnes and they're real easy to work for. She says she's a bit strict but he's lovely. Cleans his own shoes and brings coal in 'cos he says it's a lot of work for one maid.' Kate felt a stab of jealousy but she glowed with pride to hear Hetty's good opinion of Henry.

Hetty must also have relayed news to Agnes and Henry about the people in the guesthouse and told them about the death of Mr Molesworth. A few days after the funeral, a letter arrived for Mrs Molesworth containing a black-edged card engraved 'With Deepest Sympathy' and two one-pound notes.

Mrs Molesworth showed Kate and Josie the enclosed letter, in which Henry had written:

Dear Mrs Molesworth,
    My wife and I were very sorry to learn of your sad loss and offer our sincere condolences. Kate has spoken to me of your many years of devoted care for your husband, and the memory of this must be a consolation to you at this sad time.
    I am sorry we only knew too late to send a wreath to the funeral, but please accept the enclosed for flowers for the grave.
    Sincerely,
    Agnes and Henry Barnes.

Kate was unable to speak, but Josie said, 'That's lovely. Aren't they kind to send money for flowers as well?'

Mrs Molesworth stood clutching the card, her eyes full of tears. 'Eh, you never know how good people are till trouble strikes,' she said. 'Wait till our Billy sees this. He's always saying I'm just a handrag here.'

Kate swallowed. 'That shows how much they respected you, Mrs Molesworth,' she said huskily.

'I always liked him – and her too,' said the charwoman. 'But I never expected nothing like this. I'll copy it out and send it to our Florrie too, and get flowers for Charlie's grave.'

Kate felt that it was a pity that Henry was unable to

see how much pleasure and comfort his letter and gift had given to Mrs Molesworth, and to her in a different way.

Good Friday fell on 10 April and was a sunny day with boisterous winds. The library was closed, and Nell and Kate both attended early service then walked for miles in Sefton Park. 'Isn't this exhilarating?' Nell exclaimed. 'I feel sorry for anyone cooped up on such a day.' Kate agreed but felt guilty about Josie and Lottie.

On Easter Sunday most of the guests, even the woeful Miss Lennon, were out for the day, and Kate was able to give Josie and Lottie the day off. Josie and Davy went on a day trip to the Isle of Man, taking Lottie with them. The wind had dropped and they had a happy day, but when they returned Josie gave Kate a shock.

'We met Hetty and her boyfriend at the Pier Head,' she said. 'They were going to Eastham. What do you think?' She lowered her voice as Lottie was at the other end of the kitchen. 'Mrs Barnes is expecting. In June, Hetty said. She told her other day but Hetty said she'd already guessed only she couldn't say nothing until she was told, like.'

Kate felt as though she had received a physical blow and sat down abruptly. 'That's nice,' she heard herself say. Josie noticed nothing. She seemed to have forgotten about Kate's feelings for Henry and rattled on about the day.

Why has this possibility never occurred to me? Kate thought. It's what happens when people get married. I suppose I'm still trying to get used to him being a married man, she thought ruefully, and now I'll have to think of him as a father too. She tried to concentrate on what Josie was saying.

'Davy's mother is getting worse,' Josie said. 'She's carrying on that much about me that he says he can't stand no more and he's going to get a room. I told him we'd be worse off if he did. He'd still have to give her most of his wages and by the time he'd paid for a room he couldn't save nothing.'

'So will he stick it out?' asked Kate.

'Yes. He says his uncle's on at him to stand up to his mother, but it only makes her worse if he does,' Josie said with a sigh.

'Is the uncle her brother?' asked Kate.

'No, he's Davy's father's brother and he hates her. He only gave Davy the job to spite her because she didn't want Davy to have nothing to do with him, but he's fond of Davy now. Says he's like his dad.'

Kate found that talking about Josie's troubles gave her time to absorb the news about the coming baby, and she was able to tell herself that she was glad for Henry's sake. He'll make a wonderful father, she thought wistfully.

Hetty had also told Josie that Mr Barnes's sister Lucy was very ill. 'It hasn't been no good for people with TB, the autumn and winter being warm, like,' said Mrs Molesworth when they told her the next morning. 'A lot of the girls round our way are bad with it. The Bullens next door but one, they've lost every girl with it as they come to sixteen. There's only the youngest left outa six of them, and she's thirteen now. It's a terrible thing.'

'Nobody likes to say it's TB,' Josie said. 'They say they're delicate or in poor health – even rich people.'

'It's to be hoped that one doesn't leave this world as another comes into it,' said Mrs Molesworth, 'but it's very often the way.'

Kate thought that Mrs Molesworth had been changed by her husband's death. She seemed to have lost her salty humour and her optimistic outlook on life, and even her well-worn phrase 'What can't be cured must be endured', once her cheerful attitude to pain or disaster, was now uttered gloomily. Kate missed her cheerful company and wise counsel.

Billy had not been very successful at finding work at the docks, so he went back to sea. The few months of his company had helped his mother over the first shock of her loss, and he promised her that he would only sign on for short trips for a while.

Kate needed something to cheer her at this time. The news about the coming baby had been a shock and things were not going well at the guesthouse. Mildred's sick headaches had started again and she was continually finding fault with Kate and querying every penny that was spent.

Mrs Bradley was becoming a trial too. These days she seemed to be confused. She often rang her bell and when it was answered was unable to remember why she had rung. When Kate tried to consult Mildred, her aunt only snapped, 'Deal with it. That's what I've kept you for all these years.'

Mr Fallon was still worried about items in the newspaper and spoke of them to Kate. The news was dominated by the troubles in Ulster, and Mr Fallon told her that cargoes of rifles and ammunition had been landed at Larne and Bangor.

'They're afraid Carson may take over and rule the province and there's talk of martial law being imposed by the Government. Not a very safe place to live these days, Kate, but then where is safe?'

'Well, we're safe enough,' said Kate. 'It's got nothing to do with us.'

He smiled sadly. 'As the poet John Donne says, "No man is an Island" and "Any man's death diminishes me", but I was thinking less about Ireland than the Balkans. There's going to be trouble there before long or I'm a Dutchman, and if we're not careful we'll be drawn into it.'

These conversations always left Kate feeling worried, although she felt that Mr Fallon took too gloomy a view of the news. She began to buy the *Liverpool Echo* each night, feeling that the halfpenny was well spent if she could make her own more cheerful judgement on the news.

On one of the visits to Rose and Beattie, Kate tried to discuss these matters with her sister, thinking that clever Rose would be interested, but Rose said airily, 'Don't worry, Kate. Enjoy life. There are people paid to worry about such things, so let them do it. Anyway, these scares never come to anything.'

'Do you think so?' Kate said eagerly.

'Oh, yes. I did some of that with Miss Tasker. Morocco in 1905, Bosnia in 1908, Agadir in 1911 – they all came to nothing. Miss Tasker called it sabre-rattling. But why are we talking about these things on such a lovely day? Aunt Beattie's considering another cruise!' said Rose gaily.

Kate looked at her sister with admiration and immediately felt more cheerful. Mama had been right, she thought. The good fairy had given Rose everything, beauty and brains and a lovely disposition. Kate felt blessed that Rose was her sister.

The next time Mr Fallon spoke about events, Kate said firmly, 'My sister's very clever and she says this has all happened before and come to nothing. She called it sabre-rattling.'

Mr Fallon smiled sadly but only said, 'I hope your clever sister is right, Kate.'

In May Josie brought the sad news that Henry's sister had died at the age of twenty-two. 'Hetty says Mrs Barnes's mother and father have come to stay with them to look after Mrs Barnes. She's very upset and she's so near her time,' said Josie.

'She'll have to think of the new life, not the one that's gone,' said Mrs Molesworth. And Henry, thought Kate. He'll need to be comforted. He loved Lucy.

On 28 June 1914 a son was born to Agnes and Henry, bringing them great happiness and comforting those who grieved for Lucy. He was a fine healthy boy with fair hair and blue eyes, and they christened him Charles Jonathon after his two grandfathers.

On the same day, far away in Sarajevo in Serbia, the Austrian Archduke Francis Ferdinand and his wife were assassinated by a young Serbian student, Gavrilo Pricip, a member of a secret nationalist movement known as Young Bosnia. None of the happy people who surrounded Charles Jonathon Barnes knew of this event or would have believed that something so far away could affect their lives, but this was the spark that ignited a powder keg and began the Great War 1914–1918.

Most people in the country were unconcerned about events so far away. 'Them foreigners are always killing each other,' Mrs Molesworth said disparagingly. 'Our Billy says so,' and Kate turned over the pages of the *Liverpool Echo* which carried news of the declarations of war by Austria-Hungary on Serbia on 29 July, by Germany on

Russia on 1 August and by Germany on France on 3 August.

They were far more interested in a breach of promise case reported in the *Echo* and were divided for and against the girl in question. Mrs Molesworth was against the girl chiefly because she wore a blue costume and a large white hat. 'Like that one from Rupert Hill who used to chase after our Billy,' she declared, and was annoyed when the girl was awarded £75 damages.

Mr Fallon was greatly concerned about the war news, and when Germany invaded Belgium on 3 August he told Kate, 'This is it. Britain guaranteed Belgian neutrality so we'll have to act now.' Sure enough, the next day Britain declared war on Germany.

Even then Kate thought that only the regular Army and the Reservists and Territorials would be fighting, as in previous wars. She was horrified when she realised that civilians were enlisting and that Henry might go. The two young bank clerks from the guesthouse volunteered but were sent home until the Army was ready for them.

'They say it'll all be over by Christmas,' one of the clerks said gloomily. 'We might miss it just because there's no uniforms or equipment ready for us.'

'Someone should have prepared for this,' said the other. 'All those fellows wanting to fight for King and Country, and they just took our names and sent us away.'

'I wonder will Mr Barnes go?' Kate could not resist saying to Mrs Molesworth.

'If he's got any sense he won't,' she said robustly. 'He should think about his wife and child. There's soldiers trained for this sort of thing.'

Josie and Davy had been out to Seaforth Barracks, where recruits for Kitchener's Army and a large crowd outside were addressed by Lord Derby. Davy had been caught up in the patriotic hysteria fanned by the newspapers and recruitment posters, and he was anxious to enlist.

'Lord Derby said he didn't need to tell the recruits their duty as they had already responded to their country's call,' Josie said. 'He said fellows who were too old or unfit should look after the wives and children left behind. He said as long as he had a penny in the world he'd do as much for their dependants as they'd do themselves.'

'Easy said,' scoffed Mrs Molesworth. 'We'll see whether it happens.'

'I was talking to a woman whose son works for Lord Derby and she said he was a warmonger. He'd made all the single men either join up or be sacked.'

'That's not right,' Kate said. 'The men should make their own minds up.'

'She said their jobs'll be kept for them. I'm a bit sorry we went. I think it's made Davy even more determined to enlist. I don't know what to think. I don't want him to go but I want to be proud of him,' said Josie.

'That lad wants to go to get away from his mother,' Mrs Molesworth said later to Kate. 'There's a few joining up to get away from the life they've got here.'

'But most people are joining for patriotic reasons,' Kate protested. She was right. It was an exciting and different time, and many of those previously despised were gratified to know that they were now wanted and needed by their country.

Reality came with the Battle of Mons and the first Battle of Ypres in October and November. Many Liverpool men were involved, and long lists of casualties appeared in the *Liverpool Echo*. By this time Davy had tried to enlist but been rejected as unfit. His uncle shared Mrs Molesworth's view on his reasons for enlisting and told him he must get away from his mother before she ruined his life as she had done his father's.

The uncle owned some property near the shop and offered a house rent-free to Davy if he married. Josie was ecstatic and they immediately made plans for their wedding. Within a month they had become man and wife and moved into the house, a two-up, two-down in a street off Everton Road. Davy's mother refused to attend the wedding or to recognise Josie as her daughter-in-law.

In spite of that, it was a happy occasion. Josie wore a cream coat and skirt with a large cream hat trimmed with brown pansies and cherries, and Kate, as her bridesmaid, wore her blue suit. Davy's uncle gave the bride away, and it was a happy group who returned to the guesthouse kitchen for the wedding breakfast, provided by Kate. She had decorated the table with flowers and trails of smilax, and Davy's uncle said he had never seen such a spread of food. 'Your ma doesn't know what she's missing,' he joked to Davy.

Kate gave the couple a matching tea and dinner service as a wedding present, Mrs Molesworth a set of pans, Lottie a statuette under a glass dome, and the best man, a fellow cobbler, a rose-sprigged bowl and ewer and a matching chamber pot. But the most surprising present was from Mildred. She called Josie into her room and presented her with £20. 'You've been a good reliable worker,' she said, 'but this is because we're your family, as it were. I wish you and your husband a happy married life.'

'I was that thunderstruck I never thanked her properly,' Josie said. 'I never expected nothing like that and saying that about me being family, like.' She wept a little and Mrs Molesworth said encouragingly, 'Well, let's hope you soon have your own family round you. A little girl that can play with the doll your mam sent you.' Kate smiled at Josie, thinking that Mrs Molesworth always rose to the occasion and said the right thing.

It had been arranged that Josie would work in the guesthouse each day and leave in time to cook Davy's evening meal. The two bank clerks had at last received their papers and departed for training camp, but before Mildred could replace them she suffered a slight stroke. She had been to town and returned in a cab from which she had to be helped and put to bed. She was as secretive as ever and said nothing about where she had been or a possible reason for the stroke, and Kate was afraid to ask her outright.

Within a few days she was up and about, walking with a slight limp, but otherwise everything was unchanged. She still refused to allow Kate to know anything about the financial affairs of the guesthouse, but she became increasingly cantankerous and grumbled constantly about money.

Lottie complained that she could do nothing right for Mildred. 'The missus is after me the whole time,' she complained to Kate. 'Whatever I do she finds fault with it, and she's always there every time I turn round. If you wasn't so good to me I'd walk out.'

'Don't leave me, Lottie,' Kate said. 'I couldn't do without you. I'll speak to her.' More and more work was now falling to Lottie and to Kate herself, as Mrs Molesworth's ulcerated leg was worse, and Josie, who was now expecting her first child, could do much less than before. Her morning sickness persisted throughout the day, and she lost weight and all her bright colour, although she was still very happy.

'There's something wrong,' Mrs Molesworth told Kate. 'Some mornings she looks like a tallow candle. I hope that wicked old mother hasn't put a curse on her.'

Kate and Lottie did all they could to save Josie from stretching or doing heavy work, and Kate felt that without Lottie she could not have managed. She spoke to Mildred and asked her to stop harassing the girl. 'Get rid of the other two then,' Mildred snapped. 'Plenty of women who'd be glad of the jobs.'

'All right, but it'll cost you twice as much,' Kate said, determined to call her bluff. 'Anyway, the cleaning is my responsibility. You seem to want to take it over. Do you want me to do the money side instead?'

'Don't get above yourself, miss,' Mildred snarled. 'You haven't got your hands on this place yet, and maybe you never will.' Before Kate could reply she suddenly began to talk pathetically about the stroke and how she was only trying to help Kate, and Kate felt unable to say any more.

Davy's mother still refused to acknowledge Josie as his wife, and when the time came for the birth Mrs Molesworth and Kate went to help Josie. The baby was a boy, well formed but small and a strange colour, and he died within a minute of his birth.

'He only breathed and died, love,' Mrs Molesworth told

Josie gently. 'Never mind. You're young yet – plenty of time before you for more,' but Josie wept bitterly.

'She'll say it's my fault,' she sobbed. 'She met Davy and told him I'd kill the baby going out to work.'

'Take no notice, girl,' said Mrs Molesworth. 'Tell Davy to tell her you work because she leeches on to Davy for most of his wages. Tell her to go out to work herself instead.'

Josie threw her arms round Mrs Molesworth. 'Oh Mrs M.,' she said, 'you've been like a mother to me.' She turned to Kate. 'And you've been my sister and my best friend, Kate. I love both of you so much.' Kate hugged her but Mrs Molesworth seemed embarrassed. 'Don't get worked up, queen,' she said. 'Lay down. We'll tidy you, then I'll make you a drop of gruel and Davy can come and see you. He's walking up and down outside.'

'Does he know about the baby?' asked Josie, and Mrs Molesworth said, 'Yes, girl, but it's only you he's worried about.'

Within a few months Josie was pregnant again, and this time Davy insisted that she gave up work in the guesthouse. Josie was reluctant because Davy himself was often ill and off work, but he told her that he would give his mother less of his wages.

'I've been too soft with her,' he said. 'Plenty of women of her age have got jobs now, but she'd rather drain off me so there's less for us – for you, really. I'm not having you killing yourself for her.'

'It's taken him a long time to see it, but he's really turned against her now,' Josie said. 'Though really I'd rather be working than sitting at home worrying about Davy.'

'Then just come round here as a visitor,' Kate said. 'I'd be glad of your company.' Kate needed someone to confide in, as she had many worries of her own at this time.

Mildred had found guests for the two vacant rooms, but the new women, although appearing to have plenty of money, were very different from previous guests. They were noisy and arrogant, leaving their rooms in a filthy state and complaining about the food, which Kate had often queued for hours to obtain.

Jack Rothwell had already enlisted in a Pals battalion, and after the Somme offensive in July 1916 Mr Fallon told Kate that he intended to join up as well. 'Two of my finest pupils have been killed,' he said. 'Both eighteen years old. I can't stand aside any longer.'

'But at your age you don't *have* to go, do you, Mr Fallon?' said Kate.

He shook his head. 'I must, Kate,' he said sadly.

'Oh, this awful war!' Kate exclaimed. 'If only that Archduke and his wife hadn't been killed.'

'Wouldn't have made any difference,' said Mr Fallon cynically. 'They'd have found some other pretext. Wars are all about money, Kate, and stockpiles of armaments that have to be used and replaced, and old grudges and ambitions.'

Kate was uncertain how to reply, but she said quietly, 'All the more reason for you not to go, it seems to me.'

'I must, Kate,' he said again. 'I can't stand aside while boys I taught are killed. By conviction I'm a conscientious objector, but I haven't the courage to register as one. Far easier to go with the tide.'

A few weeks later he was gone, but Mildred was unable to let his room, or Jack Rothwell's.

As sorry as Kate was to see Mr Fallon go, a far worse blow had been when she learned that Henry was now in the King's Liverpool Regiment. Hetty had called to see Josie and told her that Mr Barnes's brother had been killed at the Battle of Neuve Chapelle and his mother had joined the household in Rufford Road. 'Now I've got three women telling me what to do,' she said. 'And I've had enough.'

She decided to leave and go into munitions, and Kate's source of information was lost. It was a casual remark by Jack Rothwell shortly before he left that gave her the news about Henry. After that she studied the casualty lists which appeared in the *Echo* every night, but so far Henry's name had not appeared.

In early May the ship on which Billy Molesworth was serving was torpedoed and sunk with great loss of life. Many Liverpool men were among the crew, and Kate went with

Mrs Molesworth to the Cunard offices in Bold Street, hoping against hope that Billy was among those saved, but it was not to be. Kate clutched Mrs Molesworth's work-roughened hand in wordless sympathy, knowing that nothing she could say would relieve her old friend's black despair.

Sometimes Kate herself felt almost despairing, although she told herself that she should be ashamed when she compared her troubles with those of Mrs Molesworth. Mildred spent most of the day in her room, refusing to listen when Kate tried to talk about the many problems she had, and she flatly refused to acknowledge that Mrs Bradley was becoming increasingly odd and a cause of worry to Kate.

Mrs Molesworth had not returned to work after Billy's death, and when Kate went to see her she found her in bed, being looked after by a neighbour and seeming too tired to talk.

'The rest will do her leg good anyway,' Kate said hopefully to the neighbour, but the woman shook her head.

'No, it's not her leg that's the trouble. She's just lost heart. What with Charlie going, and now Billy, she hasn't got nothing to live for, like. She doesn't want to go on.'

'She's so brave, I'm sure she'll soon start fighting back,' Kate insisted, but the woman only sighed.

'She'll never get outa that bed, girl, and maybe better for her if she don't,' she said.

Kate went back with Josie a few days later, but they were too late. Mrs Molesworth was dead. 'Slipped away in the night,' the neighbour said. 'At least she went peaceful.'

Kate and Josie were devastated. They clung together weeping, and Josie sobbed, 'She was like me mam to me. I could tell her anything.'

'She was to me too,' said Kate. 'Always helped me and gave me good advice, and she was always the same. No moods like Aunt Mildred.'

Later, after the simple funeral, Kate said sadly, 'What a life she had, Josie. Nothing but sorrow and suffering. Losing her children, then Mr Molesworth's accident and that awful ulcer. She was in agony with it from the first day I met her.

She didn't deserve to suffer so much. She was such a good woman and she did so much for everyone, as well as looking after her husband all those years.'

'But she didn't see it like that,' Josie said. 'She often said how lucky she was, with a good husband and a good son. She was never miserable, was she? We always had a good laugh with her.'

'That's true,' Kate admitted. 'And she was always interested in everyone and she had them weighed up too. I'll miss her salty comments.'

'Yes, and she got a laugh out of them too,' said Josie. 'She told me her fellow said she should be on the halls when she was taking off the missus and some of the guests. She enjoyed life, Kate.'

'Yes. It just got too much for her at the end,' said Kate. 'We shouldn't grieve for her, Josie.'

'It's ourselves we're sorry for,' Josie said, ''cos we know how much we'll miss her,' and Kate knew that she was right.

Chapter Eleven

Rose was pleased when war was declared, as she saw it as a means to an exciting new life. 'Now I can do something different,' she told Kate. 'My life is so *dull*, just waiting on Aunt Beattie and her whims, but now I can do as I like. It won't be patriotic for her to interfere.'

Kate was surprised that Rose thought her life dull. On previous visits Rose had told her of shopping sprees with friends, and of tennis teas and garden parties she had attended, but she only said, 'What will you do, Rose?'

'I haven't decided,' Rose said airily. 'Probably I'll become a VAD. Think of all those handsome officers I'd be nursing!' She giggled, and Kate thought sadly, How she's changed. A few years ago she'd have really wanted to do something useful. Remembering Rose as she was, she felt more cheerful. It's this crowd she's been in with, Kate decided. She'll go back to her old self when she gets away from them.

Although Rose spoke so flippantly to Kate, she really did intend to volunteer to nurse the troops. Many girls from middle-class families were joining the Voluntary Aid Detachment. They were trained by regular staff in hospitals and later, in France, did useful work, nursing wounded men and driving ambulances in the mud and carnage of the Western Front.

Like many other girls, Rose had a romantic vision of gliding around the wards, dressed in a becoming uniform and laying cool hands on the fevered brows of handsome young officers, who would promptly fall in love with her.

A conversation at one of Beattie's bridge afternoons swiftly brought Rose down to earth. Mrs Gilroy, a tall, commanding woman, talked of her own niece who had

165

enrolled as a VAD. 'I said it was foolish and I've been proved right,' she declared. 'The gel is absolutely exhausted, and her hands! Red and swollen like a charwoman's, and no wonder. She says she spends most of her time in what they call the sluice, scrubbing rubber sheets and *emptying* and washing bedpans. The sister hates the VADs and gives them the most menial and unpleasant tasks, and the regular staff are hateful to them. Jealousy, I suppose, because our gels are of a superior class.'

Other ladies joined in with tales of young relatives or friends enduring long hours of unpleasant work and being treated with contempt because they fainted at the sight of blood.

Rose listened, her desire to serve rapidly evaporating. She looked at her soft white hands with their carefully buffed nails, and pictured them red and swollen with hot soda water. And bedpans! She had not thought of bedpans. I could soon deal with hostile nurses or sisters, she thought, but is this what I really want to do?

She knew that she should not be influenced by selfish elderly women, but biased and garbled though the accounts were, a picture had emerged of a hard life needing self-sacrifice and endurance. Rose decided that she must learn more about the life of a VAD before making a decision.

Many of the young men who had squired Rose to various events were now serving in the Army or the Navy, and one had become an airman. One of them, Peter Bennet, came home on embarkation leave before his battalion moved to France, and Rose accompanied him to a show. Afterwards they went to a supper club and Rose told him that she was considering volunteering as a VAD.

'You're not the type, Rose,' he said decisively. 'I haven't had first-hand experience yet, but I know chaps who've been in the trenches. They're grateful to the girls who are nursing out there and they respect and admire them, but one chap said he'd hate his sister to be there, and I think that's the general opinion. There are sights there that aren't fit for girls who've led a sheltered life.'

'But I must do something, Peter,' Rose protested.

He smiled and took her hand. 'There are plenty of strong-minded women for that, Rose. You just stay the sweet butterfly you are – roll bandages or raise money for comforts for the men, by all means, but let me think of you just as you are, here waiting for me.'

Rose was alarmed. She liked Peter, but she hoped that the war would enlarge her circle of eligible young men and she was determined not to commit herself so soon. She gently withdrew her hand. 'I must think about it, Peter,' she said. 'I love my country and I want to do all I can to help her in her hour of need.'

Peter smiled indulgently and patted her hand, not realising that he was being gently fobbed off. Rose said no more about her plans and spent the rest of the evening charming Peter, giving him happy memories to take with him to France. She was pleased that society's rigid rules of behaviour had already been relaxed. Before the war she would not have been allowed such an evening alone with Peter, so she felt that already her horizons were widening. It was not the time for hasty decisions.

Kate was so fully occupied that there was no question of war work for her. As soon as Miss Lennon heard about the Zeppelin raids, she discovered a cousin living in the Cheshire countryside, and announcing that her nerves would not allow her to stay in Liverpool, she departed to stay with her.

Kate was not sorry to see her go, but her departure seemed to make Mrs Bradley's grasp on reality even more tenuous. She was becoming increasingly confused, forgetting mealtimes and having to be brought from her room by Kate or Lottie and encouraged to eat. Otherwise she sat staring blankly at the food on her plate, or looking at Miss Andrews and Mrs Burroughs, the new guests, and saying loudly, 'Who are these people? What are they doing in my house?'

The two women resented this, muttering to each other, 'Crazy old bat. Should be locked up,' and declaring that she was spoiling their meal. Kate decided that the only solution was to serve Mrs Bradley's meals in her room, although they were already fully stretched and there was no guarantee that Mrs Bradley would not appear at the dining table.

Mildred refused to help or even to admit that there was anything wrong. 'Mrs Bradley is a lady and very quiet,' she said. 'She's always been my favourite guest.'

'But her mind is failing,' Kate protested. 'We need help with her. Her relations should be told too. Have you got an address for them?'

'Nonsense,' Mildred said, ignoring Kate's question. 'She just gets a little bothered at times.'

'A little bothered!' Kate echoed. 'Aunt Mildred, she was on the front steps in her nightdress yesterday – I told you about it – and she sees me every day yet doesn't remember who I am. She's ordered me out of the house several times.'

'Leave it with me,' Mildred muttered, 'and leave me to rest.' She closed her eyes in dismissal.

'I'm sorry,' Kate told Lottie. 'I know it's not fair to you to leave you with the responsibility for Mrs Bradley *and* all the work, but I've got to be the one to queue. The shopkeepers know me and keep things for me. Aunt Mildred should help us but I can't get any sense out of her. Between the two of them I'm nearly out of my mind myself.'

'Don't worry,' Lottie said. 'If I'm cleaning upstairs I keep an eye on the old lady, and when I have to go down to the kitchen I lock her door so she can't wander round.'

'Oh Lottie, what would I do without you?' Kate said fervently. 'But I'm determined to get an address from Aunt Mildred, even if it's only Mrs Bradley's solicitor. We can't be responsible for her the way she is. She could harm herself and I'd be to blame because I didn't get help for her.'

Kate was puzzled by Mildred's behaviour. Since her stroke she rarely went to the Mission and spent nearly all her time in her rooms, taking no part in the household. Sometimes Kate wondered whether her aunt's mind had been affected by the stroke. She had always been so proud of having all her rooms full, and so discriminating in her choice of guests, but Mrs Burroughs and Miss Andrews were coarse and vulgar women who would not have been tolerated previously.

The only other new guest was a Mr Culshaw, a quiet young man who had been discharged from the Army after an accident with a gun carriage. One of his legs was shorter than the other and he walked with the aid of a stick. He worked in a shipping office. Mildred made no apparent attempt to find guests for the remaining two rooms. Kate was not sorry, as food was becoming ever more scarce, but she did worry about her aunt's state of mind.

Mildred had refused to visit Greenfields, saying that Beattie was too inquisitive, but Kate paid a brief visit there. She found Rose voluble about her own troubles. She had finally decided to enrol as a VAD, but Beattie had promptly had a heart attack. Rose's application was rejected and she was convinced that it was because Beattie had pulled strings, yet something in her manner made Kate suspect that this actually suited her sister.

The only bright spot in Kate's life now was the cheerful letters she received from Nell, who was now nursing in London. She had left the library at the outbreak of war and loved the nursing life. Her lively, humorous letters, copiously illustrated, were eagerly welcomed by Kate.

In addition to her worries about the household and her constant fear for Henry, Kate was also worried about Josie. She had suffered a miscarriage five months into her second pregnancy, and Davy had also been frequently ill and unable to work. Kate had been alarmed by the sound of his coughing when she visited Josie.

'The fog gets on his chest,' Josie said. 'The neighbours are going to bring his bed down here for me because the doctor said he should be in the one heat all the time, and them bedrooms are icy.'

The next time Kate visited, the bed was downstairs in the tiny kitchen/living room and Davy was sitting up in it, his eyes feverishly bright and a hectic flush on his hollow cheeks. 'It's done me the world of good being down here,' he told Kate. 'Josie's the best nurse in the world. I'll soon be back at work now.'

In the mirror above the mantelpiece, Kate caught a reflection of Josie's unguarded expression, and realised that her friend knew what was very clear to Kate, that Davy would never work again. The next moment, however, Josie said cheerfully, 'The doctor's made up with you, isn't he, Dave? He says the warmth and the company was all Davy needed.'

'That's good,' Kate said, wondering how Josie could manage to appear so cheerful. 'It's a lovely warm room. I suppose you have plenty of visitors.'

'Yes, the neighbours are in and out all the time,' said Josie. 'And Dave's uncle has been so good to us. He calls in nearly every day, and never empty-handed.' She picked up the basket covered with a white cloth that Kate had put down unobtrusively. 'And now you've brought us all this lovely food too. Eh, we're living like lords these days, aren't we, lad?' she said.

Davy nodded, but the action brought on a fit of coughing which was dreadful to hear. Josie went swiftly to the bed and, shielding him with her body so that Kate could not see what was happening, attended to him. Afterwards he lay back on the pillows, white and trembling. Kate wondered whether she should go or whether she could do anything to help, but Josie returned to sit beside her on the sofa.

'All right now,' she said cheerfully. 'Better up than down, as Mrs Molesworth would say.'

After a moment Davy managed to smile at Kate. 'Thank you for the food. Josie often tells me about your cooking and the lovely meals she had at the guesthouse. Very different to the orphanage,' he said.

'Yes, and Davy's felt the benefit,' Josie said, 'because you learned me to cook. He never had good meals when he was at home.'

'My ma couldn't boil water without burning it,' Davy said, and they laughed together. Kate was amazed at their courage and resilience and thought that meant that they truly loved each other. Oh God, let him get better, she prayed wordlessly. Josie deserves to be happy.

Josie had found an envelope of money in the basket. 'Hey, what's this, Kate?' she said, and Kate said briefly, 'Wages.'

'But I haven't earned any wages,' Josie protested.

Kate laughed. 'It's what they call a retainer,' she said. 'In case you decide to leave us and take your fancy cookery elsewhere.'

When she left a little later Davy was sitting up in bed again and they were all laughing, and afterwards she was thankful that this was her last memory of Davy and Josie together.

A few days later Davy had a massive haemorrhage and died in Josie's arms. Kate went to the house as soon as she could and found that already the bed and other furniture had been moved from the tiny room and Davy's coffin lay on trestles under the window, with candles burning at the head and the foot. His thin hands were folded on his breast and he looked young and vulnerable with his copper-coloured curls clustering round his brow. Josie was dry-eyed and quiet, but she wept when Kate held her in her arms.

'Mrs Molesworth was right,' she said. 'You know she said right away Davy was delicate and I'd have to look after him. Well, I did, Kate, but it was too late.'

'But you've had these few years anyway,' Kate said soothingly.

Josie dried her eyes. 'Yes, and they were good years,' she said. 'We were so happy. If only one of the babies had lived.'

'I know, Josie, but perhaps it was meant to be,' Kate comforted her. 'You were able to devote all your time to Davy.'

There was a noise at the front door, and a small woman with a ferocious expression erupted into the room. She was carrying a wooden stool, and as the girls watched in amazement she took scissors wrapped in tissue paper from her apron pocket, stood on the stool and leaned into the coffin.

She looked at Davy for a moment, then snipped off one of his bright curls and wrapped it in the tissue paper. Then, still without a word or a look at Josie, she picked up the stool and left the house.

Kate stared at Josie. 'Who?' she began, and Josie said briefly, 'Davy's mum,' then began to tremble. Kate put her arms round her and Josie wept, 'At a time like this. She hates me so much she wouldn't use anything belonging to me. Her own stool and scissors, even the tissue paper.'

Kate could only hold her, making soothing noises. She was stunned by the suddenness of the incident and found it hard to believe it had happened. 'Sit down, Josie,' she said. 'I'll make you a cup of tea. She's not worth upsetting yourself about.'

There was a tap at the door and Josie's neighbour came in. 'I seen Davy's ma coming here, and the gob on her, so I was coming in to you, girl, but before I got the pan off the fire she was out again. Are you all right? I thought she might hit you with the stool.'

'She never even looked at me,' Josie said bitterly. 'Just stood on her own stool and used her own scissors to cut a lock of his hair. She wouldn't use nothing belonging to me.'

'Bitter old cow,' the neighbour said indignantly. 'Never mind, girl. She might have took a lock of his hair but she had to go away and leave Davy with you, and he'll always be with you. Just put her outa your head.'

'I shouldn't have told her,' Josie said when the woman had left. 'Now it'll be all over the street.'

'Why worry?' Kate said. 'It's nothing for you to be ashamed of.'

'No, but it shames Davy to have a mother like that,' said Josie.

'I don't see why,' said Kate. 'We can't choose our parents. It only shows how much he loved you to defy a woman like that.'

'I don't even know mine. They might have been just as bad,' Josie said. She smiled suddenly. 'I was talking about that to Davy, about being a foundling, and he said, "I wish I was. I couldn't have done no worse than my ma." We had a good laugh and I've never worried about being a foundling since then.'

'I know it doesn't seem much comfort now, Josie, but

those happy memories will help you later on,' Kate said gently, but Josie said nothing.

Kate returned home to find Lottie in tears in the kitchen and Mildred furiously ringing her bell. 'You've got to go to the missus right away,' Lottie wept. 'Oh Kate, it's been terrible. There's been a fight.'

'A fight?' Kate echoed, but before Lottie could say any more Mildred appeared at the top of the basement stairs. 'Where have you been?' she demanded angrily. 'You're never here when you're needed. Why do you think I've kept you all these years?'

Kate stormed up the basement steps. 'If you say that to me again, Aunt, I'll tell you exactly why,' she said furiously. 'As for where I've been, I've been to see Josie. Her husband has died, remember?'

Mildred swiftly changed tack. 'I need you here, Kate,' she said pathetically. 'My health won't stand these upsets and that girl is useless in an emergency.' She placed her hand over her heart and tottered back to her room, saying, 'Deal with it, Kate. I can't be upset like this.'

Kate started to follow her, but turned instead and went down to Lottie. 'Dry your eyes, Lottie, and tell me what happened,' she said, sitting down at the kitchen table.

'It was Mrs Bradley,' Lottie said. 'I was brushing the stairs and I thought I could keep an eye on her, but she managed to slip out of her room and into Miss Andrews'. I don't know what she was doing but them two women came back and there was uproar. I'm sure they was drunk, Kate.'

'Good God,' Kate said faintly. 'What happened then?'

'They was screaming and saying Mrs Bradley was robbing them, and then Mrs Burroughs pushed the old lady against the banister. I run upstairs but I couldn't do nothing, and I knocked for the missus but at first she wouldn't come outa her room, then when she did it made it worse. Mrs Bradley just turned round and said, "There you are, Mrs Williams. Dismiss these women at once. I will not have dishonesty," and they started screaming worse than ever. I had to hold that Mrs Burroughs back.'

'Where are they now – and where's Mrs Bradley?' asked Kate.

'She's up in her room singing hymns as though nothing has happened,' Lottie said. 'And them two have gone out again but they locked their doors and said they'd get the coppers if it happened again.' Kate put her hands over her face, and Lottie, trying to comfort her, said, 'Don't worry, Kate. They'd never go near the coppers. There's something fishy about them or I'm a Dutchman.'

'I'll have to go up and see Mrs Bradley,' Kate said. 'At least she recognised my aunt. That might be a good sign.'

'Maybe,' Lottie said doubtfully, pushing a cup of tea towards Kate. 'Drink that before you go anyhow.'

Kate found Mrs Bradley sitting peacefully by her fire reading a Mission magazine. She began to talk rationally to Kate about the Missions and about her childhood. 'Mother encouraged me to save my pennies for black babies and I thought if I saved enough one would come to live with us,' she said. 'So easy for children to misunderstand, but Mother was training me to think of others.'

'Your mother was very wise,' Kate murmured. Mrs Bradley agreed and told several anecdotes about her childhood, and Kate, reassured, told Lottie that she thought the scene with the women had jolted the old lady back to reality. Her peace of mind was short-lived, however.

Later, in her bedroom, Kate had as usual quickly scanned the casualty lists in the *Liverpool Echo*, fearing to see Henry's name, but it was not there. She had then taken his card from her box and held it while she prayed for his safety before falling asleep.

She felt that she had only been asleep a few minutes when she was awakened by Mrs Bradley standing beside her bed in her nightdress. She was holding a candle and asking for Kate's help to deal with a witch doctor. 'You've had a bad dream, Mrs Bradley,' Kate said, trying to take the old lady's arm, but Mrs Bradley pulled away from her.

'Come, Derek, you must help me,' she said firmly. 'Mama always told us to help others, and Papa said you must be the man of the family.'

174

Kate decided to humour her. She slipped a coat over her own nightdress and whispered, 'Come, I'll show you the best way.' Mrs Bradley allowed her to take her hand and lead her back to her room. Once there she handed Kate the candle and allowed herself to be tucked up in bed without protest. She fell asleep within minutes, and Kate crept away, taking the precaution of locking the door behind her.

In spite of her disturbed night, she woke early and went up to unlock Mrs Bradley's door before she realised that she had been locked in. The key turned smoothly and she went quietly downstairs. She had just reached the hall when she heard a slight noise and looking up the stairs saw a man in uniform creeping down, closely followed by another. They were both carrying their boots.

As she stood transfixed, the men reached the hall. They all stared at each other open-mouthed, then the men turned and bolted through the front door. Kate stood there unable to believe her eyes.

She came to and rushed to her aunt's room, knowing that Mildred would be up and dressed. She blurted out the tale of the two men, adding, 'They must have been with those women and Lottie said they were drunk yesterday. They've got to go, Aunt, and you'll have to tell them. I'll come with you but you'll have to tell them. They'll take notice of you.'

Mildred showed no surprise, and Kate wondered whether she had heard noises on other occasions and ignored them. From her rooms at the end of the hall she would hear more than Lottie in her attic or Kate in her basement bedroom. Kate's suspicions were confirmed when Mildred said plaintively, 'We need their money, Kate. I can't get guests like I used to with this dreadful war.'

'We'll have no chance of respectable people if this becomes known as an immoral house, Aunt,' Kate said firmly. 'Come along. It must be done at once.'

The women blustered but, intimidated by Mildred's icy manner, agreed to go, only asking for a day to make arrangements. 'We've paid up to Saturday anyhow,' Mrs Burroughs said, then retreated behind her friend.

The following day two seedy-looking men arrived with a handcart, and Kate supervised the move to see that nothing belonging to the guesthouse was taken. The women started to shout abuse as they left, calling Kate a narrow-minded old maid and a bloodsucker, but when Mildred emerged from her room they slunk quickly away.

Kate and Lottie surveyed the empty rooms. 'They've done as much damage as they could,' Lottie said indignantly. 'Everything chipped or broken, even the mirrors. Well, that's seven years' bad luck for them and I hope they get it.'

'I don't care,' Kate said. 'I'm just so glad to see them go. We've got plenty of furniture. It's guests we're short of now.'

Davy's funeral was to take place on the Monday, and Kate visited Josie every day before then. Each time she found either Davy's uncle or one of the neighbours there. One neighbour accompanied Kate to the door as she left. 'She's a good thoughtful girl,' she whispered, 'having the funeral on Monday so people can get their good clothes out for it. Out of pawn, I mean,' she added as Kate looked uncomprehending.

Knowing how much it would mean to Josie, Kate asked Mildred to attend the funeral. 'You said we were her family,' she reminded her aunt, and Mildred agreed to be there.

The funeral was quiet and dignified, and Josie's fear that her mother-in-law might make a scene was not realised. She was not present at the funeral and only went to the cemetery the following day to remove Josie's wreath from the grave and replace it with her own. Josie refused to allow this to upset her, and simply replaced her own wreath without removing the one from Davy's mother. She was relieved to see or hear no more from the bitter old woman.

Kate decided to leave after the ceremony at the graveside and return home with her aunt, as Josie would be accompanied to her own house by Davy's uncle and many neighbours who had become friends.

It was as well that she did. As she and Mildred entered the house a cab drew up and Mrs Bradley descended from it, accompanied by a tall, cadaverous man in a business suit and a velvet-collared overcoat. Mildred had gone straight to her rooms, but Kate held the door wide and exclaimed, 'Mrs Bradley. I didn't know you'd gone out.'

Mrs Bradley made no reply, but the man said, 'You are Miss Williams, I think. I am James Hooper of Jones, Hooper and Prendergast, and Mrs Bradley is my client.'

Kate ushered them into the drawing room. 'I'm very glad to meet you, Mr Hooper,' she said with a sigh of relief. 'I've been asking my aunt for your address. I am Miss Drew. Mrs Williams is my aunt. I'll ring for some refreshments.' She moved to ring for Lottie, feeling nervous because of the severe gaze of the lawyer and the expression on Mrs Bradley's face, but before she could reach the bell pull Mr Hooper held up his hand.

'No thank you,' he said coldly. 'This is not a social call, Miss Drew. Why did you wish to know my address?'

Kate glanced at Mrs Bradley. 'It's rather difficult,' she said. 'Perhaps if I could speak to you privately?'

'Anything you wish to say can be said before my client,' the lawyer said frostily.

'We were worried about Mrs Bradley's health,' Kate said. 'As she had no relatives I thought—'

Her voice trailed away under his intimidating gaze and he finished the sentence for her. 'You thought she was friendless. I can assure you that that is not the case. Mrs Bradley is an old and valued client of my firm and I am here to look after her interests. My client believes that there has been systematic stealing from her room.'

'But she is mistaken,' Kate stammered. 'Those women – they've gone now, and they took nothing with them but their own stuff. I checked it myself.'

Mr Hooper stood and helped Mrs Bradley to rise. 'Be good enough to take us to Mrs Bradley's room,' he said coldly. Anger at his manner and a belated realisation of his hostility gave Kate the courage to say as coldly, 'One moment. I think my aunt should hear this.'

Mildred was sitting at the desk in her room, still in the clothes she had worn for the funeral, when Kate burst in and said abruptly, 'Aunt Mildred, that man who's with Mrs Bradley, he says he's her lawyer and that someone has been stealing from her room, and he's behaving as though he thinks it's me.'

'What!' Mildred was on her feet in an instant. She was as tall as Mr Hooper, and with her hat, which looked like a cross between a helmet and a coal scuttle, and her furious face beneath it, she was an intimidating sight as she swept into the hall where Mr Hooper and Mrs Bradley were standing. 'What's this I hear?' she demanded loudly. 'How dare you suggest my niece is dishonest?'

Mr Hooper held up his hand placatingly. 'No, no, my dear Mrs Williams,' he bleated. 'It *is* Mrs Williams? I am here to protect my client's interests, not to accuse anybody. I am James Hooper of Jones, Hooper and Prendergast, and Mrs Bradley is my client.' He inclined his head.

'You said there had been systematic stealing from her room,' Kate said angrily.

'No, no, I said my client *believed* there had been stealing,' he said. 'If we could go to Mrs Bradley's room?'

Mrs Bradley sat regally in her chair beside the fireplace and smiled round at them. 'I know my nice things are a temptation,' she said, 'but to ignore wrongdoing is to encourage it.'

Mr Hooper took out a list and cleared his throat. 'Mrs Bradley has listed some items that are missing. I may say that the list can be verified, as Mrs Bradley's mother mentioned these items specifically in her will.'

'What are they?' Mildred demanded.

He began to read from the list. 'A tea service and dinner service by Royal Doulton, a set of Toby jugs by Royal Doulton, a damask tablecloth and twelve napkins, twelve sterling silver napkin rings—'

Mildred said abruptly, 'Stop.' Mr Hooper peered at her over his eyeglasses and she said scornfully, 'Mrs Bradley has given away those things as presents over the years. The tea service to young friends who were married from this house, the dinner service to a minister and his wife when they left the parish, the other things to raise money for the Missions.

And that was when she was in her right mind. Nobody took advantage of her.'

Mrs Bradley looked bewildered, and Mildred held open the door. 'Come down to my office,' she said curtly to Hooper. 'I think you've been very obtuse.'

Kate went to Mrs Bradley. 'I'm sure you'd like a cup of tea, Mrs Bradley,' she said gently. 'I'll ring for Lottie to bring it up and you can show me the new Mission magazine.'

'Are the grown-ups cross?' Mrs Bradley asked. 'Have I been naughty?'

'No, not at all,' Kate said gently, her anger at the accusations vanishing as she soothed the old lady.

Mildred drew up her own list of the recipients of the gifts so that Mr Hooper could verify her statement, and described Mrs Bradley's state so forcefully that events moved swiftly. It was arranged that Mrs Bradley should move to a nursing home, and Mr Hooper and his wife did much to achieve the move smoothly for her.

'It's the end of an era,' Kate said sadly to Lottie as they cleaned the empty room. 'Mrs Bradley was always so kind to me. When I came here she realised I couldn't read properly and she arranged for Miss Tate to teach me. When I think how she was, so dignified, and the way she is now, I could cry. I think I'd rather be dead.'

'But she doesn't realise the way she is,' Lottie said. 'It's only other people that get upset about it.'

'That's true,' Kate said, feeling more cheerful. 'I shouldn't have said that. Life's sweet no matter what.'

Chapter Twelve

It was true that Beattie had staged a convenient heart attack late in 1916 and had pulled strings to prevent Rose from becoming a VAD, but Kate was wrong in suspecting that Rose was relieved.

Her first enthusiasm for the idea on the outbreak of war had soon waned, and for some time she simply drifted along. The war had made little impact on the household at Greenfields.

Beattie held afternoon tea parties where ladies rolled bandages and knitted for the troops as they gossiped, and Rose helped with bazaars and bric-à-brac sales to raise money for comforts for soldiers and sailors. The servants all stayed on and food was not a problem. Two young boys were taken on to help Mr Phillips extend the kitchen garden, and he also kept hens in part of the extensive grounds, and occasionally drove to farms in the countryside outside Liverpool to buy food. Beattie's wealth could purchase anything she needed at inflated prices, and she had no uncomfortable scruples about doing so.

There were no male relatives to worry about and when, as frequently happened, a friend's son or nephew was killed, Beattie wept with the bereaved mother or aunt, offering the usual platitudes, and felt that she had played her part in the war effort.

With life so little changed, the war seemed remote to Rose too. She sometimes took comforts to a hospital in West Derby, where soldiers were recovering from their wounds, but by this stage their injuries were decently covered in hospital blue, with only an empty sleeve or a pinned-up trouser leg to show what had happened.

She still had a busy social round, often accompanied by young officers home from the Front, but partly because they wanted to forget the horrors during their brief leaves, and partly because of the tradition of the stiff upper lip, the war was never talked about. Rose wrote cheerful letters in reply to their letters and field cards, and sent carefully chosen parcels of comforts to them.

Although she was too intelligent to be unaware of what was happening, and read Mr Phillips's *War Illustrated* as well as the *Liverpool Echo*, which carried reports of speeches in the Commons and long casualty lists, she had an ability to close her mind to anything distasteful. But occasionally something occurred which forced her to confront reality. One such event was in April 1915, when the SS *Lusitania* was sunk with great loss of life. Many of the crew were Liverpool men, and as Rose was driven down a street of tiny terraced houses she saw groups of shawled women, with small children clinging to their skirts, wailing in despair as the news spread.

A week later she passed down the street again and saw black crêpe pinned to almost every door, and she felt ashamed of her useless life while others suffered so much.

The memory of the tragedy troubled her for a time, but soon she was able to thrust it away. The next episode made far more impact on her. Ian Gillespie, the nephew of one of Beattie's friends, was an admirer who had often been her tennis partner before the war. He was a handsome young man with a lively, carefree manner, and Rose looked forward to seeing him when he came home on leave from the Western Front.

He had joined the Army on the outbreak of war and been sent to France in time for the first Battle of Ypres. There he had survived the gas attacks, only to be wounded in July 1916 at the Somme. After a spell in hospital in southern England he was passed fit and returned to the Front in October to find the Battle of the Somme still raging, with no apparent gain to either side. When he next came home on leave, the battle was finally over.

Rose had not seen him during all this time, and when he

came for her she was shocked at the change in him. He was gaunt and haggard, his face grey, and with a nervous twitch around his eyes. It was a lovely spring evening, and he had borrowed his father's motor car, so they drove to the countryside to the north of the city, where he stopped the car by a field gate.

At first all seemed well, and they spoke about people they knew and parties they had attended before the war, but Ian's nervous twitch became more and more pronounced, and suddenly he burst out, 'I can't believe it. Everything just going on as if the war hadn't happened. And people glorying in it. Hating the Germans and being glad they're taking heavy losses. For God's sake, our men are being killed too, just as many of them. Don't these blasted people *care*?'

He was shaking, and Rose instinctively put her arms around him. 'They do really,' she soothed him. 'They just hate the Germans because of the atrocities. You must hate them too, Ian.'

'Not now,' he said. 'They're under orders like us, and it's all mad. We hear rumours. The war could end now. The Germans were broken at the Somme but the damned old men in the War Office won't have it. They won't be satisfied until a complete generation on both sides is wiped out. They're the ones I hate.'

He was shaking even more violently now and Rose held him closer and made soothing noises, waiting for him to recover, but he went on, 'Our orders. We have to send men over the top to *walk* shoulder to shoulder in daylight, unprotected, facing machine-gun fire. If they wanted the men killed they couldn't find a better way.'

Rose was afraid to speak in case she said something that would upset him even more, and he continued, 'It hadn't stopped raining. The trenches were full of mud and water, up to our waists. We'd been there for hours, nothing but mud, dead trees, dead men. In front of me a sandbag had gone and there was a head. Not a skull – a head still with hair.'

He was crying quietly, his head on her shoulder, but he seemed unable to stop talking. 'I got my orders for us to go over the top and I couldn't do it. I put my whistle to my mouth but I couldn't blow it. I couldn't send my men out to be killed when I knew it was wrong. A sergeant came beside me. "Best time is now, sir," he said, and I blew the whistle. He knew I was funking it but he didn't know why. Now *I'm* not sure why, Rose. Was it for the men or for myself?'

Rose's mind was a jumble of emotions. Pity for him, shock because she had never before seen a man cry, a tinge of contempt because it seemed unmanly, and mixed with this, fear for herself, stranded far from home with a man in a state of collapse. Gradually, though, he became calmer.

'I'm sorry, Rose,' he said, raising his head from her shoulder, then sitting up. 'I shouldn't have inflicted that on you.'

'I'm glad you did if it makes you feel better to talk,' Rose said. 'And I'm the best one for it. I'd never repeat anything, you know that.'

'I hadn't even thought of it,' he said. He blew his nose and replaced his cap before starting up the motor car.

'Do you really think the war could end soon?' asked Rose as he drove slowly home.

He shrugged. 'They say it was the rain and the mud that finished the Somme, men drowning in trenches, but I think the Germans had had enough. Marginally less mad than our crowd, but an armistice could have been tried.'

'The newspapers say we must have complete victory to make things safe for the next generation,' Rose said tentatively, but he only replied, with a return to his wild manner, 'It's the men, Rose. My men. Decent fellows with wives and families. I don't want to be an officer ordering them out to be killed. I think I'll resign my commission and re-enlist as a private. That way I'll only be responsible for my own life.'

'Couldn't you ask for a transfer, or leave the Army altogether?' Rose said. 'You've been in from the beginning and you've done your share.' He laughed bitterly but made no reply.

When they reached Greenfields he turned to her and

kissed her gently. 'Thank you, Rose,' he said. 'Will you do something for me? Forget all that's happened tonight. Just remember all the good times we had before the war.'

Rose felt cold with fear. 'I will, Ian,' she promised. 'But those good times will come again. I'll save the first dance for you when you come home again.' She tried to sound convincing and light-hearted, but he only kissed her again gently and escorted her to the front door.

It was opened by Essy, looking grim. As soon as Rose was inside, the maid said grumpily, 'You're very late, Miss Rose. Madam has been kept awake worrying about you.'

'I'm sorry,' Rose murmured as she moved to the stairs. 'I don't want anything, Essy.'

Rose went upstairs while Essy locked the door, muttering about people being kept from their beds. She looked in on her aunt, who was sleeping peacefully, then sat by the window in her own room, feeling too disturbed to sleep. Was Ian going mad? she wondered. Or was he shell-shocked? She had only a vague idea of what that meant, and in spite of constantly hearing about Beattie's nerves had never heard of a nervous breakdown. She went to the drawer where she kept bundles of letters and cards from her admirers at the Front.

Two of the bundles, from men who had been killed, were tied with black ribbon, but she searched through the others and found a slim bundle from Ian. The first had been written soon after he arrived in France and was very enthusiastic.

I was right to join when I did. I know these are early days but I'm having a ripping time and have met several men I knew at Oxford. Not from the 'inner circle' of course, men from top public schools. *They* have a special hut and every comfort, including hampers from Harrods! But we ordinary officers do very well and it's all very exciting. Also the feeling that what we are doing is important for the future of civilisation. We can't allow the Hun to overrun the world. Some of the men are also living better than they have ever done. Good warm clothes, regular food and *work*. When I compare them with some of the ragged, hungry creatures I used to see in the poorer parts of Liverpool I feel that this war can only change lives for the better.

Rose skipped the rest of the letter and quickly read through the others, amazed to see how quickly Ian's enthusiasm had turned to disillusionment and anger at the muddle and waste of life. One written from the dressing station after he had been wounded made the deepest impression on Rose. 'The nurses are wonderful,' he wrote. 'Angels and heroines every one. Frantically busy though they are, they will find time to gently comfort the wounded or hold the hand of a dying man crying for his mother.'

Rose put the letter down and sat deep in thought. This time she would do it, she would enrol as a nurse, not drift as she had been doing all these months.

Rose said nothing to her aunt about her plan, but she did tell Essy, who was enthusiastic about it. More because she wants to be rid of me than because she approves, Rose thought cynically. Essy hid her dislike and jealousy of Rose from Beattie, but Rose was always aware of it. Now the maid suggested asking Miss Tasker for a letter of recommendation, which was willingly supplied. Rose wrote asking to enrol as a VAD and enclosing the letter, and was delighted to receive a reply asking her to attend an interview. As it was in London, Beattie had to be told.

She immediately became hysterical, clutching her heart and declaring that she was dying. Her elderly doctor was summoned and later brought an equally elderly colleague from higher in the profession to see her. Both men reprimanded Rose, telling her that she was selfish to want to nurse when she was needed at home.

'But Essy is here to care for my aunt, as well as all the servants,' Rose protested.

'Essy is only a servant herself,' the first doctor said. 'You are a relative, and Mrs Anderson regards you as a daughter. She's been good to you and it's your duty to care for her now and respect her wishes.' His colleague said much the same, and reminded Rose that there were girls without family commitments who could become nurses.

She was allowed to go to London for the interview, accompanied by a friend of Beattie's, but it was clear from the outset that she would not be accepted.

A few weeks later Kate came alone to Greenfields one Sunday afternoon, and after some general conversation with Beattie and Rose, she and Rose went into the garden. There Rose poured out her troubles to Kate, her anger and resentment that her attempt to join the VAD had once again been foiled by Beattie. 'She pulled strings again to stop me. I know she did,' she declared. 'I want to be useful, Kate.'

'Perhaps you could do as Nell did,' Kate offered. 'She was going to join the VAD but her aunt suggested she trained properly as a nurse. She's nursing people from the slums near the hospital in London, but she says they've released trained nurses to tend the wounded and at the end she'll be a properly trained nurse herself. It's a hard life, Rose, although Nell enjoys it.'

Rose could see that Kate had missed the point and said no more about nursing, only telling Kate something of what Ian had said about the Front. 'Strange to think of that going on just across the Channel, yet things are not much different from usual here,' she said. 'Only worry about fighting men and inconvenience with the blackout. I'm sure we're not in real danger from the Zeppelins.'

'But there's so much sadness and worry everywhere, with these awful submarines,' Kate said. 'So many ships sunk. It seems wrong to complain about food, Rose, when men are losing their lives, but it's getting desperate, isn't it?'

Rose listened in brooding silence and made no reply, and Kate soon left, feeling that despite her protests Rose had once again been relieved to be refused as a VAD.

Rose passed from frustration and self-pity to acceptance of her fate, as Beattie continued to play the part of an invalid, then to determination, if her role was to be that of handmaiden to her aunt and comforter to men on leave, that she would enjoy herself and take full advantage of the new freedom for women.

She embarked on a series of affairs, not only with men known to her, most of them officers home on leave, but also with men of the Army or Navy stationed in Liverpool. She skilfully shuffled them like a pack of cards so that they were unaware of how widely her favours were spread. The only one who knew about all the others was Robert Willis, the second cousin of one of Beattie's friends.

Robert was a quiet, diffident man in his early forties who was still running the family ship's supplier's business. Infantile paralysis as a child had left him with a pronounced limp, which made him unfit for military service, and he was always on hand when Rose needed an escort for some boring duty. He adored Rose, and she treated him in cavalier fashion, calling on him at short notice if her escort for the evening was forced to cancel due to service duty.

'"The crumbs that fall from the rich man's table",' he quoted wryly to her once as he escorted her to a show, but he was always available, even though she would readily cancel a date with him if it suited her.

Essy's dislike of Rose grew, but Beattie could see no fault in her darling, and Rose always showed her a smiling, dutiful face. Now that Mildred had stopped visiting her sister, Beattie often told Rose that she was all she had. 'Nobody loves me but you, Rosie darling,' she wept. Beattie had become almost a complete invalid now, grossly fat and inactive, and although she talked of cruises for herself and Rose when the war was over Rose knew that they were only fantasies.

Rose had little free time now to spend with the empty-headed young women of her set, some of whom were now married, but occasionally they met to shop and lunch in Liverpool's shopping centre. They all belonged to wealthy families, many of them made even more wealthy by the war, and well-dressed and light-hearted as they were, they drew envious glances from many of the people, drably dressed or in mourning, who passed them.

It was on an outing with two of her friends in the spring of 1918 that Rose met Kate, a meeting that was to have fateful consequences.

Rose and her friends were strolling along, giggling, among the numerous sailors, American servicemen and shabby civilians, when Rose suddenly caught sight of Kate and was shocked at what she saw. Kate's face was white, her eyes red-rimmed, with wisps of hair escaping from beneath a shabby felt hat carelessly pinned to her hair. The jacket she wore over a rusty black skirt was too large for her thin frame, and her boots were scuffed and unpolished. She wore no gloves.

Her eyes met those of Rose, and on an impulse instantly regretted, Rose looked away without acknowledging her. Kate seemed to rock for a moment with shock, then turned and sped away through the crowds on the pavement. Before Rose could turn back she was gone, swallowed up by the crowds, and Rose walked on, suddenly silent and unable to respond to her friends. 'I'm sorry. My head – I must go home,' she said, and amid cries of dismay from her companions she summoned a cab and was driven home.

She felt so distressed that she went immediately to her aunt to pour out her tale. Beattie was kind and reassuring. 'It was a mistake, Auntie,' Rose wept. 'You know I wouldn't cut Kate. It was just such a shock seeing her I didn't think, and when I turned back she'd gone.'

'Of course you wouldn't, dear. Don't worry about it. You were just taken by surprise and probably Kate's thoughts were miles away too. I expect she rushed off for quite another reason. Probably remembered something she had to do. She must be quite harassed with Mildred being so odd.'

In the past Rose had been scornful when Beattie found plausible reasons to excuse her own selfish behaviour, but now that it was for her benefit she gratefully accepted the excuses and let the soothing words flow over her.

'She didn't speak to me either, come to that,' she said, and Beattie replied comfortably, 'There you are then. You were both taken by surprise, and Kate rushed away. Living with Mildred is bound to make her behave oddly.'

'She certainly looked odd,' Rose said. 'As though she didn't give a button about her appearance.'

'Don't think any more about it, dear,' Beattie comforted her. 'Dry your eyes and ring the bell. We'll have a nice cup of tea.' Rose was pleased to obey and to take her aunt's advice, although she knew in her heart that it was wrong. At odd moments the memory of Kate's stricken face rose before her, but she thrust it away and resumed her life of pleasure.

Chapter Thirteen

As 1917 drew to a close Kate was becoming worn out by the worry and the constant search for enough food to feed four guests and herself, Lottie and Mildred. Even bread and potatoes were scarce and dear, and things became worse as the U-boat attacks on shipping increased.

People like Beattie were cushioned by their wealth, but attempts at rationing were a farce and ordinary people were becoming desperate, even rioting in some places. Kate felt that worry about food dominated her life.

After Davy's death Kate thought that Josie might wish to return to the guesthouse, and was ashamed that she dreaded the prospect of another mouth to feed, but Josie had other plans. 'Davy's uncle said I can keep on this house rent-free,' she said when Kate visited her. 'He said I'd given Davy more happiness in a few years than he'd had in the rest of his life. He's broken-hearted. Davy was like a son to him.'

'Have you seen – er, his mother?' Kate asked.

Josie replied forcefully, 'No, and I don't want to. If I never see her again it'll suit me.'

They were silent for a moment, then Kate said gently, 'But what will you do, Josie? How will you live?'

'I'll get a job,' Josie said. 'But not in service. There are jobs in shops going now. A girl from the street works in the Maypole and she'll speak for me in the greengrocer's in Brunswick Road.'

'Wouldn't you have to know about reckoning up and weighing and that?' Kate said doubtfully, but Josie said confidently, 'I know all about dealing with money after the last few years, and it'd only be like weighing for cooking. If Ivy can manage the work in the Maypole I can manage in a greengrocer's. I'm sorry about not coming back, Kate, but you can manage with Lottie, can't you? And we can still see each other.' Kate was ashamed to feel relief but told herself she would have welcomed Josie if she had needed to return.

Once Mrs Burroughs and Miss Andrews had departed, followed shortly by Mrs Bradley, only Mr Culshaw remained, and Kate felt that it was time to make a decision about the guesthouse, but Mildred refused to discuss the subject. Kate went to see Josie.

'I'm sorry about Mrs Bradley, but it's such a relief not to have to feed them. I was getting desperate, dashing about all day whenever I heard of anything, then trying to eke it out to make a meal, and it's getting worse all the time. Even things like barley and lentils that I used to help out the meat have disappeared. I think we should close until after the war, but Aunt Mildred won't talk about it. She's in one of her down moods.'

'How is she fixed, do you think – with money, like?' Josie asked.

Kate shook her head. 'I just don't know. She's never told me anything about money. It seems silly, but you know what she's like. I tried to ask but she made me feel I was being nosy.'

'Mrs Molesworth reckoned she had a long stocking,' Josie said. 'She told me once that the missus bought that house and furnished it with the money her father left, but there wasn't nothing over. Her husband never left much so all she had was the house, and that's why she opened the guesthouse.'

'She told me that too,' Kate said. 'And she said Mildred felt it was beneath her and that's why she wanted it to be high class.'

'Well, she did have nice people and they lived comfortable, so she must've charged them for it,' said Josie. 'Mrs Molesworth said although the house was high class, like, and the food was good, the butcher and the grocer never made much out of the missus. She always beat them down for price and she hated paying for servants.'

'I know,' Kate said with a smile. 'It was like getting blood out of a stone to get her to raise Mrs Molesworth's wages, or yours and Lottie's.'

'She got a bargain with you, though, Kate,' Josie said indignantly. 'She's always taken advantage of your good nature. I know she did all the cooking herself at first, but as soon as she could she threw it all on to you on top of all the rest she expected you to do, and she sat back being a lady.'

'I didn't mind that. I like cooking,' Kate said. 'And we had some good times, me and you and Mrs Molesworth, didn't we? I really miss the times when we sat round that table with our cups of tea, and the laughs we had.'

They both smiled fondly, then Josie said briskly, 'But you didn't come just to talk about old times, Kate. We've got to talk about the future. I think you're at a crossroads in your life.'

Kate smiled, and Josie went on, 'It's no laughing matter. It's the time when you've got to start thinking about yourself, and standing up for yourself. Don't just drift on. You think the guesthouse should close?'

'I think it makes sense. We could ask Mr Culshaw to find somewhere else. I've talked to Lottie and she says she'd get a job like you've done, and I could get some cleaning part time, so I could still see to the three of us and the house. My money and what Lottie could pay would keep us going. Don't you think that's a good idea?'

'And the missus would sit in her room like Lady Muck while you got run ragged,' Josie said indignantly. 'No, I don't think it's a good idea, Kate. Mrs Molesworth talked a lot to me. She thought the world of you and she was always mad about the way you was put on. She said you got the dirty end of the stick when your sister went off to live in luxury and you got taken by the missus to be an unpaid drudge. You don't owe her nothing, Kate.'

'But what else could we do?' Kate said.

Josie replied swiftly, 'You could get a proper job, Kate, even a living-in job in service but with proper time off and a set amount of work. You could have some life for yourself.'

'I couldn't just go off and leave her,' Kate protested.

'Why not? You don't owe her nothing. She's just used you and never thought about your life. I know she says she'll leave you the house and that, but who knows? She's that moody she might just leave it to the Mission or anything.'

Kate flushed. 'That's not why I feel I should stay, Josie,' she said. 'She often threatens me about the house, so I've never counted on it.' She smiled. 'Never thought about that or the future really, Josie. I've just drifted along.'

'Well, now's the time to stop drifting,' Josie said firmly. 'She must've saved plenty over the years, so let her use what she's been hoarding to pay people to work for her, but you break away, Kate. Think of the life you've had. You've never had a feller because you've never had no time to yourself.'

'That's not why,' Kate said. 'You had plenty of fellows asking you out even before Davy, but I'm not pretty like you. Fellows aren't interested in me.'

'Because you never got out and met people. Never had no sort of life, and you was too shy. You've got to let fellers know – encourage them, like. I suppose the missus frightened ordinary fellers off the way she kept saying you was her niece.'

'Oh Josie, there was no one *to* frighten off,' Kate said, but Josie said stubbornly, 'Mrs Molesworth always said the missus had made you neither fish nor fowl and that spoiled you with fellers. Too good for some and not good enough for gentlemen, or so they thought.'

They were both silent for a moment. Kate thought about Henry and the dream world she had created which had given her much happiness over the years. As though by telepathy, Josie said suddenly, 'Mrs Molesworth thought you and Mr Barnes might've got married, y'know, Kate. She said he got you a place in Bryant's and if you'd have took it you could've got married. I always thought he was in love with you, the way he looked at you and that.'

Kate blushed deeply and bent her head. 'He was kind to me when I first came when I was a little girl, and he never realised I'd grown up, that's all,' she said, but Josie insisted,

'He always treated you different, Kate. Mrs Molesworth said if the missus had let you take that place he'd have seen you away from the guesthouse, like, and Miss Tate wouldn't have got a look-in.'

Kate smiled. 'Oh Josie, you're worse than me,' she said, then, as Josie looked puzzled, she confessed, 'I'm always thinking about him. Not with me now he's married – I mean, I don't dream about *us*. I only think about him and pray he's all right. I'm terrified to look at the casualty lists in case he's on them, but so far, thank God, he's safe.'

'Have you ever seen him since he was married?' asked Josie.

'Not to speak to, but I have seen him,' Kate confessed. 'I used to hang about near the house in Rufford Road and I often saw Miss Tate – I mean, Mrs Barnes – with the baby, and when Henry was on leave once I saw him. I dodged away so he wouldn't see me. I couldn't explain what I was doing there, you see.'

'I never knew you still thought about him so much,' Josie said, and Kate said quietly, 'I've never talked about it to anyone, Josie, but it's made a lot of difference to me being able to think about him. That's partly why I'm not interested in other fellows. I'd never meet anyone as good as Henry. Not that anyone has been interested in me,' she added hastily.

'Oh Kate, all these years,' Josie said. 'I know he's a lovely man, but he'd want what was best for you. He wouldn't want you to miss having a feller of your own and a home, maybe even a family, because you was dreaming about him.'

'I can't help it, Josie,' Kate said simply. Now that she had spoken about Henry, the floodgates were opened and for the next hour they talked about him and about various incidents that had happened at the guesthouse.

'I thought of applying for the job of general at Rufford Road,' Kate said. 'But I couldn't leave my aunt, and then I thought I couldn't bear seeing them together. I'd have loved to do things for him, though, more than I could do here.'

'Remember Hetty?' Josie said. 'She loved working there, because of him mostly. He was so good to her, but his wife was a bit of a Tartar to work for. Running her finger round looking for dust.'

'She was good to me,' Kate said. 'She was a good teacher – taught me to like books. She was friendly too, never seemed to worry about class any more than Henry did, though her friends did when I went to things with her.'

'I bumped into Hetty about a year ago, but I never thought of telling you,' said Josie.

'Did she say anything about the house in Rufford Road?' Kate asked eagerly. 'I went in a shop in Kensington where Mrs Barnes got her groceries and the woman there told me the baby was lovely and the two grandmothers were living there now.'

'Yes. Hetty said she'd been back to see them but it wasn't a happy house no more. Y'know Mr Barnes's mother had come to live with them after his sister died and his brother got killed, and she was a nice quiet woman, no trouble. Then Mrs Barnes's father died and her mother came there for good. Miss Tate – I mean, Mrs Barnes – was always bossy, but her mother was worse. A real bully. Tried to take over with the baby and everything although old Mrs Barnes had always looked after him. There was always trouble and girls wouldn't stay. Hetty said she was glad she was out of it.'

'Poor Henry. He can't have much peace when he comes on leave,' said Kate, looking worried. It was now late and Kate said she must go. Nothing had been decided about her future, but Josie urged her to think of what she wanted to do without worrying about her duty to Mildred.

'Make your plans and then tell her,' Josie said. 'And don't take no notice if she starts bullying you. And tell Lottie to do the same. She could do a lot better for herself too.'

'The trouble is, Aunt Mildred's so moody, and she seems worse since her stroke,' said Kate. 'And she's so secretive about money. She won't go to Greenfields any more. Says Aunt Beattie's too inquisitive. I still go to see Rose whenever I can and we're just as close. I'm not going to stop going just because the aunts have quarrelled.'

As Kate walked home she thought how much she had enjoyed the evening. It had been lovely to talk about Henry to someone who knew him, and knew all that had happened in the past. Had Mrs Molesworth been right about that job in Bryant's? She hugged the thought to herself that Josie believed that Henry had loved her. She respected Josie's judgement. She had always been so shrewd and sensible, so what she believed must be true.

She thought no more about her future but fell asleep happily thinking about Josie's words and with Henry's card clutched in her hand.

The next day she talked things over with Lottie, then screwed up her courage and went to see her aunt to suggest again that the guesthouse should be closed. She felt unable to make her plans in secret but she was determined that this time she would not be fobbed off by Mildred.

She tapped on the door and walked in, then took a deep breath and said, 'I'm sorry, Aunt, it's just been impossible to find enough food for the guests and ourselves, and I think we should close up the guesthouse until the end of the war.'

Mildred looked at her with astonishment, and Kate went on nervously, 'I thought now while almost all the rooms are empty would be a good time,' but Mildred held up her hand.

'That's where you're wrong,' she said triumphantly. 'My rooms are not empty. I told you they are always in demand. I didn't ask for these new guests. I was approached by the butcher, Mr Dyson. He's asked me to take his two nieces, quiet, ladylike girls, he says, from his wife's side of the family. They closed up their family home last year and went to live in a hotel in Southport, but Mr Dyson thinks they should be nearer his wife. I think there are expectations. The ladies are quite wealthy.'

'But Aunt, the food. It's getting scarcer all the time with more ships being sunk. It'll only get worse. How will we manage?' Kate said desperately.

'Very well,' Mildred said with a smirk. 'Mr Dyson said he'd look after us. He won't let his nieces starve and he's got an allotment too for vegetables. *And* I've got another guest. The strangest coincidence. He'd gone into the butcher's to ask directions here and he heard something of what Mr Dyson said to me. He knew of us because he was a friend of Mr James Hughes – you remember, one of the bank clerks who lived here, and was killed at the Front.'

Kate felt like a prisoner whose escape had been barred at the last moment. She said nothing, and Mildred went on briskly, 'The Misses Barry will have Mrs Bradley's room as a sitting room and share number three as their bedroom. Mr Trent will have number six. He will arrive tomorrow and the ladies on Saturday.' She added that Mr Trent didn't want any gossip about him. 'He's doing secret work for the Army and he's been travelling about the country, but he'll be in Liverpool for some time,' she said.

'Very well, Aunt,' Kate said quietly, and went back to the kitchen. Lottie was waiting eagerly, but one look at Kate's face showed that all was not well. Kate sank into a chair and said hopelessly, 'She's done it again, Lottie. I tried to say about closing but she told me she's got three new guests.'

'She's got no right without telling you,' Lottie said indignantly, pushing the kettle on to the fire for tea. 'Why didn't you tell her you was going? If she wants guests, let her look after them herself.'

Kate shrugged. 'Because I'm a weakling, I suppose. You don't have to stay, Lot. Even if she wouldn't let you sleep here you could get a living-in job that'd be easier than here, and better paid.'

'If you're staying I am,' Lottie declared. 'I won't go off and leave you. How did she get the new guests?'

Kate related to Lottie what her aunt had told her, and Lottie said with disgust, 'She's always one step ahead. I'll bet she knew what you was going to say to her and got in first.' She sipped her tea thoughtfully. 'But when did she fix it up? She told me I could go out last night even though you was out too. I'll bet she wanted the house empty to show them the rooms. They wouldn't take them without seeing them, would they?'

Kate thought that Lottie was probably right. 'I hope this man doesn't expect things to be like when Mr Hughes was here,' she said. 'And I'm worried about the butcher's nieces if they've been used to being spoiled.'

'If he's been travelling round the country he'll know how things are, and if them women don't like it they know what to do,' Lottie said robustly. 'It's not our worry. We can always go back to our other plan,' and she and Kate laughed together.

'Oh Lottie, as long as you're staying I don't mind,' Kate said. 'I was dreading going to another job, to tell you the truth. But I don't know what Josie's going to say.'

Mildred had a sick headache on Saturday, so Kate received the Misses Barry when they came, accompanied by their uncle. Kate had made the sitting room look welcoming, with a bright fire burning and a vase of chrysanthemums on the table.

The two middle-aged women seemed shy and timid, but they made twittering murmurs of pleasure when Mr Dyson said heartily, 'There you are, girls. You'll be happy here, and your aunt and I are just round the corner.' Kate promised to send tea to their room and ushered Mr Dyson out.

Downstairs he took a damp parcel from his pocket. 'A bit of steak,' he said. 'And I'll have something from the allotment for you on Monday. Never fear, I'll look after you, miss. I'm glad to have the girls settled here.'

'Thank you, Mr Dyson. I hope they'll be happy,' Kate murmured.

'They will be,' he said confidently. 'They're as helpless as newborn babes, as I told your aunt. Never had to do anything for themselves, see.'

Kate looked alarmed, and he went on quickly, 'They're not ill or anything, just a bit lost. The last of the family, and before the war they always had plenty of servants to carry them round. Then the young ones left, and the old woman who looked after them went to her widowed sister in Wales a year ago.'

Kate said nothing, gently urging him towards the door, but he went on, 'The solicitor fellow closed the house and got them into a hotel at Southport, but they were mixing with people who might have took advantage of them. Mrs

Dyson and I thought they'd be better near us, where we can keep an eye on them.'

He went at last, and shortly afterwards the other guest arrived. He introduced himself as Gordon Trent, and gave no explanation for being a day later than expected. He told Kate that he needed a quiet billet. 'I was wounded at Leuze Wood, at the Somme. I got a Blighty one and afterwards I was seconded to Intelligence. I've got my eye on some people in Liverpool, but it's important they don't know I'm here until I'm ready to move against them.'

Kate thought it was all very exciting and assured him that his secret would be safe. His room was the smallest and darkest in the house, but he said it was admirable. He would probably be in Liverpool for some time but might have to leave suddenly.

Life soon settled into a smooth pattern with the new guests. Lottie had unpacked for the Misses Barry and had been given a sovereign by Miss Ethel and a pretty butterfly brooch by Miss Isabel, so she was now their devoted slave. Mildred kept to her rooms while she was in the house, and Mr Trent slipped in and out on his mysterious business, often via the basement entrance. He and Mr Culshaw only exchanged formal greetings or comments about the weather.

Kate often thought about her discussion with Josie about Henry, and particularly about a comment that Josie had made that there was no reason why Kate should not openly go to visit Mrs Barnes. 'You were friendly when she was Miss Tate,' she pointed out. 'No need to be just skulking round the house.'

Kate made up her mind that she would call on the first fine Sunday after Christmas, and although her courage almost failed, she found herself on the step of the house in Rufford Road, dressed in her best.

The door was opened by a tall, grim woman, but as Kate faltered out her request to see Mrs Barnes, Agnes appeared in the hall.

'Kate!' she cried, coming forward with her hands outstretched. 'How nice to see you.' She turned to the older lady. 'It's all right, Mother,' she said. 'Kate is an old friend. Miss Drew, my mother, Mrs Tate.' Mrs Tate acknowledged the introduction with an inclination of her head, and Agnes drew Kate into a room to the right of the hall.

'I – I was in the neighbourhood,' Kate stammered, but Agnes drew her down beside her.

'How nice to see someone from the old days. How happy we were, Kate, and so unaware of what was to come.' She sighed. 'This dreadful war. Will it ever end?' There was a large silver-framed photograph of Henry in officer's uniform on a side table, and Agnes picked it up. 'You know Mr Barnes went into the Army, the King's, in 1915?'

Kate nodded, unable to speak as she looked at the photograph. How handsome he was, she thought, and he looked so happy and full of life. Agnes replaced the photograph and sighed. 'His spanking new uniform,' she said. 'It looks more shabby and worn now, and so does he.'

'But he's still safe?' Kate said.

'Yes, so far. We're storming heaven to keep him so.' She took an envelope from the sideboard drawer and drew a small snapshot from it. 'This was taken on his first leave.' The photograph showed Agnes and Henry standing by a tree, with Henry holding a fat baby with curly hair and a wide smile showing two teeth.

'That's our little boy,' Agnes said proudly. 'Isn't he like his father? He has fair hair and blue eyes too.'

'He's lovely,' Kate said, but she was looking at Henry as well as the baby.

'I'm sorry he's out. In the park with my mother-in-law,' Agnes said. 'He was only eighteen months old there, but now he's quite the little man. He'll be four in June. Let me take your coat, Kate, and tell me about everybody.'

Kate reluctantly laid down the snapshot and Agnes put her coat on a chair.

'How is everybody at the guesthouse?' she asked when they were settled again and Kate told her sadly about Mrs Molesworth. Agnes looked puzzled. 'Mrs Molesworth?' she said.

'She did the rough work,' Kate explained, 'and much

more, although her leg had been bad for years. Her husband died, then her son was lost at sea, and I think she lost heart.'

'How sad,' said Agnes. 'But what about Mrs Bradley? Is she well?'

'No. Her mind failed,' Kate said. 'She got – er senile. She thought that other guests were stealing from her and often she didn't know us. She used to order me out of the house.'

'Oh dear,' Agnes cried, looking far more upset than by the news of Mrs Molesworth. 'I feel so guilty. She came here once or twice and we intended to keep in touch, but the baby and the war – What has happened to her?'

'She's in a nursing home,' Kate said. 'I believe she is happy enough living in her own world, but visits would upset her,' and she thought that Agnes seemed relieved.

'And how is life treating you, Kate? I hope you are still reading?'

Kate assured her that she was. 'I went so often to the Carnegie Library that I made friends with the librarian,' she said. 'But that was before the war. Nell's been in London for years, nursing in a big hospital, but we still write to each other and discuss books.'

'Excellent,' said Agnes. She rose. 'Excuse me, I'll just speak to the maid. No use ringing. She never answers.'

As she went into the hall, Kate heard Mrs Tate say stridently, 'Who *is* that person, Agnes?' The door was hastily closed, but Kate sat still with shock, a burning flush on her face. That person! So Agnes's mother was not deceived. She knew Kate was not of their class. What am I doing here? Kate thought, suddenly angry with herself. She looked at the framed photograph of Henry and felt ashamed. I'm pretending to visit his wife just to find out about him.

She jumped to her feet and picked up her coat, and when Agnes returned she was standing buttoning her glove. 'I'm sorry, I didn't realise the time, Mrs Barnes,' she said. 'I must go.'

Agnes seemed ill at ease and avoided her eyes. 'Must you, Kate?' she said. 'I've just ordered tea.'

'I'm sorry,' Kate repeated with quiet dignity. 'I must go. My aunt is not very well.'

'Oh dear, I'm so sorry to hear that,' Agnes said. 'Thank you for coming to tell me about Mrs Bradley. What a pity you can't wait to see Charles, but perhaps another time.' She looked down at the table and impulsively picked up the snapshot of the family group. 'Perhaps you would like to keep this, Kate? Show it to your aunt. I have several copies.'

'Thank you,' Kate said quietly, moving towards the hall.

As Agnes opened the front door she said, 'Pray for us, Kate. Henry has survived so much, he seems to live a charmed life, but I'm so afraid. I never stop praying for him.'

'I'll pray too,' Kate promised. 'For all of you.' She smiled. 'I'm sure he'll be all right.'

As she walked away from the house her smile quickly faded and she felt again the sense of deep humiliation. I feel so ashamed, she thought. I hope Agnes didn't realise why I was really there, and she was so kind. In her agitation she walked so rapidly that she was nearly home before she looked again at the snapshot of the family group. Common sense told her that Agnes had given it to her because she was embarrassed by her mother's remark and proud of her baby son, but Kate lay awake for a long time that night worrying that Agnes had suspected that Kate was in love with her husband.

She thought she was too ashamed to tell anyone – even Josie – about the visit, but the urge to confide and to show the snapshot to someone proved too strong, and she went to see Josie.

'You worry too much,' Josie said robustly. 'Sounds as if she was just glad to see you and talk about the old days, and to boast about her son. She said herself she thought you'd come to tell her about Mrs Bradley. And I wouldn't worry about the old one either. She's a right old cow, according to Hetty.'

Kate laughed. 'Oh Josie, you're a case,' she said. 'But

I shouldn't have gone there as Agnes's friend. She taught me to read and write, and took me to lectures and other things with her, but that was just to improve my mind.'

'And to get well in with Mr Barnes,' Josie said shrewdly. 'He truly never bothered about class. Everyone was the same to him, but she never really believed in it.'

'She believed in votes for women and everybody being equal,' Kate protested, but Josie looked sceptical.

'It makes me laugh,' she said. 'Everybody looking down on somebody. People posher than Mrs Barnes looking down on her, and her looking down on the likes of us. She did, Kate, although she went along with whatever Mr Barnes believed in. No wonder, though, with that snobbish old mare for a mother.'

Kate started to laugh. 'If they could only hear us,' she chuckled, 'they wouldn't believe it,' but Josie only said, 'It'd do them good.'

'Nell used to say, "When Adam delved and Eve span, who was then the gentleman?" and we're all descended from them. But we're all as bad, Josie. You know we can't get women for the rough now, not reliable ones, but Lottie doesn't like scrubbing the front steps. She thinks it's beneath her. And I'm as bad. I do them rather than ask Lottie, but I wear a rusty old skirt of Aunt Mildred's and a mob cap so nobody'll recognise me.'

They laughed about it, and Kate felt better. As time passed she rarely thought about the visit to Rufford Road, although she looked often at the snapshot of the family. Life was much easier for her now, although she sometimes felt that at the guesthouse they were all small entities revolving in their own spheres, with none of the unity there had been in the past. Fuel was scarce and fires were rarely lit in the dining room or the drawing room. There were no sociable evenings, with coffee served to the guests after dinner.

A fire was necessary in the kitchen for cooking, and in Mildred's room and the Misses Barry's sitting room, where their meals were served. The two men ate in the kitchen, but Mr Culshaw spoke little and usually went out immediately after his meal. Mr Trent never mentioned his work or the war news, but he was very interested in all that had happened in the guesthouse.

Mr Dyson kept the guesthouse supplied with meat and with vegetables from his allotment, and was repaid with gratitude from Kate but more importantly from his nieces, to whom Kate often sang his praises.

Mildred was still involved with the Mission, but the bad weather meant that she spent most of her time in her room, dosing herself from her numerous bottles of medicine, and taking no interest in the running of the guesthouse.

On one of her now rare visits to Greenfields, Kate told Rose that Mildred was now as preoccupied with her health as Beattie. 'They're true sisters,' she laughed. 'Mildred's recovered from the stroke except for her leg dragging a bit, but if there's anything she doesn't want to do or hear she collapses and takes to her bed.'

'Like Beattie,' Rose agreed. 'They're alike in that. They look a most unlikely pair, but blood will out.' Rose herself seemed unchanged by the war, as flippant and light-hearted as ever, but there was a brittle quality to her gaiety that worried Kate.

'You know so many men who are at the Front or in the Navy, Rose, you must be worried,' she said gently, but Rose replied lightly, 'No, I don't think about it. "What's the use of worrying, it never was worthwhile", as the song says. Should we go back to Beattie?'

Beattie was lying on the sofa with a small table beside her crowded with smelling salts, medicine bottles, pills and an open box of chocolates. She took Kate's hand. 'How do you think my darling looks?' she said. 'Doesn't she grow more beautiful every day?'

Rose made a gesture of impatience and rang for tea, and Kate only said cautiously, 'Yes, Aunt.'

'All those young men madly in love with her,' Beattie said. 'She says she can't choose but I know what it is. She won't leave her old aunt. I'm not long for this world, Kate. I only hope Mildred won't regret being so unkind to me when it's too late.'

She spoke in a low voice, still holding Kate's hand, but

Kate was uncomfortably aware that though Rose had moved away, she could still hear her aunt. She was uncertain what she should say. If she failed to sympathise she would seem unkind, and if she did Rose would consider her a hypocrite. She left as soon as possible.

Chapter Fourteen

Josie was now working in the greengrocer's, and in the dark days at the beginning of 1918 she often came to see Kate and Lottie after the shop closed. One foggy night, she came straight from work, as Kate had been given some liver by Mr Dyson and had invited Josie to share their meal.

'I'm glad to come here for a bit of cheerful company,' she told them. 'Everybody who comes in the shop is so miserable about the war dragging on, and the food and coal and everything scarce.'

'We can't do nothing about the war, so it's no use worrying,' Lottie said, and Kate added, 'But we're very lucky, Lottie, with the meat and vegetables from Mr Dyson and now the stuff from Mr Trent.' She turned to Josie and explained, 'The new man. He's got no food tickets but he brings things for us. A *pound* of tea and a big bag of sugar last week, and some dried raisins and two lemons the week before.'

'Where does he get them?' gasped Josie.

'I didn't ask,' Kate said. She went to the dresser drawer and took out a small parcel. 'I put some tea and sugar away for you,' she said.

After Josie had thanked her, she sniffed the savoury aroma of liver and onions and drew closer to the bright fire. 'Everything's worked out for you then, Kate, after all,' she said.

'Yes, it's all so different, but much better. Everything seems easier,' said Kate, and Lottie said eagerly, 'The two new ladies are lovely, Josie, and so is Mr Trent. Mr Culshaw's never been no trouble, and him and Mr Trent don't mind eating down here with us.'

'At first I served their meals here, then Lottie and I had ours later on, but they said why didn't we have ours with them. Mr Trent said it would be a shame if ours dried up before we had them.'

'I'm dying to see him,' said Josie. Kate had told her about Mr Trent and his job but they had never met.

Kate and Lottie began to dish up the meal. The table was already laid, and as the grandfather clock in the hall chimed, Mr Culshaw walked down the stairs from the hall and greeted Josie. At almost the same moment there was a tap on the kitchen door and Mr Trent slipped in.

Josie saw a slim young man with dark hair and eyes, and a livid scar running across his cheek. He had heard about Josie from Kate and Lottie, and when he was introduced he set out to charm her, offering condolences on Davy's death, and asking about her job in the greengrocer's.

'Josie says the customers are miserable about the war,' Lottie said as they gathered around the table

'What do you think about the war, Mr Culshaw?' asked Josie.

He looked startled, then said quietly, 'There are rumours about a big push in the spring. That may decide things.'

'At least you're both out of it,' Josie said to the two men. She smiled at them. 'Not many places with two war heroes under one roof.'

'There was nothing heroic about my injury,' Mr Culshaw said quickly. 'I was behind the lines helping wounded to a dressing station when I slipped and was run over by a gun carriage. My leg chiefly, and a rib pierced my lung, but nothing heroic, I assure you.'

Kate expected Gordon Trent to speak of his injury, but he only smiled at Josie and said, 'I suspect you're a romantic, Mrs Thomson.'

Mr Culshaw left as soon as the meal was finished, but before that Josie had talked freely to him, and they had learned that he spent three evenings a week helping at a boys' club. Mr Trent remained at the table with them, sipping tea.

'D'you know,' laughed Josie, 'I can't believe this. Guests eating in the kitchen. What does your aunt say, Kate?'

'What can she say? We haven't got coal for fires in the dining room or the parlour, and Mr Culshaw and Mr Trent don't mind, do you?' Kate appealed to Gordon Trent.

'Not at all. It's wartime and we're fortunate to have good meals and a warm room in which to eat them,' he said.

'Imagine some of the other guests though, Kate,' said Josie. 'Mrs Bradley or Mr Hayman or Miss Norton. Mind you, Mr Barnes wouldn't have minded.' She glanced at Kate. 'But the others! I thought they were like creatures from another planet when I came here. And that dining room. The food and all the dishes they used.'

'It was another world,' Kate agreed.

'When you used to sit with them on a Sunday evening I didn't know how you dared to eat,' Josie said. 'Mind you, Mrs Molesworth always said you was as good as any of them. Your mother was a Miss Green related to the Marquis of Salisbury.'

'As Rose said, about forty times removed,' Kate said.

Trent smiled at them. 'I'll leave you girls to talk,' he said, slipping away to his own room.

'You're a witch, Josie,' Kate said when he was gone. 'I've never known Mr Culshaw to talk like that. We never knew where he went at night, but he told you.'

'No, we thought he was courting,' said Lottie.

Josie laughed. 'And Mr Trent said *I* was romantic. He's nice, isn't he?'

'He must be real good at his job,' Lottie said. 'The way he just slips in and out and you hardly know he's there. You wouldn't notice him in a crowd, would you?'

Kate looked at her warningly. 'Be careful, Lottie. It's all right in front of Josie, but no one else.'

Josie laughed. 'I might have got Mr Culshaw to talk, but I didn't get much out of Mr Trent, did I? Maybe they get trained to be like that.'

In his room, Gordon Trent drew a deep breath, then let it out in a soundless whistle. That could have been nasty, he thought. That quizzing about war wounds. He'd have to do something about Josie. Make sure she didn't chatter to her customers.

He looked in the mirror at his scar, and smiled cynically as he thought of her assuming that he was a war hero, and her face if she knew how quickly he had deserted after being conscripted. It had been all right at first. His pals in London had kept him hidden until the fight with the Naylor gang. One of them had carved him with a cut-throat razor, but he had done his share of carving too. Too bad one of them was Naylor's nephew, so now the Naylors as well as the military police were out to get him. Oggy and Ginge were probably after him too, because he'd scarpered with their share of their last haul as well as his own.

He looked round the small, dark room. This was as good a place as any to lie low for the time being. He didn't need to do another job for a while, and those two stupid women had swallowed his story and were eating out of his hand. Something would have to be done about that Josie, though. A blabbermouth if ever he saw one, but he'd try talking first. No point taking more chances than need be.

He lay back on his bed and thought over the conversation. It confirmed what he'd seen in a quick shufti round the house. The furniture was all good stuff, solid mahogany mostly, and plenty of cut glass and silver in the dining room, carefully laid away now. The two canaries in the front room were loaded. Plenty of cash and knick-knacks. Jewellery. He needn't go empty-handed, even if he left in a hurry.

He could afford to wait, see how things worked out. Good pickings here, and the old aunt must be loaded too. He liked what he saw of the local prospects and he'd put a few feelers out when he was sure he was safe, maybe do a few jobs single-handed. Plenty of big houses about. He looked at his watch and got up and sluiced his face, then went back to the kitchen.

The three girls were sitting round the fire, and he hesitated on the stairs from the hall, but they welcomed him and Kate offered a cup of tea.

'I'm going in a minute,' said Josie, and Gordon Trent said

eagerly, 'That's really why I came down. I'd like to escort you home if I may, Mrs Thomson. It's foggy, and with the blackout as well it's not safe for ladies to be out alone.'

Josie was flattered to be described as a lady, and Kate was enthusiastic about the plan. 'It's very good of you, Mr Trent,' she said. 'I was worried about Josie going home on her own. You're right – it's not safe the way things are.'

As they walked home, Trent skilfully questioned Josie about Kate, and Josie chattered freely about her.

'Kate's too nice for her own good,' she said. 'The charwoman who used to work there, she said Kate was born to be put on because she thought everyone was as decent as herself. She got the dirty end of the stick when her mam died. The other sister got took off to live in a big house with their rich aunt, and Kate got brought here by the missus to be a drudge. Yet she wanted Kate to be posh as well because she was her niece. Mrs Molesworth said she made Kate neither fish nor fowl so it spoiled her for going out with lads.'

'Does Kate see much of her rich relations?' asked Trent.

'Not as much as she used to because the missus has fell out with her sister, but Kate goes to see Rose and her Aunt Beattie. Beattie thinks the world of Kate. She used to be always slipping her sovereigns and other presents, and she gave her a purse with five sovereigns in it one Christmas. The missus made her put it in the bank,' Josie said indignantly.

Before they were halfway home, Gordon Trent had learned all he needed to know about Kate's background, and he turned the talk to Davy and to Josie's own affairs. After he had left her at her door, Josie realised that he had told her nothing about himself.

She felt uneasily that there was something odd about him, and hoped that he was not becoming too interested in Kate, much as she longed to see Kate courting. Perhaps she had talked too much.

The following day was Sunday. It was the sort of mild day which sometimes comes in February as a foretaste of spring, and Josie felt more and more unhappy and restless as the day passed. She had slept badly, disturbed by Trent's questions about Davy, and finally she went out and walked through Grant's Gardens and sat down on a seat.

She had never felt able to talk about her grief for Davy. So many of her neighbours had lost sons or husbands at sea or in the trenches, and when they talked of them Josie felt an outsider. 'At least your man died in your arms in his own bed,' several of them had said. 'Not like my poor lad,' and Josie felt she had no right to grieve.

Kate would have been a sympathetic listener, but Josie was unwilling to burden her with her sorrow. Kate had such a miserable life, although she never seemed to think so, and at least Josie had known happiness and fulfilment with Davy.

The mild day was fading into a cold grey evening, and Josie became aware that the man at the other end of the seat was in deep distress. His head was bent, with his hands covering his face, and his body was shaken by silent sobs.

Josie felt unable to walk away, so she slid along the seat and touched his arm. 'Are you all right?' she asked gently.

He lifted his head and wiped his hands over his tear-streaked face. 'I'm sorry, ma'am,' he said in an Irish brogue. 'Sure, ye have your own troubles,' looking at Josie's mourning clothes.

'Have you lost someone?' Josie asked, expecting to hear of a relation killed in action, but he nodded then burst out, 'Me little sister.' Tears ran down his face again, but he wiped them with a bandanna handkerchief. 'The baby she was, a little dote. She died far from us all in the Infirmary here. I'm after coming over to take her body home to be buried.'

Josie's soft heart was touched, and she wept with him, but soon he blew his nose and sat up straight. 'It's ashamed I am,' he said. 'It just came to me that she'd be wanting her mammy, but sure, so many have sorrow now. Husbands and fathers dying far away in foreign lands or on the sea. I'm ashamed to be crying here like a child.'

'It doesn't make it any better for you that other people have troubles,' Josie said. 'How old was your sister?'

'Eighteen years old, ma'am,' he said. 'She came over with another older girl that had a job here, but Maeve met a man from Hull and went off to be near him, and Noreen was all alone here.'

'Was she ill for long?' asked Josie.

'Only the two days, ma'am, with the fever, and before we knew it she was gone,' he said. 'Mammy and the girls are broken-hearted. There's seven of them. I'm the only lad, but Noreen was ever the little dote for all of us.'

He swallowed, and Josie said sympathetically, 'There must have been a lot to arrange – for you to take her home, I mean.'

'Ah, sure, Father Donachy at home did all that for us with a priest in Liverpool here,' he said. 'From St Sylvester's parish. Father Burke. He's been very good, so.'

It was growing dark, and Josie said gently, 'I think we'll have to go. They'll be closing the gates soon.'

He stood up immediately. 'It's thankful I am for your kindness. Sure, I shouldn't be burdening you, and you with your own troubles, I can see.'

He was calmer now but he looked so wretched that Josie said impulsively, 'Would you like to come home with me for a cup of tea? At least I was at home with friends when I lost my husband.'

'Thank you, ma'am,' he said simply.

It was only a short distance to Josie's house, where she stirred up the fire and put the kettle over it. 'Have you got far to go when you get home?' she asked.

'Only Wicklow, ma'am, not far from Dublin we are,' he said, and Josie saw how he gripped his hands together at the thought of the journey to come.

'Please don't keep calling me ma'am,' she said quietly. 'My name's Josie,' and he stood up and held out his hand.

'Mine is Michael. Michael Malloy,' he said.

Josie had not lit the gas, and the little room was dark except for the light of the fire. It was easier for them to talk that way, and Michael told her more about his sister then he asked her about Davy. He seemed to assume that he had been a soldier, until she told him that Davy had died at home of consumption.

'That's why I understood what you meant when you said you were ashamed to grieve when other people had relations dying abroad. People round here think I shouldn't cry because at least Davy died at home, but I've lost him just the same as they've lost their husbands. I'm on my own as much, even more because there's so many of them.'

Once she began to speak of Davy, it was as though the floodgates were open and all that had been dammed up inside her poured out. All her loss and grief and the guilt she felt because someone had said that marriage might have shortened his life. Michael listened without interrupting her, and now it was his turn to offer comfort.

'And if it did shorten his life, sure, wouldn't that be the way he wanted it? Ye gave him years of happiness instead of a longer life of misery, that's all, and ye were his comfort to the end,' he said.

He talked of his own guilt that he had let his little sister be influenced by the older girl into going to England. 'We all blame ourselves,' he said. 'But she was so set on it, and as Mammy said, hadn't we ever given her her own way? Her being the baby and the little dote that she was.'

The kettle had boiled while Josie was talking about Davy, and Michael had quietly drawn it on to the hob, but now Josie placed a pan on the fire instead. 'We'll have a drop of soup first,' she said. 'Only vegetable, but I work in a greengrocer's so I can get plenty of those, and I got bones from the butcher's.'

Michael took out his watch and said uneasily, 'Sure, I think I should be going. Nine o'clock. Ye have to think of your good name with the neighbours,' but Josie laughed.

'Don't worry about that,' she said. 'Sit down and have some soup.'

As they ate she told him of her good meal the previous night, and about Kate and Lottie and the guesthouse, and he talked about his family, but his mind was never far from his dead sister.

'Mammy is from the west,' he said, 'County Galway, but

me da, Lord rest him, was a Dublin man. A Dublin Jackeen he used to say, but he was a grand farmer. He could always make two blades of grass grow where one grew before. I used to help him, and when we'd be coming home down the boreen Noreen would be running to meet him. I can see her now, her little fat legs and she yelling because she couldn't reach him quick enough. Tired as he was, Da would break into a trot. "The secret of life," he'd tell me. "Meet people halfway." Sure, he was great gas always.'

Before they ate, Josie had lit the gas mantle, and after having a cup of tea he said diffidently, 'Would you ever write down your name and address, ma'am? I'd like to write to thank you for your kindness to me.'

'There's no need. You were welcome,' Josie protested, but she willingly wrote down her name and address. 'I hope everything goes right for the boat home for you,' she said, and Michael gripped her hand.

'Ye've been kindness itself to me,' he said. 'May your sorrow grow less and your life be easy, ma'am.'

He went and Josie sat down again by the fire, feeling a sense of release from the burden of unspoken sorrow she had carried. She told Kate and Lottie about him on her next visit, and Kate said, 'Poor man. What a sad journey for him,' but Lottie was shocked.

'You took a chance, Josie,' she said. 'He could have been a murderer.'

'I knew he wasn't,' Josie said. 'He was a real nice man and so easy to talk to. I hope he does write to me.'

Kate was pleased to see Josie looking happier. Her own life was easier now that Mildred kept to her room except for a rare outing to the Mission, and there was less worry about food. She had framed the snapshot and put it beside her bed, and as the weeks passed, although she still read down the casualty lists in the *Echo* every night, she felt more confident that Henry would survive. Since her visit to his home she had allowed her mind to dwell on her memories of him more and more, feeling that she was doing nobody any harm.

She was often conscious of Gordon Trent gazing at her,

but he said nothing and she told herself that she was imagining that he was interested in her.

Less than a week later, Josie came in great excitement to tell Kate that she had received two letters from Ireland, one from Michael, and the other from his mother, thanking her for her kindness to her son. 'She says she has no schooling but she got her daughter to write to me because she said her heart had been scalded not only for the child she had lost but for her poor son going among strangers in his grief. She said she remembered me in her prayers and God would bless me for my kindness to Michael. Don't you think that's lovely, Kate?'

Kate smiled at Josie's sparkling eyes and broad smile. 'I do, Josie,' she said. 'And I agree with them. I think you're a good, kind girl, and you had the courage to do a kind deed, and I'm glad it's appreciated.'

Letters passed back and forth between Josie and Michael, and then one day Josie appeared at the guesthouse with a large ham. 'A man off the Irish boat brought me this,' she said. 'He said his second cousin was married to one of the Malloys and Mrs Malloy had asked him to bring me this.'

She insisted that Kate used it for dinner, saying that she had no pan large enough, and she came for the meal of pea soup, ham, potatoes and cabbage the following night. 'Food fit for a king,' Gordon Trent said.

Kate was not surprised when Michael returned to see Josie in March, nor when it was decided that he would come again to take Josie to Ireland to meet his family. The greengrocer refused her time off but she went anyway, saying that she could easily get another job later.

She came back two weeks later ecstatic about the welcome she had received. 'His mother's lovely, very gentle, and so are his sisters. There are six left now. Two nursing in Dublin, two married. One in service in a big house in Howth, and Maggie, who's still at home. They couldn't do enough for me, Kate. And they seem to be related to half the village and they all invited me in for tea. I've never drunk so much tea in my life.'

Later she told Kate more calmly about the visit. 'It was

lovely being part of the family,' she said. 'Like sinking into a feather bed. It's what I've always longed for. Michael's mother told me to call her Mammy like the rest. I told her all about being left on the doorstep. You know, I've always been a bit ashamed of it, although I think my mother must have been desperate to do it, but I didn't mind telling her a bit.'

'There was nothing for you to be ashamed of,' Kate said. 'I didn't know you felt like that.'

'She just put her arms round me and said, "Ah, the poor girl. It must have broken her heart to leave you but she did what was best for you, God help her. And you know she loved you to be sending the dolls all those years."'

'She sounds a real nice woman,' Kate said, and Josie replied enthusiastically, 'Oh, she is, Kate. I knew she would be because of Michael, but she's even nicer than I expected. They all are. I went to church with them and even the priest was nice. I might have been born a Catholic with a name like Josephine, y'know. I felt at home there.'

Kate was not surprised when Josie told her that she had arranged to take instruction in the Catholic faith, and that Michael had asked her to marry him. Kate had met him and immediately liked the big, gentle man and his tender concern for Josie. She felt that although Josie had always faced life with courage, she had been alone except for a few friends, and even though she had been happy with Davy, she had had to be the strong one in that marriage. It would be good for her to be cared for.

'Looks like Josie's fell on her feet again,' Lottie said with a sigh. She often walked out with various young men, but none of her affairs ever lasted for long.

Josie was afraid that Kate might think it was too soon after Davy's death, but Kate urged her to grasp happiness. 'It's what Davy would have wanted,' she told her, and when Josie took Michael to meet Davy's uncle, he said the same thing.

'Look after her,' he told Michael. 'She's a good girl and she gave my poor nephew the only happiness he ever had. I'd like to be there when his ma hears about it,' he added with a chuckle. 'She'll be fit to be tied.'

Michael wanted the wedding in May, but then Josie began to worry that they were rushing into it. 'We've only known each other a few months,' she said, but Michael said he'd known in the first five minutes that she was the girl for him. 'What about your family?' Josie said, and he laughed and kissed her.

'Aren't they all delighted?' he said, 'Sure, I think ye've bewitched them as well as meself.' When Josie still looked doubtful, Michael kissed her again. 'Sure, they all think it's magic. A lump like meself that never looked at a girl and I see yourself and lose me heart entirely.'

Josie smiled. 'But what does your mammy think really?' she said.

'She thinks it was meant to be, that God sent you to us to console us for Noreen. Ye have the same lovely brown eyes she had and her lovable ways, but we love you for yourself, me darlin'. Mammy thinks you're an answer to her prayers.' He grinned at her. 'Wasn't she afraid she was going to have a crusty old bachelor on her hands. She told me she loves the bones of you already,' and Josie was reassured.

It was arranged that Josie would clear her house and send her goods to Ireland. Kate would travel with her for the wedding in the second week of May, and Lottie would manage for the two days that Kate would be away. The day before they were due to go, Mildred suffered another stroke and took to her bed, so Kate had to cancel her plans and Josie travelled alone.

Mildred's speech was slightly slurred, but her mind was still clear, except that she seemed to have forgotten how little part she had taken recently in running the guesthouse. She demanded a report every morning from Kate on what she had bought and proposed to cook, and what cleaning was planned.

For two weeks she lay in bed, constantly ringing for attention or demanding details of what was happening in the guesthouse. She refused to let Lottie take any part in caring for her, saying that it was Kate's duty as her niece, and Kate felt worn out by her aunt's constant demands. She was bitterly disappointed at missing Josie's wedding and already feeling the loss of her cheerful, affectionate company.

Although Lottie was a good worker and willing to do more because Kate was so busy with Mildred, Kate had never felt as close to her as she did to Josie. Lottie was selective about her chores. She would do anything for the Barry sisters, but resented being asked to do the charwoman's work when, as often happened, she failed to arrive.

Kate missed her visits to Greenfields too, but her life had become so difficult that it was some time since she had been able to visit there. She wrote to Rose telling of her difficulties with Mildred, but promising to visit as soon as possible. She received a short note from Rose saying that her life was difficult too as Aunt Beattie was now an invalid. She sent her love to Kate, but Mildred was not mentioned.

It was at this time when her spirits were so low that Kate received a letter from the Front from Henry. It was crumpled and muddy and she opened it with trembling fingers.

Dear Kate,

I have to write to you, Kate. I know you'll understand. I am in a rest camp. We came out of the line wet and filthy, covered in mud, staggering like drunken men for lack of sleep. We passed the men who were taking our places, first-timers, young and fresh and clean and *human*. They were like another breed.

We don't feel human any more. Going blindly and insensibly to our fate which is decided by old men far away. Far away in every sense, Kate. We just dropped as we were in the camp and slept as though stunned but I am awake now and I have been looking up at the stars shining above us. What must they make of this madness? The acres of mud sown with the bodies of dead men instead of fields of wheat? But of course they have seen it all before on other battlefields down the ages. It makes me feel that none of this matters, Kate. Our brief moment of life means so little in the larger plan.

I think of you often, Kate, and the happy days in

the guesthouse. The memory of your fortitude and your ready smile that warmed my heart comforts and helps me now. God bless you always, Kate.
Henry.

Kate stood gripping the letter, torn between joy that Henry was comforted by his memories of her, and sadness that he seemed so troubled and unhappy, and so different from the Henry she remembered. She longed to comfort him, to write to him pouring out her love for him, but she was afraid. What if it fell into the wrong hands? If it was seen by men who knew he was married, or even by Agnes? I might cause trouble for him, she thought.

In the end she wrote a formal letter, saying little about her own feelings, but trying to comfort Henry and telling him she understood. At least he was now out of danger, she thought, and when he was less exhausted he would feel better. She had little time to feel either joy or grief.

Chapter Fifteen

One day, late in May, Mildred had been very demanding, and had even rung for Kate during the night to turn her pillows. The next morning Kate was wakened by Lottie from a deep sleep and stumbled into the kitchen. 'The woman's not coming,' Lottie said abruptly, and after a look at her face Kate said wearily, 'All right. I'll do the steps.'

She gulped a cup of tea, then pulled on her aunt's old skirt, and a mobcap over her hair, and went out to scrub the front steps. I'm as bad as Lottie, wearing these old clothes so I won't be recognised, she thought, as she changed back into her dress to take up Mildred's breakfast.

She suspected her aunt could do more for herself if she chose, and told her firmly that she would not answer her bell again at night. 'I need my sleep,' she said. 'There's a lot to do for just two of us,' but Mildred was even more demanding for the rest of the day. Kate felt worn out when at last the long day was over and she was alone in her bedroom.

She undressed and slipped on her nightdress, then hung up her dress before sitting down and picking up the *Liverpool Echo*. She turned first to the casualty lists as she always did, although she no longer expected to see Henry's name. He had survived so much, and for some time she had thought that he must still be behind the lines while others took their turn in danger.

The shock was all the greater when his name seemed to leap up at her from the page. Captain H. C. Barnes, King's Liverpool Regiment. The newspaper dropped from her nerveless fingers. *Oh God, no, no!* she screamed silently, then snatched up the *Echo* again to look at the lines in stunned disbelief. Not Henry, she thought wildly. Not now, after all this time. There must have been some mistake.

Her hands were shaking so much that the paper dropped from them, and she jumped to her feet and began to pace about the room, twisting her hands together frantically. The one word *no* repeated itself in her brain until suddenly reality burst upon her and she flung herself on the bed, moaning in agony and biting the pillow to stop herself from screaming aloud.

'Henry, Henry,' she moaned, thinking of his dear face, his laughing eyes looking into hers as he teased her, and his kiss on her cheek as he gave her the bouquet. For years she had tried to convince herself that she loved him as a grateful child, then as her model of all a man should be, and felt guilty if she dreamed about him, but now all her careful defences were swept away.

I loved him and he loved me, she wept. I know he did. We should have married. It was all Mildred's fault. She felt a surge of hatred for her aunt, then for Henry's wife. She stood up again and walked about, unable to lie still. I was a fool, she thought. I loved Henry and he loved me long before *she* arrived. It was just that he thought I was too young, and I was too timid.

Agnes was so bossy and pushy. She chased Henry and he was too nice and too kind to snub her. And she had the cheek to try to change him. I would just have loved him. It's my own fault. I should have done something.

She thought of the telegram arriving at Rufford Road. What did it say? When had it happened, and where? Had Henry suffered? At the thought of him dying in the mud of Flanders, of that bright spirit snuffed out, she forgot herself and was overcome again with sorrow. She lay on her bed again, her body racked with sobs until her thoughts drove her to her feet again to pace the room, too distraught to lie still.

It seemed that the night would never end, but daylight had come although Kate was unaware of it, and as she lay on the bed once again, shaking with grief and cold with shock, Lottie knocked on the door. 'The missus is ringing for you, Kate,' she called.

Kate said hoarsely, 'See to her. I'm not well.'

Lottie cautiously opened the door. 'What's up? Do you want a cup of tea?' she said, but Kate only huddled further into the bedclothes and said, 'Go away. Go away.'

'All right,' Lottie said in an offended voice, and flounced away, but Kate was back in her world of misery.

Later in the morning Lottie returned and put a cup of tea down beside Kate. 'Wharrisit, Kate?' she asked.

'A cold,' replied Kate, her face muffled in the bed-clothes.

Lottie touched the pillow. 'This is soaking. Maybe you're sweating it out of you,' she said hopefully. 'What should I do, Kate?'

'Whatever you think,' Kate replied, and Lottie went off importantly, while the weary treadmill of Kate's thoughts began again. She wept with the bitter agony of loss and the even more bitter regret for what might have been, and for the fact that she had no right to mourn.

Yet I've loved him since I was twelve, she thought, and not a day has passed when I haven't thought of him. She longed for Mrs Molesworth or Josie, for someone in whom she could confide and who would comfort her, but there was no one. Perhaps she could tell Rose sometime, but she needed someone here and now.

Sometime in mid-morning Lottie knocked and said that she was going to the shops, and a little later Kate got up and sat on the side of the bed. She felt that she was going mad. Her thoughts were skittering about like rats in a trap, and everything seemed unreal. She felt that she was living through a nightmare and the walls of the room were closing in on her. She had to get out.

She jumped to her feet and snatched up her aunt's old skirt, which lay on a nearby chair. She pulled it on over her nightdress, then thrust her bare feet into a pair of old shoes. She bundled up her hair and hastily pinned on an old felt hat, then went into the deserted kitchen and, taking an old jacket from behind the door, went up the steps to the street.

The day was bright and sunny, but Kate was unaware

of it as she walked blindly away from the house. She had been walking rapidly for more than an hour, immersed in her sad thoughts, when she found herself in Bold Street, the fashionable shopping centre of Liverpool.

The people she passed seemed like ghosts to her, until suddenly she saw Rose. She noticed nothing of the crowds around her, or of the friends with Rose, only her beloved sister, and she started towards her. Rose looked at her. Her blue eyes widened as she glanced over Kate, then she turned her head away towards her friends.

Kate stood still for a moment, frozen in shock, then she fled away in the opposite direction to Rose, running like someone demented until she reached the haven of the guesthouse. To reach her own room she needed to go through the kitchen, past Lottie, and some instinct made her go instead through the front door and up the stairs to hide away in one of the empty bedrooms.

As she sped up the stairs and along the landing, Gordon Trent slipped quietly from his room at the back of the house. They both stopped, then he took her arm and said with concern, 'What is it, Kate? Is it your aunt?' She shook her head, tears running down her face, and he drew her into his bedroom and closed the door. 'What is it?' he asked again, drawing her down to sit beside him on the bed. 'Has someone upset you?' but she seemed unable to speak.

Gently he slipped off her jacket and unpinned her hat, then put his arm around her and smoothed back her hair, which had escaped from the pins and hung down her back. As he held her, making soothing noises, she began to pour out her grief at Henry's death and her rejection by Rose.

Still holding her close, he gently eased her back on to the bed and lay beside her, holding her and gently smoothing back her hair, while Kate sobbed out her despair and desolation. Gradually his hands moved to her body, skilfully touching and stroking her, but immersed in her sorrow, Kate seemed unaware of what was happening.

He was surprised and pleased to find that under the rusty skirt and cotton nightgown she wore no underclothes. She lay pliant in his arms, still weeping, as he explored. It was only when he finally entered her that she opened her tear-swollen eyes and looked up at him in alarm, but he held her close and pressed his lips hard on her mouth.

It was soon over, but he still held her close to him. 'It's all right, it's all right, darling,' he soothed while he continued to cover her face with kisses. To Kate it all seemed part of the unreal world she inhabited, and she made no protest.

After a time he drew her up to sit again on the side of the bed, while he whispered, 'I have to go, darling. Lottie thinks you're in your room. We'll go down now and I'll get her out of the kitchen while you slip into your room. Do you feel better?' She nodded and he kissed her again. 'This is the worst. It'll get a bit easier every day now.'

Docilely she allowed Gordon to straighten her clothes and lead her down the stairs and out of the front door. 'I'll go and get Lottie out of the kitchen, then you can slip in,' he said again, then ran lightly down the area steps and into the kitchen.

Kate followed slowly. The kitchen was deserted, but she could hear Lottie's voice in the hall above. Still moving as though in a dream, she went into her own room off the kitchen and threw off her skirt and shoes, then climbed into bed and within minutes fell into an exhausted sleep.

Lottie knocked several times, but Kate slept on. At last, becoming alarmed, Lottie came into the room. She drew the bedclothes away from Kate's face and was relieved to see that she was breathing, although her face looked flushed and swollen. The skirt had fallen from the chair, so Lottie picked it up, then folded the newspaper which lay on the floor beneath, without realising the significance of it.

A little later, Gordon Trent returned to his room to tidy away the evidence and hide Kate's hat and jacket in his wardrobe. He lay on top of the bedclothes, his arms behind his head, as he thought over the events of the past few hours.

I've done it, he thought exultantly. Seized my chance. He had been working towards this, to settling here at least until it suited him to move on. He seemed to have found the perfect hidey-hole for now, but to get his hands on this

225

place and the money he'd have to marry Kate. Now it was settled. Kate would tell someone what had happened, and if she did not he would feel obliged to confess. He grinned happily.

Either way the relatives would insist on marriage. They sounded like such a strait-laced crew, the Bible-thumping old woman here, and the rich aunt in the big house. He thought over all he had learned about the set-up from Josie, and Kate's incoherent revelations earlier. She might have married the fellow who'd been killed, an officer no less, and her sister had cut her, but that was not important. It was the aunt at West Derby who held the pursestrings, and Josie had said Kate was a favourite there.

As he thought of Kate weeping in his arms, the better side of his nature came briefly to the fore and he felt unfamiliar shame, and compassion, but the moment soon passed. I treated her gently. Didn't hurt her. In fact, I comforted her, he thought defensively, and turned his mind to his prospects.

This had been a first-class place before the war, good solid furniture and fittings, and it would be again. The old aunt was on the way out and it would all come to Kate, then plenty more when the other aunt snuffed it too. Who'd ever find him here, the respected proprietor of a posh boarding house with servants and plenty of money? he thought. Not the Naylor gang, or the military police.

Not bad for Sid Maudsley, son of an East End costermonger, ex-market porter, deserter, gang member. He thought of his parents. His mother with her refrain, 'We're poor but we're honest' – where had that got them? Tatty rooms, cheap food, always scraping. Not for me, he thought. I'm rich and dishonest, and that's the way I like it. He grinned again.

Lottie was alarmed when Kate continued to sleep until the evening. She managed to rouse her briefly, and Kate drank the tea that she had brought, but Lottie was aggrieved that she asked nothing of how the other girl had managed alone, but sank again into sleep.

It was light again when Kate woke and lay looking at

the feet passing her window high in the wall. She felt light-headed and disorientated, as though she had been seriously ill for several weeks. As memories returned, it all seemed like a bad dream, until she got up and looked at the newspaper and knew that it was all too true.

She thought of Rose cutting her dead, then of Gordon's kindness. Her mind drifted over what she thought of as his strange behaviour on the bed, but returned to the memory of him holding her and comforting her. How kind he had been.

She was sitting on the side of the bed feeling faint and dizzy when Lottie came again with tea. 'You look terrible,' she said. 'How d'you feel?'

'Just dizzy,' Kate said faintly, and Lottie said briskly, 'Well, you haven't had nothing to eat. Drink this and I'll do you a sandwich, then you'll feel better. You're probably over the worst.'

For a moment Kate remembered Gordon saying, 'This is the worst. It'll get a bit easier every day now,' and her mind went even further back, to Henry smiling at her and saying, 'It's always darkest before the dawn.' Tears threatened to overwhelm her, but she gulped the hot tea and resolutely turned her mind to the present.

She managed to get her voice under control and said, 'I'm all right. How have you managed, Lottie?'

'Fine, really. D'you know, the missus got up and dressed herself. Just shows you. Mind you, she was ringing that dratted bell all the time, but I didn't take no notice mostly. I'll make you that sandwich.'

'Is there any hot water, Lottie?' Kate asked. 'I need a good wash.'

'Yes, you was sweating like a pig,' Lottie said frankly, but she brought a can of hot water.

Kate took off her nightdress, discovering that it was bloodstained and that there were also bloodstains on her legs. Too innocent to connect this with Gordon's behaviour, she vaguely thought her period had arrived. She washed and dressed in clean underwear and her everyday dress, moving as though in a dream, then went into the kitchen. It seemed unfamiliar, as though she had been away for a long time, but she ate the sandwich Lottie had made and then, still moving like a sleepwalker, washed dishes and cooked the meals that Lottie suggested.

'I haven't told the missus you're up,' Lottie said. 'I'll carry on seeing to her today,' and Kate smiled at her remotely. She felt instinctively that when this merciful numbness had passed, the pain would be unbearable, so she worked automatically and remained in her own world. The feeling of unreality persisted even when she sat at the table with Gordon Trent. His manner towards her was as formal as ever, and he made no reference to the episode in the bedroom, even when they were alone. To Kate it merged with her suffering over Henry's death and Rose's rejection. As far as possible she tried to block off that time in her mind, although she still grieved bitterly for Henry, all the more because she was unable to speak of it and her sorrow was turned inward.

She never bought the *Echo* now, or took any interest in the war news, but moved through the days like an automaton. Letters from Josie and Nell went unanswered, and she had no contact with Rose or Beattie.

As the weeks passed, Kate was often sick in the mornings although she ate very little, and her periods failed to appear, but she only thought dully that it was because of shock. She was too innocent and inexperienced to connect it with the act in Gordon's bedroom and to realise that she was pregnant.

She had grown so thin that her clothes hung on her and concealed any sign of pregnancy, and Lottie was seriously worried about her. 'You don't eat enough to keep a bird alive,' she scolded. 'And you don't seem to care about nothing. You've never got over that fever. You should go to the Dispensary, see a doctor,' but Kate only murmured, 'I'm all right.'

In the face of Kate's indifference, Mildred had decided that she was getting better. She dressed every day and sat for hours at her desk, studying her account books and totting up columns of figures. Lottie reported that sometimes there were huge ledgers on her desk which she had never seen before. 'I don't know where they've come from,' she said.

'Probably from her safe,' Kate said indifferently. 'They'll be her father's.'

'I think she's going barmy,' Lottie said, but Kate made no comment.

Mildred had resigned herself to having her meals served and her rooms cleaned by Lottie, and Kate rarely left the kitchen except to do some cleaning. Lottie looked after the Barry sisters too.

One day she confided to the young man she was walking out with that the house was driving her mad. 'I'm that worried about Kate, but she doesn't care about nothing. She's in the kitchen all the time, the missus is in her rooms, and the two fellers just go their own way. If it wasn't for Miss Ethel and Miss Isabel I'd go outa me mind.'

'You want to get outa there,' the young man advised. 'Sounds like a madhouse to me.'

'But I couldn't leave Kate,' Lottie protested.

'Why not? You've got to look after number one, girl. There isn't nobody'll do it for you. D'yer think they'll care about you if the place goes to pot? Anyhow, the war'll soon be over and there'll be plenty of places,' he added.

In July Mr Culshaw gave notice, saying that he was to be married and was renting a house in Anfield. 'He's as much of a mystery man as the other feller,' Lottie said, but she was pleased that neither Kate nor Mildred did anything about letting his room. 'Less work and one less mouth to feed,' she said to Kate, but Kate as usual said nothing. She went about her duties keeping her grief to herself, as she had kept her love for so many years.

The tide of war had turned in favour of the Allies, but the newspapers were not allowed to print much about the successes. Hopes had been raised many times before only to be dashed, and it was felt that caution was necessary. Back in 1916 when British journalists were still being refused permits to visit the Front, the French had helped them and given them information. Journalists were now using their French contacts again, and since they were forbidden to write about British success, they told instead of victorious French actions, thus forcing the British authorities to allow publication of British victories. Suddenly it became clear that at long last the war was coming to an end, but to Kate and many others the news was bittersweet.

Kate was still eating little and showing no sign of her pregnancy. Only Gordon suspected it, and he treated her with tenderness when they were alone. Now with only three of them at the table, he joined Lottie in trying to coax Kate to eat, and Lottie decided that he was a good, kind man.

Kate felt the cold, and in September she started to wear her winter coat, so that even the more knowledgeable people never suspected the truth. It was only when the butcher's wife came to call on her nieces that she saw the slight thickening round Kate's waist, in spite of her loss of weight elsewhere. Even then she found it hard to believe, and when she told her husband her suspicions he laughed at her.

'Don't be daft, woman,' he said. 'Kate! A born old maid if ever I saw one. She's never even walked out with a lad.'

'I know. I can't believe it myself. Unless she's been took advantage of.'

'No, we'd have heard about it,' the butcher scoffed. 'She'd o' been screaming blue murder.'

'Well, if it isn't that, it's a growth,' Mrs Dyson said. 'Either way, Albert, I think we should get our girls out of there. Lottie's told them she thinks the missus is going out of her mind, never moving out of her room and not seeing none of her friends, and now there's only that one other lodger, that young man. We'll have to do something.'

Josie, too, was concerned about affairs at the guesthouse, and when her letters to Kate had gone unanswered for a while she wrote to Lottie to ask for news. Lottie would have been pleased to pass on some responsibility, but she had never kept up with her reading and the thought of writing a letter, especially to another country, daunted her. She intended to write but kept putting it off.

The Dysons decided to suggest to their nieces that they opened up their house again. Both felt, although they would not admit it even to each other, that the sisters had saved a considerable amount of money by living in the guesthouse, but if there was any scandal there they might well get the blame for recommending it.

'I think this place will be closing,' Mrs Dyson said to her nieces. 'And now the war's nearly over, so they say, you'll be able to get plenty of servants. Young Lottie would go with you and look after you, I'm sure, and me and your Uncle Albert will see to everything for you.'

Lottie was approached and readily agreed, although she felt guilty at leaving Kate. I've got to look out for meself, though, like that feller said, she thought. He did it all right, scarpering as soon as I asked him about walking out serious.

'When Miss Isabel and Miss Ethel go, there'll only be the missus and Mr Trent to look after. You won't need me,' she said when she told Kate, and Kate agreed and wished her well.

In the midst of the upheaval of the move Mildred fell ill again. At first it was only her old enemies, sick headaches and dyspepsia, but soon she was running a temperature and tossing in delirium.

'I think you ought to send for her sister,' Lottie told Kate. 'I know they've fell out, but blood's thicker than water and she mightn't get over this. Then they might blame you for not telling them.'

Kate, roused from her apathy by her aunt's need, wrote a short letter to Beattie telling her of the seriousness of Mildred's illness. The reply came a few days later, a bulky letter which made it clear that Beattie would not be visiting her sister.

We are in dreadful trouble here. I am sorry about Mildred but I am very ill myself and quite prostrated. That dreadful man, that lawyer, says that all my money is gone and I must leave my lovely house where I came as a bride. He says he has been warning me for years but he was always a miserable, croaking man and I just didn't believe him. I don't believe it now. There was so much money, my dear husband was so clever. I'm sure there is some mistake or there has been some mismanagement or some wrongdoing. Rose says I must not say that.

She is very cross with me, Kate, and says I should have told her, but why should I worry her when I knew it couldn't be true? There was always plenty of money and still should be. That horrid man blames the war and my investments, but I know what I think no matter what Rose says. I'm sorry about Mildred but I am confined to bed and don't think I will ever rise from it. I shall not be sorry to leave this vale of tears.

Kate was as surprised as Beattie seemed to be that all that money had gone. What would they do? she wondered. How would Rose fare with poverty instead of the luxury she had always known? Mildred's needs, however, were too pressing to allow her to spend much thought on Rose and Beattie.

Lottie and the Misses Barry had gone, and only Kate now remained with the sick woman, but Mildred clung grimly to life. The doctor Kate had summoned was a gruff old Scotsman called from retirement by the war, and it was he who finally told Kate that she was pregnant.

Mildred was now incontinent, and Dr McAndrew arrived one day when Kate had changed the bed and was lifting her aunt back on to it. 'You shouldn't be doing that on your own in your condition, lassie,' he said, then, as Kate looked uncomprehending, he added, 'You're enceinte, aren't you? With child.'

Kate looked so stunned that he drew her out to the other room, where she now slept on a camp bed.

'Did ye not know?' he asked, and Kate shook her head. 'I'm not married,' she said foolishly, and he sighed. 'Were ye ever attacked? Molested?' he asked.

'I don't know. I don't think so,' Kate stammered, and he

said grimly, 'Ye'd know all right if ye were, lassie. I think I'd better make sure. Loosen your clothes and lie down on this bed.' Swiftly and gently he examined Kate, then said quietly, 'You're pregnant right enough, lassie. About five months. Now tell me what you were doing in May.'

As they talked, Kate suddenly connected the time when she'd lain on Gordon's bed in his arms with the fact of her pregnancy. 'You must think I'm a fool,' she said, but the doctor replied, 'No, lassie, just innocent, and he took advantage of ye.'

'No he didn't,' Kate said quickly. 'He was just kind and – and loving. He comforted me.'

The doctor patted her shoulder. 'Then ye were lucky, lassie,' he said. 'But he must face his responsibilities. Is he still about?'

'No, he's on secret work. He comes and goes,' Kate said.

The doctor said grimly, 'Well, the next time he comes, tell him I want a word with him. Who else have ye got apart from her?' and he jerked his head at the door to Mildred's bedroom.

Kate said slowly, 'Only another aunt, and my sister who lives with her, but Aunt Beattie is dying too and they are in trouble.'

'All the more reason for me to see that young man as soon as possible,' the doctor said. 'I can't get you any help, but be as careful as you can lifting her.'

By the following afternoon, when the doctor returned, Mildred was unconscious. He shook his head. 'She won't come out of this, lassie,' he said. 'Who looks after her affairs? You'd better let them know.'

'I don't know,' Kate said. 'She liked to keep her affairs to herself.'

'Then you'd better find out. Look through her papers. Are you sure there's no one you can call on?' Kate shook her head. 'And there's no sign of the young man?' Again Kate shook her head, and the doctor urged her to look through Mildred's papers right away. 'And as soon as you see that young man, send him to me,' he said.

Kate could do nothing for her aunt, and feeling guilty and shamefaced, she went into the office and began to look through the papers. The drawers of the desk were locked, but she found the keys and eventually discovered a letter from a firm of solicitors in North John Street.

She longed for Gordon's return, but he had said that with the war nearing its end he would be busier than ever for a while. She was not dismayed about the coming baby. On the contrary, she was pleased, feeling that it would be someone belonging to her. She only wished that it could have been Henry's child.

Gordon had been in a dilemma wondering whether to clinch things by marrying Kate or wait to see what happened when the old aunt finally died. Better perhaps to wait to see just what she was worth, although of course there was also the other rich old aunt too.

He thought of Kate's condition, which she surely must know about by now, and decided to keep in touch with her but do nothing in haste. He wrote from Manchester, saying that he hoped that Kate was not working too hard and trying to eat more. 'It seems the war will soon be over,' he wrote. 'Then I will be finished with this work and free to marry and settle down with you, Kate.' He gave a box number for a reply and enclosed ten pounds for his rent.

When Kate returned to her aunt after finding the solicitor's address, Mildred was moving her head restlessly and plucking at the bedclothes. Kate was bathing her face when the doctor appeared with a short, squat woman. 'This is Mrs Ludlow,' he told Kate. 'She's not a nurse but she's had a lot of experience and she can help you with your aunt.'

He took the solicitor's letter and told Kate to rest on her bed. 'She won't be long now,' he said.

Kate had only rested for an hour when Mrs Ludlow called her. Mildred was making a strange noise which Mrs Ludlow said was the death rattle. 'I've been at plenty of deathbeds,' she said. 'Nothing to worry about.'

When Mildred eventually lay still, Mrs Ludlow said briskly,

'She's gone, love. Have you got clean linen so we can lay her out?'

Kate brought the linen and did as instructed by Mrs Ludlow. As they slipped a clean nightdress on to Mildred's body she said impulsively, 'I'm so glad you're here. I had no idea what to do.'

'That's what Dr Mac said. I was in the middle of me washing but he made me leave it. Nobody doesn't dare say no to him when he's got the bit between his teeth.' She laughed.

'He's been very kind to me,' Kate said.

She soon had even more reason to be grateful to the doctor. Later in the day, Mildred's solicitor arrived, closely followed by an undertaker, both sent by Dr McAndrew.

The undertaker guided Kate through the arrangements that needed to be made for the funeral, while the solicitor went rapidly through the drawers and pigeonholes of Mildred's desk and studied her account books. He found the deeds of her parents' grave, but nothing about her husband, and it was decided that she would be buried with her parents and Kate's mother in Anfield Cemetery.

After the undertaker had gone, the solicitor opened the safe. As he studied the documents he'd taken from it he grew increasingly serious. Finally he put the papers in his briefcase, along with documents from the desk. 'Have you any money of your own, Miss Drew?' he asked. Kate told him about her savings account and the unspent wages in her room.

There was money in a linen bag in a cash box, and he took it out. 'I think this is rightly yours,' he said. 'Money owed to you in wages and disbursements, and there will be other expenses. There's forty pounds there. If you will just sign this, and then I suggest you put most of it in your savings account.' It was some years before Kate was to realise the kindness she had been shown by this usually meticulous professional man.

Before the solicitor left he told Kate that he would study the papers and the will and speak to her again after the funeral, which he would attend.

When the letter from Gordon had arrived, Kate had proudly showed it to Dr McAndrew, who had come to see her. He had seemed relieved although concerned about the box number. He was concerned that Kate was alone in the house, but she told him that she was not nervous. Secretly she hoped that Gordon might slip in to see her.

She wrote to Beattie about Mildred's death and the funeral, and Beattie sent an elaborate sympathy card and a wreath, and Essy to represent her at the funeral. Kate omitted to write to Lottie because she had told the Dysons about the funeral. Lottie was deeply offended and refused to take the time off for the funeral offered by her employers. The Barry sisters sent a wreath, including Lottie's name on the card without her knowledge.

Essy arrived early on the morning of the funeral and sat with Kate in the kitchen drinking tea. She told Kate that Beattie was taking a small house in Woolton. 'Madam wants to move away from all her friends,' she said. 'Can't bear them to pity her. I'll be with her, of course, but we'll only have a cook-general and a daily woman. Not what madam's been used to at all.'

'What about Rose?' Kate asked, and Essy sniffed.

'You may well ask. Your sister's been no better than she should be all these years, in my opinion, going about with any Tom, Dick or Harry in officer's uniform, but now if you please she's decided to marry Robert Willis. More fool him, I say.'

'Is that the older man with the lame leg?' Kate asked.

'Yes, he's hung after her for years, but he's got plenty of money, so now he suits, and she's fallen on her feet, as usual.'

'Poor Aunt Beattie,' said Kate, thinking of her aunt's kindness to her.

'Yes, nothing worse than ingratitude,' said Essy. 'I always said your sister was selfish, but madam wouldn't have it. She was always too trusting, poor lady. Well, at least she'll always have me, and Rose'll be paid back some day. God is not mocked.' Kate thought it wise to say nothing.

Essy had realised immediately that Kate was pregnant, but said nothing about it to Kate, or at that time to Beattie, and neither did Kate.

Chapter Sixteen

Rose would not have agreed that she was fortunate and felt that she had been badly treated by fate. 'Nothing ever goes right for me,' she told Robert Willis. 'Losing first my father then my mother when I was only a child, and falling into the clutches of Aunt Beattie.'

'But your aunt loves you deeply,' Robert protested. 'She's always done her best for you.'

Rose pouted. 'Best for herself, you mean. A neighbour once said Aunt Beattie wanted me for a toy, and she was right. She's taken about as much account of *my* feelings and wishes as if I really was a toy.'

Robert was a small, slight man, only inches taller than Rose due to the childhood illness which had left him lame, but he had a thin, intelligent face and a firm jaw. Much as he loved Rose, he would never agree with her if he thought she was wrong.

Now he said firmly, 'This has been a terrible blow to your aunt, Rose, having to leave this house. She feels it as much for you as she does for herself. She told me so, and that she'd always done her best for you.'

'She would,' said Rose. 'She might even believe it, but it's just not true. I have a good brain, Robert. My headmistress wanted me to go on to university. I could have been a doctor or a politician, anything, and been independent, and then none of this would have mattered.'

Tears filled her eyes and ran down her cheeks, but she never became red-eyed and blotched as Kate did, and Robert took her in his arms and tenderly wiped away the tears.

Once again he proposed to her, as he had done so often before, but this time she accepted him. 'I feel safe with you,

Robert,' she said, nestling into his arms, and although he smiled ruefully he was filled with joy. The wedding was arranged for the third week in November so that Rose could be married from Greenfields.

Rose felt it as a grievance for many years that the war ended only a week before the wedding. She went with Robert to join the exultant throngs celebrating in Lime Street, and he stayed firmly by her side throughout. She was thus unable to have the uninhibited good time she would have had with her girlfriends if the war had ended sooner.

The fact that they were officially in mourning for Mildred also overshadowed the wedding in her eyes, and was another cause for complaint. 'I was so beautiful,' she often sighed in later years. 'At any other time it would have been the wedding of the year.'

The move from Greenfields was made early in January. Robert had taken most of the responsibility from Beattie, and with a sensible man to deal with instead of a hostile and often hysterical woman, the solicitor was able to deal rapidly with the details.

Rose had stayed away from Greenfields, saying that she was too busy settling into her new home in Sandfield Park, but at Robert's insistence she accompanied Beattie to her new home in Woolton. Essy was waiting for them in the small house, which had been made as comfortable as possible with Beattie's treasured possessions. Robert remained at Greenfields to attend to matters there.

Beattie had wept all the way in the cab, and Rose had comforted her. Now Essy watched grimly as Rose assisted her aunt into the house, brushing Essy aside, then exerted herself to charm and console the old lady. 'There's so much to do in Robert's house and it's all so new to me,' she told Beattie. 'I'll need your advice, Auntie. I haven't got anyone like Essy to help *me*.' She flashed a smile at Essy, but the maid remained unmoved.

When Robert arrived to take Rose home, Beattie collapsed into grateful tears. 'What would I have done without you, Robert? You've been so good to me,' she wept. 'And my darling Rose, so kind, helping me through this dreadful day.'

She held Rose's hand, and Rose bent and pressed her cheek against Beattie's. Robert smiled proudly.

Essy watched Rose holding her aunt's hand, her husband's arm around her while he smiled tenderly at her, and thought of Kate alone in the deserted guesthouse. Her own sister, but never even given a thought by Rose. She'd treat madam the same way if her husband would let her, but for now it suited her to smarm her way round her. I'll make sure madam sees through her, though, thought Essy.

Mildred's solicitor, Mr Burton, came to her funeral, then back to the house, and as soon as Essy had gone he took out his briefcase. 'I believe that you've heard from your fiancé, Miss Drew,' he said. 'That makes my task much easier. I'm afraid that although you are named as beneficiary in your aunt's will, Mrs Williams left little but debts.'

'Debts!' Kate echoed blankly.

'Yes, if this house and its contents are sold there will be enough to pay the debts, but very little left, so I'm glad that your future is secure,' he said. Kate sat in stunned silence while he explained. 'Mrs Williams gambled in stocks and shares. According to my uncle, our senior partner, her father did also. Sometimes they did very well, at other times they lost, and I'm afraid that the war has meant that Mrs Williams has lost steadily for some years.'

'I didn't know,' Kate murmured. 'My aunt never discussed her business affairs with me.'

'A pity,' the solicitor said. 'She remortgaged the house but fortunately not for its full value, and houses will be at a premium now. I'll need to make an inventory, but that can wait for a few days.' He smiled at Kate. 'A disappointment, but fortunately your future is assured, Dr McAndrew tells me. May I wish you every happiness, Miss Drew.'

Kate smiled and shook hands, wondering what exactly the doctor had told him. No wonder Mildred would tell me nothing, she thought, but she was not worried, confident that Gordon would soon return. She had written again to the box number, telling him of Mildred's death and her debts.

For Kate, the end of the war meant mainly the end of Gordon's secret work and his speedy return to her. Dr

McAndrew called from time to time, and Kate began to dread telling him that Gordon had not arrived, although she still believed that he would.

But Kate's letter about the baby and Beattie's troubles had alarmed Gordon, and when she wrote about Mildred's tangled affairs he decided that the time had come to move on.

He cancelled the box number, emptied his safe deposit box at the bank and travelled to Hull. In a busy port with a shifting population it would be easier to merge and reappear with a new name and a new identity, he thought. He still had most of the money he had brought from London, and had added to it by robbery in Liverpool and Manchester. There would be no need to sell the stolen jewellery just yet. When the time was right he would move back to London.

Kate's pregnancy was still not obvious, although she was nearly seven months gone, but the doctor decided that something must be done. Although he and Mr Burton thought that Gordon had vanished, he said nothing to disillusion Kate. Instead he said kindly, 'You must leave here soon, Kate. I've arranged for you to stay in a mother and baby home until the child is born.'

'But what if Gordon comes back and I'm not here?' Kate said in dismay.

The doctor looked sceptical but he only said, 'You can send your new address to Manchester, and I'll also leave it with Mr Burton. You can't just drift on, Kate. Some arrangements must be made.'

'I know, Doctor,' Kate said humbly. 'I just can't seem to think straight lately.' She showed him a letter from the solicitor which told her that the house would soon be sold and advised her to make her own plans.

'Yes, well, it had to come,' he said. 'Now, the home is run by the Salvation Army, and they have a nursing home for private patients too. The girls in the home pay for their keep by doing the domestic work of the nursing home. You won't object to doing that, will you, Kate?'

'Of course not,' Kate said. 'Thank you, Doctor.'

'Good. We've got to consider the baby. You'll both be

looked after there.' Dr McAndrew added that he would arrange for her to enter the home on the following Monday.

Some of the girls in the home resented having to work for the more fortunate mothers in the nursing home, but Kate was pleased to be able to earn her keep. Mr Burton told her that after everything was settled there would be a small nest egg for her for after the baby's birth. Babies were usually adopted from the home, but Kate was determined to keep hers.

Kate's baby was born on New Year's Day, tiny and perfectly formed but stillborn. He was so tiny that he fitted into the palm of the midwife, who said sympathetically to Kate, 'God has been good to you. Even if he survived he could never have lived a normal life. Better to lose him now.' The woman who was helping added piously, 'Praise the Lord. He has given and He has taken away. Blessed be the name of the Lord.'

Kate said nothing but only held out her cupped hands, and the midwife placed the baby in them. She sat gazing at her tiny son as though to imprint his image on her brain, until the midwife took him back. 'Can he be baptised?' Kate asked. 'I'd like him called Gordon,' and the woman murmured agreement.

Dr McAndrew came to see Kate and she asked him if she had contributed to the baby's death. 'I didn't eat enough. I didn't know,' she said, but he assured her that she was not to blame.

'A baby takes what he needs from the mother even at the expense of the mother's health,' he said. 'There was something wrong from the start. I'm surprised you went so near to your full term.'

He told her that he had found her a job as an orderly in a nursing home in Waterloo. 'And before you ask, I've given Burton the address,' he said.

'Is it with babies?' Kate asked.

'No. You want to get away from babies for a while,' he said. 'It's for elderly people and rich hypochondriacs. I don't know what orderly means. Probably a general dogsbody, but it'll give you a breathing space while you look around.' Neither of them realised then that the breathing space would stretch to ten years.

Kate settled quickly into her new job, and was so willing and pleasant that she was soon a general favourite with staff and patients alike. It was only when she was alone that she grieved for her tiny baby, and for Gordon. She was now convinced that he had been killed in the course of his secret dangerous work, but she felt none of the intensity of grief for him that she had felt at Henry's death. Gradually the sharpness of her sorrow for Henry faded, and he became again a dear memory which brought her comfort.

Kate had long come to terms with her rejection by Rose. She had found the old hat and jacket in Gordon's wardrobe when she was clearing the house, and for the first time remembered how she had been dressed on that fateful day. Rose might not even have recognised her, she thought. Nevertheless, neither Rose nor Beattie had made any contact with her, and in her present circumstances Kate was too proud to get in touch with them.

She had written to both Josie and Nell to explain her silence and received affectionate letters by return of post. Josie reproached her for not telling her sooner. 'You know I would have come to you,' she wrote. 'Michael sends his love and is as upset as me that you went through that on your own. I'd like to box Lottie's ears.' Nell, who was now a district nurse, wrote that she wished she had followed her instincts and come to look for Kate, and she urged her to keep in touch. 'If not, I'll come down on you like the wrath of God,' she wrote.

The work was hard and the pay low in Kate's new job, but she had always worked hard and her wants were few, so she settled down contentedly, deciding that one phase of her life was over and this quiet life suited her. She liked the situation of the nursing home, close to the sandy shore of Waterloo. Often she walked there, gathering shells for a resident who did shell work, or watched the magnificent sunsets over the Mersey estuary. Other times when she was off duty she walked up to the Carnegie Library in College

Road. She enjoyed being able to read in peace without the constant demands of the guesthouse, and she and Nell exchanged their views on the books in their letters.

A few of the patients were arrogant and demanding, but Kate's inner serenity made it possible for her to bear with them, and she liked most of the residents. Patients and staff came and went but Kate lived there happily for nearly ten years. During that time she went twice to Ireland for holidays with Josie and her growing family.

Michael met her off the boat from Liverpool with a donkey and trap, and when they arrived at the farm Kate could see why Josie was so happy. The affection of all the family was poured out on Kate too, and Michael's mother pressed food on her every time she saw her. 'I've always been thin,' Kate protested, but old Mrs Malloy was unconvinced. Kate thoroughly enjoyed herself and was happy for Josie.

By the time of her first visit Josie had a son and a daughter, and by the next holiday twin boys had been added. Later there were two more girls, and Kate was regarded as an aunt by all of them. Kate's only sadness was the rift with Rose and Beattie, but she felt that it was their choice and was too proud to try to mend the breach.

During the years before his marriage Robert had been only on the periphery of Rose's life, and he had never met Kate. He knew that Rose had a sister who made brief, infrequent visits, but that the aunt she lived with never visited. At the time of Mildred's funeral Beattie tearfully told Robert that Mildred had been very unkind to her and had cut herself off for no reason.

Robert asked Rose about Kate, but she only said briefly, 'She's very like Aunt Mildred and I think she's become as odd as her too. She never comes here now.' Tears threatened every time Robert mentioned Kate, so he avoided the subject, thinking that a family quarrel was not his business. It was her own guilty conscience which made Rose unwilling to talk about Kate but Robert was unaware of that.

Rose believed that when she was married she would have everything her own way because Robert was so besotted with her, and he was certainly a most indulgent husband, until his principles were involved. Then he was unbending, and Rose was surprised to find herself meekly agreeing to act according to his high standards.

She had intended to drop visits to Beattie after her move to the smaller house in Woolton. 'Every time she sees me she bursts into tears. Might keep her drier if I stay away,' she said flippantly, but Robert did not smile.

'It must be very hard for your aunt to adjust, Rose,' he said quietly. 'She needs our visits. We'll go on Sunday.'

Rose was annoyed, yet her respect for Robert grew, and she quickly learned to hide the cynical, worldly side of her character from him.

Beattie was pathetically grateful for the visits, and it was second nature to Rose to charm whoever she was with, but Essy was not fooled. She watched Rose grimly and never missed an opportunity to criticise the girl when she was alone with Beattie.

Rose and Robert's first son was born in July 1920. Robert had been intensely worried about Rose during her pregnancy. He surrounded her with every possible luxury and consulted an eminent doctor about her.

The doctor was unsympathetic. 'She's a perfectly healthy young woman,' he said. 'There's no need for all this fuss. Pregnancy is not an illness. All she needs is more exercise.'

Robert gave Rose an edited version of the doctor's remarks and she was very indignant. 'Only a man would talk like that,' she declared. 'I know how ill I feel.' She wanted Robert to change to another doctor, but he told her that the man he had consulted was at the top of his profession, with top fees.

'You know I want only the best for you, darling,' he said. 'Trust me.'

Rose agreed, pleased to be able to boast of her top doctor to her friends. She was in a different set now, the young married wives of successful local businessmen, and some of them were frankly envious of the luxury surrounding Rose. 'Almost worth having a baby for all this,' one said to her, but Rose replied plaintively, 'It's easy to see that you've never had one.'

After the birth of the baby, who was christened Richard Robert, Rose was slow to recover. She had a monthly nurse to care for her and the baby, but even after she left her bed, Rose only lay all day on a sofa in a becoming gown. Robert paid the nurse handsomely to stay for another month, but the doctor told him bluntly that he was wrong.

'She's not well. She has no strength,' Robert protested.

'No,' agreed the doctor, 'and she won't have while she lies about all day doing nothing.'

'Don't suggest exercise,' Robert begged.

'No, I'm going to suggest you plan an outing. A dance, visit to the theatre, supper party, anything which will make your wife want to get up and get dressed for it.'

Robert believed that Rose truly felt ill, but he had great respect for the doctor's opinion, and he told Rose that some friends were planning a visit to the Empire Theatre, followed by a supper party. 'I don't know whether you feel up to it,' he said. 'It's not until next week.'

Rose declared that by that time she would make it, and she did. 'Mind over matter,' she said gaily to her friends, and Robert watched her indulgently.

Two years later a second son was born and christened John Arthur, after Rose's father and Beattie's husband, as Robert's father had also been Robert.

'That's all Mr Willis's doing, those names,' Essy told Beattie. 'Rose wouldn't have thought of remembering your husband and giving you that pleasure, madam.'

'No, I'm afraid she's changed, Essy,' sighed Beattie. 'She was such a loving little girl.'

'Maybe you're seeing her more clear,' said Essy. 'One thing's for sure. She's done well out of her marriage. She'll never want.'

'And she's got a wonderful husband,' Beattie said. 'Such a kind man.'

'Yes, he's pure gold,' Essy agreed, and said no more about Rose on that occasion.

It was usually Robert who brought her great-nephews to see Beattie, although Rose came occasionally and was invariably charming. She made Beattie very welcome when she visited them at Christmas or on special occasions.

As the years passed Beattie's imaginary ailments became more real, and when her increasing weight and failing heart made it impossible for her to leave her house, Robert insisted that they spent Christmas with her. The boys found their great-aunt's wheezing and her announcements that she was not long for this world alarming, but Essy was their firm friend.

In spite of these forecasts and her obvious ill health, it was still a shock to everybody when Beattie died in her sleep in November 1929. Robert was the executor of her will, so he took charge of the funeral arrangements. He consulted Essy about Beattie's wishes, and with a defiant look at Rose the maid said belligerently, 'I think Kate should be asked. Madam would like her to be there. She often talked about Kate during the last few years.'

'Kate. Your sister,' Robert said to Rose with surprise. 'I wish I'd known, Essy. I'd have tried to trace her. I wonder why Mrs Anderson said nothing to us.'

'Probably didn't want to upset Mrs Willis, sir,' said Essy recklessly.

'Me! What's it got to do with me?' said Rose. 'It was Kate who stopped visiting us. I'm sure Aunt Beattie would have said if she'd really wanted to see her. Lord knows where she is now anyway.'

'Madam would want her at her funeral,' Essy said stubbornly, and Robert promised to try to trace her.

She was easy to find, as Essy knew the name of Mildred's solicitor. Robert wrote to Kate, then went to see her. He had subconsciously expected someone like Rose, so it was a shock when a thin, plain woman wearing steel-rimmed glasses came timidly into the room where he waited. Kate's straight mousy hair had been badly cut and wisps fell over her face. Robert noticed that the hand she held out to him was red and roughened by hard work, but when she smiled the sweetness of her expression and the direct look from her large hazel eyes disarmed him, and he no longer thought of her as plain.

'Miss Drew? Kate?' he said, taking her hand.

She replied in a gentle voice, 'Yes, and you must be Rose's husband. I'm so sorry about Aunt Beattie. Did she suffer much?'

'She'd been an invalid for some time, but she died peacefully in her sleep,' he said.

'And you said in your letter that Essy was with her to the end. I'm glad about that,' Kate said simply. 'She'd looked after her for so long.'

'Essy believes that your aunt would have liked you to attend her funeral,' Robert said cautiously. 'And Rose and I would like you to be there.'

Kate's face lit up. 'I will very gladly,' she said eagerly. 'How is Rose?'

'Very well,' he said. 'Kept very busy with our two boys.' He felt uncomfortable not knowing what lay behind the rift and was afraid of saying the wrong thing, but Kate looked at him and said honestly, 'I'm sorry I didn't see Aunt Beattie before she died. My own pride, I'm afraid, because of my circumstances, but I'll be pleased to attend her funeral.'

Robert asked Kate to come to their house to see Rose and meet the boys before the funeral, and she agreed 'as long as Rose wants me to', so he arranged to collect her. Rose was not pleased, but unsure what Robert had been told, she agreed to welcome Kate.

Kate had bought a good black dress and coat and a small black hat for the funeral, and she wore them to visit Rose. As soon as the sisters saw each other the years fell away and they hugged each other and wept. Nothing was said about the years apart, or the long-ago incident in Bold Street which had caused the separation.

There was instant rapport between Kate and the two boys. She was introduced as Aunt Kate, and seven-year-old John asked innocently, 'Are you instead of Aunt Beattie?'

His elder brother, nine-year-old Richard, pushed John and smiled at Kate. 'Aunt Kate's not in place of anybody, idiot. She's here for herself,' he said, and found a place in Kate's heart which he never lost, although she deeply loved both boys.

On the day of the funeral Robert brought Essy from Woolton to Sandfield Park. She attached herself to Kate, and to Kate's embarrassment began to tell her in a loud whisper how badly Rose had treated her aunt. Kate tried to divert her by asking about Beattie's health in her later years, and by the time Essy had told her, it was time to leave for the funeral, much to Kate's relief.

Beattie's will was a surprise. Although not as rich as before, once Greenfields had been sold and her affairs settled she had been reasonably wealthy. She left the bulk of her money to be divided equally between young Richard and John, her jewellery to Rose, and her house and contents and an annuity to Essy. She also left one thousand pounds 'to my dear niece Katherine Drew', and Kate was deeply touched at this evidence that Beattie had remembered her with love.

Beattie had already given Robert her husband's gold hunter watch, his gold cuff links and pearl tiepin and his silver-backed hairbrushes, but she left him her grateful love for his affection and care for her during her last years. There was no mention of Rose, and she was furious. 'She was influenced,' she raged to Robert. 'Her house to *Essy* and that money for Kate. Nothing for me for running round after her like a lapdog for years.'

'She left you her jewellery,' Robert said mildly. 'She knew we don't need money, Rose, and she was generous to our boys.'

'But her house and furniture to Essy, who was her *servant*. It's an insult to me,' Rose snapped.

'Essy was more than a servant. You know that, Rose. She was your aunt's devoted friend for many years.'

'And my enemy,' Rose muttered.

Robert said firmly, 'I'm pleased that your aunt has left her house to Essy. She deserves it. She devoted her life to Beattie and you wouldn't want her to be left homeless, would you?'

Rose knew that note in his voice and said no more, and Robert added gently, 'At least this has brought you and your sister together again. The boys are delighted with her, aren't they?'

The two boys were weekly boarders at a preparatory school near Parkgate on the Wirral side of the River Mersey. At first Kate avoided visiting when they were home at weekends, thinking that they would wish to be alone with their parents, but the boys were disappointed if she was not there, and she was soon easily persuaded to spend Sundays at the Willis house when she was off duty.

Rose was a little jealous of the instant affection between Kate and the boys, although pleased that Kate would play boisterous games with them which she herself disliked doing. Richard was tall for his age, with straight dark hair, and features and temperament very like his father's, but John was fair and blue-eyed, an extrovert and happy child.

'They're not at all alike, are they?' Kate said one day to Rose as they sat in the garden, watching the boys.

'No. Seems to be the pattern in our family,' said Rose. '*We're* not at all alike.'

'No, and neither were Mildred and Beattie,' agreed Kate.

'They were alike in some ways,' Rose said. 'They both had imaginary illnesses and were secretive about money. And let us down because they were useless at looking after it,' she added bitterly.

'Oh Rose,' Kate protested, but they looked at each other and laughed. Rose was pleased to have her sister's companionship again. She could say anything to Kate, no matter how outrageous, things she would hesitate to say to Robert because she wanted to keep his good opinion. She was sure that in Kate's eyes she could do no wrong.

Kate's love for Rose was not as blind and uncritical as Rose supposed, but to Kate she would always be the sweet and affectionate sister she had been when they were children together. Any bitterness or selfishness Rose showed now, Kate attributed to the life she had led and the people she had mixed with since they were parted.

The sweet and loving side of Rose's character was not lost, and she showed it often to Kate in response to her sister's deep love for her. They were both very happy to be reunited.

Chapter Seventeen

Robert had been appalled to find how hard Kate worked and how menial her job was, and he urged her to leave it at once. 'There's no need for you to work, Kate, now that you are reunited with your family,' he said, but Kate told him that Beattie's legacy would make it possible for her to realise a dream.

'The money Aunt Mildred left me is there for my old age,' she said, 'but Beattie's legacy means I can afford to work for nothing but my board and lodging.' She told him of a home for unmarried mothers run by a local charity. They could not afford to pay wages, only provide board and lodging, and Kate had always wanted to work there.

'But what would you do?' Robert said doubtfully.

'Not cleaning,' said Kate. 'Helping the girls to settle in when they first come. Some of them are suicidal and they're all upset. I've been doing that sometimes in my time off. If I was there full time I could help with the babies too.'

'If that's what you want, Kate,' Robert said, recognising her need for independence. 'But remember you'll always have a home with us if you want it. I hope you'll come to us often anyway. Rose will need you, especially when the boys go away to their main school.'

Kate was warmly welcomed at the home, as they knew she had a gift for calming and comforting the girls when they arrived. They were often distraught and fearful, rejected first by the fathers of their babies then by their families. Kate drew on her own experience to help them, and she was particularly happy when she could work with the babies.

She visited Rose and Robert often, and when Richard went away to his father's old school she was there to comfort Rose. 'It's not right. He's far too young to go away from home,' Rose raged.

'But all his friends will go, and he'll be at a disadvantage later in life if he doesn't,' Robert said.

Rose replied angrily, 'Then someone should have the courage to break the pattern. We're not a flock of sheep.' Kate agreed with her, although she said nothing, but Richard made no complaint.

John was still coming home for weekends, but two years later, when he followed his brother to school, Robert took Rose away on a cruise in the Mediterranean. She had often talked of her cruise with Beattie and how much more she could have enjoyed it if she had not been at Beattie's beck and call, and Robert thought that a holiday now would console her for her sons' absence.

He was pleased to see how much Rose enjoyed herself, and she told him it had been a good idea. 'You're so thoughtful darling,' she said. When she was alone with Kate, however, she complained that it had not come up to her expectations.

'Cruises are best for young, single people. They're the ones who really have a good time, unless they're tied to a demanding relative like I was with Beattie. Now it's all too late for me, an old married woman of nearly forty,' she said tragically.

'Don't say that, Rose. I can't think of you as being forty,' Kate said. 'Although I don't think it matters anyway. I must say, I don't feel any different now *I'm* forty.'

'It matters on board ship,' said Rose.

'I'll bet you charmed them just the same,' Kate teased her. 'In spite of your great age.'

Rose smiled complacently. 'I was never short of partners for dancing or anything else,' she said. 'And a couple of ship's officers tried to flirt with me.'

Kate looked thoughtful. 'You know, Rose, Mama must have only been about our age when she died, and the aunts

254

only a few years older. They seemed so ancient to me, at Mama's funeral.'

'And to me,' said Rose. 'It was the way they dressed and behaved, too. Mildred worked hard, I know, but Beattie just sat about eating. She went out in the carriage to visit or shop, or she had tea parties here, bridge afternoons and that sort of thing, but she never exerted herself in any way. She would never have dreamed of playing tennis or swimming as I did on the cruise.' She looked at herself in a mirror with a satisfied air.

Robert had a reliable business partner but had always done more than his share in the company, so now he felt free to take Rose on frequent holidays, but they were always at home for the boys' holidays from school. Kate was a welcome visitor then.

'Why don't you go away with Mum and Dad sometimes?' Richard asked Kate one day as they sat in the garden.

'I only have two weeks' holiday,' Kate said, 'and I spent that with my friend Josie in Ireland.'

Richard touched Kate's work-roughened hand. 'Essy says you work far too hard,' he said.

Kate laughed. 'Essy's always worked herself,' she said. 'I'm glad she's having it easier now.'

'I like Miss Clarke, her lodger,' Richard said. 'She's so quiet, and she has that awful hump on her back, but she never grumbles, Essy says. She must be very clever.'

'Yes, she's head of the dressmaking department of a big shop in Bold Street,' Kate agreed. 'She's made me a lovely dress for special occasions, without a pattern or anything.'

Richard looked up in surprise. 'Mummy asked Essy if Miss Clarke would make clothes for her, but she said Miss Clarke doesn't do private sewing.'

'Then we won't say anything about my dress,' said Kate.

'No sense in rocking the boat,' Richard said, sounding so like his father that Kate began to laugh and he joined in, winking at her like a conspirator. A family holiday in Austria was planned, and Richard returned to the subject of Kate coming with them. 'You've never been abroad, have you?' he said.

'No, but I've been to Ireland and Scotland,' Kate said, smiling.

'When did you go to Scotland?' Richard asked.

'Before you were born,' Kate said. 'I went twice,' she added. 'The first time to see a doctor I used to know. He was very kind to me when I needed it most. He'd come out of retirement during the war but when it was over he was put out to grass again, as he put it.'

'What did he mean?' asked Richard.

'He had to retire again, so he went back to Scotland to the place where he was born. I went to see him then, and the second time I went it was for his funeral.'

'That must have been sad for you,' Richard said.

'No, not really,' Kate replied. 'He was very old and in pain, but he'd had a few very happy years and a good life. The last thing he said to me when I saw him on my first visit was that he'd been dealt a good hand.' Richard looked puzzled, and Kate explained, 'He thought life was like a card game. Some people are dealt a good hand and some a bad one, but you have to do your best with the cards you've been dealt.'

They sat in silence for a minute, then Richard said, 'This trip to Austria. One of the masters says this isn't a good time to go there. He says we might find some hostility. He thinks Germany is preparing for war.'

'Surely not!' Kate exclaimed. 'They wouldn't be so mad. Not so soon after the last war, and that was supposed to be the war to end all wars. Don't say anything to your mum, for heaven's sake.'

'That's what Dad said when I asked him about it. Not to say anything to Mum. As if I would! You must all think I'm daft,' Richard said indignantly.

Robert encouraged the boys to visit Essy, and on their next visit Richard spoke to her about the holiday in Austria. 'I wish Aunt Kate was coming with us,' he said. 'She's never

256

been abroad, but Dad says she knows she's welcome so she must decide.'

Essy sniffed. 'He probably knows she'd be just a handrag for your mother,' she said, then, seeing Richard's shocked face, she added quickly, 'That's how it is with Kate. It's how she's been all her life, running after other people.'

'In her work, you mean?' said Richard.

'That as well,' said Essy. 'Her mother was a spoilt girl, her father's favourite then carried round by her husband. When he got killed she just moved the burden to Kate, although she was only a child. Then, when the mother died Kate went as a drudge to Mildred.'

'I thought Aunt Mildred adopted her,' said Richard.

'Oh aye, but nobody ate idle bread in Mildred's house, least of all Kate, and because she was willing, Mildred piled the work on to her. Madam used to worry about her and try to help her. She was always kind, poor lady.' Essy wiped away a tear.

'Aunt Kate always seems happy in a quiet way, though, doesn't she?' said Richard.

'Yes, that's one way she's been blessed,' said Essy. 'She always sees the best in people and she's never sorry for herself, yet your mother—' She thought better of whatever she had been about to say, and exclaimed instead, 'Look at your John!' And she bustled into the garden, followed by Richard, and began to call John down from the tree he had climbed.

John had nearly reached the top of the tree and was now crawling along one of the branches. 'I just want to try this,' he called. 'See if I can lie along it like the cat.' He lay flat, but the branch began to sway ominously.

Essy screamed, and Richard shouted, 'Come down, you barmy coot. You're heavier than a cat and you haven't got claws.'

As John began to climb down, Essy said faintly, 'He'll be the death of me. Your mam would never forgive me if anything happened to him, but he doesn't know what fear is. I don't know what's to become of him.'

Richard laughed. 'Don't worry, Essy. He'll either be

a mountaineer or a cat burglar, but he'll enjoy himself whatever he does,' he said.

Kate often visited Essy, partly to escape from the surroundings of the home where she now worked. It was situated near the docks at Bootle, among mean streets where it seemed to Kate there were as many barefooted children and hopeless, out-of-work men as in her childhood, and she missed her walks around the pleasant area of Waterloo.

As so often happens, after first hearing about war rumours from Richard, Kate then heard them from various sources. She asked the opinion of the handyman at the home, a surly man with only one eye and a badly scarred face due to war injury. He had lost his wife and two sons in the influenza epidemic of 1919, and he agreed with her that war was unlikely.

'If my lads had lived I wouldn't let them fight, and there's plenty like me. We seen the way we was just cannon fodder in the last one and not wanted when it was over. Anyhow, the young ones now aren't mugs like we were. They know more with the wireless and that.'

'That's what I said,' Kate said eagerly. 'Nobody would be stupid enough to want another war so soon.'

'Some'll want it,' the man said. 'Them that'd make money outa it, but they can do their own fighting this time.'

Kate also spoke about the rumours when she was alone with Robert, and she was dismayed when he told her that trade was picking up and that he thought it was because the country was re-arming. 'It doesn't necessarily mean war, though, Kate,' he said. 'Just being prepared and letting other countries know that we are.'

'Joe Taggart, the handyman, says men won't fight this time. He thinks young men will remember how their fathers were treated after the last war and refuse to fight,' said Kate.

'I'm afraid I don't agree. There's still a lot of goodwill and patriotism in the country, in spite of all our troubles. Remember the celebrations for the Silver Jubilee?'

'Yes, flags and parties even in the poorest streets,' Kate agreed. 'Everyone liked King George and Queen Mary.'

'I had great respect for him myself,' said Robert. 'For both of them. Their family life and those down-to-earth Christmas broadcasts. There was real grief when he died. But it's not only royalty. In '32, when the government asked people to pay income tax promptly to help the economy, income tax offices were besieged from New Year's Day onwards by people wanting to pay.' He smiled at Kate. 'Revolution is not the English way, Kate. We'll muddle through somehow, as we always do.'

Kate smiled at him, feeling reassured, and though she was relieved when the family returned safely from Austria, she was not unduly worried while they were away.

Although Kate was sure that Robert was right and she was happy to forget the talk of another war, she found that it had revived her memories of the first, which people were now calling the Great War. During the night, if she was unable to sleep, she remembered those years when it seemed her life had been dominated by her fear for Henry and those awful casualty lists in the *Echo*. She recalled searching down them every night, and then the horror of seeing Henry's name there, and all that had followed.

Eighteen years ago, but still as vivid to Kate as if it was yesterday. The memory of Henry was always with her, but usually as a comfort, especially when she was feeling lonely or discouraged. Now, though, her thoughts were all of her terrible grief at his death.

One night as she lay unable to sleep, it occurred to her that Henry's son would be old enough to fight if war came now. She switched on the light and looked at the snapshot of Henry with the smiling baby in his arms. Impossible to think of the little boy as a man, perhaps in uniform like his father. Kate had never seen the child, as Agnes had left the district after Henry's death, and Kate later heard that she had remarried. It was a relief when daylight came and other cares drove out the fears of the night.

In December the hints of impending war were swept from the newspapers and from the minds of most people by news of a romance between King Edward VIII and a twice-divorced American, Mrs Simpson. The country was bitterly divided on the question of whether or not they should marry.

Kate had always admired the King when, as Prince of Wales, he had founded occupational centres for the unemployed, and made unannounced visits to mining villages and seen the misery there. 'Something must be done,' he had said, and she had hoped that as King he would do something about the misery she saw in the slums around the home.

Kate and Robert often discussed matters which neither of them would mention to Rose because they both felt an instinctive desire to shield her from anything worrying or unpleasant. The King and Mrs Simpson, however, was a topic which Kate could discuss with her sister, and they agreed that the politicians and churchmen involved were hypocrites in condemning the King.

'I think Baldwin and that crew are afraid he'll go too deeply into things they want covered up, like the state of the mining villages,' Kate declared. 'They want him out because he's too independent.'

Rose agreed. 'And the Archbishop of Canterbury saying it's a question of religion and morals,' she said. 'If he behaved like his grandfather, Edward VII, and married some foreign royalty for an heir and took Mrs Simpson as a mistress, they would say nothing.'

'Yes, the churchmen never condemn society people when they have these country house parties with connecting doors to the bedrooms of men and women who are married to other people, do they?' Kate said.

'Exactly. The King's got more principles. He wants to marry her,' said Rose. 'Mind you, Kate, I wouldn't agree with her for Queen, and I don't think many people would.'

'Oh, heavens, *no*,' said Kate.

Robert listened in amazement at the extent of their knowledge, but wisely said nothing.

All speculation was ended when on 11 December Edward

VIII announced his abdication in a moving message on the wireless.

The newspapers again carried reports of trouble abroad and the danger of war, but few people took them seriously. Even the sight on Pathé News in cinemas of enormous rallies in Germany presided over by Herr Hitler only amused people because of his resemblance to the comedian Charlie Chaplin.

Kate was too busy at the home to pay any attention to the news. The charity employed a cook but could only pay a pittance, and cooks never stayed very long. Volunteers who came to help were not reliable, and Kate found that she was spending more and more of her time in the kitchen.

She enjoyed cooking and was willing to help out in an emergency, but it left less time for her other duties. She wanted to be free to help the girls at the most traumatic part of their stay in the home, when their babies were six weeks old and had to be handed over for adoption.

Many of the girls when they first arrived, homeless and desperate, saw adoption as the solution to their plight, although some resisted the idea, but once their babies were born, all the girls wanted to keep them. Kate thought it was a refinement of cruelty that the babies stayed with the mothers for six weeks, to be breast-fed for two weeks then weaned by the time they were handed over for adoption.

She said so to the committee of charitable ladies who administered the home, but they did not agree. 'We must be practical, Miss Drew,' they told her kindly. 'At six weeks the babies are settled into a routine so it's easier for the adoptive mother, and by that time the girls have got over the birth and are ready to start their lives again.'

'But by six weeks the girls are attached to the babies and the babies to them,' Kate said. 'If they have to be separated it should be right away,' but the ladies told her that she was mistaken. They were acting for the best for everybody, and the rules remained the same.

All Kate could do was try to comfort the girls when the

time came for parting. 'I'm not going to hand him over,' a girl named Marie sobbed to her. 'They said he'll be going to a good home where he'll have all the things I can't give him, but how do I know how they'll treat him? Nobody can love him the way I love him. That's more important, isn't it, Kate, even if we have to live in one room.'

'It is, but how will you live, Marie?' said Kate. 'Is there no hope that his father could help?'

Marie was a quiet, reserved girl, and even when helping Kate in the kitchen she had never spoken about the father of her baby. Kate never asked questions but listened and tried to advise the girls when they wanted to confide in her.

'No. He's a teacher. His wife's been in hospital with TB for six years and he's got two little girls, seven and nine. Every penny of his salary is spoken for.'

'It's very difficult, I know,' Kate said. 'We'll have to think of what's best for everyone.'

Marie, calmer now, said, 'Don't think badly of him, Kate. We didn't mean this to happen. I only went to his house about his little girl. I was a teacher too and I felt so sorry for him. He was so lonely and we thought we could just be friends. We let our feelings get too much for us just once, and this is the result.'

'Couldn't you go back to teaching and get someone to look after the baby during the day?' Kate said.

Marie laughed bitterly. 'It's hard enough to get a job when everything's straightforward. I wouldn't have a hope with a year unaccounted for. Anyway, they won't employ married women so they're not likely to take someone who should be married and isn't,' she said.

'Will you see him again?' Kate asked.

'No,' said Marie firmly. 'This is my problem and I'll deal with it. Nick has enough to cope with. We've got to keep it from his wife. It's bad enough for her being separated from him and the children through no fault of her own, and she's got the illness to bear as well. I couldn't do anything to make it worse for her.'

Kate hugged her. 'You're a really nice, good girl,

Marie,' she said. 'You deserve to be happy. Don't give up hope yet.' An idea had been forming in her mind, but before saying anything she discussed it with Robert. After telling him about Marie, she said that she had thought of renting a small house where she and Marie could live. She would look after the baby while Marie worked. 'She's a trained teacher but she'd be willing to work at anything.'

Robert shook his head. 'It wouldn't work, Kate,' he said. 'Any job she could get would be too poorly paid to support two adults and a baby.'

'I don't mean her to support me,' Kate protested. 'I'd pay my share.'

'Yes, but the interest on your money wouldn't be sufficient and you'd have to start using your capital. That would soon be used, Kate. To make a scheme like this viable you'd have to have several girls and their babies, and there'd be numerous difficulties,' Robert said gently.

'I'd thought of that,' said Kate. 'There are other girls in the home like Marie. They would be company for one another and the babies would grow up together.'

'Kate, Kate, think this through,' Robert urged her. 'Make allowances for human nature. The girls would be very protective towards their children and jealous if they fancied you gave more attention to one than another. Then look ahead. When the children were growing up there would be quarrels. Also, although the girls might grasp at this as a short-term solution, the day might come when they would regret it and blame you. If they met another man, for instance, who wouldn't accept their child.'

'It seemed such a simple idea,' Kate said sadly.

Robert patted her hand. 'I'm sorry to have to act as devil's advocate, but I don't want you to be hurt because of your soft heart. You're very dear to all of us you know, Kate.' He smiled at her.

'Thank you,' Kate said. 'And thanks for your advice. I'm glad I was able to discuss it with you.'

'You know that if it was just a question of money I'd help out,' he said. 'I've sailed very close to the wind a few times during the past eight years, but thank God things are on an even keel again now. It's the emotional and practical problems of this idea I'm concerned about.'

'I hadn't thought ahead,' Kate admitted. 'I'm just so sorry for Marie and the other girls.'

'It does credit to your good heart, Kate, but think. It would soon be known why the girls were living with you, and the children would be branded. Other children can be cruel. Adults too, for that matter,' said Robert.

'I know. One of our girls worked in a biscuit factory and she was sacked as soon as they knew about the baby. They said it wouldn't be fair to the other girls to keep her on. She was very bitter. She said to me, "I know lots of the girls went all the way with their boyfriends. They were just more crafty than me."'

Robert was horrified that Kate heard conversations like this and wished that he could shelter her from things as he did Rose, but he only said, 'It's true what they say, "Only the good girls have babies".'

Kate saw the sense in Robert's arguments and reluctantly abandoned the scheme. Marie too had to abandon her plan to keep her baby. It was pointed out to her that she would be selfish to deprive the baby of a good home with a mother and father and every comfort just because she wanted to keep him.

'I suppose it's true, Kate,' she said sadly, 'I couldn't give him those comforts. But the thing that decided me was when one of them said that with me he'd have to go through life with the stigma of being illegitimate. If he was adopted he would never know and neither would anyone else. I've got to do what's best for him, but oh Kate, I don't know how I'll bear it when I have to give him up.'

Kate tried to comfort Marie and did the only thing she could to help. Although it was strictly against the rules she managed to learn the name and address of the adoptive parents and gave the information to Marie, who wept with gratitude.

'I won't approach them, honestly, Kate,' she said. 'But if I can just see him out in his pram and know that he's happy and healthy, it'll help me so much.'

Robert worried that Kate was becoming too emotionally involved with the girls in the home. He spoke to Richard about it when his son was home on holiday.

'The more I see of Kate the more I respect her,' he said, 'but as Essy says, she's too soft-hearted for her own good. Certainly for working in a place like that. I must try to get her to leave it.'

'Won't be easy,' Richard said. 'She's very strong-willed although she seems so gentle. Why did she and Mum fall out of touch for so many years?'

'I don't know. They never speak of it so I leave well alone,' said Robert.

Richard laughed. 'Essy often drops hints,' he said. 'But I don't think she knows any more than we do.'

Now seventeen years old, Richard had already grown taller than his father, but otherwise the physical likeness between them was striking and their minds were in tune too. Nevertheless, now that it was time for Richard to think about his future, he found that he could speak more freely to Kate than to either of his parents. He told her that they had different ambitions for him.

'Mum wants me to go to university to read law or medicine,' he said, 'but Dad's hoping I'll go into the business with him, even if I have three years at 'varsity first.'

'But what do *you* want to do, Rich?' Kate asked.

'I don't really know,' he said honestly. 'But I know I don't want to do either medicine or law. John's a better bet for that sort of thing because he's so brainy, but it seems a bit feeble just to go into the business.'

'Not if it's what you want to do,' Kate said.

'I don't know what I want, that's the trouble,' he said, looking worried.

'But you're not eighteen until July,' said Kate. 'You've got plenty of time.'

'I'll take my Higher School Certif. then,' Richard said. 'I suppose it depends partly on how well I do in that. Dad says I can have a year for a bit of travelling and other things and apply for the 1939 intake, when I'll be nineteen. I might have more idea then.'

'But at least you know what you *don't* want to do,' Kate said, smiling at him.

'You know what I *have* wondered about, Aunt Kate? Politics. You know Dad asked us to help last Christmas with that charity he's involved in? Making up grocery parcels and taking them round. It was a shock to see how some people have to live. Hungry and ragged and existing in a few rooms in falling-down houses. I'd never realised. Felt as if I'd been walking round with my eyes shut.'

'I know,' said Kate. 'It's like that near the home. Makes my blood boil. It seems no better than when I was a child, although the Corporation *are* building nice houses now out at Queens Drive and Norris Green and other places.'

'That's what I mean,' Richard said eagerly. 'I know the stuff Dad does helps, Christmas hotpots and grocery parcels and all that, but I'd like to get at the cause of it all. Get laws passed to change the system.'

He stopped and grinned. ''Ark at 'im,' he said. 'I sound a right prig, don't I?'

'No, you don't,' Kate said indignantly. 'You've got the right ideas, but remember, things aren't always what they seem. A poor woman who came in to help with the spring-cleaning was shocked by things in the home. The girls are usually from decent homes and she said to me, "We do things better round by us. If a girl gets into trouble her mam usually has a big family anyway and the baby just gets tacked on and reared as one of them. The neighbours know but they don't say nothing. They're usually rearing girls themselves and who's to know what's in front of any of us. We wouldn't dream of putting our girls out on the streets anyhow."'

'A good philosophy,' Richard said, smiling. 'So you think there are compensations in being poor, Aunt Kate? I'll remember that, but don't say anything about these ideas to Mum and Dad, will you? I'm just tossing them round in my mind.'

Kate promised, but told him to stop worrying about his options. Sooner or later he would know what he wanted to do, and there was plenty of time.

Chapter Eighteen

Marie's baby had been adopted, and she was now working as a waitress and living in a bed-sitting room in a house in Queens Road. She had promised to keep in touch with Kate.

One of the girls from the home, Wendy, had applied to the court for permission to marry, as she was only nineteen and her father had refused to allow her to wed. Her application was successful and she married the father of her child, so one story at least had a happy ending, but there were many others that Kate found harrowing.

The ladies who ran the home were concerned for the moral and physical welfare of the girls and their babies, but they felt no compassion for the young mothers. Kate felt too much and decided it was time to leave. There was another reason now. Talking to Robert about finances had made her consider hers more closely.

In theory, the small amount of interest on Beattie's legacy was sufficient for most of her needs, as her board and lodging was provided, but in practice this was not the case. She needed clothes for her visits to Rose and for her yearly holiday in Ireland. There was also her fare there and gifts for all the Malloy family.

She also bought birthday presents for Rose and her family, none of them lavish, but with her own occasional treats of cinema visits, sweets or second-hand books, Beattie's money was dwindling alarmingly.

She would need a paid job, she decided, but she would say nothing to Robert until she had found a post and somewhere to live. She knew that he would urge her to make her home with them, and she also knew that it would be a mistake.

There was still affection between herself and Rose, but Kate knew that she could never fit in to her sister's world.

Although Kate spoke clearly and without an accent and dressed very carefully for her visits to the house in Sandfield Park, she had nothing in common with Rose's friends. Their lives were filled with tennis, shopping, dinner parties and theatre visits, and Kate found conversation with them difficult on the rare occasions when they met.

On one of these occasions she overheard a conversation between Rose and a friend on the other side of a hedge. The friend said curiously, 'Katherine is your *sister*, Rose? She's not like you, is she? Where does she live?'

'Not at all like me,' Rose replied with her tinkling laugh. 'Far more worthy. She devotes her life to a charity she's interested in, a home for unmarried mothers, and she actually *lives* there. In Bootle of all places.'

The friend laughed too. 'Certainly not at all like you, Rose,' and they moved away.

Kate was furious. So that's how she explains me away, she thought. Well, she won't need to from now on. A little later, when Robert and Rose were discussing a tennis party and invited Kate, she looked straight at her sister. 'No thank you,' she said curtly. 'I've nothing in common with your friends and you must find it difficult to explain our relationship.'

Rose blushed and looked away, but then she became angry too. 'I know you despise me and my friends because we enjoy life, but if you don't want to come, why don't you just say so instead of making it my fault?' she said hotly.

Robert hastily intervened. 'I take your point, Kate,' he said. 'I'm sure you and Rose enjoy your visits more when you're free to talk to each other instead of having to make conversation with others. The boys will be home in two weeks' time. Perhaps you would prefer to come then?'

By then both Rose and Kate had cooled down and both agreed eagerly to Robert's suggestion. The incident still rankled with Kate, though, and when she visited when Richard and John were home she took a perverse pleasure in talking about the years when she and Rose had lived with their parents, and about their neighbour, Mrs Holland. She knew that Rose preferred to forget those days and talk about their grandfather and his mansion in St Anne Street, and their grandmother who was distantly related to the Marquis of Salisbury.

John, as usual, paid little attention, as he was trying to teach the gardener's dog new tricks, but Richard was interested and asked questions about Mrs Holland and his grandfather who had been killed in the Boer War. Rose, alarmed, turned the conversation to the safer topic of her ambitions for her sons.

John had received a glowing end-of-term report. He had a flair for maths and any science subject and a brilliant future was forecast for him. Richard's results in his Higher School Certificate were good enough for university entrance, and Rose returned to her wish for him to become a doctor or a lawyer.

'I'm not cut out for it, Mum,' he said. 'And it's not what I want. John would make a better doctor than I would.'

'Yes, I think John has inherited my brains,' Rose said, looking fondly at her younger son. 'I should have been a doctor, shouldn't I, Kate?'

Kate felt that she had annoyed Rose enough, so she agreed, and John left the dog and sat down on the grass at his mother's feet. 'Why weren't you then?' he asked.

'Oh John, you should know why not. I've often spoken about it. My headmistress told me that I had a brilliant brain and she wanted me to go on to university and qualify as a doctor. Lady doctors were very rare when we were young, weren't they, Kate? I lived with Aunt Beattie, though, and she refused to let me go.'

'Why didn't you just go anyway?' John said.

Rose sighed. 'You wouldn't say that if you knew how things were then,' she said. 'You don't understand because everything's always been easy for you and Richard and you've had complete freedom to do what you want. My life was very different. I was dependent on Aunt Beattie. She'd adopted me to be at her beck and call, and what I wanted didn't matter a button.'

John knelt up and pretended to play a violin, looking

soulfully into her face, and in spite of herself Rose laughed. 'You cheeky monkey,' she said. 'Your patients wouldn't get much sympathy from you.'

Richard had finished school and was happily planning a year of freedom before university when suddenly, in September, the newspaper and wireless news was all of war. By 28 September Britain had warned Hitler of the consequences if he attacked Czechoslovakia. The fleet was mobilised, and in Liverpool everyone was talking of trenches being dug in the parks and gas masks being made at Linacre Power Station. 'Even for babies,' one of the girls at the home said to Kate. 'How could anyone gas little babies?'

On 29 September the Prime Minister, Neville Chamberlain, who believed that Hitler's grievances could be settled by a man-to-man talk, flew to Berchtesgaden to see him, and returned waving a piece of paper which he said meant 'Peace in our time'.

Everyone felt immense relief and determined to enjoy life with the threat of war removed. Christmas 1938 was an excuse for extravagant rejoicing, and the spring and summer that followed seemed to people the sunniest and happiest for years.

Rose had considered joining the Women's Voluntary Service but decided instead to enjoy life more than ever. Kate made up her mind to find a job and somewhere to live after she had spent her usual fortnight in Ireland with Josie. She was always welcomed warmly by all the Malloy family. Josie and Michael now had seven children, and they all gathered about Kate, delighted with the gifts she had brought them and telling her all about school and the various animals on the farm.

Old Mrs Malloy worried as usual because Kate was so thin. 'Not a pick on you, childie,' she mourned. 'We must get some flesh on those bones before you go home.'

The day began early on the farm, and Kate tactfully stayed in bed each morning until everyone had been fed and dispersed. Then Mrs Malloy placed before her a huge plateful of bacon rashers, eggs, black and white puddings, sausages and fried potatoes, and a plateful of brown and white soda bread. 'Eat up now, child,' she urged. The food was delicious and all from the farm, but Kate was thankful that some of the younger children gathered about her. She could pass some of the food to them while their grandmother was out of the room.

All the Malloy clan expected to see Kate and offer hospitality, and Kate told Josie she would need to fast for a month when she went home. 'I could do with fasting myself,' Josie said ruefully. 'But I like my food too much.'

The slim, light-footed girl she had been was now a very plump matron, in spite of constant hard work, but Josie still had the dark curly hair and merry brown eyes, and the same happy disposition.

Kate felt closer to her than to anyone else, even Rose. Only to Josie could she talk about Henry, and only Josie had known Gordon and the full story of what had happened between him and Kate. She was the only one who knew that Kate eased her heartache about her baby by buying a toy on 1 January, the anniversary of his birth and death, and giving it to the first child she saw of the right age.

It was Josie who suggested, when ten years had passed, that Kate gave the toy instead to the Children's Hospital in Myrtle Street. 'You might get funny looks if you gave a toy to a ten- or eleven-year-old lad,' she said, and Kate laughed and agreed.

Kate and Josie were out for a walk together when Kate told her how the talk of war had revived her memories of the first war, and particularly of Henry's death.

'It must have been a terrible blow,' Josie said. 'I know how much you thought of him, and having to keep it to yourself must have made it worse. I just wish I had been there to help you. All that wouldn't have happened with Gordon if I had.'

They were silent for a moment, then Josie said quietly, 'I wonder what happened to him, Kate? Something must have done or he'd have come back to you, I'm sure.'

'I'm sure he would,' Kate agreed. 'He wrote me such a lovely letter when I told him about the baby. I'm afraid something dreadful must have happened.'

'They were dangerous times,' said Josie. 'Especially with the job he was doing.'

'That solicitor thought that Gordon had taken advantage of me then left me – I know he did. But it wasn't like that at all, Josie. That awful day I was like someone demented and he just tried to comfort me. I was so distraught, and he was so kind to me. I didn't love him but I liked and respected him, and if the baby'd lived I'd have taught him to be proud of his father. I think he lost his life for his country.'

'Like Henry,' said Josie, and Kate agreed.

'You know I said the talk of war reminded me of him?' she said. 'I was lying awake one night when I suddenly thought that Henry's son would be old enough to fight if there was a war now. I looked at the photo of him as a baby in Henry's arms and I couldn't believe it.'

'But there's not going to be a war now,' said Josie. 'Did you never hear what happened to his family?'

'I know they left the house in Rufford Road. Henry's mother died and Agnes and her mother and the baby went away somewhere. I heard she remarried but I don't know how true that was.'

'She'd have to go a long way to find anyone as good as Henry,' Josie declared, and Kate said quietly, 'I just hope he was good to the child – to Charles – because Henry loved him so much.'

'I wish your baby had lived, Kate,' Josie said. 'He'd be a comfort to you now.'

'I'm all right, Josie. I don't need comfort,' Kate said. 'I've got a lot of happy memories and good friends, especially you. It was a lucky day for me when you came to the guesthouse, and now I have Michael and all your family as well as my friends. And Rose and Robert and their boys, and Essy and Marie. I'm very lucky.'

Josie squeezed her hand gratefully. 'It was a good day for me too when I met you, Kate. You made all the difference to my life there. We had some good laughs, didn't we?'

She asked about Richard and John, and Kate told her of their plans for the future. 'Rose wants one of them to become a doctor,' she said and laughed. 'You know Rose.

She always felt hard done by because Aunt Beattie wouldn't let her stay on at school as the headmistress suggested. Now she's convinced that only Aunt Beattie stopped her from being a better doctor than Elizabeth Garrett Anderson.'

They both laughed, and Josie said, 'She went on a cruise instead, didn't she?'

'Yes, but she *was* upset at the time,' Kate said. 'I shouldn't have skitted about it. I wouldn't criticise her to anyone but you, Josie.'

Josie had her own view of Rose, but she kept it to herself and only said, 'Maybe she'll realise her ambition through her sons,' and she and Kate strolled home arm in arm in complete accord.

Richard made good use of his year of freedom by working in the French vineyards and walking in Austria and the Black Forest. Everything that he saw and heard convinced him that war was inevitable, and although he applied for university he had little hope that he would be able to go there.

When he returned home, Robert told him that an engineering works which was part of his business had been earmarked for war work, and neither of them was surprised when war was declared on 3 September. German troops had invaded Poland two days earlier, and Britain and France had issued an ultimatum to Germany to withdraw her troops or face war with them.

Rain fell all day on Saturday 2 September, a grey day in tune with the general mood. There was none of the hope of the previous year, only a sad acceptance, and as the hours ticked away on that sunny Sunday morning everyone knew that war was inevitable. At 11 a.m. the ultimatum expired, and at 11.15 Mr Chamberlain announced on the wireless that Britain was now at war with Germany.

'That's that then,' Richard said. 'I'll apply for the RAF.'

'Oh Richard, must you?' Rose said. 'Surely university students won't have to go.'

Richard laughed. 'There's conscription for all men aged between eighteen and forty-one,' he said. 'Unless on essential war work.'

'Your works will be essential war work, Robert,' Rose said eagerly. 'You can find a job there for Richard.'

'No he can't,' Richard said loudly and angrily before his father could speak. 'I'm joining the Air Force.' He stormed out of the room and Robert went to console Rose.

Kate had kept in touch with Marie, and when she left the home she had taken a bed-sitting room in the house in Queens Road where Marie lived. She had thought of applying for a job as a cook in a restaurant or a large hotel, but Marie told her she would be horrified by the kitchens. 'If people saw the state of them they'd never eat in a restaurant again,' she said. 'The working conditions are unbelievable too.'

She suggested that Kate applied for a position as an assistant in a large shop. 'You look and speak well, and that's what they want,' she said.

Kate was unwilling to tell her that she was afraid she might be seen by one of Rose's friends, and when she heard of a job in a grocer's in Brunswick Road she applied and was taken on. She had expected Rose and possibly Robert too to be annoyed by her decision, but on her next visit they were too concerned with other matters to ask many questions.

Richard had been accepted for the RAF and John had told them that he intended to join the Cheshire Regiment as soon as he was eighteen. The brother of a schoolfriend was in the Cheshires, and was now in France with the British Expeditionary Force.

Rose and two of her friends had joined the Women's Voluntary Service, and Robert was working long hours. His small engineering works had not only expanded but was now kept going continuously, day and night. He looked exhausted, and Kate left feeling more concerned about him than about Richard and John.

Nothing much seemed to be happening during the first few months of the war. Everyone had expected bombing and gas attacks to start immediately, but when they did not, children who had been evacuated began to drift home and everyone grumbled about the blackout and having to carry their gas masks everywhere.

'They frightened the life outa us for nothing,' a stout

customer in Kate's shop declared, and another customer agreed. 'My feller says we're safe in Liverpool. They can't get at us 'cos we're so near the sea and the Pennines are behind us.'

People were more concerned about the bitter weather. Snow fell after Christmas and quickly froze as icy winds swept the country, making walking in the blackout even more hazardous. 'I thought war would be exciting,' the shop boy grumbled to Kate. 'It's only boring and uncomfortable.'

People began to talk of a phony war and hope that it was stalemate and the troops on both sides would be sent home. But in April all that changed when Hitler invaded Norway and Denmark. Newspapers gave several different versions of events, and accounts of angry scenes in the House of Commons only confused and angered people.

'They must know something what we don't know,' a customer said to Kate. 'My lad's out there in France and we've gotta right to know more than what they have, but we don't get told nothing.'

Matters came to a head when a member of his own party stood up and said to the Prime Minister, 'Depart I say and let us have done with you. In the name of God go.'

Kate grieved for Mr Chamberlain, and even more when he died six months later. 'I think he died of a broken heart,' she said to Essy when she visited her. 'Poor old man. At least he got us a year to get ready.'

Essy agreed and told Kate that she and her dressmaker-lodger, Miss Clarke had made good use of the time. They were provisioned as though for a siege. 'Miss Clarke says this is what all her posh clients are doing. She's a proper clever woman, Kate. You should see the books and newspapers she reads.'

'She's got a real gift for sewing,' Kate said.

'Yes, but she's clever in other ways. She said war was bound to come and because this is an island we'd go short of food.'

'But we've got plenty of farms and factories in this country,' Kate protested.

'Yes, but she made me look at the labels on tins, and they

come from all over the world. And what about things like tea and sugar and pepper? Come and see what we've got put by.'

Kate was astounded when Essy showed her a large store-room filled with tins of meat, fish and fruit, and large catering packs of tea and coffee beans. On the floor were sacks of flour and sugar. 'You won't go hungry, that's for sure,' she exclaimed.

'No. You know, Miss Clarke never says anything about herself, but when we started this she said, "I've known what it is to be hungry and I'm not ever going to endure that again." She never said any more, mind you.' She took Kate next to one of the small bedrooms and showed her more tins and packets of food, and numerous bolts of material of every description, as well as bars and tablets of soap.

'This must have cost a fortune,' Kate gasped.

'We both put our savings into it,' Essy said, 'but Miss Clarke says we'll be glad when everything goes short. She told me not to talk about it but I know you won't say anything, Kate.'

'But don't tell anyone else, Essy. People could turn nasty if they were short and they knew about this,' said Kate.

Kate was enjoying her job in the grocery shop and the variety of women she met through it. They all had views on the conduct of the war and expressed them freely. A Coalition Government had been formed, with Winston Churchill as Prime Minister, and not many of the women approved. 'Look at all the men he got killed in the Dardanelles the last time,' one woman said. 'My eldest brother for one, and all for nothing.'

The women were sceptical too about the news reports that the British and French armies were retreating to prepared positions to lure the Germans into a trap. 'I don't think so,' a stout woman named Mrs Greaves said. 'Sounds to me as if that feller Hitler's got the run of the place. And I don't trust them Frenchies either. They're all foreigners after all.'

Kate repeated some of these comments when she went to see Rose and Robert on Sundays, and Robert laughed at them, but he looked thoughtful.

'It's a good thing Mr Chamberlain got us that year to get ready,' Kate said.

Robert pointed out that it had also been an extra year for preparations by Germany. 'And that meeting between Hitler and the French and Italian leaders and Chamberlain in '38. They gave away too much to Hitler. The Sudentenland, which was Yugoslavia's barrier against him, the big munitions factory in Pilsner and invaluable mineral deposits. I think it was a bad mistake by Chamberlain,' said Robert.

'So you agree with Churchill as Prime Minister?' Kate said.

'I don't like the man,' Robert said. 'But he might be what we need now. He might have learned from his mistakes in the last war, and he has the power of rhetoric.'

'What do you mean?' asked Kate.

Robert laughed. 'The gift of the gab,' he said. 'He's a tub-thumper and he can make rousing speeches. And he also has every confidence in himself – sure he is always right – so he'll be a strong leader anyway.'

Kate went less often now to the house in Sandfield Park, chiefly because she needed her Sundays to rest after a week of demanding work, standing for long hours, as well as her WVS work and broken nights.

She had been hurt by her realisation that Rose had to explain her away to her friends, but common sense came to her aid. It was history repeating itself, she decided. Her visits to her rich relations were now to Rose's home instead of Beattie's, and she had never expected or wanted to be included in Beattie's social life. She was content to know that Rose loved her, and so did Robert and the boys, and she loved them.

In May the truth emerged that France had been overrun. The capitulation of the Belgians had cut off the British Expeditionary Force and the 1st French Army, and British ships converged on the port of Dunkirk to take off the men.

John wrote home from school in great excitement.

Haldane's brother David was in France with the Cheshire Regiment and he was brought back to England wearing just *underpants*. David saw one fellow completely naked with *eight* watches up his arm. He said there were warships anchored and dozens of little boats taking the fellows out to them. Everything that could float was there, he said, and chaps queued in the water to be taken off the beach. Some of the little boats took men straight back to England – British and Frenchmen but mostly British. I wish Richard was flying. There were only a few of our planes to stop the Jerries bombing our fellows. I can't wait to be eighteen.

What was really a disaster was hailed as a triumph because so many men were saved, although their heavy equipment was lost. Hitler declared that he would invade England on 18 July, and Churchill made a stirring speech vowing that the country would never surrender.

Kate recognised the truth of Robert's words when she saw how people responded to the speech. Her customers, who knew little about geography, assumed that the Germans would sail up the Mersey and declared that they would be ready for them. 'Any Jerry puts his foot near my door'll wish he'd never been born,' declared Mrs Greaves, and another woman said, 'Let them come near my house and it'll be the rock they perish on. I wish that Hitler would come. I'd cut off more than his moustache.'

The manager, Mr Dutton, said quietly to Kate, 'And if one of them did and he was hurt they'd take him in and give him a cup of tea. I know these women.' Kate laughed but thought he was probably right. There had been a case reported of a crashed German pilot being taken in by a farmer's wife in Lancashire. When the Civil Defence arrived they found him tucked up in bed sipping tea. 'He's some mother's son,' the woman had said.

The women were not tested, as Hitler had to abandon his plans for invasion. Richard was not yet flying, but those who were fought heroically to drive away or destroy the German planes which came in numbers, chiefly over the south coast, to clear the way for invasion barges.

As one sunny day followed another, dog fights were

constantly fought in the skies above England, with the often exhausted RAF pilots gradually winning the battle, but at great cost. Churchill spoke for everyone when he paid tribute to the pilots, saying, 'Never has so much been owed by so many to so few.'

Richard had gone first to Regent's Park in London to be fitted out for aircrew, but had only been there a short time before moving to Scarborough, where he was billeted in a girls' boarding school. He wrote to Kate that unfortunately the girls had been evacuated before they arrived, but when he came home on leave he showed little interest in girls, although several showed interest in him.

He was an attractive young man, tall and slim with dark hair and eyes like his father and the same fine, sensitive expression and features. The RAF uniform was smart, and he wore a white flash on his cap and a badge of a two-bladed propeller on his sleeve to denote that he was training for aircrew, which made him even more attractive to the girls. He, however, talked of nothing but his training and constantly practised Morse with an Aldiss lamp and a buzzer that John had acquired as a cadet.

John was eighteen in July and immediately joined the Cheshire Regiment as a private. Rose complained that he should have applied for a commission, but he told her that he expected to have more fun as a private. 'Fun!' Robert exclaimed. 'That boy has a lot to learn,' but he was too busy to think more about it.

Rose was also busy with her WVS work, and when Richard and John both managed short leaves at the same time in November they agreed that they had never seen their mother so active and happy. Both were concerned about their father, though, and urged him to slow down.

'You've got a good manager in Stan Horrocks. Delegate more, Dad,' Richard said, but Robert claimed that it was not the actual work.

'It's all the other problems. Supply and the red tape. You never saw such a mountain of forms, all required yesterday,' he said.

Richard looked at his lined, exhausted-looking face. 'I

wish I could help, Dad. I'm almost sorry I opted for the RAF,' he said.

Robert looked alarmed. 'You're not having second thoughts, are you?' he asked. 'I thought you loved the life, Rich.'

'I do,' Richard assured him. 'I just don't want you to kill yourself before I get home.'

'Don't worry, I'm tougher than I look,' Robert said with a grin. 'You just look after yourself.

There had only been scattered raids on the Liverpool area before September, but from then, although the main raids were on London, Belfast and Coventry, the attacks on Merseyside became more frequent.

Richard and John were due to go back off leave at the end of November, but just before that the worst raid so far occurred. The warning had gone at seven o'clock but they were meeting friends for a goodbye drink and decided to ignore it, as often there was an interval before the bombers arrived. But after a quick drink, the crashes and bangs as bombs were dropped and the heavy, intimidating drone of the German aircraft overhead made them decide to start for home.

They were picking their way along the littered road by the light from burning buildings when some sixth sense made Richard pull John back. A large red-hot piece of shrapnel fell, missing John's head but landing on his Army boot. He yelped and tried to shake it off, and a passing ARP man carrying a shovel removed it.

'Is your foot all right?' Richard said anxiously, but the ARP man said crossly, 'Get in a shelter, both of youse. The money it costs to train yis and you take chances like that. Wasting the country's money.' He hustled them into a shelter, and they went in laughing at his comments. John was able to take off his boot. His sock had shrivelled away, but a St John Ambulance girl put a burn dressing on his toes. She also lent him an ancient knitted slipper to wear.

Two old women in the shelter had been interested spectators, and one of them shook her head. 'You'll never come no nearer than that to getting yer lot,' she said.

The other woman added, 'An' coming in here laffin'. Yer must have been born to be hung.'

'That's right,' the first old woman said. 'Born to be hung or born under a lucky star, like they say. Hitler won't get you anyroad, lad.'

Although Richard knew it was irrational to be comforted by the words of the old women, he often remembered them in the months to come when he knew that John was in danger.

Chapter Nineteen

Kate enjoyed her work in the grocery. She liked her customers who lived in the small houses in the area, and she liked the manager, Mr Dutton, a kindly man who used his discretion when dealing with the customers and their rations.

Several of them were old people living alone in one room, and they often told Kate that tea had been their only comfort for years. Now the tea ration was two ounces a week per person, totally inadequate for those living alone, although large families fared better because they could share a pot.

A certain amount was allowed for wastage when weighing out tea and sugar, which was also rationed, and Mr Dutton turned a blind eye when Kate gave old people double rations and saved scarce items like bacon ribs and bottles of sauce for them. Sauce was unrationed, and they spread it on bread, which saved the butter ration and made a tasty addition to their diet.

Mrs Greaves had her husband, two sons and a daughter still at home, and she told Kate that they were living better than they ever had, as were many of her neighbours. 'We've got money coming in regular now, see. The food was there before the war but we didn't have no money to buy it. My feller was down at the docks morning and afternoon looking for a half-day's work and hardly ever getting took on. It used to break my heart to see his face when he come home. Now he's working in Long Lane on munitions regular. Good money and he can hold up his head now.'

Kate thought that in many ways she too was happier than she had been for a long time, in spite of nights disturbed by air-raid warnings and fear when the raids were taking place, in addition to the irritating shortages, the blackout and the worry about Richard and John.

Marie was working at the Meccano factory in Edge Lane, which was now on war work. At present she worked days, and she and Kate pooled resources with food, and to save fuel used one or other of their rooms, where they sat in companionable silence reading or listening to the wireless or talking together as they knitted or sewed.

They usually managed a weekly visit to the cinema, and Kate said one day, 'I feel almost guilty, Marie. The country's in such a bad way and everyone worried, and I feel happier than I've been for years.'

'Why shouldn't you be?' Marie said. 'It's probably because we're independent now, and we're both doing our bit for the war. I feel better than I thought I would ever feel again.' Her baby had been adopted by a couple who lived in a large house in Woolton and one day Marie had hung about the house until she saw him wheeled out in his pram.

'He certainly has more than I could ever give him, Kate,' she said sadly when she returned. 'A big Silver Cross pram and lovely clothes. He looked happy and healthy too.' She glanced round the bed-sitting room. 'This would have been his home, and days with a childminder, I suppose,' she said. 'But I'd have given him so much love, Kate.'

'It seems that those people love him too, Marie,' Kate said gently. 'Don't go there too often, love. You'll only make it worse for yourself, and if they ever find out—'

'I know. I'm so grateful to you for the address. I wouldn't risk trouble for you. Now that I've seen him I'll just come to terms with it and get on with my life.'

She kept her promise, except that on the baby's birthday she succumbed to temptation and sent him a soft toy without any indication who it was from. Kate reflected that in some ways it had been easier for her because she knew exactly what had happened to her baby and his death had been so final.

Kate and Marie had both become members of the WVS, but Marie had to leave when she was moved to a different part of the factory on shift work. Rose was in a different unit, and it wasn't until the beginning of May 1941 that the sisters met up during their WVS work.

Since June 1940 Liverpool and other parts of Merseyside had been a target for German bombers, and from September onwards the raids became more frequent. In addition to those killed and wounded, thousands were made homeless. There were few quiet evenings at home for Kate now as the WVS organised meals and bedding for people sleeping in rest centres, or took tea to the firemen and Civil Defence workers fighting the numerous fires and rescuing those trapped in blitzed buildings.

The raids, though heavy, were comparatively scattered, so although air-raid warnings were sounded nearly every night, some districts escaped. People came wearily from shelters to prepare for work, hoping that though their district had been given a brief respite, the area that had 'bought it' was not one where their relatives lived.

All that changed when during the nights from 1 to 8 May Liverpool and district was bombed continuously and ferociously. Incendiary bombs, high-explosive bombs and land mines rained down on the city as wave after wave of bombers arrived. At times it seemed as though the whole of the city was on fire. The German bombers had no difficulty in finding their targets, mainly the docks, which handled most of the country's imports of food and goods. The small houses near the docks in Liverpool and Bootle suffered accordingly.

Like all the Civil Defence people, the Women's Voluntary Service was stretched to the limit, and Kate was on duty every night in the rest centres, where she helped to comfort homeless people with tea and food and blankets. Many had been dug out from the wreckage of their homes, and some had relations killed or missing.

Sometimes the rest centres themselves were bombed, and Kate feared for Rose when she heard that twelve WVS women had been killed at a rest centre in Bootle. But Rose was safe, and during the night of 3 May the sisters encountered one another among the chaos.

A huge bomb had fallen on nearby Mill Road Hospital,

killing or injuring patients, nurses, doctors and ambulance drivers, and everyone available rushed to help. Kate thought the scene was like something out of Dante's *Inferno*, lit by exploding cars and ambulances and burning buildings. There were screams and shouts as men scrambled over the rubble to find those buried in it. Over everything there hung a thick haze of dust, and the deep, menacing throb of the engines of a fresh wave of bombers mingled with the crump of bombs and the roar of collapsing buildings across the city.

The maternity ward had been hit, and Kate was kneeling beside a young mother who was clutching her two-day-old baby, tucking a blanket round them and wiping the woman's face, when she saw Rose. She looked calm and efficient, moving among the chaotic scenes, organising some of the WVS women who were helping and comforting the rescued, and others who were already making tea for rescued and rescuers alike.

She spoke sharply to a hysterical girl who was upsetting others, and the girl became quiet, although she grumbled to another WVS woman, 'Bossy cow, isn't she?'

'Mrs Willis is just what we need here. She's a good organiser and she gets things done,' the woman said crisply. Kate glowed with pride, and always remembered the episode and the woman's words.

Firemen and Civil Defence workers came from far and wide during that dreadful eight days and nights to help with the rescue work, put out fires and clear the streets of the rubble of collapsed buildings. They did temporary repairs to houses, only to have them bombed again and streets filled with more rubble, but the clearing-up operation continued without pause so that ambulances, fire engines and lorries could get through.

At last the raids ceased, and people could draw breath and assess the devastation of the city and how it affected them.

The house where Kate and Marie had rooms was still standing, although the roof had gone and their rooms were uninhabitable. A tarpaulin had been spread over the roof, and Kate and Marie were able to move into empty ground-floor rooms. Several of Kate's customers were dead or injured, and many more had been moved to temporary accommodation because their houses had been bombed.

The deaths that affected Kate most were those of the manager of the shop, Mr Dutton, and his wife, and Mrs Greaves and her husband and their daughter, who was an ambulance driver. The Greaves's house was still standing, but Mrs Greaves and her husband had been killed by a direct hit on the shelter they were in, and the daughter was killed on duty. The two sons, both firemen, had survived.

The death of Mr Dutton had a more lasting effect on Kate. Another manager was appointed, a slight, sandy-haired man with small eyes and a tight, pursed mouth. Kate disliked Mr Higgins on sight, and every day her feelings grew stronger. He watched her like a hawk, especially when she was serving old people, and she was unable to do anything to help them. He constantly found fault and darted suspicious glances at Kate while he complained that the coupons received were insufficient for the stock that had been used.

'I've had enough,' Kate finally told Marie. 'I don't have to stay there. I'm going to give him notice.'

She sent her notice to head office, and they replied thanking her for past service and asking her to stay for a month to help the girl who would replace her.

The girl who arrived the following Monday was a big, breezy character with a large bust and unlimited energy. Her name was Ada and she had been in the ATS but had been invalided out after an accident. 'A woman soldier!' the customers said to Kate. 'She'll be a match for that ferrety little feller. She won't be put on the way you was.' And so it proved.

When Ada asked why Kate was leaving, Kate was quite frank about her reasons, and Ada declared that if the stocks were out the manager must be helping himself.

'Mr Dutton used to let me give a bit extra to old people on their own, and *his* stocks always balanced,' Kate said. 'But this fellow's so hard with them. I can't stand it. Old Mr Johnson lost his leg in the last war, and now he can't even have a cup of tea when he needs one.'

'The bloody little creep,' Ada said. 'I'll soon sort him out.'

Kate asked if Ada's accident would make it hard for her to bear the long hours and sometimes heavy work, and warned her that Higgins could be very vindictive.

'Don't worry about me, Kate,' Ada laughed. 'I'll tell you but nobody else. My accident was that I got pregnant. The first night I was home there was a raid and I sheltered under the railway arch. It was hit and I lost the baby. Frightened the life out of the ARP man who dug me out. When he seen all the blood he thought I'd lost me legs.' She laughed heartily.

Before the month was up Kate had become very fond of Ada. She had quickly learnt the ration book system and managed to circumvent Higgins in many ways. He had weighed scant two ounces of tea into the cone-shaped bags usually used for small amounts of sweets, and one day he took one of these bags from the drawer behind him for Mr Johnson, the one-legged war pensioner.

The manager glanced triumphantly at Kate as the old man looked sadly at the tiny amount of tea, but behind him she caught sight of Ada quietly opening the drawer and sliding one of the bags of tea into her pocket. As Mr Johnson started towards the door, Ada came out from behind the counter, saying loudly, 'You all right with that crutch, sir?' and opened the door for the old soldier. As she returned she held open her empty pocket, whispering to Kate, 'There's more ways than one of skinning a cat.'

One day before the end of the month Ada asked Kate to come for a walk with her when the shop closed. Kate agreed although she was puzzled, as it was now October and the evenings were becoming dark earlier.

After clearing up and restocking the fixtures after closing, they bade Mr Higgins goodnight and set off together. After a few minutes Ada said, 'I think that feller's helping himself and I want to catch him at it. I want you for a witness, Kate.' She climbed over the wall of a bombed building behind the shop and hauled Kate over after her, then guided her to a corner where they could look down on the side door of the shop.

The moon was rising, and in the faint glow they could

see the errand boy's bicycle. 'I've been keeping watch,' Ada whispered. 'He won't be long now.' They waited, Kate shivering with cold and nervousness, until they heard the sound of the door opening. A dark blur moved to the bike and Ada stood up and shone a torch down on it.

'What's in the bag, Higgins?' she shouted. He gave a squeal of fright and clutched the bag to him, but Ada jumped down and pulled it away. 'Look, Kate!' she cried, dumping the bag in the bicycle carrier and shining the torch on the various tins and packets it contained. 'Spam, cheese, butter, sugar and tea. *Tea*, Kate.' She grabbed Higgins's shoulder and shook him. 'And not a mingy two ounces like you gave the old feller that lost his leg for this country. You bloody worm.'

She aimed a blow at his head, and as he tried to struggle with her Kate awkwardly scrambled from the bombed building. 'I ruined my stockings,' she told Marie later, 'but it was well worth it.'

'Will she report him?' asked Marie.

Kate shook her head. 'I thought she would,' she said. 'But she said she might get someone worse. She wrote out a confession and made him sign it, and I signed it too, but she said she won't say anything at present. She's a case. She told me she's got him under her thumb now so I needn't worry any more about my old people.'

Kate had applied to the factory where Marie worked but had to take a medical examination before they would give her a job. The old doctor who examined her asked her many questions about her previous work, then told her her heart was a little overstrained. 'Never mind, lassie, we'll find you a nice light job,' he said. Kate was not too dismayed. She felt well, and she told Marie that if she had been really ill she would not have been taken on.

She was employed in a converted house owned by the factory, sitting at a workbench assembling small radio parts. Deft and conscientious, she was a good worker and enjoyed the job, and the company of the five other women and two men employed there. They were from different backgrounds but all were friendly, and jokes and laughter made the day pass quickly.

The girl who worked beside Kate had been an art historian, and another of the girls, Deirdre, had been about to start at a finishing school in Switzerland when war began. There was a middle-aged woman with a stomach ulcer, a Cockney girl who had come to relatives in Liverpool when her parents were killed in the bombing of London, and a girl called Maggie who came from the roughest part of Liverpool.

Maggie's Scouse accent was so thick and mixed with thieves' cant that even Kate found it hard to understand at times. To everyone's surprise, Maggie and Deirdre were the two who had most in common and they became good friends. They were both worldly-wise in their own way, and used language that shocked the other women. They also understood each other's jokes which the others failed to see.

Of the two men, one, called Basil, was a weedy creature, happily married as he often announced, who was convinced that all the women wished to seduce him, and the other was a cheerful, slightly backward boy who did the fetching and carrying. Kate entertained Marie with stories about all of them and Marie declared that Kate had fallen on her feet.

'I was worried about you going in the factory,' she said. 'So big and noisy and such crowds of people. You'd have hated it.'

'I didn't realise,' Kate said, looking troubled. 'You've never told me this before. You must hate it too, Marie.'

'No, I'm used to it, and it's not bad in the part where I work. I've got good friends there too, as you know.'

Marie had started to go to dances occasionally with friends from work, and Kate was pleased to see that she seemed to be trying to put the past behind her. The couple who had adopted her baby had now moved away from Liverpool, which Kate thought was better for Marie, and the father of the child had also gone. His wife had been discharged from the sanatorium and advised to live further inland, so the family had moved to Derbyshire.

Kate and Marie still lived in the house in Queens Road. It had been patched up but ominous cracks had begun to appear in the walls. They talked of moving nearer their work in Edge Lane, but neither had the time for house-hunting.

As the war dragged on, they began to wonder if it would ever end. There had been a hopeful period in 1942 when the Germans under Rommel had been defeated in Africa by the Eighth Army, but Churchill had told the country gloomily that this did not mean the end of the war. 'It is not the beginning of the end,' he intoned, 'but the end of the beginning.' Marie said crossly that she was not going to listen to him any more. 'He only depresses me,' she said.

On the now fairly rare occasions when she was able to visit Rose, Kate was concerned to see how strained and ill Robert looked. He too had suffered a loss in the May Blitz, as it was now being called. His foreman, Stan, had been buried under rubble for two days, and although alive when rescued had suffered a heart attack and died after four months in hospital. The man who replaced him did his best, but for Robert no one could replace Stan as a friend and confidant as well as an employee.

In contrast Rose appeared to be blooming. She now held a high position in the WVS and told Kate that it helped her to stop worrying about the boys. Kate, though, thought that it meant more than that to Rose, who felt that her intelligence was at last being recognised and admired.

Richard had been to Canada to gain flying experience, and was now home again as pilot in a bomber crew flying Wellingtons. John was a Commando, doing all the things he had always longed to do. He had been to see Kate when home on leave, and his only grumble seemed to be that tram conductors called him Jock, because of the large bonnet with a bright hackle on the side that the Commandos wore. He described his training to Kate, warning her not to tell his mother.

'It's great,' he said. 'We row up to cliffs with muffled oars because the Jerries will expect the attack to come by land. We're in camouflage gear with our faces and hands blacked and we climb the cliffs. A bit awkward, that, because they're usually pretty sheer, but we carry our knives in our teeth so our hands are free. We've got great instructors. The stuff they can climb!'

'And where do you do this?' asked Kate.

'I can't say. In friendly places while we train,' he said, then, with belated caution, asked her not to repeat his words to anyone. Kate would have liked to know why he carried the knife, but thought it wiser not to ask.

Richard also came to see Kate when he was home on leave, and Robert visited too, but Rose had never been to Queens Road. 'I called in on impulse because I was in the district,' Robert said once. 'Rose would have come with me had she known I was dropping in.'

Kate smiled at him. 'I see Rose quite often at your house, don't I?' she said. 'I know she's very busy at present with her WVS work,' and Robert smiled back at her gratefully.

He was concerned about the state of the house, but Kate told him that she and Marie would soon find somewhere else to live. She felt that he had enough to worry about, and was distressed to see how ill and strained he looked. She sometimes went to see Essy, and she confided her worry about Robert to her.

'Yes, he's missing Stan,' Essy said. 'He could talk over his worries with him, but he makes light of them to the boys when they come home. The one he should be talking to is his wife, but he won't worry her with anything, and she can't see what's under her nose. Too busy strutting about, but we'd better not have floods of tears if she loses him or I'll tell her.' Kate said nothing. She found that was wisest when faced with Essy's implacable dislike of her sister.

When Kate saw Rose she found that her sister was worried about something entirely different. For many men marriage was out of the question, either because they were serving abroad or because they were prisoners of war, but Richard was flying bombing missions from England and John, although his movements were mysterious, occasionally appeared on leave. Neither son, however, appeared to have a regular girlfriend, and Rose was afraid that they might meet girls from another part of the country and settle down there after the war. 'I have to part with them now,' she said. 'But they should be with me for my old age. They're *my* sons, after all.'

Kate laughed. 'I know they both have plenty of dates,

but nothing serious,' she said. 'It's too soon to worry, Rose.'

She wondered whether she should tell her sister that she should be anxious about something far more important, her husband's health, but Rose changed the subject and the moment passed.

For the first time since November 1940 Richard and John were due to come home on leave at the same time. When Richard arrived he looked almost as haggard and tired as his father, but he had completed a tour of operations and was now due to be grounded. John, when he came, seemed to be bursting with health and good spirits. News trickled out occasionally of the daredevil exploits of the Commandos, and the family worried about him, but although he could say nothing about his life he was obviously enjoying it.

Although John had to go back after three days, Richard still had leave and he spent some of it at the works with his father. He told Kate how worried he felt about Robert. 'If I get through this lot, Aunt Kate, I'll go in with Dad,' he said. 'I've got no burning ambition to do anything else and I think I'll enjoy working there and taking a bit of the weight off him.'

'Have you told him?' Kate asked, and Richard confessed that he had only decided during this leave. 'Tell him before you go back,' Kate advised. 'It'll be just what he needs to cheer him up. We've all been worried about him because he misses Stan so much, and he's got so many problems and so much red tape to deal with.'

Richard did as Kate suggested, and the change in Robert could be seen immediately. Rose was pleased too, as it meant that Richard would make his home in Liverpool.

The war news was better now too. Throughout the war Kate had become used to seeing the uniforms of the sailors or soldiers from many lands as she walked along Church Street, but suddenly Liverpool seemed to be full of American soldiers. Rose invited some of them for meals, as many people did, and found them cheerful and friendly although dismissive of Richard and John's years of service and very sure of their own worth.

Just as suddenly many of them were moved, as people later discovered to the south coast for the D-Day landings. On 6 June 1944, Sally, the art historian who worked with Kate, attended a concert at the Philharmonic Hall, and at work the next day she said, 'I detest jingoism, but when Malcolm Sargent announced that the Second Front had come at last, that our troops were landing in France, I found myself on my feet singing "Land of Hope and Glory" like everyone else in the hall. It was so emotional.'

Everyone felt that the war would soon be over, and Deirdre said to Basil, 'Nearly the end of your cushy little number, darling, surrounded by nubile young women.'

'I wish you wouldn't call me darling. What if my wife heard you? She'd think we were carrying on.'

'Not to worry, darling,' Deirdre said. 'I'm a lesbian.' As none of them had heard the word before, her joke fell flat, though Maggie guessed what she meant. Kate thought she was speaking about her birth sign. Since it was not a word ever written in the newspapers or spoken on the wireless, Basil continued to fear, or hope, that he was in imminent danger of being seduced.

Robert still worried about Kate's living conditions, and he urged her to come to live with him and Rose. He said he was sure that Marie could easily make other arrangements, but Kate stubbornly resisted, and Rose was not enthusiastic about the idea either, although she said little, knowing that Kate would refuse anyway.

So much of Everton had been destroyed in the bombing that although she had lived there most of her life, Kate sometimes felt like a stranger. She was willing to move but she and Marie had not found anywhere else to live, so they were delighted when Robert told them that he had found a flat for them.

It was the ground floor of a large detached house in Lilley Road, off Edge Lane, not far from the factory where they worked, and was a pleasant flat with two good-sized bedrooms, a well-proportioned drawing room and a kitchen and bathroom. The rent was the same as they paid in Queens Road and Kate and Marie were amazed, but Robert told them the rent was protected by a by-law and could not be raised.

Neither of them was aware that Robert had bought the house and left it to Kate in his will. He had not told Rose either, as he was unsure of her discretion, but he did confide in Richard. 'When the time comes, explain to your mother and Kate that it was self-indulgence on my part. It made me feel better,' he said with a smile.

Kate and Marie were delighted with the new flat, and both felt that life was good. Marie had put her trouble behind her, and although working very hard still managed to have a good social life, and Kate rejoiced for her.

Kate worried less about Robert now, but she longed for the end of the war, when she could listen to news bulletins without fearing that Richard's plane was one of those that 'failed to return', or that John had taken one risk too many. She often thought, too, about Henry's son, wondering if he had become a soldier like his father, and if so, whether he had survived the war.

She would have been comforted to know that he was farming in Shropshire, and amazed to learn that he sometimes thought of her. When war broke out Charles was twenty-five years old and running his father-in-law's farm after the older man had suffered a stroke. He had tried to enlist in his father's old regiment but had been told in no uncertain terms to go back to the farm. 'That's the best way you can help your country,' the recruiting officer told him. 'We need all the food we can get. You can save the lives of a few seamen if we don't have to import so much,' and Charles could see the logic of it.

He threw himself into work on the farm, increasing the yield in every department and working every available hour for seven days a week, helped by his wife, and felt that he had justified the officer's decision.

Charles had been nearly five when he left Liverpool with his mother and his maternal grandmother after the death of his father and a little later of his father's mother. He never knew why his mother and his grandmother Tate decided to settle in Shrewsbury. His mother took a teaching post and

Charles was looked after by his grandmother, a cold, unloving woman who had never shown him any affection. He missed his father and was sad when his grandmother told him he would never see him again, but his mother told him that his father had died the death of a hero and he must be proud and not grieve, so he was obedient, as he was expected to be, and hid his feelings.

There had been no consolation for him in the death of his grandma Barnes, whom he had loved dearly and who had loved him and frequently told him so. He wept in bed at night and wished that she had lived and his other grandmother had died, but soon he started school and had other things to think about. He was happy at his preparatory school and enjoyed the sport, although he was not as good academically.

He was unable to pretend any grief when his grandmother Tate died when he was nine years old. His mother seemed unaffected too. She was now a headmistress, with a cool, withdrawn manner, and she simply installed a housekeeper in her mother's place. Charles was astounded when she told him in 1925 that she intended to remarry, but that it would not affect him as he had been entered for his future stepfather's public school in the Lake District. The man's name was Paul Vetch and he was a solicitor, and Charles would meet him on Sunday when he came to tea.

Paul Vetch was a quiet, colourless character, and Charles had no strong feelings about him at all. At this time he was far more interested in a discovery he had made in the attic of a tin trunk containing his father's books and papers.

It was a wet, grey day and he had been mooching about, bored and miserable, until he decided to root about in the attics. He had moved a bag of curtains off the trunk and opened it, and immediately his boredom vanished. He thought the trunk must have been packed by his grandmother Tate, as papers had been thrust in haphazardly and no care had been taken with books his father must have valued.

He stacked the books carefully and started to arrange the papers in order. Among them he found his father's diary. It had been discontinued when he married, except for an entry on the day that Charles was born, with an ecstatic account of his feelings when he first saw the baby, and minute details about his son. 'He has very long fingers. I wonder if he will be a musician,' he had written. 'Whatever he becomes he'll be the most loved child ever. I can't wait to show him to Kate.'

There was another short entry in different ink, noting that the day of Charles's birth was the day the Archduke Francis Ferdinand was assassinated, thus precipitating the war. Then, commenting on naming his son, Henry had written, 'I wish he could have been called David but Agnes wanted Charles Jonathan. I suppose I should be thankful she didn't want Ferdinand!' Charles was only eleven years old, but he decided there and then that if he ever had a son he would name him David.

It was growing dark, so he hid the diary and returned to it next morning, curious to read more about Kate. He turned over the pages until he came to the first reference to the name.

Henry had related how she had been trying to carry the heavy coal scuttle. 'It must be a sad and unsettling day for her,' he had written. 'Her mother's funeral then being whisked off to live here with the Dragon Lady, yet she only seems concerned about her sister, who seems to have come off much better. *Anything* would be better than the Dragon, but perhaps I misjudge her because she objects to my whistling. Perhaps she will be kind to the child. I hope so. She's such a brave little scrap.'

Most of the diary was concerned with Henry's work, his friends, and visits to music halls or boxing matches, and also with a boys' club where he helped, but running through it like a thread were references to Kate. He had also written about Agnes, but even when he was linked with her there were still comments about Kate. Charles was too young to analyse it, but he felt vaguely that the references to Kate were warmer than those to his mother, although his father obviously admired her.

He stacked the books and papers tidily in the trunk, but the diary he removed and concealed. He took it to school with him and often read a little of it when he was alone, and he determined that some day he would go to Liverpool and find Kate. Obviously his mother must know nothing about it, though.

Chapter Twenty

Charles settled happily in the school in the Lake District and made many friends there. His mother had resigned her post as headmistress when she married, and as Paul Vetch was semi-retired they spent much of their time travelling abroad. They always arranged to be at home for Charles's holidays from school, combining it with Paul spending some time in his office.

Charles quickly became bored at home in Shrewsbury, and when invited to visit his school friend Ben Tyland he set off eagerly. Ben's father farmed in Shropshire, and Charles enjoyed helping on the farm. 'You've got a real feel for the land, lad,' Mr Tyland told him.

This quickly became the pattern of Charles's life. A week at home during the school holidays, then the rest of the holiday spent on the Tylands' farm, where he helped out or cycled for miles with Ben and his younger sister Margaret. They took packed lunches and explored the county, singing as they rode along sweet-smelling country lanes, or making would-be knowledgeable remarks about the fields they passed.

Margaret and Ben rarely quarrelled, and as an only child Charles envied Ben and enjoyed Margaret's company. Charles kept a photograph of his father in uniform beside his bed at school, and Ben often asked about him.

One day, as they lay on a sunny hillside, Charles told Ben and Margaret about his father's diary. Ben questioned him eagerly until he realised that the diary was pre-war. 'Pity it wasn't from when he was fighting,' he said, but Margaret disagreed. 'I think it would be more interesting to know how he felt when he was a young man, living a normal life,' she said, and Charles felt that she understood.

At fourteen years of age he now looked very much like his father, with the same fair curly hair and blue eyes, and the same happy disposition with which Henry had been blessed. Ben and Margaret were both slim and dark, with grey eyes and quieter dispositions than Charles, but all three were united in their love of the land.

As time passed it became clear that Charles would not pass university entrance, as his mother had hoped, so she and Paul decided that he would be articled to Paul's law firm, although Charles himself wanted to become a farmer.

A tragedy during his last term at school decided the matter. Ben Tyland was taken to hospital with appendicitis which developed into peritonitis, and he died two days later. Charles was bereft, and the headmaster allowed him to travel back with Ben's distraught parents for the funeral.

Agnes and Paul attended the funeral too, and afterwards it was decided that Charles would stay on and live at the farm. Agnes would have preferred him to go to agricultural college if he was set on farming, but in the face of Charles's and the Tylands' grief and the comfort they gave each other, she did not insist. Although not demonstrative, Agnes truly loved Charles and wanted to do what was best for him, and Charles appreciated this and promised to visit her whenever she was in England.

As Agnes and Paul drove home, he said quietly, 'You know what will happen, don't you, my dear? Charles will marry the daughter and take over there eventually,' and he proved to be right.

Charles never attempted to take Ben's place, but his presence at the farm brought great comfort to the Tyland family, especially as he too had loved Ben. Gradually the friendship with Margaret deepened into love, and they were married in February 1934. Charles had shown the diary to Margaret and told her of his wish to call his son David, though both of them preferred to name their first son after Ben. Margaret also suggested that if they had a daughter they might call her Katherine.

Their daughter was born just before Christmas of that year and christened Katherine Margaret. Margaret worried that

Charles's mother might be hurt at the choice of names, as Margaret's own mother was also Margaret, or that she might have suspected Henry's undeclared love for Kate, but Agnes said only that she had always disliked her own name. She had evidently completely forgotten Kate and was unaware that Charles knew anything about her.

Two boys followed, Ben and David, but although they were a close and loving family, Kit, as she was known, had a special place in her father's heart. He sometimes wondered about Henry's Kate, and whether she was like his quiet, clever daughter.

At the outbreak of war Kit was five years old, Benjamin three and David six months. Kit was slim, dark-haired and grey-eyed like her mother, and was like her in temperament too. She read when she was three years old and was never happier than when she was lost to the world in a book.

Ben was like his father, tall with blue eyes and fair curly hair, and like him a natural farmer who loved the land. He was a sturdy little boy and more and more helpful on the farm as he grew. David loved all animals, and his parents hoped that someday he would become a vet. The three generations lived happily together in the roomy old farmhouse.

Margaret helped her mother to nurse her father when he had a stroke, and took over the kitchen work, the dairy and the hens, as well as looking after her young family, although her mother helped when she could. It was a relief to everyone when Mr Tyland appeared to recover, although he never regained his old vigour.

The mass of forms and regulations at the start of the war worried him, although Charles dealt with most of them, and in 1940 he told Charles and Margaret that he intended to retire and turn the farm over to them.

'Mother and I have talked it over and we think it's best,' he said. 'It would come to you anyway, so you might as well have it now.' He smiled. 'This way all the forms and that'll come to you, Charlie, God help you.'

'You're doing all the work anyway, both of you,' Mrs Tyland added. 'What with my rheumatism and Father's stroke.'

Margaret and Charles looked at each other, unable to speak. They were stunned by the suddenness of the proposal, and Charles was struggling with a familiar feeling of guilt that he was taking Ben's place. He cleared his throat and gripped Margaret's hand. 'There's something I've wanted to say for years,' he said gruffly. 'That I'm not trying to push into Ben's place. I appreciate all you've done for me but, well – this is Ben's and I'm not—'

He looked helplessly at Margaret, unable to express how he felt, but it was Mr Tyland who said, 'Nay, lad. I respect you for feeling like that but there's no need. We grieve for Ben and always will, but God was good to us. From the start you were like another son to us, Charlie, and when you married our Margaret, well – you're family, Charlie, and Ben would be glad this day.'

'I loved him too,' Charles muttered, feeling choked with memories of his dead friend.

'We know you did,' Mrs Tyland said gently. 'And Dad's right. It was a happy day for us when you and Margaret wed.'

'Yes, I wouldn't be rushing to hand over my farm if she'd married anyone else,' said Mr Tyland. 'But I know it's in good hands, and so is she. And I think we've got another farmer in the family in young Ben.'

'Yes, and with Tyland blood in his veins,' said Charles. His feelings of guilt left him and he felt free to enjoy the ownership of the farm, but it was several days before he and Margaret could believe their good fortune.

Throughout the war Charlie, as he was now known to everyone except his mother and stepfather, did the work of two men, always conscious of the recruiting officer's words that he could save seamen's lives by increasing production. His young family did all they could to help, especially little Ben, who was strong and deft at all farming tasks.

Margaret worked as hard as her husband, looking after the hens and the dairy as well as her family and the succession of Land Girls who came, married, became pregnant and left. 'I didn't think there were so many eligible men in the district,' she said ruefully to her mother, who often helped her.

Mr Tyland also helped Charlie, with good advice and by keeping a critical eye on the Land Girls and the three elderly men who worked on the farm. When the war ended all the family were tired but satisfied that they had played their part in the victory.

After many false alarms and dashed hopes, the end of the war seemed to Kate to arrive quite suddenly. She joined in all the rejoicing, thankful that Richard and John had survived, and hoping that Henry's son was safe too. Her memories of Henry were still a comfort to her, a happy land to which she could always escape.

Soon after the war ended, Kate's factory unit was closed down and the staff dispersed. They all promised to keep in touch, but Marie told Kate that it was unlikely. 'People think it'll be a classless society after the war, but George thinks everyone will go back to their own way of life,' she said.

George was a foreman at the factory with whom Marie had become friendly, and now she told Kate shyly that they planned to become engaged. Kate had met George, and she felt that Marie would be safe and happy with this kind, gentle man.

George's house had been destroyed and his wife and young son killed in the May Blitz while he was on Civil Defence duty, and Marie had tried to comfort him. He knew about her son and understood her grief in having to part with him, and Kate was delighted that the future seemed set fair for Marie.

Rose and Robert urged Kate to stay with them for a while before she thought of another job. Kate stayed for a month, enjoying being pampered, but it was clear to both sisters that though they loved each other they could never live together. Their lifestyles were too different.

Kate had saved from her very good wages, and she decided to have another month's holiday, this time with Josie in Ireland, before starting a fresh job. There she was warmly welcomed by everyone, and urged to stay permanently, but she told them that she could never leave Liverpool, although she had thoroughly enjoyed her stay and gained several pounds in weight.

Josie and Michael told her that there was always a home for her with them if she needed it, and she replied that she was grateful and happy to know it.

'Rose and Robert have offered me a home too,' she said. 'I'm more at home here than in their house. You know I love them and the boys, but it's such a different life. I'm very lucky, though, to twice have the offer of a home if I need one. Everybody's very good to me.'

Marie told Kate that there was no reason for her and George to wait to marry, as George had been rehoused after the Blitz, so in November they were married quietly in Brougham Terrace Register Office. A quiet elderly couple occupied the top flat in Lilley Road so Kate was not alone in the house.

She told Robert that she intended to look for a job in a shop as she enjoyed meeting people. He suggested Blacklers or Lewis's, large department stores which had been rebuilt after being bombed, but Kate decided she preferred a small local shop where the customers would become friends.

She found a job in a small grocer's shop in Kensington, within walking distance of the flat, and settled happily into this fresh phase in her life. She decided not to look for another flatmate, and her second bedroom was often in use for guests. Her old friend Nell, now a matron in a London hospital, came for a visit, and members of the Malloy family often came to Liverpool and stayed for a night or a month, as it suited them. They could never outstay their welcome with Kate.

She often went to see Essy, who applauded her decision to keep her independence. 'Don't ever let them talk you into living with your sister,' she said. 'It would never work.'

Essy and Miss Clarke had experienced no shortages during the war, thanks to their hoard, and they had also had plenty of fresh vegetables and eggs. Essy's cleaner had gone to work on munitions and Essy employed a young orphan named Magdalen, who lived in and shared their food. The gardener had also left, and Magdalen tidied up the garden and discovered that she had green fingers.

Essy gave her a free hand and she grew a variety of

vegetables and flowers. She also suggested keeping hens and looked after them too. She kept the house supplied with vegetables, eggs and cut flowers, and the surplus was always in demand for a market stall in Ormskirk. This continued after the war ended.

Miss Clarke developed pneumonia in 1949 and she was given the new wonder drug M&B. She seemed to be recovering, but complications set in and she died. Kate wondered if Essy could live alone, but she declared that there was no problem. 'The house is my own and I enjoy pottering round,' she said. 'And I've got plenty of friends in the church and in the Women's Guild. Magdalen is a treasure too.'

'I hope she'll stay with you,' Kate said doubtfully. 'How old is she now? About twenty?'

'Yes, but she's not likely to get married,' Essy said forthrightly. 'There are never many spare men after a war, and she's no oil painting, is she? Even without that squint.'

'But even so, she does so much. Could you manage if she left?' asked Kate.

'She won't,' Essy said positively. 'She knows which side her bread's buttered. She's got it soft here and she knows it. As long as the house is clean I don't stand over her while she does it. She can please herself and boss the woman who comes for the rough work. And then there's the garden. As long as she brings in enough potatoes and veg for the house, and the eggs and a chicken or two, she can please herself out there too.'

'Do you still sell to the market stall?' asked Kate.

'*I* don't. Magdalen does all that. She pays for the seed and stuff for the garden, and the hens' feed, and after that the money's her own. She's been selling apples and pears from the orchard too, and the windfalls and the house peelings to a pig keeper in return for sausages and a bit of pork and such. She's a good businesswoman,' said Essy.

'Does she keep *all* the money?' asked Kate.

'Yes, so she's not going to walk away from that, or do anything to make me get rid of her, is she?' Essy said triumphantly.

Kate gazed at her with awe. 'You know, Essy, I was afraid

you were being put on, but you've got it all worked out, haven't you? Everything planned.'

'Of course. I've always looked out for myself,' said Essy. 'Had to because I've no one belonging to me. There's not many people reach their three score years and ten like it says in the Bible, but I'm already six years past it, and I'm as well as many a younger woman.'

'You are,' Kate agreed. 'Although people *are* living longer – but not as long as you,' she added hastily when she saw Essy frown. 'I've heard of several people dying in their sixties lately. When I was young people were reckoned to have done well if they were fifty or so when they died. It must be all the new medicines.'

'Yes, and you should be thinking ahead about what'll happen when you're too old to work. How old are you now?' said Essy. 'About fifty-seven?' Kate nodded, and Essy went on, 'Plan your life, Kate. Do what's best for you. You've always let yourself be pushed from pillar to post. Never weighed things up and done what was best for *you*.'

'But I've been very lucky, and people have always been good to me,' Kate protested.

Essy snorted. 'That's what you like to think,' she said. 'The way I see it, you've always got the dirty end of the stick and your sister's had it easy. Mind you, it hasn't stopped her feeling sorry for herself, and she never keeps a friend, does she? Or lasts long on those committees she's always getting herself on.'

Kate smiled and changed the subject. She knew it was no use arguing with Essy about Rose, whom she still implacably disliked, but as she walked home she thought about Essy's words. It was true that Rose was unhappy. She had seemed to have found her niche in the WVS, and had been useful and successful, but after the war another woman was offered a senior position which Rose felt was her due and she resigned.

Since then she had served briefly on many committees and become interested in various causes, but always something happened to make her feel slighted or misunderstood and she left. One permanent grievance was that though several people she knew had become JPs, she had never been asked to serve on the bench.

'I know what it is,' she told Kate. 'It's because they have letters after their names and I haven't, but that's not my fault. I was denied my chance when I was young.' Kate suspected that the JPs had been selected because they had worked hard for many years for various causes, but she only said soothingly to Rose that she might be approached at a later date.

Rose hoped that John would go to university, as many ex-servicemen were doing, but John had other ideas. He was twenty-four years old when the war ended and had made many friends from Commonwealth countries while in the Commandos. He decided to see something of the world before settling down, starting with Canada, where a friend's father offered him a job in his logging business.

After he was demobbed he came home to Liverpool before setting off on his travels. Rose was tearful when he told them of his plans, but Robert approved. John had been able to tell them something of the Commandos' exploits now that the war was over. He described the raid on the Lafoten Islands and other missions which he seemed to have enjoyed but which horrified his parents. They were glad they had not known at the time of the risks he was taking.

Robert told Rose that John's plan to work his way around the world was just what he needed. 'It'd be hard for him to settle down to a steady job straight after that Commando stuff,' he said. 'Now is the time to get all that out of his system while he's still young, with no commitments,' and Rose had to agree that he was right.

John spent six months in Canada, then moved to Australia, then to New Zealand. He sent letters home regularly, and wrote from New Zealand that he would like to go to Spain but not while Franco was there. 'I may go back to Canada for a short time to see Dave, then on to the Continent,' he wrote in 1950. 'See how things are there now.'

'At least he's working towards home, away from the

wide-open spaces,' said Robert. 'Perhaps he's getting ready to settle down.'

'I wish *one* of them was,' Rose said. 'It's time Richard was thinking of marriage. He'll be thirty this year.'

'He just hasn't met the right girl yet,' Robert soothed her. 'Don't forget, dear, he's had very little time for social affairs during the past few years. It's been hard turning the business back to peacetime work, and he's borne the brunt of it and made a success of it too. I don't know what I'd have done without him.'

Rose laid her hand on his. 'I know,' she said. 'He's a good son and I'm grateful to him for the way he's spared you. I was terribly worried about you at the end of the war. I'd just like to see him married and perhaps with children before I go.'

Robert looked at her in alarm. 'What do you mean, dearest? Is something wrong? Do you feel ill?'

'Nothing more than usual,' Rose said with a sigh. 'You know my health is not good, Robert, at any time. That's why I've had to resign from some of my committees.'

Robert was relieved. He knew, although he would never have admitted it, that Rose had resigned either because younger members thought her outdated and snobbish in her ideas, or because active working members were required and she was unwilling to endure hard work or discomfort.

'She's been spoiled,' Essy told him when he visited her. 'First by madam and then by you, and Kate's always doted on her too. That's what's made her so dissatisfied.'

'You only see one side of her character, Essy,' said Robert. 'If I've spoiled Rose I've been happy to do so because she's so lovable and warm-hearted. That early disappointment about her career has affected her, and I know I'm no Prince Charming – she could have done better, such a lovely girl – but she's never complained. I don't deserve her but I'll always love and cherish her, Essy. I wish you could see her as I do.'

'She's the lucky one to have a husband like you and two good sons,' Essy said implacably. 'What about Kate, if you're talking about disappointments? She's had nothing else. No comfort, nothing but hard work badly paid, and always on her own. Never anyone to care about *her*, but you don't hear *her* whingeing.'

'Nor do you hear Rose,' Robert said with a flash of anger, and Essy quickly changed the subject.

Richard had almost completely taken over the running of the family business and Robert spent only a day or two each week there now, although he was always welcome. Richard still lived at home, and discussed business matters with his father, and Robert declared that he had the best of both worlds. All the interest of the business and none of the worry.

He looked ten years younger and his doctor was very pleased. Although Robert had told no one, the doctor had earlier warned him that his heart would not stand the strain on it for much longer, but now he had a new lease of life.

After the warning by the doctor, Robert wondered whether he should tell Rose and Kate that he was Kate's landlord and that he intended to leave her the house in Laurel Road, but he had done nothing about it. When Richard came home he consulted him about it. 'I'd really like to make it over to Kate now in case she's worrying about the future,' he said, but Richard advised against it.

'I wouldn't say anything to Aunt Kate,' he said. 'You know how independent she is. If she was short of money it'd be different but she can easily manage that tiny rent. She thinks it's protected by law so she's quite happy.'

'I told her that when I told her about the flat,' Robert said. 'The firm who collect my rents queried it but I told them it was in order and must stay at that amount. It doesn't matter to them as long as it's authorised. You're sure you don't think I should make it over to Kate now, Richard?'

'No. I think the responsibility might worry her and it'd mean you'd have to tell her about owning the house and why she's been paying so little. Might hurt her. She's very proud for all she's so quiet.'

Robert sighed. 'What a mess,' he said. 'I did it with good intentions but I'd hate Kate to think I've been deceiving her all these years.'

'She won't, Dad,' Richard said. 'I'm probably wrong about

how she'd feel. I know she's very fond of you and she'd just think you'd been good to her, but if the present system's working, why change it? She may never need to know who owns the house.'

'I don't understand,' said Robert.

'I mean you may outlive Aunt Kate, but if you don't I'll explain it all to her. Don't worry,' said Richard, and Robert was relieved to leave this responsibility too to Richard.

Chapter Twenty-One

After the war Agnes and Paul Vetch resumed their travelling abroad. In 1949 they had been for some months in Italy, where there was a small colony of English people. In late August Agnes died suddenly of a heart attack. Paul wrote to tell Charles. The funeral had taken place within forty-eight hours, so it had been impossible for her son to be present.

Charles felt more upset than he expected at his mother's death, and sorry that they had not been closer. He felt that during his early years the grim figure of his maternal grandmother had come between them, and after her death his mother's marriage and his own move to boarding school had meant that they saw little of each other.

He and Margaret had sometimes taken her grand-children to visit Agnes, but the visits had not been a success. The children had been nervous, afraid to move and damage the fragile ornaments, and Agnes, although she loved them, had been stiff and formal with them. She and Paul had always spent Christmas abroad and they had only twice visited the farm, so she was almost a stranger to the children.

Charles felt grateful to Paul, who had been a good and loving husband, and wrote asking him to stay with them. Paul replied with thanks but said that as he had no other relations he intended to stay in Italy, where the climate suited him and he had many friends. He also said that he would return to England to arrange his business affairs and sell his house, and he hoped to arrange a memorial service in Shropshire for his wife.

It was arranged very swiftly, and after the service Paul

asked Charles and Margaret to return to his house. 'Before I sell up I want you to choose anything that you can use,' he said to Charles. 'Items of your mother's, of course, but also anything else, furniture and such, as much as you can. You would be doing me a favour.'

'I'd like a trunk of my father's papers that's in the attic, if I may,' said Charles. 'And any family photographs.'

'Of course. I didn't know it was there,' said Paul. He went to a cupboard and took out a box of photographs. 'These are from before our marriage,' he said. 'Many of you as a child, and of your parents before they were married.'

'I don't remember ever seeing them,' Charles said, opening the box eagerly. There were photographs of him with his mother and some with his grandmother, but it was the earlier ones that interested him most. Photographs of his parents on their wedding day, both looking very solemn, and snapshots of his mother with a group of ladies wearing sashes.

'They were women who campaigned for women's rights, your mother said once,' Paul told him. 'Not Suffragettes. She was a great admirer of Eleanor Rathbone, MP.'

'My father was involved too,' Charles exclaimed, picking up another snapshot of a group of ladies without sashes and several young men.

'That was another group who did philanthropic work, I think. Christmas hotpots for poor children and so forth. They held bazaars and other functions to raise money for the work,' said Paul.

He looked over Charles's shoulder. 'Your mother took an interest in the young girl standing beside her. She was the niece of the owner of the guesthouse where your parents lived before they were married. The young man who owned the camera belonged to that group,' he added, but Charles scarcely heard him.

'Was her name Kate?' he asked eagerly. 'The young girl?'

'I think so,' Paul said. 'Your mother taught her to read and write, she said, and took her to meetings as her protégée.' Charles turned the snapshot over. On the back was written 'Christmas Bazaar. Agnes, Henry and Katherine Drew'. He looked again at the snapshot. Agnes and Henry looked solemn, as people did on photographs then, but Kate was smiling shyly. She was tall and thin, wearing glasses, a long coat and a large hat. Agnes wore similar clothes but looked more elegant. Her coat had a fur collar.

Paul went to a cabinet and took out a cut-glass tumbler. 'These were a wedding present from that young girl,' he said. 'Only four left, I'm afraid, but they're good quality.'

'I'm interested in that family,' Charles said. 'Could you tell me anything about them? The aunt's name, for instance?'

Paul shook his head. 'We only spoke of that time on rare occasions. When Eleanor Rathbone was in the news, for example, or when your mother spoke about the glasses.'

'I should have asked her myself,' said Charles, 'but somehow it was never the right moment.' He smiled ruefully.

Margaret had brought in coffee and Paul asked her to decide about the contents of the house. She shook her head and said firmly, 'I don't think you should make any big decisions now, so soon after bereavement. If you decide to come back to England to live, you can always buy another house, but you'll want your own things round you.'

'I won't come back,' Paul protested. 'I found the English winters very trying during the war, and my health is much better in Italy.'

'Nevertheless,' Margaret insisted, 'anything can happen. I suggest we store all your stuff – we've got plenty of room in our attics – and it'll be there if you need it.'

Paul seemed relieved to have matters settled for him, and it was arranged that Agnes's desk, dressing table and wardrobe and the furniture from his own bedroom should be sent to Charles, as well as some glass and china of his mother's. The rest of the contents of the house would be packed up and delivered to the farm for storage in the attics. Charles put the trunk and the box of photographs in his car.

They all went to a nearby hotel for a meal, then parted

with regret and promises on both sides to keep in touch and visit when possible. 'A good man,' Charles said as they drove away. 'I'm glad Mother had him to look after her. I think she was happier with Paul than she would have been with my father if he'd lived.'

'Possibly,' Margaret agreed. 'She and Paul were well suited. Judging by his diary, your father seemed a very different personality from your mother.' Charles said nothing. He knew that although there had been no animosity between his wife and his mother, Margaret had found Agnes intimidating.

When they reached home he lost no time in searching through the box of photographs, but there were no others of Kate, although many of groups of young people. Later he and Margaret sorted through the trunk and put the papers in order. They found a bundle of receipted bills which gave them the address of the guesthouse and were signed by M. J. Williams (Mrs). On the back of one of them Henry had written, 'A rent book would be more convenient but too common for the Dragon Lady. She prefers to present her guest with a monthly bill she says. Snob!!!!'

'I wish I'd looked through these more closely when I found the diary,' Charles said. 'But I was never alone in the house, and I didn't want Mother to know I was rooting about up there.'

He was constantly stopping to read different items, and it was Margaret, swiftly and neatly sorting the papers, who made the most exciting find. It was a large brown envelope under a pile of boys' adventure stories, and it contained Henry's Army papers. There were various official forms and leaflets, and inside a booklet with details of his Army service filled in with fading ink, there was a flimsy envelope.

'Charlie, here's your father's Army papers!' she exclaimed. 'There's a letter here too.'

The envelope was addressed in careful copperplate handwriting and contained a single sheet of notepaper. 'It's from Kate!' Charlie exclaimed when he drew it out. He scanned the page eagerly.

Dear Henry,

Thank you for your letter which I was so pleased to receive. I suppose that in the heat of battle there is no time to think, but in the rest camp you have time to consider how wrong and pointless this war is. I have thought so for a long time. You say that when you look up at the stars none of it seems to matter and I can understand that. Keep up your heart, Henry. I am glad that your memories comfort you. It comforts me too to remember the guesthouse and to think of you, and to think also of all the other brave men who are fighting for us. I pray every night for your safety and happiness.

Yours faithfully,
Kate.

'What a good letter!' Margaret exclaimed. 'Yet your mother had to teach her to read and write. She must have been a good teacher.'

'Yes. I'm impressed with the technical side, the hand-writing and the construction of the sentences, but it's more the content. What comes over from it. She sounds such a nice person,' said Charles.

'I wonder why the papers were in the trunk,' said Margaret. 'You'd think they'd be precious to your mother.'

'I think my grandmother packed that trunk,' Charles said. 'The way the things were tipped in higgledy-piggledy. It wasn't my mother's style and she'd have had more care for my father's things anyway. I suppose Grandmother Tate threw the envelope in without even looking through it.'

'Perhaps to spare your mother,' Margaret suggested.

'You know, Meg, I've been interested in Kate ever since I read my father's diary,' said Charles. 'But this has made me even more keen to find out more about her.'

'Why don't you take a trip to Liverpool after harvest,' Margaret suggested. 'Take Kit with you. She could have a look at Liverpool University – the outside anyway,' she laughed.

Their three children had attended the village school at first, then Kit had gone as a weekly boarder to a girls' college near the coast. Charles had no great interest in his old public school, and when both boys clamoured to be weekly boarders like Kit, the same arrangement was made for them in a boys' college.

They were all happy at school, and Kit was the star pupil at her college. When she was old enough, her parents agreed with her headmistress that she should try for university, and she told them that she would like to apply to Liverpool to read history.

'I suppose because you were born there,' she said to her father, 'I've always had a special feeling for Liverpool.'

Kit worked hard and to her delight was accepted at Liverpool. Her father had promised that he would take her to explore the city before she started at the university, and on a sunny day they set off together.

Charles wanted to learn more about his father's family, but he knew that Kit's main interest was in tracing her namesake, and he decided that this was Kit's day and she must decide what they did. He was interested in Kate too, chiefly because his father had cared for her.

They drove first to the university so that Kit could show her father the building with its corner turret and clock tower and peer into the courtyard so that he could picture her there. They drove past the two cathedrals, the Roman Catholic cathedral first, then along Hope Street to see the Anglican one. Men were working on both cathedrals, and Charles and Kit were impressed with the buildings but anxious not to be distracted from their plan of visiting the places mentioned in Henry's diary.

They looked in vain for the shop where Henry had worked, but like so much else it had disappeared in the Blitz. After finding a café for lunch they drove up past St George's Hall, where Henry had helped with Christmas dinners for destitute children, and the Empire Theatre where he and Agnes had attended shows. They went on up the steeply rising streets to Everton Road.

They were appalled by the large tracts of wasteground they passed where houses had once stood. 'I knew how heavily Liverpool was bombed,' Charles said. 'But somehow this makes it real. I didn't realise. The guesthouse may be gone, Kit.'

To his relief it still stood, although it had evidently suffered damage and been patched up. There were odd-coloured slates scattered about the roof, and the house looked dirty and neglected.

The woman who answered Charles's knock looked blank when he asked about Mrs Williams. 'I don't think there's no one of that name here now,' she said. 'Although they're in and outa these rooms like fleas.'

'It was a long time ago,' Charles said. 'About 1918. I'm trying to trace the family.'

'Oh Jeez, lad, 1918!' she said. 'You've got some hope. A lot got killed in the Blitz and people flitted – got rehoused, like, by the Corpy.'

Charles thanked her and decided to try a small general shop next. The woman behind the counter was anxious to be helpful. 'You'd need to speak to old people really, wouldn't you?' she said. 'My father-in-law might have known them. He's lived round here all his life but he's out with his pensioners' club today. They have a good time these days, the old people, don't they, and why shouldn't they? Have you come far?'

'From Shropshire,' Kit said, smiling at the woman, who lifted the flap of the counter.

'Shropshire! That's a long way. Come through and have a cup of tea,' she said.

The next moment they found themselves sitting in a comfortable room behind the shop, and the shopkeeper took a shoebox full of photographs from a cupboard.

'Look through them while I make a cup of tea,' she said. 'Grandad used to pick up photos that was blowing about after the bombing. Your friends might be there.'

'He won't mind?' Charles asked, but she laughed. 'Bless you, no. He loves showing them to people, hoping they'll recognise someone on them. He put the address of the house that was nearest where he found them on the back and made a guess at some of the names. He picked most of them up out of the rubble in the mornings after the bombing.'

They were fascinated by the photographs. There were none of Kate or Mrs Williams that they could see, but as Kit said, the guesthouse had not been bombed. As she plied them with tea and cake, the shopkeeper tried to remember other old people who might be able to help. 'I'll get Grandad to try to think,' she said. 'He's got a marvellous memory for his age, and if he can't remember anything about them he can ask the other old ones at the pensioners'. There's bound to be someone who knows something.'

'I'd be very grateful,' Charles said. 'There was a Mr Barnes and a Miss Tate living there who married later, and a Jack Rothwell.'

The shopkeeper wrote down the names and promised to ask about them. 'If you leave your name and address I'll write to you,' she said. 'Or better still, love, when you're at the university you can call here any time and talk to Grandad.'

As they drove away, Kit sighed happily. 'I'm going to enjoy being here,' she said. 'Wasn't she nice?'

'Don't raise your hopes too much, love,' Charles warned her. 'It's a long chance that we'll find Kate after all these years.'

'I know, but I want to try, Dad,' said Kit.

Charles smiled at her. 'Proper little terrier when you get an idea, aren't you?' he teased her. 'If she's to be found I'm sure you'll find her.'

While Charles and Kit were trying to trace her, Kate was lying in a hospital bed only a few miles away. The shop where she worked was an old-fashioned one run by the proprietor, Mr Robson, and his wife, with Kate and a shopboy as staff. Kate worked from 8 a.m. to 6 p.m., weighing out sugar and pulses and dried fruit before and after shop hours, and filling shelves.

In theory Mr Robson or the shopboy brought her the heavy sacks of sugar or wooden boxes of dried fruit, but they were often too busy and Kate had to do it herself. The shop was a busy one, and Kate worked hard serving customers and making up orders. She was quite happy with the situation, but she felt increasingly exhausted at the end of the day and even the walk home was more difficult.

One night she left the shop after a particularly heavy day and had only walked a hundred yards when she collapsed with sharp pains in her chest. When she woke she was in a hospital bed, with Richard sitting beside her. He put his hand on hers. 'Don't try to talk, Aunt Kate,' he said. 'Just rest.'

Within a few days she had improved so much that she was moved to a bed in a side ward. She was amazed and pleased at the number of people who visited her.

Rose and Robert came with a huge basket of fruit, and Rose wept and told Kate that she herself had collapsed on hearing about her sister. 'I've been in bed for two days,' she said tearfully. 'That's why I haven't been before this. I'm so worried about you.'

'Don't worry, Rose,' Kate said. 'I'm fine. The doctor says I should just take things easy and I'll be all right.'

'You must come and live with us, Kate,' Rose said.

Kate smiled at her. 'There's no need,' she said. 'You know it wouldn't work, Rose. Our lifestyles are so different.'

'Yes, but things are different now,' said Rose. 'I had a busy social life but now my health is so poor I hardly ever go out. You'd be company for me.'

Kate wavered, but Richard, who was also there, winked at her. He knew how much Kate loved her flat and valued her independence, and he said firmly, 'I think Aunt Kate should stay in her flat. She likes living there and she's got lots of friends nearby. The doctor says she'll be able to live a normal life, so you needn't worry about her, Mother.'

Rose's impulse to ask Kate to live with them had originally arisen out of concern for her sister, and it was only as she spoke that Rose realised the advantages to herself, so she chose to accept Richard's version.

'You must do as you wish, Kate,' she said. 'I'm only concerned about you.'

Kate felt a warm glow because her sister cared so much about her. 'I'll be fine,' she said. 'There's a pension now when a woman is sixty and I've got savings from when I was working, as well as my nest egg.' She smiled happily.

Many other people came to see Kate, including Essy, escorted by Magdalen. Essy walked with a stick but otherwise seemed as spry as ever, and as hostile to Rose. 'Don't let that sister of yours talk you into living with her,' she said. 'As soon as you were on your feet you'd be a handrag for her.'

'I wish you didn't dislike Rose so much, Essy,' Kate said. 'She's always been very good to me.' She looked distressed, and Magdalen nudged Essy.

'You don't dislike Mrs Willis, do you?' she said. 'You're just worried about Kate.'

Essy glanced at her then said to Kate, 'Magdalen's right. My tongue runs away with me. I just worry about you, Kate, because you never do what's best for yourself, only for other people, but you can't help your nature. You take after my poor madam. She was too soft too, but she had me to look out for her.'

Richard spoke to the young doctor who attended Kate, and he said that although Kate thought her age had caused her collapse it was actually heart failure. 'She has a heart defect,' he said, 'but with the tablets I've prescribed, and care, she can have many more years of life. Her age doesn't help, of course. Her generation has lived through difficult times. Two world wars and the Depression.'

'She's had a hard life,' Richard agreed. 'But she's very independent.'

'That indomitable spirit will help her now,' the doctor said with a smile.

Kate worried about letting the Robsons down, but her family and the doctor insisted on her retirement, and she was secretly very relieved to agree.

Many customers and other people came to see Kate, including the Robsons, but Richard was her most regular visitor. There had always been a close bond between them, and they felt that they could speak freely to each other on any subject.

Kate was nearly ready to go home when she told him how

she worried about the Robsons. 'They were so good to me and they brought me that lovely plant,' she said. 'I feel I've let them down, Richard. You know I'm nearly sixty, when I should retire, but Mr Robson had asked me to stay on.'

'Aunt Kate, they *exploited* you!' Richard exclaimed. 'D'you know, they've taken on two people to do the work you did. I just wish I'd known about it. And you're worrying about *them*!'

'I loved the job,' Kate protested. 'But I must admit I'll be glad to retire. I'll enjoy staying in bed in the mornings, especially when winter comes,' she laughed.

Richard smiled too. 'And don't think of giving up your flat to stay with Mother. She has visitors, and Dad's there all the time now, so she's not lonely. Turn over a new leaf when you leave here and do what *you* want to do.'

'You sound like Essy,' Kate said with a smile. 'She thinks single women should always be looking out for the main chance for themselves.'

'How is old Essy?' Richard said. 'I must go and see her. I mean to but the time just goes.'

'She's fine,' said Kate. 'Magdalen, the girl who looks after her, brought her. Essy's very shrewd, you know. She's worked out a scheme for keeping Magdalen with her, but I don't think it's just the money with Magdalen. I think she's really fond of Essy.'

'Magdalen? I think that's the name of John's latest girl, although she calls herself Magda,' said Richard.

'The nurses are still talking about the basket of flowers he sent me. The nurse who brought it in could hardly carry it. She said, "He must be very rich." I think she wants an introduction,' Kate said, laughing.

'He's making money hand over fist,' Richard said. 'Who'd ever have thought he'd be "something in the City", but he's got a real flair for it.'

Kate thought he looked despondent at the contrast between his brother's life and his own, and she said gently, 'John's been free to do as he likes because you've held the fort here, Rich. You saved your dad's life by taking over when you did. The worry was killing him.'

'I don't envy John. I was glad to take over, Aunt Kate,' Richard said. 'I'm not ambitious and I like the work and being in Liverpool.' He hesitated, then burst out, 'It's getting me down living at home, though. Sometimes I feel I can't stand much more of it. You know I love Mum, but she *irritates* me so much. Every day there's a fresh complaint, yet I know that basically she's a perfectly healthy woman.'

'She hasn't got much to do, Rich, and that's why she broods about her health,' said Kate. 'She really does feel these twinges and indigestion pains.'

'It doesn't bother Dad. Mum moans and he ladles out sympathy and it suits both of them, but it drives me mad. You know how it is. Once a thing starts to irritate you, you never seem to get away from it. It's giving *me* indigestion trying to eat my meal while I'm fuming about the moans. The trouble is, most fellows of my age are married by now and in their own homes.'

Kate agreed, and he went on, 'Mum goes on about that too – the marriage bit. I was too mad busy right after the war for any socialising, and now that things are easier I seem to have missed the boat. While I had my head down all the girls I might have married have paired off with other fellows.' He laughed ruefully.

'Still plenty of time,' Kate said easily. 'I'm sure there's a nice girl for you somewhere. You just haven't met her yet.'

'I thought I might get a place of my own anyway,' Richard said. 'But Mum nearly blew up when I suggested it. Thought it was a reflection on her housekeeping or something.'

'Well, when we were young and there were big families, some of them married, but the other brothers and sisters still lived at home, usually until they died. It seemed to work,' said Kate. 'They all had their own interests, choral societies and that sort of thing.'

'Yes, but times are different now,' said Richard. 'I think I'll have to do something. It's not just Mum. Dad's still interested in the business, although he hardly ever comes in now, so of course he wants to talk about it when I get home. I've had to make a lot of changes to move with the times, and by the time I've explained them I feel like climbing the walls. I just want to forget work when I get home.'

He began to laugh. 'Sorry, Aunt Kate,' he said. 'I'm a fine one to talk about moaners. You're just too good a listener.'

'You'll feel better now you've got it off your chest,' Kate said. 'And I think you're right. You *should* find your own place.'

There was the noise of a trolley and a nurse opened the door. 'Are you still here?' she exclaimed. 'Visiting hours finished ages ago. You'll get me shot.'

Richard jumped to his feet and apologised, then kissed Kate. 'Sorry about the moans. Hope I haven't caused a relapse,' he whispered.

A few days later Kate was discharged from hospital and Robert came to drive her home. He had arranged for the flat to be cleaned and the fire lit so the place was warm and welcoming, with flowers from Rose and a hamper of food. 'Rose wanted to be here to welcome you,' Robert explained, 'but she has a cold and doesn't want to pass it on to you.'

'She's very thoughtful and so are you, Robert,' Kate said. 'I'm very lucky.'

Robert stayed and had a meal with her, then told her gently that the elderly man from the upstairs flat had died while she was away.

'Oh dear, his wife'll miss him. They were so devoted, never apart. I think they have one daughter who's a war widow.'

Shortly after Robert left, the daughter of the couple upstairs came to see Kate. 'I was sorry to hear you'd been ill, Miss Drew,' she said. 'You heard about my father?'

'Yes, I was so sorry,' Kate said. 'Your mother'll miss him. They were always together.'

'Yes. Her gaoler,' the girl said with venom. 'He was obsessively jealous, you know. Wouldn't leave even me alone with her, and when my husband was alive he couldn't come to the flat with me. It made me so bitter when Geoff was killed. A good man like him, and my horrible old father left. Anyway, thank God he's gone first so I can make it up to Mum.'

'You'll be able to comfort each other,' Kate murmured, feeling out of her depth.

'I'm going to take her to live with me in Chester,' the girl said. 'I'll make sure she enjoys the time she's got left now he's gone. I'm just telling you because we'll be giving the landlord notice next week. I hope you get someone nice upstairs and keep better yourself.'

'I was flabbergasted,' Kate told Richard later. 'I thought they were so devoted. She was a timid little woman, mind you. The daughter seems a nice girl. She said she hoped I got someone nice upstairs.' They suddenly stared at each other, the thought striking both of them at the same instant.

'Are you thinking what I am?' Richard said. 'How would you feel about me taking the flat?'

'I'd be delighted,' Kate said truthfully. 'But what about your mum and dad? I wouldn't want to upset them.'

'I'm sure they'll see the sense of it,' Richard said. 'I'll be careful how I put it to them, but I'm quite determined.'

Kate found it difficult to sleep that night. I'd love to have Richard living upstairs, she thought. I'm so fond of him and I'd feel safe if he was near. Although she never admitted it, the collapse had shaken her confidence in herself. But what if Rose objected? I'd hate to cause trouble between her and Richard.

She tossed and turned, then diverted her thoughts to her usual resource, her happy memories of Henry. Since the war, when she'd realised that his son was old enough to fight, her dreams had been given another dimension. She often thought about the boy and wondered whether he was as good a man as his father had been. She was smiling as she drifted off to sleep.

Robert welcomed the idea of Richard taking the upstairs flat and told Rose that now she could stop worrying about

Kate, so she agreed too. It was quickly arranged, and Richard moved in two weeks later. Kate's old friend Nell, who had also retired but continued to live near nursing friends in London, was visiting, and she advised Kate to continue to treat the flats as separate establishments.

'I intend to,' Kate said. 'Otherwise Rich would be jumping out of the frying pan into the fire if he had me round his neck.'

Nell laughed. 'I might have known you didn't need advice,' she said. 'I used to wish you'd done more with your life, Kate. I've been so fulfilled with my nursing, but you always seemed to draw the short straw. Still, you've got through in spite of everything.'

Kate's eyes widened in surprise. 'I've been very lucky, Nell,' she said. 'I've always met such nice people and they've been very good to me, especially Rose and her family.'

Nell hugged her impulsively. 'You're like the sundial, love,' she said. 'You only mark the sunny hours.' They both laughed and returned to discussing their outfits for the sixtieth birthday party Rose and Robert were giving for Kate.

John returned for Kate's party with his fiancée, Magda, a slim, dark girl with a bell of shining dark hair and crimson lips and nails. She was a model, and both Kate and Nell liked her. Nell said that she had talked to Magda about her nursing. 'We talked about the district where I did my midwifery and she told me she was born there. Don't worry. If she's come up from those hovels to this she won't have any trouble turning "Johnny Head in the Air" to "Johnny Feet on the Ground",' she said.

The party was a great success. Kate was enjoying this phase of her life. She liked being able to stay in bed as long as she wished, then getting up to potter about her flat and visit or be visited by friends.

A pattern was established with Richard. He and Kate led separate lives although they often had their evening meal together and saw each other briefly every day. In spite of the difference in their ages they were good friends, with a shared sense of humour and the same taste in books and music. They enjoyed long discussions after a meal together, while Kate knitted and Richard relaxed with a cigarette.

Richard felt that he could talk to Kate as to no one else and she would understand. One night they discussed the war years, and Richard said thoughtfully, 'You know, when the war started I thought it was just an interruption and I'd soon be able to get on with my usual life. I had all sorts of plans, but I thought I was just postponing them. I was nineteen when it started and twenty-five when it finished, and I suddenly realised that the years had gone without me noticing.'

Kate nodded. 'I suppose you had too much else to think about while you were flying,' she said.

He smiled ruefully. 'Yes, but in the back of my mind there was a feeling that when we got this lot over I'd do all the things I'd planned, like hiking round Europe. I didn't realise that when it was over I'd be a different fellow at a different stage in my life, and the world would be different too.'

'And of course you had a few extra years when you weren't free, with having to sort out your father's business after the war,' said Kate.

Richard laughed. 'I'm not complaining,' he said. 'I enjoyed doing it, though it was hectic at times, but I was lucky to have it to come back to. I must sound cracked. As though I thought I was like Peter Pan and I'd go back to being nineteen when the war ended.'

'No, I understand,' Kate said. 'I know the feeling. I felt as though I'd hardly got used to being grown up and suddenly I was old. I didn't notice it happening.'

'Never! You'll never be old, Kate. Your mind's too lively for that.'

'I don't *feel* old,' Kate admitted. 'But then I don't think anyone does. You feel differently inside to the way you look on the outside. It takes some getting used to,' she added ruefully, and they laughed together.

Although each had their own friends they enjoyed the

time they spent together and unobtrusively each made life easier for the other. It was a relief to all who cared for Kate to know that Richard was near if she needed him.

Chapter Twenty-Two

Although Kit was determined to trace Kate, she had little time to spare during her first year at university. Her first term began on 6 October and on the previous day her father drove her to Liverpool to register at the university. Afterwards he took her to the female Hall of Residence in Holly Road, Fairfield, where she was to live, sharing a room with two other students.

Kit had been nervous about meeting the Warden, Miss Knight, because of the impressive letters after her name, but she proved to be kind and welcoming. They also met Kit's two roommates, Alytwyn, a Welsh girl from Anglesey, a self-confident, extrovert type, and Helen from Manchester, who was as quiet as Kit.

'I'm sure you'll be happy there, Kit,' Charlie said as they came away. 'You must go to Miss Knight if you have any problems that we can't solve, but keep closely in touch with home, won't you, love? We're all going to miss you, especially Mum.'

Kit looked tearful, as though realising her position for the first time, and Charlie hastily suggested a drive past his old home.

'It's not far from here,' he said. 'This is Kensington we're turning into, and Prescot Road is a continuation of it. Rufford Road, where we lived, is off Prescot Road. Only a short walk, really, from where you'll be living.'

Kit was fascinated by the house in Rufford Road as they drove slowly past it and parked further up the road. They walked back past the house, then up again on the other side of the road. It was a large semi-detached Victorian villa with a big garden, but Charles said it seemed much smaller than he remembered, especially the garden.

'I was just thinking what a lovely solid house and big garden,' Kit exclaimed.

Charles laughed. 'I agree, but the garden seemed enormous to me. I was only four when we left.'

'Don't you remember your father at all?' Kit said.

'Just fleeting memories. I remember him throwing me up in the air and pushing me on a swing, and I remember riding on his shoulders with my arms round his head. He had tight golden curls,' he said. 'He bought me a rocking horse. I remember that day. I wonder what happened to Dobbin?'

'Your father would have been in the Army for most of your childhood, I suppose,' said Kit.

'Yes. I only remember him in uniform,' Charlie agreed. 'D'you know, I remember an argument about that. He wanted to wear civilian clothes and Mother and Grandma Tate said he should wear uniform. I remember Grandma Tate saying something about white feathers.'

'That someone might give him one, you mean?' said Kit. 'That did happen to men in civilian clothes. I've read about it.'

They were standing across the road under a tree, looking at the house, and Charles said slowly, 'It's amazing. I thought I remembered nothing about that time, but all sorts of things are coming back to me. Some I might really remember happening, or Grandma Barnes might have told me about them.'

'Grandma Barnes? Your father's mother?' asked Kit.

'Yes, and I loved her. She took me out every day and put me to bed, and we had all sorts of little secrets from the other two.' He laughed, then his smile faded. They were walking back to the car now, and he said, 'I've just realised. I remember the day the telegram came about my father. I wasn't aware of it then, of course.'

'You wouldn't be at that age, would you? And I suppose they kept the news from you,' said Kit, but Charlie said slowly, 'I remember it was such a happy day. Grandma had bought me a little sailing boat and we sailed it on the pond in Newsham Park. She hid it in her shopping bag and when we got back Mother and Grandma Tate were standing in the hall.' He stood leaning on the car, obviously reliving the memory, and Kit watched him sympathetically but said nothing.

'I thought they'd found out about the boat. Grandma Tate grabbed me and hustled me into the dining room, and Mother took Grandma Barnes into the drawing room. I heard her cry out and I tried to go to her but Grandma Tate held on to me. I thought my mother was being cruel to Grandma because of the boat. I got away and ran to Grandma and she was crying. She put her arms round me and I clung to her and shouted at my mother that I'd asked Grandma for the boat.'

'Was your mother very upset?' asked Kit.

'No, she knew I didn't understand what had happened. With hindsight I can see that her life must have been difficult, with both my grandmothers living there.'

'It can't have been easy for your father when he came home on leave either,' said Kit.

'No,' Charles agreed. 'I remember him always laughing and cheerful, but perhaps that was just for my benefit. He had a sort of warmth about him like Grandma Barnes, but Grandmother Tate was a horror. Very strict and sour, and Mother was very reserved. She said to me once, years later, that she had always loved me but her mother thought any display of emotion was vulgar, and she was a very dominant woman. I detested my Grandma Tate.'

'I didn't detest *my* grandma, your mother, although I was a bit afraid of her,' said Kit. 'I always felt that she loved us really, although she never showed it.'

'Mother said that when Grandma Barnes died, shortly after my father, I pushed Mother away when she tried to comfort me and screamed for Grandma. She said she cried all night, the tears she hadn't shed when Dad was killed as well as because I had hurt her. I don't remember it at all.'

Charles smiled at Kit. 'That's enough of old unhappy

far-off things,' he said. 'Let's get something to eat and talk about something more cheerful.'

Kit laughed. 'Like tracking down Kate,' she said. 'I'm determined to find her if she's still alive, Dad.'

'Yes, but don't neglect your studies to do it, love,' Charlie said. 'This is a wonderful chance for you, Kit. Don't waste it.'

They would have been amazed to know that Kate was sitting in her flat in Lilley Road, only a five-minutes walk away from the Hall of Residence in Holly Road.

Kit settled happily into life at the university, in spite of a few bouts of homesickness. She enjoyed the subject she was studying, medieval and modern history, and found her spare time was fully occupied. The three roommates joined the Students' Union and were caught up in all the activities.

Alytwyn, always known as Alyt, was the group comedian and entertained them with her father's reaction to her request for the necessary five guineas to join the Union. '"Iss there no end to it?"' she wailed. '"Five guineas! Squeezing me dry you are. I neffer thought daughters could be so expensive."' Although Kit laughed, she appreciated the difference in her own father's attitude.

Alyt loved music and swept Kit and Helen off to concerts at the Philharmonic Hall and various Liverpool churches. She was more worldly-wise than the other two girls, with a reckless, happy-go-lucky attitude to life, and they learned a lot from her. Kit also learned that people were often more complex than they seemed, when they attended a performance of the *Messiah* at the Welsh chapel where Alyt worshipped, and she saw tears pouring down Alyt's face as she listened to the music.

With all these new experiences and activities, the search for Kate was postponed, although Kit was still determined to find her. She had written to the shopkeeper, Mrs Hayes, but had not found time to visit her.

It was not until just before the long vacation at the end of Kit's first year at the university that she was able to resume the search for Kate. Meanwhile Charles, who had visited Liverpool several times – once with Margaret to take Kit out for a meal, and other times alone – had succeeded in tracing his father's family. He found that his father had had a brother, Robert, who had been killed in 1915, and a sister, Lucy, who had died in May 1914 in Cheshire.

He also traced his father's father, Luke Barnes, who had been a grain merchant in Liverpool until his death at the age of forty-eight years, and was delighted to find that Luke had been the second son of a farmer in Lancashire. 'So that's where I got my love of farming, from my great-grandfather,' Charlie told Margaret exultantly when he returned home.

'I wonder why Luke didn't farm?' Margaret said.

'He was the second son. I suppose the eldest got the farm,' said Charles. 'It's fascinating, you know, Meg. My own flesh and blood. They seem quite real to me now.'

Margaret smiled at him. 'I wish Kit could find out about Kate, Charlie,' she said. 'She's really set her heart on it.'

'She will,' Charles said confidently. 'But there's too much to distract her at present. Finding her feet, making friends and doing new things, as well as the work. I tell you what, I can see now why she's so fascinated by history and why she enjoys it so much.'

'Yes, she made the right choice,' Margaret said. 'She seems really happy, doesn't she?' and Charles agreed.

Although Kit had not found time to pursue her search for Kate, she often thought about her and wondered whether the shopkeeper had learned anything from her father-in-law, or whether she had forgotten all about them. On the day before she returned home for the long summer vacation Kit impulsively set off to visit Mrs Hayes.

She was warmly welcomed and introduced to Grandad, a fat, rosy-cheeked old man. Mrs Hayes told Kit that she had meant to write to her at the university. 'I didn't know how to address the envelope, though, and I didn't want to make a show of myself or disgrace you,' she explained. 'Grandad's found this old feller. He used to fill coal buckets at the boarding house and he remembers Mrs Williams and Kate.'

'Does he?' Kit exclaimed excitedly. 'Can I talk to him?'

Grandad took his pipe from his mouth and shook his

head, and Mrs Hayes asked if Kit could come back the next day. 'He'll be out now but I could ask him to come here tomorrow. He's only in one room, y'see, and he might feel a bit ashamed, like, if you went there.'

'That'd be better still,' Kit said. 'My dad is arriving to drive me home tomorrow, so he could come with me, if you don't mind.' It was quickly arranged and Kit telephoned her father that night to tell him.

When Charles arrived he had two boxes in the car. 'One for Mrs Hayes and one for the old man in one room,' he said. 'Just some butter and eggs and ham.'

'I'm glad you're coming with me, Dad,' Kit exclaimed. 'I'd never have thought of that.'

'It was Mum's idea,' Charlie admitted. 'Just a thank-you.'

The gifts were gratefully received by Mrs Hayes, and by the old man, who was introduced as Jackie. 'No use knowing a farmer if you can't get a bit extra,' Charlie said to them with a wink. The old man sitting with Grandad was as small and shrunken as Grandad was fat and rosy, but he could tell them a great deal about the boarding house.

'Guesthouse she liked it called. Proper snob she was, Mrs Williams, and tight! As tight as—' A violent nudge from Grandad nearly knocked him off his seat, and he finished, 'as a – a drum. Kate was nice, though. She often give me a cup of cocoa or a dripping buttie when the old one was outa the way.'

'Do you remember a Miss Tate or a Mr Barnes who lived there?' Charles asked. 'They were married from the guesthouse.'

'No, not really. I only filled the coal buckets. There was another girl, Josie. She was nice too. I got told she married some Irish feller and went to live over there.'

'Do you know what happened to Kate Drew?' Kit said eagerly.

Jackie shook his head. 'No. I went in the Army in 1914, see. Me ma told me Mrs Williams died up to her eyes in debt, like, and everything got sold up. She had posh relations, though. Kate might of gone to them.'

336

The old man had been staring at Charles. 'This Mr Barnes—' he began doubtfully, and Charles said quickly, 'He was my father.'

'I thought so. You're the spitting image of him, lad. I seen him one day,' said the old man. 'I'd forgot, but looking at you brought it back, like.'

'What do you remember of him?' Charles asked eagerly, and Jackie said slowly, 'Kate was giving me a buttie on the sly one day, and someone come down the kitchen stairs. I thought it was the missus and I was going to leg it, but she said, "It's all right, Jackie. It's Mr Barnes." He was a lovely feller, a real gent but very easy, like, the way he talked to me. He never made me feel like dirt the way some posh people did. He give me sixpence. He was friendly, like, with Kate too. That's the only time I seen him.'

Mrs Hayes had been standing with her finger on her lips, thinking, and she said suddenly, 'Winnie Collins. She told me when she was in the other day that her second cousin that got left a house and loads of money – the woman she worked for was Mrs Williams's sister. I'll go and get Winnie. She only lives in the next street.'

She darted out, and while she was gone Charles took the opportunity to give each of the old men a five-pound note folded small. 'Thanks for your help. Have a drink on us,' he said. Grandad thanked him and pocketed it, but old Jackie unfolded the large white note and gaped at it. 'A five-pun note,' he said. 'I never seen one of these before. Not to have it in me hand, like.'

'Put it in your pocket, lad,' advised Grandad. He winked at Charles. 'We don't have to let the wimmin know all our business.'

Mrs Hayes returned alone. 'Winnie'd just taken her teeth out and put her slippers on so she wouldn't come, but she gave me her cousin's address. She's still alive, she says, but very old, living in luxury.'

She handed Charles an address written in shaky hand-writing. 'Her cousin's name is Esther Mills. Miss. She never got married. She should know what happened to Kate Drew.'

'Thanks very much,' Charles said gratefully. 'Is there anything—?' He let the question hang in the air, and Mrs Hayes said briskly, 'I'll give Winnie some ham and eggs. She'll be made up. She's always moaning because she never gets nothing from her rich cousin.'

They left, promising to let Mrs Hayes know how their search progressed, and Kit squeezed her father's arm. 'I'm glad you came, Dad. I wouldn't have known what to do about "mugging them", as we say in Liverpool.'

They both laughed, and Charles said, 'They didn't expect it, I'm sure, love. They wanted to help but it was just a thank-you.'

Kit giggled. 'Weren't the old men funny about "the wimmin"?' she said. 'I feel we're near to finding Kate now, Dad.'

Charles advised caution. 'You've built up a picture of Kate in your mind, but you might not like her when you meet her, love. Her life was very hard, at least in her youth, and it might have made her very sour and bitter,' he said, but Kit was not convinced.

She settled back happily into the routine of home, but before she was due to return for her second year at university she and her father had another day in Liverpool. Charles had written to Miss Mills asking if he and his daughter might visit her. He was trying to trace a Mrs Williams and a Miss Katherine Drew who had lived in Everton Road, and he had been told that she might be able to help him.

'Someone might have left Kate a fortune,' Essy said excitedly to Magdalen when the letter arrived. 'Now don't tell anyone about this. That other one's not getting any of it if I can help it.'

'The letter doesn't say anything about a fortune,' Magdalen protested. 'I think you should be careful, Miss Essy. They might be confidence tricksters,' but Essy wrote immediately, inviting Charles and his daughter to call. Magdalen determined to be present just in case.

When Charles and Kit arrived, they explained who they were, and that Charles's parents had met and married from the guesthouse. 'They're both dead,' Charles said.

'But looking through my father's papers I see that he and my mother were very friendly with Mrs Williams's niece, Katherine Drew. We've heard Mrs Williams is dead but we thought if we could find Miss Drew she might be able to tell us about my parents.'

'Kate would remember them,' said Essy. 'She ran that place for years before Mildred died. Mildred was no loss, I can tell you, and the state she left her affairs in! And poor Kate, left to clear up the mess after nursing her and working herself to the bone for her. Mildred was a gambler like her father, for all her airs and graces.'

Magdalen coughed warningly, but Essy disregarded her and went on, 'You'd never think her and my madam were sisters. As different as chalk and cheese. My madam, Miss Beattie, was beautiful like her poor mother, but Mildred was like their father in every way. She even looked like a man.'

Charles tried to slip in a question about Kate, and Magdalen served wine and fruit cake, but Essy was enjoying herself and nothing could stem the flow. They heard all about the earlier generation, the meek aristocratic mother of Beattie, Mildred and Sophie, and their father who gambled away a fortune on the Stock Exchange. She told them of Beattie's wedding and of Sophie marrying a soldier who was killed in the Boer War.

'She was the mother of Kate and that Rose,' she said. 'She kept poor Kate from school to wait on her when there was nothing wrong with her but drink, but not the other one, oh no. You'll stay to lunch,' she ordered abruptly, and they looked helplessly at Magdalen, who smiled and disappeared.

'Is Kate still alive?' Charles asked quickly.

Essy looked startled. 'Of course she's still alive,' she said. 'She often comes to see me. She's a good girl but nothing's ever gone right for her. When that mother died she went to Mildred. Nobody ate idle bread in that house and she very near worked Kate to death. My madam did her best for her, gave her gifts and money, but I suppose Mildred took them off her.'

She stopped to draw breath, and Charles opened his mouth, but before he could speak Essy swept on, 'Then when Mildred was dying poor Kate fell in with a fellow who took advantage of her and there was a baby, but it died. After that she was just a drudge in these homes for fallen women. My poor madam took the other one, Rose. She cherished a viper in her breast, as the Bible says. I'll never forgive myself that I didn't try to stop it, but I thought it would be an interest for my poor lady. Someone to dress and be company for her. Little did I know!'

'Is that Kate's sister? Is she still alive?' asked Charles.

'Yes. Why do you think everyone's dead?' Essy said pettishly. 'The wicked flourish like the green bay tree.'

Magdalen appeared and announced that lunch was ready, and Essy rose with alacrity and led the way into the dining room. They were served a delicious soup, followed by omelettes with garden peas and tiny new potatoes, then strawberries and cream. 'Magdalen has green fingers,' Essy announced with satisfaction. 'She grows these little potatoes for me, even for Christmas dinner because I like them.'

'Did you cook the meal too?' Charles asked Magdalen, and when she nodded he said, 'Then you're a wonderful cook too. This is all delicious.' He and Kit were enjoying the meal and both were glad of the respite from Essy's flow of reminiscences. There was so much to take in yet they were unable to ask the questions they wanted to.

Before the strawberries were served she started again. 'My madam always kept a good table. She was a lovely lady. Everybody loved her, she was so kind and gentle. Her husband idolised her and when he died he made sure he left her well provided for. And he knew I would always look after her. The only time we ever disagreed was over that Rose. Wicked, scheming, ungrateful girl. She broke my poor madam's heart but madam saw through her at the end.'

The strawberries were served and Charles and Kit thought it wiser not to ask any questions of Essy as she poured cream into her dish and began to eat greedily, but when the meal was finished and they went back into the other room, Charles asked again about Kate.

'She hasn't been to see me for a while. She's been very ill with overwork,' Essy said, but Magdalen, who was pouring coffee, said gently, 'She came a fortnight ago, Miss Essy. Mr Richard brought her.'

'I know. I hadn't forgotten,' Essy snapped, but it was clear that she had. 'Tell them about the legacy,' Magdalen suggested, and Essy smiled again. 'Yes, madam saw the way that Rose treated her. Her husband brought the little boys to see madam and looked after her interests but Rose was always too busy or pretending to be ill. Before she died madam said to me I had always been her one true friend.' She smiled fondly.

'The will,' Magdalen prompted her, and Essy roused herself again.

'Oh yes, the will. Rose expected to get everything but all she got was madam's jewellery, and lucky to get that. No message with it. Madam left the bulk of her money between the two boys and a thousand pounds to her dear niece Katherine Drew. She'd already given Mr Willis some things of her husband's and she left him her grateful love for his care of her during her last years. But not a word about Rose,' she cackled.

She paused impressively. 'But then – what really stuck in that one's craw – she left her house and contents and an annuity to her faithful friend and companion Esther Mills – me!' Essy gazed at them triumphantly and they both murmured congratulations. 'That showed that she appreciated all that you'd done for her,' Charles said, and Essy said venomously, 'Aye, and that she saw through that Rose Willis.'

They were silent for a moment, then Charles said quietly, 'We'd like very much to get in touch with Kate if we can,' and Magdalen said persuasively, 'Mr Barnes wants to find out about his parents.'

'What do I know about his parents?' Essy said pettishly. 'I suppose they took advantage of Kate in that guesthouse, as Mildred called it. Everyone did.' She suddenly seemed tired and Charles signalled to Kit and rose.

'Thank you very much, Miss Mills,' he said. 'You've been very kind,' but Essy already seemed sleepy.

Magdalen showed them out. 'Don't take too much notice of what Miss Essy says,' she whispered. 'She took a dislike to Mrs Willis when she was a child and she remembers those days more clearly than what's happening now.'

'Thank you,' Charles said. 'I hope we didn't make extra work for you. That was a delicious lunch.'

'I enjoyed doing it. We don't have many visitors,' said Magdalen. 'I've written down Kate's address for you.' She thrust the paper at them and said a hasty goodbye as Essy began to call for her.

Charles and Kit walked to the car feeling dazed by the amount of information that had poured out on them. 'I feel as though I've been hit by a tidal wave,' Charles said. 'What an overpowering old woman.'

'Yes. And so bitter,' Kit said. 'Imagine hating someone like that all your life. Poor Rose.'

'We should have got her address too, in case we can't reach Kate,' said Charles.

He was unfolding the paper with Kate's address as he spoke, and now he exclaimed, 'Good God!'

'What's up? What's wrong?' Kit asked, and he held out the paper.

'Look where she lives. Lilley Road!'

'Lilley Road? But that's only a stone's throw from Holly Road. It's *off* Holly Road,' gasped Kit. 'I don't know how I haven't met her.'

'You wouldn't have known who she was if you did,' Charles pointed out. 'And she wouldn't know you.'

'Oh, Dad, this is fate,' Kit exclaimed.

Charles glanced at his watch. 'It's only just after two o'clock,' he said. 'There's a phone number too. I could ring her now.'

'Oh yes, do, Dad. Find a phone box right away.'

They stopped at the first phone box and Charles found that his hands were trembling as he dialled the number. Kit stood in the box with him and she was trembling too. 'Oh Dad, I feel afraid. What if—' she began, but a voice with a slight Irish lilt answered and Charles hastily pressed Button A.

'Hello. Am I speaking to Miss Katherine Drew, please?' he asked.

'No. I'm Josie Malloy. I'm staying with Kate. She's had a fall and she's in bed for a few days,' the voice replied.

Charles hastily fed more money into the box. 'My name is Barnes. Miss Drew knew my parents when they lived in Liverpool in a guesthouse,' he said. 'They're both dead now but I was hoping to speak to Miss Drew about them.'

'God bless us. Mr Barnes and Miss Tate. I knew them too. Where are you now?' demanded the voice.

'In Liverpool for the day with my daughter,' said Charles. 'We're in Woolton now.'

'Can you find Lilley Road? Ask for the ice rink in Prescot Road and anybody'll direct you from there,' said Josie.

'Er – yes – yes,' Charles stuttered.

'Well, come and see Kate now,' said Josie. 'I'll be here to let you in. She'll be made up to see you.'

'But if she's ill—?'

'She's not ill, just shaken up by the fall, but the doctor told her to stay in bed and I'm seeing that she does. Nothing wrong with her eyes and ears and tongue, though,' she chuckled. 'Come as soon as you can.'

'Thanks. We'd love to if you're sure it's all right,' Charles said gratefully.

'Sure it is. We'll expect you when you land, then. Have you got the house number?'

'Yes,' said Charles, and before he could say any more Josie said cheerfully, 'Ta-ra then. See you soon,' and hung up, leaving Kit and her father staring at each other.

Kit hugged him. 'Oh Dad, after all this time. As simple as that.' She was almost in tears, and as they walked back to the car Charles squeezed her arm.

'Remember. Don't build up your hopes too much. Keep an open mind, love.'

'I will,' she promised, but she felt that already she knew Kate and liked her.

Chapter Twenty-Three

While Kit was experiencing her first exciting year at the university, absorbing new experiences and impressions and making new friends, Kate, living a few minutes' walk away from her, was enjoying a peaceful retirement.

There was a second-hand bookshop in Kensington where she spent many happy hours browsing. She often thought of her early days in the guesthouse when she spent her small wages on books from the stalls outside St John's Gardens in the centre of Liverpool, but had little free time to read them. Now she could buy whatever she liked, within reason, and return home to read at her leisure in front of a good fire and with a cup of tea beside her. For the first time in her life there was no need to watch the clock.

Nell came to visit several times, and on one memorable occasion Kate travelled to London to stay with her old friend. She had been nervous about meeting Nell's nursing colleagues but Nell told her that they were more likely to feel shy with her.

'It's difficult for us nurses to adapt,' she said. 'To deal with people socially rather than as patients or their relatives. You have a sort of quiet dignity, Kate, that can be very intimidating.'

As Nell knew, the thought that other people might be shy was enough to make Kate forget her own shyness and exert herself to be friendly, and she was a big success with Nell's friends. 'Now that you've done it once, I hope you'll often come to see me. I've always been a bit jealous of your visits to Josie,' Nell joked, and Kate promised that she would.

Old Mrs Malloy had died during the war, but Josie and Michael's eldest daughter was now married and living in the village and she was always willing to take over Josie's household and free her mother to visit Kate. Kate also spent two happy holidays on the farm.

Josie was the only one who remembered Henry and could talk about him with Kate. Nell had never known him and Rose had never shown any interest in him and knew nothing about Kate's secret dreams and the comfort they had brought her.

Josie also remembered Gordon, and was the only person who knew that Kate still donated a toy to Alder Hey Children's Hospital every 1 January. She sometimes wondered whether Kate realised that Gordon had abandoned her all those years ago, or whether she still believed that he had intended to return but was prevented, but with rare delicacy she forbore to ask.

Kate only spoke once to Josie about it. Marie and George had moved to Manchester and now had three children. They were living in comfort in an exclusive suburb and George now owned his own business. They seemed settled and happy. Kate showed Josie a letter from Marie in which she wrote:

> George was very keen to emigrate to Canada but I couldn't put an ocean between myself and my darling first-born son. Even if I never see him again, he is always in my heart, and as dear to me as my other children. I will never interfere and spoil his life with his adoptive parents, but I must be here if he needs me.

'George must be a very understanding man,' Josie said as she handed back the letter, but Kate's eyes had filled with tears. 'Yes, poor man, and poor Marie. I was better off losing my child like that. Marie had time to know her baby and she must always wonder whether he's happy.'

'I don't think it was easy for you,' Josie said. 'I'm just mad that I didn't know about it at the time.' She was tempted to suggest that Kate might have felt more had the baby been Henry's rather than Gordon's, but she decided on discretion.

Kate had enjoyed the winter, snug and warm in her flat with Richard in the rooms above always willing to drive her anywhere she wanted to go. The spring and summer were a delight to her as she strolled around the leafy roads near her home, watching the effect of the changing seasons and the flowers in the gardens. She enjoyed the autumn too, but one day shortly before Josie was due to arrive for a visit, she went down the two steps into her back garden, stepped on a wet leaf and fell heavily.

No bones were broken, but she was dishevelled and muddy and badly shaken. She managed to get back into the house and was cleaning off the mud when Josie arrived with Robert, who had met her off the boat.

'What's happened to you?' they exclaimed, and although she protested that she was only muddy, Robert insisted on phoning her doctor. Josie helped her to clean off the mud and made her a cup of tea. When the doctor arrived he told Kate she must stay in bed for a few days.

'I'll see that she does, Doctor,' Josie promised. She would have none of Kate's protests. 'We can talk as well if you're in bed as if you're up,' she said. 'And that's what I've come for, a talk. And I can cook as well as you, even if you did teach me.'

Kate was still in bed the next day when the call came from Charles. Josie took it in the hall, then went into Kate's bedroom. 'Did you hear that?' she cried, and Kate gasped, 'Did you say Mr Barnes?'

'Yes, our Mr Barnes's son,' said Josie. 'He said his parents were dead and he wanted to talk to you about them. I said he could come.'

'Oh Josie, when?' Kate exclaimed, and when Josie said, 'Now,' she shrieked, 'Oh no, Josie, I can't.'

'Yes you can,' Josie said firmly, although her own face was flushed and she was obviously excited. 'Keep calm. That's why I told him to come now so you wouldn't have time to get worked up.'

Kate threw back the bedclothes. 'I must get up,' she said distractedly, but Josie insisted that she stayed where she was.

'I've told him you're in bed,' she said. 'Don't make a liar of me. Get washed and change your nightie while I make your bed. Here, put Nell's present on.' She pulled a pretty nightdress and matching bedjacket from a drawer and thrust them into Kate's arms. 'Go on. Don't stand there like one of Lewis's dummies,' she said. 'But don't panic. They're driving from Woolton, so you've got time. He's bringing his little daughter with him.'

Kate stood in the bathroom, clutching the nightdress and bedjacket and staring at the reflection of her white face and terror-stricken eyes in the mirror. Oh God, what will I do? she thought. All these years she had lived on her dreams of Henry. They had fulfilled and comforted her for nearly all her life, but now this was reality. Henry's son and his granddaughter, but Agnes's too, she thought. What would they be like? How could she bear her life if she lost her dreams?

She was still standing immobile when Josie knocked on the door. 'Your bed's ready, Kate,' she called. 'I've used your posh bedlinen.' Kate woke from her trance and quickly washed and changed.

Charlie and Kit were agitated too as they drove to Fairfield. 'I can't believe this is happening,' Kit said, clasping her hands tightly together. 'Now it's so near I'm scared, Dad. I wonder what Kate's *really* like?'

'We'll soon know,' Charlie said sturdily, although he too was apprehensive.

'I wonder how much of what Miss Mills told us was true?' Kate said. 'I mean, I wonder did Kate really have a baby and it died?'

'It's quite possible,' Charlie said cautiously. 'But if she did, Kit, we don't know the circumstances.'

'Oh, I'm not condemning her,' Kit exclaimed. 'People are more sensible about such things now. I just wondered if it was true. She seems to have had enough bad luck without that.'

'I don't think Miss Mills's memory was very reliable,' said Charlie. 'The maid said as much, didn't she?'

'Wasn't she horrible about the other sister? I wouldn't

like her for an enemy,' Kit said. 'Yet Kate still visits her.'

'Duty visits, I should think,' said Charlie. 'I wonder who Mr Richard is?'

'Who knows?' Kit said indifferently, looking out of the window. 'Oh Dad, this looks familiar. Are we nearly there?'

'Not far now. Brace yourself, Katherine Margaret,' said Charlie and Kit laughed nervously.

A few minutes later they found the house, and the door was opened to them by a small, plump woman with curly white hair, but with a rosy face and merry brown eyes.

'Mr Barnes!' she exclaimed. 'Sure, you're the image of him. Come in, come in. And this is your daughter. I was expecting a little girl.' She laughed.

'Yes, this is Kit, and I'm Charlie Barnes,' he said. 'I hope it's not inconvenient us coming now.'

'Not at all, not at all,' said Josie. 'Kate's dying to see you. Give me your coats and I'll tell her.' She opened a door further down the hall. 'They're here, Kate,' she said. 'Are you decent?' then called them into the bedroom.

They saw a thin woman with neat grey hair and bowed shoulders, wearing a pretty bedjacket, with a lacy pillow behind her. Kate's face was flushed and she was sitting tensely upright, with her work-worn hands knotted tightly before her on the counterpane. When she saw Charlie, the tenseness left her and she exclaimed, 'Oh God, you're so like Henry!'

'That's what I said,' declared Josie.

Charlie held out his hand. 'Hello,' he said simply. 'I'm Charlie Barnes and this is my daughter, Kit.' Kit smiled shyly at Kate and Josie pushed chairs forward for them to sit beside Kate's bed. Kate seemed too overwhelmed to speak, and Josie said quickly, 'We're surprised at Mr Barnes having a grown-up granddaughter. We still think of him as a young man, don't we, Kate?'

Kate still seemed unable to speak, and Charlie said, 'He was so young when he was killed, but I'm turned forty and Kit's been at Liverpool University for a year.'

Kate had recovered a little from the shock of seeing

Charlie, and now she said gently to Kit, 'At Liverpool University? Do you like it?'

'Yes, very much,' said Kit shyly. 'I live at the female Hall of Residence in Holly Road.'

Josie and Kate glanced at each other in surprise. 'But that's only round the corner,' Kate exclaimed.

'Yes, it's ironic. We've been looking for you for ages, and Kit was only a few minutes away from you,' Charlie said. Kate and Josie looked puzzled and he explained, 'My mother died a few years ago and I inherited some family papers. I was interested in you before that – er, Miss Drew.'

'Kate,' Josie and Kate said together, and he smiled and said, 'Kate. When I was eleven or so I found an old trunk in the attic and my father's diary was in it. He mentioned you so often that I was curious. My mother had remarried and I was going to my stepfather's old school as a boarder. I took the diary with me. It was mostly written when he lived in the boarding house where he met my mother.'

'I heard that your mother moved away from Liverpool,' Kate said. 'After – after he was killed.'

'We lived in Shrewsbury. Moved there from Liverpool when I was about four with my grandmother. My mother's mother. I farm now in Shropshire,' said Charlie.

'And now your mother is dead,' Kate said. She seemed unable to take her eyes from his face.

'Yes. She and her second husband were living in Italy when she died. He's a good man and I think he made her happy,' said Charlie. 'He's staying in Italy because the climate suits him.'

They were both skirting round the subject of Henry until Charlie noticed the silver-framed snapshot on the bedside table. 'That photo!' he exclaimed. 'There's one like that in my box of pictures.'

Kate blushed and picked up the photo. 'Your mother gave me this when I visited her during the war – the Great War, I mean. You're the baby in it, of course. You looked like your father even then. Do you remember him at all?'

'Only odd flashes,' Charlie said.

Josie had been perched on the end of the bed, but now

she rose and said to Kit, 'Come and help me to make tea, love. Leave these two to talk over old times.' Kit would have preferred to stay, but she went with Josie to the kitchen, and Kate and Charlie were left smiling at each other.

'I can't believe we've found you at last,' said Charlie. 'I've wanted to meet you ever since I read the diary.'

'I can't imagine why I was mentioned in it,' Kate said. 'I only worked in the guesthouse, though my aunt owned it, but Mr Barnes was one of the guests.'

Charlie hesitated, then said carefully, 'You were obviously important to him. I showed the diary to Meg, my wife, and she thought so too.' He smiled. 'Kit was named Katherine after you, although we didn't think then we'd ever find you.'

'For me?' Kate said in amazement.

'Yes. You see, we read the diary so often you seemed real to us. We decided that if we had a daughter we'd call her Katherine and if we had a son we'd call him David, because my father wanted me to be called David.'

'And did you have a son?' asked Kate.

'Yes. We've got two boys, David, and Ben, who was named after Margaret's brother, my best friend who died while we were at school. Ben's very like me to look at and a born farmer, and we think David will be a vet. He and Kit are like Meg to look at.'

Meanwhile, in the kitchen, Kit was telling Josie how they had traced Kate. 'Dad knew about her from a diary of his father's he found just before he was sent to boarding school,' she said. 'And later they found a letter from Kate to his father.'

'I can't get over how like Mr Barnes your dad is,' said Josie. 'Not just the looks, but the same kind of quick, impulsive way with him.'

'Dad hardly remembers him, but he seemed a nice man, judging by his diary.' Kit added shyly, 'He seemed very fond of Kate.'

'He was a lovely man,' Josie declared. 'Funny you thought that about him and Kate. No harm in telling you now your

351

grandma's dead, but me and Mrs Molesworth – we always thought he should've married Kate.'

'So do we. Mum and Dad and I,' said Kit. Josie looked amazed and Kit blushed. 'He mentioned her so often in the diary and seemed so concerned about her. My grandmother was very cool and reserved. We didn't think that they could have been very well matched. Mum said she thought Grandmother was probably happier with Paul, her second husband. Why did he do it? Marry her, I mean, if he cared about Kate? If he was really like Dad he wouldn't have been right at all with Grandma Vetch.'

'I think the truth was, love, *she* married *him*,' Josie said. 'I think he admired her and she was strong-willed, like, and then I don't think he realised Kate had grown up till it was too late.'

'Isn't that sad?' Kit said, but Josie said briskly, 'Happens more often than you think. Fellows think they do the asking. Don't see how the girls have manipulated them until their goose is cooked. The nicest fellows are the easiest game.'

They both laughed, and Kit thought how much she liked this merry little woman and how easy it was to talk to her. She told her all about her mother and her two brothers and the farm and how her father had found that he was descended from farmers. 'Mum's a farmer's daughter too,' she said. 'Her father and mother live with us. Grandad's very frail now but they're both lovely. Have you got a family?'

'Yes, thank God. I was an orphan but I married into a lovely family and now I've got one of my own,' said Josie. 'Kate's like one of my family.'

'But she's got no family of her own?' Kit said.

'Yes. She's got a sister and brother-in-law, and two nephews. One of them lives in the flat upstairs and he's as good as a son to her,' said Josie. 'When I first met Kate I'd come from an orphanage to work in the guesthouse. She was so kind to me, like a sister, and she's been a true friend to me all my life. We'd better get this tea in to them, love. Their tongues'll be hanging out.'

They laughed and picked up the trays to carry to the bedroom, but before they left the kitchen Kit said quickly,

'I was named after Kate, Katherine Margaret, because of what Mum and Dad read in the diary.' Josie's eyes widened in surprise but before she could speak they were in the bedroom.

They found Charlie with his elbows resting on the bed and his face close to Kate's. 'Oh thanks, Josie,' said Kate. 'We're just talking about how they traced me.'

'We had no luck until a woman in a shop near the boarding house tried to help us. When we went back to her she'd found an old man who used to fill coal buckets at the guesthouse,' said Charlie.

'Little Jackie,' Josie exclaimed. 'Poor lad. He was nearly starving and I think his mother drank his wages. He went in the Army and it was the first time he ever had new clothes on his back.'

'He remembered both of you and said you were kind to him. He told me that one day Kate was giving him a dripping buttie and my father came into the kitchen and gave him sixpence.'

'Aye, he would have. That's what he was like, a lovely man,' Josie said. Kate said nothing, but her eyes shone.

'It was great to meet someone who knew you, but it was Mrs Hayes, the shopkeeper, who remembered an old lady whose cousin worked for your aunt, Miss Mills.'

'Essy!' Kate exclaimed.

'I wrote to her and we've been to lunch with her today,' Charlie said. 'Her maid gave us your address.'

'Today!' Josie exclaimed. 'You didn't let the grass grow under your feet. You're your father's son all right.'

They all laughed, and it was a happy tea party, but soon Charles glanced at his watch. 'We'll have to go, I'm afraid. It's a long drive home, but I'm absolutely delighted to have met you, Kate, and you too, Josie.'

'So am I,' said Kit. 'I can't believe we've found you at last, and just like we hoped you'd be. It's like a dream come true.' Everyone smiled and Kit blushed, but Charlie said quickly, 'It was a bonus meeting you as well, Josie. Can we come again to see you, Kate? I feel there's still so much to talk about.'

'Oh yes, do, any time,' Kate said eagerly. 'I'd love to see you both again.'

'Could I come on my own?' asked Kit. 'You see, Dad will be in Shropshire but I'm only five minutes away in termtime.'

Kate took her hand. 'Of course. As often as you like. You know you'll always be welcome. Just phone me to be sure I'm in.'

'And any of the family will be more than welcome in Wicklow too, any time,' Josie declared. 'We'd love to have you.'

While Josie went out to get the coats, Charlie said quietly to Kate, 'I'll come when I bring Kit for start of term if I may, and I'll bring the diary with me.'

Kate blushed. 'Thank you,' was all she said, but she smiled at him gratefully.

Josie went to the door with them, then returned to Kate, plumping down on the side of the bed and hugging her. 'Oh God, Kate, I'm that excited. Sure, I don't know whether I'm on me head or me heels. I just can't imagine how you must feel.'

'I feel drunk,' Kate said. 'Drunk with happiness. Oh Josie, I was so afraid I wouldn't like them, but they were so perfect. It all seems like a lovely dream.'

'It does, it does,' Josie exclaimed. 'Sure, I'm that excited I feel I'm rising in the air like a balloon.' She flung her arms round Kate again and they laughed and cried together.

Charles and Kit were equally excited as they drove home to the farm. 'I can't believe we've found Kate at last,' Kit said. 'And Josie too. Weren't they both lovely?'

Charlie agreed. 'I was getting worried about what Kate would be like,' he admitted. 'I wondered what a life like hers would have made her, but she was as sweet as a nut. I can see why my father thought so much of her.'

'Wait till we tell Mum,' Kit said. 'I hope she'll be able to meet Kate and Josie.'

'She will,' Charlie said confidently. 'We'll keep closely in touch with Kate now we've found her. When I take you back I'll bring the diary for Kate to read, and her letter.'

'Let's go before I book in at Holly Road and I can come with you,' Kit said eagerly. 'And I'll ask when I can go there on my own.'

Back home they burst into the farmhouse kitchen full of their news, and Margaret shared their excitement at finding Kate at last, and their pleasure that she was as nice as they had hoped.

'I can see why she meant so much to my father,' Charlie said later to his wife when they were alone. 'There's a sort of warmth about her. I feel that she loved my dad, Meg.'

'I'm sure he loved her,' Meg said softly. 'How happy he'd be that you've found her, Charlie.'

'It made me feel very close to him. I loved my mother, you know, and I know she loved me, but she couldn't show affection. It must have been hard for him.'

Margaret kissed him. 'Perhaps they didn't really have time to find out,' she said softly. 'They had so little time together before he was killed.'

Charlie hugged her fiercely. 'I'm so lucky I've got you, Meg,' he said. 'I wish he could have known happiness like we've had.'

'Well, at least he had Kate's company, even if he didn't know he loved her,' said Meg. 'I just hope our children meet people who can make them happy and realise it.'

'Plenty of time for that,' said Charlie, taking her in his arms.

Richard called in as usual after he returned from work, to see Kate and Josie. From their excited account of the visit, as they interrupted each other or both spoke at once, he realised how momentous it had been to them. Kate even picked up the photograph which stood by her bed.

'Charlie's the baby in this and he's grown up so like his father,' she said.

They all looked at Henry's photograph. 'He's the spitting image of him, and not only in looks,' Josie declared. 'He doesn't speak quite the same but he's got all his little ways.'

'The way he sits and the way he throws back his head when he laughs, just like Henry,' Kate said. She was quieter than Josie, but her eyes were like stars and her face was flushed with excitement, and Richard stayed and listened, and asked questions.

'He found someone related to Essy,' Josie told him, 'and went to see her this morning. Magdalen gave him this address.'

'He said Essy told him the history of the family, all about my parents and grandparents,' said Kate.

'I bet he got an earful about your Rose too,' Josie laughed. 'You know what Essy's like about her.'

'He only said she talked a lot about Beattie,' Kate said with a warning glance, and Josie remembered belatedly that Rose was Richard's mother.

'My tongue'd get me hung,' Josie said later when Richard had gone. 'But Richard never turned a hair, did he? He's a good lad. He must take after Robert.' Kate said nothing. She knew that Josie had never forgiven Rose for abandoning her.

Josie returned to Ireland the following Saturday, and the next day Richard drove Kate to Sandfield Park to have tea with his parents. Kate was looking forward to telling Rose about the visit by Charlie and Kit which filled her thoughts, but Rose showed little interest.

She now behaved like a complete invalid, and Robert cared for her devotedly. Richard urged him to encourage Rose to go out and meet people, or at least to dress and receive visitors or go for a drive, but Rose preferred just to move from her bed to her sofa every day. She wore pretty négligés and arranged herself gracefully on the sofa, although she was growing increasingly fat, and Robert was her willing slave. Kate was uncomfortably reminded of Aunt Beattie, but the similarity never seemed to occur to Rose.

On one of his visits John told his father bluntly that he was not doing his wife any favours. 'Fresh air and exercise is what Mum needs,' he said. 'Even to walk round the garden would do her good. She's never going to feel well lying around, bored and thinking about her ailments all day.'

Robert never argued, but he and Rose continued the same lifestyle, and in the end both sons realised the futility of protesting. Now Robert covered for Rose's lack of interest by asking what Charlie did for a living, and Kate told him eagerly about the farm and Charlie's wife and two sons. 'He said one of his sons was like himself and the other son and Kit look like their mother. He is *so* like his father, Henry Barnes. It's quite uncanny,' she said.

As they drove home, Richard said awkwardly, 'Don't be hurt by Mum showing no interest, Kate. I think her world has narrowed down to her problems with her health.'

'I'm not hurt, Richie,' Kate assured him. 'Your mum didn't know much about the people in the guesthouse. Aunt Mildred and I always went to Greenfields. They never came to us, perhaps because it might have been inconvenient. I always enjoyed the visits.'

In spite of her denial, Richard felt that Kate had been hurt, and he decided to spend the evening with her. They had not switched on the light, and it was as they sat talking companionably by the light of the fire that Kate told him of her feelings for Henry and how her dreams about him had been her happy refuge for so long.

'I only ever had one letter from him,' she said, 'and it was lost at the time of Aunt Mildred's death. So many people were in and out of the house. I've got other mementoes, but I don't really need anything to remind me of Henry. He's so clear in my mind, and everything that happened.' She hesitated. 'I suppose it was wrong. He was a married man with a child when he was killed.'

Richard put his hand over hers and pressed it gently. 'I don't think it was wrong,' he said. 'You took nothing from anyone. I'm glad you've had these memories, Kate. And I'm glad your visitors did nothing to damage them.'

'Oh Rich, you understand. That's what I was afraid of,' Kate said. 'But they were lovely. It was uncanny to see Charlie looking so like him, and so like him in other ways.'

'That was a bit of luck,' said Richard, and Kate went on, 'Henry would be proud of his granddaughter too, not just because she must be clever, but because she was such a nice girl. Fancy, she's been living in that university place in Holly Road for a year, yet we've never met.'

When Richard said goodnight to Kate she hugged him. 'I've never told anyone else about my dreams about Henry, although I think Josie has an idea. Thank you for being so understanding, Rich.'

'Thank *you*, Kate, for telling me. I'm proud you felt you could confide in me, and I'm glad you've had these dreams to escape to.' He kissed her. 'Henry didn't know what he was missing,' he said.

The next week was the start of the academic year, and Charlie and Kit left home early so that they could see Kate before Kit went to register. It was a brief visit but just as successful as the previous one. Charlie brought the diary and Kate's letter and explained that although the diary was only a loan he thought Kate should keep the letter.

Kate was almost in tears, but she controlled herself and promised to take great care of the diary and to keep in touch with Charlie. Before they left, she invited Kit to tea on the following Sunday.

Chapter Twenty-Four

Kate spent much of the next few days reading and rereading the diary. She felt a warm glow at the many references to her that Henry had made. Sometimes he was indignant on her behalf and seemed to have crossed swords with Mildred on several occasions. Other references were to Kate's goodness and unselfishness. Several times he recorded conversations with her.

His position as assistant manager at the shop meant that he often had problems with staff, especially female ones, and he frequently wrote about consulting Kate. 'She is so level-headed and sensible yet compassionate. I can rely absolutely on her advice.'

Richard read the diary too, and he was amazed at the apparent formality of Henry's relationship with Agnes. 'But people *were* formal before the Great War, even engaged people,' Kate said. 'Women were treated with great respect. They expected it – in their class, anyway. Christian names were not used like they are now.'

'But he wasn't formal with you, Kate,' Richard said.

'But I worked in the guesthouse,' Kate said innocently.

Richard was furious. 'But that makes him the worst kind of snob,' he exclaimed, but Kate laughed.

'I know it's hard for your generation to understand, but Henry was anything but a snob. He was friendly with everyone, too friendly, Agnes thought. She expected formality from him so that's how he treated her. Different days, different ways, Richie. We just accepted it. Anyway, according to my aunt we were as good as anybody and better than most as far as class was concerned.'

In spite of this, Richard felt that he liked Henry's character as it showed through in the entries. He could understand that Charlie could feel the same about Kate, but he had a theory about why the diary had made such a deep impression on the boy when he had first read it.

Charlie had been at the start of puberty, with all its emotional problems, his mother had remarried and he was to be sent away to school. Richard thought this might have made him feel hostility towards his mother and more ready to read a great deal into the references to Kate in the diary. He said nothing of this to Kate, and after reading the diary he was less sure of his theory himself.

Kit was nervous about her first solo visit to Kate and dressed carefully for it, donning a new blue skirt and a white blouse with Hungarian embroidery. Kate was also dressed in her best, a wine-coloured silk dress with a cameo brooch at her throat.

'You look very nice, love,' she greeted Kit, and when Kit said shyly, 'So do you,' she laughed. 'Yes, there's posh we are,' she said in a mock-Welsh accent, and the ice was broken.

Kit found Kate just as easy to talk to as Josie, and they had so much to talk about that the time slipped by unnoticed. They heard sounds overhead at one point, but Kate said, 'Only my nephew Richard. He's been playing football.'

'Mr Richard!' Kit exclaimed involuntarily, and then explained that Essy had mentioned him.

A little later they heard sounds in the hall and Richard calling, 'Only me.' He tapped on the door and opened it. 'Oh, I'm sorry,' he began as Kit jumped to her feet in confusion.

'It's all right, Rich,' Kate said. 'We were so busy talking the time just flew away,' but neither Richard nor Kit was listening to her. They stood as if transfixed, staring at each other as though they were alone.

It was only when Kate said loudly, 'Well, come in, Richard, and close the door,' that they seemed to wake from their trance. For the next hour, although they made an attempt to carry on a normal conversation, neither could resist stealing glances at each other, and it was almost a relief to Kate when Kit said she must go. Richard said he would go with her, and Kate was left alone, amazed by what had happened.

I've heard of love at first sight, she thought, but I think I've just seen it. Richard looked as though he'd been struck by lightning, and Kit was the same. She made herself a cup of tea and sat waiting for Richard to return, but it was nearly two hours before he arrived.

'Where have you been?' Kate asked.

'Taking Kit home,' he said, his voice lingering on her name.

'But she lives only five minutes away,' said Kate.

'We had things to talk about,' he said dreamily, and for the next hour Kate was hardly able to speak as Richard talked about Kit, her beauty, her intelligence, her virtues as a daughter, and his disbelief that he could have lived so near to her for so long without knowing she was there.

In the end Kate almost pushed him out, telling him that she was going to bed. He might be more sensible after a night's sleep, she thought, but she hoped this lasted for them.

She lay awake for some time, going over and over in her mind the moment when Richard and Kit had first looked at each other. If I hadn't seen it I wouldn't believe it, she thought, but I'm so delighted. Henry's granddaughter and Richard! Later she was surprised that at such an early stage she was sure that Kit and Richard would marry, but she never doubted it.

Richard came in to see her the next evening before he went to meet Kit. He was less incoherent but evidently just as deeply in love.

'I didn't believe in all this love at first sight stuff,' he said to Kate. 'But I know now that it happens. When I saw Kit it was like an electric current between us, and she says it was the same for her. We feel right together. I can't believe my luck, Kate. A lovely girl like Kit. I think this is why I could never fall for other girls. I was waiting for Kit.'

'She is a lovely girl,' said Kate. 'A sweet nature and she comes from a good family. Very devoted to each other, from what she told me. I know her father, of course, and her mother sounds nice.' She smiled. 'I knew her grandfather too.'

'Of course!' Richard exclaimed. 'I hadn't thought of that. The only thing that worries me is the age difference, but Kit says it doesn't matter.'

'I wouldn't worry about that,' said Kate. 'All that matters is that you're happy together.'

'Do you think it'll matter to Kit's parents, though?' asked Richard. 'I'm nearly old enough to be her father.'

'Thirteen years,' Kate scoffed. 'Hardly a generation gap. I've never heard of a thirteen-year-old father. But I think they might worry if she neglects her studying. They've made sacrifices for her to go to university and they're very proud of her.'

'Kit won't, Kate,' said Richard. 'We've talked about that too.'

Kit had written such an ecstatic letter about Richard to her parents that they were alarmed. Charlie wrote to Kate, saying that he and his wife were coming to Liverpool to shop and asking if they could call to see her. They intended to take Kit out for a meal and perhaps meet Richard.

Kate wrote back immediately, inviting them to lunch or at any time that suited them. She would like to talk about Kit and Richard, she wrote.

They came a few days later and there was immediate rapport between Kate and Margaret. 'This shopping is only an excuse,' Meg confessed. 'Kit seemed so excited in her letter. All about falling in love as soon as she saw him. Not like her at all. She's usually so sensible.'

'I was here when it happened,' Kate said. 'Kit and I had a lovely afternoon but we were talking so much we didn't notice the time. Richard lives in the flat above me. I heard him come in from football and go for his bath, then he came down. He knew Kit was coming but I suppose he thought she'd gone. They just stood and looked at each other as though they'd been struck by lightning. I've never seen anything like it.'

'Kit said it was like that, but she's so young and inexperienced we thought it was just romantic girls' talk.'

'*You* did,' Margaret said swiftly. 'I knew right away it was serious. I know Kit.'

'Perhaps it won't last,' Charlie said hopefully. 'He's a lot older than Kit, isn't he, and probably experienced. She's had such a sheltered life, never bothered with boys. It was always her books. We're worried about it affecting her work too.'

'Richard is not experienced in the way you mean,' Kate said more sharply than she had intended. 'He went into the Air Force when he was nineteen. He had a few dates during the war but nothing serious. Then when he came out his father was ill and the business was in such a state he was working all the hours God sends to pull it round.'

She suddenly realised that she seemed to be pleading Richard's case, and thought indignantly that she would say no more. Any girl would be damn lucky to get Richard. Margaret seemed to understand and gave Charlie a wifely look. 'It must be nice to have Richard living so near you. Kit says he's like a son to you,' she said gently.

'Yes, we're the best of friends,' Kate said briefly. They spoke no more about Richard, but talked of other matters until Meg and Charlie left for the shops. Kate had soon recovered her usual good temper and they left on friendly terms, planning to see each other again soon.

As they drove away, Margaret said thoughtfully, 'You seemed to be criticising Richard, Charlie. I think Kate felt that you were.'

'I didn't mean to,' he said. 'I'm sorry because I like Kate and I hoped you'd like her too.'

'I do, love, and all the more for sticking up for her own,' said Meg. 'The fact that she thinks so much of Richard is a recommendation as far as I'm concerned.'

They met Kit and later were joined by Richard, and both liked him immediately. Even the disparity in age seemed no obstacle now they had assured themselves that he had no history of discarded girlfriends behind him. 'He looks very young. You wouldn't think he was thirteen years older,' Meg whispered to Charlie at one point.

Richard brought up the subject of Kit's studies and said he would do nothing to interfere with them. He wanted her to get a good degree as much as they did.

'Anyone interested in my opinion?' Kit asked, and Richard took her hand and said lovingly, 'I know your opinion, don't I? We talked about it for so long,' and Kit gazed back at him just as lovingly.

'I've another reason,' Richard told them. 'My mother wanted to go to university but she was prevented and it's been a grievance all her life. I don't want Kit to feel like that – not that she ever would,' he added.

Charlie and Meg drove home both deep in thought, and it was only as they approached the farmhouse that Meg roused herself.

'I think the die is cast, as they say, Charlie. I don't think we could separate those two even if we wanted to, and I don't want to, do you?' she said.

'No, but it's early days yet, Meg. She's only twenty. She could change her mind,' Charlie said, but Meg shook her head.

'She won't,' she said positively. 'And I tell you straight, if she settles with him I'll be pleased. I can see they'll be happy together.'

Meg's mother had waited up for them, and to her Meg said frankly, 'Our Kit's head over heels, Mum, and Richard seems as smitten with her. I liked him. He's very tall and nice-looking, dark like Kit, and he's got a very easy manner.'

'And what about the aunt he lives with? The woman Charlie and Kit have been going to see?' Mrs Tyland asked.

'I got on with her right away. You'd like her, Mum. Quiet but very down to earth. Richard doesn't exactly live with her. He has the flat above hers, but I think he keeps an eye on her.'

'Sounds a nice lad. Don't you worry about Kit, Meg. That girl's a rock of sense,' said Mrs Tyland. 'If she's fallen for this lad he won't be rubbish.'

'It's just that it was so sudden,' said Meg.

'People come to marriage different ways,' her mother said placidly. 'You and Charlie were friends first and grew up to falling in love. Your dad and me – our fathers arranged our wedding because of the farms. Me and Tom were intending to hate each other but when we got to know each other we couldn't.' They laughed but Meg felt comforted.

She asked after her father. Old Mr Tyland was very frail now and almost bedridden, but his mind was alert and Charlie talked over problems at the farm with him. 'He's had a good day,' said Mrs Tyland. 'Young Ben has been in and out showing him grain samples and that. He's a good lad.'

As soon as possible Richard and Kit spent a Sunday at the farm, and everyone approved of Richard. He talked for a long time to Kit's grandfather, who had been unable to come downstairs as he'd hoped.

'My father has enjoyed meeting you,' Meg told him when they were leaving, and Richard said simply, 'He was very interesting,' but it had endeared him to the family.

'They're still in a world of their own,' Meg told Charlie as Kit and Richard drove away, and it was true that the magic still persisted for them although outwardly they seemed to have settled down. Kate often smiled to herself when she recalled that first evening and Richard's outpouring. He'd feel daft if he remembered it. It was as if he was drunk, she thought, smiling indulgently.

John and Magda were due to visit Rose and Robert, and Richard thought it was a good opportunity for Kit to meet his family and for him to proudly introduce her to them. Kate came with them, and Kit was glad of her support. She felt like a country mouse beside Magda's cool elegance, and she thought the other girl very sophisticated too.

Rose lay on her sofa wearing her prettiest négligé, with the family gathered round her and Robert in attendance. She smiled sweetly at Kit and welcomed her, and Kit thought she was charming and felt that it was sad that Rose was an invalid. She liked Robert too and was impressed by his tender care for his wife, but she was puzzled by John, although she was determined to like him because he was Richard's brother.

Richard had told her he worked in the City of London and was very successful, and he looked the part. His fair hair was carefully barbered and he wore a Savile Row suit, but he talked a lot about the climbing club he had joined. He had just returned from mountaineering in Switzerland and was planning to join an expedition to Kilimanjaro.

He was lighting Magda's cigarette, his head close to hers as she cupped her fingers round his lighter, when Rose said sharply, 'That's all very well, but when are you two going to get married?'

There was silence for a moment, then Magda blew a perfect smoke ring and drawled, 'Oh, John prefers something that's easier to get out of, and so do I. Marriage can be such a drag.'

Rose was stunned into silence, and Richard hastily asked about shows in London. Afterwards Rose ignored Magda, but the girl was unconcerned, smiling lazily and talking to other people but paying no attention to Rose. It was not a situation that suited Rose, and she made an extra effort to charm Kit. When Robert asked Kit about her course at the university, Rose saw her opportunity to regain attention.

'How lucky you are, Kit!' she cried dramatically. 'If only I'd had the chance you have now. My teachers wanted me to go to university. They were convinced that with my brain I could really make my mark in the world, become a famous doctor or scientist, but it was not to be.' She sighed and Magda smiled cynically, but Kit asked if it was because of her health.

'No, dear, because of my aunt's selfishness. My teacher pleaded with her but she preferred to have me as her lapdog, waiting on all her whims. Life was very hard for clever women then, wasn't it, Kate? We weren't free like girls are today.'

Kit felt almost guilty about her university place, but John came to sit beside her and ask her what she thought of Liverpool. 'I haven't seen a great deal of it,' she said. 'We've been in a bit of a closed shop for our first year in the university, but I like what I've seen of the city. I'm just starting my second year now. I like the Liverpool people I've met.'

'So you'd like to live here?' John said mischievously, but Kit only looked at Richard and said simply, 'I'd live anywhere with Richard.'

'Lucky Richard,' John said, but he looked thoughtful as Richard came to join them, taking Kit's hand and asking John about the expedition to Kilimanjaro. 'Does that mean you're leaving your job?' he asked.

'Yes, I always planned to when I'd made enough money,' John said. 'When the money runs out, I'll go back to it.'

'And he will too, and probably be just as successful,' Richard said as they drove home. 'He might seem wild but he's got his life planned to suit him. I think I picked a bad day to take you there, though, Kit. It isn't usually like that when John and Magda are there, is it, Kate?'

Kate, who was sitting in the back seat, agreed. 'I think your mother touched a sore spot when she spoke about marriage,' she said. 'I don't think Magda is unwilling to marry but John is. That's why she was so touchy.'

'He doesn't seem to have it on his agenda,' said Richard.

'Poor Magda,' Kit said. She was sorry for anyone who was not as happy as she was with Richard.

'Anyway, how did you like the family, Kit?' Richard asked. 'They certainly liked you.'

'I thought your parents were lovely,' Kit said. 'Isn't it sad that your mother's such an invalid and that she didn't have the chance to go to university?'

Richard's eyes met Kate's in the driving mirror, but he only said, 'Mum certainly took to you, but I knew she would.' He sqeezed Kit's hand. 'How could anyone help it?'

Kit soon realised that Richard's mother was a hypochondriac, but she never forgot the warmth of Rose's welcome, and listened patiently to her complaints when they visited her.

Kit and Richard decided that they would become engaged at the Christmas which followed their meeting, but would only marry eighteen months later when Kit – they hoped – had graduated. They realised that the waiting would be difficult and laid down rules for themselves. They were tempted to spend every available moment together, but they decided that Richard would continue to play football and have an occasional night out with his friends, and Kit would spend some of her spare time studying and some with Helen and Alytwyn. This was the theory, but in practice Richard could not resist hanging round Holly Road hoping to see Kit, and they saw each other every day, no matter how briefly.

They expected their time together to be all the sweeter because it was restricted, but sometimes quarrels blew up suddenly, like thunderstorms from a clear blue sky. Their deep love and knowledge of each other made them vulnerable. They knew how to hurt each other, but their love prevented them from using the knowledge even in moments of anger, and their quarrels were soon over.

Kate had never felt happier. Henry was always her last thought before she slept, and now she could think too about his family. She had feared that she might lose her dream world but now it took on another dimension and Henry seemed even closer to her.

Kate had visited the farm with Richard during Kit's long vacation and was popular with all the family, especially the grandparents. Rose felt unable to make the journey and Robert never left her side, but Margaret and Charlie visited them at Sandfield Park several times. Rose had gained even more weight and had difficulty in breathing. Exercise might have benefited her earlier, but it was clearly impossible now.

All the family were concerned about her, but she still managed to move to her sofa every day, and twice during the summer months even to the garden seat. Robert cared for her tenderly and her private doctor came frequently, mainly to listen patiently to her complaints and make soothing noises.

'All that fellow does is tell her to avoid stress and worry,' Richard said disgustedly to his father. 'Talk about preaching to the converted,' but Robert only said calmly, 'As long as she wants him to come I'll pay his bill gladly,' and Richard said no more.

At the start of Kit's final year, everyone was saddened when old Mr Tyland died peacefully in his sleep. Just before Christmas another blow fell when Rose suffered a heart attack. She made a partial recovery and Kate went to stay with her to help with the nursing. It was like a return to their childhood before they were parted, and Kate treasured this time together, when her loving little sister, the Rose she had known and loved, seemed to return to her.

All Rose's pretensions and grievances seemed to vanish, and to Robert she was the sweet and loving wife he had always believed she was. One day, as he sat holding her hand, she said softly, 'I'd never have been a famous doctor, would I? I've been much better off as your wife, Rob. I know how lucky I've been to have a husband like you.' She closed her eyes, and Robert and Kate looked at each other in surprise that Rose had said she had been lucky when for most of her life she had complained that nothing went right for her.

They tiptoed away, leaving her sleeping. 'It was good to hear that Rose feels like that, Kate. Perhaps now her life will be happier,' Robert said.

'I'm sure she's always thought that, but I'm glad she's told you how much you mean to her. People feel these things but never get round to saying them,' said Kate.

'To say that she was lucky,' Robert marvelled. 'I was the luckiest fellow in the world when she agreed to marry me. She could have had anybody.'

'Not anybody better than you, Rob,' Kate said. 'Thank God she seems so much better today.'

'Even her breathing seems easier,' Robert agreed.

Rose had refused to have a night nurse, and Kate and Robert shared the duties between them. At two o'clock in the morning Kate had just come to take over from Robert when Rose made a sudden sound. They both bent over her as the sound of her breathing stopped. It was so easy and peaceful that it was hard to realise she was dead.

369

'Her heart just failed,' the doctor told them later. 'It could have happened at any time.'

Robert said simply, 'I'm just thankful that she went first. That was always my fear, that I would die first, because she'd never have managed alone.'

'That's true,' Kate said. 'She'd have been lost without you. You were her rock, Robert.'

Kate felt almost unbearable pain at the loss of her sister, her last link with her childhood, and could only imagine what Robert must be feeling.

They both grieved with quiet dignity, and after a while Robert reorganised his life. He decided to stay on in the house in Sandfield Park as he had a live-in couple working for him, the wife as housekeeper and the husband as gardener/handyman. They had been evicted from a tied cottage early in the war and Rose had been told of their plight and offered them the job.

'The Hignetts will insist on staying out of loyalty to your mother,' Robert told Richard. 'When they retire I'll take a service flat. Saunders has suggested we do some travelling together later.'

'Is that the cotton broker you used to lunch with?' Richard asked.

'Yes. We often talked of travelling to some out-of-the-way place sometime. His wife died about ten years ago.'

'That's a good idea, Dad,' Richard said. 'This is the time to do it, while you're fit enough to enjoy it.'

Richard's sorrow was less for his mother than for what his father and Kate were suffering, although he had felt an exasperated affection for his mother. He admitted to Kate that Rose's frequent references to her favourite grievance – her failure to become a doctor – had always particularly irritated him.

'She needed her dreams, Rich,' Kate said. 'We all do. I know that better than anybody.'

'Yes, but you used your dreams as a refuge, Kate, and you never spoke about them. Mother used hers as a grievance and let them sour her life.'

'She was the sweetest little girl,' Kate said dreamily.

'Everyone loved her. She was so beautiful, with big blue eyes and a pink and white complexion. Her hair was like spun gold and Mama used to comb it into ringlets. She said the good fairy was present when Rose was born and gave her every gift, beauty and charm and cleverness too.'

'She left out one thing. A happy disposition,' Richard said swiftly. 'You got that, Kate.'

Richard and Kit had planned their wedding for the following August, and Robert told them that their plans must go ahead. 'Your mother would have wished it, Rich,' he said. 'The old ideas about mourning have changed, quite rightly in my opinion. For many people it was only outward show.'

'Thanks, Dad,' said Richard. 'We were a bit worried about how you'd feel about it only eight months after – after Mother's death.'

'Life must go on,' said Robert. 'I know it's a cliché, but it's true just the same.'

Richard and Kit had been house-hunting for several months and had found the house they wanted in West Derby. They had discussed it with Kate and asked her to move with them, and she had agreed. The house was newly built and well planned, with a small bungalow built on to it which was perfect for Kate. It ensured privacy for both households, yet it was a relief for all of them to know that they would be near if needed.

Richard's business was running smoothly and his father came into the office occasionally, so he thought he would spend time with Kit in Shropshire before the wedding, but she asked him to stay in Liverpool. 'We've got the rest of our lives,' she said firmly. 'This time is for Mum and Dad and Grandma.'

Richard kissed her. 'They say a good daughter makes a good wife,' he said ruefully, 'so I should be all right,' but he agreed with her.

Most of Kit's university friends had dispersed, but Helen and Alytwyn and a few others promised to come to the wedding. Meg insisted that Kate and Robert stayed at the farmhouse, but the other guests, including a large contingent of Richard's friends from Liverpool, found accommodation in the village. Richard and John, who was his brother's best man, stayed with farming neighbours overnight.

The day of the wedding was one of glorious sunshine, and the village church was packed to the doors with friends and neighbours, although neither family was numerous. Kit seemed to float down the aisle to Richard, and their happiness was almost tangible as they knelt together at the altar.

When the ceremony was over, they walked to the vestry smiling at each other as though they were alone. Meg followed holding Robert's arm, and Charlie held out his arm to Kate with a beaming smile.

Soon the organist was given a signal and broke into the triumphant strains of the Wedding March as the bridal procession moved down the aisle. Everyone was smiling at the blissful expressions on the faces of the bride and groom.

Kate felt almost as blissful as she followed the newly-weds, holding Charlie's arm. Out in the sunshine, the official photographer was fussing about the bride and bridegroom, but numerous guests were taking photographs too.

Kate and Charlie were still standing together talking, and John rushed up to them. 'Come on, Aunt Kate,' he said. 'One of you and Charlie.' Kate stood with her arm through Charlie's as John looked through the viewfinder. 'Closer,' he called, and Charlie moved nearer to Kate, smiling down at her.

She looked at him, at the face that was so like the one that had filled her dreams for so long. Fifty years, she thought, since the day of Mama's funeral when Henry first smiled at me like that. His dear spirit has been with me ever since and has always brought me comfort and happiness.

Now I'm holding his son's arm, she thought, and today our families have really been joined together. I'm so happy. I've always been lucky and had a lovely life, but I've never been happier than I am now or felt closer to my dear Henry. She smiled up at Henry's son as John's camera clicked.

'Perfect,' he called, and Kate agreed with him.

ELIZABETH MURPHY

A Nest of Singing Birds

Nicknamed 'Happy Annie', Anne is the youngest of
the eight Fitzgerald children, loved and petted by
her older brothers and sisters and secure amid their
extended family in Liverpool's Everton district. Her
childhood is blessedly free from worries: although
conditions are hard in the 1920s and '30s, Patrick
Fitzgerald's building firm provides a steady income
and there is always food on the table and the sound
of music and laughter in the house.

When Sarah Redmond introduces Anne to her
brother John, there is an unspoken attraction
between the two young people, but John goes to
Spain to fight with the International Brigade, and
when he returns, it is to find that he is a social
outcast. He is unwilling to involve Anne in his
troubles and she is too proud to admit to feelings she
believes are not returned.

Only when war breaks out do they marry and have
three children, with whom Anne hopes to recreate
her happy childhood home. But John is busy
pursuing his own ambitions and this leads to
misunderstandings and unhappiness until in the end
Anne's dream is fulfilled and she can truly describe
her home as her childhood home was once described
– a nest of singing birds.

FICTION / SAGA 0 7472 4010 8

Her Mother's Secret

Catherine King

sphere

SPHERE

First published in Great Britain in 2014 by Sphere
This paperback edition published in 2014 by Sphere

Copyright © Catherine King 2014

The moral right of the author has been asserted.

A CIP catalogue record for this book
is available from the British Library.

ISBN 978-0-7515-5430-4

Typeset in Bembo by Palimpsest Book Production Limited,
Falkirk, Stirlingshire
Printed and bound in Great Britain by Clays Ltd, St Ives plc

Papers used by Sphere are from well-managed forests
and other responsible sources.

Acknowledgements

I had a fascinating time researching early twentieth century health hydros in Yorkshire and Derbyshire. I found that they were thriving during the Edwardian era, despite some of their now questionable practices. I am indebted to the wonderful Mavis Baird of Champneys Forest Mere for her detailed knowledge of the rigorous routines from earlier years, including her reference to Russian cake. I found a recipe in *Mrs Beeton's Book of Household Management*. I am also grateful to Simon Brian of London who, as a young man, was a 'health farm patient' and remembers the Spartan regime well. Many thanks to both of you. The original Forest Mere country house has an interesting history in its own right and is in such a beautiful tranquil setting that it inspired my fictional Mereside Lodge.

As ever, my thanks also go to my agent Judith Murdoch and my editors Manpreet Grewal and Hannah Green at Sphere. Their constant help and support during the creation and production of the finished book makes the writing an enjoyable experience for me.

PART ONE

Chapter 1

Waterley Hall, South Riding, Yorkshire, 1885

'Do I look beautiful, Father?' Ruth stood in the middle of the butler's pantry and twirled around, showing off her fashionable bustle.

Seth Hargreaves leaned back in his chair, a satisfied expression on his face. 'You look more of a lady than Her Ladyship.'

'Yes I do, don't I?' It was dark outside and Ruth examined her image in the glass of the window. 'Her Ladyship is an old frump, though, so that's not difficult. Do you think His Lordship's friends will like me?'

'They won't be able to take their eyes off you.'

Ruth felt a thrill of excitement run down her spine. Lord Laughton was young and handsome and clearly rich enough to buy Waterley Hall, complete with its resident servants and surrounding farms, without worrying about the costs of renovations. His friends in the Riding came from wealthy families who lived in grand houses. Ruth's father had been butler to the old family at Waterley Hall, but that family had simply died out, and he was already a favourite of the new master.

'Won't Her Ladyship mind me being there?' Ruth asked.

'You leave all that to me. She's gone to the shipyards for a few days. It's up to you to assist His Lordship entertain his guests. I shall be serving dinner to keep a watch on you.'

'Oh, Father, I'm so excited! Who else will be there?'

'His Lordship's London friends have already arrived with their lady escorts. One or two have brought their sisters. They will be the unattached ones, Ruth, but make sure you're nice to everybody. They're all young folk like His Lordship.'

'Will they know that I'm your daughter?'

'No, why should they? You'll be presented as Miss Ruth. The guests will think you're a relation. If anybody wants to know, say you're a family friend.'

'Oh! Am I a friend of Lord Laughton?'

'His Lordship has asked for you and I'm honoured that he did. But don't let me down; I have to keep in his favour if I want the house steward position.'

Ruth was indignant. 'I do know how to behave like a lady,' she said.

She had grown up with the previous family in residence – long-established aristocrats with a centuries-old family tree that had dwindled to nothing over the years.

Nonetheless, Ruth had decided at a very early age that she wanted to be one of them, and her father had too.

'Well, His Lordship is still seen as new money so just remember everything you've learned at that ladies' college of yours. You can be a real lady if you play your cards right and this is your chance.'

'Yes, Father.'

The door opened wide and Ivy Hargreaves walked in, her arms full of clean linen. She was much younger than her husband, who had been the butler at Waterley Hall when she had arrived as head parlourmaid over twenty years ago. Ivy was a small energetic woman. She read her bible, prayed every night and walked several miles to the nearest Methodist chapel on Sundays. The previous housekeeper then had been old, arthritic and, frankly, quite dotty. From the day she arrived at Waterley Hall, Ivy had done most of her work, and done it well.

'You look very nice, my dear,' Ivy said, 'but I still don't think this is a sensible idea. Not when Her Ladyship is away.'

'Oh, Mother, don't spoil everything now,' Ruth moaned.

'It's a good opportunity for the girl, Ivy,' her father argued. 'There's no point in spending all that money on a fancy ladies' college if she doesn't mix with real gentry.'

'I'm not disagreeing with that. I just think, with Ruth being only seventeen, Her Ladyship should be present.'

'If I were the daughter of the house I'd be a debutante, Mother,' Ruth protested, 'and attending dinners and balls every night.'

'Seth,' Ivy appealed to her husband, 'His Lordship is known to have an eye for the ladies.'

'I'll be with her all the time. And what if he does flirt with my Ruth? It won't do me any harm at all when it comes to the steward's position.'

'Besides, Mother,' Ruth added, 'If I'm to marry well, it isn't enough for me to look beautiful. I have to know the right people, too.'

'Well, just remember, dear,' her mother replied, 'if you're not happy with anything, then excuse yourself and come down to me. I'll be in my sitting room all evening.'

'You don't have to stay, Ivy. You go back to the cottage and I'll bring Ruth home with me.'

'But if she waits for you she will be very late.'

'She doesn't want to miss any of the fun, do you, Ruth?' her father responded.

'No, I don't. I can talk to the ladies if the gentlemen go off to play cards or billiards. You want me to do that, don't you, Mother?'

Ivy sighed. 'Very well, dear.'

'That's settled then.' Seth Hargreaves stood up. 'Off you go, Ivy, and let me get on with the champagne.'

Ruth's pretty blue eyes lit up. 'Oh, champagne, how lovely. Don't worry about me, Mother,' Ruth said, as the two women walked out into the dimly lit passage outside the butler's pantry. 'Father will look after me.' She turned towards the green baize door that led to the main house and felt her mother's eyes on her as she walked through it and into a different life.

* * *

The reception hall of Waterley Hall was large enough for a small dance. It had a mosaic tiled floor and four fluted marble pillars on each side. Opposite the large front door, a wide staircase with gilt balustrades rose grandly to the first floor. Wood-panelled doors led off the hall to the dining room, drawing room, library and morning room.

This will be my world, Ruth thought. Not for her the world below stairs that was her parents' existence. They were respectable and comfortable as butler and housekeeper at Waterley Hall, but they were servants nonetheless. Ruth was determined to have a different life, to be mistress of a great house like Waterley, with servants of her own.

Seth Hargreaves shared his daughter's ambition; he also knew how to please his betters. He was master of his own domain in the servants' hall and ruled it with a proverbial iron rod. Servants who did not comply did not stay. The footmen may gossip in their dormitories about Ruth's elevated status to guest at His Lordship's table, but if one word of it reached her father's ear they would be 'asked to leave'. This autocratic regime had impressed the young lord, and Seth had quickly secured his patronage.

Michael, head footman at the Hall, was on duty outside the drawing-room door and opened it as soon as he saw her. 'Miss Ruth, My Lord,' he said. His face was expressionless but Ruth knew that he was in love with her. She might have considered him, too – he was a fine-looking man – if he wasn't a servant. Perfect for my future butler, she thought.

'Over here.' Lord Laughton was standing in the bay window, staring out at the driveway. He had dark hair and eyes, and features that some described as 'craggy'. But he looked very handsome in full evening dress with a tail coat and white tie. However, when she stood by his side, she realised that he was rather short. The door clicked shut behind her and they were alone. 'Turn around,' he said.

Ruth twirled for him as she had for her father. She noticed that his eyes narrowed and his fingers twitched slightly and she feared he did not like what he saw. 'Father said I looked beautiful,' she said nervously.

'He's right. Come closer.'

She did and he stroked a finger over her cheek and lips. She hadn't expected him to touch her and recoiled instinctively.

'Stay where you are!' he exclaimed.

'I'm sorry, My Lord. You surprised me.'

'And don't call me "My Lord". I'm Laughton to my friends.'

She knew that! Father had told her that! She recovered immediately and replied, 'Of course, Laughton.'

His hand travelled down over her throat to the exposed swell of her breasts. It lingered over their fullness, continued to her tightly corseted waist and returned to her breasts. She held her breath, suppressing the instinct to flee. A clock chimed somewhere, breaking Laughton's reverie. He dropped his hand and turned his attention back to the window. The first carriage was approaching.

The door opened again and Ruth's father announced

the first of the guests who had arrived earlier for a few days' shooting. His face was as expressionless as Michael's. Ruth put on her welcoming smile and prepared to do her best. Over the next hour she smiled a lot, drank champagne and joined in the conversation with suitable comments and questions.

Dinner for twenty people lasted over three hours. Everyone drank wine and voices grew louder. On two separate occasions she caught a glimpse of one of the gentlemen watching her and acknowledged his interest with an incline of her head. When her father removed her dessert plate, he whispered in her ear, 'Now, Ruth.'

She caught the eye of another lady guest, nodded, and they stood up together. 'Shall we leave the gentlemen to their port and stilton, ladies?' She smiled and led the way to the drawing room. Her mouth was beginning to ache with constant smiling.

Michael brought in coffee for the ladies and murmured to her, 'Your father sends his compliments.'

Ruth relaxed with a sigh. Father was pleased. She had performed well and the evening was almost over. Later, one of the ladies played and sang at the piano and some of the gentlemen joined them in the drawing room. His Lordship was not among them but Father came in afterwards and announced cards. Within minutes, the footmen under Michael's supervision had set up the tables and the remaining gentlemen wandered in and took their places. A few of the ladies sat down with them.

'Ruth,' His Lordship called, 'come over here and bring me luck.' Ruth didn't know how she was going to do that but she obeyed. His Lordship was in high spirits. The party broke up about an hour later except for the card table with His Lordship and his friends who were house guests, which carried on.

'Shall I retire as well, Laughton?' Ruth said.

'Certainly not. I'm on a winning streak thanks to you and these gentlemen are chasing their losses.' He raised a hand in the air and called, 'Hargreaves, more brandies, and bring sandwiches.'

The cigar smoke was hurting her eyes but Ruth kept smiling. She was tired and she was bored. Her father sent his footmen off duty and stood to attention in the shadows. The cards fell right for His Lordship. His winnings mounted and eventually the others called a halt. But the gentleman who had caught Ruth's eye at dinner was now so drunk that he could barely stand up and Father was obliged to assist him upstairs. Ruth found herself once again alone with His Lordship in the empty drawing room.

'He's a fool,' His Lordship said, referring to his drunken guest. 'He falls for it every time. I ply him with drink until he can't think straight and then I take all his money off him.' He laughed and held out his arm. 'Come here, Ruth.'

She hesitated. It was very late and she was exhausted. But she felt safe because His Lordship wasn't drunk and Father would be back soon.

'I said come here.' Laughton stepped forward, grasping her hand and pulling her towards him.

Ruth bumped against his chest and his mouth was on

hers before she could protest. He held her firmly and thrust her lips open with his tongue. This wasn't supposed to happen! He was hard up against here, pressing his hips into hers and she wanted to push him away.

But he would stop soon, she reasoned, and then she could voice her disapproval. The worst she had imagined was a brief stolen kiss in a dark corner from a single gentleman who might ask if he could take her for a carriage ride.

His mouth moved to the swell of her breasts, giving her a chance to breath. 'Please stop this, Laughton. Father assured me you wouldn't—'

'I am master here,' he growled and tore at the neckline of her gown with his teeth to expose more of her flesh.

'What are you doing?' Ruth demanded. A frisson of fear shivered down her spine. What if he didn't stop at a kiss? He ignored her question and steered her forcefully back to one of the couches.

She began to panic and push at him with her hands. 'Father will be back any minute,' she cried.

'Then we'd best hurry, hadn't we? I'm not going to hurt you so don't fight with me, Ruth.'

This made her feel easier and she let out her breath.

'That's better,' he said. 'Just relax and do as I say.'

Ruth felt that she hadn't much choice. He was strong and he had pinned her down on the couch. He sat on the edge, facing her, and then buried his face in her exposed breasts, nipping and nibbling at her flesh. She hated it but his weight pressed into her. Her frightened eyes gazed at the chandelier in the ornate plaster ceiling and she pushed ineffectually at his shoulders. One of his hands was fumbling at his clothes between them. To her horror the other reached down and under her skirts following the line of her thigh to the gap in her drawers.

'No, you can't do this! You're not supposed to do this!'

'Shut up,' he said harshly. 'I said relax. You don't want me to hit you, do you?'

'Hit me? Why would you hit me?' she cried. His fingers were between her legs and she was frightened. 'Stop it, Laughton, stop it!'

But he didn't stop. He found what he was searching for and bunched up her skirts, her beautiful new silk skirts, until they exposed her drawers. The silk covered her face but he didn't seem to notice. He was stretched out on top of her with his knee between her legs, prodding and poking at her. She recoiled and pushed her bottom backwards into the couch. Her bustle made this movement useless and her hips remained raised towards him. With a sickening grasp of the situation, she realised what he was about to do whether she wanted it or not and she could not escape from him. Her continuing protests were muffled by her skirts.

It didn't really hurt that much. Or maybe she was too shocked to feel anything. He was heavy but he didn't seem very big inside her. She couldn't see his face but she could hear him grunting and feel him pushing and pushing and pushing. She could smell him, too, or maybe it was her. It was over quickly and he flopped on top of her, groaning and panting. Then he stood up, fastened his trousers and said, 'Not a word to anyone about this, Ruth.' He wandered over to the window.

Ruth closed her legs. Her flesh was damp and sticky where he'd been. She wanted to wash him away and pulled down her skirts to cover her legs.

'Why did you do that to me?' she muttered.

'Didn't you like it?'

'No.'

'Well, it was the first time for you. You'll enjoy it next time.'

Next time? Ruth thought. How can there be a next time when I'm supposed to be wooed by a gentleman suitor? And what about him; he had a wife, for heaven's sake. He was an adulterer! She was sitting on the couch pushing her breasts back into her gown when Father returned.

He took one look at her dishevelled hair and said, 'Ruth, what have you been doing?'

'She fell asleep on the couch, Hargreaves,' Laughton answered from the window. 'Didn't you, Ruth?'

'Yes, My Lord,' she replied, hating herself for lying. What else was she to do? Admit to her father that she had allowed His Lordship to take her virtue? She felt like crying.

Lord Laughton crossed the room from the window to the door. As he passed her father he patted him on the shoulder. 'Good work tonight, Hargreaves. We'll talk about your new position in the morning.'

'Goodnight, sir.' Her father opened the door for His Lordship and closed it after him. 'On your feet, Ruth, and buck up. It's late.'

'Yes, Father.'

'And tidy your hair before I take you home. Your mother will have a fit. What happened to your gown?'

'The stitching tore. I'll take it back to the dressmaker tomorrow.'

'I've got your coat in the servants' hall. The trap's waiting.'

She followed her father back through the green baize door and shivered in the cold passage while he extinguished the last of the candles. She continued to shiver all the way home in the trap.

'You're quiet,' Father commented.

She pulled up the collar of her coat. 'I'm tired.'

'You can sleep in tomorrow. You did very well tonight. His Lordship is pleased.'

Ruth choked back her tears. Father stopped the trap at the front of their cottage and she climbed down. Mother opened the door before she reached it.

'Did you enjoy yourself, dear?' Mother asked.

'Yes, thank you,' she lied. 'I'm going straight to bed.'

'Don't you want some chocolate?'

'No thank you.'

'I'll bring it upstairs for you.'

'*No thank you*,' she cried and ran up the narrow twisty staircase to her bedroom.

She left her silk gown in a crumpled heap on the floor, put a pillow over her head to muffle her sobs and wept until she fell asleep.

Chapter 2

She heard Father rise early the following day. He fed the pony and harnessed the trap while Mother raked the fire and pumped water for the kettle. They left shortly afterwards to breakfast at the Hall. As soon as the water was warm enough she carried it upstairs to wash and put on clean clothes. Then she spread a calico sheet on the bed and wrapped the gown to take back to the dressmaker. It had cost Father a lot of money but the joy she'd felt when it arrived had disappeared and she couldn't imagine ever wearing it again. In fact, she never wanted to see it again.

She was drinking tea when she heard the first guns go off in the distance. The old family used to shoot at their lodge up near Harrogate. But the railway line had cut through the land and ruined cover for the birds.

They had been well compensated and bought up forest in the South Riding instead. The locals were pleased. They were beaters and dog handlers by day and poachers for the pheasant by night.

Father would be supervising luncheon out in the field, Ruth realised. Mother would be busy making sure that Waterley Hall was at its pristine best for His Lordship's guests. But the Hall would be quiet until the shooting party returned at the end of the day. She took down her coat and hat from the peg and set off walking.

She felt soiled and miserable but the brisk fresh air helped her to think and gave her strength. Losing her virtue was a disaster for her only if others knew and His Lordship wouldn't tell anyone. He had a crabby old wife who was easily angered. However, Ruth had to talk to someone about last night or she would go quite mad.

The only person she could trust was her mother. She had argued with Father against Ruth being there last night anyway. Also, Ivy knew more about Lady Laughton's tantrums than Father. Ruth didn't understand why His Lordship had married her until Father explained that it was a 'business arrangement'.

Lady Laughton's first husband and His Lordship had been second cousins; their fathers had owned shipyards on the east coast and steelworks in the South Riding. As partners the cousins possessed the largest industry in Yorkshire and numbered amongst the richest men in a prosperous country. A generation on from the Great Exhibition of 1851, Britannia led the world and Queen

Victoria ruled much of it. Steel and shipping basked in this wealth.

But when Lady Laughton was widowed, her husband left his share of the industry to her. His Lordship's father had been the youngest of the cousins and although the widow was much older than he, His Lordship was keen to secure total control – he could not risk her marrying someone else and taking her share with her. As it was, another cousin who had emigrated also had a share, but he was content to be a sleeping partner despite approaches from lawyers to sell.

It was rumoured that the present Lord Laughton's father had bought his title by lining the pockets of politicians in London. He was 'new money' and it showed, Father said. But Ruth was beginning to think that her father was cut from the same ambitious cloth as His Lordship. It was a trait, she guessed, that she shared. She had gone along with his plans for her to mix with the gentry and marry well. However, she had not realised the price she would have to pay.

She stood in the servants' passage waiting for her mother to hurry by. The Hall might be quiet while everyone was out shooting but below stairs was buzzing, not least because guests had brought their own servants with them. Visiting valets and footmen always caused a stir among the maids. She wondered if any of them had lost their virtue last night.

'Ruth, what are you doing here?'

'I want to talk to you, Mother.'

'About last night? Yes, I thought you might have

17

something to say to me. You looked quite worn out. Have you had breakfast?'

She shook her head.

'Wait in my sitting room. I'll be as quick as I can.'

Ruth felt safe in the housekeeper's sitting room at Waterley Hall. It was her mother's private space and even Father did not often intrude. Ruth had spent many childhood hours occupying herself in there while Mother worked. She made up the fire, took a ladies' journal from the bookshelf and settled in a comfortable chair.

The door opened and Mother came in followed by a kitchen maid with a heavy tray. The maid placed it on the table and said, 'Will there be anything else, ma'am?'

'We'll have a pot of tea and cake in an hour. I want today's cake, mind.'

'Yes, ma'am.'

Ivy lifted the lid off the tureen and a steamy spicy aroma escaped. 'It's the soup that went out to the field for His Lordship.' She sniffed the contents. 'Mmmm, mulligatawny.' She placed her hand upon a bulky white napkin. 'With warm bread from the oven. I'll have indigestion but it'll be worth it.' Then she turned her attention to her daughter. 'Dear me, Ruth, you look awful this morning. Did you drink wine last night?'

'Just a little.'

'Well, you know my feelings on that.'

'Father says I must learn about wine.'

Ivy frowned but only said, 'Come and sit to the table.' She ladled out the soup and drew out a chair. 'Now, what

18

have you to tell me? Did one of the gentlemen guests take an interest in you?'

Ruth had rehearsed what she would say . . . Yes, a gentleman had taken an interest but it wasn't the one she had expected and she . . . she . . . she didn't know what to do . . . *She didn't know what to do.* It was as this last phrase ran through her head that Ruth broke down and cried. She spluttered and sobbed and tried to speak but choked and coughed on the words. Ivy was silent. Ruth couldn't see her mother's expression through her tears but when she had hiccupped to a halt Mother was sitting staring at her with a stony face.

'What happened, Ruth?' she asked.

The hiccups hadn't stopped. 'He – he – I was . . . on the couch . . . and he was on top of me . . . I tried to stop him . . . I did try . . . but I – I . . . couldn't.' She covered her face with the clean white napkin. The tears were flowing again. She couldn't help herself.

'What did he do to you, Ruth?'

She inhaled with a shudder, but her throat was closed. *'Tell me what he did.'*

Ruth jumped at her mother's angry tone and every nerve in her body jangled.

'Did he open his trousers and push himself inside you?'

Ruth pulled the napkin down and away from her face. It was exactly what he had done and she nodded.

'Ruth, Ruth, Ruth!' her mother anguished. 'I expect it from my maids but not from my own daughter. Where was your father when this happened?'

'He . . . he . . . he was putting someone to bed.'

'We'll have to tell him.'

'Oh, please don't do that, Mother. No one need know if we don't tell anybody.'

'Except the gentleman concerned. He's ruined you, don't you see? Well, he has to take responsibility and marry you because no other gentleman will even look at you now.' Ivy stood up and paced around the room. 'I knew it! I told your father it was a bad idea when Lady Laughton wasn't here to keep her eye on things. Would he have it? Well, we'll see who was right now, won't we?' she fumed.

Ruth sobbed and hiccupped and eventually croaked, 'I'm sorry, Mother.'

'Be quiet! I'm thinking.'

The fire died down and the soup went cold. There was a tap on the door. 'Not now!' Ivy snapped. Ruth needed a cup of tea but she didn't protest. Eventually, her mother had calmed and sat down again.

'We have to tell your father because he'll know what to do. He's a favourite at the moment. Lord Laughton has made him house steward. We were planning to celebrate tonight. *Dear heaven, Ruth, what were you thinking of?*'

'I . . . I t–t–told him to stop and he . . . he wouldn't listen to me.'

Ivy let out a sharp impatient sigh. 'Well, all is not lost. At least he's a gentleman. He'll have to marry you, that's all. It's not how we wanted it but if your father can get His Lordship to persuade the gentleman to do the right thing . . . His Lordship will help us when Father tells him.'

Ruth was startled into sensibility. 'No he won't. I mean, he can't! You don't understand, Mother! It was His Lordship that did it!'

'*What?*' Ivy covered her face with her hands and cried angrily, 'Ruth, what have you done, you stupid, stupid girl?'

She ought to have known better than to expect sympathy from her pious mother and retaliated, 'I didn't do anything! He did it to me. And he seemed to think he was going to carry on doing it! It's not what *I've* done, Mother, it's what you and father have not done. You didn't warn me about that! You didn't tell me that might happen!'

Ivy stood up. 'That's enough, Ruth. I've brought you up properly to value and guard your virtue and this is how you repay me at the first opportunity. The sooner you are married the better, as far as I am concerned.'

'Yes, well,' Ruth muttered, 'as you say, who will marry me now?'

'Who indeed.' Ivy sighed.

The door opened without prior knocking and Father walked in with a picnic basket. He glanced at the table and placed the basket on the floor. His face was ruddy from being outdoors and drinking left-over sloe gin from the shoot. 'His Lordship has ordered a buffet dinner for tonight so I'll be home early to celebrate,' he said. 'Has Mother told you my good news, Ruth?'

'Yes, Father.'

Seth rubbed his hands together. 'His Lordship's had a good day and he's in fine spirits. He has a proposition for me. I'll be home as soon as he's seen me. You two take the trap with this food.' He kicked the basket. 'I'll hitch a ride or walk.'

'Are the guns back already?'

'Only one or two of the lady followers who want first dibs at the hot water.'

Ivy picked up her chatelaine. 'They'll need linen. Stay here, Ruth, and don't breathe a word to anyone.'

'Is something up?' Father queried.

'No.'

'Nothing at all.'

Ruth and her mother had answered at exactly the same time.

Ruth unpacked the basket of cold roast beef, the cook's own mustard pickle, beetroot and a bottle of wine. Dessert pears and the end of the stilton were in the bottom. The cheese smelled too strong to eat. It was last year's because it was too early for this year's to be ready yet. She laid out their tea attractively on the kitchen table and scrubbed some potatoes to bake in the oven. She was hungry now and nibbled at the beef. There was plenty. Lord Laughton fed himself, his guests and his servants well.

Father was subdued when he arrived home and opened the wine straightaway. He drank it instead of tea with his meal. They were nearly finished before he said, 'I thought he was going to offer me a new house, now I'm steward.'

'It's nice here,' Ruth said. 'I like it.'

'It was you he wanted to see me about,' he said.

Ruth exchanged an alarmed glance with her mother who shook her head silently.

'I always knew you'd catch the eye of the gentry and live in a fine house one day,' he went on. 'But I didn't expect it this way.'

'What did he say to you, Seth?'

'He's taken a fancy to our daughter, Ivy, a proper shine to her, he has. He said he'd noticed how lovely she'd grown. Well, I knew he had, otherwise he wouldn't have asked her to the party last night, or paid for the gown.'

'You told me the silk was from you!' Ruth cried.

'Be quiet, Ruth,' her mother responded. 'What do you mean, Seth? He's a married man.'

'Yes, but look at who he's wed to? Who in their right mind would want her for a wife?'

'Isn't one of the marriage vows "for better or for worse"?'

'Oh, don't go all religious on me, Ivy. He's a young blood. He wants a pretty woman on his arm and, well, we want our Ruth to mix with the gentry, don't we?'

'Yes, but not on His Lordship's arm. He has a wife.'

'He likes our Ruth. I mean he really likes her. He said he'd marry her if he could.'

Ruth saw her mother's eyes widen and looked down at the table. 'Why would he say that?' Ivy demanded. 'What else has he told you?'

'He told me I should be very proud of her as she behaved like a perfect lady last night.'

Mother seemed relieved but spoke tartly. 'Well, he would say that, wouldn't he? It's what you want to hear.'

They were talking about her as though she wasn't present and Ruth wanted to tell Father the truth about

23

His Lordship. 'Mother,' Ruth interrupted, 'please can I say something?'

'No!' Ivy answered sharply. 'Leave this to me, my dear. If you've finished your tea you can go up to your bedroom.'

'I think she has to stay, Ivy. I haven't got to the proposition yet. She's still a bit young, you see, and His Lordship's aware of that. I think it was the attraction for him. The Prince of Wales has . . . well, he has his young ladies, you know, and the upper classes take their lead from him.'

'What is this proposition, Seth?'

'It's about our Ruth, Ivy. He's made up his mind and he's determined to have his way. My position, this cottage, your position, all is at risk if he doesn't get what he wants.'

'My position as well?' Ivy queried.

But what does he want? Ruth thought anxiously, remembering that he'd implied there'd be a next time with her. Nonetheless, she couldn't imagine Her Ladyship putting up with that sort of behaviour. She was bound to find out sooner or later. Anyway, it didn't matter to Ruth what His Lordship wanted because she didn't want him. She wanted to meet a young gentleman who was free to marry her.

'You're her mother, aren't you?' Seth explained. 'His Lordship says she has to marry soon.'

'Oh, I see. He wants her out of the way.' Ivy let out her breath audibly. 'That's a relief. I was thinking the same myself earlier on today. Ruth agreed with me, didn't you, dear?'

'Well, yes, but that was because—'

'Be quiet, dear,' her mother interrupted her. 'It's because you want to marry, isn't it?'

Ruth nodded. An early marriage was probably the best option for her now; before anyone found out – or guessed – that she was ruined. Perhaps she was wrong about His Lordship and he had a guilty conscience about his behaviour towards her? If that were the case, he might help her to find a rich husband. Ruth, like her mother, began to relax.

Seth said, 'Her husband has to be a fellow who owes me a favour or two, and will stay loyal to His Lordship.'

'Loyal to His Lordship?' Ivy repeated. Ruth noticed her mother sit up.

'To keep them out of Her Ladyship's sight,' Seth explained.

Her mother and father exchanged a glance that was, apparently, meaningful to them. But not to Ruth who watched her mother's body go rigid in her chair. 'Oh, Seth, no,' Ivy said, 'you can't do that to her. *She's your daughter.*'

'She'll do as I say. So will you. It's His Lordship's orders.'

No one spoke a word for several minutes. Ruth was aware her mother's anger had moved from her to her father. Father usually ignored both of them when it suited him. His word was law in their house. Ruth wanted to ask questions but she knew better than to inflame the situation. The rule for her was 'speak when you're spoken to'.

Father stood up. He was a big man. Tall men were favoured for male servants. Their height gave them stature and authority. 'That's settled, then,' he said. 'I thought Michael, my head footman, would be right for her. I had been training him up to take over from me as butler but he's pliable so he'll agree.'

'He's not daft, though,' Mother argued. 'Michael's already asked your permission to court her and you turned him down. He'll wonder why you've changed your mind.'

'He'll comply when His Lordship pays him off with a dowry. His Lordship hasn't got stacks of hard cash to give away so it'll be a property he has no other use for. Michael won't turn down a chance to live in a country house. He likes the gentrified way of life.'

'Well, he likes the brandy bottle, that's for sure,' Ivy commented.

Ruth grew more and more agitated as she listened to her parents speaking over her head. Michael? They'd chosen *Michael* to be her husband? 'Michael's not a gentleman!' Ruth cried. 'I'm not marrying a footman!'

'Don't you contradict me, my girl!' Her father raised his voice. 'You'll do as I say. He has to be one of His Lordship's servants. You wouldn't survive as a farmer's wife and His Lordship wouldn't do it to one of his own kind.'

'Do what? I thought you said His Lordship liked me and would wed me if he could!'

Her father was losing his temper and he turned on his wife. 'Good God, Ivy,' he shouted, 'you know what His Lordship wants! Tell her, will you?'

Ivy's back was ramrod straight in the chair and her

mouth was set in a thin tight line. 'Oh, yes, Seth. I know right enough and I wish I didn't.'

'Tell me what, Mother?' Ruth asked.

Ivy didn't mince her words. It was a characteristic that helped to make her an effective housekeeper. 'His Lordship wants you in his bed, Ruth,' she said. 'He wants you to be his mistress.'

Chapter 3

Ruth swallowed. 'But I can't,' she protested. 'I'm going to marry a gentleman.' Neither of her parents was showing her any of kind of sympathy. Father was suggesting that she married one man because another one wanted her as his mistress?

'Mother?' she squeaked, but her mother was tight-lipped.

Seth went on, 'She'll be well treated. She'll have fancy gowns and hats, and her own carriage.'

'Don't be ridiculous, Seth! Do you think Her Ladyship will stand for that? As soon as she gets wind of it, she'll have our Ruth scrubbing floors or worse.'

'Well, obviously His Lordship can't have it going on here at the Hall, right under her nose. But that's where the dowry comes in. If Michael marries her, His Lordship will give him Mereside Lodge, the old hunting lodge up country. It's been no use for shooting since the railway took half the woodland. But the lake has fishing; it has been leased as a fully staffed country residence lately. Michael will have a pension and he'll be able to turn his hand to something if he wants.'

'I suppose His Lordship will take up fishing and Her Ladyship will think he's reformed,' Ivy commented sourly. 'Seth, you can't agree to this. She's our daughter, not some jumped-up parlourmaid.'

'You wanted her at that fancy college in the first place!' Seth rubbed his hands over his thinning grey hair. 'His Lordship's made his mind up, Ivy. He won't let her go and he can ruin us all if he wants. He would, too. He's a man without scruples.'

'Well, it takes one to know one,' Ivy retaliated bitterly.

'Oh, get down off your high horse, woman! We'll stay here in comfort. He's doubled my stipend. We're having another room built on and a bigger carriage.'

'Shut up, Seth,' Ivy snapped. 'I don't care about a carriage. I need to think.'

Ruth could not stomach this conversation any longer. She stood up and declared, 'Well, I don't need to think. I'm not doing it.'

'Go to your bedroom this minute, Ruth,' Ivy ordered. 'You've played your part in this too.'

'*It wasn't my fault.*'

'That's enough!' Ivy waved her index finger in the air. 'Upstairs now. I'll be up to talk to you when your father and I have discussed this matter further.'

Ruth shook her head in exasperation. This would be a discussion of arrangements, not an argument against her father's decision. She was glad of an opportunity to escape from the pair of them! Last night she had been on the edge of a new and exciting period in her life.

She couldn't understand why everything had gone so wrong. She had dreamed of a life in a gentleman's country residence just as her father was describing. Except that in her dream she would be married to the gentleman himself and not to his greedy head footman. And why? So that His Lordship could have what he wanted, regardless of her wishes?

It wasn't fair! She wished she hadn't told her mother about His Lordship now and flopped on her bed in despair. She had hoped that she might fall in love with her husband, that he would love her in return. Where was love in all of this? Was this what Mother had meant when she had warned Ruth not to expect too much from marriage? Ruth's heart sank. Mother had told her that kind of romantic love didn't last. For her, the love of God was the only enduring passion.

It occurred to Ruth that her mother might not love her as much as she loved God, possibly because Ruth didn't love God as much as her mother did. Neither did she love Michael or His Lordship! And her father was asking her to be a . . . a sort of a wife to both of them? Actually, he wasn't asking her. Ruth knew her father well. He was telling her and he expected to be obeyed. As she sat in her upholstered chair by the window staring at the darkening sky, she was no longer sure that she loved her father either.

The pony and trap were still by the front gate and when she heard the front door close she guessed her father was going out to stable it. She leaned forward to watch him. But it was her mother, clutching her prayer book, who climbed in and set off in the direction of Waterley Edge and the nearest Methodist chapel. Then Father did something he had never done before. He tapped on her bedroom door and came in with a cup of tea for her.

'Your mother'll come round eventually. She's gone to pray and she wants you to wait up for her,' he said.

'Do I have to do this, Father?' Ruth asked.

'Yes, you do.' His tone was firm.

Ruth lit the lamp, did some sewing and tried to read. The journals about London fashion had lost their appeal. She picked up her bible and put it down again. Waterley Hall had its own church in the grounds that servants were expected to attend. Her Ladyship worshipped regularly but His Lordship didn't. Neither did Ruth's father. Ruth occasionally accompanied her mother to the Methodist chapel. The commandment was the same in church or chapel: thou shalt not commit adultery.

It was dark when Mother returned and Father went out straightaway to stable the pony. However, they talked in the kitchen for a long time before Ivy came upstairs. Ruth was on her feet to open the door when her mother arrived with cups of chocolate. Ruth could see that she had been crying.

'Father says I have to do it,' Ruth said.

'Your father is a wicked man and so is His Lordship. But the damage is done and you must listen to me now. Your father will not change his mind. He's house steward now and pleased that His Lordship has chosen you. He regards it as an honour. If he had any doubts about the . . . the . . . morality of the situation, His Lordship has persuaded him otherwise.'

'What will Father do to me if I refuse?'

Her mother shook her head. 'I do not advise you to disobey your father. He can be quite unprincipled in his reprisals.'

'But I want to marry a gentleman. You want me to marry a gentleman.'

'You lost that choice when you gave yourself to His Lordship.'

Ruth opened her mouth to protest, but Ivy silenced her with a raised hand and a pointed index finger. 'His Lordship is more heartless than your father. He has the power to ruin your reputation across the Riding and he will do so if you do not give him what he demands.'

'It's not exactly giving, is it?'

Ivy look horrified. 'Ruth! Do not even think that what you have to do for him requires payment in return, let alone voice that thought.'

Payment? Goodness, she wasn't thinking of payment! That would make her a . . . a . . . She began to feel sick. That's what mother *had* thought! And that is why she went to pray in chapel. Well, what *is* the difference between a woman kept for pleasure and a prostitute?

'I wasn't thinking of payment,' Ruth said. 'I was trying to say that His Lordship took what he wanted from me without asking. I did not give myself to him willingly.'

'Well, don't ever speak of that encounter to anyone. Do you hear me? From what your father has said, I don't think His Lordship has told him that he took you down.'

Ruth's hopes were raised. 'Then if nobody knows, it won't matter. I can carry on as before.'

Her mother lost her patience and snapped. 'Are you listening to a word I say?'

'I can deny it.' Ruth shrugged.

'You can't do that if you turn out to be with child.'

Ruth's mouth dropped open in shock. 'I can't be. I mean, it was over very quickly and . . .' She pulled a face. 'Well, he isn't very big, you know.' From those whispered conversations after dark in her ladies' college she had expected something more – well, something different anyway.

Mother glared at her. 'I hope with all my heart that you are not with child, but it is not impossible, even the first time.'

Ruth was subdued by this knowledge. 'His Lordship said he would do it again to me, Mother.'

'My dear, there are ways of avoiding becoming with child. I have had enough maids through my servants' hall to know the most effective remedies. I shall take you with me to the linen suppliers in Sheffield next week and find a chemist for you. Don't look so frightened. It's only sponges and douches.'

Ruth didn't like the sound of that at all and moaned, 'I don't want to do this, Mother.'

33

'Nor do I and I have prayed for guidance!' Ivy covered her face with her hands. 'I shall continue to pray every night that you are not with child. For that would make things ten times worse. His Lordship will not want a bastard child; or its mother.'

Ruth realised that her mother was holding back her tears and Ruth felt her own throat close. 'It's not fair,' she whined. 'If I were a man I could run away to sea.'

Ivy inhaled with a shudder. 'For heaven's sake, buck yourself up! We have to make the best of a bad situation. Your father and I agree that you should marry as soon as possible. If Michael agrees to the wedding, the banns will be read at Waterley church on Sunday and we'll have the ceremony in four weeks' time. His Lordship will give your union his blessing.'

'But Michael will say yes, Mother,' she wailed. 'Does it have to be him?'

'Of course it does. He's able to run Mereside Lodge and Michael will have an income from it as well as his pension. Your father will speak to him tomorrow.'

'He's a *footman*, Mother,' Ruth reminded her.

'Your father will make him up to butler until the wedding. It won't be so bad for you. Father says he's admired you for ages. However,' Ivy leaned forward to emphasise her point, 'you'll have to keep him at arm's length: His Lordship won't want to share you.'

Ruth's frown deepened. 'But if Michael is my husband . . .?'

'Don't worry about that now. You'll have your own rooms. The upper classes always have separate bedrooms.'

Ruth's chocolate had gone cold. She didn't want it anyway. It was a rich sweet drink and her stomach felt queasy. Her life was turning upside down and she found it hard to take it all in. 'Do I really have to marry next month?' she muttered.

'Yes. It is the best I can do for you. I don't want it any more than you do. Believe me, I am more sorry than you will ever be. But, to the outside world you will be a respectable married lady whose gentleman husband owns a country residence.'

'Shall we walk?' Michael held out his arm to Ruth.

This was the second Sunday of reading the banns for their marriage and in two weeks the vicar would perform the ceremony. Last Sunday they had made a show of walking out together after church and Michael had droned on about her father coming to his senses at last. She thought he was far too full of himself but Lady Laughton was watching them so she took his arm.

'Her Ladyship is very pleased with me,' he said.

'Why, what have you done for her?'

'This, of course.' He lifted his elbow. 'Marrying you. She came up to me specially to congratulate me. I've done her a big favour.'

'I don't see how.'

'She doesn't like pretty women around His Lordship. She doesn't trust him and that new lady's maid of hers tells her everything. She heard about you at the party the other week when she was away.'

Ruth went rigid. 'What did she hear?'

'Only what I told her. I was serving at the banquet,' Michael added, 'and I saw you dressed up in silks for His Lordship.'

'It wasn't for him. He was going to introduce me to his friend.'

'Not that one who was ogling you across the table? He wouldn't have wed you. When it comes to heirs they marry their own kind. I reckon you're well out of that one, Ruthie. He can't hold his drink. Now me, I can finish up all the leftover wine and still serve the coffee without spilling.' Michael put his hand over hers and tucked his elbow closer to his body so Ruth was obliged to move nearer to him. 'Anyway, Her Ladyship will be at the ceremony and I'll get a nice bonus from her afterwards.'

Ruth reflected that everyone was benefiting from her marriage, except her. She had seriously considered running away. But without money or anywhere to go she might die in a ditch. She had learned about the Married Women's Property Act at her ladies' college. It was all very well for those who had means before they married. They could keep it for themselves nowadays. But if you went into a marriage with nothing, you stayed with nothing. She couldn't see a way out of her situation no matter how much she tried.

They strolled on in silence. Waterley Hall estate was vast, with woodland deer parks and rolling Yorkshire countryside punctuated by the blackened winding gear and growing slag heaps of coal mines. You couldn't see the pits from here. Pastures dotted with sheep and ancient forest surrounded the Hall itself.

'Where are we going?' she asked.

'The old charcoal burner's place.'

'That's a long walk into the wood.'

'The shepherd's wagon is there, waiting for repair. They've brought it down from the high pasture before the winter sets in. It'll be nice and cosy inside.'

She stopped. 'Oh, it's too far. My mother's expecting me at the Hall for tea today.'

He pulled on her arm. 'Come on, Ruthie, we're betrothed. We can have a taste of married life.'

'I don't think so.'

She saw a flash of anger in his eyes. 'Two weeks won't make any difference.'

'Yes it will. I can't.' His expression didn't change so she added, 'I won't.'

'Oh, won't you? We'll see about that.' He grasped her hand and strode on ahead, jerking her after him.

'Stop a minute! Listen. I can hear something.' Ruth wasn't prevaricating. His Lordship's wealthier friends and neighbours often rode across the estate, although they didn't hunt on Sundays. She could hear horse's hooves thudding on the ground. Someone was out riding, off the bridle path and crashing through the trees behind them. 'Out of the way!' the rider yelled.

'Good God, it's His Lordship!' Michael exclaimed.

The horse veered on to the track and they stepped aside into the undergrowth. However, His Lordship slowed when he saw them, reined in his sweating horse and swung down from the saddle. He held onto the reins, walked his horse back towards them and said, 'You're a long way from the Hall.'

'We've been to church,' Ruth explained.

His Lordship's face was shiny with perspiration and spotted with blood from a graze. He took off his tall hat and wiped the back of his hand across his forehead, streaking it with dust. He smiled at Ruth and said, 'You're walking in the wrong direction for the Hall.'

'We are just taking the air, sir,' Michael said.

'Go back now,' His Lordship ordered.

Michael did not move. He was stony-faced.

'Now,' His Lordship repeated.

'Very well, sir,' Michael said and turned round. Ruth followed suit.

'Ruth, wait,' His Lordship called.

She had to stop and face him but Michael didn't walk on either. He stayed with her and she was grateful. Ruth kept her eyes on the ground.

'Look at me when I'm talking to you.'

She obeyed.

'Come and see me at the Hall after tea.' He glanced over her head at Michael standing behind her and grinned, 'I have a wedding present for Ruth.'

She couldn't speak. She didn't want any gifts from him. She didn't want anything from him.

'Her Ladyship is talking to your mother about your wedding breakfast,' His Lordship went on. 'I shall be in my study. Five o'clock.'

'Very well, sir.'

He nodded and flicked his hands in a gesture for them to move on in the direction of the church. They did and Ruth heard him remount and spur on his horse.

Michael was gripping her hand so tightly that he was hurting her.

'Let go of me,' she said, trying to snatch her hand away.

'Bastard,' Michael hissed through his teeth. 'Bloody bastard.'

'Michael!' Ruth was shocked by his language, especially on a Sunday.

'Who the hell does he think he is?'

'He's your master, Michael.'

'Well, Her Ladyship is right. He's got a fancy for you, right enough. That's plain to see. But if he thinks he's having his *droit de seigneur* before me he can think again. Nobody's having my wife before I do.' Michael pushed her off the bridle path and into the fern undergrowth. She was so surprised that he was unhooking the waistband of her skirt before she realised his intentions.

'You can't do this here, Michael,' she protested. 'You have to wait until we're married.'

'No I don't. I've wanted you for weeks and I'm having you now. Take off your skirt.'

Ruth had some idea of what to expect and she considered a struggle. But Michael was bigger than His Lordship in every respect. He was taller, more muscular and had strong hands. When he tugged at her skirts he could easily rip them if she resisted, and his fingers on her arm were tight enough to bruise them. She told herself he was practically her husband and therefore he had a right.

His face dripped sweat on to her forehead. All she could see over his shoulder were the dried-up fronds of dying ferns scratching at her hair. His weight pressed her down while he jabbed at her. He seemed to have some difficulty getting inside her until he probed around with his fingers. Then he went on for longer than His Lordship. And all she could think about was that she hadn't put in a sponge and whether or not she would tell her mother.

Chapter 4

Ruth was silent afterwards, all the way back to the church and onwards to the Hall. Michael talked about himself and how he would be well off when they were wed. He'd have Mereside Lodge, anything he could make from it and an account with a bank. Ruth wondered miserably what she would have that she could call her own? Michael didn't seem to notice she was quiet. Her mother did, though, later, when they were having tea in her house-keeper's room in at the Hall.

'Well, have you nothing to say about that, Ruth?'

'About what, Mother?'

'Do pay attention, my dear. Lady Laughton has asked me to take five o'clock tea with her in the drawing room so we can talk about a wedding breakfast for you. It won't be in the drawing room, of course, but here in the servants'

41

hall.' She picked up a plate. 'I shan't have my piece of cake now. You have it.'

'I'm not hungry.' Ruth's fingers were winding round each other nervously. 'Mother, His Lordship wants to see me in his study at five.'

Mother frowned. 'Calm down. You will have to see him when he says so. He'll be nice to you, I'm sure. Your father says he's very keen on you.'

'Well, can you . . .? I mean, if he does it to me can you put the sponge in afterwards?'

Mother looked shocked at first and then very sad, as though she was going to cry. She swallowed and answered, 'I don't know but I suppose it's better than nothing. The douche is for afterwards. Try not to worry about it now. He won't do anything like that here, not with Lady Laughton at home.'

But he did; on the button-backed maroon leather chesterfield behind the locked door of his study. Ruth's eyes roamed over the high shelves of books until he'd finished. He was quite admiring of her; her hair, her eyes, her lips and her breasts, especially her breasts. 'I told you it would be easier the second time,' he said.

He did have a wedding present for her, as well. It was a sapphire set in gold and threaded on a gold chain. He fastened it around her neck, underneath her gown and put the velvet lined box back in his desk drawer. 'Make sure to wear this on your wedding day,' he ordered, and sent her away.

She went home with her parents in the trap that evening. Ruth asked Father to bring the hip bath up to her bedroom and Mother helped carry the hot water.

'I'll stay and help,' her mother said.

Ruth stood fully dressed in her bedroom and shook her head. 'I can take care of myself, Mother. You and Father have done your . . . your best for me, but you are not responsible for me any more now that I have a . . . a patron.' Ruth managed to raise a weak smile. She was aware that her mother was holding back her tears.

Ivy said, 'You must understand that I have to keep Lady Laughton's approval. After your marriage, you will not be able to return here, no matter what.' She raised her eyes to the ceiling. 'Lord help all of us if Her Ladyship finds out the truth.'

Ruth supposed that Michael wouldn't be too pleased, either, when he realised that he'd been duped into this marriage. 'Do what you have to, Mother,' she said. 'I'm learning fast about what I have to do. The ladies' college has prepared me well.' Ruth saw that her mother wasn't quite sure how to take this remark so she added, 'I shall be a perfect lady at all times for His Lordship and . . . cultivate his favour for as long as I can.'

But Ruth was thinking, If I don't I'll end up on the streets, because no one will want me when His Lordship's finished with me, least of all Michael. In this instance the ladies' college might be more useful than mother ever imagined. She remembered a girl who was known to be the daughter of a 'kept women'. In some respects she had seemed wise beyond her years about marriage and money, but her mother had prepared her well to understand the needs of men. Ruth was just beginning.

She fingered the sapphire hidden under her gown and

thought, His Lordship will pay well for me. I'll make sure he does, in jewels and horses and anything else I can sell in the future. It crossed her mind that she was more her father's daughter than her pious mother's.

She said, 'I won't ever come back here, Mother. And I shan't expect you to visit me. You and Father may carry on as before. I know how to make my own way through life now.'

'Dear Lord,' Ivy whispered. 'What have I done to you?'

Ruth shrugged and muttered, 'What's done is done.'

Mother left, fishing in her pocket for a handkerchief and Ruth heard her take the trap over to the Methodist chapel that night.

Ruth refused to go for a walk after church the following Sunday, arguing that she had too much to do before the wedding. She sent sketches and torn-out journal pages to her dressmaker with instructions to arrange delivery to Mereside Lodge of everything except her wedding gown. For that she chose a modest high-necked affair in dusky pink with long tight sleeves and a bustle. The small private church was full. Lady Laughton occupied the front pew alone, with Mother and Father behind her. The remainder of the congregation included Michael's widowed father, his spinster aunt and Hall servants. Ruth was relieved that Lord Laughton had stayed away.

It was a fine autumn day and they lingered amongst the gravestones in the churchyard afterwards. Lady Laughton spoke to the vicar first and then came over to Ruth and Michael and their respective families. She ignored Ruth's father but said something complimentary to her mother. Then she turned to Michael and gave him an envelope.

'Thank you, My Lady,' he said and tucked it away inside his Sunday-best jacket.

Her Ladyship left immediately in her carriage. Michael extracted a leather-covered hip flask from his pocket and took a swig. He offered it to her father who declined and said, 'I have beer and cider set up in the servants' hall.'

Michael shrugged. He was a fine-looking man, tall and straight, but Ruth noticed he had developed a swagger about him recently. 'We won't be there,' Michael said. 'His Lordship has lent a carriage to take us to the railway station.'

Ivy was surprised. 'Are you leaving now?'

'His Lordship gave me tickets for a first-class carriage in the railway train.'

Ruth was as surprised as her mother but maintained her composure. She was becoming quite adept at that these days. 'I shall want my travelling coat, Michael,' she said.

His aunt stepped forward. 'I've put everything in the carriage for you, Ruth.'

They walked towards the waiting carriage. Before Ruth climbed in her mother took her to one side. 'This is goodbye, then,' Ivy said. She leaned forward to make a show of kissing her daughter on the cheek and whispered, 'Encourage him to drink and he won't bother you in the bedroom.' It was the last piece of advice her mother gave her.

Michael didn't need Ruth for encouragement to drink. The picnic basket, prepared by the Hall cook, contained bottled beer and he had brandy in his luggage. It was a long journey by carriage, two railway trains and another carriage at the end. Night was drawing in and Michael's brandy was finished when they arrived at Mereside Lodge.

The house appeared to be a respectable size and set beside water: the fishing lake, Ruth realised. She looked forward to seeing it in daylight. A manservant opened the front door to them and Michael pushed past him and looked around. There was a decanter and glasses sitting on the hall table, intended to warm travellers coming in from wintry weather. Michael poured himself a drink and sat in a chair with his legs stretched across the tiled floor. 'This is the life for me,' he said. His speech was slurred and his eyelids drooping. The manservant stood by and watched as he drank.

Apart from Michael, Ruth liked what she saw. A chandelier of about twenty candles suspended from a high ceiling illuminated the spacious reception hall and grand oak staircase leading to the first and second floors. She heard a movement on the stairs and looked up. His Lordship, dressed in a tweed Norfolk jacket and trousers, stood at the top. He was smoking a cigar.

'Pour the gentleman another drink,' Ruth said to the manservant, indicating Michael.

His Lordship walked slowly down until he reached the last few steps. Michael's attention was diverted by his manservant and the decanter he carried towards him.

When the manservant moved aside, Michael had sight of His Lordship. He was visibly shaken.

'What the blazes is he doing here?' he demanded.

'Don't you know?' Ruth said. She actually felt sorry for him. But she had been used in a similar fashion and had to come to terms with it. He would have to find his own way through.

Michael tipped the brandy to the back of his throat and held out the empty glass.

Ruth nodded at the manservant who stepped forward to refill the glass. 'See him safely to bed,' she said, and turned towards the stairs. She gave His Lordship her widest smile. 'Good evening, Laughton,' she said, 'how lovely to see you.'

'Good evening, Ruth. Come this way.'

Four Months Later

'Where is your husband, Ruth?'

'He doesn't stay in the house when you are here.' And very rarely at other times, she thought. But it suited her so she did not complain. Michael had a carriage and pair with a groom to drive him.

'Where does he go?'

Anywhere he can drink his brandy in solitude, Ruth thought. But she said, 'He's employed a woodman to manage the forest. He spends much of his time with the man's family on the other side of the estate.'

She was sitting in her morning room. Laughton had joined her after a gallop in the icy air and a gargantuan breakfast. Ruth was unable to stomach food at present.

Laughton stood at the bay window that looked out over the lake. 'There's profit in wood,' he commented. 'Michael was a good choice of your father's.' He moved to the fireplace and added a few coals. 'I'm moving abroad, Ruth.'

Ruth's heart stopped. Surely he had not tired of her already? Yet it had not seemed so last night, although he had commented that she was thinner. It was the morning sickness. She wondered how long she could keep it a secret from him and how he would react when he found out. She wondered, also, when he'd be going abroad and how long he'd be away. She fingered the sapphire ring he had given her and then the matching bracelet. She wore them all the time when he was here, even at night; actually, especially at night, when he demanded she wore nothing else. He liked her that way.

He pulled her to her feet and ran his hands up and down the curve of her corseted waist. 'I want to be the envy of my club, Ruth. I want you on my arm at the races to show them how beautiful you are. I can't do that in Yorkshire, let alone the rest of England. I'd be shunned by every society host.'

'Do you mean you want me to go abroad with you?' Her mind was churning with possibilities.

'France,' he said. 'I've got stock over there that I don't want Her Ladyship to know about. I'm liquidising it to buy a stud farm in your name.' His eyes gleamed as he added, 'Racehorses.'

'This is quite a surprise, Laughton.'

'A pleasant one, surely? You'd like to own a string of racehorses, wouldn't you?'

'I should, Laughton. I should.' She hoped the sale would be completed quickly and before her baby began to show. She could disguise it with her gowns, but not so easily between the bed sheets.

She gave a light laugh. 'But oughtn't you to be breeding heirs instead of horses?'

His tone changed and he answered harshly, 'I'll not bed her and why should I? She's too old anyway.' He glanced at her shrewdly. 'What is it, Ruth? Your father assured me that you knew better than to yearn for a bastard. Don't let me down. I won't stand for that.'

'Of course not, dearest. When shall we leave for France?'

'Soon. Very soon. Her Ladyship has found out about this arrangement and there's going to be a hell of scandal. It could cause lost orders, a drop in share prices and God knows what else, so I'm leaving the country.'

'Does Her Ladyship know it's me?' she squeaked.

'That's what I'm trying to tell you,' he replied impatiently. 'Get your maid to start packing. She can come with you if you want, but she'll have to learn French.'

But Ruth's mind wasn't in France yet, it was still in Yorkshire. Everyone would know it was her! She would be blamed as the temptress who had caused the rift in His Lordship's marriage and the name of Hargreaves would be dragged through the gutter. His Lordship was running and so should she. But her parents would remain at Waterley Hall. They had nowhere else to go. Their home, their livelihood, their future depended on the patronage of the incumbents. She had to hold herself rigid so that her trembling did not show. 'What will happen to my mother and father when you leave Waterley Hall?' she asked.

He wasn't interested. 'Not now, Ruth,' he said. 'I've more important things to think about. We'll break the journey in London until I've completed my negotiations with the French. I'm staying at my club and I've reserved a suite for you at The Admiral.'

'It's all arranged, then?'

'I'll be in the library writing letters until luncheon. I suggest you do the same.'

He fondled her face and kissed her. She had come to the conclusion that his affection for her was genuine although he did not say he loved her, not ever. He treated her well, as long as she behaved as he wished. But he was intolerant of argument if she transgressed so she was obliged to obey him. However, she feared for her safety when he found out about the baby, as he would – eventually.

She had no way of knowing whose baby it was. She believed she had conceived very early in her marriage, perhaps before the ceremony. Michael drank less between Laughton's visits and when he was sober he insisted on his marital rights. He made a practice of muttering disparaging remarks about His Lordship both during and after their intimacy. It was clear that Michael no longer wanted her; he only wanted to punish Laughton. If he hated her enough to use her in this way, she could not rely on Michael's protection when Laughton discarded her.

Michael was not a contented man but he knew better than to challenge His Lordship directly. He was aware how much power His Lordship had and how far-reaching it was. But Michael had independent means thanks, in part at least, to her father. He might be persuaded to offer her parents a home at Mereside Lodge.

Ruth wished she had more time to accumulate the

means of escape. She had jewellery, carriages and horses but not money. A bank note from His Lordship here and there for notions from the draper would not pay her passage home from France. If only she didn't have the baby and could wait! One thoroughbred sold without his knowledge would get her to America and anonymity. She heaved a sigh. If only she didn't have the baby, she would not need to flee.

She unlocked her writing desk, took out her address book and flicked through the pages. Not many of her ladies' college friends had volunteered their details to a butler's daughter. But the girl whose mother was a baronet's mistress was there. Ruth hardly knew her and turned the page quickly. Finally she closed the book, took a sheet of writing paper embossed with *Mereside Lodge, Forest Chase, Yorkshire, NR*, and dipped her pen in the ink.

Dear Mother, I hope this letter finds you and Father in good health.

You will know by now that His Lordship is leaving England. I shall be going with him. I imagine this will please you as I am aware that my living arrangements give you much pain. However, I fear that you and Father will be required to quit your positions and your home. Michael may have a place for you here, although I have not had time to discuss this with him. I suggest that Father writes to him.

I have to tell you that His Lordship treats me well and I have no complaints. However, the worst has happened.

*In spite of my vigilance I find that I am with child and
I do not know who the father is.*

Ruth stopped and reread the last sentence. It was a
shockingly immoral sin to confess to her religious mother
and she guessed it would cause her acute distress. But
what had her mother expected? She needed her mother
to realise how desperate she was. Ruth screwed up the
page and began again, changing the sentence to:

*I do not know whether the father is my husband or His
Lordship.*

She continued.

*A child will be an encumbrance to His Lordship and so
shall I. He will not want me or the child even if he believes
that my baby is his. Michael hates me as much as he hates
His Lordship and, now he can afford it, he drinks brandy
for most of his time.*

*I shall not humiliate you with my presence at Waterley.
However, I know that you have helped housemaids in my
situation in the past and I am asking you to do the same
for me. I shall be at The Admiral Hotel in London from
next week. If you can furnish me with a name and address
of one or two ladies who might assist me in any way, I
can prepare myself.*

Prepare myself? She thought. For what? For any solution
that presented itself. She wasn't the only girl without means

53

to land herself in trouble and it was never the men who paid the price. Some of these girls received help. Ruth simply wanted to be helped in the same way by people she could trust.

She sat back and reread her words. She was still their daughter and not yet twenty-one. Father had handed responsibility for her to His Lordship. Did that responsibility include an obligation to love her and care for her? She guessed not and reflected that neither Mother nor Father had demonstrated much love towards her, anyway; or indeed to each other. Their lives were driven by ambition for her father and religion for her mother. But they were her parents and Ruth felt she had no one else, no one at all, to turn to.

She signed the letter,

Your loving daughter, Ruth.

It was the only letter she wrote. She folded it and slid it inside one of the embossed envelopes, then hesitated. If a scandal was about to break, correspondence from Mereside Lodge would be suspect. She lit the tiny oil burner, picked up a stick of red sealing wax and watched it drip in blobs onto the closed envelope flap. She pressed the brass seal into the wax. No one would dare break a seal to examine the contents.

She placed it on a brass tray in the reception hall for a servant to carry to the post office then went for a long walk around the lake. Even in late winter, when the surrounding trees were bare twigs against the sky, it was beautiful and she would be sorry to leave. A few geese landed, disturbing the glassy water and she watched an ever-extending circle of ripples until they faded. Her existence as the scandalous mistress of Lord Laughton might fade in the same way if she lived abroad. No one would know her in France and she could start her life afresh.

But she had to decide about her baby first.

No matter how hard she prayed, Ivy could not find it within herself to forgive her husband or her daughter for their easy acceptance of their immoral ambitions. In her view, the thunderclouds of scandal that gathered over Waterley Hall were God's vengeance on the sinners.

Seth realised quickly that his days as house steward were numbered when he heard of Lord Laughton's plans to leave the country. He expected a cottage and a pension but neither was forthcoming. Lady Laughton dismissed him without notice and with some pleasure. Seth's resentment festered. On the day he received an official notice to quit his cottage he suffered a seizure that left him without the power of speech and the use of an arm and leg.

Ivy was unmoved. This was the wrath of God and Seth deserved it. She persuaded the doctor to place him in an almshouse for his last few months. Then she drove the trap and her belongings to Waterley Hall where she installed herself in an attic servant's room while she waited for Lady Laughton's decision on her position as housekeeper.

In this frame of mind, when Ivy received her daughter's letter, forwarded to the Hall, she regarded her with-child predicament as 'just deserts'. She marched into the kitchen, threw the letter on the cooking-range fire and watched it flare up with some satisfaction.

Of course no one wanted this child! The mother did not want it. His Lordship would never own it and Michael was too drunk to care. These wicked people deserved everything they got. Ivy stared at the flames until they died back to embers. Then she collected her prayer book from her sitting room and went outside to harness her trap. Waterley Hall was nearer to the Methodist chapel than the cottage. God was on her side.

PART TWO

Chapter 5

Waterley Edge, South Riding, Yorkshire, 1905

'Lettie, come here a minute.'

'What is it, Gran?' Lettie was sitting at the kitchen table cleaning the knives. She put down her buffing cloth and jumped to her feet. At nineteen, she had plenty of spare energy to use up and her grandmother relied on her for much of the rough work in the manse.

Gran closed the kitchen door behind her. 'The Reverend has a special meeting of the elders this afternoon. They'll be in the dining room from three o'clock.'

'I'll make sure it's ready.' Lettie cleared away the knives and stored her cleaning materials in the scullery cupboard. She folded the sheets of newspaper that had protected her carefully scrubbed table top and placed them on the pile for fire lighting.

Reverend Ennis did not have a wife. He was married

to his vocation as Methodist minister for Waterley Edge chapel and he depended on Gran to organise his life for the benefit of his calling. Gran was an intelligent old lady. As a young woman she had been a housekeeper to a lord in a large country house. She ran the manse with the same discipline. Lettie wore a serviceable cotton dress and housemaid's apron. Her long light brown hair was pulled back, plaited and left down her back or pinned up under a plain cap.

Lettie wondered what the meeting was about. 'Has someone passed away?' she asked.

'The Reverend buried him last month. He left a legacy for electric light in the mission hall. I hope they put it in here as well.' The manse had gas lights in the main rooms at the front, but still used oil lamps in the kitchen and bedrooms at the back of the house.

'So do I,' Lettie agreed. 'It will help your eyes.'

'There's nothing wrong with my eyes.'

Lettie disagreed but did not argue. 'Shall I sit in with you and take notes?'

'Not today, it's Friday. You'll have to stay in here for the egg man.'

'I could write up the minute book for you afterwards,' she offered.

'Thank you. You are such a help to me these days.'

Lettie would have done anything for her grandmother. Gran had looked after Lettie since she was a baby and brought her up to 'do everything properly' in the manse. But since she had left school, Lettie had been concerned about Gran's advancing years and anxious to shoulder much of the work herself. Consequently, Lettie hardly ever met people of her own age and, although she could never admit it to Gran, she was growing restless with her life at Waterley Edge.

She was secretly pleased that she didn't have to sit through the elders' meeting and tried not to let her excitement show. Thomas called with the delivery on Fridays. Normally Gran was present to pay him for the week, but mission duties always came first. Lettie liked Thomas. He was fun. She remembered him as one of the bigger boys at school. He lived in town and every time she walked the two miles to market she looked out for him cavorting around out on his delivery bicycle. He freewheeled down the hills with his legs stuck out in front of him and he made her laugh.

He was not what she would call handsome, but he was tall and strong, with thick dark hair. He worked for Mr Adley, a local smallholder, and when he wasn't delivering, he was on Adley's market stall selling eggs and vegetables. Last week, when Lettie walked to town for some sewing thread from the draper's, he had stopped to talk and asked her to go to the Midsummer Fair with him. He would be expecting a reply today.

Lettie collected a feather duster, broom and dustpan from the scullery. The dining room was already clean because it was summer and she hadn't lit a fire. 'Gran,' she asked, 'can I go to the fair on Saturday? Thomas has asked if he can take me.'

'Thomas?' Gran queried. 'Is that Thomas from chapel?'

'Thomas, who brings the eggs,' Lettie explained.

'You mean Thomas the delivery boy? What was he doing speaking to you? Who on earth does he think he is?'

He's not a delivery 'boy', Lettie thought. He's a young man, just as she was now a young woman, even if Gran wasn't aware of it. Why shouldn't Thomas want to walk out with her?

'I know him from school.' Lettie waited patiently for Gran to reply and, when she didn't, prompted, 'Well, can I go with him?'

'No, you most certainly cannot. His father's a coal miner and he's a roughneck. I'm surprised you even considered it. And you a Sunday school teacher, too.'

Lettie frowned at Gran's reaction and commented, 'Some of my Sunday school children have fathers who are coal miners.'

'Yes, well, their families are chapel folk. I haven't brought you up to mix with roughnecks.'

It had not occurred to Lettie that Gran would think Thomas wasn't good enough for her. But that's what she had implied.

'You stay away from that sort,' Gran warned. 'They're trouble, all of them.'

Lettie pressed her lips together to conceal her irritation. Thomas wasn't a coal miner anyway! And even if he was, it wouldn't have mattered to Lettie. She suppressed a sigh, wondering what she could say to Gran to change her mind. 'Mr Adley must trust him because he collects the money,' she muttered.

Gran scowled as she counted out some coins and piled them neatly on the kitchen table.

'Please, Gran.'

'I've said no and don't you go encouraging him. Now, remember to put the remains of the joint in the meat safe when you take the eggs down the cellar.'

'Yes, Gran.' Lettie was already a capable housekeeper and didn't have to be reminded what to do, but Gran still thought she did. Gran was full of wisdom and common sense but she could not shake off her habit of giving orders to servants and tradesmen – and to Lettie. It was her way and Lettie shrugged off her disappointment about the fair.

As she removed and folded the chenille table covering in the dining room, Lettie told herself she didn't mind missing the fair. But she did feel cross with Gran for her reaction to Thomas. The Reverend rarely interfered with Lettie's upbringing but if he did he sided with Gran. They were both too strict with her and she was becoming restless about her future. She stood back to admire her work. The mahogany table top shone. She arranged eight chairs neatly around it and checked that the sideboard had clear space for the tea tray.

Gran came in with ashtrays. The Reverend did not smoke tobacco but the elders were prosperous and one or two brought cigars. 'What time do you want tea for the gentlemen?' Lettie asked.

'The Reverend said three o'clock. Put out your jam sponge on the glass cake stand. It's going to be a long meeting.'

Lettie could see that Gran's eyes were already tired. 'He's lucky to have you to take the minutes,' she commented. 'Why can't he get a lay preacher to do it?'

'Because I do it for him and don't you be cheeky.'

'Well, I don't think your eyes are up to it.' Lettie had mentioned this before and Gran usually disagreed with her.

This time her grandmother didn't reply, so Lettie thought she might be right. She'd noticed that Gran didn't see colours as well as she used to and it was she who had suggested electric light in the manse as well as the mission hall. Lettie had noticed, too, that Gran had to stop for breath at the top of the stairs and she often asked Lettie to 'run and fetch me' items from upstairs.

The Reverend was a busy man. He was closely involved in miners' welfare, the almshouse and the orphanage. He worked tirelessly to raise funds for the mission, looked after his own pony and trap, and even kept a pig at the bottom of the garden. He relied on Gran for everything a housekeeper and clerk might do, including making sure that his chapel accounts were in order. Gran was more than happy to oblige as she was dedicated to chapel herself and she had always had Lettie to help her.

Lettie was not as devoted to chapel as her Gran was, but she had inherited her grandmother's quick wits and common sense. The manse at Waterley Edge was well run and comfortable – some said too comfortable for a manse – and most visitors appreciated their efforts. The ham and bacon from Reverend Ennis's pig was particularly desirable as Gran cured it herself in a zinc bath in one of the outhouses.

Gran took off her apron and said, 'I'm off to tidy myself up now. The cake is in the pantry.'

Where else would it be? Lettie thought uncharitably. She was used to Gran's ways but the old woman's reaction to Thomas had rattled her. She put away her broom and took her mending into the drawing room at the front, from where she could keep an eye out for Thomas. She had first noticed him from that window, pedalling down the road on his big black bicycle with its large basket in front of the handlebars.

She had simply wanted to go to the fair to have a little fun and maybe find out more about Thomas. She thought Gran was being unreasonable because she wouldn't even give Thomas a chance to show her he wasn't a roughneck. Maybe if she asked him to attend chapel Gran would approve?

Lettie had a big earthenware mixing bowl ready on the kitchen table for the eggs and, when she saw Thomas climb off his bicycle and wheel it down the path at the side of the house, she went to open the back kitchen door.

'Hello, Lettie!' He was carrying a large basket and looked past her into the gloom. 'Where's your gran? She's not ill, is she?'

'No, Thomas, she's at an elders' meeting. Your money's ready.'

'Thanks. Have you got a bowl for the eggs?'

'On the kitchen table. Why don't you come in and have a cup of tea?'

'Are you sure your gran won't mind?'

No, thought Lettie, I'm not sure, but she had to tell him she couldn't go to the fair and replied, 'It won't be for long.'

Thomas had a twinkle in his dark eyes as he grinned at her. 'While the cat's away, the mice will play.'

Lettie laughed. He was a friendly and cheery young man and made a welcome change to the sober and serious business of life in the manse. Not for the first time, she wondered what it would feel like to be kissed by him. Well, actually, she had been curious for a while about being kissed by a man, properly, on the lips. 'Kettle's on,' she said. 'Do you like sponge cake?'

'Yes please,' he replied. He counted out eggs from his basket and placed them in the bowl, then he deposited a newspaper-wrapped parcel on the table and pulled out a chair. 'You've some early runners, young carrots and lettuce hearts in there for the Reverend this week. He deserves the best on a Sunday after all his preaching.'

'Are you a chapel-goer?' she asked.

'Not me.' Thomas grinned. 'But a lot of Mr Adley's customers are and they like to know we look after the Reverend.'

Adley's market garden was one of the biggest in the area and his stall in town was popular because his prices were affordable to miners' and steelworkers' wives. His first-rate produce never went to market, though. He reserved it for his best customers who had regular deliveries and could pay full price.

'Did you ask your gran about the fair?'

'She said no.'

'Oh.' He looked disappointed and stared at her sadly for a moment.

'I'll just put these away, then,' Lettie muttered and

picked up the cooling mutton joint next to the bowl of eggs. It was on a big meat plate and heavier than she'd expected so it tipped slightly. 'Oops,' she commented.

Thomas darted forward. 'Shall I carry it for you?'

'I can manage, thank you. You mash the tea. The kettle's just boiled and the tea is in the pot.'

Lettie carried the meat carefully down a flight of stone steps that led to the cellar. There were two cellars under the manse: one for storing coal with an iron-grid covered opening in the ceiling for deliveries, and the other with a stone slab counter for keeping food. It was always cool in the cellar, even in a summer heatwave. A small amount of light penetrated down the steps through the open door at the top. She deposited the meat plate in the gauze meat safe and checked that the door catch was securely fastened. Then she turned and bumped straight into the bowl of eggs in Thomas's hands.

'Oh, you made me jump! What do you want down here?'

'I brought these down for you. Where shall I put them?'

'Over there next to the cheese dome.'

Thomas deposited the bowl carefully. 'I don't want to break any,' he said.

Lettie stepped to one side and watched him. He had to keep his head bowed in the low-ceilinged cellar. His wide shoulders seemed to fill the space. Normally there was plenty of room for her and Gran but Gran was tiny and Thomas was big so she was very aware that he was standing close to her. He seemed reluctant to return to the kitchen.

'Thomas?' she said.

'What is it, Lettie?'

'Will you kiss me?'

'Oh, I don't know, Lettie. I'd like to, but—'

'Please. There's nobody here.'

Lettie hadn't kissed anyone before, let alone a young man. Gran sometimes gave her a hug on her birthday and told her how much she loved her and she had only ever seen the Reverend shake hands with his congregation, even the women.

'All right, then, if you're sure.' Thomas stood in front of her and put his hands gently on her upper arms.

Lettie closed her eyes, puckered her lips and waited. When his mouth touched hers his lips were parted and as though by instinct her mouth opened too. She heard a growling noise in Thomas's throat and his grip on her arms strengthened. His tongue pushed between her lips and into her mouth and she felt her body tingle with excitement. Then he pulled her body against his and, startled, she pushed him away. 'Phew, Thomas, I didn't expect that.'

His face was flushed. 'Haven't you been kissed before?' he said. He sounded as surprised as she was but they were both brought back sharply to their right senses by a shadow in the doorway at the top of the cellar steps.

'What's going on down there?'

Lettie's hand flew to her mouth. 'Oh Lord, that's my gran!'

'I thought she was in the meeting!' Thomas whispered.

'She was.'

'Leave her to me,' Thomas whispered and dashed towards the steps. 'It's only me, Mrs Hargreaves. The egg bowl was too heavy for Lettie to carry down the cellar and she was showing me where to put them.'

Lettie grimaced. It was the truth but it felt like a lie to Lettie and she hoped Gran would believe him.

'Lettie! Are you down the cellar as well?'

'Yes, Gran.' Lettie stood beside Thomas and gazed up at the silhouette of Gran. 'Is something wrong?'

'Get yourself up here now.'

'Yes, Gran.' Lettie pushed passed Thomas and ran up the steps.

'What were you doing down there?'

'Nothing!' Lettie felt her cheeks grow hot.

'Then why have you gone red?'

Lettie put the cooling back of her hand on her cheek. She couldn't say she was hot from standing near the range. 'I must be sickening for something.'

Gran made an impatient sound in her throat. She wasn't stupid, nor did she have any time to waste. 'Don't make excuses. That Thomas is taking liberties with you.' Gran raised her voice and called over Lettie's shoulder, 'Up here this minute, young man!'

Thomas arrived in the kitchen with a serious expression on his face. 'I heard what you said, Mrs Hargreaves, and it's not true. I was only doing Lettie a favour.'

Lettie watched Gran's face set into her sternest expression as she replied, 'I don't believe you. You're all the same, your sort.'

'Gran!' Lettie was shocked. Thomas might have told

half a fib for her sake but there was no need for Gran to be so rude. 'It was my fault, Gran!' she cried.

'No, Lettie, it wasn't,' Thomas argued. He spoke directly to Gran. 'Mrs Hargreaves, I'd like to walk out with your Lettie. I want to take her to the Summer Fair and she wants to come with me. She says you won't let her.'

Lettie's eyes widened with delight. Thomas had said he wanted to walk out with her! No one had ever spoken up for like that before. He was very serious and polite and Lettie held her breath waiting for Gran to reply.

But Lettie's hopes were crushed as Gran replied, 'She's right. I won't. She's not going anywhere with you and don't you come near her again. D'you hear me?'

Thomas's mouth turned down at the corners.

'Well, do you?' Gran repeated.

'Yes, Mrs Hargreaves.'

'Get yourself off on your rounds, then.'

Thomas turned to Lettie and whispered, 'I'm sorry.' She smiled nervously but he wasn't smiling. He was cross and she hadn't seen him angry before. He took the coins on the table and left.

When he had gone, Gran turned on Lettie. 'I told you not to ask him in! Did you encourage him? Well, did you?'

'No, I didn't! Not like you think, anyway! But so what if I had? Most girls my age have sweethearts. Why shouldn't I?'

'You did encourage him! I knew it!'

'I like him, Gran,' Lettie protested.

Gran looked harassed and went on, 'You and I need

to sit down for a proper talk. I have to get back to my meeting now. Dear Lord! I only came out to say there are seven of us at the meeting. You'll need an extra cup and saucer on the tray.'

'But you've already told me. Look, I've put out seven like you said!'

Gran looked at the tray on the table and muttered, 'So I see.' Then she added firmly, 'Well, I saw Thomas out of the window and I wanted to make sure you were safe.'

'Thomas isn't dangerous!'

'You don't know anything about him.'

'Well, how can I if you won't let me walk out with him?'

'He's not suitable for you, Lettie.'

'You mean he's not good enough for me!'

'That's exactly what I mean. His father works down the pit.'

'But he's not a miner like his dad!'

'He's not chapel either.' The mantelpiece clock chimed. 'I'll talk to you about this after supper. The Reverend will be writing his sermon in his study so we can use the front room. We'll have it to ourselves.'

Gran picked up the tray. 'I'll take this in. You make the tea and bring it through with the cake.' She left in a hurry, leaving Lettie without further explanation.

Chapter 6

It's not fair, Lettie fumed. Thomas had done nothing wrong! She had asked him for a kiss and, although her first kiss had been brief, it had been exciting and she'd like to repeat it. She wanted to walk out with a man who would kiss her goodnight on the doorstep. Now, she wished she had not pushed him away. It had felt thrilling being close to a man. She remembered the smell of him and it had pleased her. Gran could not keep her cooped up in the manse like a child all her life!

Lettie brooded on what she had missed – the travelling bioscope show, a dance band in the town hall and now the fair. At first she had accepted that she couldn't go to dances in town because they had barrels of ale and cider for sale and chapel didn't approve of drink. Lettie understood that, but her gran took it further. Lettie wasn't allowed to go to any of the things that other young girls enjoyed, for example Sunday-afternoon walks in the Municipal Park or even village barn dances if they weren't chapel ones. She thought that it was time to make a stand. This was the twentieth century, after all!

The elders' meeting was long and Gran was tired by evening. Once the gentlemen had left, Lettie cooked the Reverend's six o'clock tea while Gran put the dining room back to rights. As soon as the Reverend disappeared into his study Gran insisted on her 'talk' with Lettie in the front room.

'I've done my best to protect you, Lettie, but you have to understand that a lady's reputation must be safeguarded. Young men do not always behave as you would want them to and you have to know them very well before you can trust them,' she explained. 'When I was in service, young ladies were not allowed to meet young gentlemen anywhere without a chaperone present.'

'It was different then. Gentry had to marry who their parents chose for them. And I heard that even the maids and footmen had to ask the butler's permission to walk out with each other in the old days.'

Gran's expression was stony. 'Who told you that?'

Lettie shrugged. 'I don't know. Somebody from the mission, I expect.'

'What else did they say?'

Lettie was puzzled. 'About what?' she queried.

Gran seemed to shake herself and pull herself together. 'Oh nothing,' she said. Her mouth smiled but her brow

73

was frowning. 'You mentioned sweethearts this morning. Is that what you want: a sweetheart?'

'Not particularly,' Lettie muttered. Sweethearts usually married each other and Lettie couldn't imagine herself married to anybody yet. She didn't yearn for a husband and babies as some village girls did. Nonetheless she added, 'But why shouldn't I wish to marry one day?'

'I haven't said you shouldn't but I do expect you to choose someone suitable.'

'By suitable you mean chapel?'

'Eric from chapel is a schoolmaster.'

'And I suppose that makes him better than Thomas from Adley's?'

'Yes it does. He will be a faithful husband to his wife.'

Lettie wanted to say 'he's too dull to be anything else' and searched for words that didn't sound rude. 'He's . . . he's . . . he's a bit, well, serious about everything.'

'He has sober habits and that is in his favour. I should welcome him at our table.'

Lettie didn't know what to say. Eric was a few years older than she and had been to grammar school and Training College. He was a bony, wiry sort of fellow who taught at Waterley Board School and gave bible classes at the mission in his spare time. Lettie's face must have shown dismay at the thought of him because Gran shook her head and clicked her tongue, adding, 'Lettie, what is happening to you? You were always such a good little girl.'

'I've not been a little girl for a long time, Gran.' But when Gran spoke to her like this she felt like a little girl and sometimes she thought that Gran wanted to keep her looking like one. Her best blouses and skirts were plain, her hats unadorned, and she really ought to stop wearing her hair down her back like a schoolgirl. 'I want to go out and see a bit more of life,' she added.

'I thought you were happy here helping me to look after the Reverend?'

'I am and I love you both, but . . . but . . . oh, I don't know . . .' Lettie lapsed into silence. She didn't want to say she was bored with the manse, bored with the mission hall and bored with Eric and his ilk.

'You'd like some excitement in your life?' Gran suggested.

Lettie looked up quickly with a smile. 'Oh yes, Gran. Yes please.'

'I'll tell Eric to ask you to the next barn dance we have in the village. He'll take good care of you.'

Lettie's heart sank. Why would she want to go anywhere with a man who had to be prompted to invite her?

'I'd rather go to the fair, Gran.'

'No, dear, not the fair, there are too many . . .'

'Roughnecks?' Lettie finished the sentence for her.

Gran smiled. 'I knew you would see sense in the end.'

Then why don't you trust me? Lettie thought with a sigh. She tried to understand Gran's concern. Gran was her only living relative. She was also her guardian, a duty that Gran shouldered responsibly and diligently, which Lettie appreciated. But she wondered if her parents would have been so strict with her.

'I had a word with the Reverend while you were

washing up,' Gran said. 'He doesn't mind if I go elsewhere for his eggs and vegetables.'

'You can't give up Adley's! They're the best in town.'

'Actually, Boundary Farm is better. They supply . . . well, they supply Waterley Hall.'

'But that's Lord Laughton's estate and you hate him.'

'Who told you that?'

Lettie couldn't answer because nobody had. It was simply a feeling that she had developed over the years. Gran always shut down conversations about the Laughtons or their large house and grounds, not that there was ever much to say because Lord Laughton was never home and his wife was a recluse. Fortunately, Gran did not wait for her reply. She went on, 'The Reverend knows the grower there and he often has a surplus. Boundary Farm doesn't deliver, though.'

'Then don't cancel Adley's,' Lettie pleaded. 'Mr Adley will want to know why.'

'And I shall tell him.'

'You mustn't do that! Thomas will get into trouble.'

'He is already in trouble, my girl, and deservedly so.'

'Please don't do it, Gran. It was my fault. Honest.'

'I won't have you taking the blame. He took advantage of you while my back was turned.'

Lettie knew that it wasn't true and chewed on her lip as Gran went on, 'You are too young to know how deceitful men can be.'

'Thomas wasn't deceitful! He was honest with you!'

'I shall be the judge of that. I have spoken to the Reverend and he understands why I cannot have that boy calling at the manse.'

'Well, I'll shop at Mr Adley's market stall instead. I can walk to town every other day and carry the shopping home.' Lettie thought this was a splendid idea as she had plenty of surplus energy to use up.

'Yes, I do believe more walking will be of benefit to you, which is why I agree with the Reverend. He will change his supplier to Boundary Farm and you will walk over two or three times a week to fetch the order.'

This wasn't at all what Lettie wanted and she protested, 'Gran, please don't cancel Adley's order.'

'My mind is made up. You will not see or speak to that miner's son again.'

Lettie blew out her cheeks. She knew that Gran and the Reverend meant well, but she liked Thomas and she was determined not to give up his friendship. She didn't want to meet him in secret, but if she had to, she would; at least until she could persuade Gran to change her mind about him. 'You're not being fair, Gran,' she muttered.

'You'll thank me one day.' Gran rose to her feet and added, 'The matter is closed. Off you go to bed and ask for guidance in your prayers tonight.' She frowned at Lettie. 'Be patient, Lettie, and the Lord will show you the way.'

The following Monday, Reverend Ennis asked her to 'step into his study' after his midday dinner of cold mutton with bubble and squeak. He wasn't sitting at his desk, but in a comfortable chair by the fireplace. It was too warm for a fire and a polished brass fire-screen stood in the hearth. He indicated the chair opposite him. 'Sit down,

77

Lettie. Your grandmother has asked me to have a word with you.'

She was pleased to sink into a comfortable chair. Monday was washday and she had been turning the mangle in the wash house for most of the morning. Then she hung out all the sheets while Gran started the Reverend's dinner before running upstairs to change into a dress fit for Reverend's study.

Normally, Lettie had little formal contact with the Reverend because she ate in the kitchen with Gran and he took his meals in the dining room. Sometimes in the week, when he had finished his chapel work and put on his corduroys, he would join her and Gran at the kitchen table for a cup of tea and a slice of cake. But the conversation was usually about the weather or the Reverend's pig, which was fattening in a sty at the bottom of the garden. He never discussed chapel business or the fortunes of the nearby pit, and gossip about local people was frowned upon.

He opened their conversation. 'You are looking delightful in that summer frock, my dear. Your grandmother and I have noticed what a pretty young woman you have become.'

Lettie blinked. She hadn't expected him to compliment her on her appearance. 'Thank you, Reverend,' she said.

'It is natural for you to catch the eye of young men, but you must be careful of your reputation, my dear. Young men are not yet accustomed to the freedoms that ladies insist upon nowadays.'

Oh Lord, Lettie thought, that's what this is about. 'Gran had a talk with me about young men after . . . after I

78

asked Thomas to step into the kitchen,' she said. 'I am nineteen, sir, and I can stand up for myself.'

'You still have much to learn about the ways of the world. Your grandmother has told me that you have thought about marriage. I think that is very sensible of you. Her mind will rest easy when you are safely married. Do you have a young gentleman in mind?'

'No, sir. I only mentioned to Gran that some girls of my age already have sweethearts. I wasn't thinking particularly of myself.'

'You are not against the institution of marriage, surely?'

'No, sir.' It was not generally a topic for conversation in the manse. Lettie had formed the opinion that Gran's husband, who had passed away years ago, was best forgotten and the Reverend maintained he was married to his vocation.

'Very well,' he went on. 'Your grandmother and I shall help you find someone. We have discussed it and I am prepared for you to have a young man call on you at the manse on Sundays for tea.'

Her eyes widened. She could ask Thomas and Gran would see him in his Sunday best. A smile spread across her features. It would be fun to sit in the kitchen and talk, eating scones that she'd baked for him. She wanted to know much more about Thomas.

The Reverend was satisfied with her reaction. 'I can see that my decision pleases you. However, there is a condition. Your grandmother must approve of the young man. Then you may entertain him in the drawing room if I am not using it for chapel business.'

Lettie tried not to let her disappointment show because she was grateful to the Reverend. It was his home, not hers, and it was very generous of him to allow her to use his front room as her own. But if she couldn't ask Thomas for tea, there was no one else. She said, 'Thank you, sir. But I don't have a follower to invite yet.'

'You will have, my dear. Be assured of that.' He gave her one of his rare smiles.

On the Wednesday afternoon, Lettie accompanied Gran to the chapel ladies' committee meeting at the mission hall. The ladies were wives of successful or important men in Waterley Edge who, of course, attended chapel. Officially, Gran was clerk to the group but it was Lettie who took the minutes and made the tea. Mrs Jones, who always took charge, brought a cake that her housemaid had baked. Before they set out, Gran glanced over Lettie's dress and hat. They were her Sunday best, as was befitting for her to wait on these ladies, especially Mrs Jones whose husband was a book-keeper for the Corporation in the nearby town.

'I think you ought to have a new outfit for best,' Gran said. 'I'll give you enough money to choose the stuff from the market tomorrow. You'll be able to make it up for chapel next week. Eric Jones will be there with his mother and father.'

Any other time Lettie would have been excited at the prospect of a new frock and ribbons for her best hat. But the implication that it was for Eric Jones's benefit took all the joy out of it. However, as she walked to town the following day, she realised that if she asked Thomas to come to chapel on Sunday, he would see her in her new outfit as well.

But Thomas wasn't on Adley's market stall. Mr Adley's son was serving and he had a queue. She joined it at first to ask when Thomas would be back, then realised his temper was frayed as he dealt with his customers. She didn't need eggs or vegetables and she didn't want to risk his sharp tongue so she moved away. Thomas was probably out on a delivery anyway.

But she chose her material with Thomas in mind and was pleased with some good white cotton for a blouse and a length of fine blue wool for a skirt. She had enough money left over for lace ribbon to decorate the front of her blouse. As she carried home her parcels, she had in mind a picture she had seen in a ladies' journal with a nipped-in waist and full sleeves. Gran would help her, although she'd have to do all the tiny stitching herself.

But Gran was no help with her hair. It was always plaited down her back. Lettie had tried winding the plaits round her head, but it made her look plain, like a governess. She wanted her hair piled high and framing her face, as in the picture. It can't be that difficult, she thought, and, on impulse, bought a packet of hair pins.

The skirt was straightforward but her blouse was tricky because it had a wide collar and fine pleats on the sleeve heads and down the front. Gran was disappointed it wasn't ready for Sunday but Lettie didn't mind. She hadn't seen Thomas to invite him to chapel yet. During the following week, Gran was happy for her to spend the hours sewing in her bedroom and Lettie used some of the time undoing her plait and piling up her hair.

When the next Sunday arrived her new outfit was finished and Gran insisted that she wore it to chapel. Lettie still hadn't set eyes on Thomas and wondered if he'd taken Gran's words to heart and given up on her. She'd be cross with him if he had! It was a fine day so maybe he'd be out for a walk after his Sunday dinner?

She pinned her summer hat with its new ribbon on top of her piled-up hair. It wasn't quite the look she wanted but she was satisfied with her appearance in the mirror. She was a proper young woman now.

Gran was waiting in the hall as she came downstairs. 'Goodness me!' she said. She seemed shocked and Lettie wondered if she'd cut her skirt too short. But ladies could show their ankles these days and she was wearing boots.

'Don't you like it?' she asked.

Gran seemed lost for words. Eventually she said, 'You've made yourself look very nice, dear.' As she opened the front door, Lettie heard her mutter, 'I suppose Eric is a trustworthy fellow.'

Lettie had forgotten about Eric because he had taken no notice of her last Sunday. Anyway, Gran had this notion about men in general. You couldn't trust them unless they were proven to be reliable, like the Reverend; and Eric, of course, because he was a schoolmaster.

She did turn a few heads when she walked into chapel and took her place in one of the front pews. During the service she even caught Eric staring at her. He didn't looked away either but sucked in his cheeks as his eyes darted over her. She didn't smile at him. Finally, the organ music faded, leaving the echo of its vibrations ringing in Lettie's ears, and gradually the congregation filed out into the bright morning sun.

One or two of the young women chatted to Lettie in the yard while Gran talked to Mrs Jones in the gloomy porch. When they emerged into the sunlight, instead of saying goodbye to each other and going their separate ways they both walked towards her.

Mrs Jones was a brisk buxom lady and Lettie frequently wondered whether she knew that her husband had a liking for patting the bottom of any young woman within his reach. One of them had said he'd gone further and put his hand up her skirt as well but Lettie didn't believe her. Mr Jones was respectable. He had a responsible position at the Town Hall and took care of the collection after each service. His was very proud of his clever son Eric. But Eric was a serious young man who was no fun and hardly ever smiled, and to Lettie's dismay he was now walking over to join his mother.

'Ah, there you are, Eric,' Mrs Jones began. 'I was looking for you. Your father will be a bit longer with the Reverend. You remember Lettie from Sunday school, don't you? Why don't you two go for a walk round while I talk to Mrs Hargreaves?'

'Very well, Mother.' Eric tugged at the cuffs of his jacket and crooked an elbow for Lettie to take his arm.

Lettie noticed that he didn't look at her. His eyes were scanning the chapel yard as the worshippers began to disperse to their homes. Perhaps he'd prefer to walk with someone else? She glanced at Gran who looked pleased and nodded at her, so she felt obliged to stand by his side. However, she didn't take his arm.

'Where do you want to walk?' he asked.

Nowhere with you, she thought but said, 'I don't mind.'

'We'll follow the path around the chapel.'

Lettie didn't think this was a good idea as it was always mossy and damp underfoot at the back of the building. She had a good look at him. He was taller than she and quite thin so that his collar looked too big for his neck. He had straight brown hair, darkened by pomade, small brown eyes and thin lips. Until today, Lettie had only ever spoken to him in Sunday school bible classes at the mission hall next door and she didn't think they had much in common at all.

She said, 'You don't have to take me for a walk if you don't want to.'

'Don't you want to come with me?' He sounded put out.

She didn't answer but she was conscious of the fact that Gran and Mrs Jones were watching them so, when he jutted his elbow towards her, reluctantly she took it. He headed along the cinder path that went alongside the chapel building.

They walked in silence for what seemed like an age to Lettie. She felt irritated by Eric. He was so stiff and starchy, and he didn't make any effort at conversation. They turned a corner of the building and were out of sight of the worshippers.

'Shall we go the other way? It might be slippy underfoot round here.'

'I shan't let you fall,' he said and placed his elbow against his body, trapping her arm.

She wanted to take her hand away but knew it would seem ungrateful and rude. It won't be for long, she thought, and said, 'I enjoyed the sermon today.'

'Did you? I could have done better myself.'

Lettie blinked with surprise. She had never heard anyone criticise the Reverend's sermons before and added, 'He didn't go on for too long.'

'I suppose you just wanted to get outside and talk to your friends.' He sounded critical.

'No I didn't. But why shouldn't I?'

She felt his arm stiffen. 'Do you answer back like that in the manse?'

Lettie's eyes widened. Well, yes she did, sometimes, she realised, but only to Gran and never, ever to the Reverend or one of his visitors. They turned a second corner and were now behind the chapel in the shade of several large trees. 'Shall we walk back now?' she suggested.

He clamped his elbow even closer to his side and he was strong.

'That hurts. Let me go, please,' she asked reasonably. When she tried to pull her hand out he took hold of it in his large bony fingers and held it in place.

'Mother said earlier to look out for you today,' he said.

'She spoke to you beforehand about me?'

'Your grandmother asked her, presumably because you told her to.'

'No, I didn't,' she denied.

'Well, what about all this . . . this dolling-up? You've

85

not done your hair like that before.' He indicated her appearance with a casual wave of his arm.

He thought it was all for his benefit. He must think that it was her idea and she wanted to walk out with him! Lettie frowned at him but he didn't appear to notice. He pushed her to one side and into a corner formed by the chapel wall and one of its flying buttresses. The sun never reached this side of the chapel. Ferns had taken over from grass and the stone wall felt damp against her back. Annoyed, she tried to push by him but he stepped to one side to stop her. Then he stood in front of her with his legs apart making it quite clear to her that he wasn't going to let her go.

With hindsight, Lettie realised that she ought to have made her views about Eric clearer to Gran. But it was too late for that now. She stared past him, over his shoulder at the tangled leafy branches of the trees and said, 'Well, I didn't do it for you. I think there's been a misunderstanding, Eric.'

'Not on my part, there hasn't,' he answered. His face loomed in front of hers so quickly that she squealed. Her squeal was immediately silenced by his mouth clamping over hers as he tried to kiss her. His teeth clashed with hers and his lips pressed so hard on her face that her head connected with the rough stone behind it, pushing her hat forward. Her instinctive objections were muffled in her throat. He put his hands on the swell of her breasts and then forced the lower half of his body hard on hers. She was pinned to the wall as he squeezed her flesh with his fingers and pushed his hips backwards and forwards against her.

Surely he must have been aware that the noises in her throat were a protest and that her eyes were wide open with fear? His eyes seemed glazed and looked straight through her as he kept pushing at her. Then he made a gravelly, groaning noise, slowed and stopped. He lifted his head and leaned, no *sagged* against her, breathing heavily.

She tried to push him off and waited for him to apologise. Instead, he muttered in her ear, 'That is your fault.'

Indignation caused her to blow out her cheeks. They were hot with embarrassment. 'How is it my fault?' she demanded.

'You flaunted yourself at me,' he replied.

Lettie had only done the same as other young women her age and if he thought that making herself look pretty was 'flaunting' then something was wrong with him! But Gran and the Reverend were as proud of Eric as his parents were. He could do no wrong in their eyes and he believed it of himself too.

'I didn't ask you to do that! You forced yourself on me,' she protested. All she wanted to do was get away from him so she went on, 'Now would you please step aside so I can go back to my gran?' She felt hot and bothered and knew she must look it as well. What on earth would Gran think if she emerged into the sunlight dishevelled and flushed? She placed her palms on her cheeks to cool them and said, 'Don't you ever do that to me again.'

He stared at her with raised eyebrows as though she had gone mad and said, 'Oh, be quiet and put your hat straight.'

She thought him rude but nonetheless tidied her hair as best she could, using one of the dingy rear windows of the chapel as a mirror. He waited until she had smoothed down her dress then held out his arm for her. She ignored it and tried to walk past him but he poked his elbow at her.

'You'd better take my arm,' he said. 'If we don't walk back together, they'll think I've been up to something.'

'Well, you have,' she replied irritably, but did as he suggested, feeling frustrated and cornered into a fib by his behaviour. She didn't care whether he was a schoolmaster or not, he took liberties and she didn't like him. She'd rather walk out with a miner's son who at least treated her with some respect.

Chapter 7

Lettie emerged into the sunshine hoping her cheeks did not appear as red as they felt. The last of the congregation had left. Gran and Mr and Mrs Jones were talking to the Reverend. Gran appeared pleased with herself. 'Here they are!' she called. 'My, they make a fine couple, don't they?'

Lettie realised that everyone heard this and protested, 'Gran!'

'Now don't be modest, dear.'

Lettie glanced around the small group. Everyone was smiling. Gran went on, 'You will come to the manse for tea today, won't you, Eric?'

'Thank you, Mrs Hargreaves, I should like that,' he replied.

Lettie resigned herself to this done deed, which seemed

to be what everyone wanted except her. 'Will you and Mr Jones come too?' she asked.

'Another time, dear.' Mrs Jones smiled. 'The Reverend has a double baptism this afternoon and we are expecting a large gathering. They have asked the mission ladies for tea in the hall.'

'It'll give you and Eric a chance to get to know each other,' Gran commented.

Lettie thought that she already knew more than she wanted to about Eric Jones. It shocked her that someone as outwardly pious as Eric could behave as he had. What was even more surprising was that Gran had been taken in by him. Hadn't Gran warned her, not so long ago, that men could be deceitful? Not chapel men, it seemed, only miners' sons. Lettie was cross. She wondered what words she could use to describe Eric's conduct towards her.

'Come along, dear,' Gran said, 'we have to get the Reverend's dinner on and the joint will need basting.'

As they hurried on ahead of the Reverend, Gran commented, 'Nice family, the Joneses. Mrs Jones works very hard for the mission and Mr Jones audits the manse accounts, which you do for me, of course. Nothing is ever too much trouble for either of them. What did Eric have to say for himself?'

'Nothing much.'

'Well, he has always been a quiet lad who keeps himself to himself. I suppose you can expect that with him being the studious sort. He's going to be a headmaster of the village school, you know.'

'No, I didn't.' Lettie preferred not to talk about Eric

because she could still feel the imprint of his fingers poking at the flesh of her breast, and the rough stone of the church wall on her back as his weight pressed against her.

But Gran went on about him. 'He'll be starting there after the summer and live in the school house. Have you ever been inside the school house? It's got front and back parlours and three good bedrooms as well as a box room. Make sure you give him a nice tea. You can make a sponge cake and some scones for him while the oven's on.'

'But I don't like him, Gran,' Lettie said.

'You haven't spent enough time in his company. He comes from a good hardworking family. You'll have a nice house and clever children, what more does a girl want?'

A man she respects and loves, Lettie thought, but didn't say it. Instead she replied, 'I don't think he likes me either.'

'Oh, I believe he does. In fact, I'd go so far as to say he's quite taken by you now you're a bit older. His mother told me he wouldn't need any persuading to come to tea.'

'You'll be there, won't you?'

'Well, I would be as a rule, but I've just been invited to attend this baptism. There'll be folk coming that I haven't seen in a while and they'll have travelled a long way. Besides, the mission ladies will need a hand giving them tea.' Gran beamed at her. 'It'll give you a chance to show Eric what a good little housekeeper you are.'

Lettie felt trapped. If she disagreed, Gran would be upset and annoyed and if she agreed, everyone, including

Eric, would get the wrong idea. She pressed her lips together in frustration. At least she had enough time to prepare what she would say to him. She had already made her feelings known to him so she only had to repeat herself to put him off for good. 'What time will you be back?' she asked.

'Why do you want to know that?' Gran queried. She sighed and went on, 'Sometimes, Lettie, I really worry about you. Eric has to see what a well-behaved young lady you are. I do hope I can trust you not to let me down in that respect. I don't want a repetition of that Thomas incident in the cellar, my girl.'

What about Eric? Lettie thought. He's the one who can't be trusted. Lettie considered telling Gran about his behaviour behind the chapel now, but with Gran in this frame of mind Lettie knew she wouldn't come out of it very well. Gran had already made up her mind that Eric could do no wrong. She felt irritated by Gran's injustice towards first Thomas and now her, so there was a touch of irony in her tone when she replied, 'But shouldn't I have a chaperone?'

Gran's serious expression became stern. 'Not all young men are like that Thomas. I blame myself for not speaking to you earlier about roughnecks. I assumed the fact that you lived in the manse would protect you from his sort.' She leaned over and patted her hand. 'Eric is chapel, my dear. The Reverend speaks very highly of him. He'll look after you.'

That made Lettie feel marginally better. If the Reverend thought well of Eric than she supposed he could be trusted to behave himself in the manse. And if Eric had agreed so readily to come to tea, perhaps he had been keen to walk out with her for a while. This possibility came as a shock to Lettie because she had not considered herself to be desirable in that way. Yet his actions behind the chapel had shown her he was . . . well . . . desperate to get his hands on her, quite literally.

Perhaps he was secretly in love with her and had had to wait for Gran's permission to court her? And perhaps that was a silly fantasy more likely to have occurred in one of the novels she read. Besides, it didn't alter the fact that she had never really liked him and his actions today had confirmed her opinion of him.

She liked Thomas. He was, she thought, clever in a different way from Eric. Thomas hadn't been to college but he was sharp and she reckoned that it wouldn't matter what kind of scrape he found himself in, Thomas would find a way out. On top of that he was fun. The thought of him made her smile.

'That's better, Lettie,' Gran responded. 'You are pretty when you smile.' Gran stared at her for a moment and repeated, 'Really very pretty indeed.' She looked down at the floor and muttered, 'Just like your mother, too pretty for her own good.'

Lettie wanted to pick up on that comment immediately and ask about her mother but Gran added briskly, 'Must get on, there is so much to do and you have to start your baking for this afternoon.'

This set Lettie thinking about all sorts of sabotage such as making the scones heavy or not leaving the sponge in the oven long enough. But it was not her way to waste good ingredients and Gran would be furious if she did.

I know what I'll do, Lettie decided as she creamed together butter and sugar for the cake. I'll make enough to take some to Thomas on the market stall in town.

She beat away at the mixture until her arms ached.

Eric arrived punctually and complimented Gran on the charm of the entrance hall at the manse. The Reverend had already left for the baptism and Gran was anxious not to be late. Lettie helped her with her hatpin in the hall and Eric held open the front door for her.

'Thank you, Eric. I know I can rely on you to take care of my granddaughter in my absence. Make yourself at home in the drawing room.'

'That is most kind of you, Mrs Hargreaves. Thank you,' he said.

'It's the Reverend's home, you must thank him.'

'I shall.'

Eric followed Lettie into the front room and walked over to the fireplace. It was too warm for a fire and the brass screen was in place.

'I'll go and put the kettle on.'

'Is there no one else here?'

'No. Do you think there ought to be?'

'Don't you have a maid for the scullery? Mother has a girl for the rough work.'

'Gran and I do everything in the manse.'

This seemed to impress him. 'Go on then,' he said, shrugging. 'But hurry up.'

'Tea will be in about half an hour,' she said when she

returned. She thought he might have offered to carry the tray in but he didn't. He sat proudly on the Reverend's couch with his legs splayed and a satisfied expression on his face. She wondered what he had to be so smug about and wandered over to look out of the window.

'Come away from the window and sit down over here,' he said firmly.

It was an order, she thought, and not a request, but the purpose of his visit was conversation so Lettie obeyed. She chose a fireside chair.

'No, over here with me on the settee,' he said.

'I'm comfortable here, thank you.'

'Well I'm not.' He got up, took her hand and yanked her to her feet. 'If you want to walk out with me you'd better learn to do as I say!'

'Who said I wanted to walk out with you?'

'Your grandmother did. She told my mother and she invited me here.'

'I thought you would have realised how I felt about you after this morning.'

'Oh that. You haven't been kissed before, have you? You'll soon learn. I'll show you if you come over here like I say.' He tugged on her arm so she fell against him, turned her round deftly and pushed her onto the settee. She scrambled to her feet. 'Aren't we supposed to have our tea and make conversation first?' she said.

'Your grandmother might be home by then,' he stated. 'Are you sure there's no one in the back?'

Lettie half laughed. He couldn't be serious about this. Surely he was not going to try to kiss her again, not after the last time? She was looking at his face, his shiny jumpy eyes and slack jaw. His regular features were not unattractive but at that precise moment they repulsed her. She kept her chin down so he couldn't kiss her in case he tried. That's when she saw his hands fumbling between them and they weren't on her because they weren't standing close enough. One hand was covering the bulge in his trousers and the other seemed to be wrestling with buttons in front of her and in full view! Lettie could barely believe her eyes and turned to exit the room as fast as she could. But he cut across her path and she tripped over his foot, only saving herself from falling by grasping the back of the settee.

He reached the door first and placed himself with his back against the door. 'Don't pretend to be stuffy with me. The word is out that your grandmother wants you married before you get yourself into trouble. We may as well find out as much as we can about each other while we have the chance.' She noticed his chest was rising and falling rapidly and she glimpsed a bulge of brown flesh pushing from his trouser opening. She spread the fingers of both hands in front to prevent him coming any nearer and said, 'You must stop this at once, Eric, and let me out.'

She heard him turn the key in the lock behind him and when he moved away there was no sign of it. He slid his hand in his jacket pocket presumably with the key and said, 'Come on, Lettie, I'm not courting a girl who won't do what I want.'

'Then that is just as well, Eric, because I have no desire for you to court me.'

'Don't play hard to get with me, Lettie. Your grandmother told my parents she wanted this and the Reverend agreed with her. You won't do any better than me in Waterley Edge. You might be the lass that all the fellows lust after but when it comes to marriage none of the toffs will consider you.'

'Marriage? Who said anything about marriage?'

'You'll have to marry soon. Who's going to look after you when your grandmother's gone?'

'I am quite capable of looking after myself, thank you.'

'No you're not. You won't last a week in the bottle factory and you've got no parents. You'll be a spinster of the parish, living in lodgings and asking for help from the mission.'

'I can find work.'

'Taking in washing and going out scrubbing for other folk? As my wife you'll have a lass to do that for you. And you'll be invited to sit on the mission hall ladies' committee.'

Her heart sank because some of what he said was true. She didn't have a proper occupation and Lettie could think of nothing more boring than arranging jumble sales and sewing circles for the mission welfare fund. It was noble work and she admired the ladies who did it, but she wanted to do something more challenging, something in the world outside the mission and the village. She didn't comment so he added, 'I thought your gran would have explained all that to you.'

'She warned me that some young men can't be trusted and you have shown me that she is right.'

He frowned and his face darkened. When he spoke he sounded exactly the same as her old headmaster in school. 'That's twice in one day I've been on the receiving end of your sharp tongue and it is quite enough. I can see you'll need taming if you're to be my wife.' He chewed the inside of his cheek. 'In school, the boys have the cane but I keep a leather slipper for the girls.'

Lettie was astounded. 'You would use a leather slipper on me?'

'As I say to the children, it depends entirely on whether or not you disobey me.'

He was quite serious. And to think that Gran approved of this potential match! She tried to appeal to Eric's reasoning. 'Why would you wish to marry a girl who has to be beaten into being the wife you want?'

The lines on his forehead deepened as though he was genuinely puzzled by this remark. 'I shall not need to because, as my wife, you will obey me.'

'Should I love and honour you as well?' she returned quickly, but her intended irony was wasted on him.

'I shall expect no less of you,' he replied.

'Then you ought not to marry me because I cannot meet your expectations.'

She saw anger flash in his eyes and suppressed a sigh. For an educated man he could be very obtuse. She spoke slowly and clearly. 'Eric, I do not love you.'

She ought to have saved her breath. He dismissed her argument with a wave of his hand, and sounded very confident when he responded. 'You will. I shall see to it.'

She wondered how he was going to do that, shuddered, and closed her mind to the possibilities. 'I shan't. I didn't ask for this, it was Gran's idea.'

'She's your guardian, isn't she? You have to do what she says. She knows what's best for you and you won't do better than me, not with you being an orphan and . . .' he hesitated before finishing, 'and all that.'

And all what? she thought. Her indignation must have shown on her face because he quickly added, 'Oh, don't worry, I shouldn't be ashamed of you standing by my side in chapel. I mean your grandmother is well respected and you are the prettiest girl at the mission. Besides, Mother and Father approve of you so everyone is satisfied.'

'Except me,' she said. 'I do not like the way you have behaved towards me. Shouldn't you at least wait until we are engaged?'

'We'll have an announcement in a few weeks, but a fellow likes to know a girl will' – he gave her a secretive little smile that sent a shiver down her back and lowered his voice – 'will suit his needs before he makes her any promises.'

And vice versa, Lettie thought. She regretted her irony about 'waiting until they were engaged' because now, heaven forbid, he presumed she had agreed to an engagement.

He stared at her thoughtfully for a few moments, and then said, 'You're not young but you've had a sheltered life here with your gran. You need to get used to being courted.' She was hugely relieved when he fumbled with his buttons again and closed up the gap in his trousers.

'Nonetheless,' he went on, 'I don't like to waste my time. You might be the prettiest girl in Waterley Edge but you have no background to speak of so you won't get a better offer than mine. I can wait.' He sat down heavily on the couch and tossed her the door key. 'I'll have my tea, now,' he said.

Lettie could think of nothing more to say to him and endured a gruelling hour of his conceit where conversation was limited to Eric's criticism of her scones and hints of shortcomings in her upbringing. She became quietly angered by this censure of her grandmother, which, she guessed, he must have realised eventually. After an extended silence he praised her cake. But, as he ate three pieces, this didn't help her mood because there would be none left for Thomas after she had put some by for Gran and the Reverend and she wished she hadn't eaten her slice. Her jam sponge was good, everybody said so.

She resisted blowing out her cheeks and heaving a sigh as he passed his cup across for a second refill. 'I'll refresh the pot,' she said, picking it up and moving swiftly to her feet.

She was in the kitchen before he could comment further and was standing at the range when she heard him follow her. He came up very close behind her and placed his hands on her waist. He stroked her hips, following the curve of her waist and bottom and she felt his breath on the back of her neck.

'You'll suit me very well, you know,' he whispered. 'It's a pity your grandmother will be home shortly. As soon as I'm installed in the school house, we can announce our engagement then you'll be able to come and take tea with me there, where no one will disturb us.'

Lettie splashed boiling water onto fresh tea in the pot and pushed away the uncharitable thoughts that flitted across her mind of where she'd like to splash it on him. She didn't want to waste her time any more than he did but decided that argument with him was futile. She needed to convince Gran and the Reverend that an engagement to Eric was a bad idea. She had to get them on her side.

Gran sensed an atmosphere between her and Eric when she came in from the baptism. Eric left shortly afterwards and Gran confronted her in the kitchen. 'Eric didn't look very pleased when he left. I hope you made an effort with him, my girl,' she scolded.

'I told you I didn't like him and I'd be hopeless as a headmaster's wife.'

'No you wouldn't and you'd have a good life.'

'Yes, but not the life I want.'

'Well, what do you want?' Gran was cross with her.

'I don't know yet; just something more than the mission ladies' committee!' Gran looked wounded and Lettie immediately regretted her words. 'I'm sorry, Gran; I didn't mean that, honestly.'

'I think you did,' Gran replied. 'You're headstrong, Lettie. Dear Lord, I've done my best with you but I hope you're not going turn out like your mother.' Gran shook her

101

head sadly and went upstairs to take off her best hat and coat.

Gran rarely mentioned Lettie's mother, except to say that she 'had gone' or 'been taken from her'. But a comment recently about being pretty and now a second one concerning her behaviour had made Lettie question some of the things Eric had hinted about her background.

Chapter 8

Lettie used up the last of the eggs in her baking the following day. Gran hadn't checked them before she did last week's order so she didn't object to Lettie walking into town to buy some more from the provisions merchant in the high street.

She was nearly there when she heard a bicycle bell and turned quickly. Thomas was freewheeling down the hill towards the market square, but not with his feet stretched out in front of him as usual. He applied his brake and slid to a halt beside her. He was not on the Adley's delivery bicycle. This was some old bone-shaker she hadn't seen before. He climbed off, swinging one of his sturdy legs over the saddle. She was about to ask him where he'd been these past two weeks when he demanded, 'What have you said to your granny about me?'

'Nothing!' she answered. 'I am sorry about Gran but she was only trying to protect me.'

'You don't need protecting from me! What does she think I am?'

Thomas didn't expect an answer. He had a quick mind and he would easily have worked out why Gran didn't approve of him. He went on, 'She doesn't even know me!'

'I'm hoping to change that. She and the Reverend have agreed that I can have a . . . a foll—' She stopped. She mustn't presume too much and continued, 'A friend to call on me at the manse.' She gave him a hopeful smile. 'Providing Gran approves, of course.'

'Which rules me out, then.'

Her smile faded. 'I know. I'm sorry.'

'I'm the one who's sorry! Your granny wrote to Mr Adley and cancelled the Reverend's order. And she said why so old man Adley told me to leave.'

'Oh no,' Lettie groaned. 'I did ask her not to tell him. Will he change his mind?'

'Don't be daft!' Thomas was clearly upset and went on, 'My dad's furious with me.'

Lettie felt awful and repeated, 'I'm sorry.'

'Me too. He says I've got to go down the pit like my brothers, so my mam is mad with me an' all. She was really proud of me when I started at Adley's.'

'Gran gave me a telling-off as well. But I did make her see that I am old enough to walk out with someone if I want.'

'I should think so. I know girls your age who are married.'

'She's just over-protective. It's been hard for her bringing me up on her own.'

'And she's done a good job with you. You're a credit to her, but she ought to trust you more.'

Lettie agreed. She hesitated before adding, 'She would, I'm sure, if you were . . . that is . . . well, Gran said that you weren't suitable because you were not "chapel". If you came to chapel on Sunday, she might change her mind about you.'

'That's impossible! My mam and dad would never forgive me. We're Roman Catholic.'

'Oh. I didn't know.' Lettie was disappointed. She remembered an awful rumpus in the village when the eldest son of a well-to-do Roman Catholic family took up with a chapel girl. They married eventually but she had to take instruction and become a Roman Catholic too.

'I'll tell you what, though,' Thomas said, 'my dad wouldn't have judged you like your granny judged me! He'd have given you a proper chance to say your piece. Your granny just got rid of me as fast as she could.'

Lettie felt obliged to defend Gran and replied, 'She only has my interests at heart. She thinks any lad who's not chapel is not to be trusted. At least she knows I'm a grown-up now. I thought she was going to keep me a little girl for ever.'

'You ought to try and get way from that manse for a while.'

'And that's impossible for *me*!' she responded. Oh heavens, if their conversation carried on in this way they'd just end up squabbling and Lettie didn't want that. She pasted a bright smile on her face and asked, 'Which pit will you be working at?'

He tapped the side of his nose with his forefinger. 'Wait and see. I've got my own ideas. Are you off to the market?'

'The grocer's in the square, but I was going to come and look for you.'

'Were you?'

She nodded.

'That's nice of you to say so. I like you, Lettie.'

'Do you really mean that?'

'Yes.'

'Do you . . . do you lust after me, Thomas?'

'Lettie!' He glanced around. 'If you're going to say things like that, keep your voice down. Why are you asking me that?'

'Oh, it was just something that somebody said.'

'About you?'

'Never mind.'

'Who said it, Lettie?' Thomas insisted.

'It doesn't matter but he said that all the lads lusted after me. Is it true?'

'*He* said? Who said?'

'Is it true?'

'No, of course it's not. You don't flaunt yourself like some of the lasses. But you are very pretty and lads notice that in any girl.'

'Thank you for telling me,' she responded and he shrugged.

It was a shame that Gran had taken against Thomas

because Gran was so very wrong about him. He was decent and honest and she was determined to change Gran's mind.

'I'd best be on my way,' she added.

'Well, I'll look out for you. Ta-ra.'

'Ta-ra.'

Lettie felt better after seeing Thomas. She could talk to him about anything.

Later that week, Reverend Ennis asked to speak with Lettie again and this time she could guess what it was about.

'Your grandmother is concerned about you, Lettie,' he began. 'You were seen in town with that delivery boy.'

'If you mean Thomas, we were only talking.'

'Did he try to kiss you again?'

'He wouldn't,' she protested, 'not unless I asked him.'

'So did you ask him to kiss you in the cellar?' the Reverend queried.

Lettie blushed.

'And did he really kiss you?'

'Sort of, I pushed him away.'

'But he persisted?'

'No.'

'No? Didn't he want to kiss you?'

'Not at first, and then he did.'

'And your grandmother interrupted him.'

'No! I told you, I pushed him away.'

'Yet you had asked him to kiss you,' the Reverend pointed out. He suddenly looked grave and said, 'Your grandmother is disappointed that you don't want Eric Jones to call on you again.'

I'm not, Lettie thought and chewed on her lip, wondering whether to tell the Reverend the truth about Eric. She decided not to as it might not do her own reputation any good at the moment.

'Eric is a fine young man,' the Reverend went on.

When she didn't comment, he sighed. 'Lettie, you must begin to think about your future. Your grandmother will not live for ever and it would please her immensely to see you safely married quite soon.'

'I don't want to marry Eric Jones,' she stated.

'So I gather. But you must understand that you are an orphan with no means of support. A husband is your best option for the future.'

'I can work. I can be a housekeeper, like Gran.'

'It's far better for a young woman to keep her own house for her own husband.'

Lettie pressed her lips together. She hoped he wasn't going to browbeat her into changing her mind about Eric. He could be quite dominating in his sermons. He continued, 'I have suggested a solution to which your grandmother readily agreed. I have a sister in Wales, with a growing family who would welcome you to live with them for a while.'

'Gran agreed to that?'

'It was her idea. She is worried about you.'

'I don't mean to worry her, but sometimes, I feel . . .' She didn't want to say bored because it seemed rude. Anyway she had plenty to do, but somehow it wasn't enough for her. 'I feel restless.' She sounded inadequate and looked down.

'Yes, we thought as much. Your grandmother asked if I could find you a position where you might be more fully occupied; in another mission, perhaps.'

'I should have to leave Gran if I did that!' Lettie was shocked. She wouldn't dream of leaving Gran now she was getting old.

'Don't you want to meet new people?'

'Well, yes, but—'

'It was your grandmother's suggestion.'

'Gran wants to send me away?'

'She herself argued that it would be a positive experience for you to live in a proper family for a while, with other young ladies of your own age, and young men, too.'

'You mean she wants me to leave the manse and go and live with your sister in Wales? I couldn't do that. I can't leave. Gran can't manage without me.'

'She says she can, with a girl from the village for the rough work.'

It wasn't domestic help that Gran needed most but the Reverend wasn't aware of that. She said, 'Gran hasn't told you, has she?'

'What are you talking about, Lettie?'

'Her eyes are going. She'll deny it if you ask her but I know I'm right.'

The Reverend looked away from her and gazed at the fire-screen for what seemed to be a long time. When he turned back to her his expression was serious. 'Yes,' he said, 'that would explain one or two things that have happened recently.'

'And she always has to stop at the top of the stairs to catch her breath.'

'Indeed?' He frowned. 'I had not noticed that.'

'Please don't say I told you. She'll be cross with me.'

'But she ought to have told me herself.'

'Why? I can do everything in the manse that Gran does,' Lettie volunteered eagerly. 'She has trained me properly, just as she did her maids when she was young. Please don't send me away, Reverend. Gran needs me more than ever now.'

He gave a slight nod as though he agreed, but grimaced as he said, 'I know you think she does but the manse is not your responsibility. I agree with your grandmother. Your interests will be best served if you move away from Waterley Edge. I have several nieces and nephews doing excellent work with missions in the Welsh valleys.'

Her heart sank. She admired the Reverend and his good works, but she really did not want a future in a Methodist mission. And she most certainly was not going to desert Gran.

'What would happen to my grandmother if I left her?' she asked.

'You do not have to concern yourself with your grandmother. She has many friends at the mission here to help her and you are too young to be tied to looking after an old lady.'

Lettie had never considered Gran to be a burden and protested, 'But I want to look after her!'

The Reverend remained resolute. 'Her eyesight is failing, and from what you tell me, perhaps her heart as well. I shall apply to the chapel welfare fund for her to see a physician. You do not have to worry about your grandmother, Lettie.'

But Lettie could be stubborn when she wanted and responded, 'Of course I do. She's my gran!'

'The mission ladies will look after her and my family will look after you.' The firmness in his tone made Lettie hesitate. Apart from Gran, the Reverend was the only person in the world for her to turn to and she respected his views. She did not doubt that he had her welfare at heart, nor did she doubt that this was all about keeping her away from Thomas.

'But I want to stay here where I have friends,' she argued.

'Do you mean Thomas?'

She refused to deny it and replied, 'He's a friend, yes.' He's the only one who seems to talk sense, she thought.

'You'll make new friends in Wales and forget about that delivery boy. He is not the sort of fellow that your grandmother wishes you to mix with, especially as he is not one of my congregation.'

Lettie knew that well enough. An awkward silence followed until the Reverend asked, 'What would you like to do with your life, Lettie?'

She hadn't given her future any serious thought because helping Gran had been her life so far. She didn't care to think about a time when Gran wouldn't be with her. She imagined that, one day, she would marry and have children. Meanwhile, Lettie took pride in everything she did and keeping to the high standard that Gran demanded. She wanted to manage the household perfectly just as Gran did. Gran had been appointed as a housekeeper at Waterley Hall when she was relatively young because she had been first-rate at it.

'You are a very good Sunday school teacher,' Reverend Ennis prompted.

Her headmaster at school had suggested, with his help, she could train to be a schoolteacher. But the women she had known as teachers either had married after a couple of years or were fusty old spinsters, and Lettie didn't want to turn out like them. There must be something more exciting that she could do?

'I don't want to be a teacher,' she replied.

The Reverend stood up. 'Well, you should think seriously about it. I shall write to my sister in South Wales and we shall see what can be done for you.'

A letter; is that all it took to change the course of her life? What was so wrong with Thomas anyway? She liked him and he liked her and she'd have much more fun with him than stuck in the school house with someone like Eric.

After tea that evening, Gran wanted to know how she had got on with the Reverend. They were tidying the pantry and Lettie was on the steps checking labels on bottles of preserves.

'Do you really want me to go away, Gran?' she said.

'Only if you won't reconsider Eric Jones,' she answered. 'He might give you another chance. His mother said he was quite taken by you, but thought you were a bit young.

I take responsibility for that and I don't regret it. You have plenty of time to become an adult.'

'*I don't like him.*'

Gran became impatient. 'He's a fine man, established in a good profession and a regular chapel-goer. You caused me and the Reverend a good deal of embarrassment when you refused to even consider him. *I'm* not getting any younger and *you* haven't got many options.' Gran put a hand to her breast. 'Oh goodness me, you've set off my palpitations. I'll have to sit down.' She staggered into the kitchen and sank onto a chair.

'Gran?' Lettie clambered down from the steps, thinking, What palpitations? 'What are you talking about, Gran? How long have you been having turns like this?'

Gran was catching her breath in gasps. 'It's nothing. Make me a cup of tea and I'll be fine.'

Gran couldn't blame this on the stairs but Lettie recognised when Gran was refusing to discuss something and obeyed silently. After Gran had drunk the tea and said she had recovered, Lettie queried it. Gran's face was ashen and Lettie suggested that she ask the Reverend to call the doctor.

'Nonsense, I'm as fit as a butcher's dog – always have been. Now, I do think it's a good idea of the Reverend's for you to go to his relations. It's a long way to South Wales but you'll be with people I can trust. You'll have to earn your keep, though. But you're a good little house-keeper so you won't be a burden to them.'

'You mean I'll be working for the Reverend's relations in South Wales?'

'For his sister; she has a big family and needs an extra pair of hands. Her eldest daughter is a schoolteacher. She'll be a good influence on you.'

Lettie considered she would be doing exactly the same work as she did at the manse but without her gran. It was the last thing Lettie wanted. Yet how could she say that when everyone had been so obliging? It was very kind of the Reverend to arrange this for her and she would be seen as extremely ungrateful if she refused. It seemed that he had decided on her future already and she wondered if Gran agreed wholeheartedly.

'The Reverend said it was your idea.'

'I asked him for advice and he recommended his family. He has an older brother too who is also a preacher and their chapel community is much bigger than ours. It is an extremely generous offer.' Gran's face was still pale but she took hold of Lettie's hand. 'The Reverend is as worried about you as I am.' She hesitated before adding, 'I had not intended to tell you but he . . . he will be your guardian if I should be taken by the Lord before you are twenty-one.'

Lettie was taken aback. Gran never spoke of her death and rarely mentioned her guardianship. It was something she avoided in conversation because Lettie always wanted to know about her parents and Gran wouldn't talk about them.

Gran went on hastily, her expression serious, 'I hope that it does not come to pass. But if I am called to God, I need someone I trust absolutely to care for you.'

Lettie stared at her. Gran would surely live for many

more years? She had been like a mother to her and the Reverend like a . . . a . . . Lettie realised with a start that the Reverend gave her the attention he would bestow on his own daughter. Her heart began to thump. 'The Reverend has agreed to be my guardian?' she commented. 'Why is he so kind and generous to me, Gran?'

'Why should he not be?' Gran's tone was sharp but her tired eyes were wary. Whenever Lettie asked questions that Gran didn't want to answer, Gran's conversation became guarded.

Lettie considered her words carefully. She was a young woman now and her life was changing. She wanted to know who she was. 'He's . . . he's not my father, is he?' she asked quietly.

Chapter 9

Her grandmother's jaw dropped open and her eyes widened. 'Good gracious me, no!' She was horrified. 'How dare you suggest such a slur on the Reverend?'

Lettie was frantic for a minute in case Gran had another attack. But Gran calmed down quickly and said, 'Whatever has given you that idea?'

Lettie hunched her shoulders. 'Why else would he care so much about me?'

'Because he is a good man, and believe me, Lettie, there are some who are not in this world!'

Lettie did believe her. Eric was one of those who were not, she thought, and from the information she had gleaned from Gran about her grandfather, he was another. She wondered what her own mother and father had thought of him and wished Gran would tell her. Over the years, when Lettie had asked after her parents, Gran had been evasive about them and the most she ever got in reply was: 'They've gone, both of them. It upsets me to talk of the past.' So Lettie had learned not to pursue her queries.

But some of the things Eric had said raised questions in Lettie's mind. Who was she, really? He had implied that Lettie's lineage was less than wholesome and she had wanted to challenge him on his comments. She couldn't do that, of course, unless she was in possession of the truth herself. What was the truth about her past? Perhaps now was not the best time to ask? But Lettie felt she had a right to know and Gran was getting on in years.

She was a Hargreaves so her father had been Gran's son or, or . . . her mother had not married. Lettie spoke quietly and clearly, 'Who was my father, Gran? You've never said. Was he a good man, or didn't you approve of him?'

Gran closed her tired eyes and kept them shut as she replied. 'He . . . he lost your mother and he could not look after you. I . . . I took you away for your own safety.'

That made sense to Lettie. While Gran was in this mood, she responded with the question that had smouldered in her mind for years, and since Eric's comments it now burned to be answered. It was the taboo question, the one you never asked because you might not like the answer. She kept her voice low. 'But they were married, though, weren't they? I'm not a . . .' She wanted to say 'bastard' but did not wish to shock her grandmother further and her words trailed away.

Lettie felt embarrassed by the look of horror that Gran gave her. Gran placed both her palms on the table and pushed herself to her feet. 'No you are not. Your mother was married when you were born and that is all you need to know,' she stated. 'Now, my dear, that's enough questions for now. Finish tidying the pantry for me. I really must get on with next week's orders.'

Gran had made it clear that the matter was closed. Lettie took the hint and moved on to a more mundane conversation. 'We need more laundry blue for the sheets. We'll be having a washday before the grocer does his rounds. Shall I walk into town tomorrow and get some?'

'All right. Take him the list for next week's delivery. You won't need the trap, but don't go looking for that delivery boy because he's not at Adley's any more.'

'Yes, Gran.' Lettie had use of the Reverend's pony and trap whenever he wasn't using it, but she preferred to walk anyway.

She set off the next day for the two miles to the grocer's shop on the high street. Waterley Edge used to be a separate village from the town, but they were more or less linked now by streets of houses for coal miners and steelworkers and their families. A horse rider passed her at a canter and she stood back to let him by. The horse was beautifully groomed and its gentleman rider sat tall in the saddle. She didn't recognise him as he looked down at her. He took a hand off the reins to raise his bowler hat. She bowed her head in acknow- ledgement and watched him for a few minutes. He was new to the area; probably a visitor to one of the big houses built in the surrounding countryside for furnace and factory owners. He glanced back at her over his shoulder and she smiled.

Half a mile further on she noticed the horse tethered outside the cemetery and saw the man wandering through the burial ground, bending down to read the gravestones. She wondered why he was so interested in the dead and shivered. She was so intent on watching this stranger that she didn't hear a bicycle approaching until he rang his bell and distracted her.

'Thomas!'

He was out of breath. 'I was at the bottom of the hill,' he panted.

He'd said he'd look out for her and she was pleased to see him, but worried at the same time in case anyone saw them together and told Gran. She didn't want to upset her again.

'I'm not supposed to talk to you,' she said.

'Well, I haven't got much time either. How are you getting on with your granny?'

'She wants to send me away to South Wales.'

'Phew, that's a long way. She must be really worried about you staying here.'

'I don't know why. I haven't done anything wrong.'

'She thinks you might. This is a bit drastic, though, you won't know anybody.'

'I'd be living with the Reverend's relations.'

'Oh, I see. Won't your granny miss you?'

'Yes and I'll miss her. Except that I won't because I'm not going. She can't make me.'

'Yes she can. You're not twenty-one yet. What did she say when you refused?'

'I haven't told her yet.'

Thomas frowned. 'It sounds as though you've a row brewing there.'

'I know. That's why I haven't said anything. I don't want give her palpitations.'

Thomas sympathised and said, 'If you really have to go, I'll come with you and get a job in a Welsh coal mine.'

Lettie didn't take him seriously but it wouldn't have surprised her if Thomas did do just that. She glanced sideways at the graveyard. The stranger was writing something in a small notebook and it dawned on her what he was doing. He was looking at names and dates on the headstones. Was he an orphan like she, and searching for his father? Even if he wasn't, Lettie felt an immediate empathy for the man and it occurred to her that she could do the same.

'I shan't go,' she said to Thomas. 'I have things I want to do here.'

Thomas smiled. 'Is one of them to give me another kiss?'

'Stop it, Thomas,' she hissed. 'I'm in real trouble because of that kiss in the cellar.'

'You liked it, though, didn't you?'

'If I want to stay in Waterley Edge I'll have to find some way of persuading Gran to let me. So you've got to keep away from me – a least until this fuss dies down.'

'All right, Lettie,' he soothed. 'I was only joking. We're still friends, aren't we?'

She nodded and said, 'I'm sorry. Gran's not well and I'm a bit anxious about her.'

'Now I'm the one who's sorry. When I'm settled, I'll let you know where I'm working and you'll be able to get a message to me if I can do anything to help. Promise me you'll do that?'

'I will. Thanks, Thomas.'

He turned his bicycle round to face downhill. 'Ta-ra, then.'

'Ta-ra.'

She walked on but her mind wasn't on her errand. It was on where she might find her mother's grave, or her father's, or even her grandfather's. They wouldn't be in the cemetery she'd just passed because that was an over-flow from the parish church in town and Church of England. Gran was a Methodist. She'd start with the chapel burial ground.

But the more she thought about it the more she real-ised that they probably weren't around here because Gran never visited them. Lettie decided to choose her moment and ask Gran where they were. By the time she returned to the manse with the laundry blue she was quite anxious to talk to Gran before the Reverend wrote his letter to South Wales.

Gran was very tired by evening and Lettie was loath to say anything to upset her. So she tried to be calm when she asked, 'Gran, can you ask the Reverend not to write to his sister in Wales just yet?'

Gran was sitting in her rocking chair by the kitchen fire, her eyes closed. Lettie knew she wasn't asleep. Lettie ought to have been reading by the oil lamp on the kitchen table but she just couldn't concentrate until she'd had this out with Gran.

'Why should I do that?' Gran answered without opening her eyes.

'I really don't want to go to South Wales and I don't want to be a teacher either.'

Gran opened her eyes. 'Don't be awkward about this, Lettie. I know what's best for you.'

No you don't! Lettie wanted to say, but instead she said, 'Teachers turn into fusty old spinsters. I might want to marry and have babies instead.'

'Well, you can still do that. But you have refused Eric.'

'I don't mean with him!'

This seemed to startle Gran and she sat upright causing her chair to rock. 'You haven't done anything silly with that delivery boy, have you?'

'Silly? Oh, you think we have . . .' Lettie blushed in the lamplight. 'Oh no, I don't mean that. I mean . . .' What did she mean? It was so ungrateful of her to say that she simply wanted to do more with her life than work in a mission. She said, 'I was thinking about what you were doing at my age.'

Gran had told her she had been responsible for most of the housekeeping at Waterley Hall because she was head parlourmaid by eighteen and the housekeeper was too old to manage anything on her own.

Gran looked past her and out of the window. 'I was the youngest housekeeper in the Riding when I was appointed; probably the youngest in the county. Your grandfather was butler at the time and then, years later, he became the new master's favourite.' Her expression soured. 'As thick as thieves, they were, but I didn't know that then.'

This wasn't the way Lettie had expected the conversation to go but she took an opportunity and asked lightly, 'Where is Grandfather buried?'

'Why do you want to know that?' Gran asked wearily.

'Well, I don't think he's in our chapel cemetery. You or the Reverend would have shown me.'

'No, he wasn't chapel so he stayed on the Waterley estate where he belonged,' Gran said. Her tone was sharp and Lettie bit back a barrage of questions. Gran was tired. She was an active lady, so much so that it was easy to forget how old she was in spite of her failing sight and her palpitations. She grew weary by nightfall. 'Shall I make some hot milk and honey to help you sleep?' Lettie suggested.

'Thank you, dear.' Gran rocked her chair and pushed herself out of it. 'Bring it upstairs and leave it outside my door.'

'Do you want me to brush out your hair?'

'Not tonight. I shall be too long at my prayers. Make sure you pray for guidance in yours, too.'

'Yes, Gran.'

Lettie mixed the warm nourishing drink in a stoneware mug and carried it carefully upstairs. She bent down to place it on the worn floorboards. A glow from an oil lamp was visible under the door and around the frame. Lettie could hear Gran at her prayers. The sound of her own name caused her to stop and listen.

* * *

Dear Lord, thank you for your leading me to Reverend Ennis and showing me the way forward to repentance. I beseech you to call my granddaughter Lettie to your service. Lead her towards an honourable life and give me the strength to bear our separation.

Please, Father, do not ask Lettie to suffer for her mother's sins. They were my sins too and I beg you to forgive me for them. Watch over my dearest Lettie and keep her pure and safe. Give her the wisdom to choose a more virtuous path than her mother . . .

Gran made a choking noise that muffled her words and then there was a silence followed by *Forgive me Lord.* Gran was weeping! Gran never cried and Lettie had to resist the temptation to dash into her bedroom and comfort her. But prayers were private and Lettie crept away, wondering if she had heard correctly. She could only guess at the sin her mother had committed that Gran blamed herself for. The answer seemed obvious and it would have brought shame on all the family. But Gran had been very firm when she said that Lettie was not born out of wedlock.

Yet she could not forget Gran's prayers. Lettie's mother had sinned in some unforgiveable manner and Gran was worried that Lettie was in danger of doing the same. Was she turning out to be like her sinful mother? Lettie thought not. Just because she had asked Thomas to kiss her didn't make her wicked! Of course she was aware what it might lead to – Eric had made that clear enough – but Lettie would not have allowed *that*; not before marriage. She heaved an impatient sigh. She didn't want to be a teacher or work in a mission either. No wonder Gran was worried about her.

Lettie did pray for guidance that night. Finding out a little about her father and mother had only whetted her appetite for more. She *had* to know what her mother had done and who her father was, who *she* was. Gran may be unyieldingly obstinate about revealing some parts of the past but the Lord might be more accommodating.

As Lettie lay awake in bed later that night, she realised that one of her prayers had been answered. Boundary Farm was on the borders of the Waterley estate. Waterley church and graveyard were about halfway between Boundary Farm and Waterley Hall. When she walked over to collect eggs and vegetables for the manse she could continue on to look for her grandfather's grave.

Boundary Farm had been standing for generations, some said longer than Waterley Hall itself. It was a well-worn stone building with a slate roof and a collection of wooden and brick outbuildings at the rear for horses and storage. But the main advantage for its occupant, Mr Osborne, was a large walled garden sheltered from the cold winter winds and enough acres for him to erect glass houses. He had a few small fields of staple vegetables but the larger areas from the old farmstead were leased to a nearby farmer as grazing pasture and growing crops for winter feed.

Mr Osborne was well known amongst the local gentry

for growing apricots and grapes as well as figs and berry fruits. The pick of his crop went to the kitchens of Waterley Hall but as the only resident was old Lady Laughton other larger residences in the Riding benefited from his produce. His wife greeted Lettie at the kitchen door when she arrived swinging her shopping baskets.

'Are you Lettie? I've been expecting you. Your mother housekeeps for the Reverend, is that right?'

'My grandmother,' Lettie corrected.

'I'm Mrs Osborne. Come with me to the barn and you can see what we have this week.'

'The Reverend said he knows you don't deliver but said to ask if Mr Osborne could take round a sack of potatoes when he's next in the village.'

'I'm sure he can.' Mrs Osborne was distracted by a young gentleman dressed for riding, leading a saddled horse from the stables. 'Good morning, sir.'

'Good morning, Mrs Osborne.' He stopped and took in Lettie's appearance, nodded briefly and added, 'Miss.'

He wasn't local, not even English, she thought, and replied, 'Good morning, sir.'

It was the same gentleman that she had seen wandering in the parish graveyard in town. He was well attired for riding, in jodhpurs and high leather boots, a brown woollen waistcoat and hacking jacket. Not very old, she thought, he had an even-featured face with an outdoor complexion and none of the whiskers that were so fashionable for the gentleman. She watched him with interest as he mounted the horse and clattered out of the cobbled farm yard.

'Handsome young fellow, isn't he?' Mrs Osborne remarked and walked on. 'This way, m'ducks.'

'Does Mr Osborne do livery as well?' Lettie queried.

'Dear me, no! He has his hands full with the gardening. The gentleman is lodging with us for the summer. That's his own horse and he looks after it himself.'

Lettie looked back at the young man over her shoulder and was embarrassed to see him doing the same to her as he cantered away. She filled her two shopping baskets, handed over payment and prepared to leave. 'Is it far to Waterley Hall church from here?'

'A good couple of miles in that direction, towards the house. Why do you ask?'

'Can I leave my baskets here while I walk over there?'

'Well, it's a fine day for the walk but I thought you were chapel, like, with you living in the manse.'

'I am but my grandfather wasn't and I think he's buried in the graveyard there. He was a butler to His Lordship before he died.'

'Well I never! Fancy that. Put your baskets in my scullery then and by the time you get back my scones'll be coming out of the oven.'

Lettie picked a posy of wild flowers on her way. She found the small church easily. The surrounding cemetery was tidy and dominated by ancient stone tombs, dark and mossy with age. They bore names and titles she did not recognise and none, apparently, for Lord Laughton's ancestors. She wandered around the smaller headstones and crosses, saddened by inscriptions such as *faithful servant* or *dearly loved sister* and eventually came across

Seth Hargreaves, House Steward, Husband of Ivy and Father of Ruth. This must be her grandfather! House steward? That was more important than butler. But it must be him because Gran's name was Ivy. Their daughter, presumably the daughter who had sinned and who was Lettie's mother – *her mother* – had been called Ruth. Lettie felt excitement bubble through her. Was her father buried here as well?

Lettie had never in her memory heard the name Ruth pass her grandmother's lips. She guessed that Ruth had died as a young woman and it hurt Gran to talk of her. She gave an involuntary cry and put her hand to her mouth as it occurred to her that her mother may have died in childbirth. The dates on her headstone would tell her, if only she could find her mother's grave. And it might give her father's name too so she would know who she really was. What would it say? *Ruth —, husband of —, mother of Lettie*, if Lettie was her full name. She hadn't questioned that before because everyone called her Lettie, even the Reverend.

She placed her posy at the base of the inscription on her grandfather's headstone and offered a short prayer. Then she searched the graveyard again for a Ruth and found one. This Ruth, however, had been a tenant farmer's dairymaid, and a much-loved sister of a coachman at the Hall, but there was no mention of her being a daughter, mother, wife or even widow. Disappointed, Lettie returned to her grandfather's headstone and frowned. Why did it not say *Beloved Husband* or *Loving Father* on his headstone? She looked at the dates. He had been much older than

Gran and died a long time ago. It was highly unlikely that anyone who remembered him apart from Gran was still alive.

Lettie walked back to Boundary Farm, confused and puzzled by her churchyard visit. Instead of answering her questions it had raised more in her mind and she was impatient for answers. Consequently she was in a restless mood when she collected her baskets from Mrs Osborne's scullery.

'Thank you, Mrs Osborne,' she called through the open door. 'I'll get off home now.'

Mrs Osborne cried immediately, 'You'll stay for a cuppa, won't you? It's not often I have company these days. My nippers are all grown and gone now and I do miss them. Did you find your grandfather?'

Lettie put down the baskets and went into the kitchen, which smelled appetisingly of baking scones. Mrs Osborne was a kindly lady and Lettie realised she was being rude by not acknowledging her hospitality. 'Thank you,' she said, 'I did find him. But I was surprised I couldn't find any Laughtons.'

'Lord Laughton's a newcomer. His father wasn't born a lord but he was as rich as one. When the old Waterley title died out the estate had to be sold and Queen Victoria, God rest her soul, had just made him a lord because of what he'd done.'

'Why, what had he done?'

'He'd made a pile of money out of steel and ships. His son and heir still does, an' all. An industrialist, they call him. They also say that he only bought the Waterley estate because he liked he sound of Lord Laughton of Waterley. He's never here, though.' Mrs Osborne glanced out of her kitchen window. 'Oh, there's Mr Boyer back. He'll be wanting some tea.' She rose stiffly to her feet. 'Scones'll be ready now.'

'Shall I take them out for you?' Lettie volunteered. It was one of the tasks she always did for Gran.

'Bless you, no, m'ducks. I can manage my baking.'

Lettie glanced out of the window and her attention was riveted by the sight of horse and rider as the stranger swung easily out of the saddle and led his horse to the stable. Behind her in the kitchen, Mrs Osborne groaned as she straightened up. Quickly, Lettie picked up a cloth, took the hot baking tray from the older woman and placed it on a wooden pot stand.

'Ta, m'ducks. I'm as stiff as a board these days.'

Lettie smiled. Her grandmother was more supple than Mrs Osborne and Gran must be ten or fifteen years older than her. Lettie realised that she was lucky to have her gran at all.

'He'll see to the beast first and then have a wash,' Mrs Osborne said. 'You couldn't carry the hot water up to his room for me, could you? My legs are not what they used to be.'

Lettie jumped to her feet. 'Of course I can. Is the jug in the scullery?'

'Use one of the brass hot-water cans on the floor. He has a washstand in his room so you'll see where to pour it.'

Lettie filled the can from the brass tap in the boiler

beside the fire that heated Mrs Osborne's cooking range. 'Which room?' she asked.

'It's straight in front of you at the top of the stairs.'

Lettie carried the heavy hot water upstairs and into Mr Boyer's room. It must be the best room in the house, she thought when she opened the door and light flooded from a large window onto the dim landing. A mahogany desk had been positioned under the window with one of those round-backed leather-studded chairs that she had seen in the municipal offices. The desktop held writing implements, books and leather folders of papers. Even with the desk, the room was large enough for a big mahogany bed, matching wardrobe and ottoman for blankets. There were heavy brocade drapes at the window and a counterpane on the bed in the same material. The effect was stately and comfortable. Lettie placed her can on the marble-topped washstand and then poured the hot water carefully into the decorated china ewer standing inside a similar gilt-edged wash basin. The hot steam rose to her face.

She was favourably impressed by the room and moved to the window to look at the view. As expected it was probably the best in the house, overlooking the front drive that led down through pasture towards the Waterley Hall road. Sheep grazed the lush grass. Their woolly coats were beginning to emerge again after early-summer shearing. She watched a couple of late-born lambs springing about, still trying to suckle their mother who kicked with her back legs and tossed them away with her head. So much for motherhood, she thought wryly.

The ewe's behaviour upset her and for a few minutes she was distracted, thinking about her own mother and wondering who she was. And who am I? she thought. Her dreaming was interrupted abruptly.

'My documents are private. Kindly leave.'

Chapter 10

The strong male voice left her in no doubt who was speaking and she turned away from the window quickly, clutching the warm metal jug.

'Beg pardon, sir.' Should she say she was looking at the lambs and not prying into his papers?

He had already removed his jacket, thrown it on the bed and was taking out his cufflinks. 'Kindly leave,' he repeated without looking at her.

His imperious tone reminded Lettie of Eric and she frowned, wanting to stay and defend herself. As well, she experienced a really strong urge to watch him roll up his sleeves. Discretion got the better of her and she obeyed silently, closing the door behind her. She walked slowly down the staircase wondering if his arms were sinewy like Eric's or brawny like Thomas's. The image of his capable fingers, manipulating the crisp cotton of his cuffs remained with her until she reached the kitchen. Mrs Osborne was laying his tea tray on the table.

'He's already washing,' Lettie said, wondering whether to tell her about his remarks.

'Yes, I heard the front door.'

'I . . . I was still in his room when he arrived.' Mrs Osborne didn't comment so she went on. 'I was watching the sheep out of the window and he thought I was looking at his desk.'

'Oh, I see. He likes to keep himself to himself. Was he angry?'

'He asked me to leave. I'm sorry, Mrs Osborne.'

'No harm done, I'm sure. I'll explain when I take in his tea.'

'I'd better get back. Gran will wonder where I've got to.'

This time Mrs Osborne didn't argue. 'All right, m'ducks. We'll have that cuppa another time.'

She's not happy with me, Lettie thought as she collected her baskets and left by the back door. She couldn't have read anything because all the books and binders were closed. But she had glanced at his desktop before she noticed the sheep so perhaps she was guilty of prying. She hurried along the path that led from the back of Boundary Farm to the wide track at the front, stopping briefly to admire the mellow stone of the handsome bay windows. A movement through the glass caught her attention.

Mr Boyer was standing in the bay and Mrs Osborne

appeared beside him to hand him a cup of tea and a plate of buttered scones. Lettie looked away quickly and lengthened her stride. As she walked away she felt two pairs of eyes burning into her back. The baskets grew heavy but she did not slacken her pace and was quite hot and bothered by the time the manse was in sight. Then she slowed. Why should she be so concerned about a stranger? He had hardly noticed her and a simple glance at the items on his desk was not, surely, such a terrible sin. She took a few deep breaths to calm herself and decided not to mention Mr Boyer to Gran.

'You were a long time over there,' Gran commented as Lettie placed her baskets on the quarry-tiled floor of the scullery.

'Mrs Osborne asked me to stay for cup of tea. She wanted a chat. I think she's lonely now her children have left home.'

'You might be right about that,' Gran considered. 'They say her husband spends all his time talking to his plants.'

'I didn't see him at all. I . . . I,' Lettie hesitated, wondering whether to mention her visit to the graveyard. But she had to if she wanted to know more about Grandfather and Ruth. 'I walked over to the Waterley church and looked for Grandfather's grave.'

Gran stopped lifting the vegetables into the stone sink. 'Did you find it?'

Lettie noticed that Gran didn't look up from examining the leeks. 'Yes,' she answered. 'It was very neat and tidy.'

'It's private to the estate and has gardeners tending all the graves.'

'I left a posy at his headstone and said a prayer.'

Gran turned on the big brass tap in the wall and water spluttered out into the shallow stone sink. 'These leeks are bigger than Mr Adley's.'

'Don't you want to talk about Grandfather, Gran?'

'No, I don't. I am sorry to have to tell you this but he was a wicked man and he is best forgotten. Now, can we get on with these vegetables?'

It was not a very charitable thing to say about her late husband but it would explain why he was not 'beloved'. What on earth had he done? Gran had said he'd been butler at Waterley Hall when they married. How does a wicked man reach the heights of house steward? There was so much more Lettie wanted to know but she recognised when Gran had closed down a conversation. Questions about Ruth would have to come later and she bit her tongue in frustration. Perhaps Gran might volunteer another snippet of information in a few minutes?

After a lengthy silence Lettie gave up waiting and said, 'These have got more muck on them than Adley's. I'll take them outside to give 'em a good scrub. You go and start on the Reverend's tea.' She took down her heavy sacking apron from the hook beside the sink.

The Reverend, like most ordinary folk in the Riding, had his dinner in the middle of the day and a substantial high tea in the dining room at six o'clock, often with a visitor connected to chapel. Lettie and Gran ate about half an hour later. Her chance came at the kitchen table when she and Gran had finished eating. The kettle was already boiling and Lettie stood up to make a fresh pot of tea.

'Why was Grandfather so wicked? What did he do?' she asked as she brought the pot to the table. Gran was cutting a piece of apple cake and she dropped the knife on the glass cake stand with a clatter. The pain on her face was so evident that Lettie regretted bringing up the topic again and she went on quickly, 'Oh, I'm sorry, Gran, but it's just that it's so long ago now, it really doesn't matter to me if he was sent to prison or something.'

'It was nothing like that. He was a favourite of Lord Laughton.'

'It says he was house steward on his headstone.'

'Ill-gotten gains,' Gran muttered.

Lettie could see she was becoming anxious by Lettie's questions. 'Don't upset yourself, Gran,' she said. 'You don't have to tell me.'

'You wouldn't understand if I did.'

'I might.'

Gran shook her head. 'Your innocence is your virtue.'

Lettie picked up the fallen knife to cut a piece of the cake and slide it across to Gran on a small plate. 'I may be innocent in comparison with some of my old school friends but I'm not a child. I read newspapers and I hear gossip in the mission hall.'

'What have you heard?'

'Nothing, nothing at all about Grandfather.' Although Eric had implied that there was gossip about her. She repeated, 'It was a long time ago, Gran, and nobody remembers him.'

'I do! I conspired in his wickedness and for that I shall shoulder the blame as much as he. I was a dutiful wife and a loyal servant. I obeyed my husband and my master against my conscience and I pray every day to the Lord for forgiveness.'

Lettie was astounded. It was the most Gran had ever said about the past and now Lettie understood why. Gran had been involved in the wickedness. 'What did you do?' she asked.

'Do not concern yourself with the past, my dear. When you move permanently to South Wales and live with the Reverend's family, you will mix with decent people and forget all about Waterley.'

'Move *permanently*? I thought it was just a visit!'

'There is no future for you in Waterley Edge. The Reverend has promised that, when I pass on, his family will take care of you.'

'But I don't want to go.'

'You have to; for my peace of mind. Lettie, you must understand your position. I am an old lady and I have only a small amount of money to leave you. We have a home here with the support of the Reverend and by the grace and favour of the church elders. When I am gone, the Reverend cannot have a young unmarried woman residing in the manse. You will have to live somewhere else.'

The Reverend was like a father to Lettie but she understood that for propriety's sake the elders would not permit her to stay, even as his housekeeper. Nonetheless, she protested, 'But that could be years in the future!'

'It is best to make the changes now.'

'Do you want to be rid of me for some reason?'

'Of course I do not and it will hurt me more than I can say to be separated from you. But I believe it is the Lord's will that you go.'

Lettie remembered her grandmother's prayer. She would feel the separation as much as Gran. 'Is my pain the Lord's will too?' she said. 'Does He wish me to abandon you when I know you need me more than ever, and then suffer that regret for the rest of my life?'

'I shall have the support of the mission. Truly, I am only doing what I think is best for you, as I have always done. Your head has been turned by the first young man to give you attention and—'

'This has nothing to do with Thomas! If it were I should go willingly because he has said he will follow me to South Wales anyway. I do understand my position as an orphan but I am sure I can find work here to support myself when I have to.'

'Doing what, may I ask?' Gran demanded.

'I don't see why I can't be a housekeeper as you were.'

'That is not a good idea for you and we have talked enough on this. Please can you pour my tea before it goes cold in the pot?'

Lettie did so and then picked up a tray to clear the Reverend's dining room. He had dined with a guest and they had already retreated to the drawing room. She stacked the tray with dirty dishes and left it on the hall table while she tapped on the drawing-room door. The conversation stopped when she entered and the

Reverend glanced up. 'Can I get you anything else, sir?' she asked.

'No thank you, Lettie.'

'Would you like another lamp?'

'I'll help myself from the scullery if I need one. I suggest you make sure your grandmother has an early night. She has been looking tired of late.'

'Very well. Goodnight then, sir.'

'Goodnight, Lettie.' He returned to his conversation.

She retreated gratefully, wondering if the Reverend had any information about her grandfather and decided not. He had much more pressing matters to deal with, many of which were confidential. Her duty was to look after Gran and not exhaust her with constant questions on a past she would prefer to forget. Lettie felt guilty about her selfishness and vowed in future to avoid anything that caused Gran anxiety. She would have to try very hard to be satisfied with what she knew for the time being.

A few days later Lettie was walking back from Boundary Farm with a basket full of vegetables when she saw Thomas leaning against the wall of the Miners' Arms with a tankard of beer in his hand. He wore heavy pit boots, a leather jerkin over his working clothes, and was black all over from coal dust. Goodness, if the day shift at the pit had finished already it was later than she'd thought. She quickened her pace, looking forward to exchanging a few words with him.

As soon as he saw her hc pushed himself away from

the wall and stood up straight. 'Hello, Lettie,' he said. 'I thought I might see you. The landlord said you pass here on your way to and from Boundary Farm.'

'You can't do anything in this village without everybody knowing. The Reverend has his vegetables from there, now.'

'I heard. He was a bit hard on Mr Adley, I thought, because he'd already got rid of me.'

Close up, Lettie took in the whole of his blackened appearance and the word 'roughneck' crossed her mind. 'Have you started down the pit already?'

'I'm not down the pit. I'm working for Toogoods and I've found him two new customers from my Adley's round.'

Mr Toogood was a big name in coal haulage in the Riding and he was expanding, setting up coal yards near railway lines that brought in wagon loads of coal direct from the local pitheads. He had caused quite a stir when he bought a motorised vehicle for deliveries and had his name painted on the doors.

Lettie swung her head round to where the Toogoods wagon stood by the kerb, still carrying about twenty sacks of coal. 'Are you their new coalman?'

Thomas raised his glass in a toast. 'That's me. The landlord here always has a pint waiting for when I've filled his cellar.'

Lettie stared again at the wagon, which was huge compared with a bicycle. 'Do you mean you can drive that thing?'

''Course I can. Mr Adley had a motor car for when

he delivered to the inn and big houses in town. I used to back it up and turn it round for him reg'lar. One day I'll have my own.'

Lettie was impressed. 'I bet your mam is pleased.'

'And my dad.' He drained his tankard, adding, 'I needed that,' and placed it on a window ledge. Then he rapped on the window and said, 'I'd better get going. These sacks are for that row of farm cottages on the Sheffield road.'

Not Boundary Farm, she thought. They had coal delivered at a discount price direct from the pit, the same as Waterley Hall. The Reverend, too, had his delivered from the pithead on a cart pulled by two heavy horses. The pit owners were generous because they appreciated how well the mission looked after miners' families when they had troubles. The driver shovelled it off the back of the cart and a couple of lads from the Reverend's congregation shovelled it into the cellar for him.

Thomas walked by close to her as he returned to his truck and she shrank away from the coal dust that covered him. 'It washes off,' he commented. 'Have you got your gran to change her mind about me yet?'

'Give me a chance!' Lettie retaliated. But she knew it was a lost cause. Gran wanted her to be a schoolteacher or marry one. The fact that Thomas might have his own motor wagon one day would count for nothing in her eyes. Once a roughneck, always a roughneck was Gran's opinion. 'Was the fair any good?' she asked.

'It was better than last year. They had a new ride that sent you round and round as well as up and down. I went on it three times. Listen, I can see you this Sunday

142

afternoon in the park if you like. Most of your village will be there because the colliery band is playing. I'll meet you by the bandstand and it'll look like a coincidence if anybody is watching.'

'I'll try,' she answered. She stayed to watch him crank the engine into life, climb up into the driver's seat and rumble away down the road.

A young woman came outside for his tankard and stood beside her to watch him drive away. 'Friendly sort, isn't he? Are you sweet on him?'

Lettie didn't answer. She was thinking about how she could get away from the manse on Sunday afternoon to go to the park. The woman prompted, 'Well, are you? I bet you are.'

Lettie thought about it. If being sweet on someone meant he was your sweetheart then she wasn't and she said so.

The woman didn't believe her. 'You're that stuck-up lass from the manse, aren't you?' she said. 'You'd better not be seen hanging about here. Chapel don't hold with us lot.' She snorted ungraciously. 'My dad's the landlord here and he says Reverend Ennis calls his ale "the demon drink".'

The woman went inside with the tankard and Lettie gazed down the empty road. She hadn't been called 'stuck-up' to her face since schooldays. But she guessed these names stayed with you for ever. She was more concerned with what Gran would think if she found out that Thomas drank beer in an ale house. It wouldn't do him any favours at all in her eyes. But it must be thirsty work heaving sacks of coal off the back of a wagon and up-ending them down cellar grates all day, so what was a working man to do?

Following morning service on Sunday, the talk outside chapel was about the colliery band in the Municipal Park and that it would be all right to go because they would be playing hymns. Both the Reverend and Gran approved so Lettie agreed to meet with others from chapel after dinner and walk to the park. She put on her new outfit with a ribbon bow at the front and another on her straw hat. After that unfortunate Sunday afternoon with Eric she had stopped being adventurous with coiling her hair but decided to pile it high for her day out. She was in a hurry and, annoyingly, her hair would not behave itself so in the end she brushed it out down her back. It was pretty enough but it made her appear younger than she was, which was even more noticeable when she joined the others from chapel for their walk.

The park was busy with men and women parading up and down in their summery finery making Lettie feel insignificant in comparison. Also, the other girls of her age had their hair coiled under flower-trimmed hats. Several wore skirts showing their ankles and matching short jackets that skimmed their waistlines. She eyed them with interest as she made her way to the bandstand. Rows of chairs were lined up all around, many already taken, and she scanned the gathering crowd for Thomas. He was standing up in the middle of a row and waved as soon as he saw her. Goodness, how clean and neat and tidy he was! She wished Gran could see him now.

'Oh, someone has saved me a seat,' she said to the others and detached herself from the group to weave her way through the crowd and shuffle down the row. 'Thomas, how did you get such good seats?'

'I came really early. Is your gran with you?'

'No, and she doesn't know I'm meeting you.'

'Will you tell her?'

'I'll say I saw you here but I don't think it will help. She's made up her mind about you and can be very stubborn when she wants.'

They sat down together and talked about the people they knew in the band and said which hymns they wanted to hear. Thomas was very easy to be with, she thought, and she felt safe with him after Eric. She stared at his profile for a while. He kept his eyes facing forwards but she noticed he smiled and that made her smile too.

'Who's that lady in the middle, a few rows down?' he said. 'She seems to know you.'

Lettie's eyes dodged between the large hats in front of her and realised it was Mrs Osborne, waving at her impatiently. She returned the wave and that seemed to satisfy her for she turned back and settled in her seat. Lettie noticed that even Mrs Osborne's grey hair was piled up elaborately underneath her hat, and her hat was trimmed with an ostrich feather. She fingered her long straight locks pensively as the band filed onto the circular stand with their shiny silver instruments. When they began to play, more folk gathered around the seating and stood to listen. After the finale, Thomas whispered, 'I enjoyed that, did you?' Lettie nodded and he added, 'Good, I'm glad. When do you have to be home?'

'I'm meeting the others by the gates at six.'

'Oh, we've plenty of time yet. Shall we go for a walk?'

The rows of chairs emptied gradually but when she and Thomas shuffled to the aisle she was waylaid by Mrs Osborne who materialised beside her, determined to talk.

'Wasn't that grand? We must ask the Corporation to make it a regular thing.' Mrs Osborne turned pointedly to Thomas. 'Good afternoon, young man.'

'This is Thomas,' Lettie said and went on quickly, 'We were at school together a few years ago and met each other just by chance.' Actually that was the truth, she thought, as it was chance that had brought them together, but it hadn't happened today.

Mrs Osborne nodded in Thomas's direction and he replied with a polite 'Good afternoon', then she turned back to Lettie. 'Will you be over tomorrow?'

'Not until Tuesday. It's washday tomorrow.'

'I'll look forward to Tuesday then.' Mrs Osborne gazed around. 'Now where is Mr Osborne? He'll be inspecting the flower beds, I expect. He didn't want to sit down. He can't keep still for two minutes at a time.' Mrs Osborne chatted on about the weather, her husband's glasshouses and her grown-up children. Lettie listened patiently until the older lady looked around and said, 'You haven't seen our Mr Boyer, have you?'

'Mr Boyer? Is he here, too?'

'He hired a trap, you know, to bring me here. Wasn't that kind of him? I find the walk into town too far these days and I can't ride in Mr Osborne's cart in my best frock, can I?'

'No, Mrs Osborne.' Lettie smiled. She glanced sideways at Thomas, who was waiting patiently. The crowd was thinning and through a gap she saw Mr Boyer, standing in the shade of a large oak tree, formally dressed in a dark suit and bowler hat with a black cane in his hand. 'Mr Boyer is over there,' she said. 'He's waiting for you at the other side.' She considered waving to attract his attention but didn't. He was a gentleman and it was hardly a ladylike gesture. And he would see her with Thomas if she did.

'We're going this way,' Thomas said and touched Lettie's arm with his hand.

Mrs Osborne noticed and her eyebrows moved up very slightly. 'I'll see you on Tuesday, then. Come after you've done your ironing and ask your gran if you can stay for a cuppa.'

'All right, Mrs Osborne. Bye, then.' Mrs Osborne turned round to search for her lodger and ride home.

Thomas tugged lightly on Lettie's hand. 'I thought we'd never get away from her.'

'She likes talking, that's all.'

The walkers continued to thin as many went straight home after the band finished playing.

'Shall we walk on the grass?' Lettie suggested. She liked the feel of the soft turf underfoot. 'We could cut across to the shrubbery.'

'Oh, I don't know.' Thomas slowed his pace. 'Let's stick to the path.'

Lettie was surprised. Several younger folk were walking that way and she watched them. Several *couples*, she noticed; not families with children and grandparents. There were lots of twists and turns and secluded corners in the shrubbery and Lettie guessed the reason for its popularity. She felt a blush rising and looked down. Thomas would be thinking she was very forward and she had to put that right.

'All right,' she said and shrugged, 'but I wasn't going to ask you to kiss me again.'

'You don't want me to kiss you anyway, do you?'

Chapter 11

No she didn't, not after Eric. She hadn't told Thomas about Eric so she asked, 'Why do you say that?'

'I don't think you wanted *me* to kiss you in the first place. You just wanted to be kissed.'

He was right and Lettie didn't know what to say so she kept quiet. Thomas went on, 'You still want to be kissed, though, don't you?'

'No! Well, yes, I do, but things are different now.'

Kissing led to other things. Thomas knew that, so did Gran and her warnings echoed in Lettie's ears. She liked being with Thomas and she had wanted to know what kissing was like and it . . . he . . . all of it . . . had surprised her. Proper kissing was . . . was . . . oh, she wasn't sure but it was something that she wanted to be special, with someone special, very special, with someone she . . . Lettie stared at the other couples walking across the grass. Were they all special to each other, or were they, as she was, simply finding out?

Thomas was nice, he was fun, but he wasn't, well, he wasn't special in the way she wanted him to be and if she asked him to kiss her again he would think he was.

He said, 'There's no wonder your gran is worried about you. She's protected you too much from ordinary life. In some ways you're still a child. You even look like my little sister today.'

'No, please don't say that! Gran doesn't let me come to the park as a rule.'

'That's what I mean! You need to grow up. I'm sorry, Lettie. I don't mean to be rude, but you should know what I think.'

They walked on in silence for a while until Lettie said, 'I want you to always tell me the truth, Thomas. Promise me you will.'

'That's easy. My dad brought me up never to tell lies.'

'Are we still friends, then?' she asked.

'Friends? I suppose so; for now.' He let out a sigh through the corner of his mouth. 'Shall we walk up to the fountain and make a wish?'

'All right,' she agreed.

She felt uncomfortable for a while. Thomas had under-lined what Gran had said about the value of going to Wales and living with other young folk in a proper family. Then Thomas began to talk about the Toogoods and she relaxed. In fact, she thought that Thomas was making an effort to be especially nice to her for the rest of the afternoon. He gave her a shiny new penny to throw in the fountain.

She tossed it high, watched it sparkle in the sun and fall with a plop into the clear water. As it sank she closed her eyes tightly and wished hard. She wished for something she had not prayed for. Guidance from God was all very well but she wanted to do something with her life that was more interesting than mission work and she wished for that; for something more exciting in her life.

When she opened her eyes Thomas was smiling at her and she smiled back.

'Come on,' he said. 'It's a long way back to the entrance.'

'We'd best separate before we get there.'

'I'll disappear at the bandstand. I can see the gates from under the trees.'

'Thank you for asking me here this afternoon. I've had a lovely time.'

'Me too. How often do you walk to Boundary Farm?'

'Two or three times a week, generally.'

'I'll look out for you by the inn when I'm delivering over that way.'

'All right,' she replied. 'Ta-ra, then.'

'Ta-ra, Lettie.'

The others questioned her about where she had been on her own and she gave them a half truth, saying she'd managed to get a seat at the bandstand and met up with Mrs Osborne from Boundary Farm. They all agreed that she had been lucky to get away from her before dark. They were in family groups and hurrying home to help their fathers clean and polish boots or help their mothers put laundry to soak for washday tomorrow. Lettie was no exception for this task and did it all herself because Gran was usually too tired by Sunday evening.

Gran and the Reverend had retired to their bedrooms when Lettie came in from the wash house. She ate the jam tarts that Gran had left out for her and poured warming milk from a pan on the edge of the hob into a cup. Then she rubbed lanolin cream into her hands to cure the wrinkling, blew out the lamp and took her milk upstairs by candlelight.

Eric had made her cautious about young men. She was sure she didn't want anything more to do with him, but she wanted to stay friends with Thomas. He had been kind to her this afternoon. But the more she thought about it the more she realised he had treated her like his little sister and she wasn't sure that's what she wanted. It was all very confusing and she couldn't talk to Gran about any of it. She wished she had a sister or even an aunty as the other young people in the mission did. She fell asleep eventually, wondering what advice her mother would have given her if she'd lived.

Gran insisted on using the wooden dolly to move around bed sheets in the wash tub even though she had to sit down every ten minutes to catch her breath. During one of her short rests Lettie asked, 'Gran, when I pick up the eggs and vegetables from Boundary Farm would you mind if I stayed to have a cup of tea with Mrs Osborne? She can't get out as much as she used to and I think she misses the company of her children.'

'I'm sure she does.' Gran stood up and nodded to herself. 'That's very thoughtful of you. It's just the kind of thing the Reverend expects of his mission ladies. You'll do very well in South Wales.'

Lettie tried not to frown. 'Has the Reverend written to his sister yet?'

'I haven't asked him. Can we get these sheets on the line before we have to stop and do the dinner?'

Lettie turned the mangle for most of the morning and it was hard work, but dinner was easy on Mondays. Cold meat and pickles with bubble and squeak and a rice pudding that was already in the oven. The Reverend came through the kitchen after his dinner to pick up the bucket of peelings for his pig. He never failed to say he had enjoyed his dinner, even when it was nothing special. Gran and Lettie were still finishing their pudding at the kitchen table. Lettie made a pot of tea for the Reverend to drink in his study when he came back, and a pot for her and Gran after they had done the washing-up. You could set your clock by the routine, Lettie thought. The following day at exactly the same time, she gulped back her scalding tea to set off with her baskets for Boundary Farm.

There was no sign of Thomas at the inn and no tell-tale coal debris around the grating in the yard. Lettie walked on slowly and looked back frequently until the inn was out of sight. Mrs Osborne was pleased to see her and her kitchen was full of the delicious smell of boiling jam. 'Aren't we lucky with the weather this year?' she said. 'Mr Osborne's fruit garden is bursting.'

'That reminds me,' Lettie responded, 'Gran says if you ever have any of your jam to spare, the Reverend will take it. Just put it on his bill.'

'I most certainly will. Did your gran say you could stay for tea?'

Lettie nodded enthusiastically.

'You can help me with the labelling when the jars have cooled. Let me have a little sit-down first.'

Lettie gazed out of the kitchen window for signs of a horse and rider but the yard was empty. 'Was Mr Boyer cross with me for being in his room last week?' she queried.

'Well, he asked who you were and where you were from. I persuaded him you weren't prying.'

'Where's he from, Mrs Osborne?'

'I don't rightly know, except that his family came from round these parts years ago and he was born in Canada. He's well-to-do, though.'

'How do you know that?'

'Oh, you can always tell by what folk expect and how they behave. I was at Redfern Abbey before I married Mr Osborne. Lord and Lady Redfern are proper gentry, you know, not like these newcomers in Waterley Hall.'

'I thought Lord and Lady Laughton had been there for years.'

'Bless you, m'ducks, not really. He was the first Laughton to live there. The Earl and Countess have been at Redfern Abbey for generations.'

'My gran doesn't like Lord Laughton.'

'Mrs Osborne rounded her eyes. 'It doesn't do to say

154

it around here, even though plenty would agree with her!' She squeezed Lettie's hand in a friendly way. 'He's lived abroad for years but his lady wife is still at Waterley Hall. Mind you, folk don't like her either. When the pig man came for his swill he said another of her maids had walked out after only a week and gone back to the mill. It's not like it was in the old days when young lasses had no choice. They can get factory work round here and even jobs at the pithead. They think they'll like being a maidservant and wearing a clean dress and pinny, but she's a right tartar is old Lady Laughton.'

'Do you know her, then?'

'Not me, m'ducks. Mr Osborne does. Why?'

'I was wondering whether, in the future, I might apply for a position at Waterley Hall.'

'After what I've just said? Years ago, Lady Laughton wanted me to be her lady's maid, like I was at Redfern Abbey, but Mr Osborne wouldn't hear of it. He knew what she was like.'

'You were a lady's maid? That sounds exciting.'

'Oh, it was. I've been to their shooting lodge in the Dales, and their London residence, and, of course, we came here to Waterley Hall once. That's when I met Mr Osborne.'

'Did you? How romantic.'

'Yes, I suppose it was. He was head gardener and Earl Redfern came looking for him to ask him how he grew his grapes. Now, it's not done to poach good servants from other estates and Earl Redfern wouldn't have dreamed of asking, but if Mr Osborne had wanted, he was sure he could have gone to Redfern Abbey. We'd talked about it, you see, me and Mr Osborne, because we'd hit it off straightaway. When His Lordship here got wind of us, he offered Mr Osborne Boundary Farm tenancy if he stayed. Well, it meant we could wed and have children straightaway, and have a proper house to bring 'em up.' Mrs Osborne looked pensive for a moment. 'Mr Osborne said he was like that, Lord Laughton. He reckoned his money could buy him anything he wanted, even folk.'

Lettie didn't know what to say, but Mrs Osborne voiced her thoughts for her and added, 'Well, I suppose he could and he did. But me and Mr Osborne got what we wanted as well.'

'He must have been there when my grandfather was house steward.'

'Aye, but Mr Osborne answered to the land steward.'

'Would he mind if I asked him about grandfather?'

'He's never says much, m'ducks, and he won't talk about the old days. Best forgotten, he reckons.'

'Oh.' Lettie was disappointed and after a pause said brightly, 'This is a lovely home, Mrs Osborne.'

'Do you like it? I'm glad your granny has let you stay for tea. It can get lonely here because Mr Osborne won't have me go anywhere near Waterley Hall – he never has, nor my girls – and we're a long walk from the village. It's nice having a young lass around the house again.'

'You've got Mr Boyer.'

'He's different. He's a lodger, well, a paying guest, Mr Osborne calls him. Will you want to stay for tea every time you come over?'

'If I have the time. I'd really like to hear about Redfern Abbey.'

'I could tell you a tale or two, that's for sure.' Mrs Osborne rocked her chair to stand up. She groaned. 'My knees are playing me up again. Come along, Lettie, let's see what we have for the Reverend's basket today.' She walked awkwardly to the door then called over her shoulder, 'Fill the kettle and put it on the range for me, would you, m'ducks.'

Mrs Osborne allowed Lettie to choose which vegetables and fruit to take, including some luscious ripe gooseberries that were the Reverend's favourite.

'He's a lucky man, is the Reverend Ennis, to have you look after him as well as your grandmother.'

'He's a good man,' Lettie commented, echoing her granny's words. She remembered Gran's request for jam and added, 'He really likes your jam, Mrs Osborne.'

'He's not the only one, m'ducks. I'll tell you what; if you write me out the labels you can take some of my latest batch with you. Will you be able to carry all this?'

'Oh yes, it's not far and I stop by the inn for a rest.'

'Not for a glass of ale, I hope,' Mrs Osborne said. 'The Reverend wouldn't care for that at all.'

Nor Gran, Lettie thought; nonetheless, it was another thing, like kissing, that she wanted to try.

'I'll call you when the tea's mashed,' the older lady added.

Lettie sat at Mrs Osborne's writing table in her wide entrance hall and painstakingly wrote on tiny pieces of paper in her best handwriting: *gooseberry*, *strawberry*, *blackcurrant*, all followed by 1905. She had good handwriting – her teachers had told her so – and she did not hurry. She heard the door through to the back kitchen open and close but did not look up as she finished the label. She was concentrating on adding a wavy line underneath.

Then she sat back and let out a sigh. 'There,' she said, 'all done. Shall I stick them on the jars for you, Mrs Os— Oh!' As she turned to speak she realised it was not Mrs Osborne standing behind her. It was Mr Boyer. 'Oh, I beg your pardon, sir, I thought you were someone else.'

'Clearly.' He placed his hat and riding crop on a side table by the front door and took a leather binder tied with tape from under his arm. 'I am looking for Mrs Osborne; do you know where she is?'

'Is she not in her kitchen?'

'I have just come from there,' he explained with, she thought, exaggerated patience.

She stood up, gazed at him with serious eyes and replied, 'I was not aware of that, sir. As you see, I have been occupied with my own tasks.'

He glanced past her at the desktop. 'Well, now you've finished, can you occupy yourself in looking for her and when you find her ask her to bring tea to my room today.'

'Very well, sir,' she replied. She bobbed a curtsey, something she had never done to the Reverend or any of his guests, turned her back on him and went through the kitchen door with a wry grin on her face. She wondered if he realised that she was mocking him. She was not a servant at Boundary Farm and even if she were, he did not warrant a curtsey. This was not Waterley Hall and he was not a lord! He could be, though, she thought, because he dressed as one of the gentry and had a confidence and a presence that made people notice him.

The kitchen was empty but Mrs Osborne came in from the scullery with a bowl of eggs in her hand. 'I nearly forgot these. Did I hear Mr Boyer's horse in the yard?'

'You did and he wants his tea upstairs.'

'Oh drat! He'll be working on his papers again.'

'Shall I carry the tray upstairs for you?'

'Would you, m'ducks? I'll have to take it into his room after the last time but, yes, it would be a great help.'

'He spoke to me as though I were your maidservant. Is he always so abrupt with folk?'

'It's just his way. He's come over here looking up his family roots and I don't think he likes what he's finding out.'

'Oh.' Lettie felt again the empathy that she'd experienced when she saw him in the cemetery. Maybe his family had been in the workhouse or prison. Perhaps Gran was right and it's best not to know about your forebears. But Lettie knew what it felt like to be desperate to find out, to give you a proper sense of who you were and maybe to give you a family, like Mrs Osborne's – far flung, but people that you loved nonetheless.

She carried his jug of hot water to wash and then a laden tea tray up to the landing for Mrs Osborne to take into his room. 'I'll open the door for you,' she said as she deposited the heavy tray in Mrs Osborne's hands. She held open the door and called, 'Your tea, sir,' then immediately closed it. She wasn't the least bit interested in his papers; she had her own antecedents to explore. And, she realised, she had to stay in the South Riding to make a start.

Later, when Mrs Osborne returned to the kitchen, they drank tea together at her scrubbed wooden table, and ate a piece of the seed cake, made for Mr Boyer's tea. 'This is delicious,' Lettie commented.

'It's a favourite of Mr Osborne.' She placed a gauze cover over the remainder to keep the flies away.

'Your hair looked lovely when I saw you in the park, all coils and swathes,' Lettie commented. 'How do you get it like that?'

'Ways and means, m'ducks.' Mrs Osborne smiled. 'I could show you how to do yours the same if you want.'

'Oh, would you?'

'I used to do Lady Redfern's hair all the time.'

'She must have been sorry to lose you.'

'Well, I trained up a nice young woman to take over. She was a lot like you, actually; lively and bright.'

'Will you show me how to do it today?'

'I'll have you looking every inch a lady, m'ducks. I use plenty of rolls and pads as my hair is thinning, but yours is beautiful and thick so I won't need so many. I can't do it in the kitchen, though. How do you want it to look?'

They went upstairs to a small dressing room at the end of the landing. It had a washstand and a small table with a mahogany-framed three-sided mirror standing on it and an upholstered chair. There was a fireplace, a tin bath hanging on the wall and a mahogany towel rail. 'My girls used this room all the time,' Mrs Osborne said wistfully. 'Sit yourself down.' She opened the drawers in the table and took out combs, hairpieces and wool pads, and a china bowl of hair pins. 'From what you've said, you've seen a picture of a Gibson Girl.'

Lettie watched, captivated by Mrs Osborne's deft fingers and, indeed, her own image in the mirror, as her hair took shape. Mrs Osborne kept making appreciative noises in her throat.

'You've got lovely hair, m'ducks, and a very pretty neck,' she said. 'In fact, I'd say this style is a great improvement. It's made you look like the young lady that you are.'

'It's . . . it's beautiful,' Lettie breathed. 'Thank you so much.' Lettie stared at her reflection. 'Do you think I could get a position as a lady's maid somewhere?'

'You might, for a family with a few daughters growing up. You'd certainly be above stairs, a parlourmaid, say. It's usually the head parlourmaid who looks after the daughters.'

Lettie fingered her hair. 'I wonder what Gran will think.'

'Well, leave it up and see. You can keep the padding and the extra hairpiece. You'll need it to do it up yourself. You'll be wanting extra-long hatpins as well. I'll see if I've got any to spare.'

Lettie wished Thomas could have been there to see her. This might change his mind about her being not-grown-up! She decided to walk home without her hat and placed it on top of the vegetables in her basket. As she hurried away from the farmhouse she stood for a moment and looked back fondly at the worn stone frontage. Mr Boyer was visible in the bay window of his bedroom. He was standing in front of his desk, she thought. He must have noticed her but he didn't move; neither did she. She felt pleased that he'd seen her with her hair done up. She didn't look like a servant girl now!

She wondered who his family were and whether they had lots of servants where he came from. To her knowledge there was no one in this part of the Riding called Boyer. It sounded foreign to her, but then he was from overseas according to Mrs Osborne. Canada, she mentioned. Didn't they speak French in Canada? Whoever Mr Boyer was, he was a fine horseman; that much she had noticed in her short association with him.

Lettie was so engrossed in her thoughts about Mr Boyer that she didn't realise she had hurried passed the inn until it was too late. She stopped in her tracks for a second. She had forgotten about Thomas and the coal wagon. He wasn't there, was he? She would have noticed. She would, wouldn't she? Unless he had taken the wagon round the back where it was nearer to the cellar grating? She glanced behind her and there was no sign of either. She put her hand up to touch her hair and wondered what Thomas would have thought of it. But she dare not linger as it was getting late. She shrugged and walked on. There'd be other days to see him.

Chapter 12

Gran was busy laying the table in the dining room when Lettie dumped her baskets on the scullery floor. 'I'm home,' she called.

She heard Gran's footsteps in the hall. 'Where on earth have you been until this hour? I was worried about you.'

'I stayed for tea with Mrs Osborne. You said I should.'

'Yes, but for all this time? I know she likes a chat but— Oh my goodness me! What have you done to yourself?'

Gran was in the kitchen as Lettie straightened up from emptying her baskets. Lettie patted her hair. 'Do you like it? Mrs Osborne did it for me.'

'She did that to you? And you let her?'

Lettie's pleasure in her new appearance drained away. 'I asked her to. I thought it would make me look more . . . more grown up.'

'Grown up? You like some music-hall actress. For goodness' sake, don't let the Reverend see you.'

'But Gran, all the ladies in Sheffield wear their hair this way. It's the fashion.'

'Don't be ridiculous! This is a manse, not some hippodrome.'

She had not expected Gran to be cross with her and Gran's agitation alarmed her. Mrs Osborne had spent ages on her hair and Lettie didn't want to undo all her handiwork but it seemed wise to offer. She said, 'Oh, all right then. I'll go upstairs and brush it out.'

'You haven't time now. The Reverend's been given a brown trout for his tea and I want you to gut it for me.' Normally, Gran did that herself. But the last time she cleaned a trout the Reverend's plate came back littered with a large number of tiny bones that Gran had missed. She simply had not seen them because she couldn't. Lettie had tactfully suggested turning up the lamp on the scullery wall. 'That's a waste of oil,' Gran had said. 'You'll have to clean them in future.'

'It's in the sink,' Gran added. She gazed at Lettie and clicked her tongue. 'Ridiculous,' she repeated.

Lettie blew out her cheeks and lifted an apron carefully over her head. She had been thinking of suggesting to Gran that she apply for a position at Waterley Hall instead of going to Wales. Clearly, now was not a suitable time to mention it. Perhaps Gran would be calmer after she had had her tea? 'What are we having?' she called as she slit the trout's belly.

'I've only time to do cheese and pickles for us,' Gran called back. 'Is the fish ready yet?'

Lettie placed the head and trimmings on an old tin plate for the mission hall cat and took the filleted trout into the kitchen for Gran to fry.

'I took a letter from the Reverend for Wales to the post today,' Gran said.

Lettie realised she had to say something now and it seemed easier if she didn't have to face her grandmother. She took down pots from the dresser to lay one end of the kitchen table for their tea. 'I'm not going to Wales, Gran.'

'I beg your pardon?'

'I don't want to leave you. I don't want to go.'

'And I'll not allow you to throw the Reverend's kindness back in his face.'

'But he isn't being kind if I don't want to go.'

'Sometimes you have to be cruel to be kind. It's for your own good. You have no idea what an opportunity this is for you.'

'There are opportunities here!'

'What opportunities? The bottle factory?'

The spat between them was over quickly. Gran served up the trout in silence and took it through to the Reverend. When she came back she said, 'He has everything he needs now. You can clear away after he goes into his study. I'm not having the Reverend see you all dolled-up. You'll be wearing lip rouge next.'

No I won't, Lettie thought rebelliously. She began to cut the bread, aware that Gran was watching her. 'I could find a position somewhere in the Riding,' she said.

'A teaching position? How?'

'Not teaching, Gran. I'll go into service.'

'You will do no such thing!'

Having mentioned it, Lettie was anxious to explain her reasoning and rushed on, 'But you were very good at it and you've taught me well, so why shouldn't I? I've been thinking about it since I heard there was a vacancy at Waterley Hall—' She stopped suddenly, bewildered by the look of horror that was spreading across Gran's features. 'There's nothing wrong with working in service. I could be a lady's maid and travel,' she finished lamely.

'You will not go to Waterley Hall.' Gran almost choked on her words and put one of her hands on a chair back to support herself.

Lettie immediately picked up the teapot to pour her a cup. 'Sit down, Gran, and tell me why not? Both you and grandfather were in service there and I know that Lady Laughton—'

'Lady Laughton?' Gran glared at Lettie. 'What do know about her?'

Gran's anger silenced Lettie for a moment and she decided to drop the subject. Now was not the time. She finished pouring and moved the milk jug nearer to where Gran was still standing. Gran repeated her question and after a further silence added, 'Well?'

Lettie gave a defensive shrug. 'Only that she is looking for a new maid.'

'Who told you?'

'Mrs Osborne.'

Gran looked sideways out of the window. The nights were drawing in and it would soon be dusk. 'I should have known it was a mistake to let you go anywhere near the Waterley estate. What else has she said about Her Ladyship?'

'Nothing, except that she's a grumpy old lady. Mrs Osborne doesn't know her but Mr Osborne told her. She doesn't seem to be very well liked.'

'Then why do you want to work for her?'

Lettie found this a difficult question to answer without being totally honest and risk upsetting Gran further. The truth was that she wanted to find out more about grandfather – to find anyone who might have known him. She felt a huge sense of urgency to do this before – she shook her head slightly and gazed at her grandmother – before all of these people grew old like Gran. 'I don't,' she answered, 'but neither do I want to go to Wales and I have to do something with my future.' Her answer sounded petulant and feeble. Lettie wished she could explain it more.

'And you would rather fetch and carry for a bad-tempered mistress than be part of a respectable family who will give you a chance to be a pupil teacher in a mission school?'

Lettie looked down at her hands. The answer was yes and put like that it sounded pathetic. 'She might remember you . . . and . . . and grandfather; maybe even my mother and father.'

Gran closed her eyes for a second and sat down with a bump. She put a hand to her breast and began to breathe heavily. When her eyes opened they were wide and wild and her breathing was laboured.

'Gran! What's wrong? What's happening to you?'

Gran's eyes rolled as she struggled to get her breath. 'Fetch the Reverend,' she gasped.

Lettie dashed out of the door yelling, 'Reverend Ennis, come quick! It's Gran!'

He wasn't in the dining room or his study. She guessed he had finished his tea and gone out for his evening constitutional. He often walked after tea when the weather was fine. She rushed back through the kitchen, where Gran was slumped in her chair. 'I'll get you some water,' she said and hurried into the scullery with an earthenware mug.

After a few sips of water, Gran recovered a little. 'I'll help you upstairs to bed,' Lettie said.

'No, it was only my palpitations. I've had them before.'

Lettie frowned. 'But never as bad as this.'

'It's nothing and I'm better now.'

'Well, you don't look it. I think you should go and have a lie-down. I'll bring you some tea on a tray.'

'Well, don't tell the Reverend. I don't want to worry him.'

'You ought to have the doctor, Gran.'

'I'm not ill. Now stop fussing and give me hand up.'

Lettie helped Gran to the bottom of the stairs where Gran said, 'Bring me a chair. I'll sit down a minute before I go up.'

'I really think the Reverend should know you're not well.'

'Nonsense! When he comes in, just tell him I'm overtired. I'll be as right as rain in the morning.'

Lettie waited several minutes for her grandmother to

gather her strength until Gran sent her away to clear the dining room before the Reverend returned. It took Gran a long time to climb the stairs, even with Lettie's help. Eventually Lettie tucked her into bed, propped her up with pillows and said, 'I'll fetch you something to eat. What do you fancy?"

Gran shook her head. 'I can't eat anything. A glass of my tonic will do. Bring me one, will you, dear?'

'Of course I will.'

The next day, Gran's complexion was as grey as her hair and when Lettie took in her early-morning tea she was still in bed. Normally Gran would be up and dressed and lacing her boots.

Gran turned her head on the pillow. 'I think I might have caught a chill or something. Can you help me out of bed, love?'

Lettie placed the cup and saucer carefully on her bedside table. 'Gran, you're really poorly. I've got to tell the Reverend.'

Gran clutched at Lettie's arm. 'Give me your hand, Lettie. I need the po.'

'Can you hang on another minute? I'll fetch the commode from the closet.'

'Good girl.' Gran sank into her pillow.

As soon as Gran was settled back in bed, sitting up and drinking her tea, Lettie said, 'You will let me ask the Reverend to send for the doctor now, won't you?'

Gran nodded and Lettie hurried away to start cooking his breakfast.

For the whole of the following week, Lettie was so busy that she barely had time to think about Waterley Hall, or Mr Boyer, or even Thomas. It was clear to the doctor, the Reverend and now Gran herself what Lettie had known for a while: Gran could not continue in her present role. She was ordered by the doctor to stay in bed and rest.

Lettie stepped into Gran's housekeeping shoes, which fitted her well, and the mission ladies rallied round. By the second Monday, with a washerwoman in for the laundry, her fresh vegetable supplies getting low, and a desperate need to get out of the manse for a change of scenery, Lettie picked up her baskets and set off for Boundary Farm.

Mrs Osborne came out of her kitchen to meet her on the path. 'Ee, m'ducks, how are you? I heard about your granny. How is she now?'

'She's not her normal self yet and the doctor says she's not to do anything strenuous. The Reverend's looking for another housekeeper.'

'Doesn't he want you to take over from her? I'm sure you'd do a grand job.'

'He wants me to go to Wales and train to be a teacher when there's an opening for me. Gran does too.'

Mrs Osborne looked impressed. 'I see. I didn't know you were clever, although I should have guessed. You're like my eldest lad. He has quick wits, too.'

'Is he a teacher?'

'He has green fingers like his father. He's already in charge of the glasshouses at Redfern. He knows all about how they work and how the plants grow and he gives talks at the local institute.'

'You must be very proud of him.'

'I'm proud of all my children, m'ducks. I'm a fortunate old lady.'

Lettie thought that her children were the fortunate ones to have Mrs Osborne for a mother. She smiled and said, 'You're not old,' and they both laughed.

Lettie said she couldn't stop for tea as she had to get back for the Reverend, which was partly true. But with the washing taken care of and cold ham for tea, there was no real rush. If she reached the inn early she might catch Thomas, if he was in the area and if he was looking out for her. Too many ifs and buts, she thought, and pressed her lips together. She hadn't seen or had word of him since before Gran had had her turn and she wanted someone of her own age to talk to.

She hovered outside the inn for over ten minutes straining her ears for a sound of his lorry until the land-lord's buxom daughter came out with frown on her face.

'If you're waiting for that coalman again you're too early. Go away and come back in half an hour.'

'I'd rather wait,' Lettie replied.

'Well, my dad would rather you didn't. We're not some four-ale bar, y'know, with women hanging about outside.'

Lettie blushed to the roots of her hair. 'But I'm not—'

'I know you're not, but our customers don't. Now shift yourself.' The young woman stood her ground until Lettie moved away reluctantly. She went back the way she had

171

come and found a low stone wall to sit on that she hoped was out of sight but within earshot of the inn.

She heard the coal lorry rumble down the road, felt a flutter of pleasure and moved to where she could watch Thomas grasp the iron chain and lift off the heavy cellar grating in the inn yard. He must be quite strong, she thought, although he didn't look stocky like a miner. He took each sack of coal on his back to the open grate and up-ended it into the inn cellar. When he had finished and was enjoying his pint of ale, she stepped forward.

He didn't seem very pleased to see her. 'You're a stranger these days.'

'My gran was taken poorly. I thought you would have heard.'

He shook his head. 'No, I haven't. Is she better now?'

'She had to have the doctor.'

'It's not serious, is it?'

Lettie nodded. 'I've been doing everything at the manse. This is the first time I've been out for a fortnight.'

He stepped closer and she could see the coal dust clinging to his skin. She noticed the sympathy in his eyes and immediately felt better. 'I had no idea. Is she in bed, then?'

'She's got to stay there and rest. It's her heart, you see.'

'Oh, Lettie, I am sorry. No wonder I haven't seen you out and about.'

'I didn't want to leave her at all at first but it's going to take her a long time to get better.'

'You're not doing everything on your own, are you?'

'Oh no, some of the mission ladies help out occasionally.' But not often, she thought. Mainly, they visited and chatted to Gran and then left to look after their own families.

'Well, you need a bit of fresh air every now and then. Can you get to the park on Sunday afternoon?'

'Not really. I've got to look after the Reverend as well and Sunday is his busiest day.'

'I'll come round and take you out for a walk.'

Lettie thought that was really kind of Thomas but worried about being seen out with him and word of it getting back to Gran. 'The Reverend might see you,' she muttered.

'I'll wait until he goes to evensong. Take your granny her tea and I'll meet you in the lane behind the pigsty.'

It would be something cheering to look forward to and life wasn't very cheerful for her at present. 'All right, but I don't want anyone to see us.'

'They won't, I promise.'

He smiled and his teeth flashed white against the ingrained coal dust on his skin. 'You look as though you could do with a hug.' She could and she loved him for realising it. He went on, 'Don't worry, I've got four sisters and I know better than to risk dirtying your frock.'

Lettie smiled.

'That's better,' he said.

'How do you do it?' she said.

'Do what?'

'Always raise my spirits.'

'I take after my dad. His glass is never half empty, it's

always half full. So is mine.' He continued to smile at her. 'You might think yours is empty now, but it's not. Things will get better for you.'

'I hope so.' She heard a horse approaching and so did he.

'Best get on with my round,' he said. 'See you on Sunday.'

Four sisters, Lettie marvelled! He had brothers as well. They were a big family and they seemed to be happy. Lettie wished she had brothers and sisters; and a mother and father like Thomas. Goodness! That sounded so disloyal to Gran.

Gran knew the value of brothers and sisters, too. The Reverend's family in Wales would fill a gap in Lettie's upbringing and she ought to go and live with them. But she had to stay here now for Gran. And she had to find out as much as she could about her own family before it was too late. Nobody understood the desperate urgency she felt to do this. People got old and . . . She gulped back the thought. And they died and then it was too late . . .

Thomas cranked the lorry's engine into life and swung himself into the cab. The horse rider approached and Lettie realised she and Thomas had been in full view of the road. She hoped he'd realised they were just friends, passing the time of day. But it was Mr Boyer and she hadn't made a favourable impression on him so far. The words of the innkeeper's daughter ran through her head. *I know you're not, but our customers don't.* She blushed at the thought and put her hands on her cheeks defensively. She felt a piece of gritty coal dust clinging to her skin and looked down at her dress to see a small dusting on the front. It had blown up from an eddy in the yard. She tried to brush it away and only made it more noticeable by smudging.

Mr Boyer reined in his horse as he reached her and stared down. 'Good day, Lettie,' he said. His expression turned from curiosity to distaste. Did he really think she was a woman of easy virtue who hung about outside inns looking to pick up men to pay for her services? She felt she had to explain herself and stuttered, 'T–Thomas is a friend. He delivers coal to the inn.'

'So I see.'

She couldn't think of anything else to say. What was wrong with her? She was not usually tongued-tied. She glanced around for her baskets, located where she had dumped them and hastily took a step in that direction. Her sudden movement caused the horse to shy.

But Mr Boyer had control of the reins and turned the horse's head away from Lettie. She was left standing in the empty inn yard, feeling dusty and dishevelled, watching the well-groomed rump of the horse as it walked away. Mr Boyer sat high in the saddle, haughty and erect. His horse gave a swish of her tail as though swatting Lettie away like a fly.

Lettie slumped against the wall. Why did she feel the need to explain herself to this man? She guessed it would make no difference to him anyway. He'd probably made up his mind about the kind of girl she was – and what he had seen today had simply supported his views. Her anger simmered. He was wrong about her and just as bad as Gran in his prejudice!

Nonetheless, she hoped he wouldn't say anything about the incident to Mrs Osborne because she valued that lady's good opinion of her as much as she did her gran's. She wished she didn't have to arrange to see Thomas on Sunday against her Gran's wishes. But he was such a breath of fresh air in her life. She wished also that Gran were more like Mrs Osborne and then she could talk about him. Oh, why was everything so difficult!

Lettie stood in the middle of the empty inn yard and scowled until a farmer rolled out of the back bar towards the privy and leered at her. Hurriedly, she picked up her baskets and scuttled away, feeling inexplicably ashamed of her behaviour. When she arrived home, she was glad that Gran was upstairs in bed and did not see her smudgy face and dress before she cleaned it up.

Chapter 13

As Sunday evening approached, Lettie became more and more apprehensive. She looked forward to getting away from the manse for an hour or so, but where could she and Thomas walk without someone seeing them together? The lane was busy at certain times of the day because miners used it as a short cut from the pithead to the village. But the pit closed on Sunday so perhaps it would be quiet.

It was, but it wasn't deserted. When Lettie let herself out of the back garden gate, she saw a man and woman strolling along. He had his arm around her and her head rested on his shoulder. As soon as they saw her, he loosened his hold and they moved apart so Lettie looked down and pretended to be fixing the gate latch until they had passed her. The shrubs and trees lining the lane were hawthorn, holly and elderberry – too scratchy, she thought, for anyone to hide in them. But Thomas appeared from between them, glanced in each direction then called, 'Over here, Lettie.' He was clean and spruce and smiling.

She inhaled unsteadily and hurried towards him. He held back the thorns, making a pathway through the scrub. 'This way,' he added, 'there's a gap in the fencing ahead of you. Go through and I'll follow you.'

'But that field belongs to the old Farmer Watson. He doesn't like people on his land.'

'He'll be in church so he won't know, will he?'

Lettie hesitated. 'He has a big dog, Thomas.'

'It's chained up in the farmyard. I checked.'

She stopped. 'Even so, I don't want to trespass.'

'I'll go first, then. There is a footpath round the edge. We'll be all right as long as we stick to it. Mind the thorns on your frock as I squeeze by.'

There was plenty of room as it was obvious that others had used this way and broken away branches to form a makeshift track. Thomas helped her through the broken fence into the field. A few cows were grazing idly and over the other side a family group was gathering early blackberries from the hedgerow.

'Who are they, do you reckon?' Thomas said.

'I don't know but they're bound to be villagers. It's too early for town folk to be out blackberrying. I'd better go back.'

'Do you have to? It's a fine evening and you look as though you could do with the fresh air.'

'What do you mean?'

'Only that nursing your granny and housekeeping for the Reverend seem to be wearing you out. You've got dark circles under your eyes.'

'Have I?' Lettie had hardly looked in the mirror recently. She had gone back to plaiting her hair and as soon as she woke in the morning she was too concerned about Gran to worry about her appearance.

He took her hand in his and gave it a gentle tug. 'Come on, Lettie, we'll walk as far as the barn. They might be gone by then.'

She followed Thomas along the path around the edge of the field, enjoying the scent of wild honeysuckle. One or two of Farmer Watson's dairy herd looked up from their chewing. The group picking berries increased in numbers, effectively putting a stop to Thomas's plan.

'Shall we sit by the barn until they've gone?' he suggested.

'I'd rather not. Let's go the other way to the canal bridge.'

'There'll be a lot of couples on the towpath.'

Lettie groaned. 'It's no good. It doesn't matter where we go, somebody will see us.' She heard him sigh. 'I'm sorry,' she muttered.

'I'm the one who's sorry. All we're doing is going for a walk and this secrecy is daft.'

She remembered Mr Boyer's reaction to seeing her outside the inn. 'People can get the wrong idea.'

'Well, your granny can,' he responded tetchily.

'She's ever so poorly, Thomas. I daren't upset her now.'

He sighed again, more sympathetically this time. 'I know. Do you want to go back?'

'Yes, please.' But she didn't really. She wanted to ask Thomas about his family and where she might discover more about hers. He seemed to know so much more than she did about, well, about everything that she hadn't learned from books. All Lettie seemed to have learned apart from how to housekeep were stories from the Bible; but only the ones suitable for Sunday school. She wasn't interested enough to root around for the forbidden tales. Thomas had tried his best to raise her spirits and she was upset that he seemed displeased.

They said goodbye in the lane behind the pigsty. 'Will you look out for me at the inn?' she said hopefully.

'If that's what you want.'

He didn't sound very enthusiastic and she wondered if they were still friends. It was the first time he hadn't cheered her up and Lettie went indoors feeling disappointed and frustrated. She made a cup of tea for Gran and took it upstairs. Gran was dozing but she woke as soon as Lettie walked into her bedroom.

'Did you have a nice walk?'

'Yes thank you, Gran.'

'Where did you go?'

'Not far. There were people out blackberrying already.'

'They're early this year.'

'Yes.' Lettie helped Gran to sit up and plumped her pillows.

'Did you see anyone you know?'

'Just a friend.'

'You will be careful who you talk to, won't you? You ought to think again about Eric.'

'We've already discussed him, Gran.'

'Yes, but that was before I was taken poorly and I'm worried about what you'll do when I'm gone.'

'Don't say things like that.'

'I have to. Somebody told the Reverend he saw you speaking to a coalman in the inn yard the other day. What were you doing in the inn yard, Lettie?'

'I was on my way back from Boundary Farm and the coalman was doing his delivery as I went by.'

'Was it the same one that brings out coal from the pithead? I didn't know you knew him.'

'I don't. It wasn't him anyway.' Perhaps now was the time to own up to Gran. 'It was Thomas, Gran. When Mr Adley got rid of him he went to work for Toogoods. He can drive a wagon, you know.'

'Oh, Lettie,' Gran groaned, 'and you stopped to talk to him. What were you thinking of?'

'I was only telling him how pleased I was that he'd got another job. I wish you'd give him a chance, Gran. He's not a roughneck, honest, he isn't.'

Gran looked weary; worn out and grey. 'You haven't listened to a word I've said to you, have you?'

'I have. But you're wrong about Thomas.'

'Well, you don't want to be settling down with the first lad who turns your head.'

'I never said I wanted to settle down with him.'

'Well, you shouldn't be leading him on, then, because he'll think you do.'

'No, he won't!' Lettie felt quite irritated that Gran had made this leap in her imagination. 'We're friends, that's all.' But she wasn't even sure about that any more.

'Young fellows want more than friendship with a girl.'

Eric Jones certainly did. She wondered what Gran would say if she told her about Eric's behaviour. 'Maybe,' Lettie shrugged.

Gran handed the cup and saucer to Lettie. Then she closed her eyes for a minute and kept them closed as she spoke. 'Men do, you know. They want everything and they'll want it before they wed you if you'll let them.'

Lettie didn't need to be told that after her experience with Eric. 'I do know about these things, Gran. You don't have to worry about me.'

'Oh, but I do. You don't know how persuasive men can be, and how dishonest.'

'The Reverend isn't like that.'

'He's different, and you . . . well, you always see the best in folk.'

Until they prove otherwise, Lettie thought. She said, 'Is that such a bad thing?'

'No, but you can't let them have their way with you. You mustn't ever, not with anyone, not before he marries you.'

Lettie's eyes widened. What on earth had brought this on? Even in her most rebellious mood Lettie wouldn't dream of doing anything like that!

'Gran, you know I wouldn't.'

'You say that but men can be persuasive. They're crafty. They say they love you when they don't and then it's too late.' Gran reached out her hand and placed it over

Lettie's on the bed sheet. 'I want you to make me a solemn promise. I mean it, Lettie, I want you to swear on the Bible. Fetch it from the bookcase.'

Lettie carried the heavy book over to the bed. She often read from it to Gran when she asked. She placed it on the bedcover.

'Put your hand on it and promise.'

'Promise what, Gran?'

'Swear by almighty God with your hand on His holy book, that you will never, ever, have relations with a man before you wed him. I shan't rest easy unless I know you mean it. Promise me, Lettie,' Gran repeated.

Lettie didn't think it was necessary and felt cross that Gran didn't have enough faith in her without this little show. But Gran was a poorly old lady and Lettie loved her, so she placed her hand on the Bible and made her pledge. Gran seemed hugely relieved afterwards. Her head lolled to one side on the pillow, she closed her eyes and dozed.

Lettie sat with her, staring out of the window. Something in the past had happened to make Gran behave in this way and Gran had stated quite firmly that Lettie wasn't born out of wedlock. She supposed she might well have been conceived before marriage because that was a common occurrence. Or, Lettie realised, perhaps it was her mother Ruth who had been on the way when Gran made her vows at the altar? Was that why she thought grandfather was wicked? Surely that wasn't such a wicked thing to do? But it seemed a much more likely explanation to Lettie.

*   *   *

Gran's health improved slowly and Lettie continued to nurse her and run the manse, leaving her little time to think about herself. One or two of the mission ladies came in occasionally but they had their own homes to run as well as their welfare visits. Mrs Jones, however, had a housekeeper and a girl for the rough work so she had more free time and was only too pleased to help out for the Reverend. Mrs Jones was a good cook, her baking especially, and her pies and cakes were a welcome addition to the Reverend's pantry. She eased Lettie's workload significantly but she came with a special purpose of her own. Lettie soon realised that Mrs Jones had not given up the notion of a match between her Eric and Lettie.

Lettie's move to Wales was postponed until Gran was on her feet again. Secretly, Lettie didn't believe Gran would ever be back to her full strength but she went along with the possibility for Gran's sake. Apparently, the Reverend and Mrs Jones were of the same mind because at one of her visits, the older lady mentioned quite casually, 'The Reverend will have to find himself a new housekeeper one day.'

Lettie was drying her hands in the scullery. 'Please don't say that to Gran, will you?' she said anxiously. Mrs Jones's visits gave Lettie an opportunity to walk over to Boundary Farm and she had been looking forward to it until that remark.

'Of course not, my dear. We all want her to get better. It's you I am thinking of. You've shown everybody what a good little housekeeper you can be. You're a credit to your grandmother.'

'Thank you, Mrs Jones.'

'You know, my Eric was very taken by you.'

Lettie was pinning her hat on in the hall. Mrs Jones, with her fashionably elaborate grey hair and intricate blouse, came up behind her so that Lettie could see her image in the mirror. 'We rushed you a bit,' Mrs Jones went on, 'but you will suit him very well. We all understand that you've lived a sheltered life here at the manse and my Eric will look after you.' Mrs Jones smiled and raised her eyebrows.

Lettie had two hatpins in her mouth, which prevented her from replying.

Mrs Jones continued as she strolled away towards the kitchen, 'When your grandmother is better, you must bring her to tea with me and Mr Jones because Mr Jones would very much like to meet you properly.'

Lettie fixed her hat, and bit back her response, scowling at herself in the mirror. From what she knew about Eric and his father, they were two of a kind and the Joneses were the last family she wanted to associate with, let alone marry into. But she couldn't refuse to take Gran for tea with them when she was well enough. She replied, 'Thank you, Mrs Jones, I'll ask Gran.'

Mrs Jones stopped with her hand on the kitchen door-knob. 'Oh, I've already done that. She's looking forward to it.'

Lettie felt cornered and her anger bubbled as she walked briskly to Boundary Farm. She wanted to unburden her irritation in some way, to talk to someone, and Mrs Osborne was a willing listener. Lettie asked her if she would show her how to do her hair again, but not quite so elaborate this time so she could pin her hat on to go home.

Mrs Osborne was delighted. 'Are you meeting that coalman at the inn again?'

'How did you now about him?'

'Mr Boyer saw you. You shouldn't be loitering outside an inn, m'ducks. I had to explain to him that he was mistaken about you as you lived in a manse and went to chapel.'

'Thomas is a friend,' Lettie said defensively.

'Well, he's a nice enough lad but you're a right lovely lass, well brought up and with your wits about you. You'd be a good catch for him and you could do better, m'ducks.'

Not Mrs Osborne as well! Lettie thought she would have been less critical of Thomas than Gran. 'I said he's just a friend,' she repeated. 'But I've been told that I have got a . . . a suitor.'

'Not this Thomas, then?'

'No. It's someone I don't really like. He seems to be keen on me, though. I've said no to him once already.'

'Oh, that's a fellow for you. They're all the same. If he's set his cap at you, he won't give up easily. You see it's all about you being *his* woman for all the world to see.'

Lettie frowned. 'He was very persistent and, well, he, you know . . . wanted to kiss me . . . and more.'

'Did he now? Your grandmother has told you that if you let him have his way with you, he's landed you at the altar as far as he's concerned?'

'Oh, I wouldn't do anything foolish. Honest I wouldn't.

186

Gran has made me promise not to, not before I'm married anyway.'

'So you do know what I'm talking about?'

'Y-y-yes.'

'And that even a gentleman can be very persuasive.' *Persuasive* – Gran had used that word, too, Lettie thought. Mrs Osborne continued, 'He'll tell you he loves you and all that.'

Lettie was decisive. 'Well, if he did and he was lying I wouldn't marry him.'

'Ah, but if you were in the family way, m'ducks, you'd have to get wed, wouldn't you?'

Goodness! Mrs Osborne didn't mince her words. 'I suppose you would,' she answered.

'There's no suppose about it, m'ducks.' Mrs Osborne smiled. 'That's what he'd be hoping for; hooked and in his keep net.'

Lettie wasn't happy to be likened to a salmon or a trout but she understood Mrs Osborne's meaning. It went some way to explaining Eric's behaviour towards her.

'Or worse, m'ducks,' Mrs Osborne went on, 'if he decided he didn't love you after all and threw you back into the stream.'

'Well, how do I know if he really loves me?' she demanded.

'How do you know if you really love him? It cuts both ways, m'ducks. But you'll know when it happens, believe me. Shall we do your hair before tea?'

Lettie spent a pleasant hour padding and pinning up her hair herself under Mrs Osborne's helpful guidance.

'You have a good eye for making the best of yourself,' the older lady said. 'And you're always clean and tidy. Have you thought any more about Waterley Hall? Lady Laughton is definitely looking for a new maid. I asked Mr Osborne to make sure. But,' Mrs Osborne lowered her voice as she continued, 'she's a crotchety old biddy and it's more of a nursemaid than a lady's maid she needs these days.'

'I'd like to apply but I can't leave Gran yet.'

'I thought the Reverend was getting his mission ladies to rally round?'

'Mrs Jones is helping out. She makes pies for the Reverend for me to warm up in the oven so I can see to Gran.'

'Is your granny not up and about yet?' Mrs Osborne frowned and pulled down the corners of her mouth.

Lettie chewed on her lip and shook her head. 'The doctor says she has to take her time. Before she took poorly she was planning to send me to Wales to stay with the Reverend's sister but I'm not going now. I didn't want to go anyway. I wanted to stay here and find out about my mother.'

'Don't you know anything about her?'

'Not really. Gran won't talk about the past. It upsets her.'

'Perhaps it's best if you don't find out then, m'ducks.'

'But if Gran is hiding something then it only makes me more curious. I know my mother was called Ruth yet I can't find out where she's buried. She's not with grandfather in Waterley Hall churchyard.'

'She must have moved away when she was wed. All my girls did. There might be nothing for you to find out around here.'

Lettie didn't argue. But she thought there might be a servant still at Waterley Hall from the old days when Grandfather was butler. If there was he would remember him, and Gran too. Long-serving maids and footmen who hadn't married were sometimes allowed to stay on when they grew old if the alternative was the workhouse, especially if they could still see to sew or clean boots. A position at Waterley Hall would enable Lettie to ask questions.

Chapter 14

Gran's pallid colour remained despite all the bed rest, doctoring and nurturing care from Lettie. It was even tiring for her to sit out of bed to eat her dinner; not that she ever ate very much. Summer was turning into autumn and one day, at the Reverend's suggestion, Lettie lit a fire in the Reverend's front room. She and Mrs Jones helped Gran down the stairs for a change of scenery. But it was far too exhausting for Gran and her palpitations returned. She took her medicine, which calmed her down, but she couldn't summon up the strength to climb back upstairs so Lettie had to make up a bed on the couch for her. The Reverend was so concerned he called the doctor in again. The doctor recommended a proper convalescent home for Gran, at the seaside.

'We have a Methodist one in the East Riding,' the Reverend said. 'It's near Filey, I believe. I'll make enquiries.' He went into his study and Mrs Jones accompanied the doctor to the front door.

'Well, I guess I'll have to go,' Gran confided to Lettie, 'if it's the only way I'll get my strength back. I'm not ready to meet my maker just yet.'

'It won't be for ever, Gran.'

'I hope not but you won't be able to stay here without me. The Reverend will have to find a new housekeeper.'

Lettie was fighting back her tears, none of which were for her own dilemma. If Gran thought that about herself she was aware that she had, if anything, become weaker during the last few weeks. 'I'll ask if I can come with you,' she said.

Gran gave a rare, though weak, smile. 'I'd like that. I'm sure the Reverend will know a family you can lodge with. Then I can see you every day.'

Lettie managed to return her smile. 'I'll talk to him tomorrow.'

'Whatever he says, dear, you must promise me you'll do as the Reverend asks. He will be your guardian when I'm gone.'

'That won't be for a long time yet, but I promise.'

Gran lay back and closed her eyes. 'You're a good girl, Lettie. I'm proud of you.'

At Mrs Jones's suggestion, the Reverend sent a neighbour for Eric to carry Gran upstairs to bed. He was very polite to her in front of his mother but kept smiling at Lettie in a manner she could only describe as a smirk. Lettie was thankful he was busy with his new school. He could not stay long and Lettie soon forgot about him.

She sat through the night with Gran, dozing from time to time in a fireside chair. Instead of being the resilient old lady that Lettie loved so dearly, Gran seemed to shrink before her eyes into a fragile birdlike creature. Her body had worn itself out, but her mind was still active and Gran was a fighter. 'I'll be fine as long as you're with me, Lettie,' she murmured frequently.

Reverend Ennis was sympathetic but he was hard working and his duties never diminished. When Lettie spoke with him in his study the following day, he was thankful for a solution and agreed to contact the mission in the East Riding to find lodgings for Lettie. 'Think of it as a holiday,' he said to her.

'I shall be able to read to her every morning as well as evening,' Lettie responded. 'She enjoys that. Have you finished with your newspaper?'

He hesitated. 'Er, no, not yet.' He glanced down at the wastepaper basket where it rested,

Lettie frowned. It wasn't yesterday's paper – she had read that one to Gran last night. She bent down to retrieve it. 'It must have fallen off your desk.'

The Reverend took it quickly from her grasp. 'Thank you, Lettie. I'll finish it after supper.' He paused. 'The doctor said your grandmother tires easily so I hope you don't keep her awake too long.'

'She insists that I read all of the paper to her. She does like to keep up with the news, sir.'

'Even so, she is very ill. Give the readings a miss tonight.' He nodded at her, expecting her agreement.

'Very well. She will be happy to hear that I can go with her to Filey.'

Gran was put out when Lettie said she wouldn't be reading. 'The Reverend asked me not to,' she explained. 'The doctor advised him. You have to rest.'

Gran grunted. 'What about a bible reading, then?'

'Not tonight, Gran. I'll ask the Reverend about that tomorrow.'

'Don't bother. I'll ask him myself when he comes in to say goodnight.'

In the past she had read to Gran by lamplight in her bedroom and learned what was happening in the Riding at the same time. No matter how tired Lettie was, it was still a part of the day that she looked forward to and she was as disappointed as Gran. She tidied the bedroom, picked up Gran's supper tray and stood in the open doorway.

'Goodnight, Gran,' she said. The doctor's sleeping draught was taking effect and she would be fast asleep by the time the Reverend tapped on her door later.

Lettie always waited in the kitchen until the Reverend retired. He was an early riser so he didn't sit up late. As soon as she heard the landing floorboards creak she raked out the fire ashes, and placed the kindling for tomorrow in the hearth. Then she crept into his study to retrieve the discarded newspaper intending to read it by lamplight in her own bedroom. It wasn't anywhere to be seen.

Her disappointment drove her to search the scullery

where clean old newspapers were kept to be torn into squares and threaded on a string for the privy. She carried her lamp through but it wasn't there either. She found it eventually outside the back door under the pig bucket to be added to the straw bedding in the sty. Well, the pig can sleep on it after I've read it, she thought.

As soon as she saw the front page her attention was riveted by the picture and headline.

LADY LAUGHTON DIES

The grainy photograph was of a much younger Lady Laughton, severe and formal, looking like a smaller version of old Queen Victoria before she died. Lettie sat down at the kitchen table and read, surprised to find out that she had been much older than Lord Laughton and previously married to his cousin; second cousin, it said. That meant their fathers had been first cousins. Between them the cousins owned the Laughton South Riding steelworks and east coast shipyards where Lord Laughton's fabled wealth came from. As a young woman, the newspaper reported, Lady Laughton had led a charmed life that was, sadly, beset by tragedy and she had withdrawn from public life many years ago.

No wonder she was a crabby old lady, thought Lettie, as she pieced together the scraps of information. She had had three daughters with her first husband, none of whom had survived infancy. 'Poor woman,' Lettie said out loud.

Her marriage to Lord Laughton, as everyone knew, was childless. It didn't say but Lettie guessed she had been past her childbearing years when she married him. Good heavens, she thought. It was known for older men to marry young women and although one or two gossips raised their eyebrows nobody questioned the sense of it, especially if the man had an income and his own home. But for an older woman to marry a younger man was almost unheard of! Well, they hadn't lived together for years so Lettie reckoned the marriage hadn't worked.

'I don't expect they loved each other,' she said to the kitchen shadows.

There was more about Lady Laughton's father who had been in shipping in the days of sail. He had transported raw pig iron from Russia and Sweden across the North Sea for the South Riding steel industry, where the abundant coal had contributed to making Sheffield the steel capital of the world. And at the end of the paragraph, Lettie read a telling sentence that made her think the Reverend knew what he was talking about when he preached that riches don't bring happiness. *She was his only surviving child and heiress to his fortune.* Lady Laughton's life had been an unhappy one, she thought. Even the rich have their tragedies.

She read the article again. Gran had never liked the Laughtons but she had worked for them as a younger woman. She would want to hear about Lady Laughton's death yet the Reverend had seen fit to keep it from her, from them both actually. He hadn't wanted Lettie to see it either, or he would have left the newspaper in the scullery for the privy.

Lettie blew out her cheeks. It would bring back memories for Gran, perhaps very distressing memories, so she respected the Reverend's wisdom. She put the newspaper back under the pig bucket and decided not to mention it.

But of course Lady Laughton's death was big news in Waterley Edge and gossip was rife in the town as well. The Reverend could not stop his mission ladies from talking so eventually Gran heard about it from one of them who came to visit. It was Monday, the day that Lettie helped the washerwoman. She was turning the mangle when the Reverend came into the wash house.

In the steamy heat, Lettie's face was red with effort and she was in her oldest gown covered by a sacking apron. The Reverend seemed quite taken aback by her appearance as she wiped her wet hands down the apron and pushed her damp hair under an equally damp cap.

'Is something amiss, sir?' She stepped outside, glad of the cooling breeze.

'One of my helpers said your grandmother had a bit of a turn when Lady Laughton's name came up in their conversation. I have sent her to fetch the doctor. You must come in and sit with her until he arrives.'

The washerwoman nodded in agreement and Lettie went indoors with the Reverend. He went on: 'She has taken one of her powders and is resting but it really is best not to speak to her of Waterley Hall or its former occupants at all.'

'Of course,' Lettie agreed. 'Do you know what happened, Reverend?'

'What do you mean?'

'What happened in the old days to make Gran hate the Laughtons so much?'

'You ought not to listen to gossip, Lettie. Your grand-mother has assured me she has told you all you need to know. If she chooses not to say more it is for your benefit. Look forward to your future, Lettie, not backwards to the past.'

But Lettie found that difficult when she was unsure of who her father was and therefore who she was. Why shouldn't she want to find out about her own parents? Surely she had a right to know where they were buried. However, she managed a smile and said, 'Very well, sir.'

The doctor said Gran wasn't any worse, but she wasn't any better either and exposing her to more anxiety might make her condition deteriorate. He lectured Lettie on keeping her calm at all times. Lettie agreed with every-thing the gentleman said. However, Gran was Gran and she couldn't change her nature. Her mind was still active and it needed occupying.

The Reverend decided that from now on Lettie should devote most of her day to Gran. Mrs Jones would take over his housekeeping and employ help. Lettie was relieved of some of her chores, notably the cleaning, ironing and scrubbing out, and this gave her plenty of time to spend with Gran. She was able to make sure the sick room was always fresh, keep Gran's hair looking dressed and tidy and prepare all the little delicacies that were Gran's favour-ites. And have time to sit and talk to her.

'Did you know about Lady Laughton?' Gran demanded one evening.

Lettie felt uncomfortable. 'I saw it in the newspaper. It was the one the Reverend asked me not to read to you.'

Gran sounded critical when she said, 'I wonder what Her Ladyship will have to say for herself when she meets her maker.'

'Surely she wasn't all bad?' Lettie ventured.

'No and I'll not speak ill of the dead. She didn't have a happy life and now she's gone.'

That echoed Lettie's own sentiments. 'Money isn't everything,' she said.

'Huh. Tell that to your grandfather. When's the funeral?'

'Soon, I think.' Lettie hadn't taken note of the date, although she did remember that present and former servants were invited to attend the service. 'Shall I ask the Reverend?'

Gran shook her head. 'I couldn't go anyway. It'll be in their private church.'

'I expect there will be enough mourners to fill it.'

'I mean I'm not strong enough to travel there and stand for any length of time yet.'

Lettie, aware that she ought to move their conversation away from Waterley Hall, said, 'The doctor's advised fresh air if you're well wrapped up. He suggested I take you out in a Bath chair when the weather is fine. The Reverend is trying to get hold of one for you. I can take you to chapel or to the mission hall.'

Her grandmother stared at the window. 'I'd like to see the old witch lowered into the ground.'

'Gran!' Lettie was shocked. 'That isn't very charitable of you.'

'No and neither was she. It wasn't my fault her husband left her but she dismissed me all the same. Nevertheless, I ought to pay my last respects.'

'Shall I go on your behalf? I'm sure folk will understand.'

'No, they won't!' Gran tried to sit up in bed. 'I don't want you there! It's bad enough you sneaking up there to find your grandfather's grave without you publicly mourning any of them.'

'But – but – I thought – please calm down, Gran. Remember what the doctor said.'

Oh dear, somehow Lettie had said the wrong thing. Gran had brought up the subject so what should she have done? Made some excuse to go out of the room? Yes, she should have done that; that's what she would do next time. Meanwhile Gran had started to breathe heavily and this increased her anxiety, which made her breathing more laboured. Lettie became alarmed. 'I'll mix you a powder,' she said. She poured some water into a glass from the carafe on her bedside table.

Gran shook her head wordlessly and waved her hand to say no, but Lettie ignored her. She hurried round the bed to Gran's marble-topped washstand, opened one of the packets, tipped it into the water and stirred it vigorously with a spoon.

'Come on, Gran, doctor's order.' She supported her head while, thankfully, Gran drank the draught. She gasped and choked as she swallowed. Lettie fretted as she held her hand and stroked her brow until, eventually, Gran's breathing calmed. It seemed like an age to Lettie and when it was over Gran looked even older and greyer, more tired and worn out. Lettie made her comfortable and when her powder took effect and Gran was dozing, she went downstairs, tapped on the study door and went straight in.

The Reverend looked up from his desk and peered at her over the reading spectacles perched on his nose. 'What is it, Lettie? I'm very busy.'

'I know and I shouldn't disturb you if it wasn't important but Gran's had another turn.'

The Reverend rose to his feet.

'She's sleeping now,' Lettie added quickly. 'But she looks much worse. Please can I fetch the doctor?'

'Of course. Call in the mission as you pass and send round one of the ladies. I'll sit with her until you get back.'

'Thank you, Reverend.'

Later that evening, Lettie took a tray of tea into the front room where the doctor was speaking to the Reverend and Mrs Jones.

'Come and sit down, Lettie,' Mrs Jones said. 'I'll pour.'

'Thank you.' Lettie was grateful to sit down for a few minutes. 'How is she, Doctor?'

'Sleeping, but she needs someone with her all the time now.'

'I'll stay with her,' Lettie said. 'I can sleep in the chair.'

'She is lucky to have you,' the doctor said. 'She's too ill for convalescence and anyway she is now too weak to travel. Rest and light nourishment is all she needs at present.' He drank his tea.

Mrs Jones took his empty cup. 'I'll ask if there's a room at our House of Help in town.'

The doctor shook his head. 'A move like that will put

too much of a strain on her heart, and they couldn't give her the nursing that she has here. She's more comfortable with those who love her.'

'Will she get any of her strength back, sir?' Lettie asked quietly.

The doctor leaned forward. 'With you to care for her, my dear, she is in the very best hands. It is important for you to keep up her spirits,' he glanced at the Reverend, 'and pray for her.'

A cold hand clutched at Lettie's heart. Gran wasn't going to get better. The Reverend had said prayers for Gran every Sunday since her first attack and it hadn't helped. She said, 'She'd like to go to chapel on Sundays. She misses it.'

'You could try but it might be too much for her. Did you manage to locate a Bath chair?'

Reverend Ennis answered, 'Yes, one of our elders has one in his outhouse. He will deliver it tomorrow.'

The doctor smiled. 'I'm sure that will do her as much good as anything I can prescribe. Give her what she wants.'

Lettie could hardly speak. This was much worse than she had realised. Gran might be, might be . . . might be . . . she stifled a sob rising in throat and croaked, 'How much time does she have left, Doctor?'

'It is very difficult for me to say in your grandmother's case, Miss Hargreaves. Her mind is strong but another attack like this one will further weaken her heart and it can only take so much.'

'Is there anything else I can do to help her?'

'You must keep her quiet. Any anxiety at all could precipitate another attack. I'll leave you some of the powders that help to calm her and a script for more.'

'Thank you.'

They stared silently at each other until Mrs Jones said, 'Would you care for another cup of tea, Doctor?'

He stood up. 'Thank you, no. I have two more patients to visit this evening.'

The Reverend accompanied him to the front door and Mrs Jones began to re-stack the tray. 'Don't worry, my dear,' she said, 'we're all here to help you.'

Lettie stared at the gas light, hissing on the wall. Installing the electric had been postponed while Gran was ill. She was all the family Lettie had. She had always been here for her, looking after her, teaching her, guiding her, chastising her and occasionally, yes occasionally, praising her.

'Why don't you?' Mrs Jones was speaking to her from the doorway, holding the loaded tray in her hands.

Lettie roused herself. 'Beg pardon, what was it you said?'

'I said why don't you go to bed and get some proper sleep while I see to these. I'll sit with her tonight and someone will be in to give you a hand in the morning.'

'You're all so kind.'

'It's what the mission does. You should think about joining us when . . . well, think about it anyway.'

Lettie nodded, sighed and stood up. She felt drained of all her energy and had to drag her feet up the stairs. But when she was in bed she found it difficult to sleep.

Gran wasn't going to get better. The doctor had all but said those words and that, with Lettie's care, she could still enjoy her last few weeks.

Lettie doubted it. Gran had needed to be kept busy and involved in chapel affairs. How satisfied would she be with little to look forward to except sitting in a Bath chair at her bedroom window and watching the world pass by? Of course, no one need tell her how poorly she was and Lettie could continue to make plans for her future. But Gran still had her wits and she knew her granddaughter well. Lettie would find it difficult to keep the truth from her. She fell asleep worrying.

Fortunately she did not have to carry the nursing burden totally alone as Mrs Jones arranged a supply of older ladies to sit with Gran and read to her. All understood the strict instruction to avoid any reference to the Laughtons or Waterley Hall. But the effect on Lettie of this ban only served to inflame her curiosity about the past and there was absolutely no possibility of questioning Gran now. She considered asking the Reverend what he knew but on reflection realised that her interest was likely to worry him and he had enough to deal with. Chapel work had not reduced because Gran was ill. If anything he had more to do and during quiet times, when others relieved her of her sick-room duties, Lettie sorted out meetings for the Reverend, kept the chapel accounts in order and informed Gran on her work. Chapel business was a safe topic of conversation.

Occasionally Lettie opened letters for the Reverend and placed them in neat stacks according to the type of response needed. At the end of each day she tidied his desk and emptied his wastepaper basket, retrieving the newspaper to take to her bedroom for later reading before it was put out for the privy or the pig.

Each week brought speculation from a reporter on the future of Waterley Hall and its former occupants. Would Lady Laughton's estranged husband attend her funeral? Would he return to Yorkshire or sell up in favour of his self-indulgent life in London and abroad? Who would buy Waterley Hall if he sold it? Lettie wished that she had time to visit Boundary Farm where, she was sure, Mrs Osborne would have some answers.

One Tuesday afternoon, when Gran was sleeping after her dinner, Mrs Jones came into the sick room and said, 'Mrs Osborne is downstairs.'

'She's here! Does she want to see Gran?'

'She's asking after you. She brought vegetables and fruit with her. I've shown her into the drawing room. Go down and thank her. You can make her a cup of tea while I sit with your grandmother.'

'Thank you. Gran's had a powder. She'll sleep for at least an hour.'

Mrs Osborne gave Lettie a hug and was so sympathetic that she wanted to cry.

Lettie sniffed. 'Gran's asleep at the moment. Did you want to see her?'

'I did, but I can wait until she wakes. I've missed your company, m'ducks.'

'Would you like some tea?'

'Oh, don't bother with all that yet. Come and sit here

beside me. Who is looking after you?' Mrs Osborne emphasised the 'you'.

'Oh, I'm all right.' Lettie yawned. 'Beg pardon, Mrs Osborne. I do most of the nights with Gran so the other ladies can be home with their families.'

'You sit up all night with her?'

'She likes to see I'm there if she wakes, and I don't want her falling out of bed. I usually read the Bible to her until she falls asleep and then I read to myself until I doze. The clock chimes in the hall always rouse me, though. When she wakes I help her to sit on the commode while I make the bed. Then I give her a drink or a powder if she wants one.'

'Can you go back to your own bed then?'

Lettie shook her head. 'It's hard for her to breathe so she has to stay sitting up. She might choke if she lolls over.'

'I see. She's really very poorly, then. Folk said she was. It must be tiring for you.'

'I don't mind. She's my gran and I love her. The Reverend lets me keep the lamp burning and I catch up on my reading.'

'You must know your bible backwards by now.'

'I read the newspaper mainly. I can just about stay awake for that!'

'How long do you think you'll be able to keep it up, m'ducks?'

Lettie didn't answer. She hadn't given the future a second thought. Mrs Osborne raised her eyebrows expecting an answer and Lettie shrugged. 'As long as it takes,' she said.

'You'll have read what's been going on at Waterley Hall, then?'

'We don't discuss it in the manse. It upsets Gran.'

'Well, it's the talk of Waterley Edge, and in the town, too.'

'Has Mr Osborne heard anything?'

'Oh aye, m'ducks. He doesn't say much, as you know, but he reckons His Lordship will come home now she's gone. It's whether he'll bring his floozy with him that folk really want to know. He can marry her now, of course. Oh dear me, look at your face. I've shocked you, haven't I?'

Chapter 15

Lettie was astounded. 'I hadn't heard anything about a floozy,' she murmured. No wonder Gran didn't approve of him, she thought.

'Well, Mr Osborne says that's why he left Her Ladyship in the first place. He and Lady Laughton never got on. They didn't even like each other, apparently.'

'Then why did they marry?'

'Isn't that obvious, m'ducks? She owned half of the fortune. His Lordship couldn't risk her being wed to somebody else and that somebody else muscling in on his empire. Mr Osborne says she never forgave her first husband for dying on her or her second one for going off with his floozy.'

'My gran thinks they were both as bad as each other.'

'Your granny's a wise old lady.'

'Yes, but when you go up to see her, you mustn't mention any of this. Promise me you won't. It was hearing about Lady Laughton that brought on her attack. She'll ask you as well so you have to be prepared to make an excuse and change the subject. We really don't talk about the Laughtons in the manse.'

'Well, if you say so, m'ducks.'

'I'll go up with you. I try to get her to sit in the Bath chair in the afternoons and wheel her to the window.'

'I can give you a hand with that.' Mrs Osborne put her head on one side. 'How are you getting on with that young fellow of yours?'

'Thomas? I've barely seen him since Gran took bad.' They hadn't parted on very good terms so she guessed he'd lost interest in her.

'Not the coalman. Didn't you say you had a follower?'

'A follower? Oh, you mean Eric, Mrs Jones's son?'

'Is that the young man? Isn't he the new head teacher at the village school?'

'I've really not had time to think about him, Mrs Osborne,' Lettie replied decisively. 'I've had other things on my mind.'

'I see. Out of sight, out of mind.'

Lettie supposed that was true because she hadn't thought about Eric since he'd called to carry Gran upstairs and the only time she'd remembered Thomas was when the coal was delivered last week. She had wondered how he was getting on at Toogoods and had experienced a pang of disloyalty towards him because she had spoiled their last afternoon together. On the whole she preferred not to talk about either of them and said the first thing that came into her head. 'Has Mr Boyer gone home to Canada?'

'Mr Boyer?'

As soon as Mrs Osborne repeated his name with her querulous tone, Lettie wished she hadn't asked. The truth was, thoughts of Mr Boyer had frequently crossed her mind, especially in those long wakeful night-time hours. She was intrigued by his presence and attracted to him despite his cold and distant manner.

She gave what she hoped was a nonchalant shrug. 'I just wondered if he was still staying with you at Boundary Farm.'

'Well, he is and he isn't, so to speak. He still has the front bedroom but he's been away more than he's been in there lately and Mr Osborne said he saw him at Waterley Hall when the lawyers were in talking to the servants.'

'I wonder what that was about.'

'It's whether they've still got positions there, m'ducks. Mr Osborne is a tenant so he's seeing a lawyer himself about his lease. You never know what'll happen when there's been a death. Shall we have that cup of tea, after all?'

Lettie rose to her feet. 'The kettle's already on the hob. Mrs Jones will come down and tell me when Gran wakes up.'

'I'll come through with you and tell you all about my girls.'

Two shopping baskets overflowing with early-autumn vegetables and fruit sat on the kitchen table.

'Goodness, Mrs Osborne, it's like the Harvest Festival already! The Reverend will be pleased.'

'I'll unpack them for you. Where shall I put them?'

'Just pile them in the scullery sink. Not the fruit, though. Did I see some grapes?'

'They're for your grandmother. They were Lady Laughton's favourite.'

'I'd better not tell that to Gran. How did you get here with all this?'

'Mr Boyer bought that trap he hired and he allows Mr Osborne to use it when he's away.'

'That's very kind of him.'

'Yes it is, isn't it? He's a bit stiff and starchy sometimes but underneath he's a thoroughly decent fellow.'

'Have you any idea what his business is in the South Riding?'

'I wish I did, but I know better than to poke my nose in where it's not wanted.'

Lettie took this as a mild rebuke and changed the subject. 'Is Mr Osborne with you, then? Will he join us for tea?'

'He's gone on into town. He'll call for me on his way back.'

Mrs Jones left as soon as Gran woke and Lettie spent a pleasant afternoon with Mrs Osborne and Gran, who was cheered by her chatter and enjoyed the grapes. Lettie left them to each other's company while she went downstairs to deal with the vegetables and clean out Mrs Osborne's baskets. Before Mrs Osborne left Lettie promised her she would find a couple of hours soon to visit her on the farm. 'It'll do you good to get out,' she said and Lettie agreed.

As she tidied the scullery at the end of the day she noticed the latest newspaper at the top of the pile. The Reverend must have taken it straight out there instead of placing it in the wastepaper basket and when she turned it over she saw why. The headline shouted at her.

LORD LAUGHTON RETURNS TO WATERLEY HALL
Speculation that absent landlord will return to his native Yorkshire

Lettie gazed at the grainy print of a photograph and guessed it had been taken a few years ago when Lord Laughton was much younger. He looked very handsome in his country tweeds, a shotgun in his hand and a couple of black gun dogs at his feet. A line of servants filled the background. He certainly appeared to be a wealthy and aristocratic country gentleman. Lettie took a minute to scan part of the lengthy article on his achievements then tucked the newspaper underneath the bib of her apron, planning to read it in bed before she went to sleep.

But the lady who was due to sit with Gran that night sent word to say her husband had been taken poorly and she couldn't leave him until the doctor had been. Lettie could have asked the mission to send someone else but it seemed an imposition as they were all busy ladies. She was already here and volunteered to sit up again. She had her paper to read for when Gran fell asleep and, sensibly, left it in her own bedroom until Gran's powder took effect.

She crept along the landing to retrieve it as soon her grandmother's breathing slowed into the slumbering rhythm she recognised. When she returned, Gran looked peaceful. Lettie stroked her brow very gently, pushed back a straying lock of grey hair and bent to give her a light kiss on her forehead. Gran didn't stir. The new powders were stronger. The doctor had said that quiet rest was Gran's best treatment now. Lettie spread the newspaper on the counterpane and drew the lamp closer.

As she read she realised that Lord Laughton certainly lived life high off the hog. He and his late cousin, Lady Laughton's first husband, had built on their fathers' earlier fortunes in steel-making and shipbuilding. The report mentioned another cousin, too, who had married and left the country.

And then, right at the very end of the piece, the article told of the 'questions on everyone's lips': whether Lord Laughton would return to Waterley Hall and whether he would be alone or with his 'constant companion', an unnamed woman who had been seen with him at several race meetings in France and Germany.

Goodness, Lettie thought, surely this was not the floozy that Mrs Osborne mentioned? If it was then there was little wonder the Reverend did not wish her to see this article. He preached a very moral code in chapel and Gran echoed it. Was that why Gran would not have Lord Laughton's name mentioned? She smoothed the newspaper, stared at his photograph and wondered when it was taken.

In the background a line of footmen stood by the steps

leading to the front door of, she assumed, Waterley Hall. She took a closer look at the caption. *Lord Laughton with some of his loyal servants*. Were Gran and her grandfather among them? Her heart began to thump. Perhaps her mother or father was in the group as well? She fingered the picture lightly. It was hard to make out their features but she supposed a servant would recognise themselves or a close relative. She desperately wished she knew someone other than Gran who had been employed there and considered, again, approaching Mr Osborne. She sat back in her chair and yawned. Her eyelids drooped. The lamplight flickered and she focused her attention on moving shadows jumping across the wall. She yawned again. Then she closed her eyes for a minute intending to finish reading the newspaper . . . in a moment . . .

The next thing she knew was the sound of Gran making peculiar gurgling noises in her throat. Startled, she half rose to her feet. 'What is it, Gran? What do you need?' she cried.

The lamp still burned brightly. Gran's eyes were rolling, apparently helplessly. Her pillows were slipping away to right and left and she was trying to sit up but couldn't. Her breathing was difficult. Lettie stood up and attempted to get her upright again. Gran's bony fingers were clutching at the newspaper as though she were clinging onto it for her life. It was crumpled, scrunched up, even torn in places.

'Reverend!' Lettie called. 'Come quick!'

Gran lolled over towards her and the newspaper slipped to one side. Lettie managed to retrieve the pillows and pushed them behind Gran as best she could. But Gran could not help herself to sit up. Her body was limp and her eyes had closed. For a second, Lettie thought that she had died until the gurgling in her throat resumed. She eased her back onto the pillows and the gurgling stopped.

'Say something, Gran,' Lettie pleaded.

Nothing was audible. No movement of her lips was visible. Where is the Reverend? she thought frantically. Lettie watched for what seemed like an age, trying to detect any movement that suggested breathing. Then she knew that the Reverend, or indeed the doctor, could not do any more for Gran now.

'Oh Gran,' Lettie breathed. 'Dearest Gran.' She leaned forward and took Gran's fragile form in her arms, cradling her gently against her soft bosom. 'Dearest Gran,' she repeated. 'I love you so much.'

Lettie inhaled suddenly and realised it was a sob so she pressed her lips together and sniffed. Gran's hair was awry and she wouldn't want anyone to see her looking so dishevelled. Lettie combed it for her, neatened the ribbon ties at the top of her nightgown, straightened the tumbled pillows behind her and tidied the bedcover. She looked more peaceful now and in her mind she could hear Gran say, *That's better, Lettie, much better*. The newspaper slid to the floor and Lettie bent to push it out of sight, under the bed with a stray pillow, before she went out onto the landing to tap on the Reverend's door.

He didn't take long to rouse and within a minute or so he had put on a heavy dressing gown and carpet slippers and was standing by the side of Gran's bed.

'I think she's gone, sir,' Lettie murmured.

'Yes, my dear. I'm very sorry.'

'Shall I fetch the doctor?'

'It's still dark. I'll get dressed and go. Will you be all right on your own?'

Lettie didn't reply. *On her own.* Without Gran she had nobody; no family, except the Reverend who was good and kind to her because that was his vocation. But he didn't love her like her gran had loved her. Gran had been the mother that Lettie had never known.

'I could fetch Mrs Jones or one of the others . . .' The Reverend prompted.

'No, there's no need,' she answered. 'I'd like to be alone with her for a while.'

He nodded and left quietly.

Lettie spoke softly as she continued to smooth the bedclothes. 'I know I haven't turned out exactly as you wished but I know you will be watching me from heaven and I shall do my best to make sure you are proud of me. I promise.' Then her tears began to flow and she tried to pull herself together but it was difficult. It was a long time before the Reverend returned with the doctor. She heard the side gate and went to the window to look. They were walking round to the back of the house. The sky was already streaked with grey and she heard the clock chime.

The doctor was very kindly when he confirmed what she and the Reverend knew already. Lettie simply stared at the wall as she tried to stem her tears.

'Why don't you go downstairs and get the fire going

for some tea,' the Reverend suggested so she nodded silently and went down to the kitchen, glad of a routine to be getting on with.

Both gentlemen joined her before the kettle had boiled. The fire was drawing well and the teapot was ready.

'I'll bring it into your study when it's ready, sir,' she said.

'It's cosier in here,' the Reverend replied and pulled out a couple of chairs for himself and the doctor.

The doctor put his black bag on the kitchen table and took out some folded paper packets. 'These will help you sleep, my dear,' he said. 'I want you to take one now and go straight to bed. Keep the others for night-time when you can't get off. They'll help.'

'What will happen now?' she asked.

'You will go to bed and sleep.' The doctor smiled.

'I mean, what will happen to Gran?'

The Reverend answered, 'I'll arrange for your grandmother to be taken to the Chapel of Rest until the funeral. She left a will with her last wishes about burial, my dear. I have it in my study.'

'Oh. Can I see it?'

'Of course. When you are feeling stronger we shall have a long talk.'

The kettle began to bubble on the hob and the Reverend stood up to make the tea. 'Shall we have some of those fancy biscuits that your grandmother kept for the elders' meetings?' he suggested.

Lettie got up. 'I'll fetch them.'

When she returned with the biscuit barrel from the

dining room the Reverend had prepared a small tray for her and the doctor was stirring a powder in a small glass tumbler of water.

The doctor handed her the tray. 'I want you to take this upstairs to your bedroom, put on your nightgown, have your tea and biscuit and take the powder. Then climb into bed and I promise you'll feel better when you wake up.'

'Do as the doctor advises, Lettie,' the Reverend added. 'I'll take care of everything else.'

She inhaled a shuddering sob and then stifled a yawn and obeyed. She hadn't realised how exhausted she was. Her legs felt like the lead weights in window sashes and she had to summon all her strength to climb the stairs. In spite of the hot tea she felt cold and the sheets chilled her further as she fell into bed. Her last thought was of how cold her feet were and then she sank into slumber.

Daylight forced its way through the crack in the curtains when she woke, disorientated and with a dry mouth. After a second she remembered and lay there quite still, trying to quell the rising tears. When she got out of bed she found warm water in her ewer. Someone had been in to bring it and presumably to check on her. She wondered what time it was and waited for the clock to chime. But it only chimed the quarter hour so she turned back the covers and went to look out of the window. The sky was overcast although it was bright enough to be the middle of the day.

Her hands shook as she washed and dressed. She stood outside Gran's room for several minutes before she turned the knob and opened the door. The bed was empty, stripped of bedding, and the curtains at the window remained closed; and would until after the funeral. It was the custom. The room needed a good fettle now, Lettie thought.

She walked over to the commode and closed the lid. The pot had been taken away along with the miscellany of medicine, spectacles and pot-pourri on the bedside table and washstand. Gran's bible was still there and Lettie picked it up. She wasn't as devoted to God as her grandmother and had sometimes questioned the Reverend's sermons but had never said as much. Nonetheless this bible was so much part of Gran's life that if felt as though it were part of her. Lettie hugged it to her body and her tears flowed again.

'Is that you, Lettie?' she heard the Reverend call up the stairs. Putting down the bible, she went on to the landing.

'Come down and get something to eat. Mrs Jones has cooked a dinner and saved you some in the oven.'

It was so difficult to stop the tears and her legs now felt like jelly. She grasped the handrail as she went downstairs. The Reverend was waiting for her.

'I heard you get up. How are you, my dear?'

The Reverend didn't usually address her as 'my dear' but the doctor had called her that as well, she recalled. 'A bit shaky,' she answered. 'I slept quite heavily.'

'That would be the powder. The doctor said you would feel fine once you've come round. Mrs Jones has just gone and she left a tea tray laid up. She'll be in tomorrow as well, so you don't have to worry about a thing.'

'I . . . I'll turn out Gran's room. You'll need it for your new housekeeper.'

'There's no hurry, my dear.'

'I'll sort out Gran's belongings as well. She would want them to go to the mission – her best tweed coat and—' She couldn't go on.

He smiled sympathetically. 'Yes, my dear. We'll talk about that after the funeral.'

'When will it be?'

'Next week. There'll be a large attendance. Mrs Jones is arranging a tea afterwards at the mission hall.' He kept the gentle smile on his face. 'Why don't you go and eat your dinner now? I've finished my reports and I'll be seeing to the pig if you need me.'

He went upstairs to change into his old clothes.

Lettie did feel better after a lovely meal of meat and potato hash followed by stewed apples. The kettle simmered on the hob and the teapot stood ready. Lettie made some tea and walked down the garden with a steaming mug for the Reverend. He was leaning on the wall of the sty and scratching the pig's back with a stick. The pig seemed to really enjoy that and he snuffled and rolled on his side in the mud. Lettie smiled.

The Reverend had always kept a pig and he never gave it a name. You couldn't eat a pig that you'd given a name. She hoped the new housekeeper would be able to salt it down in just the way the Reverend wanted for his Christmas table. She left his mug of tea on the

219

wall and he acknowledged her with a wave of his stick. Then she went back indoors to finish her tea and gather together some cleaning materials.

The bed was stripped and the mattress smelled of rosemary and lavender. Lettie rolled up the rugs to take outdoors and beat, and as she knelt on the floor she caught sight of the stray pillow under the bed; and then the crumpled newspaper. She stretched to retrieve them. The distorted headline brought those last few moments of her grandmother's life flooding back. Lettie relived the image of Gran, her wild rolling eyes, her fingers gripping the flimsy paper. And then she realised that Gran must have seen it. She had not been clutching it as the straw clutched by a drowning man. She had been tearing at it to destroy it.

Lettie remembered the report she had been reading when she dozed off. Gran had read it – or at least the headline and picture caption – and had . . . had what? Lettie would never know except that Gran had found the strength in her fingers to scrunch up the page. She stifled a cry in her throat. She had allowed Gran to read the very thing that the Reverend had advised against.

Lettie realised with a shock that Gran's final, fatal attack had been brought on by what she had seen in the paper and it was her fault! She had taken the paper into Gran's room despite the Reverend's warning. She had been the one to disobey. She had caused her grandmother's death.

Chapter 16

She screwed up the newspaper, rocked on her knees until her sobbing subsided and then attempted to smooth it out again on the waxed floorboards. She tried to think rationally. Gran had been seriously ill and could have gone at any time. But Lettie could not excuse herself from the blame. Seeing this picture and this headline had shortened her grandmother's life. It had been her actions that had brought on Gran's attack. Why had she hated Lord Laughton so much? Why? Lettie had to know.

She folded the newspaper carefully and placed it on the bed with the other things-to-keep. As she swept and dusted and polished, Lettie considered the questions she might ask the Reverend during their talk after the funeral. What had happened in the past to cause such hatred and anger in a steadfast God-fearing woman?

Gran's funeral was a large though not ostentatious affair. The chapel was filled to overflowing and mourners stood six deep at the burial. Tributes were small, floral arrangements or cards with purple ribbon and personal messages saying lovely things about her gran.

Lettie wanted to stay and read them all and asked the Reverend if he minded.

'You must be at the mission hall to receive the mourners, my dear. Allow them to express their condolences to you.'

Lettie nodded in agreement. This was the first funeral she had attended and she had never felt so lonely. Gran used to say that women never went to funerals when she was a girl but it was different now. Lettie had a black skirt and a dark grey blouse and wore a long black coat of Gran's that was fashionably short on her. Mrs Jones lent her a black hat and said that Eric would walk with her in the procession. In spite of the way she felt about him she was grateful for that gesture on the day. He was familiar with the service and order of events and she only had to keep her hand on his arm to be sure of doing things correctly. He behaved so well it crossed her mind that it was a pity she didn't like him.

Lettie found the occasion exhausting and would have preferred to grieve alone. She lost count of the numerous kindly folk who offered her their condolences. She couldn't remember the names of many, although she knew most of them by sight. Mrs Jones seemed to be in charge and she directed mourners to the tea and cake. The hall was crowded and stuffy and Lettie needed air. However, after about an hour, one or two of the elders left and others took this as their cue to say goodbye. Very soon, the stragglers who were left finishing the cake were more interested in talking to each other than to Lettie or the Reverend.

The Reverend whispered in her ear, 'Why don't you go and spend a few minutes by the grave on your own?'

'Thank you, sir.'

She slipped away and spent a tearful hour reading the many grateful messages on the tributes. She knew the strength of Gran's commitment to chapel but had no idea that Gran was so much appreciated in the village and even further afield in the town. Alone, Lettie reflected on the past and on Gran's more recent revelations about her late husband.

'I don't know what Grandfather did but you never forgave him, did you?' she murmured, adding, 'And the Reverend preaches forgiveness.' Lettie inhaled shakily, her sobbing over for now. She bent down to retrieve the small posy of wild flowers that she had picked and arranged for her gran. There were many similar tributes and one less would not take away from the display of affection and respect. She said, 'I am doing this for you, Gran, because you were too poorly to do it yourself. I hope you understand.' However, she wasn't entirely sure that Gran would approve of her actions as she set off for the private churchyard on the Waterley estate.

She took the short cut through woods and pasture, avoiding the road past the inn to Boundary Farm. The path was muddy in parts and the grass was wet so that when she arrived her boots had lost their shine and the hem of her skirt was soggy and soiled. She had walked briskly and felt her cheeks must be glowing in the cool air.

Grandfather's grave was much easier to find the second time and she stood at the foot of the simple grassy plot, alone with her thoughts for a long time. She heard the whine of a hinge and looked back at the gate. No one was there so she thought she must have imagined it. Lettie wasn't given to fanciful notions of spirits and visitations so this did not worry her. She bent to place her posy at the base of the headstone. Now she was here she didn't know what to say. The prayers she knew by heart were the ones she recited to the children at Sunday school and none seemed suitable. And then she considered it was God that Gran should ask to forgive her, and not her late husband.

The headstone ought to say more, she thought, and wondered if she could instruct a mason to add more words. The Reverend had already asked her about Gran's headstone and Seth Hargreaves was her grandfather, after all. 'What can I say about you?' she murmured and finally heaved a sigh. 'I just wish I had known you.'

'*Do you?*'

The voice was very close and it surprised her. She jumped and inhaled so sharply it sounded like a shriek.

'Oh! Where did you spring from?' she cried.

'The church,' he stated.

It was Mr Boyer. He must have returned to Boundary Farm. He had stepped from behind her and into her field of vision. He looked at her face briefly and added, 'It's you, I see.'

Lettie regained her composure quickly. 'Good afternoon, sir.'

He nodded an acknowledgement but did not walk on.

Was he waiting for her to speak? She wondered what he was doing here and assumed it was for the same reason as she. She said, 'I saw you searching the town cemetery last month. Are you looking for someone?'

'Is that what you were trying to find out when you were reading my papers?'

'I was not reading your papers,' she protested mildly. Goodness me, he still remembers, and he isn't being very friendly at all. She turned away from him and back to her grandfather's headstone, expecting him to leave.

'You wouldn't have wanted to know him, believe me,' Mr Boyer said.

Why would he say that? She whirled around. 'Did you know him? He . . . he was my grandfather.'

He looked astounded for a moment then recovered. 'That man was your grandfather?'

His tone was disparaging and Lettie felt herself blushing but she ignored the sneer. What business was it of his, anyway?

'Did you know my grandfather?'

'Of course not! How old do you think I am?'

Lettie was put off by his abrupt manner. Mrs Osborne had said he was a gentleman but he certainly wasn't behaving very much like one now. However, if he had some knowledge of her grandfather she was prepared to overlook his brusqueness on this occasion. 'But you know something about him? Please tell me. Please. You see, his headstone seems so . . . so bleak and I want to add a few words about him – something truthful – about the man he was.' She sounded emotional but did not care. It was how she felt at the moment. She lowered her voice and hunched her shoulders. 'There are no endearments and there ought to be.'

'Well, the truth is never wrong,' he said. Then he added, as if it were an afterthought, 'It is the telling of the truth that is right or wrong.'

He seemed to be mocking her in some way and she wasn't sure what to make of him. Was he saying that it was right not to add anything if it had to be the truth? This implied that Gran had been right not to tell her anything. She felt she should walk away from him but was not ready to leave Grandfather's grave yet. He had imposed himself on her and she wanted him to go. But not before he had explained himself. 'What do you know about him, sir?' she asked.

'Why don't you ask your grandmother?'

His question felt like a knife in her stomach. Her voice cracked and the tears threatened. 'I can't. I buried her today.'

His demeanour changed in a second and his sour expression turned to one of compassion. Was this the same face that had scorned her a moment before? 'Forgive me,' he said. 'I had no idea.' He looked past her to the posy of flowers resting at the base of the stone. 'I have intruded on your grief and for that I apologise most sincerely. Good afternoon, miss.' He turned and walked away, out of the graveyard without looking back.

Lettie was ready to collapse. Her legs seemed unable to support her and she placed a hand on the headstone to steady herself. Whatever Grandfather had done it was a long time ago and, surely, forgotten by all concerned. Perhaps *Rest in Peace* was the most fitting inscription for him.

She retraced her steps slowly across the pasture and through the woods to the manse. The Reverend had begun to worry about her absence and was relieved to see her. He urged an early night with one of her sleeping powders. Tomorrow, he planned to discuss the future with her. She supposed he meant Wales. It had not been possible when Gran was taken ill. Now, of course, it was an obvious choice and thoughts of the Welsh coalmining valleys jumbled with curiosity about Mr Boyer and her grandfather filled her mind until she fell asleep.

'Come in and sit down, Lettie my dear. Have you eaten breakfast?'

'Yes, thank you,' she replied, surprised at his interest in such detail about her welfare.

'Good. Mrs Jones has already found someone to take over from her for the next month. She will move in later today.'

'But I said I could manage until you found a permanent replacement.'

'No, my dear. You must allow her to do that. You have to leave chapel and manse affairs to others and think seriously about your future. As you know, your grandmother was keen for you to seek new pastures.'

'Did you write to your sister in Wales?'

'I did. And then I wrote again when your grandmother took poorly so no firm decisions were made. We – that is, you – must decide now.'

'Are you giving me a choice, sir?'

The Reverend was valued in Waterley Edge for a practical approach to his pastoral duty. His guidance was welcomed when his worshippers suffered crises in their lives. He was used to such interviews as this but Lettie thought he was considering his words extra carefully. She was prepared to listen but had mentally prepared herself for a disagreement. She added, 'I understood that you agreed with Gran so I suppose you still want me to go.'

'It would, in my view, be the best course of action for you. However, it has to be your decision and I shall not rest easy if you choose before, well, before I have discharged my duty towards you.'

My goodness, he does sound formal. He was an educated man with a good command of language as anyone might expect of a preacher. But now he was beginning to sound more like a lawyer than a pastor! Did he want to dispense with his responsibility towards her altogether? Gran had talked to her about her wishes so she said, 'Gran told me you would be my guardian when she . . . she . . .' Her voiced trailed away.

'None of us expected her to leave us so quickly, my dear. But, yes, she did confide in me with regard to your guardianship.'

'I could not wish for anyone else, sir. When I asked

Gran why you cared so much about me she told me it was because you are a good man.'

He smiled in a kindly fashion. 'It is my vocation, Lettie.'

And, she realised, he has a whole parish of worshippers to care for. He ought not to have his time taken up by one unfortunate orphan. 'I shall not be a burden to you. I told Gran I would find a position. I am convinced that I can.'

'So am I, my dear, which is why your grandmother wanted you to train for a proper vocation. You have a little money that she had saved for you, precisely for that purpose. What have you in mind?'

Not a teacher! She had to say it and wondered if he would argue with her. He was a clever man and credible in his arguments. He waited for her to respond and she said, 'I . . . I was thinking of applying to Waterley Hall before Her Ladyship died. But no one is quite sure what will happen there now. The newspaper said—'

'You really must put that idea right out of your mind. Your grandmother would not have approved.'

But that was because it holds secrets, Lettie thought defiantly, secrets about her past. Nonetheless, she had loved Gran and the Reverend was her guardian so she would have to abide by his wishes. Yet, he had said that she must decide for herself. She took a deep breath and said, 'I really do not want to be a teacher, Reverend. I am sorry to disappoint you but I don't want to go to Wales, either. Truly, I don't.'

'Why not? What do you have against the Welsh valleys?'

'Nothing at all, sir. It's just that I want to know who

I am. I have to. It's an urge in me that I cannot quell. Gran gave me a little information and warned me against further enquiry. But that has only made me want to find out more and I believe the answers must start here in Waterley, with my grandfather.'

The Reverend rested his forehead in the palm of his hand for a second. 'In some ways you have just made this interview much easier for me. Your grandmother said that you might be told when you reached twenty-one. I disagreed with her. You are an intelligent young woman and I think that you are mature enough to cope with it now.'

Now Lettie wanted to put her head in her hands. 'Cope with what, sir?'

'The truth, my dear.'

She felt an unusual shivering sensation spread through her body and swallowed. He knew something. She said the words that burned into her brain since she heard them yesterday: 'The truth is never wrong. It is whether you tell it or not that is right or wrong.'

'That is a very philosophical statement. Did you think of it yourself?'

'I wish I had.'

'Eric, then? He is a very well-read young man.'

'No, not Eric.' Eric wasn't interested in meaningful discussion with her, Far from it!

'Thomas, then? His father can be quite philosophical, I hear. He writes poetry.'

She shook her head. 'A gentleman I met at Mrs Osborne's.'

Reverend Ennis frowned. 'Another gentleman? I believe

your grandmother did speak fully with you about the dangers of being taken in by the flatteries of young men.'

'She did,' Lettie stated and considered, actually, that Mrs Osborne was much more help in explaining the actions of young men; as indeed the Reverend's sister in Wales might be. 'Do not concern yourself, sir. He did not flatter me.' Quite the opposite, she thought.

'Well, whoever said it was wise. It is precisely that dilemma that prompts me to go against your grand-mother's wishes regarding your guardianship.'

This was a blow to Lettie and she floundered, lost for words for a moment. 'You . . . you will not be my guardian?'

He shook his head and a surge of disappointment washed over her. 'I am deferring my decision until I have gathered more information. When we talked of your guardianship your grandmother told me . . . certain facts of your background. She wanted me to promise to keep them from you.'

He knew something! Lettie's frustration deepened. The Reverend would not break his promise to Gran.

The Reverend had not finished and he went on, 'I replied that as your guardian I should have to consider what was in your best interests at the time.'

I wonder how Gran reacted to that, Lettie thought. She would not have been pleased.

'I am aware that your upbringing in the manse has been sheltered. You are not as . . . as worldly as some of the young women in the parish whose behaviour causes their parents endless worry.'

Well, those young women had been out in service or at the bottle factory for several years at her age, Lettie thought. If Gran had not felt the need to stop her from doing things that other nineteen-year-olds did, she may well have known what to expect from Eric Jones! She refocused her attention on the Reverend's speech.

'However,' he went on, 'your sense of right and wrong is well developed and I believe you can be trusted to behave in a proper manner, given a little more freedom.'

Lettie's eyebrows shot up in surprise. 'Did you say that to Gran?'

'I did not. I conveyed to her that I am prepared to act as your guardian and she passed away with that knowledge.'

'Thank you, sir.'

'However, I find my conscience is not at ease when I am aware that there is someone else with a better claim than I for the role.'

She wasn't sure she had heard him correctly. 'Beg pardon, sir, but could you say that again?'

'I understand this will come as a shock to you. It was, indeed, a surprise to me. In my role as your preacher as well as your guardian, I must do what I believe to be in your best interests.' He stopped to focus his attention on her face. 'Who am I to say that I will make a better guardian than your own father?'

Chapter 17

'My own father? But my father is dead.' What on earth is he talking about? she wondered.

'No, my dear, he may not be. He was estranged from your mother before you were born.'

Lettie's jaw slackened. 'Are you saying my father may still be alive?' she muttered. 'Surely not?'

'He has never owned you – that is, taken responsibility for you – as his child.'

'Then . . . he did not . . . want me?' This realisation devastated Lettie. 'Did he know about me?' she asked.

'I can only repeat what your grandmother told me a few months ago, when we discussed your guardianship. You see, I pressed her for information – any information on possible living relations, however distant. Blood is always best in matters of guardianship. She told me that your father had not passed away as she had led you to believe.'

'He may be alive?' Lettie sagged into her chair. 'My father may be alive and neither of you thought I should know?'

'Your grandmother has had no contact with him for nigh on twenty years.'

'But he's my father! Why didn't she tell me about him?'

'She spoke of him in a dismissive way. He was a man influenced by money and position, and, it seems, by your grandfather, too.'

Lettie sighed in frustration. 'Grandfather again! Well, Gran hated him so it's not surprising that she disliked my father as well. Even so, to have no contact with him whatsoever, it's . . . it's . . . it's just not fair.' Dear Lord, she had lost her mother and Gran had deprived her of her father too! Of course Gran must have had her reasons, but she thought it was a cruel thing to do. However, she could not say that to the Reverend. He was trying to make amends.

He said, 'Your grandmother was talking of when he was a young man. He may have changed with the years.' He paused before adding, 'If he is still alive, of course.'

Lettie stared past him and out of the window. 'If he is, he will remember my mother,' she murmured. Then she stood up smartly and said, 'I must find him, sir. You would not have told me about him if you did not believe that I have to search for him.'

'Not necessarily, my dear. I said I had to do as my conscience dictated. You must exercise caution in this

234

matter. If your father is alive, he may have another wife and family. He may not wish to be reminded of you after all this time.'

'But he's my father—'

'He is a father who has never set eyes on you, let alone held you in his arms. Believe me, Lettie, since your grandmother passed away, I have prayed every single day for guidance in this matter. Now I pray for the Lord to guide you.' The Reverend continued in this vein, advising caution, prayer and reflection before action.

But Lettie was not listening as well as she ought. Her mind was racing. Her father's estrangement was to do with Grandfather. It had to be. Had he been a wicked man in the same way as grandfather had been? After Mother died, did Gran take her away from both of them because of what they did? She spoke her thoughts aloud and demanded, 'Do you know where he might be, where I might begin to search?'

Lettie's anxiety mounted. What if she were too late? There was not a moment to waste! The Reverend was very good at keeping calm in situations that were highly charged with all kinds of emotion and he remained unmoved; or at least he appeared to.

'You must be patient. I understand that you have many questions and I shall endeavour to answer them. I have already written to Lady Laughton's lawyer—'

'Lady Laughton? What has she to do with my father?'

'If you will allow me to finish, I shall tell you. Your grandmother said your father was butler at Waterley Hall before . . . that is, when Lord Laughton was in residence.

He was young for such a position but I guess he served His Lordship well and, of course, your grandfather was in a powerful position as house steward.'

'I knew it! I knew it was something to do with Grandfather! Lady Laughton dismissed all His Lordship's servants when he left her. Where did my father go?'

'That is precisely the question I have asked of Waterley Hall trustees. The estate must have kept records of their employees and I have asked them for information on all the indoor male servants in their service.' He smiled at Lettie. 'I await their reply.'

Lettie knew from the mission hall minutes that lawyers took forever to answer letters, especially from people who had not retained their services in the first place. She tried to quell the growing trembling inside her. What if they wouldn't say? What if her father had gone overseas? What if, heaven forbid, he had died? She could not bear that thought; to have lost him after all this time, after all the years when she might have known him and . . . and loved him. Gran must have been aware that someone had knowledge of his whereabouts. Why didn't she say?

'Did . . . did my grandmother ever try to find him?'

'I'm afraid not. He was part of a past that she stead-fastly refused to acknowledge. It was only your future that concerned her, which is why she involved me.' He sat back in his chair. 'However, *if* your father is still alive, *if* I find him and *if* he is a suitable person to be your guardian, and *if* you and he desire it, I shall be happy to support both of you. My dear,' he looked directly into her eyes, 'you do understand that you must prepare yourself for the possibility of unwelcome news?'

'You mean he may have died?' That would be so dreadful to bear, especially now that Gran had gone.

'Do not forget that at some time in his life he had given up his right to be your father and he must have had a reason.'

Lettie closed her eyes. She had so much to think about, so much to plan, and all of it dependent on 'if's. If, if, if! How would she ever sleep until she had the answers?

The Reverend let the silence go on. He took a key from his waistcoat pocket, leaned down, and unlocked a drawer in the pedestal of his desk. Then he placed a battered metal cashbox on the surface in front of him and smiled.

'We shall decide on your long-term future when we have more substantial information about your father. At present I do not even know his name.'

'It will be Hargreaves, of course,' Lettie exclaimed. 'Gran told me. It's what they do in big houses. The family become accustomed to calling their butler by one name and they do not change it when he is replaced. Grandfather was Hargreaves to Lord Laughton before he became house steward, so father would have been addressed as Hargreaves too.'

'How confusing.' The Reverend frowned.

Lettie shrugged. 'Not to the family.'

'Well, I expect the records give his own name as well. In the meantime, I have more cheering news. Your grandmother had a savings account that now belongs to you.

I am your trustee and I have decided to give you a quarterly allowance to spend as you wish so that you may become used to more independence.'

Lettie's eyes widened with gratitude. 'Thank you, sir. Gran allowed me a little money of my own, but I usually had to ask her for it.' And justify why I needed it, she thought and added hastily, 'Not that I minded.'

'Your grandmother felt her responsibility for you keenly. Your well-being was always her only motive.'

Lettie nodded briefly to show that she agreed. But she had already overheard a couple of the mission ladies talking about Gran being 'over-protective'. She remembered that one had said about Lettie, *She's not The Princess Royal*, whilst the other had responded, *No, but she is a lovely-looking lass,* and this had amused Lettie because how could someone with a tendency to freckle in the sun be called 'lovely'?

She assured the Reverend that she would account for her spending and told him about the small tin box kept in her bedroom containing her pencil and pocket book and where she noted her purchases. The Reverend seemed satisfied with his decision, counted out banknotes and coins and placed them in a small leather pouch. Banknotes! Goodness, she would have to take very great care of them. The coins jingled in a most satisfactory way as she felt the weight of the purse in her hand. She climbed the stairs to stow it away safely. Then she offered her services to the temporary housekeeper who responded briskly, 'I don't want you under my feet all day. Go away and help in the mission or something.'

Lettie was hurt by this rebuff and it must have shown in her face, because the woman changed her tone and went on, 'I'm sorry about your grandmother, lass, but your heart won't be in it with me in charge now. Besides, you've done enough for other folk lately. Why don't you go off and spend a bit of time on yourself for a change?'

Well, why don't I? Lettie echoed silently. Because she didn't know really where to start as the only young people she knew were chapel-goers. Although they were pleasant enough, their lives revolved around chapel life, which was not where Lettie saw her future. She sat in her bedroom and stared at her reflection in the mirror, fiddled with her hair for a minute and said out loud, 'Mrs Osborne.' Yes, Mrs Osborne, she thought. She treats me as she would her own daughters. I shall ask her to show me her journals, the ones with pictures and drawings of Gibson Girls. She grew excited as she planned her afternoon.

After dinner, eaten alone in the kitchen, Lettie asked the new housekeeper if she needed vegetables or eggs. She replied that her husband's allotment would be able to keep the Reverend supplied, so Lettie set off without the encumbrance of her baskets. She hardly noticed the walk. Her mind was on whether or not to tell Mrs Osborne about her father. Mrs Osborne was such a gossip. The Reverend had made it clear that his searches might all come to nothing so she decided to keep it to herself for now.

She realised quite suddenly that she had gone past the inn and felt a pang of disappointment that she hadn't seen Thomas. She didn't have any such qualms about telling him about her father because he could keep a confidence. She missed Thomas. They weren't walking out together or anything but she did not want to lose his friendship altogether and determined to look out for him on the way back.

Mrs Osborne was delighted to see her. 'They were saying at your grandmother's funeral that you'd be off to Wales as soon as the Reverend fixed it up for you. He hasn't asked you to step into your granny's shoes, then?'

'He wants me to be a teacher. Gran did too.'

'Well, it's a fine occupation for a spinster, if that's what you want to be. Mind, I reckon you wouldn't stay that for long. A bright young woman such as you will soon be snapped up. You could do quite well, you know.'

Lettie grew excited. 'Do you think so? I am thinking of going into service. Apparently titled ladies are desperate for lady's maids.'

Mrs Osborne raised her eyebrows. 'Got your ideas set on a young master, have you?'

'No. Why do you say that?'

'Didn't I just tell you you'd soon be wed?' Mrs Osborne shook her head good-naturedly at Lettie's puzzled expression. 'Oh, I see,' she went on, 'you thought I was talking about being snapped up for a position, didn't you?'

'Yes. Isn't that what we are talking about?'

Mrs Osborne laughed. 'Aye it is, m'ducks. Take no notice of me and put the kettle on.'

Lettie noticed Mrs Osborne hadn't laid up the tray for Mr Boyer's tea. She felt an acute sense of disappointment she wouldn't see him leading his horse across the yard. 'Has Mr Boyer gone away again?' she asked.

'No, m'ducks. He's out all day today and doesn't know when he'll be back. I'll be cooking his tea at eight o'clock tonight.'

'That was bedtime for Gran.'

'Aye and it was dinner time for Lady Laughton. That's how they have their meals up there. They don't have dinner and tea like we do.' Mrs Osborne put on her artificial aristocrat's air and added, 'She had luncheon at one thirty, ah-ah-afternoon tea at five and dinner at eight o'clock at night, a proper dinner an' all. I ask you, what time is that to be eating your dinner?'

Lettie laughed at her affected accent and said, 'Didn't they do that when you were at Redfern Abbey?'

'Yes but the Earl and Countess were different there somehow. They only fussed about meal times when they had guests. They were a proper lord and lady; not like these jumped-up Laughtons.'

Lettie pressed her lips together to suppress a smile. Mrs Osborne looked embarrassed and went on quickly, 'I shouldn't have said that, should I? But Mr Osborne said Her Ladyship was always complaining about something.' She paused to reflect on this and added, 'His Lordship had been generous, though, but then he was, with them that were loyal.' Mrs Osborne lowered her voice as though she might be overheard. 'You couldn't say that of Her Ladyship. Nothing was ever good enough for her.'

'My grandmother didn't have a pleasant word to say about either of them.'

'She wasn't on her own, m'ducks. But the old lady has gone now and what's left of the servants are wondering what the future holds for them.'

'Have some of them left already?'

'I gather so from Mr Osborne. The newspaper report said Waterley Hall was empty apart from a few servants.'

'It also said Lord Laughton was coming home.'

Mrs Osborne shook her head. 'That won't be until the shooting has finished in the New Year.'

'But there are servants still living there?' Lettie's mind raced. Maybe she wouldn't have to wait for the lawyer's letter? One of the servants might remember her father, might even know where he went when he left? She experienced a frantic urgency to question them before they disappeared to other positions.

'There's a bailiff and a gamekeeper, and a few indoor servants. They are mostly them that have been there for years.'

'Do you know if anyone up there could tell me about becoming a lady's maid?'

'I don't know. The last one left a while ago and Her Ladyship never replaced her.'

'Well, who looked after her then?'

'I've no idea, m'ducks. Nannies were sometimes drafted in at Redfern but Lady Laughton never had call for one of them at Waterley Hall. A head parlourmaid would do it if she had the knack, otherwise the housekeeper could always be trusted. They still have jobs up there, keeping the place spick and span just in case His Lordship arrives unexpected. Why don't you go up there and ask? I'm sure they won't mind.'

'I think I will.'

'Well, have a cup of tea first. I've had a letter from my eldest at Redfern.'

Over tea, and scones leftover from the day before, Mrs Osborne talked about her children and their children. Lettie was interested but listened with only half an ear as she imagined what she would say to the housekeeper at Waterley Hall. Mrs Osborne didn't seem to notice. After she had done the washing-up, Lettie came though from the scullery drying her hands on a towel and glanced at the kitchen clock. 'I'll have to get off now,' she said, 'but thanks ever so much for cheering me up.'

'It's a pleasure, m'ducks. Come again soon.'

'I will.'

If she hurried, there was still time to reach Waterley Hall, find the housekeeper and get home to the manse before the lamplighter came round for the gas lamps. The path forked just before the church. She carried straight on past fields of grazing sheep towards a jumble of outbuildings comprising stables, barns and a few poorly built brick buildings that looked empty and neglected. The rear of the house rose above this, grandly in comparison but probably not as grand as the Georgian frontage. Lettie had not actually seen the front yet, only a picture of it in the newspaper.

Everywhere looked shut up and dingy. The air of damp neglect made Lettie feel sad. She watched for several minutes until one of the doors on the ground floor opened and a man and a woman came out, sat on a wooden bench and lit cigarettes. They were in dark clothes and she guessed they were servants. They chatted with their heads together for a while then went back indoors still smoking their cigarettes. After a few more minutes, Lettie gathered her courage, walked up to the door and rapped on it as loudly as she could. She repeated her knocking after what seemed like a long time and the silence continued. She tried the large tarnished brass knob and the door opened so she stepped inside into a passage that had several doors leading off. One of the doors was slightly open and light from the gap fell onto the stone-flagged floor in front of her. She pushed it open further.

She was in a large scullery with wooden sinks on one wall opposite a large dresser laden with heavy crested china. A young girl in a dark serge dress and plain white apron looked up startled. 'Who are you?'

'Lettie. I've come to see the housekeeper.'

'Are you from the village?'

'Yes,' she answered truthfully.

'Oh good. We can use another pair of hands for tonight. Some o' the toffs are here; well, they're not really toffs, more professional gentlemen. Been here all day, they have, and expecting us to do for them like we used to for Her Ladyship. But most of the servants have found themselves positions and there's only a few left. My auntie's roped me in for the kitchen but Mrs S hasn't got anybody now.'

'I see,' Lettie responded. 'Where do I find Mrs S?'

'Don't let her hear you calling her that! She's in her room.' The maid went back to checking and counting plates.

'I don't know where the housekeeper's room is,' Lettie said.

The girl gave an impatient grunt. 'I'll show you but you'll have to help me carry these. Tell me if you spot a crack, will you? They're only supposed to be used in the servants' hall but one of the toffs has taken the butler's keys now he's gone an' all, so we're using 'em for upstairs. Mrs S is not happy about that at all, I can tell you. Here, take these and follow me.'

Lettie staggered under the weight of the heavy crockery until she placed it in a dumb waiter at the end of the passage as she was directed. Then she retraced a few steps and knocked on the housekeeper's door.

The housekeeper was surprised to see her but didn't question her reason to be present or, indeed, ask her name. 'You're here at last! Have you got a uniform?'

Chapter 18

Lettie shook her head. 'I'd like to talk to you if I may.'

'Later.' The housekeeper pulled her towards the window and examined her outfit. 'Well, your skirt will do and I'll lend you a blouse. Can you wait at table?'

'Yes, but I think I should explain.'

'No time for that now. We'll talk about your references if you can do the work. The trustees are here and everything is taking longer than expected so they've asked to be fed. It's early for dinner, I know, but I can't give a servants' tea to upstairs, can I? As it is, I'm having to use the servants' china because they won't let me have the keys. All the years I've been housekeeper here and I can't be trusted with the keys, not until after the inventory, they said. Where have you worked before?'

Lettie had already decided it was in her interests to

play along with the misunderstanding and answered, 'In the Methodist manse at Waterley Edge.'

'That's good enough for me tonight. You'll know how to mind your manners. You'll take the dishes from the dumb waiter to the sideboard and I'll serve. But you'll have to help with handing round the soup and clearing away so be on your best behaviour.'

'Yes Mrs S . . .?'

'Sinjun. It's spelt as St John and pronounced "Sinjun". Yes, I know you haven't heard of it before but you'll get used to it.'

Actually I have, Lettie thought, because I've read *Jane Eyre* and there's a St John in there and my teacher told me how to say it. 'Where can I wash my hands, Mrs St John?' she asked.

There were four of them present to cook and serve dinner to three gentlemen, which seemed more than enough servants to Lettie. Mrs St John left her to change into a plain high-necked, long-sleeved blouse and then cover most of it with a pretty lace-trimmed apron while she went to talk to the cook. Lettie stood in the dim draughty passage and waited until the housekeeper came out of the kitchen. Then she followed her up plain wooden stairs to a small landing. The dumb waiter full of crockery was waiting. It didn't have a door, only a wooden box opened at the front that was hoisted up and down a shaft with ropes around pulleys.

'Take those dishes and put them on the sideboard through there,' Mrs St John ordered.

Lettie smiled to herself. She sounded like Gran and it

was strangely comforting in the unfamiliar surroundings. Lettie obeyed and began to enjoy herself. She opened the door and faced a high black folding screen. Waterley Hall dining room, on the other side, was long with tall sash windows along one wall. She paused with her arms full to gaze out over the parkland stretching into the distance. The nights are drawing in, she thought. It will be dark when I get home. She heard Mrs St John call down the dumb waiter shaft behind her.

A polished wooden table and enormous sideboard dominated the room. Lettie reckoned there were twenty chairs around the table and more pushed back against the wall. Three places were laid at one end for dinner. Her footsteps echoed on the floorboards as she walked across to deposit the china. She stood to attention at the sideboard while the housekeeper walked slowly around the dining table checking the settings of shining silver and sparkling glass. Without looking up, Mrs St John said, 'Go and get the next load from out there.'

Lettie went back to the dumb waiter. The screen that hid the servants' entrance was ornately decorated in the Chinese style on the dining room side. The curtains at the windows were of a heavy brocade. Lady Laughton may have been a recluse but she did not live like a hermit.

Lettie returned with a large silver tureen of steaming soup. It smelled delicious but it was so heavy and hot that she almost dropped it before reaching the sideboard. She checked that everything was to hand on the sideboard while the gentlemen came in and sat down. They were talking, in low voices, about the late Lady Laughton and how prudent she had been during her lifetime. Lettie had not heard anyone speak of her in those terms before. The gentlemen sounded as though they approved of her careful control of affairs.

Mrs St John whispered in her ear, 'Carry the tureen on the tray to each diner in turn and I shall serve it. No talking and don't look at them.'

Lettie concentrated on not slopping the soup around as she followed the housekeeper cautiously to the end of the long table. The conversation ceased as they approached.

'Will you take soup, sir?' Mrs St John enquired.

Lettie was gazing at the back of the head of the man at the top of the table and thinking that he had lovely thick hair, although it could do with a tidy from the barber. He turned and glanced at the tureen and then at Lettie. Her eyebrows shot up. It was Mr Boyer.

His serious expression turned to one of consternation but he recovered his composure quickly and spoke tersely to Mrs St John. 'What is this girl doing here, madam?'

'She's my new maid, sir.'

He took his napkin from his lap, placed it on his waiting soup cup and sat back in his chair. 'She is not. She cannot stay.'

Lettie stood mortified and embarrassed as Mrs St John stammered a little and then said, 'Very well, sir.'

Mr Boyer rose to his feet and apologised to the others. 'Please excuse me, gentlemen. This is unexpected and I must deal with it.'

'But must you do it now, Boyer?' one of the others complained. 'We are all of us hungry.'

'I assure you that Lady Letitia would not want this girl in Waterley Hall.'

He relieved Lettie of the tray without looking at her and took it back to the sideboard. Mrs St John appeared unsure of what to do next. She said, 'Mr Boyer, forgive me, sir, but I only have a cook and kitchen maid in the house.'

'You may place all the dishes on the sideboard and we shall serve ourselves. This girl must leave Waterley Hall immediately. Mr Osborne will still be at work in the orangery. Send the kitchen maid to find him and he will escort her to Boundary Farm.'

'Very well, sir.' Mrs St John took a firm grip on Lettie's elbow and steered her towards the screen and door to the back stairs. As soon as they were out of earshot, she hissed, 'What have you done?'

'Nothing, honestly.'

'Well, he knows you from somewhere so you must have done something.' Mrs St John took her to the kitchen, pushed her into a corner and sent the kitchen maid to find Mr Osborne. Then she had a conversation with the cook, which Lettie could not hear.

Lettie was cross. She had done nothing wrong. Mr Boyer knew her from Boundary Farm only and Mrs Osborne had explained who she was. Oh, and there was the misunderstanding outside the inn with Thomas, and their exchange at Grandfather's graveside. Was this because of who her grandfather was? Lettie thought incredulously.

It has to be, she reflected. Grandfather was one of His Lordship's favourites. If Mr Boyer was one of Lady Laughton's trustees then he was duty bound to champion her cause and discredit His Lordship's supporters.

Lettie experienced a profound sense of disappointment. When Mr Boyer had been at Grandfather's grave and she'd told him about Gran, he had been contrite and she'd seen a flash of kindness and sympathy that . . . that she had cherished. Now that was gone. She was, once again, someone he despised because of who she was. Dear Lord, she prayed, who am I? Help me to find my father – and myself.

Mrs St John returned. 'Come with me,' she directed.

Lettie followed the housekeeper to her sitting room. It was comfortably furnished with a good fire in the grate and she invited Lettie to sit in one of the upholstered fireside chairs.

Mrs St John took the other and said, 'I've nothing against you, but I'm ordered to stay with you until Mr Osborne takes you away. You'd best tell me everything.'

Lettie told her about crossing Mr Boyer's path at Boundary Farm.

'Is that all?' the housekeeper commented.

Lettie grimaced and went on. 'I ran into him in the Waterley church graveyard and he was . . . well, he was bothered when he found out who my grandfather was.' The housekeeper frowned so she added, 'He worked for Lord Laughton when His Lordship was a young man.'

'Who was your grandfather?'

'Seth Hargreaves. He was butler when Lord Laughton

251

arrived here, and later his house steward. It was years ago. My grandmother told me.'

'Oh, that explains it.' The housekeeper appeared to relax and raised her eyes towards the ceiling. 'Those gentlemen are Her Ladyship's representatives.'

Lettie was very conscious of why she had come here in the first place and took advantage of the moment. 'I never met my grandfather. Do you know anything about him?'

Mrs St John shook her head. 'If it was in Lord Laughton's day it was before my time here. Anyway, if your grandfather was one of His Lordship's staff, Her Ladyship would have got rid of him. She cleared out all his servants after His Lordship left her.'

'Is . . . was Her Ladyship Lady Letitia, then?'

'She liked us to call her that. She was Lady Laughton by rights but it was common knowledge that she hated His Lordship, especially after he went off with . . . well, after he went off. She wouldn't have folk use his name in her hearing. Now, I expect the last of us will be given notice when His Lordship comes home.'

Lettie blew out her cheeks. 'What a waste of a beautiful house and grounds. They had all the money they needed so why couldn't they be happy here, living with each other?'

The housekeeper shrugged. 'Because she was older than His Lordship, I suppose. They never had any children. It's children that make a marriage in my opinion.'

'And love,' Lettie murmured.

She hadn't said it for the housekeeper's ears but she

heard her. 'Oh, there was love all right,' Mrs St John responded caustically. 'If we believe what Lady Letitia told us, His Lordship loved *her* shipyards and *his* women.'

Women? Not just one floozy then, Lettie thought. Perhaps Grandfather had been the same? That would explain why Gran described him as wicked. And Grandfather had had an attractive young wife in Gran. Poor Gran.

Mrs St John went on, 'That's what rich folk do to get richer. They marry more money.'

'But husbands don't get to keep their wives' money these days.'

'That's right. Half of Waterley Hall belonged to Lady Letitia and His Lordship wants all of it back.'

Well, he'll have it, Lettie thought, now that his wife has died, unless, of course, she's left it to someone else. Lettie's curiosity got the better of her discretion.

'Who are those gentlemen upstairs?'

'You do have a lot of questions, don't you?'

'Well, Mr Boyer has been staying at Boundary Farm for a while now. He's come all the way from Canada.'

'I'm not sure where he fits in. The other two are from Her Ladyship's bank and one of them is a legal man.' There was the sound of heavy boots in the passage and Mrs St John stood up. 'That's Mr Osborne. You'll leave with him now.' She sighed. 'I'm sorry you can't take the position here. You have the right manner and I could do with a useful pair of hands.'

'I should like to talk to you about your early days here, Mrs St John. Can I visit you?'

'No you cannot! You heard Mr Boyer. Her Ladyship, God rest her soul, would turn in her grave.'

'Was her name really Letitia?'

Mrs St John ignored her question and addressed the gardener. 'Don't come into my sitting room in your boots.' She grasped Lettie's arm and pushed her out of the door. 'Just take this one home with you.'

Lettie went out into the evening air with the taciturn Mr Osborne, her mind in turmoil. She attempted conversation. 'They're a rum lot at Waterley Hall, that's for sure.'

He did not comment.

'Mr Boyer is one of Her Ladyship's trustees.'

Still he made no response.

'I hope I haven't made you late for your tea. I didn't do anything wrong, you know. It's Mr Boyer, he's taken against me.'

'Aye,' he said. That was all.

She did not linger at Boundary Farm, but apologised to Mrs Osborne for causing her any embarrassment. 'Mr Boyer was there,' she explained, 'and you know what he thinks of me.'

Mrs Osborne raised her eyebrows and turned to her husband. 'You never said he had business at the big house.'

'Nowt to do wi' me,' he replied and went outside again.

'I am sorry,' Lettie repeated.

'You'd best get off home, m'ducks, and keep your visits to Tuesday and Friday like before.'

Lettie was frustrated but agreed. Anyway she had a question for the Reverend, which she presented him with in his study after breakfast the following day.

'Do you have my birth certificate in Gran's papers?' she asked.

'I have searched for it and it's not there.'

'It must be somewhere.'

'What do you want to see it for?'

'It's my name, that's all. Is it really Lettie?'

'Why would it be anything else?'

'It might be short for something.'

'Such as?'

'Well, Letitia, for example.'

'It's possible. But I do baptisms for babies called Maggie and not Margaret or Beth instead of Elizabeth. You may have been baptised Lettie.'

'Baptised! Of course! Did you baptise me as a baby? It will be in chapel records.'

'I didn't. Your grandmother assured me you were already baptised when you arrived.'

'Well, it would have been a chapel baptism and not the parish church. Is there any way I can find out, sir?'

The Reverend widened his eyes and spread his hands. 'Short of searching every Methodist chapel baptism record in Yorkshire, no, and that assumes you were baptised in Yorkshire.'

'Then that's what I shall do.'

'Your birth will be registered, my dear. I can make enquiries on your behalf.'

'Oh, would you? Thank you, sir.'

'Letitia, you think? Where have you got that idea from?'

'Lady Laughton was called Letitia. I . . . I thought I might have been named after her.'

'Now why on earth would you think that?'

'It's what you said about my father. You don't suppose that . . . that he and Lady Laughton were – you know – that I could be her . . . her . . .' She dare not say what was on her mind but the Reverend was not stupid.

He finished the sentence for her. 'Do you seriously believe that your father had an illicit affair with Lady Laughton?' She had not seen him quite so shocked with her before. But it was a stupidly fanciful notion and now she felt foolish.

He stood up, clearly alarmed. 'Put that outrageous idea right out of your head. It has no credence whatsoever! Your grandmother assured me that you had a mother and father and they were married; to each other.'

'I'm sorry,' she said.

'Sit down, Lettie.' He resumed his position behind his desk. 'I was not planning to tell you this until I had more information but I can see that these questions are eating away at your rationale. You are normally such a well-balanced young woman.'

A nervous tremble clutched at Lettie's heart. 'What have you found out, Reverend? Please tell me.'

'I have received a reply from Lady Laughton's representatives with an address that might be of help.'

'You have an address for my father?'

'No, I'm afraid not. Records were not kept as well as they ought to have been after Lord Laughton left and there were several upheavals amongst the servants. Their records show only one Hargreaves and he was Seth Hargreaves, house steward. They did not have a butler. It seems that your grandfather continued in that role as well.'

Lettie was disappointed until the Reverend went on, 'However, they did have the names of footmen employed by your grandfather, all of whom resigned or were let go when Lord Laughton left.'

'They may have known my father!'

'It is possible. I shall make further enquires. Do not raise your hopes at this stage. They did locate a forwarding address for a footman, a fellow called Powell, but it is from many years ago. I expect that he has moved on from there. However, I shall write at once to find out before you get any more of your silly ideas.'

Lettie didn't think it was silly. These things happened in great houses. She thought it was perfectly feasible that the lady of house, if disliked and rejected by her husband, might have had an affair with a handsome young servant and subsequently given birth to a child who was brought up on the estate. Except . . . She realised the flaw in her thinking. Her Ladyship had been much older than her husband and probably too old to bear children. Yes, it had been a silly idea.

'Will you tell me what the letter says, sir, so that I may help?'

'Not until I have made further investigations about this gentleman. The church is a useful organisation for such enquiries.'

Lettie had to be content with waiting and she tried her best to be patient. But she could not sleep that night. If her father was still alive, she had to know where he was and this Mr Powell might have the answer. A sense of urgency overtook her. She must find him before it was too late. Dear heaven, it might already be too late! But he may have told stories to his family, tales of his time in service at Waterley Hall. Someone might remember!

She gazed at the ceiling in the darkness. There was a bright moon – a hunter's moon. It kept dimming behind clouds and while she counted seconds for it to reappear she decided to start her search that minute. The house was silent. She crept on to the landing in her slippers and robe, listened for the soft steady snoring of the Reverend, and then stole downstairs first to the scullery for a candle and, quiet as a mouse, into the Reverend's study.

She found the letter, which came from the Waterley Hall land agent who had access to estate papers. The request had been passed on to him from Lady Laughton's lawyers.

The footman's name was Powell and he had removed to Mereside Lodge, Forest Chase, Yorkshire, NR. Yorkshire! It was a big county and NR was North Riding. There was no indication of the position he took up at Mereside Lodge. But the Hall had kept his records, which, Lettie guessed, indicated that he had been a respected servant, deserving of a reference then or later.

Was he still at Mereside Lodge? Was he still alive? She could barely wait until morning to act on this information.

The following day she walked into town with her shopping basket for the market and took a detour to the railway station where she asked the ticket clerk if she could catch a train to Forest Chase.

Chapter 19

'Forest Chase, miss? Yes, it's Harrogate way. You go from here to Sheffield and then change onto the line for Leeds and York. It'll stop at Mereside Halt, Forest Chase and then Stainthwaite.'

'Mereside Halt? What's at Mereside Halt?'

The ticket collector took off his peaked cap and scratched his brow. 'Mereside Halt? I don't rightly know these days, miss. There used to be a hunting lodge before the railway line opened. Set by a lake for fishing, I believe; the Mere, they called it.' He shrugged. 'It must still be there but we don't get many folk from these parts asking for it. Is that where you want to go?'

'How much will it cost?'

'First or third class, miss?'

She had her allowance from the Reverend, more than

enough for several third-class tickets. She walked away pensively, wondering what to do next. It was a long way to Mereside Halt and if she did go by railway train she would have to travel alone. But they had guards on the train to look after you and it was the twentieth century.

If only Thomas still worked at the Adley's stall on the market. She could go and ask him about travelling on railway trains and if he'd heard of Mereside Lodge. She needed a friend to talk to but didn't want to mention her search to anyone from chapel. They wouldn't understand and, anyway, nothing might come of it. Besides, if the Reverend found out he would be cross. He had been so wise and kind to her, she didn't want to disappoint him again.

As she came out of the railway station she noticed the gritty frontage of the coal merchant's office with the coal yard behind where goods trains from the pithead unloaded. It belonged to Toogoods now. Mr Toogood was setting up all over the Riding, wherever he saw an opportunity. She peered through the wrought-iron gates but there was no sign of Thomas or his wagon. A small mountain of coal waited to be bagged and a couple of hefty men were shovelling it into sacks on a weighbridge.

'Is Thomas here?' she called through the railings.

They stopped, straightened and wandered over. 'Who are you, then?' one replied. He grinned at her cheekily and his teeth contrasted sharply with his grimy skin.

'I'm looking for Thomas. He drives the lorry.'

'Aye, we know who Thomas is. What do you want him for?'

'I want to talk to him.'

'What about?'

'I think that's my business, not yours.'

'Ooh, touchy, aren't we?'

The other man said, 'He's out on the wagon. Ask in yon office. Gaffer'll know when he's due back.' He inclined his head towards the small sooty brick building that housed the merchant's office in the corner of the yard.

'Thanks.'

The door to the office opened directly onto the roadway, with another door at the back that led to the coal yard.

The gaffer was a small man with hardly any hair on his head and a pair of spectacles perched on his nose. He was sitting at a worn writing table. 'Yes, miss. What can I do for you?'

'Can you tell me when Thomas will be back?'

He pushed his pencil behind his ear and took a long look at her. 'I can but I don't see why I should. Have you come on behalf of your mistress?'

'No, sir. I'm not a customer. I'm a friend of Thomas's and I want to talk to him about something.'

'Not in my time, you don't. He finishes at half past six.'

She couldn't wait that long. The station ticket office might be closed by then. 'It's very important,' she said. 'I could talk to him while he waits for the wagon to be loaded.'

The gaffer took hold of his pencil again and looked down at his papers. 'Half past six, miss. Good day to you.'

She stood and watched him add up his figures for a moment then turned for the door. As she lifted the latch she heard him say, 'Who shall I say wants him?'

She swivelled around. He had not looked up from his invoices. 'Lettie Hargreaves,' she answered. 'Thank you, sir.' He still didn't look up and she left without another word.

It was a big decision to make without speaking to anyone about it but she did. She went back to the railway station ticket office and enquired about journey times then purchased a third-class ticket to Mereside Halt. Her intention was to go there the next day. She would be very late getting home and racked her brain to think of what she would tell the Reverend to explain her absence. Her grandmother had always taught her to tell the truth. But Gran had not always practised what she preached, if only by omission. Lettie considered this option. It reminded her of Mr Boyer's words about telling the truth and she couldn't decide whether she would be right or wrong. Mr Boyer would know everything about travelling and she wished he was here so that she could ask him.

She was beginning to understand why he was so set against her. It was probably for the same reason that Gran was so set against her grandfather and Lord Laughton. Even so, where was her father in all this? The now-familiar sense of urgency to find him overtook her. If she found this Mr Powell, and he had, indeed, been a footman at Waterley Hall he might be able to tell her about her mother too! This was something she had never, ever, even in her wildest flight of fancy, imagined was possible.

Every time her thoughts turned to Mr Powell, she felt an excitement bubble inside her, a thrill that shivered through her body and buzzed in her head. She might find out something, anything, about who she really was, and perhaps why she couldn't settle at the mission in the same way that Gran did. She prayed feverishly that Mr Powell was still alive and living in the North Riding.

Lettie completed her market shopping making extra purchases she thought she might need on her journey, and hurried home anxious to prepare for her long day of travelling. The Reverend was out at a meeting where he would be given supper afterwards and would not return until late. The temporary housekeeper had prepared a tray for Lettie and left it on the kitchen table with some soup on the range. As she washed up afterwards, Lettie realised that she would not see either of them in the morning before she left to catch the early-morning train to Sheffield. She sat down, thought long and hard, and wrote a note for the Reverend to say where she had gone and what time she would be home and asked him to forgive her impatience. The dining table was already laid up for his breakfast and she placed her folded sheet of paper on top of his table napkin.

She was amazed that she slept at all because she was frightened of not waking up in time. But she was exhausted from excitement and she must have dozed as she didn't hear the Reverend come in. She woke very early before the hall clock chimed five and dared not turn over for another half-hour in case she overslept. So she dressed quietly and crept downstairs with her small carpet bag already half full of items for the day. She added food from the pantry and let herself out of the back kitchen door. At the railway station she sat and yawned in the waiting room until the train arrived.

Sheffield railway station was big and she had to go over a footbridge to another platform for the York train. It was crowded. Factory men and women crammed into the third-class carriages only to spill out a few stops down the line for the mills and factories where they worked. Lettie got a seat but it was none too clean and very hard on her bottom. She felt grubby and dishevelled when, much later, she alighted with her bag at Mereside Halt.

The guard walked along the platform calling, 'Mereside Halt.' Lettie climbed out quickly in case the carriage started to move again but she needn't have. The guard was heaving large wickerwork hampers out of his guard's van and arranging them on the platform. After he had waved his flag and climbed aboard, the platform was deserted. Steam from the engine cleared and she was totally alone, except for the hampers, secured by leather straps and neatly stacked.

Mereside Halt did not have a ticket office or a waiting room and lavatory. It was simply a painted wooden fence separating the platform from a track through the trees that she hoped connected with a road around the corner. For the first time Lettie thought that this journey might not be a very wise undertaking after all.

If Mereside Lodge was a hunting lodge as the ticket officer had said, they would, of course, send a carriage or a motor car to collect visitors from the railway train.

Even a servant might be met by one of the outdoor staff with a cart. She was neither visitor nor servant, and she was uninvited. She unlatched the gate in the fence, went through and closed it behind her.

It was, actually, a very pleasant morning. A warm sun was out, lighting up trees and shrubs that had never been dulled by smoke from factory chimneys. Birds were chirruping around her and the ground was dry underfoot. She threaded her way through woodland to find a well-hidden spot to relieve herself. She had a damp flannel in her bag wrapped in a piece of oilcloth and used it to wipe over her face and hands. Then she adjusted her corset, smoothed down her skirt, re-pinned a few stray locks of hair and emerged on the track feeling fresher.

There has to be a proper road at the end of the track, she thought as she set off with a determined stride. There was and she stood for several minutes looking in both directions for any sign of humanity. Then she heard the steam whistle of a train, another one, approaching the Halt. Perhaps it will stop and set down a passenger! She hurried back down the track and waited. It came from the York direction and a young woman let herself out of third class. She was smartly dressed in a maroon skirt and a dark grey fitted jacket with a jaunty little hat perched high on her fashionably piled-up hair.

'Excuse me, miss,' Lettie said as she went by, 'are you going to Mereside?'

'I am. Have you been sent to meet me?'

'No, I'm afraid not. I'm a stranger to these parts and

I was hoping you were familiar with the area and could show me the way.'

'Are you here for the wedding, then? I am.'

'No, I came from . . . from Sheffield for the day. It's my first visit to Mereside.'

'Oh, I was born here,' the young woman replied airily. 'I live in York now.'

'May I walk with you?' Lettie asked.

'If you want to; who do you know here?' The young woman didn't wait for an answer. 'I know most folk in Mereside, 'cos my mam does for the vicar's wife and my dad's the sexton.'

They were church people! Lettie felt comfortable in her presence. 'Is Mereside Lodge the vicarage then?'

'Mereside Lodge? I'm talking about Mereside Church in the village.'

Lettie was confused. 'Oh, Mereside is a village.'

The young woman frowned. 'Ye-e-es. What did you think it was?'

'The ticket clerk told me it was a hunting lodge by a lake.'

'Ooooh, you mean Mereside Lodge up the hill. The lake's the other side of it. It used to be a hunting lodge years ago before they built the railway line. At least, that's what my dad says.' The woman paused and took a closer look at Lettie. 'They'd have sent a carriage for you if they were expecting you. Who are you?'

'I'm looking for Mr . . . er . . . I'm looking for the butler or the housekeeper.'

The young woman blew out her cheeks. 'Are you going

for a position there? Well, I don't want to put you off but my ma wouldn't have me anywhere near the place. She's not a prude or anything because she lets me stay in lodgings and work in a draper's shop in York, but she wouldn't let me go to Mereside Lodge.'

Lettie wondered why and frowned, an expression that the young woman misunderstood totally. 'Don't get the wrong idea of me. I haven't been dismissed or anything. They've let me have a day off today to be maid of honour at my sister's wedding.' The young woman quickened her pace. 'I've got to rush. There's a lot to do. When we get to the road, you go the opposite way to me. Good job it's nice weather 'cos it's a long walk. Actually, I'd go back to the Halt if I were you and wait for the cart from the Lodge. It'll be along to collect the hampers soon.' She broke into a run. 'I've got to dash. Ta-ra.'

'Ta-ra,' Lettie called to her back, 'and thank you.' She retraced her steps for a second time, wondering what was so unseemly about taking a position in a hunting lodge; unless it wasn't a hunting lodge any more. If much of the forest had been swallowed up by the railway line it may simply have reverted to a gentleman's country residence.

When she reached the Halt she went back to the platform and looked more closely at the labels tied to the rope handles with string. They were addressed to *Mereside Lodge, Mereside Halt,* but they were printed with details of the senders — big stores in Leeds and Sheffield with names that Lettie had heard of. Goodness, she thought, you didn't shop at those places without deep pockets. She didn't have to wait much longer before a horse and cart arrived to pick up the hampers and she asked the driver to take her with him to the house.

He was a stocky, ruddy-faced countryman, wearing thick outdoor trousers and a long battered jacket that had deep poacher's pockets. 'They never told me I had a passenger,' he said.

'I'm not expected.'

'No and you're not a guest either. They'd have sent a carriage for you. Who are you and what do you want?'

'I have business with a Mr Powell, if he still resides there.'

'He doesn't like unexpected nosy parkers and neither do I. You could be one of them newspaper men.'

That means he exists and he is still here! Lettie made a supreme effort to contain the exciting thrill that spread through her.

'Well, quite clearly I am not,' she said reasonably. 'I was, until very recently a . . . a housekeeper in a manse.'

'Oh, well, if you're here for a position, you'll be welcome if only by us lot. Can you climb up yourself?'

'Of course.'

'Go and get on the cart, then,' he replied, and waved her away.

The horse had moved a little way down the track to graze and had taken the cart with him. Lettie scrambled aboard but the driver was such a long time that she climbed down again to go back and offer her help. He was bending over one of the hampers buckling the leather straps that secured it.

'Can I assist you in any way?' she called.

'You can mind your own business,' he answered, rather rudely she thought, and started to drag the hampers towards the gate in the fence. She held the bridle as he hoisted them onto the cart then climbed up beside the driver. He didn't voice his thanks or attempt conversation so Lettie decided to stay silent as well. The horse plodded down the track and along the road to Mereside Lodge.

It was a pretty country house, large but not palatial, built of stone with some half-timbered elevations and gabled windows in the roof. The roof itself was tile, not slate, a warm red that nestled comfortably in the surrounding trees. A high stone wall stretched in both directions to right and left of the house until it disappeared into the trees. Bee boles containing woven straw beehives punctuated the wall at regular intervals.

'Whoa.' The surly driver stopped his cart. 'This is where you get off.'

'Oh! Shouldn't I go in the servants' entrance?'

'All newcomers have to go in that door.' He jerked his thumb in the direction of a sturdy but small wooden door at one end of the building. It was not the main front door. That was in the middle and protected by a porch with more red tiles on its pitched roof.

She climbed down, reached for her bag and muttered, 'Thank you.' The driver flicked the reins and the horse moved on. Lettie watched the cart disappear down a track by the wall, which, she presumed, led to a gateway. A few birds flew around twittering in the still air and Lettie sensed an atmosphere of quiet tranquillity about the house.

She straightened her shoulders and walked purposefully towards the small door.

As she passed the porch she noticed it had a beautiful red, black and white tiled floor laid in decorative pattern, but it was sorely in need of a good scrub and polish. Perhaps the owner was elderly like Lady Laughton and the servants were taking advantage. Certainly if Mr Powell was still here he would be of advanced years. The windows at this end, the servants' entrance she assumed, needed a coat of paint and there was a patch of green moss high on the stone wall beneath a dip in the guttering. She pulled at the wrought-iron ring and waited, staring at the graining on the small oak door. A maidservant answered, which surprised Lettie for she had been expecting a footman. The maid was a young woman, not a girl, of her own age perhaps if not older.

'Good morning, miss,' Lettie said. She had already decided to be totally honest about who she was and what she wanted. 'My name is Miss Hargreaves and I am looking for a Mr Powell.'

The maid's eyes rounded. 'Is he expecting you?' As an afterthought she added, 'Madam.'

He's here, Lettie thought excitedly. He's still alive and he lives here! She took a deep breath to quell her nervousness. 'I am afraid not but I am prepared to wait if he will see me.'

The maid's mouth turned down at the corners. 'He won't see you today. We're expecting Lord— I mean we are expecting an important guest.' She took a closer look at Lettie, taking in her boots, skirt, coat and hat, and went on slowly, 'And only the one party is due. Are you one of his servants?'

Lettie shook her head. 'If Mr Powell is busy, may I speak with the housekeeper?'

The maid grimaced.

Lettie glanced at the high wall stretching in both directions and hiding access to the domestic offices and suggested, 'Shall I go round to the servants' entrance?'

'No!' The maid chewed on her lip. 'If you're not with His Lordship's party and you haven't got an appointment you'll have to leave.' She began to close the door.

Lettie took a step forward onto the threshold and the door stopped against her boot. 'I've come a long way on the railway train and it's vital that I speak to Mr Powell.'

The maid frowned at her belligerently. 'He won't see you,' she repeated.

Lettie returned her fighting look. 'I am not going away without speaking to *someone*.'

The maid seemed to struggle with her thoughts for a moment. 'If you wait here, I'll fetch Dr Bretton. What name shall I give?'

Lettie told her and once again faced the closed door, for what seemed like a long time. Her initial euphoria turned to worry that if a doctor was coming to speak to her, Mr Powell might be ill. She prayed he was not. Eventually, the maid returned, opened the door and said, 'Come with me, Miss Hargreaves.'

PART THREE

Chapter 20

Mereside Lodge, Forest Chase, Yorkshire, North Riding

Lettie stepped into a lobby with plain plastered walls and a black and white chequered tiled floor. There were coat hooks on the wall and a small table at the end next to a closed door. Another door was open on one side. It led to the main entrance hall for the house and she glimpsed a square, wood-panelled room with a high wooden counter along one side and a rack of pigeon-holes with hooks on the wall behind it. Keys hung from some of the hooks and there was correspondence waiting in the pigeon-holes. A smartly dressed young man appeared from a room behind the counter and stared at her through the open door.

Lettie had seen this arrangement only once before, in the Waterley Arms in Waterley Edge back home. The Waterley Arms was an old coaching inn and in the game season it was full of visitors on their way to one or other of the Yorkshire estates for the shooting.

This wasn't a private house at all, she realised. It was a country hotel. A very discrete and private hotel, she thought, as she had no inkling of its function when she approached.

The maid pushed her across the entrance hall and into a small sitting room. A brass plate on the door said 'Morning Room'. Lettie's boots were silent on the thick Turkish carpet. 'He'll be along in a minute,' the maid said and left her alone.

It was a long minute for Lettie. The room contained very comfortable, upholstered furniture, bookcases and polished inlaid writing tables. And it had a view of the lake from its bay windows. This was the mere, she realised. Surrounded by trees, Lettie was mesmerised by its tranquil beauty. She stood at the window and watched a skein of geese descend from a clear sky and land on the glassy water, skating along the surface and making ever-expanding ripples.

'Miss Hargreaves? I am Dr Bretton. How may I assist you?' His English was good but he had a foreign accent of some sort. French, possibly, she thought, certainly not a drawl like Mr Boyer.

'I was hoping to speak with Mr Powell,' she replied. 'Will that be possible? I do hope he isn't ill.'

'May I ask the nature of your business with him?'

'Oh, it is a personal matter, sir, and I don't even know if he can help me. You see, I am looking for my father and I believe Mr Powell knew him as a young man.'

Dr Bretton stared at her. 'As a young man, you say? Mr Powell has lived here for many years so how would Mr Powell have known your father?'

'It would be from his time at Waterley Hall. It's in the South Riding near Sheffield and my grand . . .' She hesitated, aware of her grandmother's reaction to digging up the past. 'My father may have been a servant to Lord Laughton at the same time as Mr Powell was a footman.' She swallowed anxiously. 'At least, I think Mr Powell was a footman. He may remember him . . . and . . . and know what happened to him.'

'You are speaking of a very long time ago.'

'Twenty years, I should guess, sir.'

'Well, I'm afraid that I cannot help you. I have no knowledge of Mr Powell's early life. Nor, I suspect, have any of the people here.'

'Is Mr Powell ill, sir? I really should like to speak to him.'

Dr Bretton shook his head. 'That is quite impossible, Miss Hargreaves. I'm afraid you have had a wasted journey.'

Lettie could have wept with disappointment. She was exhausted from her travelling and had been tense with expectation. In spite of the Reverend's warnings she had allowed her hopes to be raised and now they were dashed.

Her voice trembled. 'He isn't going to die, is he? He can't! Not before I've had a chance to ask him about my father! I've prayed for Mr Powell to be still alive and to remember him. He's my only hope.' She swallowed a threatening sob.

'He is your only hope for what, Miss Hargreaves?'

She must have sounded garbled. But the strain of losing Gran, finding out about her father and then this journey all alone had taken its toll on Lettie's nerves. 'My grandmother told me my parents were dead, you see, but after she passed away Reverend Ennis – he's my guardian – told me that my father might still be alive and . . . and this Mr Powell left Waterley Hall about the same time as my father. You see, when Lord Laughton went to live abroad, Lady Laughton got rid of all his servants.'

Lettie shuddered. Her nerves were in shreds. Anxiety and exhaustion on top of her grief now got the better of her. Her throat closed and tears threatened. She fumbled in her coat pocket for a handkerchief to wipe her nose. 'Please excuse me, sir,' she muttered.

She was aware that Dr Bretton was watching her as he waited for her to compose herself. Finally, he stood up and said, 'I'll ask my nurse to speak to you.'

A nurse! Lettie was startled back to her senses. Oh, goodness me! Did Mr Powell need a nurse? He must be very ill. 'I'm too late,' she wailed. 'He's going to die, isn't he?' The misery and distress must have shown on Lettie's face because the doctor stood up and came over to her chair and looked closely at her face.

'You cannot stay here, Miss Hargreaves. Nonetheless, I can see that you are fatigued from your journey. You may rest on the couch until Miss Fanshaw is available. However, you must promise not to stir from this room.'

'I promise, sir. Thank you, sir.'

'Miss Fanshaw is very busy but she is well acquainted with Mr Powell. She may be able to help you.'

278

Lettie was trembling with anticipation. She had come this far. Even if it took her all day she was determined to find out whether Mr Powell had known her father. She gazed out of the window for a long time then stood up to examine a glass-fronted bookcase. It contained leather-bound volumes in sets, grouped according to their author. Some were tales of adventures in parts of the world Lettie had barely heard of. But others were novels by Mr Scott, Mr Dickens and Mr Hardy.

She recognised some of the titles and was tempted to take one out and read as she waited. *Tess of the D'Urbervilles* was there! Gran had said it was 'not fit for decent folk' and she shouldn't read it, which only made Lettie want to read it more and she had to wait a long time for the lending library copy. Poor Tess. She thought she was someone she wasn't and was duped by a gentleman who took advantage of her innocence.

As a child, Lettie had not been concerned about who she was. But now the need to know was dominating her life. It had become an itch that she couldn't scratch and it was always there, controlling her actions. She stood by one of the writing tables, drumming her fingers on its surface. Finally, the door to the morning room opened and the young woman who had answered the front door came in with a tray. 'I've brought you some refreshment, miss. Dr Bretton said that you may have a long wait and to make sure you had everything you needed.'

'Thank you. I should like to read if I may.'

'Of course you may. The bookcase isn't locked. There's a bell-pull by the fireplace if you want anything else.'

This maid was about the same age as herself and Lettie thought she detected a little sympathy in her eyes. 'Is Mr Powell very ill?' she asked.

The maid did not have to stop and think about her reply. 'Miss Fanshaw will answer your questions.'

But Lettie wasn't put off. 'You can trust me. I'm not from the newspapers or anything.'

The maid hesitated before responding. 'I am not supposed to speak to you.'

She remembered what the young woman at the Halt had told her. She could be in a house of ill-repute! Lettie looked pointedly at the tray and then back to the maid's face. 'Well, I shall have to trust you if I drink that. It could be drugged and you could be part of the white slave trade for all I know!'

'We most definitely are not!' The maid was, quite clearly, appalled and her dark eyes flashed. 'How dare you make such a suggestion,' she hissed.

Lettie immediately regretted her outburst. 'I'm sorry, but, please, you have to understand that I'm looking for my father and I believe Mr Powell knew him as a young man.'

Lettie saw that the maid wavered before answering. But her response was firm. 'I'll lose my position if I say anything about anybody here. But I can tell you this: don't believe the village gossip because they're wrong. Mereside Lodge is a respectable establishment and I am proud to be employed here.' She opened the door to leave, paused on the threshold and pointed to the tray. 'And that is very good. It's Dr Bretton's own restorative and you don't want to know how much we charge for it.'

She was gone from the room before Lettie could press her further. Lettie sat down for her 'tea'. It was very welcome. When she poured it from the pot it was an unusual khaki colour and the debris in the tea strainer was definitely not tea leaves. It was similar to one of the herbal infusions that Gran used to make to calm her nerves. The tray had honey and not sugar as a sweetener. From the beehives, she guessed. She tried a little of it on a spoon and it was delicious – and scented, she noticed. There were two dark-coloured baked biscuits on a matching tea plate. Lettie picked one up and sniffed it. It had a crest baked into the surface so she reckoned it must be special and, curious, bit into it. It was bland and gritty on her palate. She expected it to be sweeter than it tasted but it wasn't unpleasant. She sampled the brew and had to add all the honey to disguise its bitterness.

She was deciding which book to read when the door opened again and a mature woman dressed in a plain grey gown entered. Lettie would have assumed she was the housekeeper if Dr Bretton had not described her as a nurse.

'Miss Hargreaves? I am Miss Fanshaw. Are you feeling better?'

'Yes thank you, ma'am,' she answered truthfully.

Miss Fanshaw took one of the comfortable armchairs by the window and gestured to an adjacent one. 'Please come and sit down. I understand that you arrived at the

Halt unexpected and alone. If I may say so, that is a foolhardy action for a young woman.'

Perhaps so, Lettie agreed but said, 'I do have a good reason to come here.'

'So I hear. Why don't you tell me?'

Miss Fanshaw had a brisk manner that reminded her a little of Gran. She had a pleasant face, not especially beautiful or pretty but her features were even and although she had the lines of ageing, her skin was exceptionally fine. So much so that it was at odds with her greying hair.

'I'm searching for my father,' she repeated. 'I had been led to believe that he had passed away and found out, only recently, that this may not be true.'

'But why have you come here, Miss Hargreaves?'

'To speak with Mr Powell.'

'How could he possibly be of assistance to you?'

'I believe that he was a servant at Waterley Hall at the same time as my father.'

Miss Fanshaw's face remained composed. 'Assuming that to be true, how did you know that Mr Powell was here?'

'The Waterley estate land agent wrote to my guardian and told him that a Mr Powell took a position here many years ago when he left the service of Lord Laughton.' Lettie noticed surprise register on Miss Fanshaw's face. But she did not interrupt. 'It was about the same time as my father left. Lord Laughton went abroad and his servants had to find other places.'

Miss Fanshaw looked at her with widened eyes for a

moment then she seemed to compose herself and her features relaxed. 'They told you that he took a position here?'

Lettie thought that she almost smiled and responded eagerly. 'He would have been a footman, I think.' She raised her eyes to the decor and spread her hands. 'He may even have been the butler here. Mereside Lodge is a beautiful residence but it is much smaller than Waterley Hall.'

Lettie waited for a response of any sort and received only another silence.

'Mr Powell might remember where my father went.' Lettie stopped speaking again and wished Miss Fanshaw would say something – anything to indicate how she was reacting to Lettie's story. She wondered whether to mention her grandfather or not and decided that perhaps the whole truth was needed here. 'Of course with Waterley Hall being so big Lord Laughton had a steward. He was my grandfather, Seth Hargreaves. Mr Powell will surely remember him.'

Miss Fanshaw held up both her hands in a desperate gesture. 'You need not go on, Miss Hargreaves. You are very convincing.'

'You believe me?'

'I did not say that. Mereside Lodge is a very exclusive establishment and we pride ourselves on protecting the privacy of our . . . our visitors. I cannot tell you anything about anyone here.'

Lettie sagged into the chair. 'But I only wish to ask Mr Powell if he knows where my father went. You could ask him for me.'

'How do I know you are not a newspaper correspondent?'

Lettie was taken aback that anyone would think she was capable of such a situation. 'Well, I am not a gentleman for a start!'

'No, I do not believe an editor has sent you. But who are you really? You have wheedled your way in here no doubt looking for some titbit of information to whip up into a scandal.'

'I have told you the truth!'

'Our visitors require privacy, Miss Hargreaves, and if you knew anything at all about Mereside Lodge you would realise that our discretion is everything. You will not move from this room until I have arranged for you to be taken back to the Halt in good time for the railway connection to Leeds.'

Lettie's thoughts were tumbling to make sense of this information. Mereside Lodge wasn't a country hotel. It was a clinic of some sort. No wonder she couldn't get past the front entrance! Mr Powell was a patient here. She had so many questions but for the moment she could only hope that he would get better. After a weighty silence she said, 'Very well, Miss Fanshaw. Thank you for seeing me. May I leave a letter for when Mr Powell is well enough to read it?'

'You ought to have written in the first place.'

Miss Fanshaw was right and Reverend Ennis had advised her to wait. But neither of them was her, and had just discovered she had been deceived all her life by someone she loved and trusted. 'May I?' she repeated.

Miss Fanshaw waved her arm at a writing desk underneath one of the casement windows. 'You may. I shall send a maid to sit with you and escort you back to the Halt.'

Lettie closed the flap on the envelope and leaned back in her chair, satisfied that she had made her request to Mr Powell clear. The writing desk was a beautiful piece of carved mahogany furniture, designed to hold writing implements and an old-fashioned blotting block that she had rocked gently over her letter before folding it. The notepaper and envelopes were fine quality paper, with *Mereside Lodge, Forest Chase, Yorkshire, NR* embossed in blue. She noticed wax and a spirit burner for seals, a practice that was totally unnecessary now people used envelopes fastened with glue. A king or royal duke might seal documents with an imprint of his ring. She picked up the brass seal and examined the end. It was, she thought, an engraving of stag antlers, perhaps from the coat of arms when the house was a hunting lodge.

On impulse, Lettie lit the candle and picked up the stick of red wax. She melted the end and let it drip over the envelope flap to form a blob. Then she pressed the end of the brass seal into it and blew out the candle. It showed that she had written it here and was, she thought, an indication of her serious intentions. When the maid arrived in her hat and coat, Lettie gave her the letter, which she in turn left with the young man in the entrance hall. She then followed the maid to the side door.

'What's your name?' Lettie asked as they walked to the Halt.

'Cutler.'

'I mean your Christian name. I'm Lettie.'

'Agnes Cutler.'

'What is going on here, Agnes? Is it some kind of clinic?'

'I'm not allowed to talk about it.'

'Well, it's a long walk to the Halt, so what shall we talk about?'

Agnes didn't reply. Lettie continued, 'I met a girl from the village at the Halt and she said her mother and father wouldn't let her work at Mereside Lodge.'

'She doesn't know what she's talking about. I don't take any notice of gossip.'

'What do your parents say, then?'

'I haven't got any parents.'

'Are you an orphan, too?' Lettie knew what that felt like. She went on, 'I thought I was until recently. Then I heard my father might still be alive. That's why I'm here.'

'You don't think he's here, do you?'

'No, but how would you feel if you found out your father wasn't dead after all and you had the name of someone who might have known him? Mr Powell was in service with my father. He could help me find him.'

Agnes turned to face her. 'Is that true?'

'Of course it's true. I don't tell lies. I was brought up in a Methodist manse.'

'Did you write that in your letter?'

'Yes. Mr Powell will get to read it, won't he?'

'I don't know. Miss Fanshaw'll probably reply for him.'

'Can he not think for himself?'

'He's fine when he's well, but sometimes when he is not . . . well, we're all anxious about . . . our imminent visitor.'

Lettie sighed. 'It's not the King, is it?' Lettie wasn't really serious but Agnes was. She stopped abruptly and answered firmly. 'No it's not. Can we talk about something else?'

They walked on in silence for a while until Lettie asked, 'Have you worked here since you left the orphanage?'

'I had a position in a well-to-do household first. It was a below-stairs position and I wasn't very happy but I couldn't see a way out until I'd been there long enough for a reference. Then two winters ago a visiting dowager fell ill and needed someone with her round the clock so I was sent upstairs to help.' Agnes seemed to relax as she told her story. 'She was . . . well . . . oh, she was really tiresome. Nothing was ever right and no one else wanted to sit with her so it was always me who had to cope with her.'

'Oh you poor thing, how did you do that?'

'I just tried to do everything she asked and when she complained I always apologised.'

Lettie laughed. 'Is that all?'

'Why is that funny?'

'It sounds so easy but it can't have been.'

'No it wasn't, I can tell you. It paid off, though. When she was feeling better and I was back below stairs, she sent for me and told me if I wanted a better position she could help me. She's a regular patient at Mereside

Lodge. She knows the—' Again Agnes stopped talking abruptly.

A patient? Lettie thought. Her presumption had been correct. It was a clinic. 'Does this lady know Mr Powell?' Lettie asked.

But Agnes reverted to her formal voice. 'I'll see that Miss Fanshaw gets your letter. It's the best you can hope for. Listen, when we reach the track to the Halt, I'll leave you. You'll have a long wait for the train but I have some errands in the village for the patients. The villagers might disapprove of Mereside Lodge but the shopkeepers and the blacksmith make a good living out of us.'

They said goodbye to each other and Lettie was left with the impression that Agnes was more than just a parlourmaid. She walked briskly to the Halt then paced up and down the platform, wrestling with her thoughts. Instead of feeling pleased that she had located Mr Powell and written to him, she was dissatisfied that she had been close to the answers to her questions and was now on her way home. What was she to do with herself while she waited for Miss Fanshaw to reply? And what if she didn't write?

A stack of empty hampers awaited collection and she sat down with her thoughts until she heard the steam whistle of the approaching train. The big black engine hissed to a halt and clouds of steam swirled around the platform. No one alighted apart from the guard. She stood up while he stacked the hampers in his van and then waited patiently for her to climb aboard.

She couldn't do it. She had come so far in such a short

time; she could not leave without answers to her questions.

'All aboard, miss,' the guard called.

Lettie turned smartly away from the train and with a straight back marched through the white gate and away from the platform. She heard the huge steam engine huff and puff, and then grind into motion. It was too late, now, to change her mind and she continued walking, pushing all practical considerations out of her head.

Chapter 21

The road between Mereside Lodge and the village was deserted. She turned towards the village and as she approached it, passed a row of farm workers' cottages with slate roofs and then a pair that were thatched with pretty curtains at the windows and well-kept front gardens. When the green came into view, Lettie realised that Mereside was a well-to-do village with a row of shops along one side of the triangular patch of grassland. A church and school stood on another side and an inn on the third with a blacksmith's forge next door. There was a carriage and pair outside the inn. She was walking past the church when she saw Agnes step out of the draper's shop and join a cluster of women who were intent on chatting. Lettie quickly dodged into the churchyard and behind a yew tree, away from view. She wasn't sure why she was hiding except that it didn't seem sensible for Mereside Lodge to know she had not left as they wished.

She heard organ music from inside the church and remembered the girl off the railway train earlier, home for her sister's wedding. Lettie's heart began to thump. She had no wish to be caught out as a vagrant. Wedding guests would be milling around the churchyard soon. She moved to behind a beech hedge and stayed out of sight until the bride and groom emerged as husband and wife. Eventually, the party moved off and straggled across the green to the inn. It was Church of England and not Methodist but Lettie slipped inside while she worked out what to do. Her immediate reaction was one of delight. The flowers were enchanting, making a plain interior attractive and inviting. She chose a pew in the darkest corner and knelt down to say a prayer.

What had she done? Only stranded herself in a place she did not know! She must be out of her mind and thanked the Lord for keeping her safe until now. It had been a foolish idea to take the train to Mereside Halt in the first place without any sort of invitation or introduction. A young woman travelling alone was asking for trouble and she was lucky that Mereside Lodge wasn't some country hideaway established for race-goers and gamblers. Heavens, it could house activities just as sinister as the white slave trade and she had willingly gone inside! Her thoughts ran riot, but prayers helped. They anchored her jumbled ideas and made sense of her actions. She was determined not to leave Mereside until she had met with Mr Powell. Anything less would mean that she had wasted her journey.

It was cool inside the church and she went out into the sunlight to warm up. Across the green, the wedding party took up everyone's attention and the sun was already in the western sky. The days were getting shorter as autumn approached and with a clear sky the night was likely to be chilly. She hadn't passed a farm or a barn and she didn't know how much a night in the inn would cost.

There might be someone in the village who took in lodgers but she would have to knock on doors and ask. It was that or a church pew for her bed tonight! A landlady would, quite reasonably, wish to know her business in Mereside and what could she say? Certainly not 'I have business with Mr Powell of Mereside Lodge' if she wanted to be seen as respectable! Why hadn't she listened to Reverend Ennis and waited?

Gran had often advised her that a Methodist chapel was the best place to shelter in a storm, whether real or inside her head, and it seemed to Lettie that a church was the next best thing to a chapel. She returned to her shadowy spot and sat on hassocks with her knees drawn up and her back against the cold stone wall, hiding quietly until the vicar returned and went into his vestry to change. He went out again through the main door.

She was in luck. He did not lock the vestry and a winter cloak hung on a hook on the wall next to an umbrella. She wrapped herself in the cloak and returned to her pew, then finished the last of her oatmeal biscuits and apples and tried to sleep. The church clock chimed every quarter of an hour, but she must have dozed for while.

When she woke she felt refreshed. Her leg had gone to sleep and she got up to stretch and walk round. It was eerie in the silent empty building and she was glad of the flowers at the ends of the pews to cheer her. She massaged her leg then returned the cloak to its peg in the vestry. Her eyes were used to the darkness by then and she went outside to look at the clock. It was almost half past one and another four hours at least before folk started moving about.

She sat on a low wall and shivered. She didn't want to go back inside the church and spend the rest of the night huddled on the church floor. She wouldn't freeze to death out of doors at this time of year. But, more importantly she decided to return to Mereside Lodge, to walk back under cover of darkness and, somehow, find her way to the domestic offices at the rear until the household woke up. If she couldn't get to see Mr Powell via the front door, she would find another way.

She jumped at every rustle and squeak at first. But when she became accustomed to the nocturnal comings and goings of small animals and birds she relaxed. Even the fox seemed more scared of her than she was of him, although he did stop and stare at her for a minute.

She became aware of a low rumbling noise a long time before she identified the sound. It was a motor vehicle on the road behind her making slow progress in the dark. She darted off the road into a clump of trees and crouched down as it rumbled passed her. A motor vehicle was an unusual sight out here in the middle of the countryside and this was a delivery wagon like – good heavens! She straightened up, startled by the name on the door. She ran forward for a closer look at the name inscribed on the coachwork. It *was* a Toogoods wagon, just like the one Thomas drove, but it was empty of coal.

As she stared after it, it stopped in the middle of the road and the noise of the engine died away. The door to the driving seat opened and she retreated to the shadows of the trees.

'Wait!' the driver called.

He sounded just like Thomas. Thomas? Surely not?

'Wait,' he repeated, 'I'm looking for someone.'

'Thomas?'

'Lettie? Is that you? Oh, thank God. Are you all right? You're not hurt or anything?'

'No, I'm well. What are you doing here?'

'I'm searching for you! What do you think I'm doing! The foreman back at the yard told me you'd been in the office asking for me and then Reverend Ennis came looking for you.'

'Oh no. I didn't mean to worry him.'

'Well, you did. You left him a letter and he thought I might know more about it. We were all worried about you. Even my foreman got the wind up when the Reverend turned up at the yard. He knew your gran because he used to work at the Waterley Edge pit so he let me take the wagon to find you. What's all this about, Lettie?'

'It was something the Reverend said about my father. He might still be alive, Thomas, and if he is I have to find out.'

'Oh I see. I thought your gran said your parents were dead?'

'Not exactly. She never actually said they were dead, just that they'd gone.' Lettie shuddered suddenly and felt weary.

Thomas took up her hands and rubbed them between his palms. There were rough and covered in calluses but they were large and warm. 'You're cold,' he said. 'Come over here and stand by the engine.'

'You haven't got anything to eat, have you?' she asked.

He reached under the driver's seat and brought out a battered tin box. 'Try one of my mum's pasties.'

'Oh, thank you.'

'I've got some cold tea in a bottle if you're thirsty.'

'Thank you,' she repeated. 'God must be listening to me. I prayed in church for help and here you are. How did you know where I'd be?'

'Reverend Ennis told me what you'd put in your note to him and then the lads in the yard had seen you at the railway station, so I asked about you in the ticket office. What are you doing wandering around in the middle of the night?'

'I've been up to Mereside Lodge. I think it's a private clinic and there's a patient there who might have been at Waterley Hall at the same time as my father.'

'Have you spoken to him?'

'They wouldn't let me see him.'

'Were you surprised? I'm not. You could be anybody.'

'They let me leave a letter for him.'

'Then come home with me until he replies.'

'I can't. I'm too close to give up now.'

'You won't be giving up. You'll be being sensible.'

'I don't want to be sensible! I want to find my father! Nobody understands how it feels to be so close to something you have always wanted. I'm not leaving until I've seen Mr Powell. I'm not.'

'Lettie, you have to. I can't stay with you. I've promised to have the wagon back for morning. If I'm not in the yard at six o'clock loading it with coal, I'll be on my bicycle again.'

'Then you must go home now! You can't lose another job because of me!'

'Well, come back with me, then! I'll ask if I can borrow the wagon on Sunday and bring you over for the day.'

She shook her head. 'You're so kind, Thomas, but I've made up my mind. I am going to see this Mr Powell before I leave.'

'Please, Lettie. Let me take you home.'

She shook her head.

An owl hooted and, in the distance, the church clock chimed. 'It's a long way back, Lettie. I've got to set off now.'

'Then you go. I've already spoken to one of the maids up there. She's an orphan like me and understands why I'm here.'

'You're determined to do this, aren't you?'

'Yes.'

'I'll drive you up to the house then.'

'No, you can't. That thing makes too much noise.'

'Then I'll walk you up there, but *come on*.'

Lettie smiled in the dark. She knew she could rely on Thomas. 'Thank you,' she said. 'Keep to the trees. I want to find my way round to the back.'

The wall around Mereside Lodge stretched as far as Lettie could see it. 'Give me a leg-up over there,' she said. 'There's a tree the other side.'

'Are you sure about this? They might have dogs.'

Lettie hesitated. 'I don't think so. I didn't hear any earlier on.'

'I don't want to leave you.'

'I know what I'm doing. Help me up.'

He cupped his hands and she placed her boot in them, reaching for the top of the wall and hoisting herself up. She sat astride and whispered, 'It's easy. I can climb down the tree.'

'What's on the other side?'

'Just gardens.' She sat there watching for movement or a light. 'It's quiet.' She looked down at Thomas's anxious face. 'Thank you,' she said. 'I'll be all right now. It's a clinic. They take care of people. You'd better be off. Please tell Reverend Ennis that I'm safe and well.'

'But you're not!'

'I am,' she argued. 'As soon as I've spoken to Mr Powell I'll catch the railway train home.'

'Well, I hope this Mr Powell is worth it. I'll call in at the manse to see you on Sunday and if you're not there I'm coming to find you.'

'You're a good friend, Thomas.'

She stayed astride the wall as he walked away. A few minutes later she heard the low rumble of the motor engine and listened as the sound grew fainter and fainter until the air was silent again. She shivered, wavered for a moment, and then dragged herself onto a sturdy branch and climbed carefully down the tree. She brushed the flakes of bark and leaves from her clothes and yawned, suddenly feeling very tired. From the top of the wall she had noticed a summerhouse and she headed towards it. It wasn't locked and contained several pieces of wickerwork furniture. She piled the cushions onto a couple of chairs and placed them facing each other to make a bed. It was more comfortable than the church pew and she slept for a few hours.

Daylight woke her and she sat up quickly, alert for any sounds. But all was quiet. She stretched and yawned, wondering what time it was. There wasn't a soul in sight from the summerhouse windows. Nonetheless, Lettie decided she would be less noticeable if she were round the back of Mereside Lodge where the domestic offices must be situated. She replaced the furniture as she had found it and headed for a section of straggly shrubbery. The garden, she noticed, was neglected and untidy, which was a shame because it was laid out with flower borders and beds and could be quite beautiful.

From the cover of the shrubbery, Lettie was able to see the collection of buildings at the back of the Lodge. The nearest were the stables and coach house and they were as much in need of attention as the garden. But her eyes were drawn to a long building that formed a rear wing of the main house. Lettie identified a boiler room at the end by its chimney stack already giving out smoke. Outside a young man was shovelling coal from a heap into buckets and lining them up by the building. A maid came outside and called him in, presumably for his breakfast.

Lettie was considering her next move when she almost jumped out of her skin as a heavy hand grabbed her shoulder.

'What are you doing nosing around here?' She whirled round to see the surly man who had collected the hampers from the station the day before.

'I . . . I—'

'You come with me.'

His hand stayed firmly on her shoulder and he steered her towards the stabling where a gnarled and stooping stable hand was leading out a pony. 'Who's she?' he asked.

'She's trouble. I got a ticking-off from Fanny for bringing this 'un from the Halt yesterday.'

'Did she see owt?'

'Dunno, but she were supposed to be on her way yesterday so tek her with you when you go down for the hampers. See her into the railway carriage afore, y'know, you check owt. She's got eyes in the back of her head, this one.'

The stable hand grimaced. 'What shall I do wi' her till then?'

'Put her in the tack room and lock the door.'

'You can't do that to me!' Lettie protested. 'I came back to see the housekeeper.'

They ignored her and the gnarled old man let go of his pony, gripped her arm and tugged her in the direction of the coach house.

She tried to shake free and protested, 'I'm not going and you can't make me.'

'Shut up.' The other man gave her a hefty shove in the back.

She stumbled and fell to her knees, causing the old man to jerk sideways, swear and spook the pony. It reared its front legs, snatching the reins from the man's grasp. For a moment both men let go of Lettie, fearful, as she was, of receiving a kick from the frightened beast. Lettie saw her opportunity. She scrambled to her feet and ran in the direction of the coal heap and a door that she knew was open. They didn't follow her and she guessed they were more concerned about the pony than her. But she was left with a distinct impression that both of these men were up to no good.

The boilerman who had been shovelling coal and the maid who had called out to him were just inside the open door lolling against the wall and drinking mugs of tea. They were so interested in each other than they didn't notice her until she was virtually in front of them, catching her breath.

'Good morning,' she said brightly. 'Is the housekeeper's room this way?'

'What housekeeper? We haven't got a housekeeper,' the maid answered. The young man handed his empty mug to her and returned to shovelling coal.

'The butler then or whoever is in charge of the servants. I . . . I'm looking for a position.'

'Are you?' The maid gave her an interested glance. 'Can you start today?'

Lettie did not hesitate. 'Yes.'

'You'll want to see Fanny, then. That's Miss Fanshaw to you.'

Not her, Lettie groaned silently, she'll send me away again. 'Is there no one else I can talk to?' A crashing sound came from inside the house. 'Good heavens! What was that?'

The maid looked miserable. 'It's the scullery maid. The new cook uses her as an assistant cook and the poor girl isn't up to it.'

'Shall I go and help her?'

'Can you cook?' the girl asked.

'Have you got a clean apron? I can make a start in the kitchen while I'm waiting for Miss Fanshaw.'

'Would you? I don't know what Fanny'll say but to be honest if she doesn't get more help in, I'll be off an' all. Follow me.' She started to walk down the passage.

'Are servants always leaving, then?' Lettie asked. But the girl went through a door that she left open and returned a few seconds later with a fresh white apron and a hat.

'I'll put the hat on for you.' It was shaped like a close-fitting bonnet without a brim and had to be pinned to her head, squashing down her piled-up hair. 'Cor, you look different! Go and see what Cook wants. If she asks where I am, tell her I'm helping Agnes.' The girl pointed towards a door opposite and pulled on her own cap as she carried on down the passage towards the green baize door that separated domestic offices from the main house.

The kitchen was a huge high-ceilinged room with walls covered in white tiles. It was filled with the aromatic odour of sausages sizzling on the cooking range. But the light was poor as, Lettie noticed, all the windows needed cleaning. They were opposite the door and looked out on to the coal yard and, beyond that, the stables. Hastily, Lettie closed the kitchen door behind her, wondering if her earlier captors had followed her.

'Good morning, Cook.'

Cook did not turned around from her sausages. 'Where've you been? The men'll be in for their breakfast soon. Pick up those oven trays and lay out the bacon then bring me the frying pans for the eggs.'

Lettie tied on her apron, which, fortunately, covered most of her dress. The long scrubbed table appeared to be divided into three with polished silver serving dishes at one end and older tarnished ones at the other. A bowl of soaked prunes, another full of eggs and a pile of ready-sliced bacon were in the middle directly behind the cook. Lettie arranged the bacon on an oven tray and carried it to the range.

Cook's face was ruddy from the heat. 'Oh, you're new. About time too, what's your name?'

'Lettie.'

Cook examined the bacon and nodded. 'Put that in the top oven. Where are my frying pans?'

Lettie responded swiftly.

'Well, put them on the hotplate then,' Cook said. 'They won't heat up with you waving them around in the air.'

Lettie obeyed. A kettle was bubbling away and she suggested making the tea.

'Yes and carry it into the servants' hall; they'll be gasping for it by now.'

Lettie's recent visit to Waterley Hall had given her an idea of how servants' quarters were organised in a large household and Mereside Lodge wasn't as big. She stood in the passage with the heavy teapot and milk jug on a tray. Someone had closed the outer door and it was dark. But she reckoned that the scullery and pot store was the same side as the kitchen; so the housekeeper's and butler's rooms were likely to be opposite alongside the servants' hall. She stood with aching arms until the green baize door swung open and a liveried footman came through. It was the same one she had seen in the entrance hall yesterday.

Luckily he didn't recognise her in her kitchen maid's cap. 'I'll take that,' he said and did, disappearing through a door opposite as quickly as he had arrived.

Lettie returned to the kitchen and Cook immediately ordered her to take in the prunes and porridge. 'And tell them the bacon's not ready yet.'

Well, this is it, she thought. Someone is bound to recognise me now. As she picked up the bowls of prunes, the maid came in, quite out of breath and said, 'Fanny says Mr Powell wants his breakfast now.'

'Miss Fanshaw to you,' Cook snapped. 'Show this new girl what's needed, then.'

The maid groaned. 'Agnes wants me to help her.'

Lettie glanced at the silverware and linen stacked on

the table. 'I don't need to be shown,' she said and began to lay up one of the silver trays.

'He must be feeling better this morning,' Cook muttered. 'Hand me those dishes for the sausages.' Cook fried a dozen eggs in two huge frying pans and transferred them to shallow earthenware dishes warming on her hotplate. Then she dealt with the bacon before turning round to check Lettie's silver trays. She had completed half a dozen of them.

'Very nice. Have you done this before?'

'My grandmother was a housekeeper in service and she taught me.'

'Very nice,' Cook repeated. 'You'd best keep your apron clean for taking them upstairs. I'll get on with the servants' breakfast.'

'What about Mr Powell's breakfast?'

'It's in that bowl on the dresser. Squeeze the lemons into the glass jug, put three of those biscuits under the dome and fill the silver jug with hot water.'

'Is that all?'

'Dr Bretton's orders.' Cook shook her head. 'I can't see how half-starving a body will help it get well.'

Me neither, Lettie thought. 'Shall I take it up to Mr Powell?'

'Give it to Agnes or Miss Fanshaw then come back for your own breakfast before it gets cold.'

'Which room is he in?' Lettie asked. Her heart was beginning to thump with excitement and fear. She'd be bundled out as soon as she was recognised but there was a chance that she might get to see Mr Powell before that happened and it was worth the risk.

'Facing the lake but his name's on the door.'

'Is that on the first floor?' she asked.

It was and Lettie went out into the passage with Mr Powell's breakfast tray.

Chapter 22

She pushed open the green baize door with her bottom and found herself, as anticipated, at the rear of the entrance hall. She probably should have used the back stairs but she wasn't sure where they were and the entrance hall was deserted. She walked quickly towards the staircase that rose and turned out of sight. It was carpeted. Mereside Lodge had beautiful Turkish carpets in the rooms she had seen. The tray was nowhere near as heavy as those she had carried into the dining room at the manse but she was careful not to spill anything.

At the top of the stairs she turned to her left, past one of the fluted wooden pillars, remembering where the windows were located from outside the Lodge. Guessing which might have the finest view she peered at the white name card sitting in its brass holder on the outside of the door.

Lord Laughton. The shock nearly caused her to drop the tray. Lord Laughton! Here! Her mind raced. Was he ill? Was that the reason he was returning from abroad?

She heard a doorknob turn and huddled with her back to the door hoping she was shielded from view by the pillar. Someone came out of a room on the other side of the stairs and went down to the hall. Lettie leaned forward to see Miss Fanshaw hurrying away. Forgetting Lord Laughton, she crossed the landing to find Mr Powell's room and knocked on the door.

'Come in.' His voice sounded weary.

Lettie's heart was thumping in her mouth as she leaned down to turn the doorknob. Her feet crossed the carpet silently. It was not a huge room but it had a fine bay window that looked out over the lake. The bedroom furniture was heavy mahogany and a fire burned in the grate. Mr Powell was sitting in an upholstered chair at a round table positioned in the bay window. He had his back to her but she noticed that his hair was white. The soft furnishings in the room gave it a hushed comfort that Lettie found calming.

'Your breakfast is here, Mr Powell,' she said quietly.

'Is that you, Agnes? Speak up, will you?' He leaned forward to push some documents to one side.

Against all her grandmother's training of never looking directly at the faces of those you were serving, she did. He was not as old as his white hair indicated although he had lined features and dark shadows around his eyes. He had been handsome, she thought, for he had a straight brow and nose, good cheekbones and jawline, although his sallow skin now sagged. He did not appear to be in good health. His eyes were a dull blue and when he caught sight of her, they opened wide. 'Good God,' he exclaimed, 'you startled me.'

'I beg your pardon, sir.'

'Who the devil are you?'

Every muscle in Lettie's body seemed to seize. She could hardly breathe. She had to be honest. 'I'm a new maid, sir.'

'Oh, I see. Your eyes, the way you speak, it reminded me of—' He stopped and glanced over the tray as she placed it before him. 'No brandy?'

'Shall I fetch you some, sir?'

He gave a short dry laugh. 'You would risk Miss Fanshaw's wrath? You have more courage than I.'

Lettie stood motionless, gathering her courage and formulating the words in her head. As she did, he waved a hand and said, 'That will be all.'

'Very good, sir.' She didn't move. She couldn't. Her legs seemed frozen to the spot. Ask him! What can he do to you? This is your chance, ask him now!

'Mr Powell.' Her voice was light and breathless.

'What is it, girl?' He twisted his head in her direction. 'What do I call you?'

'Mr Powell, please forgive me for this intrusion but I must speak with you. You see, I'm searching for my father and you may have known him as a young man. I believe he was in service for Lord Laughton when you were a footman. Can you help me, sir?'

There, she'd said it, and she had rehearsed it in her head so many times that it came out word perfect and she was satisfied with her delivery. 'Please, sir,' she added. 'You are my only hope.'

Within seconds the room seemed to be in chaos. Mr Powell shot to his feet and turned on her with a terrifying expression of disbelief and horror. 'Who are you?' he cried.

At the same time the bedroom door flew open, Miss Fanshaw rushed in and demanded, 'What are you doing in this house? How dare you come back here? Sneaking in, unannounced, who do you think you are?'

Mr Powell echoed her last question. 'Answer her, girl. Who are you?'

'I'm Lettie Hargreaves,' she answered. 'My grandfather was Seth Hargreaves.'

Mr Powell's face drained of the little colour it had, leaving a pasty, yellowing complexion. He sank into his chair. 'Dear God, is this true? Who sent you here?' There was desperation in his eyes as he turned to Miss Fanshaw. 'Did he send her, Frances? He means to get what he wants, doesn't he? What shall I do?' He looked pleadingly at Miss Fanshaw, whose face Lettie could only describe as a mixture of fury and anguish.

Miss Fanshaw was beside him with one arm across his shoulders and the other covering his hand. 'She's nothing to do with him, Michael,' Miss Fanshaw soothed. 'She's a nobody and I'll get rid of her. Calm down and take your breakfast. Dr Bretton will call in as usual.'

But Mr Powell would not be calmed. His voice had a hard edge to it. 'If he's sent her she is not a nobody. What is the old goat up to now? Oh God, I need a drink, Frances. You have to let me have a brandy, just a small one, only the one, I promise.'

Miss Fanshaw knelt down beside him and cupped his hand between hers. 'You know I can't do that. What would Dr Bretton say?' Then she twisted her head to look at Lettie over her shoulder, her face flushed with anger. 'Get out of here,' she ordered.

'I need a brandy, Frances. Just one,' Mr Powell pleaded.

'Get out this minute,' Miss Fanshaw repeated harshly.

Lettie obeyed.

Agnes was hovering outside the bedroom door. 'It is you! I knew it! I said it was you in the kitchen!' she exclaimed. 'Miss Fanshaw would have told me if she'd taken on a new maid. You should have gone home yesterday on the railway train.'

'Would you have, when you were so close to discovering someone who might know where your father was?'

'Miss Fanshaw was livid after she realised you'd wormed your way back here. She'll call the constable. She will, so you'd better leave now.'

'I can't.' Lettie shook her head decisively. 'Mr Powell recognised my grandfather's name. He is the man I am looking for.' Lettie grimaced. 'I am sorry if I've upset him. I . . . I think I did give him a shock. He . . . he said something about a brandy.'

'Some patients take it with their morning tea,' Agnes replied. 'If Dr Bretton recommends it.'

Lettie didn't comment at first but it was clear to her that Mr Powell had really wanted his brandy. There had been a desperation in his eyes that made Lettie frown. She recalled what the Reverend and Gran said about men who liked their drink too much. He was one of those folk for whom 'one drink was too many because ten were not enough'. She murmured more to herself than to Agnes, 'He's a drunkard.'

After a moment Agnes added, 'Miss Fanshaw has given everyone strict orders never to serve drink of any kind to Mr Powell. He . . . he has been very poorly with the drink habit in the past and we have got this important visitor due.'

'Would that be Lord Laughton?'

'How do you know?'

Lettie pointed along the landing. 'His name's on that door.'

'You shouldn't be up here prying. I'm instructed to keep an eye on you.' Agnes gave her a little push towards the staircase, adding, 'And I want my breakfast.'

The servants' hall was smaller than Lettie had expected, but then she had seen only the one at Waterley Hall. It had a wooden floor and a fireplace flanked by two armchairs with a clock sitting on the mantelpiece. There was also a worn, spotted cheval mirror, an upright piano plus stool and an old sideboard where the servants helped themselves to food. The room was dominated by a long dining table covered with a white tablecloth. Lettie counted eighteen chairs around the table and they were all in use as different servants came and went constantly. Lettie realised that some of them were nurses. Eventually, the chaos eased, leaving Cook seated at the end nearest the sideboard with Lettie and Agnes, and a few outdoor servants including the two men from the stables further down the table.

'That's her!' one said. 'A right little madam, she is, she broke into the summerhouse.'

'Is that true?' Agnes queried.

'It wasn't locked so I slept inside.'

'All night?'

'Not exactly,' Lettie replied. 'I spent the first half of the night in the village church.'

'You don't want to believe a word she says,' the other man said. 'She told me a pack of lies yesterday.'

'I did not!'

Cook intervened. 'Now then, I don't want arguments in here. If you've got any complaints, speak to Miss Fanshaw. She's in charge now.'

'Only because she says so!' the man continued. 'How do we know it's what Mr Powell wants? He's been poorly for weeks. How do we know she hasn't drugged him with one of her fancy cures?'

'They burned her sort as witches in the old days,' the stableman added.

'Oh shut up, you two!' Agnes responded angrily. 'We have enough dealing with village gossip without you adding to it! Miss Fanshaw is a proper nurse. She nursed injured soldiers in Africa, in the war out there.'

'We managed well enough afore without her interference,' the man muttered.

Agnes retaliated. 'Haven't you got a carriage and pair to spruce up for when His Lordship's train arrives?'

Cook stood up and raised her voice. 'That's enough from all of you. If you outdoor lot have finished you can get off now. Dinner's at twelve sharp for everybody today.'

The outdoor servants rose to their feet and one of them said, 'Grand breakfast, that. At least summat's improved around here.'

'Aye and the sooner that new butler gets here, the better,' Cook muttered.

Agnes waited until they had closed the door behind them before she went to the sideboard to help herself. Lettie followed her. She was very hungry and helped herself to porridge, bacon, sausage, egg and a hunk of bread. The kitchen maid she had met earlier came in and sat next to her.

'I hope I haven't caused you any trouble?' Lettie whispered.

The girl glanced at Cook and Agnes with their heads close together deep in conversation. 'Cook said she didn't care who you were because you showed some gumption in the kitchen.'

'When's His Lordship arriving?'

'It must be today because Cook's planning seven courses for dinner tonight.'

The girl ate quickly and went back to her duties leaving Lettie on her own with Agnes and Cook. They stood up to leave.

Cook said to her, 'Come with me and wait in the kitchen for Miss Fanshaw. She'll be down in a minute to check the patients' breakfasts.'

'What can I do to help while I wait?'

'Trying to be nice won't make any difference to Miss Fanshaw. But I'm not going to turn down a useful pair of hands. Can you make meringues?'

Lettie hadn't made them often although both the Reverend and Gran had praised hers. As with her sponge cakes, she didn't stint on the beating. Meringues were easy as long as you left them long enough to dry out. She walked over to the oven range, opened the lower door and put her hand inside. 'That's just right now, but if it gets any hotter, they'll colour.'

'Get them in as soon as you can. I'll be roasting venison by teatime.'

Lettie became engrossed in her task and was piping the meringues into nests, as Cook had directed, when Miss Fanshaw came into the kitchen. Her task called for concentration and a steady hand so, although she heard their lowered voices, she didn't allow herself to be distracted until she had finished. She straightened and passed the back of her hand over her forehead.

Cook said, 'Very nice. I'll see those into the oven. Off you go with Miss Fanshaw.'

Lettie wiped her hands on a tea-towel and followed the starchy Miss Fanshaw across the passage through a door with a brass label 'Housekeeper'. It was a comfortable little sitting room with a fire laid but not lit. There were no pictures, journals or needlework bags. In fact, the room appeared to be unused.

'Sit down.' Miss Fanshaw indicated a dining chair at the small chenille-covered table. 'You are a very determined young lady,' she began, 'but so am I and my main concern at present is Mr Powell.'

'I am sorry that I upset him, ma'am. Please assure Mr Powell that no one has sent me, least of all my grandfather who has been dead for many years.'

'Mr Powell was not speaking of your grandfather. He had not expected to hear from anyone bearing the name Hargreaves. Your arrival has been a great shock to him. His journey back to health is a long and difficult one and . . .' Miss Fanshaw's composure faltered and, for a second, Lettie glimpsed the compassionate side to her nature. But it did not last and her firm tone returned quickly. 'You are jeopardising his recovery. I assume you are one of His Lordship's servants who he has sent ahead of his party in secret. Now you must tell me why.' Miss Fanshaw glared at her and added, 'I am waiting.'

'I have nothing to do with Lord Laughton or his party. I have explained it to you and to Mr Powell. I believe he remembers my father from his days at Waterley Hall. Please, Miss Fanshaw, I beg you to let me speak to him. You see, I didn't know my father was alive—' Lettie continued with her well rehearsed little speech until Miss Fanshaw interrupted.

'He will see you.'

Lettie stopped, open mouthed. 'Beg pardon, ma'am.'

'Mr Powell will see you. He is inclined to believe who you are.'

'I am speaking the truth.'

Miss Fanshaw passed her hand over her brow and frowned. 'Unfortunately, it is the truth that is difficult for him to face. He has spoken very little of his past and the brandy bottle is an easy friend.'

'I didn't know. I'm sorry.' Lettie looked down at her hands resting lightly on the plush table cover.

She heard Miss Fanshaw sigh and then say, 'Cook wants you to stay and help her with tonight's banquet.'

'May I?'

'Do you not have a home to go to?'

'Not any more. I have no family left and I must find an occupation or . . . or marry, I suppose.' Lettie gave an involuntary shudder as she considered the latter with Eric Jones.

'Your clothes indicate that you are not destitute. Surely someone will be wondering why you have not returned?'

Reverend Ennis, she thought. But she had explained everything to Thomas and she trusted him to tell the Reverend.

'Well, Miss Hargreaves? There is a telegraph office in the village.'

'I have already sent a message to my guardian.' Miss Fanshaw assumed she meant a telegraph message and Lettie did not enlighten her. 'When will Mr Powell see me?'

'He has treatments throughout the morning as do most of the patients here. He rests after lunch so you may speak with him at tea. He takes tea at five o'clock in his room.'

'Thank you, ma'am.'

Miss Fanshaw stood up. 'You will not set foot out of

the servants' quarters until then.' She clicked her tongue. 'This is most tiresome. We are very busy and cannot watch over you every minute of the day.'

'Will you let me help where I can? I was an assistant housekeeper until recently and I can cook.'

'Yes, I noticed your meringues.' Miss Fanshaw stared at her while she decided. 'Very well,' she said at last. 'I shall inform Cook and you will take your orders from her.'

'Thank you, ma'am.'

'Make sure I do not regret this decision.'

'May I ask a question, ma'am?'

'What is it now?'

'What sort of clinic is Mereside Lodge?'

'It is a private one and none of your business.'

Miss Fanshaw left Lettie in the kitchen with Cook who seemed to be enjoying preparing the forthcoming dinner. Lettie spent most of her day picking over, peeling and turning vegetables and fruit. Cook gave the responsibility for the servants' dinner to Lettie, which consisted of boiling a whole brisket of beef and making two huge baked rice puddings. There were no complaints and Lettie gained the impression that meals had improved since Cook had taken over.

'Where were you before here?' Lettie asked her.

'I worked in the kitchens of an Earl and Countess once,' Cook replied. 'The cooks never ate with the rest of the servants there. We had our own dining room.'

'Was that your last position?' Lettie asked.

'No, m'dear. My last master was a Bradford mill owner.

He entertained local gentry from miles around. I used to cook dinners of several courses every night and they drank a different wine with each dish.'

'Will they do that tonight?'

'His Lordship will expect it. He's starting the cure tomorrow.'

'The cure?'

'The cure. It's what they do here.'

Lettie's imagination ran riot. 'A cure for what?'

'Gout, rheumatism.' Cook shrugged. 'Hydropathy can help lots of illnesses.'

'Hydropathy? What's that? I've never heard of it before.'

'The gentry go for it in a big way. Turkish baths and not much to eat, as far as I can make out. It's very popular with gentlemen who've lost their vigour, if you get my meaning.'

'I'm sorry, I don't.'

'Well, the ancient Romans had steam baths; and cold ones, and rubs and pummelling—'

'It sounds painful to me.'

'Invigorating, I'm told. They don't have much to eat either. Folk used to "take the waters" and now they have hydropathy. My last master used to go to an establishment in Harrogate. Haven't you heard of the Matlock House Hydro in Derbyshire? The King goes there.'

'I shouldn't think the King would take kindly to lemon juice and biscuits for his breakfast.'

'You'd be surprised. Now, I think those meringues will have to come out before they colour. Take them into the pastry room until I need them.'

'How many guests are you expecting for dinner?'

'Not many. His Lordship and another well-to-do gentleman who apparently telegraphed to say he was arriving today. Dr Bretton and Miss Fanshaw will be attending and one or two patients who have finished their treatments, and Mr Powell, of course. He's the host.'

'Mr Powell is the host? I thought he was a patient.'

'Mr Powell is the master here. He owns Mereside Lodge.'

Chapter 23

Goodness, thought Lettie, Mr Powell must be a rich man. Perhaps he wasn't a footman and my father was employed by him at some time. She felt her excitement bubble. If he had been Father's employer, he would be sure to know where Father went.

Lettie passed the afternoon in the pastry room lining tiny tin baking moulds with shortcrust and cutting sponge cake into shapes for decorating desserts. The time dragged slowly until Cook called her out to put on a clean cap and apron.

'Agnes says Mr Powell wants to see you and you're to take his tea. I want you back here in time to do the servants' high tea. They have it at six o'clock. It's cold meat and pickles tonight, followed by fruitcake and cheese, but the valets and footmen will want it punctual so don't be late.'

'Of course not, Cook,' Lettie said automatically. Less than an hour with him! Her mind was full of questions for Mr Powell about her father.

The tray was laid up with afternoon tea for two people. Agnes had made a plate of delicate cucumber sandwiches, which were hidden under a silver dome. Lettie carried it carefully up the main stairs and tapped on Mr Powell's door. Miss Fanshaw opened it. 'I've brought your tea, ma'am.'

Miss Fanshaw checked over the tray and nodded as though satisfied. 'You may speak with Mr Powell for half an hour. I shall wait outside on the landing.'

'But what about your tea?'

'It's for you and him; half an hour only.'

'Yes, Miss Fanshaw.'

Lettie stood inside the bedroom door. The stunning view of the mere distracted her for a moment. 'It's Miss Hargreaves, Mr Powell. I've brought your tea.'

'Bring it over here by the window, where I can see you.'

Lettie unloaded the tray, aware that he was watching her closely. 'Shall I pour it for you, sir?'

'Please; and for yourself.'

'Thank you, sir.'

He offered her the plate of cucumber sandwiches and took one for himself. 'Now, sit down and tell me who you are really and why you are here. I want the truth.'

Lettie tried to relax but it was difficult. Her mouth dried but she had to answer his questions. 'I told you the truth this morning, sir. I was orphaned as a baby and brought up by my grandmother. She was Ivy Hargreaves. She passed away recently and my guardian—'

'Stop.' He held up his hand to silence her. 'Ivy Hargreaves has died? When was this?'

'Last month. Did you know her? She was housekeeper at Waterley Hall for many years.' He stared at her as she sipped her tea.

'What has she told you about her life before you were born?'

'Very little, sir. I understood it was a period in her life that she put firmly behind her. I am sorry to say that she had no affection for my grandfather.'

'Yes, I shared her sentiment.'

'Oh. You were acquainted with both of them? Did you know my father, sir? Have you knowledge of his whereabouts after he left Waterley Hall?'

He continued to gaze at her, not in a curious way but more in a thoughtful, almost affectionate, way. She thought he must feel sorry for her and cold fingers seemed to encircle her heart. He was going to tell her that something awful had happened to her father! He seemed to be undecided what to say.

She pressed him to respond. 'Please tell me anything you know about him, sir. There is no one else for me to ask.'

A frown furrowed his brow. Why would he not answer her? Perhaps her father had done something truly wicked. But she had prepared herself for the worst. At least she had *tried* to brace herself for bad news. Lettie could feel her heart beating louder. Is that why Gran hadn't told her? It had hurt Lettie to discover that the grandmother she had loved so dearly had not been totally honest with her. She knew Gran as a religious, somewhat pious woman. But in Lettie's experience, she had been intolerant of those who strayed and could be a harsh judge of others. Lettie hoped she would not be so quick to condemn others.

She found it difficult to sit still and sprang to her feet to stand at the window. Directly below there were gardeners at work with wheelbarrows full of debris, tidying flower beds and shrubberies. A few patients strolled along the paths. One of them was tall and straight. He reminded her of Mr Boyer in the way he walked. The truth is never wrong, Mr Boyer had said, only the telling of it. *Or the not telling of it.*

She turned to face Mr Powell. 'Was he sent to prison, sir?'

Mr Powell blinked and appeared genuinely startled. 'My dear girl, is that what you believe happened to your father?'

'I should rather know the truth about him, sir, however unpalatable.'

Mr Powell covered his face with his hand, drawing his fingers slowly down his features. His chest began to rise and fall as his breathing quickened. Lettie realised that she was distressing him with her questions and became anxious about his well-being.

'Shall I fetch Miss Fanshaw, sir?'

He shook his head. 'She cannot help me with this. I must get through this alone and I shall.'

'But if you are not well, sir, you need medicine or a doctor.'

He sat back in his chair, closed his eyes for a moment and then asked, 'Would you hand me my cup of tea.'

Lettie obeyed. 'Shall I leave you, sir?'

'Stay. I am quite well. It is strange that you speak of prison in connection with your father. His life was a kind of prison but be assured that he was not a criminal. His chains were of a wholly different nature.'

He knew something! There was some secret about her father's life and he knew it! Lettie hardly dare breathe as she waited for him to continue.

After a couple of minutes he seemed more composed and went on. 'Sit down, Lettie. You gave me quite a shock when you told me your name this morning.' He examined her features. 'You have your mother's eyes. Did your grandmother not speak of her?'

'Rarely. She was steadfast in her refusal. I believe it caused her too much hurt.'

'Yes, Ruth caused everybody a lot of hurt.'

He knew her mother! 'How, sir? Will you tell me about her? How well did you know her?'

He clasped his hands together and squeezed them together so firmly that his knuckles went white. He gazed past her out of the window and his features turned grim. 'I loved her once and she became my wife.'

The bitterness in his voice was evident to Lettie. Her eyes widened and she swallowed, causing her to cough. She picked up her napkin to cover her mouth as the

324

realisation dawned on her. A burning, feverish sensation spread over her arms, back and neck and enveloped her head. It blotted out the tea table in front of her and the stunning view from the window.

She took a gulp of tea. 'Are you my father, sir?'

He gave a harsh ironic laugh, more of a grunt really, and commented, 'How can I be called your father when I did not even hold you as an infant in my arms.'

'Please tell me the truth, sir. Are you my father or was I, as I have always suspected, born out of wedlock?'

This seemed to bring Mr Powell back to his senses. He took a couple of deep breaths and turned his head to face her. His features had softened and his tone was kinder. 'You must never think that of yourself. Your mother and I were married in the sight of God. We were husband and wife when you were born.'

'But I am Lettie Hargreaves, not Lettie Powell.'

'That was your grandmother's wish. She took you away from me and I allowed it. It was for your own good.'

'Don't say that! Gran used to say that to me, and sometimes she was wrong!' Lettie's emotions were rising, taking over, and tears threatened but she composed herself quickly and added, 'How could it be for my own good if you were my father and you were alive?'

'I was no father to you. I was chained to the brandy bottle. It was – it is – my weakness and I should be long dead if it weren't for Miss Fanshaw's ministrations.'

Lettie had seen the outcome of this weakness in men and women at Waterley Edge. It ruined the lives of whole families and she understood why everyone who attended chapel was encouraged to 'take the pledge' and promise never to indulge in the 'demon drink'.

She was silenced for a minute and regretted her uncharitable thoughts about Gran. Of course Gran had had her best interests at heart! A drunken father could not bring up any child without its mother.

'Was it the loss of my mother that turned you to the drink, sir?' she asked.

He closed his eyes and gave a weary sigh. 'She was never really mine. She . . . she belonged to another and . . . There is so much you do not know.'

'Then will you enlighten me, sir?'

'Another day,' he said. 'We shall continue our conversation another day. I am dining with Lord Laughton tonight and I must prepare myself. It will be an ordeal for me after so long.'

'Of course,' she realised. 'There will be wine.'

'Frances – that's Miss Fanshaw – will be at my side.'

Miss Fanshaw will look after him. Lettie considered that their relationship was more than that of patient and nurse. She didn't want to leave yet but she rose to her feet and began to stack the tray. 'This has been a shock for me too, sir – er, Father. May I call you Father?'

'Please don't; not yet. It has to be our secret – ours and Frances's, until – well, for a few weeks yet. Promise me that you will not speak to anyone of our relationship within the servants' hearing. Valets pass on servants' hall gossip to their masters and I should prefer Lord Laughton not to know that you are here.'

'What has our connection to do with him?' Her initial

euphoria from finding her father was waning and she remembered being escorted from the premises of Waterley Hall when Mr Boyer discovered her presence.

He said, 'Please be patient, Lettie. Patience is something that Frances has taught me. Will you promise?'

Lettie suppressed her disappointment. Patience had not been one of her merits lately but she would try to keep her word. Perhaps a busy night in the kitchen was what she needed? She would not have time to dwell on the emotions and questions mushrooming through her heart and her head and taking over her reason.

'Very well,' she said. 'But I do look forward to the time when I may address you openly as my father.'

'So do I, my dear. Would you ask Frances to come in?'

She bent down and kissed her father lightly on his forehead. He seemed surprised and put his fingers on the spot. Then she picked up the tray and went out onto the landing.

Frances appeared from the shadows in front of Lettie. She seemed very anxious. 'How is he?' she asked.

Lettie considered again that her father was more than simply a patient to her. For her to find out that an inter-loper who has disobeyed her so flagrantly was his daughter would be a shock to her, too. 'He has something to tell you,' Lettie answered. Lettie had no idea how Frances would take the news and added as an afterthought, 'I shall be in the kitchen tonight as planned, helping Cook.'

In the servants' hall later, the outdoor servants enjoyed the attention as they informed everyone about the vis-itors they had collected that day from Mereside Halt.

The coachman was a much pleasanter person than the carter who collected the hampers. He was a recent addition to Mereside Lodge, like Cook and the new butler, Mr Norwich, who had arrived on the same railway train. Mr Norwich had taken his place at the head of the table and carved the cold remains of an aitch bone of beef for the servants who were now his responsibility. Under Gran's tutelage, Lettie had carved many hot and cold joints of meat during her years at the manse and watched him with interest. He did it well.

The coachman said, 'Lord Laughton was not pleased about sharing the coach. The two gentlemen from first class were not travelling together. We ought to have taken a second coach.'

Lord Laughton's valet added, 'Yes, they had a quite an argument. He should have gone on the luggage cart.'

'Don't be ridiculous,' Mr Norwich interrupted. 'He was a gentleman.'

'Are you sure? He didn't have a man with him.'

'He's an American,' the valet commented, as though it explained everything.

'Well, he's in one of the best suites,' Mr Norwich said. 'And his name is Laughton. I'll talk to Mr Powell about a second coach in the morning.'

'It was a family quarrel, I expect,' the valet muttered. 'I didn't realise he had any family left.'

'All right, that's enough gossip,' Mr Norwich said. 'We have much to do tonight. My head footman will act as valet to Mr Laughton and Lord Laughton's footman will be with me in the dining room. Any mishaps outside the kitchen, report directly to me. Cook will prepare cocoa for when we've finished.'

The valets and footmen went off first and Lettie followed Cook into the kitchen. Cook was relieved the new butler had arrived and said, 'At least I'll have somebody who knows what they're doing serving my lovely dinner.'

'What will happen about the patients' dinner tonight?'

'If they're taking the cure, it's pretty frugal and served early – often in their rooms. Miss Fanshaw will see to them but she has to dress for dinner so you can help her. I'll only need you for sauces and carrying.'

While Lettie was taking round patients' dinners under silver domes she checked name plates on the doors and found Mr Laughton's next to Lord Laughton's. *Alexander B. Laughton*, it read. A relative but perhaps not a friend of Lord Laughton by the sound of it, she thought.

The evening was fascinating for Lettie and, thankfully for all, uneventful. It was a lengthy meal that began at eight and went on until eleven. The servants were kept busy until after midnight. Lettie strained sauces in serving boats, cleaned up any smudged edges of dishes and carried them carefully to the white-gloved hands of waiting footmen. It was exhausting but it took Lettie's mind away from her own concerns for a few hours. She didn't really notice how tired she was until the last of the Rockingham china, Waterford crystal and silver cutlery had been locked away in the butler's pantry.

Mr Norwich assembled everyone in the servants' hall to thank them. He had a bottle of brandy and some glasses and Cook brought in a pot of tea and a jug of cocoa. The valets were with their respective gentleman. The kitchen maid and boot-boy, who had spent most of their time scrubbing cooking pots and washing tableware in the scullery, lit lamps and went off to their beds. Agnes and the footmen followed shortly afterwards, leaving Lettie with Cook and Mr Norwich sitting around the table in the servants' hall.

'Ought I to go up with Agnes?' Lettie suggested.

Cook replied, 'Miss Fanshaw asked for you to wait for her.'

Lettie stifled a yawn.

'Lord Laughton appeared satisfied with dinner,' Mr Norwich said. 'I've served him before in London and he is difficult to please.'

'Did they talk of anything interesting?' Cook asked.

'A good butler does not gossip about his employer,' Mr Norwich replied. But Lettie noticed he grinned as he said it.

'I'm not asking you about Mr Powell,' Cook protested, 'but I know something is in the air. Miss Fanshaw was quite keyed up.'

'Well, the atmosphere was icy between Lord Laughton and Mr Laughton. Dr Bretton managed to keep the conversation civil. He was speaking of recommending Mereside Lodge to his medical colleagues for their patients.'

'That's good, isn't it?' Lettie commented. She wasn't really interested and was trying to summon up the energy to go to bed.

'Not if Lord Laughton gets his way,' Mr Norwich said. 'He wants to buy the Lodge and, apparently, Mr Powell needs the money. Keep that to yourself. I don't want to alarm the servants.'

Lettie heard footsteps in the passage and turned to see Frances in the doorway. She looked beautiful, in a grey chiffon frock with a lace bodice and matching chiffon and lace jacket that skimmed her waist. Her hair was piled high and decorated with grey velvet ribbon and she wore grey kid shoes with a heel. She was carrying a lighted lamp.

'Miss Fanshaw!' Mr Norwich scrambled to his feet.

'Oh, do sit down, Mr Norwich, I'm not the lady of the house,' she said.

She could be, though, Lettie realised. She was more than ready for her bed, stifled a yawn and queried, 'Where shall I be sleeping?'

Miss Fanshaw said, 'I am sorry I've been so long. It has been a . . . a difficult evening for Mr Powell.'

'Will the lass be staying?' Cook asked. 'She'll be an asset. Don't you agree, Mr Norwich?'

'I do but I shall need sight of a testimonial,' he answered.

'That won't be necessary,' Miss Fanshaw said. 'Mr Powell will vouch for her.'

Cook raised her eyebrows. In response, Miss Fanshaw gave her a rare smile. 'Come with me, Lettie, I'll show you to your room.'

They went through to the main house and climbed the wide, carpeted staircase until they reached the first landing. Miss Fanshaw said, 'Michael – your father

– told me about you. We have no secrets from each other.'

'You are lucky, Miss Fanshaw. It seems that my life has been one huge secret since I was born.'

'Well, it was a shock for me. Do call me Frances when other servants are not within earshot.' She led the way. 'You are on the second landing, next to me.' As they climbed she went on, 'We have to keep quiet about it for now. I hope you understand.'

'Well, no actually. Father said it was to do with Lord Laughton. Is he ashamed of me?'

'No, of course not! Michael will tell you all in good time. For now he has other issues to consider.'

Such as the future of Mereside Lodge, Lettie realised. They reached the second landing and stopped. Frances opened one of the bedroom doors and said, 'You are in here, Lettie. My room is next door if you need anything.' They went inside. Two lamps were already burning, one on a dressing table and the other on a bedside table.

'Thank you.' It was the biggest bedroom Lettie had ever slept in. 'It looks very comfortable,' she said. 'Mereside Lodge used to belong to the Waterley estate, didn't it?'

'It was the hunting lodge, yes.' Frances took a deep breath. 'You may as well know. His Lordship gave it to your father many years ago and now he wants it back.'

'He *gave* it to my father? Then why must he give it back?'

'His Lordship is prepared to buy it and . . . and he is aware that Michael has need of a large sum of money.'

Lettie noticed that Frances looked embarrassed as she said this.

'Is Mereside Lodge losing money?'

'It is not as straightforward as that, Lettie. Lord Laughton wants Mereside Lodge for his own reasons and he is ruthless. He is also influential and powerful. It is a mistake to cross him.'

'Will Father sell?' she asked.

'I don't know. All I know is that Mereside Lodge could be the best hydro in Yorkshire. But it won't be if Lord Laughton gets his hands on it.' Frances sat down on the edge of the bed and added, 'Mereside Lodge is Michael's life's work!' She sounded emotional but after a few seconds pulled herself together and stood up. 'There is hot water in the ewer,' she said. She picked up a clean towel from the washstand and handed it to Lettie. 'Sleep for as long as you wish. Agnes has laid out nightwear and clean clothes for you. She will bring your tea in the morning and fresh water.'

'I'm not used to servants waiting on me.'

Frances smiled and it lit up her face so that, in spite of being exhausted, she looked pretty. 'You will be thankful in the morning,' she said. 'Shall I pull the curtains?'

'I'll do it. You must be very tired yourself.'

'I am. Goodnight, Lettie.'

'Goodnight, Frances.'

Lettie washed and put on the long nightgown. It was made of the softest cotton and trimmed with lace. Lettie was past her tiredness now. She had too much to think about to sleep. She wrapped a shawl around her shoulders and went over to the window, staring into the blackness, waiting for her eyes to become accustomed to the night. Her room overlooked the garden where the summerhouse was located. She was high up but she noticed a tiny intermittent glow of a cigar as one of the gentlemen walked in the garden. She wondered who he was, outside in the night air.

It was unlikely to be a patient; Lord Laughton perhaps or Dr Bretton or the American gentleman. She understood why the doctor was interested in the future of Mereside but what was the American gentleman's part in all this? Although he was a Laughton it seemed that he and His Lordship were not on good terms. Were these 'important visitors' simply vultures circling her father and his financial embarrassment, waiting for rich pickings? It must have been an ordeal for Father and she wished she had been at his side, helping to fend off these foes. As she stared into the darkness she felt a strong protective urge to fight for whatever her father wanted.

He's my father. She repeated the words softly, enjoying the warm feeling it gave her. Would she ever get used to saying them? It had been hard, at first, for her to understand why her grandmother had kept him from her. But Gran had wanted to protect her, perhaps too much, and Lettie appreciated that she was driven by love. She had never doubted that Gran loved her and knowing she was loved had given Lettie strength as a child. She wondered if her father might love her in the same way.

She realised that it was the thing she craved above all. A family that cared for her, not because it was their duty as it was in the church, but because they loved her, she belonged to them and loved them in return. She thought fondly of Thomas, of his belief in himself and his friendliness. She admired him for those qualities. He came from a big family, not well-off but hardworking and happy. Lettie wanted that for herself one day, when she fell in love. She wanted to fall in love and hoped it would happen to her. But the face that came to mind when she imagined herself in love was not Thomas's. It was Mr Boyer's: handsome, foreign and intriguing. She shook her head and rebuked herself for her foolishness.

Frances was in love with her father, Lettie had decided. She was convinced about this and wondered why she was so certain. Was Father aware of it? How did anyone know if someone truly loved them? She gave a shivery sigh. Life used to be so much simpler at the manse. She yawned and stretched. The tiny glow in the garden beneath her had stopped moving around and she realised the lamp in her room was making her visible to whoever was smoking his cigar in the garden beneath her. She pulled the curtains quickly, turned down her lamps and climbed into a soft feather bed.

Chapter 24

She woke to the sound of her bedroom door clicking softly and sat up with bleary eyes. Her room was empty and dark but chinks of bright light squeezed in around the curtains. She had slept late and a welcome aroma of freshly made tea drifted in her nose. A tray waited for her on the bedside table. She examined the biscuit. It was a special one with the crest. She had never seen them in any of the shops she frequented. No doubt they arrived by railway train in one of the hampers. She sat on the edge of the bed to eat her biscuit and drink the tea, noticing steam rising from the ewer on her washstand. It was time to get up.

Agnes had laid out a dark grey skirt with a matching tie, and fresh white blouse. Her own clothes had disappeared and she had noticed the evening before that they were grubby and crumpled. Agnes's choices were plain but they fitted her and were clean. She washed and spent more time than she ought to have on piling up her hair. She couldn't find her boots until she opened her bedroom door and found them sitting outside, nicely polished. Nonetheless, she wasn't a patient or an honoured visitor so she went down to the kitchen by the back stairs.

'Oh, there you are,' Cook said. 'You've missed breakfast but there's porridge keeping warm on the hotplate. Miss Fanshaw wants to see you in the housekeeper's sitting room when she's finished in the bath house.' Cook examined her clothes and added, 'Well, you can't help in here in those. That's what the upstairs maids wear.'

'I can't sit about all morning, either.'

'Can you sew?'

'Of course.'

'The sewing room is across the passage.'

It was a small, well-lit room lined with cupboards that reached the ceiling and dominated by a large table in the middle piled with linen and assorted items of servants' uniforms. Lettie found a well-stocked workbox and tackled some of the aprons that needed stitches here and there until it was time to see Frances.

Her hair was fuzzy and her face reddened from the steam in the bath house but Frances was more cheerful than the previous evening. They exchanged a few pleasantries then Frances said, 'This telegraph message came for you,' and handed it over.

Lettie opened the seal and read it. 'It's from Reverend

Ennis.' *Go to mission at Forest Chase stop Will send help*, she read. 'How far is Forest Chase?'

'It's the next stop on the railway line. Why?'

'The Reverend wants me to go to the Methodist chapel there. He's my guardian.'

'He must be worried about you.'

'It was rather foolish of me to set out alone for Mereside Lodge, but I had to come. You saw how I was.'

'Yes, and I understand why. Will you go to Forest Chase?'

'I don't know. I want to do what is best for Father.'

Frances chewed on her lip. 'Your presence is an added strain for him.'

'Do you think I should leave?'

'I do not want you to leave but . . .' She shook her head slightly. 'I want him to get well and you don't understand how difficult it has been for him to get this far.'

'I do. At least, I am aware that he has to take the pledge if he wants to stay alive.'

'He told you about the drinking?'

'It was the reason he gave me up.'

'I am so fearful that he will slip back into his old ways.' A tear glistened in Frances's eye. 'I couldn't bear to see him suffer again.'

'I want to help him, Frances,' Lettie urged. 'I do understand. I was brought up a Methodist in a pit village. He is lucky to have you, you know.'

Frances shook her head and murmured, 'I am the lucky one.'

She is definitely in love with him, Lettie thought, and this cheered her. They were allies in making Father better.

Frances stood up briskly. 'I have to check the energising drinks for patients.'

'May I assist you?'

'I'm sorry. Not until Lord Laughton has departed.'

'What shall I do for the rest of the day?' Lettie didn't look forward to staying in the sewing room for the afternoon.

'You are not a servant,' she glanced over her gown, 'although you are dressed as one. Your own clothes will be ready tomorrow.'

'Well, I shall have to occupy myself with something.'

'Go for a long walk. It's a couple of miles or so around the mere. It will clear your head and you will see why your father loves this place.'

Lettie needed the time to make sense of her thoughts. It was a fine day and warm for the time of year but she took her coat and pinned on her hat. She wandered across the pasture and stared at the calm water, occasionally rippled by a bird landing quietly on its surface.

Reverend Ennis had offered her an escape route if she wanted but she wasn't at all certain that she wished to take it. Of course he wasn't aware of her father's situation and she could well have spent a second night in the draughty church or summerhouse. No doubt the Methodist minister at Forest Chase would be expecting her and she ought to do as her guardian advised. At the very least she must reply to his telegraph.

A pathway took her away from the mere, through a

small wrought-iron gate in the wall and back to the road that led to the Halt. Deep in thought, she walked slowly, remembering how Thomas had risked his job to find her and had promised to make the journey again on Sunday. He must care for her quite a lot to do that.

The road seemed shorter than before; the track to the Halt was soon behind her and the church spire in view above the trees. The green was peopled with village housewives carrying shopping baskets, some trailing children pulling at their skirts. They glanced at her curiously as she walked by and one or two wished her good morning. She returned their greetings but moved on purposefully to the post office.

The postmistress was helpful as each word in a telegraph had to be paid for. She gave Lettie a scrap of paper and pencil stub to plan her message. What should she say to ease the Reverend's mind? *Safe stop Father alive stop Staying here stop Letter follows stop Lettie.*

She exhaled audibly as she paid for it. Sending this message to the Reverend had somehow confirmed her decision that she wanted to be involved in her father's life and help in any way she could. Satisfied, she turned to walk into the sunshine and found herself face to face with the very last person she expected to see.

'Mr Boyer! What are *you* doing here?' Heavens, she thought, how rude I must sound! Why shouldn't a foreign gentleman be travelling the more attractive parts of Yorkshire?

He raised his hat and bowed his head. 'Good morning, Miss Hargreaves.'

This was remarkably civil of him considering the way they had parted at Waterley Hall. She acknowledged him with a bow of her head, murmured an inoffensive 'sir' and waited for him to step aside so that she could pass. He didn't move and neither did she. She could have walked around him but her feet wouldn't budge and she guessed they – no, *she* – didn't want them to.

She was, she realised, unduly pleased to see him and to hear his rich voice and unusual vowels. True, his manner had been offhand and aloof but not all the time and his apology on the day of Gran's funeral had been sincere. And, she considered, although his reaction to her serving soup in the dining room at Waterley Hall had been a shock, there was something about him that appealed to her, something *physical* that stirred her senses as a woman. She was, when in his presence, very conscious that she was a woman.

He did not take his eyes off her face and they were penetrating eyes that seemed to pierce hers, making her unusually tongue tied. She looked away, desperately searching her mind for something to say to him. 'Mrs Osborne will be sad that you have left Boundary Farm.'

'My horse remains in the stables there.'

Oh. He intended to return then. Lettie wondered briefly if she would do the same. Waterley Edge seemed a long way away at present. The post-office door opened and a customer came in with a shopping basket over her arm. They both stepped to one side to give her more room.

Lettie said, 'Are you lodging at the inn? This is a beautiful part of Yorkshire, don't you think?'

'I do.'

'Did you travel here by the railway train?'

'I did.'

After a further silence Lettie realised he had not forgotten their parting and did not wish to make further conversation with her. Disappointed, she said, 'Well, good day to you, Mr Boyer.' But still he did not stand aside, or move to open the door for her. She would have to walk around him.

'I should like to speak with you, Miss Hargreaves.'

'You were anxious for me to leave your presence at our last meeting, sir.'

'I had my reasons and I wish to account for my behaviour.'

'There is no need, sir. I was simply trying to find my father and I believed one of the older servants at Waterley Hall might remember him. But I have found him now.'

'So you have discovered who you are?'

'I have.' She said it with some satisfaction and relief. Although she still had many questions for her father, her desperate urgency for answers had eased. She added, 'After growing up believing I was an orphan and then losing my only living relation, I have been blessed with someone who is my family. Do you know what that feels like, sir?'

'I cannot say that I do. You seem to have taken it very well. But you are a Hargreaves and you are strong. Do I take it that you are comfortable with the knowledge?'

'I am.'

Mr Boyer's face took on a guarded expression. 'You have met your father, haven't you?'

'I really don't see how it is any of your concern, sir, but yes, I have.'

'You must be cautious, Miss Hargreaves. You do not know him well and his behaviour in the past—'

She interrupted him. 'He told me about his past.'

Mr Boyer seemed concerned by her reaction. 'I understand your loyalty,' he said. 'He is, after all, your father, but where has he been all your life?'

'Mr Boyer, I really do not care what you think. My father and I have much to discover about each other. He has had his difficulties but now he has reformed.'

'He has not! He is the same—' He stopped as a customer at the post-office counter turned round to see who was raising their voice. He spoke more quietly and added, 'I really must speak privately with you. He has told you only his version.'

There was an insistence in his tone that made Lettie hesitate. 'Do you have a different story, sir?'

He kept his voice low. 'Not here. Will you take some refreshment at the inn with me?'

The nearest Lettie had been to an inn was in the outside coal yard on her walk to Boundary Farm. Her first thought was that the Reverend would be horrified and Gran would turn in her grave. The alarm must have shown on her face because he added, 'I am not suggesting we drink ale in the public bar. Will a pot of coffee be suitable for you?'

'Very well,' she agreed.

'Shall we?' He opened the post-office door for her, followed her into the sunlight and they set off the short distance to the inn. He must have rooms there, she thought. Perhaps he came for the wedding. She repeated her earlier question. 'Are you staying at the inn?'

'I thought you were.'

'My father asked me to stay at Mereside Lodge,' she explained.

'He did? Then he was pleased to see you? Perhaps he has mellowed towards you with the years.'

His comment stung. 'He gave me up because his situation meant that he was not able to look after me himself! That does not mean he did not love me!'

'I do apologise, Miss Hargreaves. My remark was ill-judged. Forgive me.'

'Do not be so quick to criticise, Mr Boyer. You have been mistaken about me in the past.'

'But I have known who you really are for a while now.'

Why should he be interested in who she was? Who was she to him? She stopped on the steps of the inn and said, 'Did you follow me into the post office?'

He didn't answer her question but offered his arm to climb the steps and said, 'I think we ought to continue this conversation in a more private place.'

She didn't take his arm. 'I shall not accompany you to your private rooms, sir. If that is what you expect then we must part here.'

He seemed mildly amused, which annoyed her. 'Surely you do not believe my intentions are dishonourable? I am not Lord Laughton.'

She did not move until he added, 'There is a small

parlour overlooking the rear garden. We shall not be alone but we may converse in private.'

Satisfied, she went inside, down a central corridor, to a small comfortably furnished room with a very pretty window made up of many small panes. Mr Boyer selected a couple of comfortable armchairs next to a low table. He waited for Lettie to settle before he sat down and ordered coffee. He had an air of quiet confidence that impressed her.

'You have the advantage of me, Mr Boyer,' she said. 'You appear to know who I am but I have little knowledge about you.'

'I am sure Mrs Osborne told you of my connection with the late Lady Laughton.'

'Actually, she didn't. It was Mrs St John. She said you were a trustee of Lady Laughton's estate.'

'It is an inherited duty. I am a distant relation, very distant.'

Lettie wondered why he had added 'very'. A relation was a relation and even more precious when you didn't have a family of your own. She said, 'I should be very pleased to discover I had relations, however distant.'

Her response caused him to raise an eyebrow. 'Would you, even if one turned out to be Seth Hargreaves?'

'My grandfather could not have been all bad.'

'You have a forgiving nature.'

'Perhaps that is because I don't accept the judgement of others readily! I prefer to draw my own conclusions. Don't you?' she challenged. Lettie thought he might. In spite of their apparent differences in background, she felt he might share this sentiment. She went on, 'My grand-mother was quick to condemn. It was a weakness in her character.' Lettie felt herself blushing for thinking and speaking ill of Gran and looked away.

'Maybe she had good reason to censure her husband.'

Her head twisted back sharply. 'Why do you say that? What do you know?'

'Seth Hargreaves was a confidante of Lord Laughton and everyone is aware of how badly he treated his wife.'

'Is it true that Lady Laughton owned half of the Waterley estate and Lord Laughton's industries?'

He raised his eyebrows so she added, 'Mrs St John told me that as well.'

'It was a third, actually.'

The coffee arrived and Mr Boyer had to move his legs out of the way for the landlord to set it down on the table. He was supple, she thought, a good horseman, tall and straight in the saddle; not especially muscular but agile. She had thought of him in these terms before and dismissed them as girlish whims. But in closer proximity to him it was these aspects that made her aware that she was not a girl any more. She was a young woman with all the aspirations it entailed. She wished she was wearing her own clothes instead of Agnes's.

He poured the coffee and offered her cream and sugar. She stirred her cup thoughtfully. 'Lady Laughton had a reputation for being a difficult old lady.'

'How diplomatic of you! She was an angry, bitter woman. She hated her husband with a vengeance because he only married her so that no one else would get their hands on the companies. Sadly, her bitterness extended to any and all of Lord Laughton's kin.'

'Did that include you?'

'She never met me and I kept it that way. My father's life was ruined by her efforts to disinherit him. Lady Laughton's one-third share was only a lifetime interest for her. Now she has passed away, her share reverts to the two remaining cousins and that is what she hated. She wanted to leave her share to her kin rather than to any of the Laughtons and couldn't because it was entailed.'

Lettie listened with interest, but didn't see that it was her concern. She wondered why he thought it was. Perhaps he just needed to talk. She understood that and responded, 'Are you saying that Lord Laughton has to share Lady Laughton's one-third with your father?'

'With me,' he corrected. 'My father is dead. My grandfather was the third cousin who left England for Canada as a young man, with his share. My father spent the latter years of his life fighting legal battles with the Laughtons and since he passed away I have spent all my time researching this whole sorry affair. That is how I know about you.'

'You're not making sense to me.' Lettie frowned. She didn't see how she fitted in to this at all.

He misunderstood her query and said, 'It's quite simple really. Lord Laughton and I each owned a third and now each of us has half of the remaining third.'

Lettie was good at figures. 'You own half of Waterley estate?'

'Including all the shipyards and steelworks. I'm proud

of my father and grandfather for their pioneering spirit, but I am sorry to say that I am a Laughton.'

'You told everyone your name was Boyer.'

'It is. It's my mother's family name.' He smiled. 'Alexander Boyer Laughton. My friends call me Alec. May I call you Lettie?'

He's *Alexander B. Laughton*, she realised. 'You are the American gentleman at Mereside Lodge?'

'Canadian. It's a common error among Europeans.'

Lettie had a sinking feeling about this information. She'd have preferred him to remain as Mr Boyer, rather than heir to half of the Laughton fortune. The knowledge of who he was seemed to distance him from her and she found that depressing. And she still didn't see why his family affairs were her concern. The coffee was finished and she felt it was time for her to leave. She said, 'Will you return to Canada soon?'

'Not until His Lordship and I have resolved our dispute. Of course, Mereside Lodge is at the centre of our disagreement.'

The mention of Mereside Lodge grabbed Lettie's attention. This did concern her. She remembered the servants' report of an argument at the Halt when they arrived.

'Lord Laughton does not give up easily,' Mr Boyer went on. 'He has not changed, believe me. He wants total control and he has decided to buy me off by giving me Mereside Lodge as compensation.'

'But Mereside Lodge doesn't belong to him!'

'Why should that stop him? He is used to buying his own way and he knows that Mr Powell needs money.'

'That is what I don't understand! Frances has told me he needs money but if Mereside Lodge is sold, he hasn't got a hydro to invest in, so what does he want the money for?'

'His divorce, of course. Mr Powell has to pay for his divorce, in order to marry Miss Fanshaw. Divorce is an expensive affair.'

Lettie was taken aback by mention of divorce. It was almost unheard of in Waterley Edge. 'I . . . I didn't know that my father was seeking a divorce.'

Mr Boyer sat back in his chair and frowned. In fact, he appeared to be genuinely puzzled. 'You said you knew who you were,' he murmured. His eyes widened and, for a gentleman normally so confident, he seemed at a loss to go on.

She added, 'I had no idea he had married again.'

His puzzled expression turned to one of dismay 'Dear God,' he muttered, 'what have I done? I assumed that you knew.'

'Knew what, sir?'

He didn't answer and his dismay appeared to degenerate into despair.

Chapter 25

'Mr Boyer – Alec – if this concerns me, I should like to hear what you assume I know already.'

'I have said far too much already. I . . . I don't have a right to say more. You must ask your . . . your father to tell you.'

Her frustration made her cross. 'But you have to tell me! My father has been reluctant to speak of the past and I am equally reluctant to press him. You know that he is not strong.'

'Even so, he is the person you must ask.'

'But what if he won't say? My grandmother kept *him* a secret from me all her life.' Lettie realised she was shaking and dangerously close to tears.

His reply gave her a crumb of comfort. 'You have hardly given him time yet. Speak to him, Lettie.' He seemed to be pleading with her and there was desperation in his eyes. 'Your sudden appearance was a shock to him. He is embarrassed by his relationship with Frances when he already has a wife.'

'My grandmother would turn in her grave if she knew!'

'Perhaps she did know? And that is why she kept him a secret.'

That made sense to Lettie and she calmed a little.

Alec took in a breath to speak further then seemed to change his mind.

Lettie sat with her thoughts for a minute. Alec had been honest with her but was drawing a line under further involvement and she didn't want that. She wanted to be involved with him. But what was she to him, apart from someone caught in the crossfire of his family feud? She said, 'Very well. I shall not compromise you with my questions any longer. You have been most kind in your considerations.'

'I fear I have not. I feel the need to make reparation.'

'For what? You have given me an insight into a past that I craved about.'

'On the contrary, Lettie, I have stirred a hornets' nest. I judged you to be strong enough but now I am not so sure. Is there no one else, no other relation you can turn to?' His eyes were questioning but he seemed wary of her response.

'I have my father. It is enough.'

Alec didn't respond immediately. He continued to frown and his eyes darted over her. She was not very well acquainted with him but he seemed fearful of something.

Finally he said, 'I have made a mistake in speaking with you. Your grandmother was right. It is better not to know anything than only a half truth.'

An odd feeling was spreading over Lettie and she began to feel lightheaded, as though the floor was falling away from beneath her. What did Alec mean? Her father had only given her a half truth? She could not bear it if this had been a wild-goose chase. 'I wish I'd never come here and started this search,' she muttered.

His face twisted in anguish and he seemed to be wrestling with his thoughts. 'This is my fault. I am to blame and I shall make amends. But there is only one person I am aware of who has the right to answer your questions and it is not me. You must ignore everything I have just said to you.'

Exasperated, she burst out, 'But I cannot!' She shook her head repeatedly. A sense of frustration and despair settled over her.

'And I cannot continue this conversation with you. I am truly sorry. It was not my intention to distress you in this way.'

But Lettie was distressed. She was exhausted after a tiring evening and late night yesterday, and troubled by her father's difficulties. As well, the worries of recent weeks had taken their toll on her. She felt shivery and tearful and didn't wish to break down in front of Alec. He had gained her respect and she wanted him to think well of her.

He gazed at her and there was sympathy in his eyes. 'You have turned quite pale, Lettie.'

'I feel unwell. I should go . . .' She was going to say 'go home' but she wasn't sure where home was any more. It didn't matter anyway and Alec seemed to understand.

He said, 'I'll order something to revive you first.' He raised an arm and called for the landlord. 'Bring a brandy for the lady; quickly, my good man, and do you have a carriage and driver available for hire?'

The brandy arrived and he handed it to her.

'I can't drink that,' she protested weakly.

'Take it as you would a medicine,' he urged, 'in one gulp.'

It was just a small amount and she tipped it to the back of her throat. The fiery liquid made her catch her breath and gasp, but its warmth soon spread through her veins. She began to feel better and composed herself after a few minutes.

'Another brandy?' he asked.

'Thank you, no. I'm ready to leave now.'

He said, 'I've ordered the inn carriage to take you back to Mereside Lodge.' Then he added, 'I shall ride with you as far as the Halt, if you have no objections.'

The landlord came to say the carriage was ready at the front steps. Alec offered her his hand to stand up but she didn't need it. However, she appreciated his help to step up into the carriage. It was a lightweight open trap, high off the ground with a flimsy step. 'Hold her steady,' he called to the driver at the pony's head.

He climbed in after her and unfolded one of the woollen blankets to wrap around her knees. As he leaned over to tuck in the edges his face came close to hers. He didn't have any whiskers and she caught the scent from his skin. It was an earthy, masculine aroma that excited her. He lingered and she could have stretched her neck a fraction and kissed him. Embarrassed that she wanted to, she shifted her position.

'Keep yourself warm,' he said, 'and when you get to the lodge, ask Miss Fanshaw for one of her new reviving drinks from America. They really do work.'

'Where to, sir?' the driver called.

'Stop at the Halt to set me down and then take the lady to Mereside Lodge. Ask for Miss Fanshaw and stay with her until she arrives.'

'Very good, sir.'

'I am not ill,' Lettie protested.

'Your colour has not returned yet.'

As the carriage approached the track though the trees to the Halt, he called again to the driver, 'I'll walk from the road. The train is not due yet.'

'Are you leaving?' Lettie queried. He had no luggage with him.

'I said that I would put right the distress I have caused you. I shall be away for – oh, a couple of weeks, perhaps. But I promise I shall return.'

'What shall I say to Frances?'

'I'll telegraph. Take care of yourself, Lettie.'

He climbed down and waited for the carriage to set off again before walking down the track. Lettie watched him until he had disappeared. She didn't know what to make of him. He was a law unto himself. But she was very much aware that she would be counting the days until he came back.

Frances put her to bed with a cup of calming camomile tea. She slept for a short time and woke feeling refreshed. Lettie had a long letter to write to Reverend Ennis and she went down to the morning room to find paper and pen. She smiled at a footman on duty in the entrance hall as she went in. She was alone but a few minutes later Agnes came in.

'What are you doing in here?' Agnes said.

'I have to write to my guardian. Frances – I mean, Miss Fanshaw – said I could.'

'Oh, did she? I suppose it's all right then. She told me you were above stairs now. What are you going to do?'

'I'm not sure yet.'

Agnes glanced over her serviceable skirt and blouse. 'Well, you'll be asked by the patients to serve tea dressed in those clothes.'

'I won't be long. I want to take this to the post office today.'

'Shall I bring you some tea? It's a bit early but I can make some.'

'May I have some of that new American drink?'

'Have you tried it before? It is not to everyone's taste.'

'Why, what's in it?'

'It's a herbal tonic made from the coca plant mixed with an extract of kola leaves. It's guaranteed to revive you.'

'I'll try it, then.'

355

In her letter, she thanked the Reverend for sending Thomas, apologised for causing him distress but hoped he would understand her hastiness. She explained her father's situation and it clarified her thinking about him and Frances and Mereside Lodge. Agnes arrived with her drink as she was in the middle of her letter; she left it on the table and retreated quietly.

When Lettie had finished writing she knew what she wanted to do. She was determined to help her father and Frances in whatever way she could. Why should he give up his life's work because Lord Laughton did not wish to share Waterley Hall with his cousin? But she suspected her father's future happiness depended on marriage to Frances as well. She sat back, gazed out at the mere through the window and said aloud, 'Father must not sell. There has to be another way.' The drink restored her energy and she ran upstairs for her hat and coat then set off to post her letter.

On her way back she saw the cart from Mereside Lodge making slow progress up the road with hampers from the afternoon train. She remembered her arrival at the Halt and the length of time the carter had taken to load them. Curious, she turned off to walk down to the Halt but stepped off the road into the trees and approached the platform unseen.

A pony pulling an old governess cart was tethered outside the gate in the fence and she recognised the stable hand from Mereside Lodge. He was heaving two hampers into the cart. He covered them with sacking, unhitched the reins and climbed into the driver's seat. Lettie stayed out of sight as the pony ambled away but she followed it as it bounced its way along a rutted bridleway through the woodland. It was heading away from Mereside Lodge.

Halfway to the village and under cover of the trees she watched the stable hand transfer packages, including a whole ham wrapped in muslin, from the hampers to a couple of men with a handcart. She could not recall seeing a ham boiling or roasting in the Mereside Lodge kitchens so far and now she knew why. A banknote and coins exchanged hands.

Lettie was cross with what she saw but not especially surprised. She had suspected something underhand was going on when she arrived. However, fearful of discovery, she hurried in the opposite direction towards Mereside Lodge. She dawdled when she reached the road and waited for the returning governess cart to catch up with her, raising her hand to hail a lift.

'How fortunate you came along, my feet are quite worn out,' she commented cheerily as she climbed up the steps at the rear of the cart. The stable hand did not reply and she noted that the empty hampers had disappeared; presumably he had left them at the Halt for the railway train guard to load into his van. She wondered if Father was aware his servants were stealing from him. Probably not, but she decided not to increase his anxiety by discussing it with him when she was quite capable of doing something about it herself.

Back at the Lodge, she climbed the stairs to the second landing thoughtfully.

Agnes had sponged and pressed her clothes and returned

them with a note from her father. It was an invitation to join him for dinner in the small dining room at nine, after the patients had returned to their rooms for the night. This was a late hour for Lettie who was used to keeping manse hours. She dressed carefully and spent half an hour on her hair. When she looked in the mirror she imagined Mrs Osborne advising her and thought fondly of her afternoons at Boundary Farm. She had met Alec there and had been intrigued by who he was. She realised now that her interest in him had been more than curiosity. It had been, and remained, a deeper appeal. Lettie was lost in thought when Frances knocked on her door to ask if she was ready.

Frances was transformed into a graceful woman when she was not wearing the plain grey outfit of a hydropathic nurse. She was poised and charming in a delicate blue floating dress with an overskirt and long jacket, and feathers in her hair. Lettie thought that she was a perfect antidote for her father.

'Your father has told Dr Bretton and Agnes that you are his daughter,' Frances said. 'They will keep it to themselves for the present.'

They went along the landing together. Father and Dr Bretton were waiting in the hall below, looking unnervingly formal in evening dress with white ties. Lettie urged Frances to go on ahead of her while she lingered at the top of the stairs to compose herself. She took a deep breath, straightened her back and took hold of the banister rail. It was a grand staircase, wide with carved wooden balustrades, and Lettie felt grand – elegant and grand – as she walked down. She could hear her father speaking to Dr Bretton.

'Is everything satisfactory for Lord Laughton?' he asked.

'I believe so,' Dr Bretton replied. 'It is hard to tell because his manner is quite obnoxious.'

'I did warn you, Take care. His bad opinion can be damaging.'

'Well, he has been recommended to my regimen and he is following it closely. He says he will marry again soon and is determined to renew his vigour.'

'Really?'

'His wants an heir and his mistress is young enough.'

'He's going to marry his mistress?' Her father sounded surprised.

Dr Bretton nodded. 'He spoke of her during his consultation. She lives in France, I believe.'

'Dear God, no! Not her! He can't bring her back with him!'

Frances had joined them and intervened. 'Michael, dearest, hush now. Your daughter is here.'

Her father stopped talking and turned round. He looked much improved this evening but she noticed that he swallowed at the sight of her. She had tried very hard to impress him and now she wasn't sure that he liked what he saw. Nevertheless, she smiled and said, 'Good evening, Father.' She loved the sound of that and went down the last few steps quickly.

'You look very lovely, my dear.' He bent to kiss her gently on each cheek.

'Thank you, Father. Good evening, Dr Bretton,' Lettie responded.

They exchanged pleasantries and went into the dining room. She had not overheard much of their conversation but neither gentleman had referred to Lord Laughton in sympathetic tones. Rather the opposite, she thought. They didn't seem to have much respect for him at all.

The small dining room at Mereside Lodge was for patients taking the cure who did not wish to dine in their rooms. It was a square, wood-panelled room, well lit by oil lamps. Each table had a silver candelabrum to set off the white linen and crystal. The effect was of a restful grace, disturbed only by the sound of cutlery on china. The food, though, was very plain and had little in common with the banquet that had been served in the main dining room the evening before, or indeed the menu that evening for those not taking the cure. In the small dining room patients could order only vegetables or salads with grilled fish or an omelette if their regimen allowed it. Some simply took the consommé and did not linger to be tempted further.

'We occasionally have dinner in here after the patients had finished,' her father explained as they sat down. Lettie recognised the footman who took their order.

The ensuing silence felt awkward to Lettie and she guessed that her presence was limiting their conversation. 'How long will Lord Laughton stay?' she began.

'I don't know,' her father answered.

'Until he gets what he wants, I imagine,' Frances added quietly.

'Well, will you sell to him, Father?' Lettie asked.

Three pairs of enquiring eyes turned in her direction. 'How do you know that I am considering it?' Father queried.

'I . . . I met Mr Laughton at the post office in the village and we took coffee together at the inn.'

Frances raised her eyebrows. 'You went to an inn with a gentleman you are not acquainted with?'

'Oh, but I am acquainted with him! He has been staying at Boundary Farm near Waterley Edge. We had an . . . an interesting conversation.'

'What has he said to you, Lettie?' her father asked.

'Not much, except that he's entitled to half of Waterley estate and Lord Laughton has offered him Mereside Lodge instead.'

'They argued about it – at least, Lord Laughton did – all through dinner yesterday,' Frances complained. 'It was quite exhausting.'

Dr Bretton added, 'If part of the estate had been willed to others he'd no business giving any of it away in the first place.'

'Well, he did. I have the title deeds. He had Lady Laughton's willing consent at the time. She wanted . . .' Her father hesitated. 'She wanted me out of Waterley Hall and agreed to sign.'

The memory appeared to trouble her father, causing Lettie to hesitate with more questions. Frances took up the conversation, 'Mr Laughton is not at all like his cousin. I thought he was very civil.'

'I sincerely hope he is not going to stir up more trouble with His Lordship,' her father commented.

Lettie grimaced. 'I think it's too late to hope for that, Father. He has little regard for either Lord or Lady Laughton. He told me that his father spent most of his life in legal battles with one Laughton or the other.'

'Considering you are a stranger to him, he seems to have told you a great deal.'

'He appeared to think I should know. Actually, I think he was explaining his involvement as a kind of apology for his earlier behaviour towards me. He took a dislike to me at first, especially when he found out who my grandfather was.'

Her father exchanged a questioning glance with Frances. She returned a faltering smile. Their soup arrived accompanied by the gritty biscuits that Dr Bretton called crackers and crumbled them into his consommé. Her father waited until the footman had disappeared before asking Lettie what else Alec had divulged.

'Not much that I haven't told you already.' She took a deep breath. 'Well, I . . . I do know why you want the money.'

She saw her father glance at Frances who tried to maintain her cheerfulness. 'Selling up is the only way for us to be together in the way we wish,' she said and added firmly, 'You have to tell her, Michael.'

Lettie noticed that her eyes were sad and she realised that her father had already made up his mind to sell. 'But what will you do if you leave here?' she demanded.

'We'll have enough left over for a guest house at the seaside,' Frances answered. She appeared to be happy with this solution.

Her father, too, managed a smile and Lettie realised that the only time he seemed happy was in Frances's company. He loved her and he needed her and it was clear to Lettie that Frances would do anything for him. That's love, she thought. They wanted to be together as husband and wife. Father was estranged from his wife but Frances, clearly, was not prepared to live with him as his mistress and play the part of the Lady of the House at Mereside Lodge. Lettie admired her for that stance.

'You have already decided to sell,' Lettie stated.

'We don't want any more battles.'

'Then Lord Laughton has won!' she exclaimed. 'You can't let him do that. He's a bully and it's not fair!'

Chapter 26

'I shall have Frances as my wife. That is worth any amount of money.'

Lettie was forced to agree with him. But her sense of injustice was strong. 'You can't give in without a fight!'

'Yes I can.' Her father put down his soup spoon. 'I am worn out with fighting,' he said.

This silenced Lettie for a moment as she realised he had been fighting his own personal battles for most of his life. Yet Mereside Lodge *was* his life! A guest house in Scarborough was hardly the same.

'But Frances isn't,' she exclaimed and swivelled to face her. 'Are you?'

Dr Bretton intervened, 'You would be a notable loss to hydropathy, Frances. And Michael is not ready for a major upheaval. He needs more time to complete his recovery and this is the best place for him.'

'Father will recover, won't he?' Lettie asked him anxiously. She was very aware that her sudden appearance had come as a shock to him and he had been tempted back to the brandy bottle.

'Your arrival has been my biggest test in recent months,' her father admitted.

'I know and I am sorry. I want to make amends.' She turned to Dr Bretton. 'Is there anything I can do to help with Father's recovery?'

'Very little, Lettie. He must do it for himself.'

Frances added, 'But you can do what I do and be there for him when the temptation is greatest.'

'That is enough about me!' her father interrupted. 'May we not enjoy our dinner? Our new cook has proved to be an excellent choice and Mereside Lodge will continue as a hydropathic establishment until the deed of sale is signed.'

'If Lord Laughton is going to give it to his cousin, Mr Laughton may wish for it to continue as such,' Dr Bretton commented. 'I know he was favourably impressed.'

'Did Mr Laughton take the cure?' Lettie queried.

'He planned to but that was before he was called away. However, I did have an interesting conversation with him on the merits of radioactive tonic water.' Dr Bretton warmed to this topic as a footman cleared the soup plates. 'Healing waters from natural springs have been scientific-ally proven to possess radium emanation. There is a company in San Francisco selling ceramic water dispensers lined with radium ore. The tonic eases pain from gout and rheumatism.'

Lettie had no idea what he was talking about, but Frances did. 'The water cures at Bath and Harrogate involve drinking the water as well as bathing in it. We ought to have our spring water tested for radioactivity.'

'I'll see to it,' Dr Bretton said. He poured water from a jug into their drinking glasses.

Lettie hesitated before she drank. It did taste slightly different from the water at the manse and didn't lather as well either.

Lettie had noticed that the table was not laid with wine glasses. Her eyes roamed round the room. All the tables were the same. Quite a contrast, she thought, with the selection offered by the butler the previous evening. He must have made the choices for her father.

Mr Norwich came in with their Dover sole on a large silver platter, which he offered to each of them in turn. The footmen followed with neatly turned and beautifully presented vegetables. After they had left, her father commented, 'Mr Norwich was worth waiting for. He was an under butler in the household of a duke. When I watch him at work I remember my days as a young man.'

Lettie wanted to know more about those times and asked, 'Did you enjoy your years in service, Father?'

'I did. It was my vocation. Whilst I am here, Mereside Lodge will be run as a gentleman's country residence ought to be.'

Lettie resisted a strong temptation to voice other questions running through her mind, judging it to be unwise.

Instead she said, 'I should like to learn about hydropathy, if I may. The patients take steam baths, I understand.'

'Perhaps the two of us might spend tomorrow afternoon together?' Frances responded. 'I'll show you the bath house and treatment rooms.'

'I should like that very much.'

Lettie went to sleep that night contented that, although she still had much to discover about her father and Mereside Lodge, she had made a friend of Frances. They had had a difficult start because of her rash impulsiveness and Lettie wanted to make it up to her. She now felt some easing of the impatient urgency she suffered at first. Father had, she thought, accepted Lettie although there was obviously some residual anxiety about her existence. It was an apprehensive time for her as well, but she was young and strong, whatever Alec Laughton had implied earlier.

Would he be the owner of Mereside Lodge in future? When he had told her about Lord Laughton's plans, he had not seemed predisposed to go along with them. Where had Alec gone, she wondered, and with what purpose? He said he would telegraph so perhaps Frances would tell her tomorrow; if she asked.

She met up with Frances at the end of morning treatments in the palm court, a conservatory adorned with large glossy green plants and colonial bamboo furniture. A straggle of patients wearing bathrobes were exchanging comments on their treatments and waiting for luncheon. They were mainly gentlemen smoking cigars and enjoying the view. Lettie followed Frances along a corridor of windows to the bath house. As they walked Lettie commented on how much she had enjoyed dinner last evening.

'Your father did, too,' Francs responded.

'Have you ever met Father's wife?' Lettie asked.

'No, never, they have lived apart for many years.'

'It must have been a short marriage. She cannot have loved him very much.'

'He believes that she did not love him at all.'

'Then why did she marry him?'

'I really do not know and he will not speak of it. I assumed at first that she was a maidservant and she married him for his position but he once said that she was a woman of independent means.'

'And you are sure she is still alive?'

'Oh yes. She lives abroad and that makes a divorce even more difficult. Lawyers are so expensive and it is, of course, not a gentlemanly thing to do. There has to be a . . . a third party. Michael has to have evidence of – you know – her . . . her adultery, and the newspapers these days are so aggressive in their reporting. It will not be easy for any of us.'

'Doesn't she want the divorce as well?'

'I imagine so but I don't know yet. We cannot instruct a lawyer without the means to pay him. I have offered to allow her to cite me as the guilty party but Michael won't hear of it. He gets angry because it would be a lie. He insists that she is the guilty one.'

Lettie noticed that talking of divorce was making

Frances anxious so she didn't pursue the conversation. They reached the bath house and this cheered Frances as she explained to Lettie what went on in a twentieth-century health hydro and how modern science was improving on the old methods.

The bath house was a long low building containing rooms of different sizes for various hydropathic treatments. The atmosphere was warm and oppressively humid in some areas. Frances had a team of assistants – female hydropathic nurses and male bath attendants who administered treatments to their patients and kept the bath house clean. An aroma of scented oil filled Lettie's nostrils.

The steam rooms were lined with white tiles and fitted with similarly tiled benches. They had adjacent cubicles for cold water treatments, which sounded quite brutal to Lettie. Some of the cubicles had long bathtubs, permanently situated with their own piped water supply and drain hole, for sulphur mud or peat treatments.

Mereside Lodge had taken delivery recently of some patented 'sitz' baths from Germany. Lettie thought they were attractive hip baths until she learned that, although the water in the sitz bath was warm, the treatment consisted of sitting in it with the feet in icy water. This sounded unpleasant enough, but the treatment also required that the patient then move to a cold sitz bath with the feet in warm water and alternate between the two. Excellent for gout and rheumatism, France advised.

The larger baths used for immersing the whole body in warm ocean salts or seaweed seemed a much better proposition. Lettie was undecided about the massage tables but totally enamoured of a delightfully warm and dry room at one end containing a row of comfortable couches with pillows and blankets for patient relaxation at the end of their treatments. Frances knocked on a door labelled 'Consultations' and a voice answered, 'Come in.'

Dr Bretton was sitting behind a desk reading a journal by the light of an oil lamp with a glass chimney. He had a pair of reading spectacles hooked round his ears.

'Are we disturbing you?' Frances said.

He stood up. 'Not at all. Come in and sit down. I have been reading about a new design of sitz bath that is divided into two halves and holds the hot and cold water in one utensil.' He took off his spectacles, massaged his eyes with his fingers and muttered, 'We must seriously consider putting in electric light.'

Lettie glanced around the room for a gas mantle on the wall and queried, 'Why don't you have gas lights at Mereside Lodge? We had them in the downstairs rooms at the manse.'

Frances replied, 'It costs far too much to lay the pipes. They don't have gas lamps in the village either.'

'The Reverend is having electric light in the mission hall at Waterley Edge.'

'But electric is dangerous,' Frances said. 'I mean, it can kill you, can't it?'

'Only if you touch it,' Dr Bretton replied.

'But you can't see it so how would you know?'

'It travels along wires inside rubber tubes. We ought to consider it, Frances. I have been reading about patient treatments using electric.'

'It does cost a lot, though,' Lettie explained. 'I used to write up minutes for the elders' meetings and I saw the figures. Our chapel had a legacy to pay for it.'

'I'll talk to Michael about it. More treatments mean more patients,' Dr Bretton said.

'And now we have better servants we can take more patients,' Frances added.

'Perhaps we can make savings, too?' Lettie suggested. Neither Frances nor Dr Bretton queried the fact that she was including herself in the future of Mereside Lodge. She went on, 'Those daily hampers from Leeds and Sheffield must cost a fortune. I know how much a whole ham costs.'

Frances shook her head emphatically. 'Michael will not compromise on his daily deliveries of provisions. He insists on the best suppliers. Patients expect the same high standards that they have in their own country residences.'

'Do you ever check that they are sending you the full order?'

Frances raised her eyebrows and looked helpless for a second. 'I cannot do everything, Lettie! I never have a minute to spare on some days and I am a hydropathic nurse not a housekeeper.'

'We do have a housekeeper, normally,' Dr Bretton explained. 'Unfortunately, the last one turned out to be most unsuitable. She came with testimonials but we think they were not genuine.'

'I can housekeep,' Lettie suggested. 'My grandmother used to be a housekeeper at Waterley Hall and she taught me everything. I've never used half of what I learned but Gran said I should know anyway.'

Frances smiled. 'Lettie, managing a manse is hardly the same as here.'

'I had the mission hall and chapel accounts to look after as well. I checked all the ordering and invoices and kept the books balanced for the Reverend.' Lettie felt excited by the thought of being involved in her father's venture.

'Someone to help with housekeeping records would be useful, Frances,' Dr Bretton pointed out.

'You cannot do housekeeping and nursing,' Lettie added. 'Of course, I'll only do it if Father agrees.'

'You are far too young for such a position,' Frances said.

'I'm not suggesting I am the housekeeper, or even that you call me housekeeper. Cook and Mr Norwich would probably walk out if you did. But I could be your assistant, Frances, doing the housekeeping work for you until you have made a new appointment.'

Frances was undecided until Lettie added, 'I should be acting on your instructions all the time.' Lettie recalled the meticulous minute books recording mission business and suggested enthusiastically, 'I'll write a full report for you and Father every day.'

'Well, I can't say that I don't need your help,' Frances said slowly then added more briskly, 'Very well. You can start with the laundry lists.' She stood up and went on, 'We'll leave Dr Bretton to his reading and I'll show you where the keys are. The linen cupboards are next to the housekeeper's sitting room.'

'I know. I did some sewing in there.'

They went out of the bath house through the servants' entrance at the opposite end from the palm court and passed the laundry, which had completed most of its work for the day. As they skirted the coal yard to return to the servants' hall, Frances muttered, 'Coals are getting low again. Michael will have to send word to the coal merchant.'

Lettie reflected that Toogoods wouldn't need a reminder to deliver supplies. They knew how much coal their customers used and replenished their cellars on a regular basis. Life was different in the countryside. They didn't even have the gas light here.

'Who is your coalman?' she asked.

'I can't recall his name but I'll show you where I keep the invoices and record books.' Frances led the way into the housekeeper's sitting room and said, 'Wait here while I fetch some refreshment.'

Lettie sat by the unlit fire, her gaze wandering over the bookcases with interest until Frances returned with a pot of aromatic coffee on a tray.

'The house servants are eating their dinner. We'll have ours at second sitting with the hydro nurses and bath attendants so I've brought cake to keep you going,' Frances said. 'Do you like cherry cake? It's just out of the oven.' She placed the tray on a small table between the two fireside chairs.

'I like all cake,' Lettie replied. 'Shall I pour?'

Frances outlined how she managed the housekeeping and pointed out where the relevant books were kept. 'I'm

373

afraid I haven't kept the linen records up to date, and the invoices haven't been sorted for over two months. But every one is there, so you can find out anything you need to know. The previous housekeeper ordered food supplies as well.'

'I gather she didn't stay long,' Lettie commented.

'Michael had to let her go. I agreed with him but I haven't been able to replace her yet.' Frances looked unhappy for a moment, then said more cheerily, 'Now Mr Norwich has joined us, he will order his own supplies and Cook can manage food provisions. They can be trusted. Both come with good references that Michael has checked himself.'

Lettie didn't comment but she guessed the old house-keeper had been in collusion with the outdoor staff to steal food. Frances's record-keeping was, indeed, in a sorry state and Lettie decided she would begin with stock-taking and inventories.

After tea, Frances took her into the butler's pantry. Mr Norwich was poring over his own inventories. He was very pleased to learn that he would be receiving regular housekeeping returns from Miss Fanshaw in future and Lettie itched to get started.

The following day, Lettie was unexpectedly called away from her task by Frances who said, 'Your father has had a visitor who insists on meeting you before he leaves. He's waiting in the morning room.'

Intrigued, Lettie took off her apron and tidied her hair. A mature gentleman, plainly dressed and wearing an ecclesiastical collar, was waiting for her. He stood up as soon as she entered the room and approached her with an air of briskness.

'Are you Miss Hargreaves?' He appeared to be examining her appearance in some detail.

'I am, sir.'

He nodded. 'Yes. You match the description I have. Excellent! My name is Reverend Pryce from Mereside Church. Your guardian has requested that I place myself at your service.'

'Reverend Ennis asked you to come here?'

'Actually, no. It was his colleague from the Methodist chapel in Forest Chase. We are acquainted. Your guardian sent word that you were here and requested that I confirm you are well and it is your wish to remain here. A gentleman who claims to be your father received me and gave me such confirmation, but I must hear it from you.'

'The gentleman is my father, sir, and please be assured that he speaks the truth. I have written to the Reverend to explain this.'

'Yes, yes, but he is concerned, and rightly so. Mereside Lodge is not an establishment for young girls.'

'That is nonsense!' Reverend Pryce raised his eyebrows and Lettie searched for words to redeem her rudeness. She remembered the words that Agnes had used about the Lodge's reputation and added, 'Forgive me, sir, but this is a respectable house, whatever you may have heard.'

His mouth turned down at the corners but he responded positively. 'Very well. I have done my duty and shall report my findings as requested. Good day to you.'

'I'll show you out, sir.' She opened the morning-room

door, followed him out and handed him his hat and cane from the hall closet. When she held the front door she said, 'Thank you for taking the trouble to find me. I am sure some of our . . . our guests will be pleased to attend your Sunday services if you advise us of the times.'

'Indeed?' he answered with a query in his voice.

'Guests at Mereside Lodge are here to improve their health, sir, and I am sure my father has a high regard for their spiritual well-being too. I shall arrange the carriage for evensong.' She wondered if she'd had been too forward, but smiled anyway. 'Good day to you, sir.'

He raised his hat to acknowledge her as he walked down the steps and she closed the front door softly. There was so much to be done at Mereside Lodge and she looked forward to returning to the servants' hall and catching up with Agnes. Agnes was in charge of the upstairs maids and an important ally of any housekeeper.

Engrossed in her new challenge, the days flew by. Alec had telegraphed to say he was going abroad and would return to Mereside Lodge within the month. Lettie counted the days on the calendar in the housekeeper's sitting room and her mind registered the date every day. Occasionally, when she was walking alone by the mere and heckled by the geese, she allowed herself to daydream about him. She imagined hearing the approaching thud of hooves behind her as he rode up to sweep her up onto his horse and carry her away to she knew not where.

It was a girlish fantasy and she reproached herself for it afterwards. But she believed his chivalrous nature to be real. He was a gentleman in every sense of the word and he would protect his chosen lady to the death. Sadly, she thought, that lady was not likely to be her. Alec's lady would be more akin to one of the elegant aristocratic creatures who came to Mereside Lodge to recover from a hectic and exhausting season of parties and balls.

Chapter 27

Michael gained in strength every day and cheered notice-
ably when several new patients arrived. Lettie assumed
they had been influenced by Lord Laughton's presence.
His Lordship took the cure for a week and, against Dr
Breton's advice, insisted on a further week. Lettie was
curious about him and she saw him once, in the palm
court.

She had been asked by Frances to make a needlework
repair on the ribbon of a satin bedroom slipper for one
of the lady patients. The lady was elderly, not titled but
connected to a baronet's family through her marriage,
and Lettie was instructed to take the slippers to her in
the palm court at teatime. They were very pretty embroidered slippers and Lettie wrapped them in clean muslin
to return them.

Palm court was a popular venue for patients taking the cure. It had a restful ambience and a relaxed dress code. Those on strict regimens could remain in their hydropath bathrobes and take tea amongst the greenery, perhaps sharing conversation with new-found acquaintances. Afternoon tea did not vary. The traditional beverage with milk or lemon as patients wished, or a herbal alternative, a few very dainty cucumber sandwiches, even in winter when the cucumbers came from glasshouses, and a slice of Russian cake.

Lettie was intrigued by the Russian cake. It was the same every day and baked in loaf tins by Cook to a special recipe without butter, solely for patients taking the cure. The ingredients of eggs, flour and a mix of minced dried fruits were assured to keep sluggish digestions in working order. One slice at teatime was obligatory for the cure.

Lettie delivered the slippers and was admiring the plants when she was distracted by a commotion from one of the gentlemen. She overheard a patient comment, 'Lord Laughton again. When is he going home?'

Lord Laughton was a gentleman of middling years with greying hair and whiskers. He was running to fat, Lettie noticed, and it made him look like King Edward. He must have been handsome as a younger man but his face was deeply lined so that his expression was angry even when he was calm. He did not seem to care that he had disturbed other patients by his demands. A young footman, one of Mr Norwich's recent additions, was standing in front of him with a silver tea tray.

'You heard me! Dundee cake and a glass of whiskey to wash it down,' His Lordship demanded.

'Your order card has light diet on it, sir,' the footman replied.

'I've had enough of that. Fit as a fiddle now, everything in good working order.' He threw a coin on the tray and said, 'Whiskey, a large one.'

The footman placed the tray on a low table. 'I beg your pardon, sir. I cannot accept a tip. House rules, sir.'

Lord Laughton added another coin. 'You'll fetch me a whiskey if you want to keep your position.'

'I'll ask Mr Norwich. Excuse me, sir.'

As the footman walked by Lettie, he said, 'He's always complaining about something. And he knows about the tipping.' The young man added indignantly, 'I am not a waiter.'

Lettie agreed that Lord Laughton should have known better. Father was proud of his 'gentleman's country house' traditions at Mereside Lodge. Guests in country houses presented monetary gifts to servants discreetly in envelopes at the end of their stay. Of course His Lordship knew! She recalled a comment of Mrs Osborne that Lord Laughton thought he could buy anyone, and grimaced. Well, he's not buying my father's life, she thought crossly, not if I can help it. She spoke quietly to the footman. 'Mr Norwich won't change it without Dr Bretton's say-so. I'll fetch him.'

Lettie explained the situation to Dr Bretton and he went to speak to His Lordship immediately. She hovered in the background, half hidden by the large glossy leaves of a magnificent rubber plant. Dr Bretton suggested that Lord Laughton dispensed with the cure as he had advised earlier. One week was the normal prescription. Eventually, His Lordship agreed to continue the discussion in Dr Bretton's consulting room, to the relief of other patients.

It was a minor incident yet it made Lettie determined that her father would not give in to His Lordship's demands to sell. Mereside Lodge was her father's life, and now hers as well. But his divorce was equally as important to him and he ought to have both. At the manse she had had to account for every penny that was spent. It appeared that no one had applied the same principles here for a long time and Lettie resolved to change that.

Lettie spoke with her father on most days. She ate her breakfast and dinner in the servants' hall but took tea or dinner with her father, either in his room or in the small dining room for patients. She preferred tea when they were alone as Frances and Dr Bretton were present at dinner and the conversation different. Alone with father, she talked fondly of her grandmother and childhood at the manse, and saw that this gave him pleasure. But for Lettie, questions about her mother were constantly on her mind. However, although she remained intensely curious about her mother, she had to be satisfied, for the present, to have found her father.

As he gained in strength he talked of earlier years at Mereside Lodge, at least those he could remember. He had 'given up the drink' several times on the advice of his physician and more than ten years ago had visited a famous hydro in Derbyshire frequented by the then Prince of Wales. It was there that he met Frances, fell in love, and with her help began his slow and very rocky road to recovery. But, following that visit, his vision for the future of Mereside Lodge had remained steadfast. He sold his thriving woodland concern to pay for the bath house and other changes. Frances contacted Dr Bretton, a colleague from her years as a nurse in Africa, and persuaded him to join them.

On one occasion Lettie outlined her ideas for savings. Michael readily accepted her request to investigate coal supplies and it made her think of Thomas. He could advise her and she wondered if he would drive over in the coal wagon one Sunday as he had promised. She realised that she missed him.

'Father,' she asked one evening, 'why do you buy York hams from a London supplier when they come from Yorkshire?'

'I only have the very best quality, my dear. London stores supply the great houses of our lords and ladies.'

'But I could go direct to the pig curers for the very same hams.'

'And how would they get here? London stores deliver every day on the railway.'

'The provisions merchant in Mereside village has York ham. His wife cooks it and he slices it, weighs it out and sells it to his customers. In fact, he could probably supply you at a saving.'

'I have no intention of reducing my standards. I should rather close down.'

'I agree with you, Father, but will you let me look into it?'

'If you wish. Frances says you are proving to be a good housekeeper.'

'Gran taught me well.'

He gazed out of the window. 'Yes, she was a good woman. But your grandfather was powerful. He controlled his own home as he did the servants' hall at Waterley.'

'Tell me about my mother,' she said softly.

Pain washed over her father's face and he closed his eyes.

'I'm sorry, Father. I didn't mean to upset you.'

'It's not your fault. Your grandmother and I were as one in that respect. Why should a daughter suffer for her father's evils?'

Lettie didn't understand and said, 'I . . . I haven't suffered, Father.'

'I believe you have,' he replied, 'and it has been because of my actions. However, I was not speaking of you.'

'Then who?'

'Your mother. She suffered from your grandfather's ambition. It ruled him and infected her and I . . . I went along with his ways. I was weak, I see that with hindsight.'

'But you are strong now! You have conquered your weakness.'

She realised that he was distressed and immediately talked of other things: her arrangement for Sunday worshippers at the village church, and the governess cart. She said, 'I should like to buy some notions from the draper's in the village and I thought I might use the old governess cart in the stables.'

'Certainly. The stableman will take you.'

'I am able to drive myself, Father. Now I am Frances's assistant, I often want to make small purchases. May I not have the governess cart for my own use?'

'Why, that is a splendid idea! It will need some renovation. I'll speak to Norwich about it.'

'Thank you. I wasn't aware Mr Norwich was responsible for the outdoor staff as well.'

'He has to be for the present. I used to have a steward, a reliable fellow who managed all the servants for me.'

'Where is he now?'

'I couldn't pay him, you see. But he was loyal. He stayed as long as he could, but he had a family to support . . .'

'Well, that won't happen again. We have more new patients expected this week. Lord Laughton may be difficult but his presence here has helped.'

'No, my dear, His Lordship has not helped at all. We are constantly offering patients extra services to apologise for his behaviour. It was his cousin, Mr Laughton, who recommended us to his London acquaintances.'

Lettie's heart lifted. If that were the case then Alec did not want Mereside Lodge to close! When Father sold to Lord Laughton, it might remain as a hydro, with Father and Frances and Dr Bretton and . . . *and me*, she realised happily. Nothing would change and soon she would see Alec again.

'When is Mr Laughton returning?' she asked.

Her happiness was short lived. Father replied, 'He has written to say he has been delayed. The letter was posted overseas.'

She realised that travelling was a part of Alec's life and he would return home to Canada as soon as his business with Lord Laughton was finished. She found this a depressing thought and sighed unconsciously.

'Are you sad about our new patients?'

'No, of course not, it's . . . it's good news for the hydro.' She rallied her thoughts. 'I . . . I want to examine our coal costs. Is Mr Norwich in charge of the boilerman as well?'

'He is. I shall not make any further appointments now. Mereside Lodge will need an engineer in future even if the hydro closes. A house of these proportions must have electric light and a motor vehicle.'

'But it will still need coal for the boilers and fires.'

'Everybody needs coal,' her father said with a smile.

Lettie agreed and her thoughts turned to Thomas. She wanted his advice so it was with some delight that the following Sunday afternoon, when she said 'Come in' after a tap on her door, Thomas walked in to the house-keeper's room.

'Well, look at you, Lettie Hargreaves, the housekeeper already.'

'Thomas! How lovely to see you. Sit down.'

'I like the grey outfit.' He grinned, referring to her

dark, serviceable housekeeper's dress. 'It makes you look, er, um . . .'

'It makes me look what?' she prompted.

'Your age,' he said, 'but in a nice way; grown up and capable.'

She wasn't flattered and she frowned.

'It's what you are,' he added quickly. 'It's you, especially with your hair done up like that.'

When she didn't reply he went on, 'Reverend Ennis told me you were staying on here and I said I'd be back if you didn't come home so here am I.'

'So here you are,' she repeated and decided not to dwell on what he thought about her appearance. 'And I am very pleased to see you. Reverend Ennis sent a spy from the local church to check up on me.'

'I know. I've called into the manse several times and he told me. He was worried about you and he couldn't leave the mission. You found your father, then? I'm happy for you, Lettie. What kind of place is this?'

'Oh, I've so much to tell you.' She closed her account books carefully, pushed them aside and began.

After about half an hour he said, 'Do you know that you look different when you talk about here. Your eyes light up and you smile a lot.'

'I'm happy here, Thomas. Whatever happens to Mereside Lodge, Father will marry a lovely lady and he will be happy too. I'll have a family.' After she had said it, Lettie realised how satisfying that sounded to her. Thomas wouldn't understand. He had always been surrounded by a large and loving family. But she hadn't and she smiled to herself every time she thought about it. She couldn't help herself.

'I'm thirsty now,' she said. 'And you must be hungry after your long drive. Let me get you some refreshment. Tea? Or coffee? The coffee here is very good.'

'Then I'll have coffee please.'

'With cream?'

'No, ta. Have you got sugar?'

'Of course we have! Wait here.' Lettie went off to the still room next to the scullery.

Agnes was laying up tea trays for the patients and Lettie explained who Thomas was as she warmed a silver coffee pot.

'We were all wondering,' Agnes replied, 'because he came round the back in a motor wagon. You go back and talk to him. I'll bring your coffee. Large slices of cake?'

'And sandwiches, he'll be hungry.'

Agnes lingered to serve Thomas his coffee and hand round sandwiches and cake. 'Can I fetch you anything else?' she asked.

'No thank you,' Lettie answered, aware that the patients' teas were waiting.

'I'll come back for the tray,' Agnes volunteered.

'No need, you've a lot to do out there,' Lettie said.

'It's no trouble,' Agnes replied as she left.

After the door had closed, Thomas commented, 'Do the maids always wait on you as well?'

'No, they don't. I'm not even the housekeeper, just an

assistant, and I normally do everything for myself.' Agnes knows that, she thought.

Thomas pulled down the cuffs of his Sunday suit and straightened up in his chair. 'Perhaps she thinks I'm somebody important.'

'She saw you arrive in the coal wagon, that's all, so don't get above yourself,' Lettie commented, smiling. 'And speaking of coal, I may be able to give you an order for Mr Toogood. How much will he charge a ton for regular deliveries here?'

'To here? I don't know. It'd have to come from a pithead via a yard around these parts.'

'Well, has he got one?' Lettie got up to find a piece of paper, an invoice for the Lodge's latest load of coal. She waved it in front of his face. 'Can he beat this price?'

'Keep it still, then.' Thomas took hold of the document and read it. He blew out his cheeks. 'That's a bit dear, isn't it?'

'I thought so too. And the Lodge uses a lot.'

'It doesn't look that big a house to me.'

'It's not, but we have the bath house. You know, Turkish baths and so on, every morning.'

'I know about them. My dad says they're supposed to be good for you.'

'They are, especially when you've been ill like my father has.'

Thomas gave her a sympathetic look. 'He'll need you and Frances on his side for ever.'

'I know. He's got us, both of us.'

'He's a lucky man. Tell me more about this place. My dad'll be fascinated.'

Lettie spent another very pleasant hour with Thomas before Agnes came back for the tray. 'Your father was asking where you were today,' she said to Lettie.

'I sometimes have my tea with him, if he feels up to it,' Lettie explained to Thomas.

'And I've kept you from him,' he said. 'Go and see him for half an hour.'

'What about you?'

'Well, I'd like to see the size of the boilers here before I leave.'

'I'll find one of the men to show you after I've seen father.'

'I can do that for you, Lettie,' Agnes suggested.

'Thank you, I'd like that.' Thomas smiled and stood up. 'Have you worked here long, Agnes?'

As Agnes returned Thomas's smile, Lettie felt excluded from this hasty arrangement. Before Agnes could reply Lettie asked, 'Will you be able to stay for servants' tea? It's at five o'clock on Sundays.'

'Yes please! I've a long drive home.'

'I'll take him to the servants' hall,' Agnes volunteered. 'We'll wait for you in there.'

Lettie had little choice but to agree. 'Well, if you're sure, Thomas?' she muttered.

'Don't neglect your father for my sake,' Thomas said. 'I'll be in good hands with Agnes.'

Lettie knew that and watched them walk out of her room with a frown. Thomas was *her* friend. He'd come to see *her* and she wanted to show him round. But Father was asking for her so she quelled her feelings and gave some attention to her appearance.

She was late arriving for tea in the servants' hall, which, on Sundays, was cold cuts with fresh and pickled vegetables followed by fruit cake and cheese. She wasn't hungry anyway and went straight over to Thomas and Agnes who were deep in conversation.

'Did you see the boilers?' she asked brightly.

'I did, and I had a talk with your boilerman. You know that invoice you showed me?'

'Ye-e-es,' Lettie answered.

'Is that every fortnight?'

'Every week.'

'You do get through a lot of coal,' he responded with raised eyebrows.

Agnes stood up. 'I've got sewing to organise this evening. It was nice to meet you, Thomas. You'll come again, won't you?'

'If I'm invited,' he answered. When Agnes had left the room he added, 'She's a lovely girl, isn't she?'

'I like her. She's a good friend as well as being reliable.'

Thomas lowered his voice. 'I wouldn't say that about some others employed here.'

'What do you mean?' She knew the answer, of course.

'Even if those boilers are going all day and night, you wouldn't get through that much coal every week. Where else do you use it?'

'Nowhere. It's the same with the food deliveries,' she whispered. 'Stuff goes missing before it even gets here. Come back to the housekeeper's room. I want your help.'

Lettie told him what she had seen with the food hampers.

'If you know who it is you'll have to get the constable in,' Thomas concluded.

'I can't do that because it'll get in the newspapers and cause a scandal and that won't do the Lodge's reputation any good at all. Father can't afford to lose any patients but he says I can look at all costings. I've got a better idea.'

'Watch your back, Lettie. These people have no scruples.'

Lettie put his mind at ease by outlining her plan to change suppliers and the way provisions were delivered and remove the opportunities for stealing.

'Yes, but you'll need someone to find you new suppliers – someone like me who knows the traders. And he'd need a motor vehicle out here.'

Lettie gave a short laugh. 'Do you mean you?'

Thomas was surprised, thought about it for a moment and said, 'I don't see why not. I'll ask Mr Toogood about the coal order. What with all these mill and factory owners building their big houses and living like the gentry, he has interests all over the Yorkshire coal fields.'

'You must have impressed him to let you borrow the coal wagon again.'

'Reverend Ennis asked my foreman if I could. That reminds me, he sent some of your things from the manse.' He stood up. 'I'll fetch them in, and then I'd best make a start for home. Can I say goodbye to Agnes before I leave?'

'I'll find her for you.'

But Agnes was already outside, cutting spikes of lavender for the linen cupboard. By the time Lettie caught up with her she was sitting on a garden seat with her trug of scented flower stalks, near to where the coal wagon was parked. Thomas was sitting next to her.

Lettie gazed at them and frowned, pressing her lips together in thought. She recognised her Gran's old travelling box on the ground by the wagon and walked over to it. Thomas and Agnes joined her a minute later.

'Where do you want your box?' Thomas asked, bending down to pick it up. He heaved it onto his shoulder.

'Leave it in the passage,' Lettie said. 'The footmen will carry it upstairs.'

'It'll take two of them,' Agnes commented as she watched Thomas walk away.

Left on their own, Lettie and Agnes stared at each other in silence until Agnes said, 'I have to check on the maids in the sewing room,' and followed Thomas indoors.

Lettie waited by the wagon until he came out again. She was trying to make sense of her feelings. Thomas was *her* friend but there was no doubt in her mind that he was attracted to Agnes, and that Agnes was welcoming his attentions. As Thomas cranked the engine into life, climbed into the driver's seat and waved goodbye, she noticed that Agnes was standing in the open doorway, watching them.

Chapter 28

Lettie walked over to the stables to see the coachman. He was supervising renovations on the governess cart. The last coat of varnish was dry and it looked very spruce. The coachman had selected a pony for it and he showed her where the tack was hung. Mr Norwich had made him ostler, in charge of all the horses, carriage and carts – and the men who worked them.

The carter and stableman were not happy but Mr Norwich had already made his presence felt, outdoors and indoors, as the most senior servant at Mereside Lodge. Cook and the head gardener, who were rulers in their own realms at Mereside Lodge, respected his word. And Cook was very popular with the outdoor men because she looked after their stomachs.

The carter appeared as they were admiring the trap.

'You'll need one of us to tek care of it fer you,' he said.

The coachman replied for her: 'I've a lad from the village starting next week. You and the stableman are needed with the heavy horses, clearing woodland and watercourses round the mere.'

'What about the hampers waiting fer fetching from the Halt?' the carter demanded.

'Oh, I'll collect those in future,' Lettie answered.

'You can't lift them on your own.'

'Then I'll take the new stable hand.' She paused before adding, 'Ordering is different now so I'll know what to expect.'

The carter grunted and wandered away. Lettie thanked the coachman and looked forward to speedier journeys into Mereside village. She went indoors to tidy the paperwork that she had been doing when Thomas arrived. The door to the laundry store and sewing room was open and the maids were packing away. Agnes had been supervising running repairs on uniforms, and repairing worn bed linen from patients' rooms for its second life in the servants' attics.

Lettie fingered the fabrics spread out on the table. 'Do they make their own dresses?' she asked.

Agnes looked up from her task. 'Not any more. They're sent over from a factory in Leeds.'

The room was warm because a fire had been lit to heat up the flat irons. They were cooling on the fender. 'If we have the electric light, I can buy flat irons that work off them,' she commented.

'Really?' Agnes continued checking the linen and sewing box contents. After a few more minutes she sent off the maids and locked the cupboards. Then she turned to Lettie and said, 'Can I ask you a question about Thomas?'

Lettie closed the door and sat down at the sewing table. 'You like him, don't you?'

Agnes didn't reply. Instead she asked, 'Do you have an understanding with him?'

Yes! No! Yes! Lettie didn't know what to say at first. But Agnes expected an answer and the directness of her question made Lettie think seriously about her relationship with Thomas. It wasn't what Agnes thought. It was a friendship, a close friendship, because Lettie didn't have the privilege of brothers and sisters. And her so-called friends from the mission were not the ones she would choose. She chose Thomas as her friend and she did not want to lose him; which, she realised, was the reason why she was jealous of Agnes's interference.

'Yes, we have,' she replied.

'He says not,' Agnes responded.

'Why ask me if you know!'

'Because we are friends and I do not want to spoil that!'

'Then stay away from him!'

Agnes drew out a chair and sat down opposite her. 'I don't want to.' She looked directly into Lettie's eyes. 'He will be here again, won't he?'

Lettie felt uncomfortable. If she was honest with herself, she didn't *love* Thomas. And he had spent as much time with Agnes as he had with her that afternoon. She didn't want to lose him as her friend. If she made an enemy of Agnes and . . . and Thomas preferred Agnes's company to hers . . . Oh, that didn't bear thinking about! Yet it had been clear to Lettie that Thomas was instantly attracted to Agnes; and she to him.

She took a deep breath and started again. 'Yes, we do have an understanding but it's not what you think. We are friends, close friends, and for my part I want to keep it that way.'

'He said the same about you when I asked him.'

'You didn't waste any time, did you?'

'I know my own mind, Lettie.'

'Yes you do,' she agreed, 'and I want us to stay friends as well.'

'So do I.'

'And so does Thomas.'

'He said that to you?'

Agnes nodded.

He didn't waste any time either, Lettie thought. She didn't own him and she wanted him to be happy. Nonetheless, although it was hard for her to say it, she did: 'Well, good luck with him, Agnes.'

Lettie managed a smile. She felt that she was letting something precious slip away from her. She wasn't devastated but she was sad because their friendship would never be quite the same in future.

'Thanks, Lettie. I didn't want to quarrel with you.'

Agnes seemed happier and Lettie left the sewing room.

*   *   *

The following day, after her dinner in the servants' hall, Lettie changed into her best outfit and went over to the stables in the sunshine. She harnessed the docile pony herself, backed him into the shafts and secured the reins. She hadn't driven a trap for a while and the seat seemed higher than the Reverend's, but the rudiments of driving returned and her pony was well behaved.

The draper's in Mereside village was run by two spinster sisters who fashioned gowns from the fabrics they sold and displayed them in their shop window for sale to ladies whose husbands could afford them. Lettie purchased her threads and enquired of one of the ladies if she had used one of the new treadle machines for sewing.

'Certainly not,' she replied. 'Our garments are hand-made, every one of them.'

'And they are very beautiful. But I am from Mereside Lodge and the sewing room has a pile of bed sheets waiting for sides-to-middle. Perhaps you know of a local girl who can help?'

The sisters exchanged a glance. 'We offer that service to larger households. If you would care to bring your linen here I am sure we can come to an arrangement.'

'Then I shall,' Lettie replied. 'Expect me tomorrow afternoon. Good day to you.'

One of the sisters came around the counter to open the shop door for her. 'Good day, Miss . . .?'

'Hargreaves; Miss Hargreaves.'

Feeling confident, Lettie went next door to the provisions merchant, stared in the plate-glass window for a minute then opened the door. The interior was large and much more impressive than anything she had seen in Waterley Edge, or indeed their nearby town. The floor was tiled in a black and white chequered design, strewn with sawdust. There was a ladder-back chair to sit on, and two glass-fronted counters displaying cheeses and a variety of cooked meats. A wall of mahogany shelving held bottles, jars and a few cans of preserved goods, some of them with labels in a foreign language. Lettie gazed around in awe.

A young man in shirtsleeves and a waistcoat covered by a long white apron stood behind a polished mahogany-topped counter with brass edgings and corners. 'Good morning, miss,' he said.

'Is the proprietor available?'

'That would be my father. He's not here today. Can I help you?'

'I am looking for a supplier of lemons.'

'Lemons?' He climbed a small ladder to reach down a preserve jar from one of the higher shelves, wiping it free of dust before placing it on the counter. 'Best there is, miss. They come in from Italy.'

'I am looking for fresh lemons, they must be fresh.'

The young man's eyes widened for a second. 'Not much call for them around here. We'll be having oranges in from Spain in a few weeks' time.'

'Lemons,' she repeated.

He took the pencil from behind his ear and picked up a notebook. 'My father will get them for you, miss. He prides himself on supplying every request. What name shall I give him?'

'Miss Hargreaves, Mereside Lodge.'

He stopped writing for a second and then continued, 'The Lodge, eh?' he said. 'I'd heard there were a few changes going on up there. Is there anything else I can help you with, Miss Hargreaves?'

Lettie glanced at the fresh provisions displayed under glass domes on the counter. 'I'll take some York ham and . . . Wensleydale, I think. Yes, some Wensleydale cheese.' She watched as the young man sliced and weighed out her purchases and then wrapped them neatly in clean crisp paper. 'There's no need to send them on for me. I have my trap outside.'

'I'll carry them outside for you, Miss Hargreaves.' The young man walked round his counter and opened the door for her. Then he stowed her packages safely in the trap and helped her into the driving seat. When he handed her the reins he said, 'It's a pleasure to serve you, Miss Hargreaves.'

'Thank you.' She smiled. 'I'll call again when your father is home. Good day.'

Lettie flicked the reins gently and set off for the Halt. She was on the platform before the railway train with the hampers was due. Shortly after she arrived another small carriage appeared on the track behind her, the driver wearing the livery jacket of the inn. He waited on the platform too and when the railway engine hissed to a steamy halt, both went directly to the guard's van. The guard handed out two hampers, a travelling trunk and a valise.

Lettie's hampers were light enough for her to handle as they didn't contain hams. Quails eggs, cucumbers and cinnamon sticks were not heavy, although dried fruits for the Russian cake were. The driver from the inn was kind enough to offer help and she did not refuse him. A lady and gentleman, who had alighted from first class, walked out in front of them to their waiting carriage.

Lettie had been so concerned about her hampers that she had not taken any notice of the passengers. But, as she looked up, she saw the gentleman help the lady into their carriage and recognised Alec. Her heart gave a peculiar little lurch. He was so tall and handsome, so smartly dressed, that she experienced an immediate pang of envy for the lady who accompanied him. He appeared to be very attentive towards her and Lettie wished she had seen more of her. She wore a large feathered hat that shaded her features from the sun. But even without seeing her face, Lettie's overriding impression was that she was a lady of elegance and fashion.

'Who is the lady?' she whispered.

'She's a guest at the inn, miss.'

'She isn't a local lady, then?' she queried. But he didn't answer her because he had moved away to collect his passengers' luggage.

Alec didn't even glance in her direction before he climbed into the carriage after the lady. It was hardly surprising, she shrugged. Lettie may be wearing her best outfit and feel confident that the village traders had taken her seriously, but she felt dowdy in comparison to Alec's companion. The thought depressed her. She wanted Alec to think well of her. Perhaps, intent on the comforts of his companion, he had not even noticed her. If he had, he hadn't acknowledged her and this depressed her further.

Who was the lady? The answer dropped into her mind like a stone in a well, plummeting to its depths. She was Alec's wife. He had a wife and why would he not have one? He was a gentleman of means, educated and well-travelled, and the most attractive man she had ever set eyes on. His wife had accompanied him from Canada and remained in London while he completed his business in the North of England. She stood at the rear of her trap waiting for the inn carriage to move off and felt her new-found poise drain away.

When she reached the road, the inn carriage was well on its way to the village and Lettie considered that Alec must be staying at the inn with his wife for . . . for how long? For the time being? Until her father had agreed the sale with Lord Laughton and His Lordship had left? Yes, of course, although Lord Laughton was a relation of Alec's, His Lordship was an unpleasant gentleman and Alec was protecting his wife from His Lordship's domineering behaviour.

Father will know! Lettie realised. Alec, surely, has tele-graphed her father about his return. As far as she knew, Alec had not given up his suite at the Lodge. She flicked the reins eagerly and called, 'Gee-up!' The pony ignored her and she was obliged to quell her impatience.

Michael and Frances did not change for dinner every evening and instead took supper on a tray at their own convenience in Michael's room. Frances was in the still room preparing it when Lettie found her.

'Is that for you and Father?'

'And you, if you can join us. Michael has something to tell you.'

'What about? Do you know?'

'I do, but I shall not say. What have you got there?'

Lettie placed her packages on the wooden dresser.

'I've brought something from the village for him to sample; York ham and a tomato from the hamper. Is there any Dundee cake left? I have Wensleydale, too, and it goes particularly well with Cook's Dundee.'

Lettie thought that Frances was not as excited as Father about the news. He stood by the window gazing at the mere as the daylight faded and announced, 'I have decided that I shall not sell to Lord Laughton. My life is here.'

Lettie was overjoyed. She leapt to her feet and went over to hug him. It was an impulsive gesture and he was surprised. But he hugged her back and he looked pleased. 'Does Dr Bretton know?' she asked.

'I've been having discussions with him and Mr Norwich and we are in agreement. We can make Mereside Lodge profitable.'

'And Frances?' Lettie turned round to face her. She was smiling but her eyes were sad. 'How will you pay for the divorce?' she asked.

Michael stretched out his hand towards Frances. 'Frances has been involved in all our decisions. It will be hard for both of us, but we have agreed to wait.'

Frances came forward. 'We are quite used to waiting

now. Installing the electric light is important for a twentieth-century hydro.'

'I wish there was another way,' Lettie said.

'Michael and I are together,' Frances argued, 'not as we would wish to be, but we have hopes for our future.'

It was a bitter-sweet celebration, Lettie thought, although they were as happy as they could be in the circumstances. She was happy for them and pleased with plans for the changes at Mereside Lodge. Father approved the quality of her ham and cheese and questioned her about the village provisions merchant.

'I expect Lord Laughton will be angry,' Lettie commented later.

'He is. He was the first to know,' Michael nodded.

'He's leaving for Waterley Hall tomorrow,' Frances added. 'He and Mr Laughton can take their squabbles there.'

'Has Mr Laughton given up his suite as well?' Lettie queried.

'Actually, he hasn't,' Michael said. 'Why do you ask?'

'I saw him today,' Lettie explained. 'He arrived at the Halt this afternoon.'

'He isn't here,' Frances stated.

'No, he went to the inn. He was with a lady.'

'But he has a suite here! How strange. He'll call or write to inform us, I'm sure.'

'I hope so,' Michael added. 'There is the matter of his bill.'

Lettie's eyes widened. 'He wouldn't *not* pay you, Father!' she exclaimed.

Michael and Frances looked at her, surprised at her outburst. 'These things do happen,' Frances pointed out.

'Alec is an honest man,' Lettie stated indignantly. But she noticed Frances and Michael exchanged a questioning glance and this irritated her. She knew him better than they did.

They retired shortly afterwards and the following morning after breakfast in the servants' hall, Agnes came into the housekeeper's room with a message for Lettie to see her father immediately.

He was dressed and standing in the middle of his room. But he had a helpless look in his eyes and he was clutching an opened letter.

'Frances is packing,' he said. 'She says she cannot stay, it wouldn't be decent.'

Lettie couldn't believe her ears. Frances was having a crisis of conscience? After all this time? 'Of course it's decent!' Lettie cried. 'Your relationship is respectable. Heavens, your rooms are on separate floors!'

'You don't understand. She's here! She's in the village, staying at the inn!'

Baffled, Lettie stared at him.

'My wife,' he anguished. 'My wife has come back.'

Chapter 29

Lettie blew out her cheeks and sat down on the nearest chair. She collected her thoughts for a moment and said, 'But that is good, Father, because you can talk to her about your divorce.'

'Not without Frances by my side. I can't do anything without Frances. You must go and persuade her to stay!'

Lettie raced upstairs. Frances was adamant that she should not be in the same house as Michael while his wife was here. Lettie argued that his wife wasn't at Mereside Lodge yet and anyway Frances couldn't leave her team of hydropathy nurses. And if Mrs Powell moved into Mereside Lodge then Frances could live in the village until she left. Surely Michael's wife did not want to return permanently? Did she?

She was such a distant person in his life that, in Lettie's

mind, she hardly existed. Yet she did, and her father was in a close relationship with another woman while he had a living wife. Apart from the impropriety, which would have horrified Gran, it would cause a scandal if it got out, and that would not do the hydro's reputation any good at all.

Frances left a packed suitcase in her room, ready to quit at short notice, and went down to the bath house. Lettie reported back to her father. He was relieved and gestured to the letter lying half folded on table. 'You will have to meet her.' He seemed very depressed about this and added, 'I'll . . . I'll organise it. I'm sorry, Lettie. I am so sorry.'

It was a setback for her father and Frances, she agreed. She glanced at the letter. The beginning was innocent enough, enquiring about his health and so on . . . *I should like to arrange a meeting with you. We have much to discuss . . .* But the words that riveted her attention were in the engraved heading on the notepaper. Mrs Powell was residing at the inn in Mereside village. Mrs Powell was the lady that Alec had brought to Mereside!

This was Alec's doing. It was something to do with him, and Lettie wanted him to explain himself. She left her father writing his response to the letter and went to her room for her coat and hat. She didn't stop to change out of her dark grey housekeeper's dress but hurried to the stables for her trap.

At the inn she asked to see Mr Laughton. The landlord took her name and called his wife from the back. 'There's a Miss Hargreaves to see Mr Laughton. He's just ordered refreshment in the back parlour.'

'Thank you,' Lettie replied. 'I know the way.' And she set off down the carpeted passage.

'Just a minute, miss!' the landlord called after her.

She ignored him. The small parlour was empty apart from Alec and Mrs Powell. Alec was sitting in the same chair he had used when he had brought her here. Lettie slowed and stared. Mrs Powell was less flamboyantly dressed this morning with a smaller hat that showed her features. There was something vaguely familiar about her face but she was ....she was much older than Alec, and much older than Lettie had imagined. Of course she was! She was her stepmother! This realisation made Lettie stop and take a breath. Alec was on his feet as soon as he saw her, and the landlord caught up with her as well.

'Sorry, sir,' the landlord apologised, 'this lady barged in before I could—'

'She is welcome, landlord,' Alec said. 'Bring another cup with our coffee, if you please.' He hesitated then added, 'And brandy, I think.'

He stood in front of Lettie, effectively blocking her view of Mrs Powell. His face was serious but not angry, she thought.

He went on, 'Sit down, Lettie. This meeting was supposed to happen later this week. But I should have known your father would tell you and you would not wait.' He stepped back to allow her to sit down and gestured towards his companion. 'This is—'

'My stepmother,' Lettie interrupted. 'I know.'

Alec frowned, a painful anguished frown. Lettie looked at her stepmother and was shocked to see that she was distressed. Her eyes were brimming and her mouth was trembling. She was shaking her head very slightly.

Alec kept his voice steady and addressed the older lady. 'The deception has gone on for too long. You must tell her the truth now.'

'The truth?' Lettie queried. Dear Lord, not more lies, more secrets, more revelations about her father. 'Are you not Mrs Powell?'

The lady composed herself. She was, Lettie realised, very beautiful and had a grace and poise that Lettie wished she possessed. And she *was* vaguely familiar. Perhaps she had seen her picture somewhere.

The lady inhaled and straightened her spine, something Lettie did when she needed to gather her courage. 'I am Mrs Powell,' she replied. 'I am your mother.'

'Stepmother,' Lettie corrected gently. 'My mother is dead.'

Mrs Powell continued to shake her head very slightly. 'I am your mother and I am alive. You are my daughter. You were born in France and I baptised you Collette.' She looked down and to one side. 'Your grandmother said the name was too fanciful and, when she took you away, she called you Lettie, Lettie Hargreaves.'

Yes, Gran would do something like that, Lettie thought irreverently, and swivelled her eyes onto Alec. 'Is this true?' He nodded. 'And you knew? All this time, you knew?'

He spread his hands in a gesture of helplessness. 'When we were speaking together, here in this room, I thought you knew too. I assumed you knew every-thing about your parents – your real parents – but I was wrong. When I realised I had made a mistake I believed there was only one person who could correct it and that was your mother.'

'Alec is right,' Mrs Powell said. 'You see, it was my secret and when you were born your grandmother insisted that it should remain so. She did not want you to suffer because of me.'

Lettie's father had spoken of her 'suffering' as well. 'Are you really my mother?' she asked.

'I am.'

'Then why did Gran deny your existence to me? All my life I believed you were dead! I don't understand. Didn't you want me?'

Lettie's heart was thumping and her eyes were filling up. She'd had a father and mother all along! She understood why Gran had taken her from her father. But to deprive her of her *mother* for all these years?

Her tears began to spill over. She swallowed and then sniffed. A handkerchief appeared and she clutched it. She shot a grateful glance at Alec and she wiped her nose. Her . . . her mother was doing the same with a delicate lace-edged hanky that fitted her fragile beauty so very well.

Alec moved away, behind her, and she heard him speak to the landlord. He reappeared with a tray and placed it on a nearby table and said, 'Tell her, Ruth. Tell her everything. I shall make sure you are not disturbed.'

'Don't go, Alec,' Lettie begged him. 'You know all this anyway and . . . and I . . . I want you to stay.' It was more than that, she thought. She needed him to be there. He seemed to understand her and how much the truth meant to her.

'Ruth?' he queried.

'Yes, stay,' Ruth agreed.

He poured coffee and handed it round then sat down again as Ruth related her story.

'Before I tell you,' she began, 'I want to say how much I regret what happened. I was young – younger than you are now – and ambitious, like my father. I was, I thought, destined to marry a gentleman of means. I was unaware that more powerful influences were at work.'

Lettie's coffee went cold as she listened. She was shocked, she couldn't deny it, and she tried not to let it show. But hiding her feelings was not one of Lettie's strengths. She had little wonder that Gran had kept this scandalous, sorry affair from her. Knowing Gran as she had, it must have been very difficult for Gran to come to terms with her daughter's life. Lettie understood why chapel had become so important to her.

'When I fled to France,' Ruth continued, 'I believed I was the only person that wanted you. I asked your grand-mother for help. She misunderstood my plea and thought I wished to be rid of you.' Ruth choked slightly on her words, but she went on, 'I felt that I was trapped and, whatever happened to me, I wanted to be sure you would be well cared for.'

'I was,' Lettie said. 'Gran did her best for me.'

'She didn't reply to my letter and I was desperate. I wrote to her again from London and pleaded with her to find me someone trustworthy and reliable. I can't

411

remember what I wrote, but she had a change of heart, arrived at The Admiral and travelled with me to France.' Ruth stopped talking for a moment and inhaled with a shudder.

'A brandy?' Alec queried.

'Yes please,' Ruth answered.

'Lettie?'

She nodded. 'Just a tot for me.' Lettie was thinking that it was not surprising her father turned to drink. Michael had all her sympathy. She said, 'Well, Lord Laughton is free to marry you now if you will divorce Father.'

'Laughton does not want to marry me! He was angry about . . . about you, and he lost interest in me a long time ago. His current mistress is some Italian countess, I believe.'

'But you stayed in France.'

'Yorkshire folk have long memories for scandals and my concern was always for you. Lady Laughton was as powerful and vindictive as her husband. I have, however, wanted to make contact with you for many years.'

'I wish you had.'

Ruth didn't reply. She looked as sad as Lettie felt. What a waste of those years, Lettie thought. She said, 'You will divorce Father, won't you? He has Frances now.'

'I'll do more than that. Alec has explained Michael's position and his own in relation to Laughton. I shall make it as easy as I can for Michael to divorce me. The lawyers will work something out and I shall pay them for both of us. Michael was deceived by all of us and I owe him that, at the very least.'

412

Lettie found this offer difficult to believe and wondered if it was an empty promise. 'Divorce is very expensive!' she exclaimed. 'How can you afford it?'

'When Laughton left me, he took his racehorses and left me the farm. It was purchased in my name anyway and I was wise to his ways by then. I had my own horses and some valuable jewellery and objets d'art as investments for my future. I learned to farm. I live a simple country life but I have wealth. Be assured that I can afford it.'

'Then you must go and tell him now,' Lettie urged. 'He and Frances will be so pleased. Frances means such a lot to Father and it is very awkward for her to be thought of . . . to be a . . .'

'To be what I was?' Ruth embarrassed Lettie by finishing the sentence for her.

'I – I'm sorry,' Lettie muttered. 'This is difficult for me, as well.' She was finding it impossible to call this woman her mother. Yet she had had no such qualms with her father.

'I am the one who is sorry,' Ruth replied. 'You did not choose your parents.'

'Nor you,' she said, and a spark of sympathy glimmered in her heart. Ruth's story concurred with Gran's opinion of her grandfather. Lettie was overcome, quite suddenly, by a surge of tearfulness. She sat in silence to compose herself. No one spoke. The only sounds came from the inn reception along the corridor.

Finally, Alec broke the stillness. He said, 'There is something else, isn't there, Ruth?'

'I don't think so,' Ruth answered.

413

'There is the matter of Lettie's father.'

'Alec, please! Michael is her father.'

Alec stood up. 'Wait here.'

'Where's he gone?' Lettie asked.

'I don't know but we ought to do as he asks.'

They stared at each for a couple of minutes then Ruth said, 'Your grandmother decided what was best for you and I had made too many mistakes to argue with her. You grew up untainted by the scandal that kept me in France. Very few people know the truth.'

'Alec does and he found it out for himself.'

'He has his own reasons for searching out the truth. He was very insistent that I came back to Mereside Lodge with him. He said he wouldn't leave the farm without me. Have you any idea why?'

Lettie didn't and she shrugged. 'He's a gentleman so I trust his reasons are honourable. He's an admirable man, which is more than I can say about some.'

Ruth raised her eyebrows. 'You have no idea at all why he came for me?'

'Have you?'

Ruth seemed mildly irritated by her response. 'But he did it for you, of course! He did it for you because the truth is important to you and . . . and because he loves you. Didn't you know?'

Lettie blinked. Well, yes, she knew the bit about the truth, but not . . . but not the . . . the rest. Was this true? Her heart began to stir with a peculiar fluttering. She opened her mouth to ask Ruth how she knew, but Ruth's attention was already diverted by Alec as he returned.

He carried a folder – one of the leather ones Lettie had seen on his desk at Boundary Farm. He undid the ties and took out some pictures, sepia photographs, all of the same lady, and handed them round. He said, 'Lettie has your eyes, Ruth, but don't you think there is a greater resemblance to this lady?'

Ruth agreed. So did Lettie and she asked, 'Who is she?'

'Lord Laughton's elder sister, late elder sister.' He turned to Ruth. 'You did know he was Lettie's father, didn't you?'

Ruth covered her face with her hands and groaned. 'We all knew, as soon as you were born. The likeness was obvious then. You have grown more like me, I am pleased to say.'

Lettie was aghast, 'But you have let Michael believe . . .'

'He knows. We have lived the lie to protect you from the . . . from my disgrace.'

From the truth, Lettie realised, from the stigma of illegitimacy.

Ruth added more harshly, 'Well, who would want Laughton as a father?' She sounded stronger now.

'But Michael has accepted me . . .'

'None of that dreadful scandal was your fault,' Ruth stressed. 'Why should you have to suffer the repercussions? Your grandmother provided a way out for you. She took you home and brought you up as her orphaned grandchild.'

Lettie gazed at her, at this woman who was her mother, and whispered, 'Have you any idea how much I have dreamed and wondered about you?'

Lettie saw the pain cross Ruth's features but she did not flinch from her reply. 'Of course I have. Not a day has passed when I have not thought of you, of how you had grown, and of how much I loved you. I gave you up because I loved you.'

Lettie could not make a response. She was exhausted, emotionally drained, and confused. She was confused about her feelings for this woman who was her mother.

Ruth went on, 'I have many regrets about my past, not least of which was agreeing with your grandmother that I should never be part of your life. I should have liked to have made up our differences and I am so very sorry that she has passed on.'

'Did Alec tell you?'

Ruth nodded and fell silent.

Lettie hadn't drunk her coffee or tot of brandy but her head was fuzzy. She needed to think, she needed air, and she needed a walk to clear her head. Ruth had made mistakes, but then who hadn't? She looked at Alec. There was much about him that she did not know, yet that didn't seem to matter to Lettie. She needed him. Was Ruth right in her observations about him? Love meant wanting to spend the rest of your life with someone. How on earth could Alec love her knowing that she was Lord Laughton's daughter?

She stood up and said, 'I need to think. May I meet again with you later, Ruth?'

'Of course you may. Why not join us for dinner tonight?'

'Us?'

Alec answered, 'This is a difficult situation for your

mother as well, Lettie. I shall stay at the inn for her until she has resolved matters with Michael.'

'Very well,' Lettie agreed. 'In the meantime, I should like to ask a favour.'

'Anything,' Ruth said.

'Please don't go up to the Lodge to see Michael. You will upset Frances. Michael is writing to you and I am sure he will come here.'

Alec offered to drive back to the Lodge. She thanked him and told him she had her own trap now. He accompanied her outside and helped her climb in then unhitched the pony for her.

'Thank you,' she said once again as he handed her the reins. She was glad that he was there, that he was staying at the inn for Ruth, and she was sincere when she added, 'Thank you for everything.'

An expression of relief crossed his features. 'It was a gamble for me to bring Ruth here. I did it for you and I wasn't sure that you would be pleased. But I was very sure that you deserved the truth.'

He held onto her hands as he passed across the reins and she felt his strength flood into her. *I love him*, she thought. She pressed her lips together to stop them trembling. *I want to spend the rest of my life with him*. They stared at each other until he stepped back to allow her to drive away.

She drove the trap back to Mereside Lodge, left it at the stables and took the path around the mere on foot. It had a calming influence on her muddled emotions. Her real father, a man that few people had any kind of regard for, had not wanted her. It was clear in her mind that, lord or not, she did not want him either. She felt that she understood Michael and his battles and admired him for the man he was.

But her mother? How did she feel about her mother? I don't know, she thought. Then, she knew so little about her, aside from her part in a scandal that had happened years ago. She had criticised Gran for her quick judgements on people and vowed not to do the same herself. So what did she really know about this woman who was her mother? Heavens, she knew more about Alec and that was little enough!

A cackle of duck and geese, squabbling over territory, disturbed her thoughts. She plodded on through the trampled undergrowth following the curve of the bank, her mind returning constantly to the man who had precipitated this present situation. She wanted him here now, walking beside her. Alec's presence gave her strength and she didn't want him ever to go back to Canada. Yet Canada was his home and he would wish to return. But just the thought of him leaving left her feeling empty and alone.

She walked all the way round the mere and sat on one of the rustic wooden seats in sight of the bath house. It was near the end of morning treatments and servants' dinner would be almost ready. She was hungry but did not want to speak to anyone; not yet anyway. She heard someone approach and guessed she would have to make an effort. She glanced sideways to see Alec sitting down at the far end of the bench.

'I'll just sit here and wait for you,' he said. He stretched out his legs and stared at the geese on the mere.

After a few minutes she said, 'When are you going back to Canada?'

'I haven't decided. My half of Waterley Estates will keep me occupied for months. I'm gearing up for some battles with Lord Laughton.' He sounded as though he looked forward to the fight and that made her smile.

'What about your family?'

'My brothers? They are taking care of our agricultural concerns back home. They packed me off willingly to sort out the English part of our father's legacy.'

'You have brothers, how lucky.'

'And aunts on my mother's side, with cousins.'

He's very lucky, Lettie thought, except for his titled Yorkshire cousin. She said, 'I suppose I am related to you as well.'

'Oh, I think that's stretching it a bit; third cousins at one remove or something. Not what you would call family at all, really. Would you prefer it to be different?'

She liked the fact that he was different from Lord Laughton. He was foreign and with fresh ideas. She turned to face him and shook her head.

'I would,' he said, and shuffled along the smooth wooden seat towards her. 'I want us to be much closer. I want us to married. I love you, Lettie.'

She ought to have been elated because she loved him too. But all of his recent disclosures to Lettie had, invariably, come with a sting in the tail. She said, 'How can you love me when you know who my father is?'

'I'm following my heart, Lettie, and my heart is telling me all I need to know. What is your heart saying to you?'

'It's saying I love you too.'

He put his arms around her and kissed her, hesitantly at first and then, when she offered no resistance, deeply and longingly and satisfyingly. When they parted, out of breath, he stayed close to her with his arm around her shoulders, watching the ducks bobbing and foraging in the shallows of the mere.

Eventually he said, 'I am meeting with Michael for luncheon today. I want to buy a piece of land from him, well away from the Lodge on the edge of his estate. I'm going to build a house on it. What do you think?'

'For you to live in?'

'For us both to live in. That's if you'll marry me. Will you marry me, Lettie?'

Lettie sat up straight to look at him directly. He was smiling and so was she. 'Of course I'll marry you.'

'I have to ask Michael's permission first. Do you think he will object? I am Lord Laughton's cousin after all.' He was making light of it and there was a twinkle in his eye as he added, 'If he does object I shall bribe him with an offer to pay for the electric in the Lodge.'

'But he won't need a bribe if he sells you some land,' she pointed out.

'I know.'

She smiled again, feeling confident in her future, married to Alec, helping Frances and Father in his hydro and . . . and . . . where did Ruth fit into her life? 'You'd better go or you'll be late for your meeting,' she said. 'I'll see you tonight for dinner at the inn.'

He kissed her again and left reluctantly. She stayed watching the waterfowl until she was sure that servants' dinner was over. Then she helped herself to a piece of cold pie and ate it in the housekeeper's room. She did not want to be distracted from her thoughts about Ruth and what she would say to her that evening.

So, she spoke with confidence when she arrived at the inn for dinner. She wore her Sunday-best outfit and dressed her hair carefully. She had finished with her frantic searching. She had her answers and although she did not like some of them, she knew, at last, who she was and, more importantly, what she wanted. She wanted what she believed she had: Alec, her father and Frances and the challenge of Mereside Lodge; and one thing more.

Lettie and Alec and Ruth dined well at the inn. They celebrated Lettie's as yet unofficial engagement to Alec with French champagne. Ruth, Lettie realised, had a taste for it.

'We shall not make a proper announcement until you have settled your divorce arrangements with Michael,' Alec said to Ruth.

'Anyway, he has to court me first,' Lettie stated proudly. 'I look forward to that.'

'I'm very pleased for both of you,' Ruth smiled.

Lettie returned her smile and commented, 'Earlier today, you said that we cannot choose our parents. But I believe that I am an exception, and that I can.'

A wary look came into Ruth's eyes. 'What do you mean?'

421

'I mean that I can choose who my father is and I choose Michael, as you did.'

'With Frances as your mother?' Ruth queried.

Lettie noticed the wariness had returned to Ruth's eyes. She said, 'Frances is my friend. You are my mother. You.'

Lettie reached across the polished-oak table with her fingers. Ruth's hand closed over them, held them and squeezed them gently.

'Thank you,' Ruth said.

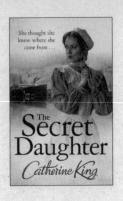

She thought she
knew where she
came from . . .

The
Secret
Daughter
Catherine King

A gripping novel set during the run-up to the launch of Titanic.

Loss

Phyllis Kimber's entire future is called into question after
her father is killed in Earl Redfern's employ. But the earl
knows something about Phyllis that means she will always
be looked after.

Lies

As lady's maid to Martha, Phyllis is the American heiress's
only confidant in England: she knows Martha doesn't love
the recently widowed Lord Melton, the man Martha's
socially ambitious father is determined she marries, but
there's another secret — a secret that makes Phyllis give up
everything to protect her friend.

Loyalty

Martha begins making preparations to return to America
with Phyllis, her father and new husband on the *Titanic*
but the burden of deception eclipses Phyllis's hope for a
new future. As she struggles to protect Martha, Phyllis
must decide where her loyalties lie, unaware of the undis-
covered secrets in her own past and of the tragedy that is
about to unfold on that fateful crossing.

Available now.

Out of tragedy, came her strength and hope.

Sacrifice

When her mother passed away, Meg Parker was forced to sacrifice her chance at love for the sake of her family. She hopes she will be able to live a full life once again after her father remarries – until tragedy strikes a second time. Suddenly, Meg is facing a darker future altogether.

Struggles

Lady Alice Langton is travelling the Yorkshire Dales, spreading the suffragette message. Florence Brookes, the daughter of a prosperous grocer, accompanies her, impassioned by the cause but seeking distraction from her own troubles. Appalled by their lack of domestic skills, Meg decides to flee her old life and joins the two women as their maidservant as they make their way to London.

Strength

When Meg is reunited with her old flame, she is hesitant about her feelings for him – not least because of the rift this causes between her and Lady Alice. It's not until Florence's actions land them in jeopardy that Meg realises she must find the courage to make a heartbreaking choice.

Available now.

Find out more about **Catherine King**'s books at

www.catherineking.info

Or you can follow her on Twitter

@cathkingauthor

And keep up to date with

@LittleBrownUK
@LittleBookCafe

To buy any Catherine King books and to find out more about all other Little, Brown titles go to our website

www.littlebrown.co.uk

To order any Sphere titles p & p free in the UK, please contact our mail order supplier on:
+ 44 (0)1832 737525

Customers not based in the UK should contact the same number for appropriate postage and packing costs.